ALL QUIET IN PEKING

FINAL CURTAIN CALL

LIU HEPING

Translated by
Christopher Payne

SINOIST

ACA Publishing Ltd
University House
11-13 Lower Grosvenor Place,
London SW1W 0EX, UK
Tel: +44 20 3289 3885
E-mail: info@alaincharlesasia.com
www.alaincharlesasia.com
www.sinoistbooks.com

Beijing Office
Tel: +86(0)10 8472 1250

Author: Liu Heping
Translator: Christopher Payne

Published by Sinoist Books (an imprint of ACA Publishing Ltd) in arrangement with Guangdong Flower City Publishing House Co., Ltd.

Original Chinese Text © 北平无战事 (Bei Ping Wu Zhan Shi) 2019, Guangdong Flower City Publishing House Co., Ltd, Guangdong, China

English Translation text © 2023 ACA Publishing Ltd, London, UK

ALL RIGHTS RESERVED. NO PART OF THIS PUBLICATION MAY BE REPRODUCED IN MATERIAL FORM, BY ANY MEANS, WHETHER GRAPHIC, ELECTRONIC, MECHANICAL OR OTHER, INCLUDING PHOTOCOPYING OR INFORMATION STORAGE, IN WHOLE OR IN PART, AND MAY NOT BE USED TO PREPARE OTHER PUBLICATIONS WITHOUT WRITTEN PERMISSION FROM THE PUBLISHER.

This novel is entirely a work of fiction. The names, characters and incidents portrayed in it are the work of the author's imagination. Any resemblance to actual persons, living or dead, events or localities is entirely coincidental.

Paperback ISBN: 978-1-83890-547-7
eBook ISBN: 978-1-83890-546-0

A catalogue record for *All Quiet in Peking (Book Three): Final Curtain Call* is available from the National Bibliographic Service of the British Library.

FINAL CURTAIN CALL
THE ALL QUIET IN PEKING SERIES
BOOK 3

LIU HEPING

Translated by
CHRISTOPHER PAYNE

SINOIST BOOKS

LIST OF CHARACTERS

Fang Buting - governor of the Central Bank's Peking branch
Xie Peidong - brother-in-law of, and assistant to, Fang Buting. CPC underground agent
Fang Meng'ao - colonel in the National Revolutionary Army Air Force, instructor at Jianqiao Aviation Academy and captain of the Peking Economic Inspection Brigade. Son of Fang Buting and brother of Fang Mengwei
Cui Zhongshi - deputy treasury director at the Central Bank's Peking branch, CPC underground agent
Fang Mengwei - Fang Buting's youngest son, deputy commissioner of the Peking Police Bureau and deputy director of the Investigation Department of the Peking Garrison headquarters
He Qicang - vice-chancellor of Yenching University and economic adviser to the Kuomintang government
He Xiaoyu - Yenching University student and Vice-Chancellor He Qicang's daughter
Xie Mulan - Yenching University student, daughter of Xie Peidong and cousin of Fang Mengwei and Fang Meng'ao
Chiang Ching-kuo - eldest son of Chiang Kai-shek, also known as Comrade Jianfeng
Zeng Keda - inspector-general of the Ministry of Defence's Bureau of Reserved Cadres

Hou Juntang - deputy director of the Air Force Operations Department
Lin Dawei - former staff member of the Air Force Operations Department, CPC Underground agent
Fu Zuoyi - commander-in-chief of the North China Headquarters for the Suppression of Communist Insurgency
Xu Tieying - director of the Liaison Office of the Communications Bureau of the Kuomintang Central Membership Committee, chief superintendent of Peking Municipal Police Bureau
Du Wancheng - general auditor of the Ministry of Finance, head of the Five-Member Working Group
Ma Linshen - deputy director of the Kuomintang's Central Commission on Citizens' Food Distribution
Wang Benquan - secretary of the Central Bank
Ma Hanshan - deputy director of the Peking Citizens' Food Distribution Committee, and director of the Civil Affairs Bureau of Peking Municipality
Gu Weijun - Chinese ambassador to the US
Yan Chunming - professor, and head of the Communist Party's Student Committee at Yenching University
Cheng Xiaoyun - second wife of Fang Buting
Wang Yunwu - minister of the Ministry of Finance
Liang Jinglun - Yenching University professor, assistant to He Qicang and leading member of the Iron and Blood Congress of Nation Saving
Shao Yuangang - member of the Youth Aviation Brigade

CHAPTER 1

"Daughter..."

He Qicang's voice shattered the calm in his room, causing He Xiaoyu to lift her head in the direction of her father. She'd been standing next to the chair in which he was slumped, lost in her own thoughts as she had so often been before. Her father's voice had seemingly come from some far-off place. But there was a note of familiarity in his tone. She'd heard him speak like that before, back when she was in primary school. He'd not called her "daughter" since at least that time.

"You're startled... daughter." He said the word again. "Bring a stool over here, just here. Put it in front of me."

He'd never asked her to do anything like this before. Ordinarily, she just waited on him, occasionally rubbed his shoulders and back when needed... but she was always standing behind. She'd washed his feet, too, in the past, and massaged his calves, but always to the side of him. They'd shared words, of course, as a father and daughter are wont to do, but never up close and intimate, a distance had always to be maintained. Not once had she ever been asked to sit in front of him. Never.

But, as a dutiful daughter, she now did as she was told, even if she made sure to place the stool at what she thought was a respectable distance away.

He Qicang arched his head to look at his daughter and smiled as he'd never done before. "Ah, the teacher in front, the grandson at one's knees... us Chinese. This is something a father needs to pass on to his grandchildren, but not today. Come closer. Yes... there, put the stool there. Now sit."

He Xiaoyu obliged, moving the stool closer to her father, but then she hesitated, remained standing. She'd never previously dared to look at him as he was now asking her to do, to say nothing about sitting down in front of him.

He Qicang stretched out his hand. Xiaoyu reciprocated. He gripped hers tight in his hand. For Xiaoyu, it felt as though he'd grabbed hold of her heart just as tightly. Somehow, she knew he was waiting for their eyes to meet. But she resisted, not wanting to look at him like that, even though she had little choice but to do so.

"Dad..."

She sat down quickly, their knees bumping together, but neither of them spoke. A silence ensued, forcing her father to shift his gaze away from his daughter and up towards the ceiling as though he were scanning it for something.

"Dad, if you want to ask me something, go ahead."

"Then I will. Do you remember what I asked you once before, that if Fang Meng'ao and Liang Jinglun were both arrested but I could only save one, which one would you choose? You never answered me then. And afterwards, I regretted putting you on the spot like that. There are so many questions that will forever be unanswered because there are no... no answers. That's why they shouldn't be asked."

"Dad." He Xiaoyu closed her hand firmly around her father's. "No, it was right for you to ask. And as your daughter, I should have answered."

"Then... you have an answer?" He Qicang stared at her.

"Yes, I'm ready to tell you."

He Qicang was stunned, unable to hide the cowardice on his face. "I don't want to hear. For there's no answer that would be any good, none whatsoever."

"There is..."

He Qicang stared at his daughter.

"I hope... hope you can save Liang Jinglun."

"Why?"

"Because you can't do without him."

"And Fang Meng'ao?"

"I'll take him something to eat."

He Qicang smiled once more and then seemed to nod his head and shake it at the same time. Dazed, he stared after his daughter.

―――

On the first floor of the Foreign Languages Bookstore, Zeng Keda sat bewildered and transfixed on Fang Meng'ao. "Come on, there's no need, Comrade Liang Jinglun has already spilled the beans. He's told us everything about his work for the Communist Party."

"I'd still like to hear it." The stubbornness in Fang Meng'ao's voice was unmistakable. "Read me his pledge to join the Communists, please. I want to hear Professor Liang's words... just once."

All Zeng could do was direct his attention towards Liang Jinglun.

Liang seemed to squirm a little under his stare and then averted his eyes so that they fell on Fang Meng'ao. "I can read it. But before I do, tell me, Captain Fang, why do you so want to hear those words? What's your aim?"

"I'll tell you once you've finished."

"All right then." Liang stood and scanned the scene in front of him. "I, Liang Jinglun, voluntarily joined the Communist Party of China and hereby pledged the following oaths to it. One, I swear to fight for the cause of communism my entire life. Two, I uphold the interests of the party above everything else. Three, the party's discipline is infallible. Four, I fear no hardship and will forever serve the party. Five, I aim to be a model for the masses. Six, I will keep the party's secrets. Seven, I have absolute faith in the party. Eight, I will continue the fight despite any and all setbacks, and I shall never betray it."

"Finished?" Fang Meng'ao's eyes bore into the man.

"Yes." Liang met his gaze unwaveringly.

Neither man paid any attention to Zeng Keda.

"Mr Liang, please sit." Meng'ao continued to watch him as he returned to his seat, only standing after the other man had sat down. "I asked Mr Liang to read his oath because I'm not the kind of man who could do so myself, so I sincerely hope you won't ask me to do the same. Inspector Zeng, could you explain how Mr Liang and I are to co-operate hereafter?"

"I prefer to be pragmatic." Zeng Keda felt the need to stand now that Fang Meng'ao had returned to his seat. "Now, I would like to convey the specific details and steps concerning the plan for the 'Peacocks Flying Southeast'."

In the courtyard of He Qicang's home, Xie Mulan sat on the stone steps, her arms wrapped around her knees. She was mumbling under her breath: "'Moon over the West River: Mount Jinggang…' I remember this poem by Mao Zedong." Staring up at the moon as it shone through the night sky, Xie Mulan recalled how not so long ago Mr Liang had taught her the words. "'Below the hill fly our flags and banners, above the hilltops sound our bugles and drums. The foe encircles us thousands strong, steadfastly we stand our…'" She suddenly stopped her recitation. Her sharp ears had caught the sound of the drawing room doors being pushed open. It was He Xiaoyu. She dipped her head between her legs and grasped hold of them a little tighter, feigning sleep.

Moonlight illuminated the path from the drawing room to where Liang Jinglun resided, showering He Xiaoyu in the same glow. Xie Mulan, however, was still pretending to be asleep. A few more moments passed before Xiaoyu walked over to her, leaned low and told her to get up. Mulan was perplexed at first, unable to comprehend why Xiaoyu was herself pretending not to know that Xie was only faking.

But she couldn't hold her tongue: "You knew I wasn't really sleeping. Why pretend to be merciful?" There was a noticeable sulky tone in her voice, even as she kept her head buried between her legs.

"Go on up," Xiaoyu continued. "My father is waiting for you."

"Uncle He is… is waiting for me?" She raised her head swiftly. "Does he want to talk about Mr Liang?"

"Most likely, I imagine."

Xie Mulan stood and looked into the face of He Xiaoyu. The

weak moonlight made it difficult to gauge what kind of mood she was in. For a moment, she felt a twinge of cowardice, but then couldn't help herself. "So, should I go up and see him or not?"

"Decide for yourself."

"You go first, but not like you're escorting me."

"Then how about you escort me?" With those words, He Xiaoyu strode away.

"Please, let's walk together." Xie Mulan reached out and grabbed her hand, pleading with her not to be left alone. He Xiaoyu didn't resist. She couldn't be sure if she was holding the younger girl's hand, or if it was the other way round. But together, hand in hand, they walked off in the direction of the smaller building on the other side of the courtyard. The moon lit their way. He Qicang's eyes followed them from the window above.

The two young women walked up the stairs to stand outside He Qicang's room, and there they stopped. They could see him standing before the window, and they were both embarrassed. He Qicang turned his head and smiled. "Ah, you two..." Before saying anything further, he ambled back over to his chair and sat down. "Watching you both under the moon's gentle light, a quaint verse came to mind. Would you like to hear?"

They didn't respond but strode over to the stool that had been placed in front of his chair.

Still laughing to himself, He Qicang continued his questioning: "You've still not got an answer for me, hmm?"

"Dad, just go ahead." He Xiaoyu understood what her father was up to.

"But I don't want to waste my time. Once I've finished, you have to tell me who wrote it, all right? And who they wrote it for. Yes, that's important. Mulan, you answer."

Xie Mulan was a bright girl. She'd worked out the older man's intention, so all she did was respond with a nod.

"All right then, I'll recite it." He Qicang was from Jiangsu, but at this moment he made a great effort to mimic the accent of an Anhui native. "'The wind in the sky blows hard against the clouds, the moonlight shines on both me and you. I ask you about last year, why you hid behind that closed door? Who hid, who hid, that was last year's me.'" He Qicang stared at Xie Mulan.

"Who doesn't know that poem? Mr Hu Shih wrote it for his wife." Xie Mulan understood her uncle's intention, which spurred her on and gave her courage. "It's a classic example of an old courtier's poem, nothing special about it."

"Oh?" Her response intrigued him. "I'd like to hear you explain this... this point of view."

"Well, isn't it clear enough? The poem, such as it is, is about the lives of a husband and wife, the lines a matchmaker would use to convince parents. Uncle He, you and all those others went to Harvard and got your PhDs there. Are you all so traditionally minded, so conservative?"

He Qicang let loose a boisterous laugh. "A good answer, yes indeed. Good criticism, too. Ah, yes."

The mirth shown by the older man prompted the two girls to respond in kind.

"Dr Hu Shih advocated the overthrow of cultural traditions, that's true, but those very same traditions were mired deep in his bones and not so easily eradicated." He Qicang had stopped his laughter by now. "But you know what? Most of us, of that generation, well, we're the same, whether or not we studied overseas, got doctorates, it doesn't matter. I know for sure, however, that none of us want you to return to those traditions. Here, I'll quote you something else, another few lines that will explain things better. They're written by an English chap, quite an outstanding fellow, actually. The answer will be what kind of conservative values you oppose. And whatever they are, I'll support you. You have my word."

"All right, test us then. We'll give you an answer for sure." Xie Mulan couldn't hide her growing excitement.

"OK." He Qicang straightened himself up and readied his voice. His face took on a look of extreme seriousness. "'There may be dark days ahead and war is no longer confined to the battlefield, but we can only do what is right as we see it and reverently commend our cause to God. If one and all be resolutely faithful today, ready for whatever service or sacrifice it may demand, with God's help we shall prevail.'"

Such an impassioned quotation!

Xie Mulan could feel a shiver down her spine. So, too, could He Xiaoyu.

"So he spoke these words? What's their meaning?"

Xie Mulan was disgusted with herself, for she could not think of an answer. All she could do was shift her eyes towards He Xiaoyu in the hope that she might know. A moment passed. Then two. Finally, in a quiet voice, Xiaoyu offered a response. "Ge... George the Sixth said these words. It was his first speech... the declaration of war on Nazi Germany."

"That's right." He Qicang smiled and chuckled once more. It was a young man's laugh, despite his age. "Mulan, you just levied some criticisms at your uncle, yes? Now it's my turn to do the same. Such a famous speech, and yet you couldn't identify it. I've another question for you, one you must answer. Otherwise, my dear, I won't be able to help you. Do you understand?"

"Go ahead, ask."

"How's it that George the Sixth became King of England?"

"I know that!" Her answer was immediate and excited, her arm held high in the air as though she were in a classroom and eager to answer the teacher's question.

He Qicang laughed again. "You don't need to raise your hand, girl. Just answer."

Xie Mulan lowered her hand but kept standing straight. A split-second later, she began her answer. "Because his older brother, Edward VIII, abdicated so that he could marry the woman he loved."

"Who was this man, and why did he do such a thing?"

"He was the Duke of Windsor, heir to the throne. He loved an American and not his homeland!"

"Nonsense, that's just popular opinion and nothing else. Try again."

"It's... uh." Xie Mulan grew nervous as she fumbled for a better way to explain Edward's abdication. Then, after seemingly hitting upon the answer, she continued, quoting the Hungarian poet, Sándor Petőfi: "'Freedom and love my creed! These are the two I need. For love, I'll freely sacrifice my earthly spell. For freedom, I will sacrifice...'" She paused at this point, thinking that what she had said was also wrong. Embarrassed, she tried to continue. "That's not it either. Uncle He, please tell us the right answer."

"All right, Xiaoyu, you listen as well." He Qicang shielded his smile and looked at them solemnly. "At that time, not so many years ago really, the First World War had not long ended and Europe was enjoying a period of relative peace. Edward thus pursued love and freedom from the demands of his position, hence his abdication in 1936, which was really quite something, one could say remarkable even. But, and this is important, if he'd done such a thing just a few years later, at the beginning of the Second World War, well then he'd have been in the wrong, he was king after all, and that meant his own life, love and freedom could only be secondary to his role as king, his responsibility to his country and its people. Now, whether a nation is prosperous and strong, whether its people are blessed and happy, that depends on its leader, more so if it's a man who's judged by whether he can provide for his family and ensure their happiness. Us Chinese though... ah, how's it we've hoisted so much responsibility onto our women and children? How could we have let their happiness slip away? I suppose, maybe... Gu Yanwu. I'm sure you've heard of him, he was a Confucian philosopher during the Ming-Qing transition, from the same town I'm from as it happens. Anyway, I guess he said it best: 'The rise and fall of a nation concerns everyone!' As a nation, we've gone through so much these past years, so many hardships, saving it from extinction. It should be man's work. There's not much else to get happiness from in times such as these, so you should seek happiness in love at least. Before you came up here, Xiaoyu was here, we spoke. I understand what she was trying to say. Xiaoyu, if you love Fang Meng'ao, then you shouldn't be concerned with anything else. You need to love with all your heart. Mulan, if you love Liang Jinglun, then the same is true for you, love with all your heart. I'll do what I can, help how I can. I'll stand next to you and support you, no matter what."

"That's an odd bloody pair!" The loudness of his voice clearly conveyed Fang Buting's sense of urgency and worry. They were in the drawing room. Cheng Xiaoyun's hand was still on the telephone receiver she'd just placed back, but Fang's shriek forced her eyes first in his direction, then towards Xie Peidong.

"The car's ready, I'm off." Before his words were finished, Fang Buting was already walking out of the room.

"Buting!" There was clear concern in Cheng's tone as she called out after him. He pulled up, stopped and waited. "Vice-Chancellor He has told us it's their wish, for… for love… the freedom to choose it at least. He didn't interfere, he told us that, he hoped, too, that we would do the same and not get involved…"

"The vice-chancellor is a bookish fool, as you well know!" He'd kept his back to Xiaoyun as she'd pleaded, but now he spun around, fury in his eyes. He realised then, in that moment, that his attempts to be calm and cool-headed were a farce. That just wasn't who he was. He shifted his focus to Xie Peidong. "My own favourite pupil a bloody spy! And right beneath my nose… playing at politics. And I was completely unaware, duped. All day long prattling on about democracy and freedom, and what's this now, free love? Mulan's been pushed into the fiery pits of hell, that's what…"

Xie Peidong's own heart was even more troubled than his friend's. It was just that he couldn't find the words to voice that worry. All he could do was just stare at Fang Buting.

"It's like this. Xiaoyun, you go and see him, talk to him about Meng'ao and Xiaoyu. I'll pay Liang Jinglun a visit."

"Governor, Fang Buting… sir," said Xie Peidong, finally breaking his silence. "What's the point of going to see Liang Jinglun?"

"He's a party princeling, isn't he? I just want to ask him if the planned currency reform for Peking is to proceed or not, and to offer my cooperation… if he stays the hell away from Mulan!"

"That ought to work," said Xie Peidong, being sincere. "It's just that Liang Jinglun is right now with Meng'ao. It's better if you don't go, Governor…"

"You're an idiot, too. I'm surrounded by fools." Fang Buting directed his gaze towards Cheng Xiaoyun. "Telephone him. Tell Meng'ao to get over to He's place. Just say the vice-chancellor wants to see him. Do it!"

Xiaoyun picked up the receiver. "What number?"

Exasperated but running out of energy to be angry, Fang Buting complied: "Yenching University, the Foreign Languages Bookstore. The operator will have the number."

"Understood."

"You're still here?" said Fang, turning to Xie Peidong. "Tell Xiaoli to get the car. Xiaoyun will accompany me, at least to the university. I'll get off at the bookstore, and she'll go on to He's place."

"Understood." Xie rushed out without uttering another word.

The telephone that rang on the first floor of the Foreign Languages Bookstore came as no surprise. Many wanted to speak to Fang Meng'ao, but for Liang Jinglun, he couldn't help but feel suddenly left alone, abandoned.

Zeng Keda also needed to depart, and he didn't dwell on why He Qicang had instructed Fang Meng'ao to go. Nor did he say anything about Fang Buting arriving and wishing to speak to him about something or other. All he did was extend his hand and wave goodbye.

Liang Jinglun, however, didn't grasp what Zeng's wave was for and interrupted the other man's departure. "Comrade Keda, you're also leaving?"

A streak of embarrassment crossed his face, if only for a second, before he replied in earnest: "Comrade Jinglun, in the current situation… things are hard, yes, but the organisation will always be behind you. You can count on that. Now, however, you must accept the ordeal you're about to endure. Talk to Fang Buting, talk to him well." He extended his hand to shake Jinglun's, but there was no other hand to clasp.

"Of course I'll do what's expected. I'll face whatever ordeal I must. But I had hoped you would stay, Comrade, that we would talk to Fang Buting together."

"What? Me, talk to Fang Buting?" He withdrew his hand.

"Then your instructions, Comrade, at least give me those. How am I to talk to Fang Buting?"

"As the vice-chancellor's representative, discuss, in all seriousness, the planned currency reforms."

Liang Jinglun's eyes glazed over, betraying the desolation he felt.

"How, with all that's happened, how can I represent the vice-chancellor's interests?"

"What do you mean?"

"The vice-chancellor is a public figure, a democracy activist, while I'm a member... a comrade... of the Iron and Blood Congress."

Zeng Keda directed his eyes towards the floor for a moment, then lifted his face. "Does Fang Buting know?"

"I'm not sure. All I can say for certain is that he suddenly wanted to see me. But I can't think it's because he wants to discuss currency reforms."

"It doesn't matter what he wants to talk about, you just focus on the money... the reforms planned." Zeng Keda understood the confusion the younger man must be going through, but at the same time, he knew he mustn't get caught up in it. And with that, he turned to leave.

He didn't get far, however, before he halted his departure once again. Turning slowly, he was surprised to see that Liang Jinglun had already walked over to the window and now stood with his back to him. "Comrade Jinglun."

The other man was slow to rotate, slow to meet his eyes. "I've just told you, yes? The organisation is behind you, always, and now I speak on their behalf to reaffirm the directives Comrade Jianfeng gave us in March: 'At present the Kuomintang is wholly and thoroughly corrupt, it has no means by which to wage war and it has lost the support of the people. What's more, the Communists' efforts to turn China red aren't a match for this great nation. China's future should be... *is* with us. We're the ones who've sacrificed our youth for her. Once we properly organise, then blood will be spilt and heads will roll!' Join forces with Fang Meng'ao, see that the peacocks do indeed fly southeast."

"And if Fang Meng'ao really is a Communist? What then?"

"You don't need to worry about this particular problem. Comrade Jianfeng's instructions on this matter were clear: 'You must doubt and suspect everyone. A person who is suspected can still be used. The key is to use them well.'"

"And how do I do that?" At that moment, Liang Jinglun's own stubbornness was clear.

"Study Comrade Fengjian's words, and don't let matters of love get in the way!" These last words were deliberate on Zeng Keda's part. He had to lay bare the fact that he knew what secrets Jinglun kept in his heart. They worked too, for Liang was stung by what Zeng had said. Then Zeng's eyes softened. "Mencius said it, didn't he? Whenever heaven tasks a person with great responsibilities... as a comrade, you're only representing yourself. Let me tell you one more thing." Liang Jinglun remained quiet, his eyes transfixed on the other man. "The barbarians are still at the gates, so how can one think of family!" He paused for a moment, then added: "Aren't you a man character? Why suffer thoughts of love!"

Zeng Keda turned and left. This time, there was no hesitation.

As he reached the bottom of the stairs, he spied two students from the Chiang Kai-shek Student Society. It was clear they weren't just standing there as hall monitors, or guards, but more as though they were anxious to report something to Liang Jinglun. He couldn't think what, but as soon as they saw him descend, they straightened up and gave their Youth Army salute.

Quickening his pace, Zeng Keda waved at the youths. "It's exhausting, I know, but make sure you look after Comrade Liang Jinglun."

"Comrade sir, yes sir!"

One of the student guards, a young man by the name of Ouyang, added: "The students, everyone, they've all gathered at the library, waiting for Professor Liang to arrive to arrange things for tomorrow."

Zeng Keda halted his steps. "You two ought to send some of your comrades there first, to make sure there are no members of the Communist Youth League stirring up trouble and trying to manipulate the situation. For the time being, Comrade Liang Jinglun is occupied. It'll be a little while before he's able to come."

"Comrade sir, yes sir!"

———

Not just in Peking, but throughout China, university libraries tended to be large and imposing, none more so than the Yenching repository, which possessed the most extensive collection of materials in the country. Even the reading hall could hold hundreds of people. During the summer months of 1948, despite all the hardships and conflict ravaging the country, those students graduating were still able to receive their diplomas and enjoy the standard ceremony, all because of American money and the guarantees it had made to support Yenching University. Those students yet to finish had no cause to worry either, no need to hurry along with their theses. There would be time for that. But on that night, at 9 pm, the library shouldn't have been filled with so many students. Library administrators were there, assistant administrators, the place was abuzz with activity, books registered, loaned, returned. Those who'd checked out their books sat to the left, those who hadn't sat to the right. Others leaned against shelves and perused the titles they were holding. Still others wandered back and forth, unsure of what books to focus on. And in spite of the great numbers, it was quiet, deathly quiet, a tradition imported from America and now considered a tradition in China. No words were exchanged among the many readers, only their eyes were permitted to convey what was on their minds. Everyone was waiting, waiting and watching.

No one knew who might be a Communist, other than those who were already card-carrying members. Nor did anyone know who might be a Kuomintang true believer, other than those who'd already committed.

They were all students, however, they shared that at least. And despite what all of them might think about their personal political affiliations and their opponents, they were all waiting for Liang Jinglun.

But Liang was nowhere to be seen. Unfortunately for him, he was still stuck in the Foreign Languages Bookstore.

A rather meek library assistant broke the silence: "Director Yan, you've returned?" Surprised by what they had heard, multiple pairs of eyes shifted towards the main door. They'd all received the news several days earlier that the library director, Yan Chunming, had resigned from his post and all his duties. He had, apparently, told the administration that he was returning to Tianjin and Nankai University.

And yet, here he was.

Some of the surprised onlookers were Communists, others were Nationalists. They were members of their respective student committees, stalwarts to the cause, both the reds and the blues. Amid their number were several who had no clue who Yan Chunming was.

Yan Chunming's response to their unasked question was brief, and to the point: "Still some things to take care of, work to finish and hand over to my successors. Keep at it, keep those heads buried in those books."

As in the past, the director brought up his previous experience as an exchange student in France, and how he'd used his scholarship money to buy a leather Louis Vuitton bag. This purchase was made in the previous century and so the leather was noticeably aged, which only made it more distinct. He was quiet as he strode past the bookshelves and tables. While he wouldn't have been concerned by the eyes that followed him, he hadn't really seen them in the first place, had paid them no attention. All he did was nod in the direction of the students, his eyes hidden behind thick glasses whose main function appeared to be acting as a barrier to the world. He reached the end of the reading hall and stepped into the corridor that lay beyond. Then he fumbled in his pockets and pulled out a set of well-used keys. At the end of the hallway was the rare books collection, a room he had frequented for work, and for naps.

A knobbled hand reached out to grab the telephone that had suddenly sprung to life in the north room situated near the Jingchun Botanical Gardens. The hand belonged to Liu Chuwu.

"It's me." It was clear the person had only recently arrived. "Boss Zhang."

It was only two sentences, but Old Liu was genuinely surprised: "He left just a minute ago. Everything's been arranged, let's let things play out... I've used the party, vouched for his courage, his credentials have been assured. It's, it's just no one has called him back to campus... I've got to look into this. Once I do, I'll report back to you."

Old Liu hung up the phone and for a moment remained motionless, seemingly baffled. This lasted for only a moment, however, and then he shouted: "Little Zhang!"

"Here." The door was pushed open from the outside and the strapping lad who whispered his presence stepped in.

Old Liu's eyes were anything but frightening. "Did you send someone along with Professor Yan?"

"Yes, as instructed."

"Who, dammit? He's over at the Yenching Library now!"

"That's, that's not possible."

"And why not? If anything happens to him, I swear to hell it'll be you who pays for it! Now get the fuck out of here!" Liu fell silent again as he thought things over. Finally, he extended his skeletal hand for the telephone and dialled a number.

Yan Chunming was sitting in the rare books collection room. He seemed dejected and dispirited, intent on ignoring the phone. Let it ring, he thought. He was more inclined towards the books, great stacks that he could stack even more. Yes, tidy up his desk, take out a handkerchief. Yes, wipe the surface clean.

But the telephone was more obstinate than him, ring followed ring, again and again, incessant, demanding. With one hand he continued to clean his desk, with the other he reached out and lifted the receiver. "You've reached Yan Chunming. I'm cleaning the rare books collection room. If you must say something, please be brief."

Old Liu felt as though he'd had a hammer slammed into his chest. His breathing became ragged, and it took some effort to calm himself down. "Professor Yan, I've just come across a very old, rare, precious you could say, volume dated to sometime after the fall of the Han Dynasty. It's got a grand-sounding name, *Songs*... or something... yes, *New Songs from the Jade Terrace*. I think you should come and collect it, quickly... Understand?"

Yan Chunming's voice was eerily serene: "Mr Liu, there's nothing of value from the Han Dynasty, nor immediately after. I shan't be coming over. I can't leave here..." He stopped himself mid-sentence, stunned by the ferocity by which Liu banged down the receiver. He stared for a moment at the telephone he was still holding in his hand, unsure of what to do. Finally, he replaced it on

15

the switch hook. Whatever comes shall come, he thought to himself. All he could do was face it as calmly as possible.

More students had streamed into the reading hall, and more were approaching its doors. Intentionally or not, both the Communist student advocates and their Nationalist counterparts began to surreptitiously scan the growing crowd. A few sets of eyes seemed to fall on their target, on one particular person. He had a canvas rucksack slung over one shoulder, and in his hand he carried an electrician's valise. He pushed his way through the swarm of students, past the reading tables, deeper and deeper into the throng of bodies.

It was Old Liu, the university janitor.

He scanned the crowd of students, looking at faces and poses, and then walked in among a group standing to one side. They were Kuomintang adherents, students of Chiang Kai-shek. Without introducing himself, he simply asked where Yan Chunming's office was. One of the students sized him up for a moment, then gestured towards the far end of the hall. "Walk that way. His office is just past the doors there at the end."

"Thanks," was all he said before swiftly walking off.

He didn't get very far, however, before an administrative officer who'd seen him enter the hall called out to halt his steps: "What's the matter? Who's called you over here?"

"Professor Yan called. Evidently, the light in his office isn't working. At least, that's what the maintenance office told me. They said I need to take a look at it."

"Ah, all right then. On your way." Old Liu carried on but was held up again by the administrator, who had some additional words for him: "Listen, you're going into the rare books collection. Be careful."

"Understood."

When Liu was out of earshot, the administrator beckoned to the Kuomintang student Liu had questioned when he came into the hall. "He's the campus janitor, yes?"

"Yes, he's been to our dorm before to fix the lights." In what was no more than a whisper, he added that Liu had told him Professor Yan's lamp had apparently been acting up and that the maintenance office had dispatched him to take care of it.

Old Liu entered the rare books collection room and locked the door behind him. Paying no attention to Yan Chunming, he strode over to the bookshelf positioned below the ceiling light fixture and climbed up on top of it. Deftly, he unscrewed one of the light bulbs.

"There's nothing wrong with it, you know."

"Whether it's blown or not, I don't know. Come over and take a look yourself."

There was little else Yan Chunming could do but comply with Old Liu's request. He did not, however, climb up on the bookcase, but rather stood to its side, choosing not to look up at the other man. Liu continued his work. Crouching down, he gently tapped the light bulb he'd removed on the shelf. The tungsten filament was dislodged almost immediately. The bulb was ruined. Still crouching, Liu reached into his valise and pulled out a new one. In a quiet, threatening voice, he let Yan Chunming know of his displeasure. "You've gone against our instructions. What the fuck are you trying to do?"

"I... I've got responsibilities."

"Responsibilities?"

"Yes. Many responsibilities."

"And these are?"

"Uni... university committees. Liang Jinglun was under my direct leadership. I didn't observe any Nationalist leanings on his part, no connection to the Kuomintang whatsoever. Whatever the seriousness of the consequences of this lapse on my part, I should confront them myself."

"Confront... confront them yourself!" Old Liu straightened his legs and quickly replaced the light bulb. He leapt down from the shelf and turned towards Yan. "As a rep for the Ministry of Industry in North China and Peking, I hereby order you to vacate these premises. In other words, get your fucking arse out of here."

Yan Chunming said nothing. Nor did he show any sign of leaving.

Old Liu paid no heed to his inaction. He simply reached into his valise and pulled out a foot-long steel pipe. Then he turned his attention to the window and the iron bars that graced it. "Once I'm gone, you exit by the window. Right away. There'll be someone waiting for you." And with that, he marched over to the window himself.

"No, don't pry it open." Yan Chunming's voice was low, but firm nonetheless. "I can't go."

Liu stopped and spun around. "What did you say?"

"Here, I am the organisation. Tomorrow, we're due to get our rations, and I'm the only one who can oversee that. The authorities won't work with anyone else. I'm responsible for student health and well-being, for their safety. Once tomorrow's past, I'll follow whatever instructions the organisation lays down."

"Tomorrow you'll be arrested. Do you understand? How will you follow orders, then?"

"Then I'll be arrested."

Old Liu sucked on his teeth, betraying his growing exasperation. "And the Kuomintang's punishment, their brutality. You'll face that?"

"I don't know." Yan Chunming remained calm. "Perhaps it's best I don't let them grab me."

"You'll flee?" There was a degree of doubt as Liu's eyes bore into him.

"I... I can't. I'll just throw myself into the lake."

"What? Are you toying with me, citing something from *New Songs from the Jade Terrace*? You're that bloody cultured, are you?" Liu recognised the image Yan was sketching with his words. He knew it was a line from that collection.

Desolate, Yan Chunming laughed. "There's nothing cultured about it. Mao said it best, this is an uprising, the violent action of one class against another."

Old Liu couldn't help but be startled by Yan's words. "What violent action are you talking about? What violence are you capable of, huh? Who the hell told you to rise up?"

"I told myself. Please, Comrade Liu... Comrade Zhang Yueyin. Forgive me, and please tell our superiors what's been on my mind. If the situation can be dealt with safely tomorrow, I'll submit to whatever the organisation has planned. If I'm arrested, I'll end my life before they ever get the chance to throw me into a Kuomintang prison."

Liu tilted his head to one side to size up the professor, this Yan Chunming. All he saw, however, was the thickness of his glasses. The poor bastard, it seemed, was terribly short-sighted. You couldn't even see his eyes through the lenses.

"I've... I've made other mistakes, you know," Yan Chunming continued. "Make that clear to the organisation. You know, when I was with you earlier, I took advantage of the moment you stepped out to take your gun."

Liu reached instinctively to his waist, groping in vain for his weapon. His second reaction was more abrupt, less controlled. He grabbed Yan Chunming's wrist, hard. "Where is it? Hand it over. Now!"

Yan Chunming was calm. "I... I can't."

"The balls!"

"I... I need it to make sure I'm not arrested, to keep our secrets. Your gun is my insurance, the party's, too. It's got nothing to with, as you put it, balls."

Liu let his grip loosen. The tone of his voice softened as well. "Comrade Yan Chunming, we're only ever cogs in the machine, small parts of the whole, we do what our superiors tell us to do. Please, hand me my gun."

Yan shook his head. "And an individual must submit to the circumstances he finds himself in. Please, Comrade Liu, don't say anything else, just go..."

Liu's eyes fell on Yan's attaché case on the table.

"The pistol's in a safe place, I've locked it up. No one but me knows the combination."

Liu scanned the rest of the room. Fucking rare books collection, so many fucking locked cabinets! Big, small... everywhere. Liu began to realise, however reluctantly, that he wouldn't be getting his gun back. No one but Yan could get it now. His eyes returned to the other man. "Comrade Chunming, do you know what the party will do once they learn of this?"

"After they understand what's happened, I imagine they'll remember me as a martyr. And if they don't understand, then I suppose they'll just put my title on my file, Professor. Nothing more."

"Fine." Liu was perturbed at his ability to command a subordinate but felt there was nothing else he could do. "You won't listen to me. That's fine, I'll get Comrade Zhang Yueyin to come. Don't destroy the organisation you profess to be committed to… and don't turn around." With those words, Old Liu grabbed his valise, replaced his tools inside it and headed through the door.

"Comrade Liu," said Yan Chunming, trailing behind him. "If you're intent on calling Comrade Zhang here, then I'll come clean right now. I'll tell the entire student body who Liang Jinglun is really working for!"

Old Liu spun around. "You… you'll destroy everything if you do!"

"I don't think so. Nor do I fully understand what you're trying to get at. I just want to follow orders. That's why I need to stay here. I need to keep my eyes on Liang Jinglun."

Liu remained glued to the ground. He didn't want to look at Yan Chunming again, so he directed his attention to the broken tungsten filament he was holding. That's when Yan stretched out his hand. "What're you doing? What've you got in your hand?" Both his hands now clasped Liu's. "Comrade Liu, I've… I've never used a gun before. Teach me, please. Is… do… um… do I just put the bullets in? Will it work just like that?"

Liu yanked his hands free. "You bookish fool!" He stepped towards the door.

"Do you really think I'll be arrested?" His voice was no more than a whisper.

"Aren't there a lot of books here?" Liu's hands paused on the latch to the door. "Find out for yourself. Surely you've got books on West Point don't you, books about infantry and the training that takes place at the Baoding Military Academy, at Whampoa…"

―――

Fang Meng'ao was busy kneading dough to make noodles. He was in the kitchen, a wide open space adjacent to He Qicang's drawing room. He Qicang was plumped on the sofa, his eyes fixed on the younger man covered in flour. Cheng Xiaoyun was seated next to him. On another much longer sofa, He Xiaoyu and Xie Mulan sat, their eyes also trained on the man in the kitchen. Fang Meng'ao continued to knead. His work was furious. As he added the baking soda, he kept his hands pumping. The bag of flour that sat at his feet was nearly half empty. The mound of dough he'd already kneaded resembled a small hill.

"Shall I use all the flour?" His question was directed at He Qicang.

"I imagine you've kneaded enough. We've only got to send it to a couple of other homes. What do you think, Xiaoyu?"

"Enough, yes. If you make any more, we'll have no way to cook it all."

"Let them sit for, what, fifteen minutes or so? That should be sufficient, yes?"

"I would think so."

"All right then, wash your hands and come over here."

Fang Meng'ao cleaned his hands and joined the rest of them in the drawing room.

Xie Mulan stood and relinquished her seat almost as quickly as Fang Meng'ao left the kitchen. He Xiaoyu did the same. "Please, here, take my spot. I'll go and make a start on the steamed buns."

"Not for fifteen minutes at least," interjected He Qicang. "Sit, all of you."

The two young women returned to their seats while Fang Meng'ao stood nearby. He Qicang wanted him to stand for what he was about to say. "Now listen to this old father, you've a beautiful singing voice. A bel canto, as the Italians say…"

"Dad!" Xiaoyu cut him off before he could say anything further. Now was not the time, she thought, to get one of them to sing.

"Don't interrupt." He gestured towards his daughter for her to remain silent. "In the West, as in China, there are traditions to be admired, just as there are modern things to be marvelled at. There are an equal number of things to disdain. When I was in England, I often went to see Shakespeare productions. In the US, it was Broadway. I enjoyed both. At the same time, I still adore Peking Opera. Mulan."

"I'm here," and she stood up at once.

"Ah, my dear, you don't need to stand." He waved for her to sit. "Did you know China has its own Edward the Eighth?"

"I didn't."

"Perhaps my comparison is not wholly on the mark, perhaps it's impossible to say that China had a monarch who closely resembled Edward the Eighth, but his pursuit of love above all else does bear an uncanny similarity to Edward's. Xiaoyun, you ought to be able to guess who I'm referring to. Tell us, please."

"I'll guess that it was the Zhengde Emperor of the Ming, yes?"

"Absolutely." He Qicang smiled and looked at the two girls. "Do you know, this... this is what I most liked about your Auntie Cheng. I could be thinking about just about anything, and she would always be able to guess what it was. Xiaoyun, Meng'ao has recently helped me with so much, shouldn't we sing a tune from *The Wandering Dragon Toys with the Phoenix*? It's Zhengde's love story after all!"

From their previous telephone exchange, Cheng Xiaoyun knew what kind of mood He Qicang was in, but she was surprised, and quite moved, too, that he would choose this method to show Fang Meng'ao how he was feeling. The old man was well-intentioned, she thought, but would Meng'ao understand?

"Master He, you've made clear you rather enjoy Peking Opera, but I don't believe Meng'ao is that much of a connoisseur of the stage."

"You mean he's not a fan?" Everyone looked at Fang Meng'ao.

Grasping the mood of the older man, Fang Meng'ao readily answered: "I wouldn't say I don't like it, it's just that I've not had the opportunity to listen to it all that much."

Turning to Cheng Xiaoyun, He Qicang seemed satisfied with the answer. "You see... he never said he disliked it."

"Shall we sing all of it?" Xiaoyun asked, standing up. "Do you think you'll be able to?"

"I don't think I can manage the whole opera. No, that would be too much." Despite these words, He Qicang had raised himself from the sofa. And unlike many times before, he wasn't using it to support himself. Rather, he stood strong and firm on his own. "Let's start from 'The curve of the moon.'"

"Yes, let's."

Despite the lack of musical accompaniment, it was as though they'd been transported to the stage. Their feet became light, and they carried themselves as those on a dance floor, moving in rhythm to the music the orchestra was ringing out.

> *Oh beautiful curved moon high up in the night sky, please tell me where the lord resides.*

Xiaoyun and Mulan were enthralled. So, too, was Fang Meng'ao.

What struck them even more was when He Qicang followed in song thereafter.

> *Sister, you need not ask anything more, for all under heaven is mine from yore.*
>
> *I fear, Lord, you lack in reason, for one ought not to take such liberties on humble houses.*
>
> *But noble homes, my dear, invite wanton and often mischievous strangers, especially so when affected shyness serves only to make one even more alluring; the beauty of the Chinese crab apple tree when it flowers holds the talent for true romance.*
>
> *Those flowers come but from those trees, and I fear my lord is but making fun of me; busily trying to get my blossoms to fall, only to discard them when they float to the ground.*
>
> *Sister Phoenix, you do me an injustice, you ought not to carelessly throw such flowers away. Quick, instruct my soldiers to gather them up, quick, quick, without delay.*
>
> *My lord, you're still yet teasing me, but when the time comes, you'll only hide yourself away.*
>
> *Let heaven take care of the land below and let this humble soldier carry you off to the ends of the world...*

The room went quiet once their performance came to an end. There was tension in the air. The Air Force uniform Fang Meng'ao was wearing was now more striking than ever before. Of course, he understood the gist of the ballad, he knew that "lord" and "soldier" could only refer to himself. It was a challenge to conceal the moistness of his eyes.

Xie Mulan appeared afraid. He Xiaoyu, on the other hand, seemed moved, stunned by her father's performance.

Somehow, Cheng Xiaoyun was able to read the situation. She extended her arm to give support to He Qicang, and then sought to change topic: "Professor, my word, you sing as well as Ma Lianliang. Please, take a rest. You must need it."

He Qicang held his position, however. "That's a lie and you know it. I'm only a little better than Fang Buting, certainly no more adept a singer than that. He can't keep the beat either, he's always stepping on his partner's heels. Call him. I'd like to know what he went to talk to Liang Jinglun about. I wonder… quite baffling, wouldn't you say? Call them both to come."

Cheng Xiaoyun stared dumbstruck for a moment. So, too, were the three younger adults in the room. Everyone was silent, unsure of what to say or do. A moment later, He Qicang picked up the telephone himself, but before he could begin to dial the number, Cheng Xiaoyun seemed to be awoken from her stupor. "Let me, please. I'll call." And she took the receiver from his hand, not really waiting for him to protest.

"Uncle He," said Fang Meng'ao. "I must return to barracks, I need to see to the distribution of rations tomorrow."

He Qicang understood at once. He had no desire to see Fang Buting, at least not here. Nor did he wish to see Liang Jinglun. He Qicang looked him up and down, and said: "Yes, go. Xiaoyu, please see him to the door."

As Fang Meng'ao reached the gate to the inner courtyard he stopped, turned and looked at Xiaoyu. "I kneaded all that dough especially for you. You know that, don't you? Tonight, with Mulan, enjoy some steamed buns. Don't go out, don't go and get your rations tomorrow either."

"What did you discuss with Mr Liang? You've not told me anything, not a single word."

"What can I talk to him about? I asked him if he were Red, if he belonged to the party, but he wouldn't say, wouldn't admit to anything. So that's that. Oh, I did tell him something else, about you and Mulan. I said one of you was my fiancé, the other my cousin… and that neither of you would be participating in any further student activities."

"What?" Her voice failed her for a moment before she gathered her strength and spoke, low but firmly: "Who gave you the right?"

"Comrade Cui Zhongshi." He shifted his gaze to the moon hanging in the night sky. His eyes sparkled more brilliantly than the moon itself. He Xiaoyu's heart skipped a beat. Her eyes followed his, timidly, as she too looked at the white orb in the darkness above.

"Go back. You've seen me to the door. Now, look after yourself, and Mulan, too." His attention turned to the jeep parked nearby. Its engine sputtered to life, the gears shifted and Meng'ao was on his way. A moment later, however, he put the vehicle into reverse and drove up alongside her. Then he stretched out his hand and gestured for Xiaoyu to come closer. She could do nothing but oblige him. With a smile on his lips, he told her he'd forgotten to tell He Qicang he enjoyed his performance. "Please let him know from me that it was wonderful, especially those two particular lines."

"What lines?"

"The last two."

Her face flushed with embarrassment. The jeep pulled away, unrushed and at half its usual speed.

On the second floor of the Foreign Languages Bookstore, Liang Jinglun was alerted to a ringing phone. No one knew who was calling. Fang Buting, who was seated next to the table, waited calmly, unhurriedly for him to return. A moment later, a sound echoed from the stairwell and Liang reappeared.

"Sit. Let's continue our chat." As before, Fang Buting didn't deign to look at the younger man.

"I can't. I had no answer for you before, and I still don't."

Fang's eyes fell penetratingly on Liang. "Was it the Communists who called you away just now or Zeng Keda?"

"You don't want to guess." There was a tone of indifference in his voice. "It was Professor He who telephoned, actually. Your wife took the call. They want us both to come over quickly."

"Good." Fang lifted himself out of his chair. "Since you don't seem inclined to answer my question directly, and since I don't really need you to admit to being a Communist or a Nationalist, all you need to understand is that I've got my eye on you and I won't let it slip. Just make sure you don't involve my family in whatever it is you're up to. What you do has no connection to me. Come on, let's go to He's. And when we get there, I hope you'll make clear to Mulan that besides the teacher-student relationship, there's really nothing else between you. Do you think you'll be able to honour this request?"

"I… I don't believe so. At least not now." Again, his tone was one of indifference.

"Eh?" Fang Buting's eyes took on a sudden look of severity.

"Because I can't accompany you to He's home, not now anyway. Tomorrow, we're supposed to provide rations for universities across the city, but the arrangements are woefully lacking, and if things are better organised, well, that could very well lead to another wave of student protests. When that happened before, your son, Captain Fang, exacerbated an already tense situation. At this moment, the students are gathered in the library waiting for me. Don't you think it's best for me to remain here, to try to resolve things *before* they escalate?"

Liang had ripped the scab off a still-open, festering wound.

Fang looked at the younger man. This pup who'd been to America, obtained a PhD there, a man who now seemed to be playing both sides of the political divide, who often walked around with an air of darkness about him, he'd dredged up something cold from the depths of Fang's heart. Fang had to be careful not to let the other man see the look in his eyes. He had to hold on to the seriousness in his voice.

"Incidentally, since you brought it up, I should tell you, it's quite likely that my son is no rival to you, but I stand behind him. If you don't believe that, keep on the same track you're on and see what happens. I abhor getting involved in politics. My area of interest lies in banking, finance and… well… you've studied economics, you should understand, my young friend, the economy is the base of everything. It can determine politics, not the other way round. I want you to remember that. They're advantages there for you and for your planned currency reforms. Remember that as well."

Fang Buting picked up his bag and hat that he'd placed on the table and prepared to depart. Before doing so, however, he had one more thing to say. "Tell your superiors, they don't want to tangle with my family. Leave them alone. I'll co-operate with you on the distribution of Nationalist funds, and provide assistance in pushing through the currency reforms. Now go."

With those last words, Fang Buting departed. But it was those last words that were rather odd, for it was he who left, not Liang Jinglun.

In the span of a day, in one particular room, explosive titbits of information had been revealed. First, Zeng Keda had revealed his secret political affiliation to Fang Meng'ao, and now Fang Buting had essentially done the same. Liang Jinglun watched the back of the older man as he descended the stairs, gradually disappearing out of sight. Once more, he couldn't escape the feeling that he'd been stripped bare and left naked, exposed. The small, twenty-five-watt bulb seemed as bright as the noonday sun.

As he stood there wondering about the day's events, an echoing of urgent footsteps could be heard. It was one of the student hall monitors running towards him.

"Fang Buting's left?"

Ouyang's voice was rapid: "Yes, he's just got in his car."

"So, has something happened? Is that why you came running?"

"Yes. Yan Chunming's returned."

"Who? Where?"

"Yan Chunming... he's just come... the library..."

"Is he looking for me?" He knew almost immediately that his voice betrayed a growing lack of composure. He had to be wary. "Everything you know... tell me... now."

"Sir, yes sir, as soon as Yan Chunming entered the library, he went straight to the rare books collection. He didn't greet anyone, didn't say anything."

"The two of you, get over there now. I want you to watch each and every movement he makes."

"But sir, our orders are to protect you."

"And I don't bloody well need it!" It was rare for Liang Jinglun to be so animated, but this new development seemed to call for it. "Now go!"

"Sir, yes sir." There was little emotion in the young guard's voice. He simply spun around and went down the stairs.

Liang Jinglun paused for a moment, stunned and unsure of what to do. Then he walked over to the door and shut it, thinking all the while he should distance himself from all that was going on, while realising that he could not.

The streetlight near the rear gate to Gu Weijun's mansion illuminated only the narrow stone path that stretched its way through the neighbourhood. As a result, the figures cut by Zeng Keda and his aide-de-camp, Wang, were indistinct and mostly covered in shadow. The young barracks officer who stood stationed at the gate was similarly shrouded in darkness. His voice, however, cut cleanly through the night: "Inspector Zeng. Xu Tieying and Wang Puchen have arrived."

Zeng halted his approach and turned to the officer. "When? Did they come together or separately?"

"They arrived at twenty-one hundred hours. They came together."

"Did they come in one vehicle or two?"

"One sir, Xu Tieying's car."

Zeng turned towards Wang. "It seems Chen Jicheng has made a move. Have the radio transmitter ready, I may have to report this to Comrade Jianfeng at any moment."

"Sir."

With that, Zeng Keda marched inside.

Wang remained outside for a moment longer. "Officer, the ration distribution scheduled for tomorrow... are our men ready?"

"Yes sir, ready sir. One company is on site. Another has taken up position around the distribution zone. The final company is on standby, ready to deploy wherever needed."

Wang acknowledged the information with a nod of his head, before issuing additional commands in an almost whisper: "You must remember this, soldier, your first duty is to ensure the safety of Captain Fang's inspection unit. Got it? I don't care if guards from HQ, or troops from the Fourth or Eleventh Corps show up, if anyone at all interferes with the inspection team, you have the authority of the Ministry of Defence to arrest them. Understand? If you discover Communist insurgents, don't apprehend them on site, but contact Inspector Zeng and request instructions. Whoever he tells you to arrest, that's who you grab. Got it?"

"Sir, yes sir. Understood sir."

With those words, Zeng's aide-de-camp took his leave.

―――

Zeng Keda stood beneath a ceiling light to ensure the blue letter-headed paper on which the general headquarters had issued its orders could be read more easily. Xu Tieying was seated in an armchair further inside the room, sipping tea. Wang Puchen was on the opposite side of the room, seated comfortably in his own armchair and smoking a cigarette. There was no ashtray, so he was using the lid of his teacup to tap away the ash. Each time he tapped the end of his cigarette, he'd cough a little as well.

Zeng placed the orders gently on the table.

"Finished reading?" There was a distinct and noticeable coldness in Xu Tieying's voice.

Zeng turned around, but he didn't walk over to the large sofa that had seemingly been left for him to occupy. Instead, he pulled out a dining chair from the table and moved it over towards where the tea set had been laid. He appeared polite, and yet also terribly casual and unconcerned. But there was a definite purpose behind his actions. The chair he'd chosen stood higher than the armchairs, giving him a somewhat raised and exalted position of dominance over the other two men.

Xu Tieying continued, his eyes purposefully neglecting to make contact with Zeng. "We've both signed our names. Inspector Zeng, if you've no dissenting opinion, please do the same. Deputy Commander-in-Chief Chen is awaiting receipt of our signatures."

"I don't believe I'll sign it."

"We must be united in action. I fear... it's not... not appropriate for you not to sign, don't you think?" Xu Tieying couldn't help but look at Zeng now.

"I think it is." Zeng met Xu's gaze steadfastly, before looking to

Wang Puchen. "Chief Xu, as the main investigator for the Security Bureau, it makes sense for you to sign those orders. That goes for you as well, Mr Wang. You're in charge of the central station, after all. But I represent the Ministry of Defence, and we don't fall under your jurisdiction."

"When the meeting was called, you weren't there, so you don't know. Deputy Commander-in-Chief Chen has already reported these orders to the capital, to Nanking."

"Which Nanking?" Zeng Keda stood up and walked over to his desk to pour some water.

"It's already been steeped. Here, this's your tea." Wang Puchen was staring at his back, but it was clear from his voice that he was trying to ease the growing tension in the room.

"Since when have we had such thorough agreement among the leadership, such unity of thought?" Zeng Keda held the teacup in one hand, while in the other he lifted the thermos of hot water. His eyes squinted in the direction of Wang Puchen and what he was doing with his cup lid. "Mr Wang, like what the Ministry of Defence has done, the Intelligence Department ought to supply you with a new operations manual. If one can't do without cigarettes, surely one can't also do without plain, boiled water, no?"

This wasn't just turning into an unfriendly exchange, but an increasingly unreasonable one, too. There'd been a cloud of gloom hanging above Xu Tieying since the start, but once he heard the pin click on Zeng Keda's pistol, he simply lifted the teacup to his mouth, imbibing the liquid at the same time as he chewed the tea leaves.

Zeng Keda smiled coldly and poured the water.

Wang Puchen's first attempt to defuse the situation had clearly failed, so he resorted to a fit of coughing. He stood up and stamped his still burning cigarette out in the teacup lid. He seemed intent on leaving.

"Mr Wang." Zeng Keda's voice made him stop. "I apologise. What I just said was not directed towards you. Should you wish to have more tea, another cigarette, please go ahead."

His mood improving almost immediately, Wang returned to his armchair. Carrying the cup of water in his hand, Zeng Keda walked back to his seat as well. "Would you like me to add some water to your cup, Chief Xu?"

"Your signature. I'd like to return to this."

"As I've already said, I have not received orders from Nanking to make any arrests tomorrow. I hope, too, that if you can take the big picture into consideration, you won't follow through on the orders from the Peking HQ. The most important thing at this moment is stability."

"That's our hope as well, stability, but the Communists are doing everything they can to ensure things won't be stable. We actually just received new intelligence. They're planning to instigate fresh student protests tomorrow. Tell him, Mr Wang. It was your department that came by this intelligence, after all."

There was great seriousness in his eyes when Zeng Keda turned them towards Wang Puchen.

Zeng's stare was met by another fit of coughing. Again, it was Wang's attempt to dial back the tension in the room. Gradually, his cough eased, but he still wouldn't speak. He needed to drink a little more tea, soothe his bruised throat. Finally, he felt he could elaborate: "This evening, the formerly missing Professor Yan Chunming of Yenching University suddenly reappeared on campus, in the library. Shortly thereafter, a succession of student leaders went into the rare books collection room to see him. An analysis of this intelligence report indicates in no uncertain terms that Yan Chunming is a Communist operative placed at Yenching to stir up student protests."

This last detail was especially shocking to Zeng Keda.

Yan Chunming was Liang Jinglun's superior, he knew this already. He'd learned this titbit of information from Liang himself. What's more, he knew, too, that Yan Chunming had secretly travelled to Tianjin, which further meant it was highly likely that he visited a so-called liberated zone. While he was away, Liang Jinglun had been placed in temporary command of Communist activities on campus. He knew all of this, so how was it that Yan had suddenly returned?

Zeng thought things over a little more. "Do you... do you have specific intelligence that says Yan Chunming has returned specifically to stir up trouble?"

"No," said Wang Puchen, hesitating a moment, "but it's clear the Communist Party ordered him to return, in which case something must be planned."

"But what? We need more precise information."

"More precise information would only add superfluous details," Xu Tieying cut in. "We all know what happened on the fifth of July. We were too passive then, far too passive. And it's going to happen again tomorrow, and not just in Peking. Things are planned in Nanking, too. If we don't act now, we certainly won't be able to do so tomorrow, and the situation will easily get out of hand. Inspector Zeng, the Ministry of Defence is tasked with rooting out corruption. Part of that – you might say the most important part – is dealing with the Communists and their efforts to stir up violence in Peking. Tackling corruption mustn't become a tool for the Communists. We can't let them exploit that campaign for their own benefit. Surely our hard work, our toil and pain can't be made into something our enemy enjoys."

"Chief Xu, I'm afraid I don't understand. How's it our drive to weed out corruption can benefit the Communists?"

"You really don't understand?"

Zeng Keda turned to Wang Puchen. "Mr Wang, you reported on what you uncovered, yes? On what the Communist leader Peng Zhen stated on the sixth of May?"

"In the first instance, it was reported to the Intelligence Bureau, whereupon Chief Mao presented the information to the president."

"And what did the Intelligence Bureau determine... once they had analysed the documents, of course?"

"The documents are still being... analysed. They've not yet come to any concrete conclusions."

"Well then, let me elaborate, if you will, on the concrete instructions issued by the Ministry of Defence. In our Nationalist-controlled areas where the Communists have sought to ignite their fires, they've all withdrawn to, as it were, watch the havoc they instigated from afar. Now, contrary to what you may think, some of us indeed prefer to stoke those flames to make them burn even brighter."

Now it was Xu Tieying's turn to ask for clarification.

"Those documents – Peng Zhen's words – they were already

incredibly clear. Their plan is to conceal their operatives and conserve their strength and then, by the safest means possible, transport party members to their so-called liberated zones... which means, doesn't it, that they don't have the strength or support to instigate further student protests, yes? So why are some of us so afraid of potential student marches? To speak lightly, we're talking about the otter that foolishly drives the fish it wants to eat into deep water, or the eagle that wishes to feast on the sparrow and yet succeeds only in chasing it deeper in the forest. To speak seriously, we're talking about those who use the cause of anti-communism to hide their own depraved corruption. Comrade Jianfeng has made his orders plain: our greatest objective is to win the hearts and minds of the general populace, especially in the big cities. Then, once things are stable behind the lines, we can muster our full strength and meet the Communists on the battlefield... for the final, decisive fight. We must be resolute in stamping out corruption, that's our main objective. And so, too, is the distribution of rations tomorrow. I hope, therefore, that you two will follow through and see that Comrade Jianfeng's orders are carried out. That means we don't need to inflame the situation, no sweeping, mass arrests. Chief Xu, now do you understand?"

"Yes, completely." Xu Tieying stood and turned towards Wang Puchen. "Now, about my secretary. How did the interrogation go?"

Wang coughed again, raised his teacup to his lips and drank a mouthful before answering: "I don't recall receiving orders to interrogate Secretary Sun."

"Should we still be concerned about him?"

Wang could only direct his attention towards Zeng Keda.

Comrade Sun Chaozhong, a nationally outstanding young cadre trained by the Communications Bureau, do you mean to say he is above suspicion, uncorrupted, incorruptible? He's done no more than implement policies to save the nation, quell rioting and ensure stability... executed Communist agents like Cui Zhongshi... had you and Ma Hanshan imprisoned. Now, true Communist agents have reappeared, but Inspector Zeng has assured us they will not – cannot – instigate further protests, and that we are not to arrest anyone. He's stated, moreover, that the Ministry of Defence has issued such specific orders. If that is the case, I would request

Inspector Zeng to ask Mr Chiang Ching-kuo, yes, ask him directly to confirm such orders. Or perhaps that's not necessary, perhaps Inspector Zeng is representing Mr Chiang and has letters to that effect, has been given such authority. Otherwise, we'll just have to follow the orders we've been given by the northern commanders."

A great welling of disgust rose up in Zeng Keda. At almost the same moment, the telephone rang. Lifting himself up from his chair, he strode over to the table. "Professor Zeng?" The words issuing from the receiver came as a shock to Zeng, for it was Liang Jinglun on the other end of the line. Why had Liang called? Was it to report on his conversation with Fang Buting? Or was it to ask for instructions on how to deal with the reappearance of Yan Chunming?

Of course, with his current company, Zeng could say nothing on either matter. Instead, he held the speaker close to his mouth and instructed the younger man to ring back in ten minutes, he was currently engaged. These words uttered, he replaced the receiver and walked back over to his seat. "Mr Wang," he announced, "Chief Xu has just now explained quite clearly his point of view. What is your appraisal of the situation?"

Again he coughed to delay his response and collect his thoughts, and then he pulled out a cigarette as he had done so often before. He placed the butt end on his lip, ceased coughing and answered: "I praise harmony above all else."

"And just what does that mean?"

"Please, Inspector Zeng, request instructions from Mr Chiang on whether Secretary Sun should be first released. As for Yan Chunming, a known Communist agent, wait until rations have been distributed tomorrow and then arrest him... in secret."

Zeng's voice was remarkably calm. He turned to Xu Tieying. "We've heard Mr Wang's opinion. Do you agree?"

"You didn't solicit my opinion when you arrested my secretary. Do you need it now to release him?"

"Then let us both request instructions, hmm? I'll contact Comrade Jianfeng, and you reach out to Deputy Commander Chen for advice. The most important thing is for nothing to happen tomorrow. No student protests. Agreed?"

Xie Tieying and Wang Puchen stood up. No words were

exchanged. Xie simply marched out through the door. Wang followed, but was sure to shake hands with Zeng before taking his leave. Zeng took care to accompany him to the door, and to instruct Wang, who had been standing in the hallway during the entire discussion, to escort him out. Once he was sure the two men had been ushered well beyond earshot, he shut the door and dashed over to the telephone.

Zhang Yueyin had received Old Liu's telephone call, had learnt of Yan Chunming's return to Yenching University, and had been so shocked by this unexpected development that he had little choice but to rush over to the Jingchun Botanical Gardens to speak to Liu in person.

"I've already drafted the telegram," said Liu, handing it to his superior. "Inspect it. The request for instructions is at the top. You, Comrade Yueyin, you just need to sign it and send it, as soon as possible, to Comrade Liu Yun."

There was no emotion on his face. He simply received the telegram and looked it over:

The orders with regard to Yan Chunming have not been followed <break> He has returned to university without permission <break> He is armed <break> Fearful his actions will lead to blood being spilt tomorrow <break> Ask for disciplinary actions to be taken <break> Instructions on how to deal with these developments requested <break>
  Liu <end>

"Damn," Zhang Yueyin spat coldly, his eyes fixed on Old Liu.

At first, Liu was unsure what to say, how to respond, but his stupor ended almost as quickly as it had begun: "I request this be transmitted immediately to our superiors. Please, Comrade Yueyin, put your name to it."

"I'm in charge of labourers in Peking. I'm your superior." He had never been this harsh before with Old Liu. "Such a serious act of misconduct... failure to follow orders... and now you've called me over here to... to what... sign this telegram *you've* written?"

Liu struggled to think of an explanation.

"I don't want to hear it!" Zhang Yueyin had never before forbidden a comrade to speak, especially not one like Old Liu. "Comrade, what am I to do with you? You've flouted organisational procedures before, you've bypassed the chain of command more than once. Still, you're here repeating to me that Yan Chunming has not followed orders, he's disregarded organisational discipline." He held the telegram in his hand. "I don't want an explanation. Get me a match."

Old Liu was dumbstruck. He'd not expected such harsh criticism from Zhang Yueyin. There was nothing he could say, no explanation he could give. All he could do was fetch the matches as requested, as ordered. The only hiccup was that normally he didn't smoke, and all the lights in the Botanical Gardens were electric. Where the hell was he to find one? He rummaged around the room, pulling open drawer after drawer, all to no avail. As a last resort, he pulled open the sliding door just an inch and shouted: "Little Zhang. Find me some matches, boy!"

"Yes, I'm here," came the answer. The matches followed a second or two later, pushed in through the crack in the door.

Old Liu had forgotten that his helper was a smoker. It was difficult to blame him. The unexpected severity of Zhang Yueyin's words had left his mind confused and somewhat distraught. He pulled the door shut again and handed the matches over.

"You strike it."

Old Liu complied once more without a word, striking the match against the side of the box. After it sparked and caught fire, he held it up to Zhang, who proceeded to set the telegram alight. He held on to it as the flames devoured the paper. Then, finally, when there was nothing but a small corner left, he let go and the ashes tumbled to the floor. "I don't want to hear any talk about a review, a self-criticism. Tell me directly, what your opinion is on these matters." Zhang Yueyin sat down on a nearby chair and waited for the old worker to respond.

Old Liu racked his brains before speaking. His eyes were careful to avoid Zhang Yueyin's. Finally, he spoke. "Yan Chunming is already aware of Liang Jinglun's political persuasions, nor can he keep this under wraps. Once they see each other, I'm sure Liang

Jinglun will perceive this, and as soon as he does, as soon as he knows we know, our plans are, to be frank, in the shitter. It's quite likely blood will be spilt tomorrow. To my mind, we need to adopt emergency measures now. Comrade Yan needs to leave. We can't let them see each other."

"Now? Don't you think it's already too late?"

"Perhaps." There was resentment in his voice. "But what other options do we have? We must take urgent steps to at least mitigate the disaster."

"And what emergency measures do you have in mind?" Zhang Yueyin's tone made clear the seriousness with which he was asking this question. "Are these measures to be taken against our enemies, or our own comrades?"

Old Liu was taken aback and remained silent for a moment. Zhang's words had so perfectly hit the mark, had exposed Liu's own plans to take armed action that he couldn't think of anything to say. Nor did Zhang say more. Instead, he reached into his bag and pulled out a pen and paper. Old Liu just stood and watched the other man, his eyes growing wider and wider. Using his left hand, Zhang began to write. Quickly and with purpose. On finishing, he passed it to Liu. He'd written a letter, not just a telegram. As he read the words, Old Liu's eyes opened even wider. His hands gripped the paper.

Comrade Liang Jinglun,
Comrade Yan Chunming has openly violated organisational decisions, and he has returned to the university without permission. Moreover, he is armed. We believe he's under the misguided assumption that he is acting out of some extreme form of personal heroism. He is not. His behaviour is a direct violation of the spirit of the Central Committee's Sixth of July Instruction. I am giving you specific orders to act on our behalf. Stability must be maintained. Avoid any unnecessary bloodshed at all costs. This letter is to be shown to Comrade Yan Chunming. It orders him to hand over his weapon and cease any and all actions. Ensure Comrade Yan's safety.

Old Liu was stunned, pondering over the implications of this letter. Zhang Yueyin had already taken the paper back from him and placed it in an envelope. "On the eve of our final battle, the next step is to seize control of the city. There're a thousand things to do. We need men, good men we can trust. Comrade Cui Zhongshi has already made the ultimate sacrifice. We've lost a remarkably talented man who understood economics. We can't lose Comrade Chunming. At present, the only appropriate measure open to us is to make sure Liang Jinglun believes that we don't suspect him. In the interests of having Liang Jinglun continue to play both sides, Yan Chunming cannot be arrested."

Zhang handed the envelope to Liu. His face was serious, solemn. Taking receipt of it, Old Liu's mind carried him off to thoughts of Zhuge Liang and the brocade pouch he had long ago given to General Zhao Zilong.

"Don't delay. Tell your assistant, Zhang, to head over to the university library straight away. He must ensure the students fall in line under Liang Jinglun. Once confirmed, he's to leave."

"Sir, yes sir! Zhhaaannnggg!"

CHAPTER 2

It was past ten o'clock at night. The moon was high in the sky, and the streets were bathed in an electric glow. After his telephone conversation with Zeng Keda, Liang Jinglun refused in no uncertain terms to be accompanied by any of the students from the Chiang Kai-shek Student Society who had been waiting outside the Foreign Languages Bookstore. He would go to the library on his own. He marched off determined, but as he passed through the corridor that cut through the Chinese-style building on the way to the library, he stopped to take in the grassy lawns that stretched on either side of the building. Liang enjoyed quiet time by himself to just observe his surroundings. He was fond of loitering among buildings and green spaces, doing nothing other than watching his environs. These varieties of grass had been recommended by Harvard and they were nurtured like those in the US, trimmed so that they looked more like a green rug that you could walk softly over, lie down upon, bathe in the sunlight or sit in the shadow of a tree to read. If you became thirsty, the sprinklers deployed to feed the lawn would serve equally well in quenching your thirst. Each time he strolled along these grounds, he couldn't help but feel transported back to his days as an exchange student at Harvard. There would be a yearning in his heart to return there. When in the future would China be like this? he would wonder.

But standing here on this night, in the dark, his mood changed.

It was impossible to get rid of the sound of Zeng Keda's voice over the telephone, and the instructions he gave him. "Allow Fang Meng'ao to learn political loyalty. You must join forces to implement our plan, to see the Peacocks take flight. This was of greatest importance to Comrade Jianfeng. Have faith in the organisation, trust Comrade Jianfeng. If Fang Buting knows, we'll start an investigation immediately and ensure he doesn't talk. As for whether the Communist Party knows your true colours, you must go and meet Yan Chunming, observe his reaction. Then you'll be able to ascertain if they know or not. Time is of the essence. We must be resolute."

He continued on his way to the Chinese-style building and the library within it. Shadowy forms seemed to be lurking behind the trees that bordered the further reaches of the lawns. Students, he surmised. Finally, they came into the clear and walked towards him. One group were members of the Communist Student Federation, and under normal circumstances, he would never suspect that they knew he belonged to the Iron and Blood Congress. On the other side, members of the Kuomintang Student Federation appeared. Again, he wouldn't dream they knew of his Communist Party allegiances. But these were not normal times. Liang suspected that both groups knew he was playing both sides, and so he paid neither any attention whatsoever. His only response to their appearance was to hurry his pace.

Seeing his reaction, the students called out after him: "Mr Liang!" A girl's words carried forcefully on the air, louder and clearer than any megaphone they could imagine.

Liang Jinglun trembled and his brow knitted. Fang Meng'ao had simply greeted him, Fang Buting had threatened him directly, but now, at this moment, Xie Mulan's high-pitched voice froze him to the spot.

In what seemed like a great swirling of wind, Xie Mulan bounded up alongside him. "What... who called you here?" he asked in a voice not much more than a whisper. His eyes avoided hers.

"Uncle He." She matched the pitch of his voice, but it was difficult for her to disguise her excitement at finding him.

Liang finally allowed himself to look at her.

Mulan, however, bowed her head, choosing not to meet his

gaze. Her voice was still low, but rapid. "I'm not supposed to see you. At least, that's what most of them think. But Uncle He got angry at this and told me to find you."

Worry and anxiety tore at Liang's heart. But he had to hide this from her. "Then go and wait with the other students. You can't... no... you can't stay with me."

He turned away, but Xie Mulan tugged hard on his sleeve. Liang looked around, no longer able to disguise the seriousness in his eyes.

This time, Mulan met his stare, her own eyes confident, sure. She didn't say anything at first, but Liang Jinglun soon felt her push something into his hand. A letter. Then she moved close and whispered into his ear: "It's from the General Academic Committee. It's their letter." And just like that, her tone changed. She now acted like a courier dispatched by the higher-ups. "Read it, straight away."

He was fairly close to the main gate. The lights there would be just sufficient to read the letter. He scanned the area for anyone else. No one drew near. Liang Jinglun shifted his attention. He couldn't be concerned with Mulan or the manner in which she was acting. He opened the envelope and pulled out the letter – orders from Zhang Yueyin!

"The person who gave you this?" He'd never looked at Mulan the way he did now.

"Gone..."

"Someone known to you?"

The excitement she'd felt before had diminished. She shook her head. "N... no."

Liang Jinglun adjusted his demeanour, softening a little. His voice was low: "What did he say?"

"He just told me it was from the General Academic Committee, and that I needed to give it to you right away."

Liang chuckled quietly, and then slipped the letter inside his jacket. "It's certainly not from them. Go on into the library. Read something. There's nothing more to say right now."

Liang Jinglun started to walk away. Mulan remained where she was, her heart beating rapidly, unevenly. Moments passed and slowly she began to regain her composure. The lights shining from the main gate made her eyes sparkle. She was sure. The letter had come from the General Academic Committee. A second later, she strode through the gate herself in the same direction as Liang Jinglun. Some distance behind her, the students who had walked out from beyond the trees watched her shadow disappear, and then they followed after. She felt their eyes on her, but she wasn't afraid. Only a sense of pride welled up inside her.

"Here to report, sir!" Little Zhang had completed his task beautifully, had returned to the Botanical Gardens, and was now finding it somewhat difficult to contain his excitement. "I gave the letter to a student, a female student. She's Fang Buting's niece, cousin to the Kuomintang Auditor General. I handed it to her, and then I observed her passing it on to Liang Jinglun. It was all by the numbers, Comrade Liu… sir."

"I should execute you now, you fool!"

The ferocity of Old Liu's response caused a shiver to run up his assistant's spine. A look of terror came over him.

Zhang Yueyin's brows furrowed. "Comrade Liu, don't say another word."

It took great effort, but Old Liu swallowed down the venom that had rushed up into his mouth. Urging himself to calm down, he gave Zhang further instructions: "Go to the south courtyard, give the pistol to Cui. You're to remain there, confined to quarters as it were, until I arrive."

Little Zhang was still at a loss, so surprised had he been at Old Liu's reaction.

"Go!"

"Sir!" Still dazed, Little Zhang departed.

"He's just been transferred here, yes?" Zhang Yueyin still stared at Old Liu, blaming himself for the impatience shown by the other man.

"Yes. He was sent to help with the rather monumental task at hand, specially dispatched from the East China Field Army. They're good fighters, of course, but they don't know how to deal with… the more cultured types. Fuck, he's ended up causing more trouble than anything else." Old Liu now directed his full attention to

Zhang Yueyin: "Contact Comrade Liuyun. Report what's happened, request he be disciplined. That'd be the proactive thing to do."

Zhang Yueyin picked up the bag that had been on the table. "Reports, reviews, that's my business, not yours. The comrades dispatched by the organisation from the East China Field Army can learn, they need to be introduced to the complexity of Peking's current situation, brought up to speed. No more assignments for the time being."

"All right, understood." There was really nothing else Liu could say. He'd been put in his place, as it were. Nothing left to do but escort Zhang Yueyin to the door.

"Understand this as well, I mean it. We don't have the authority to execute a member of the East China Field Army, even if we wanted to."

Liu smiled, embarrassed. "I know. What I said, it was in a moment of anger. That's all."

"That may be true, but such talk will have to go into your file."

"I accept your criticism."

"It's not a criticism." And with those words, he left.

In the rare books collection room, Yan Chunming was busy tidying up, placing books in the filing cabinet in their proper places. "I've criticised you?" He turned his head at hearing these words and his eyes fell on Liang Jinglun, who was staring at him intently. Each time Liang saw Yan like this, he couldn't help but feel disappointed. The glasses he wore, with their thick lenses, obscured his eyes; his face, too, resembled glass, never showing any signs of emotion. "Spit it out. Tell me what's on your mind." Liang Jinglun acted as though he had not received instructions. He wanted to sound things out for himself, get a feel for what was on the other man's mind.

"Peking University, Tsinghua, Peking Normal, the other schools, too, they all have their designated places to distribute rations. Go on, go to all of them tomorrow. How will they manage them, how will they control what's going on?"

"The Nationalists made those plans, as the higher-ups well know. Have you received any other specific orders?"

"My orders were that I return, work with you. And take advantage of the fact that Yenching has the backing of the Americans. And should conflict arise, then we would act, confront the Kuomintang authorities directly. And at all costs, other institutions are not to be implicated."

"Confront them how, exactly? And what of the student federations?"

"Did I say we were to sacrifice the student federations? Now listen." Yan Chunming walked around his desk and returned to his seat. His eyes were unflinching as he looked at Liang Jinglun on the other side of the table. "I said *we* would confront the Kuomintang authorities. I'm not talking about the students, I mean you and me, the two of us. We can give them our lives if necessary, which should be enough to prevent any more bloodshed. Comrade Liang, our Communist revolution, the liberation of the masses, our independence, this is the final battle, the last stage. And on that battlefield, there are countless revolutionary comrades sacrificing their lives every day. Death comes to all of us, it's one inescapable fate. And that death, that sacrifice, it can either be the most important thing, or it can mean nothing whatsoever. Well, I think that we, too, us intellectuals, our underground vanguard, we should be prepared to take the same test as every other party member."

Liang Jinglun had not expected to hear Yan speak this way. His words were strange. They didn't seem to match the man. "This is… what you're talking about… you've got a martyr complex." Liang began to believe what had been written on the paper Mulan had given him. "The party orders are what they are. And they're what I obey."

"Then be prepared for what will happen. Now, go and talk to the student federations, each of them. Let them know, but remember, talk to them separately. Don't muddle things up. Whatever happens tomorrow, we can't have anyone expose themselves." Yan Chunming stood and extended his hand to shake on it. Liang Jinglun complied and the two men clasped. As they did so, however, Yan froze, seemingly dazed. Liang would not let go.

Liang Jinglun maintained his tight hold of Yan's hand. "Comrade Chunming, has it occurred to you, me and you, we're already on the cusp of bloodshed? Do you think the student federations will be rational, reasonable? Do you really think we will avoid confrontation?"

Yan Chunming was startled at Liang's grip, ultimately realising there was nothing else to do but strengthen his own hold. "We're both professors here at Yenching. If things do deteriorate, if the situation becomes extreme, then the Americans will come and the Kuomintang won't dare to have anyone killed. Understand? Now go."

Liang Jinglun finally released his hand, but he did not depart. Instead, he sat down. "Comrade Yan Chunming, please give me the gun you took."

"What?" Yan Chunming was alarmed by Liang's words.

"I'm here representing the senior leadership. You must hand over the pistol. Immediately."

Yan Chunming remained stunned, unable to say or do anything. Without saying anything himself, Liang pulled out the letter he'd been given and handed it to Yan. He received it robotically, his eyes unmoving, fixed on Liang's face.

"Comrade Yan Chunming, please read. But do so quickly."

Yan pulled his spectacles down from his eyes and brought the letter close. Liang watched as the words had their effect, transforming the man's face. The distortion was expected, normal. The blankness that followed seemed expected, too. Normal. Although the handwriting was unfamiliar, Yan Chunming knew for certain whence the letter came. Old Liu was the only person who knew about the gun; it was his, after all. Yan knew then, too, that his actions had startled Liu's superiors in the Ministry of Labour, but he never suspected for a moment that his superiors would decide to rein him in with such a letter. Liu had tried to take the weapon back already and had failed. Was he now to turn it over to Liang Jinglun? It felt as though both his heart and mind were being tossed about by a vicious ocean storm.

"I... I need... want to explain things to the higher-ups." As soon as he said the words, he knew he would never be permitted to do so.

"Comrade Chunming, you should understand something, right

now. Our task is not to question, but to obey the orders we've been given. That means you need to give me the gun. And then you're to wait here. Once new orders arrive, I will relay them to you."

Yan Chunming's hand trembled. Then he pushed his glasses back up his nose and reached towards the desk and the bag that lay there. Lifting out his keys, he walked over to the locked cabinet. Liang's eyes followed him intently. As the lock clicked, Liang moved forward to receive the pistol. He looked it over for a minute and then put it back. "Let's leave it here. Keys?"

Yan Chunming handed Liang the keys. Quickly, Liang locked the cabinet once again and proceeded to remove the one specific key to the lock. After that, he handed the ring back to Yan. "Comrade Chunming, I do my utmost to see that our orders are carried out, which means making sure that nothing happens tomorrow. If that goes to plan, I shall, as representative of our academic committee, report to our higher-ups and see that you're transferred. Under your leadership here at Yenching University, we've instilled the spirit of revolutionary sacrifice. We've not inculcated a selfish desire for martyrdom."

It was Liang Jinglun's turn to extend his hand. Yan Chunming returned the gesture but trembled slightly as he did so.

This was all as it should be. Laing Jinglun tried his best to lighten the mood. "Trust in the party, have faith in me. And take care of your own person. Be safe." He placed the key into his pocket and turned to leave.

As the door was pulled closed from the outside, Yan Chunming reached for the telephone. He dialled a number, held the receiver close to his ear, but all he heard was the engaged signal.

Only the light over the guardhouse was illuminated; the remainder of the barracks was dark. It had been that way since earlier in the evening when, after the captain had returned, he'd ordered the larger, tungsten-iodine floodlights to be shut down. With no artificial lights, the barracks took on the hue of the moon. Chen Changwu had ordered nine soldiers from the Youth Aviation Brigade to stand to the left of the main gate. Shao Yuangang had ordered another nine to stand to the right. Just beyond the entrance, the lights of the motorcade shone brightly. The younger soldiers standing guard all carried rifles.

Chen Changwu leaned close to Guo Jinyang and said: "The rations have arrived. I'll inform the captain."

"Good."

Chen walked briskly into the inner rooms of the barracks.

"Attention!" the lead guard roared from beyond the gate. His subordinates responded immediately, their weapons at the ready, their legs slamming together in unison.

The first vehicle to approach was a large truck converted into a troop carrier. The rear was filled with young soldiers, each with live rounds in their rifles. The troop commander sat in front and saluted as the vehicle drove past. But their speed did not drop; the vehicle simply motored straight inside. Guo Jinyang, Shao Yuangang and the soldiers from the flight brigade standing on either side of the gate conformed to military protocol and returned the gesture. This was followed in turn by the troops in the truck bed, all of them saluting as they passed each other.

The second vehicle to enter the barracks carried the rations. Guo Jinyang was startled on seeing it, and then he smiled and chuckled to himself. There was Section Chief Li standing on the running board, his hand holding tight to the railing inside the truck, his face travel-worn and weary looking. All in the name of the party, the nation! The third truck followed, again carrying rations, this time with Section Chief Wang hanging on in the same manner as Li. Unfortunately for Wang, the abundant girth of his midsection made the pose much more difficult to pull off, and he seemed close to tumbling down onto the ground. Needless to say, he didn't convey quite the same image of determination as Section Chief Li.

Vehicle after vehicle motored past, all of them stock full of rations. Finally, the last truck pulled through the gate. This one, like the first, was filled with eager-faced young soldiers. In the cab, however, sat Xie Peidong.

Fang Meng'ao watched the glare of the vehicle lights. As the first truck pulled to a stop, the troops riding in the back pushed open the rear guard and leapt down. One of the young men waved, and the driver stepped on the accelerator, manoeuvring the truck further into the base. The commanding soldier strode up to Fang Meng'ao and saluted. "Sir, Captain Fang, here to report, sir. The first batch of rations has been delivered, sir!"

"Hard work, eh soldier?" Fang Meng'ao did not return the salutation but rather offered his hand to shake. A handshake was much more intimate than a salute, and the young man extended his hand readily, thrilled by the gesture. As they clasped hands, however, he noticed Fang Meng'ao's brow wrinkle, his eyes squint and stare at something behind him. The soldier turned to see what it was and saw the second convoy vehicle stop, bottlenecking the remaining trucks behind it. Chief Li was still perched alongside the driver's cab door. Once he saw that Fang Meng'ao had seen him, he hopped down and forced himself to smile. "Captain Fang…"

"You're holding things up." Fang's voice was curt and cut Chief Li off.

"Eh?" Surprised, Li turned and saw what had caused Captain Fang to greet him so coldly. "Oh," he mumbled under his breath before running over to the driver's window. "You dumb bastard! Who told you to stop here? Move it, come on. Further in you damn fool!"

It was clear Section Chief Li had given the order to stop where the truck had, but now he cursed the driver to hide his own incompetence. The driver, despite being a civilian, knew the man's character and the futility of saying anything in response. He simply shifted gears and angled the vehicle further into the barracks courtyard. The third truck rumbled in after. Section Chief Wang, still hanging on precariously, leapt down, but unlike Li, he did not stroll over to Fang Meng'ao. He instead planted his feet firmly on the ground and remained next to the transport.

The passage clear, the vehicles proceeded in one after the other. Chief Li remained restive, barking orders and waving his hands like a traffic cop. Despite the scene a moment ago with Captain Fang, Li excelled at directing the vehicles to where they should go, finally lining them up in neat formation, each truck parked next to another. Once complete, he walked confidently over to his superiors. As he did, he passed by Chief Wang and whispered: "You've not made your report yet?" He smiled and continued to walk towards Fang Meng'ao. Wang seemed to grasp the meaning of Li's words and hurried after him. Watching the scene unfold, Chen Changwu and Guo Jinyang laughed to themselves. They were fully aware of how adept Section Chief Li was at stirring up trouble.

"Lights!" Chen shouted towards the guardhouse.

The floodlights positioned at each corner of the barracks walls came alive once more, bathing the grounds in artificial daylight. The remaining escort troops jumped down from their vehicles, marched to the walls and stood at guard. Twenty inspectors in turn strode over towards the stores of rations, and they, along with the civilian representatives, began the requisite check-marking of forms.

"Report for Captain Fang." Under the floodlights, Section Chief Li's face came into full view, matching the uncouthness of his voice. Standing in front of Fang, he delivered his report: "Sir, captain sir, a thousand tonnes of rations have been transferred. This batch weighs a hundred tonnes. Please have the inspectors verify the amount, then we can deliver it to the distribution sites. Please clarify, Captain, sir, there are still nine more deliveries. Should all of them be transported here first for inspection?"

"Your men have been responsible for transporting these thousand tonnes?" Fang Meng'ao had already seen Xie Peidong alight from the last vehicle of the convoy.

It took a minute for Li to muster his thoughts before replying: "Sir, yes sir. We brought the rations all the way from Tianjin, sir. We didn't stop, sir."

"And your paperwork?"

Li paused for a moment before driving his hands into his pockets. Startled by what he found, or rather what he didn't, he spun around. That's when he noticed Chief Wang was still some distance behind him. "Hey," he called out, "the paperwork…"

"These are rations transferred from the Peking branch. Why would we have the paperwork?"

Under his breath, Li cursed the other man. Then he slapped his forehead as though realising his error. "Ah, I'm all mixed up. Assistant Manager Xie should know, yes?" No sooner had he tried to deflect responsibility to someone else, Xie Peidong walked up to them. "Ah, and here he is now, Mr Xie. Captain Fang would like to see the paperwork."

Xie Peidong continued his approach, but he did not immediately respond.

Turning to the young soldier who had been standing nearby, Fang directed him to take charge of security instead of loitering too close to him. Saluting quickly, the soldier walked off. Xie Peidong had already drawn close by the time the young man left, but Fang seemed not to care, for he started to walk into the barracks offices. Xie Peidong followed.

―――

The floodlights beyond radiated into Fang Meng'ao's room, bathing it in an artificial glow just sufficient for him to see the man who had stepped in soon after he had. Since what lay outside was even more easily seen, Fang Meng'ao refrained from turning on the light. Pointing to a chair, he gestured for Xie Peidong to sit down. Xie had never been inside Fang's room before and so he couldn't help but look it up and down before sitting. Registering everything he saw, Xie finally directed his gaze towards Fang.

His guest seated, Fang Meng'ao pulled another chair from against one of the walls and positioned it facing Xie Peidong. From where he sat, he could see the door to the building, as well as the windows on either side.

"Here's the paperwork, a thousand tonnes in total." Xie passed the file to Fang.

"How will it be distributed?"

"Students from each university in Peking, plus those from the northeast, that's fifteen thousand in all, each will receive seven and a half kilos. Each professor will get double that. Family members will be given the same amount as the students."

"And the city's residents?" Fang Meng'ao laid the papers on the table next to him. "There are hundreds of thousands of common people in the city. Are we not bothering with them at all?"

"The residents of Peking already received seven and a half kilos per person last month. They have to wait until the fifteenth. After that, there'll be more rations available for them."

"That's only three days from now. Will another shipment of that size be ready?"

"That's what they're worried about. The American relief vessel is stuck in Shanghai, the Nanking government is pressuring the Central Bank to raise the funds, and hopefully by tomorrow there'll be three and a half million US dollars ready to be paid into the Chinese branch of the American Commercial Bank and Trust... as compensation."

Fang Meng'ao rarely had occasion to sigh as long and as loudly as he did at hearing this information, but he held his tongue, and instead raised himself up from his chair and walked over to the window. He saw how close the building was to the barracks' drill grounds. He saw, too, under the great floodlights Guo Jinyang, who was standing next to the field. Guo's presence ensured that his current discussion with Xie Peidong was not being eavesdropped upon. A few moments later and he returned to his chair. "You and me, two Communist agents, here doing the bidding of the Kuomintang. Is that what we're doing?"

"Yes," said Xie Peidong, "before, it was me and Comrade Zhongshi. We were in the same boat in which you now find yourself... and he said the same thing."

Fang Meng'ao let his head droop, then turned to look out the window once more.

"Comrade Cui Zhongshi had raised this with the upper levels of the party. He'd hoped we'd be sent to work for the regional bank directly. I regret not taking his argument to the higher-ups, even if there's little point. Besides, he was of more use in the Peking branch than anywhere else. No one else could do what he did."

Fang Meng'ao turned to stare at Xie Peidong again. "And did this include getting me involved?"

"Yes, it did. If he were to depart, I would still at least have you to contact. Once he was exposed, I was the only one who could carry on the work he'd been doing... to save myself. Of course, I didn't want him to go, I needed him in front, to take the bullet instead of me."

Fang Meng'ao narrowed his eyes. Xie Peidong seemed somewhat vacant, as though he wasn't really there. Finally, Fang opened his mouth: "This is not what I meant."

"It doesn't really matter what you meant. Things are what they are. You know, most believe it's just the Communists battling the Nationalists, a fight for control over China. But tell me, has anyone ever really thought about what happens after, about where we're all going to sit? The higher-ups exaggerate my importance. Deputy Chairman Zhou has already told me this, that once the New China is established that I should take up the position of deputy head of the People's Bank. That's a position higher than what your father now holds."

"That's not how I look at you." Fang Meng'ao knew that this man sitting in front of him, his uncle, was being ironic, deliberately mocking himself. "If you were to have become an official, you wouldn't have been able to return to the party in 1927."

There was finally a glimmer of light in Xie Peidong's eyes, a look of gratification. He shifted the chair a little closer. "What did you say to Liang Jinglun today?"

"I asked if he was a Communist."

"And what did he say?"

"He admitted it."

"He did!"

"Well, he didn't admit it himself. Zeng Keda arrived, and he put all the cards on the table. He told me about Liang's dual affiliations, his work for the Communists and for the Iron and Blood Congress. Tell me... this's Liu Lanzhi."

Xie Peidong quickly thought everything over and then blurted out: "They aim to shift things ahead and print the Nationalist currency earlier than planned. Do you know what kind of situation you're in?"

"I know some of it. Jiao Zhongqing and Liu Lanzhi must still be in a pickle themselves. Liang Jinglun and I were both trying to push back against this embrasure, this hole in the wall..."

Xie Peidong was surprised to hear Fang Meng'ao talk like this. He was impressed and couldn't help but let his eyes show it. Unfortunately, the feeling was fleeting as the heaviness he'd felt before reclaimed him. "Would you like to know what the party hopes you'll do?"

"Uncle Cui has already sacrificed himself. I suppose I could be next, or perhaps you. If I see him, I guess I'd have to talk things over."

"That's not what the party hopes," said Xie Peidong, growing serious. "You don't want to hear the orders Deputy Chairman Zhou gave himself?"

Fang Meng'ao trembled a little before slowly sitting down.

"Let me pass on the gist of things." Xie also stood. "The Kuomintang's so-called efforts to stamp out internal corruption, their push for currency reforms, they're attempts to shore up the economies of the areas they control, especially where things have already collapsed… they're trying to rebuild the public's trust in their government, which is why we've launched our final push across each and every battleground. The central authorities believe that no matter what the Kuomintang tries, their fate has already been sealed, that there's no stopping the birth of the New China. The Nationalist-held cities today will be the heart of industry in the New China, and the residents of those cities will be the people who establish our new nation. Thus, in order to protect the industrial base of the cities, and the people in them, we've had to infiltrate the Kuomintang itself. That's why we're here, comrade, that's why we have to participate in seeing through these so-called currency reforms. We can't clash with what they're planning, we must co-operate, bide our time and quietly wait for the arrival of new instructions from our superiors."

"But… am I capable of seeing these things through?"

"Of course you are."

"Should we transport military supplies?" It was clear to Fang that Xie Peidong had not thought of this question. "Central Command has agreed to let me take charge of the flight brigade, to transport the people's belongings, but if open conflict breaks out, my orders will be to help General Fu Zuoyi in the transportation of fifty thousand men and supplies. Tell me, when this happens, will Deputy Chairman Zhou still have Chairman Mao's support?"

"I've… I've not received any orders on this matter." Xie Peidong was full of admiration for Fang Meng'ao for having brought up this problem. "But according to my knowledge of the two men, I'm sure they've already thought of this, have already considered it thoroughly. That said, I will report directly back to them, bring to their attention the issues you've raised, as well as your own point of view."

"Will you be able to tell them everything?"

"We all swore the oath once we joined the party, loyalty to it above all else."

"Then I would like to give you all, including Deputy Chairman Zhou, my particular opinion. Uncle Cui clearly demonstrated his loyalty to the party. What he did was sincere and for the party. Allow me to show my respect for what he's done. But over the two years that he helped train me, kept your identity concealed, and then, when death was set to claim him, he swore he was not a Communist, and nor was I. Well, I know he did that to protect me. Have you protected me just so that you could use me, get me to fly your planes into the liberated areas?"

Xie Peidong's eyes grew wide.

"In the first year of the War of Resistance, the Air Force didn't have a single plane. The Eighth Route Army, the New Fourth Army had never even had planes before, they'd only ever fought the Japanese on land, as so many soldiers had done before. After Chennault formed the Flying Tigers in 1941, that's when the Pacific theatre of World War Two truly erupted, and we had planes of our own. We were good, too, beautiful fighters streaking through the sky. We knew what we were fighting for then, to save our people. But after we won, so many people lost their way, like me... Before I came to Peking, I had a wingman. He went by the nickname 'The Eagle', he fought the Japanese Zeros, had flown over the Hump. There was never any ambiguity about what he was doing. Afterwards he got involved in illicit trade, as did the whole Kuomintang Air Force. I had planned to save him, get him out, but by the time I tried, it was already too late. I want you to report all of this to Deputy Chairman Zhou. It's not just about the planes, it's about the men who fly them, they're the key. Chiang Ching-kuo had seen this. Now you're taking risks in using me, making me take those risks. Do you think the party can put their faith in me... just a little more than they have?"

"As a party representative, as a representative for Deputy Chairman Zhou, I can assure you it does. The party has complete confidence in you."

"This is not necessary. You perhaps trust me to serve the people, but you've never shown belief in my ability, in my judgment. You're an important person, a member of the inner circle. Can I ask you something? The final push against the Kuomintang... on how many fronts will that push be launched?"

By now Xie Peidong understood clearly Fang Meng'ao's mood. His answer was as sincere as it could be: "The party would like to hear your opinion on these matters."

"At the Hangzhou airbase, I'm the lead instructor. Now let me tell you, the commander of the Kuomintang Air Force has set a key subject to study, to analyse the Communist plans for their final assault. In forty-six, the administrators of the school, including the vice-chancellor, presented their analysis to their superiors. They said the attack would be in the northwest, the target Yan'an. I was the only one who said something different, in class. I told the students it wouldn't be Yan'an, it wouldn't be in the northwest at all, but rather it'd be elsewhere, a three-pronged attack."

"And those three fronts?"

"One line of attack would be launched in the southeast, another in the northeast and the third in the north itself. One more thing. At the time, Uncle Cui was still grooming me. As soon as I presented this analysis, the vice-chancellor cancelled my classes, believing that I was talking nothing but nonsense. In June of this year, I was unwilling to bomb Kaifeng, and for that they wanted to court martial me, but once Chiang Ching-kuo saw my file, yeah, it was perhaps then, when he saw my analysis, well, they were given new life... and great importance... along with me. It certainly wasn't only because my father managed the Peking branch. They wanted to use me to get at him. The Kuomintang can use all its power to fight us for influence over the young, for control of talented individuals, but the only person who'll remain is Chiang Ching-kuo."

Xie Peidong remained silent for a while, mulling over what Fang Meng'ao had said. Once he'd collected his thoughts, his voice became quiet. "Tell me some more about your analysis of this three-pronged assault, especially where it's being launched in the north. If it involves in any way how you've been deployed, I need to report it straight away."

"In the northeast, the campaign should be launched in Liaoshen. Down south, the target should be Xubeng. I can't be certain about the north, but I reckon it's Pingjin. The most important thing about the northern campaign is location. Pingjin matches well with Liaoshen, and so does Xubeng in the south. If the party decided to strike first in the northeast, or in the south, then Deputy Chairman Zhou, Chairman Mao, too, will agree that I should help Fu Zuoyi in his efforts to transport people's goods out of the conflict zone and relocate them safely to Pingjin. And there they'll stay, unable to leave, unable to head south."

A look of astonishment and consternation flashed across Xie Peidong's face, but then he smiled and sighed. "I think the party – no, that's not right, not the party, me – I don't think I've got to know you well enough. In fact, I'm sure I haven't. Tell me, why didn't you share any of this with Comrade Cui?"

"Uncle Cui didn't only speak to me about faith in the party, he also told me to keep things concealed. Nor did he talk to me about any concrete plans or missions. So how could I?"

"I'll take responsibility for that. Now, however, I need to inform my superiors of what you've just told me. Deputy Chairman Zhou will surely give us further instructions… and an answer to you specifically." Xie stood up from his chair and exhaled slowly. "I've no other orders to pass on. From now on, you're tasked with seeing through Chiang Ching-kuo's plans. As indispensable as you are to us, the same is true for your position in the Iron and Blood Congress. They can't do without you either."

"So, you'd rather not talk about Xiaoyu and Mulan?" As he said these words, Fang Meng'ao suddenly felt that Xie Peidong was as pitiable as Uncle Cui.

Slowly, Xie turned to look at Fang. "I'll find the opportunity to speak to her and make her listen to you. As for Mulan, she's not a party member, so it can't show any concern for her. Nor can I."

"And what about me?"

Xie Peidong sighed again. "Your father is looking after her."

"Him? How?"

"I'd better explain. Before I came here, your father had already gone looking for Liang Jinglun. He figured out Liang was a double agent working against the party. He also suspected Chiang Ching-kuo had personally seen to his placement near Vice-Chancellor He."

Fang Meng'ao was alarmed by the revelation and looked towards the window to collect his thoughts. He pulled out a cigarette and lighter, intent on having a smoke to settle his conflicted heart. He flicked up the lighter lid and the flame burst to life. But no sooner had he done this than he closed the lid again. He put the cigarette back in its pack. "My dad is something else, isn't he? Shrewd old man. But he can't take on the Kuomintang by himself. He saved Uncle Cui before, even made sure Xie Tieying's secretary was protected. He's no match for Liang Jinglun, though, nor the Iron and Blood Congress."

Xie gave a small laugh. "You understand him... certainly better than anyone else."

Fang turned away from the window, put the lighter and pack of cigarettes inside his pocket, and picked up the paperwork that still lay on the table. "Give this to the civilian authorities. Get them to take hold of the rations, then get back to see my dad. If all the cards are on the table, Liang Jinglun is for sure waiting to talk things over with you. Tell him not to get involved with anything I'm doing, nor should he be concerned about Mulan and Mengwei. At all costs, there should be no conflict with the Iron and Blood Congress. There's nothing he can do about any of this, nor can he fight against it. All he can do, all he has to do, is trust you."

Fang Meng'ao's sincerity caused a pang of regret to well up in Xie Peidong. "Yes, it's been nearly twenty years. He's always trusted me. To be honest, if you were to ask what kind of man I feel most sorry for in this life, it's a man like your father. But thoughts like these go against the principles of the party, they're not to be shared."

Fang Meng'ao wanted to offer a comforting smile, but his face would not obey. "Uncle, there's no need for thoughts like these. You're an extraordinary man, Uncle, and a great asset to the party, a true believer. I always listened to Uncle Cui. Now I'll listen to you."

"To the party." Xie avoided the younger man's face as he said these words, then turned to leave. "I'm off."

"Zeng Keda ought to be here." Fang's eyes were trained on the window. "I'll see you out."

Walking behind the older man, he couldn't say why, but his mind suddenly recalled Zhu Ziqing's famous essay *The Retreating Figure*. But was the figure he saw departing that of the party or his father? It didn't matter. In times like these, blood relations were of little concern.

As expected, Zeng Keda did show up. He was standing by the gates of the barracks watching the convoy trucks being unloaded.

"Why didn't you tell me Inspector Zeng had arrived?" Fang Meng'ao's attention was on the young barrack's commander.

Zeng smiled and explained: "I told him not to tell you. I guess you've been working hard, eh, Mr Xie?"

"Yes, as expected."

"Will you be able to get the other nine hundred tonnes sorted tonight?"

"The best we can hope for is to get the vehicles here."

"I'd say don't bother with that. Why not just send the already loaded trucks on to where they need to be? You don't need to handle all the details yourself. After all, you're no spring chicken any more. You should go back and rest. Oh, and if you get the chance, please pass along my gratitude to Fang Buting. On behalf of the Ministry of Defence's inspection team, I thank him for his service."

"He makes a good point. Perhaps you should return." Fang Meng'ao met Xie Peidong's eyes.

Zeng's meaning matched what Fang Meng'ao had said only a few minutes before, but that didn't stop Xie Peidong from growing ever more certain that Fang had some sort of sixth sense. He nodded his head. "Well then, since there is seemingly this concern for my personal health, I'll pass the matter of the distribution of rations on to you two, and do as Inspector Zeng suggests."

Turning to the barrack's commander, Zeng ordered him to take his own vehicle to escort Xie Peidong home. The young soldier complied immediately and walked over to Zeng's jeep that was parked near the gate. Holding the door open for Xie Peidong, the commander saluted once Xie was seated, then jumped in behind the wheel and motored away.

"There's something I need to discuss with you." Zeng's words to Fang Meng'ao came shortly after Xie's departure, and the two men entered the same building in which Fang and Xie had just spent time discussing the present situation.

Once in the building, Zeng Keda turned to face Fang Meng'ao. "A meeting needs to be called," he announced. "Tomorrow, the rations will be distributed. Chen Jicheng and Xu Tieying intend to arrest Communist agents."

"Should I play along, to further demonstrate I'm not a Communist?"

"That's not what I'm getting at. I've just received information that the party reps in Peking have made Liang Jinglun responsible for tomorrow. He's been ordered to keep control of the situation. If Chen Jicheng and Xu Tieying really do intend to arrest anyone tomorrow, the first person taken into custody will be Liang Jinglun."

"Does the party have its doubts about Liang?"

"There's no way to determine this. It might just be because of Liang Jinglun's connection to He Qicang, or to John Leighton Stuart. The Ministry of Labour is under the direct control of Zhou Enlai, and his handling of things has always been to make sure if you're there, then so am I, and vice versa. Besides Comrade Jianfeng, no one else can hope for anything else. Unfortunately, there are still so many people asking for favours. The currency reforms must be implemented without delay. We're trying to maintain stability, while all they want is chaos."

"What does Mr Chiang think? Does he agree with their plans to make these arrests?"

Zeng Keda laughed bitterly. "Who dare disagree with the order to arrest Communists? The important thing is that tomorrow is just not the right time."

"Then how can we prevent them from doing so?"

"Nothing, aside from making sure the students don't cause a

59

ruckus. Another thing, Xu Tieying has informed the authorities and the president of his doubts concerning the arrest of his secretary. He's called into question the apprehension of him while the Communists have been left unmolested. He says he just doesn't understand it."

It was Fang's turn to laugh. "Ah, so he's targeting me directly. When they executed Uncle Cui, they said he was a Communist. Afterwards, when he was confronted about it, Xu Tieying claimed that Cui wasn't Red, but that was just their way to keep concealed their own corruption, by killing anyone who might know about it. Right now, the only two men who know anything about what they've done are Secretary Sun and Ma Hanshan. If Sun is released, shouldn't Ma be as well? But if they're both freed, how does Cui Zhongshi's death tie up the case?"

"Don't keep nagging about what happened to Cui Zhongshi. After all, it involves your father as well as Soong and Kung… and the party. Bringing it up again will negatively impact the currency reform plans. That's Comrade Jianfeng's opinion on the matter. He asked that I make this clear to you."

"Then the anticorruption campaign is just a slogan."

"No, not a slogan. It's a matter of vital importance, as it's seriously draining their cash reserves, which is why they're coordinating their currency reform efforts with us. In the end, the bill will have to be settled."

"Then what do you want me to do? And don't beat around the bush."

"Release Secretary Sun… tonight. That'll hopefully make Xu Tieying think twice about carrying out arrests tomorrow."

"Fine." An evil smile crossed Fang Meng'ao's face. "I'll release Ma Hanshan, too. The pair of them can go free."

"But the order for Ma's arrest came from the Ministry of Defence. It won't be easy to explain his release to the authorities in Nanking."

"It was Chen Jicheng who wrote the order. Xu Tieying and the Nanking government colluded in carrying it out. Cui Zhongshi died, Chen and his cronies made off with so much, and afterwards Xu thought to divvy up Hou Juntang's stock. Ma Hanshan knows about all of this. The rations will be distributed tomorrow. They only need to hear about Ma being released. When they do, they won't dare try to stir up trouble. If they do, I'll get Ma to deal with them."

Zeng muttered to himself, then seemed to come to terms with what Fang had said. "Fine, good. There are only a couple of hours left before the rations will be given out. Go, now, to Xishan prison and see to their release. I'll ring Wang Puchen and tell him to expect you."

"Shouldn't you first report all of this to Mr Chiang?"

"I will. Let me handle it."

Fang Meng'ao slapped the heels of his boots together and formally saluted Zeng Keda. Then he grabbed the keys for his jeep off the table, as well as a cigar and lighter. "I'm off."

Before Zeng Keda could fully recover from his surprise at having Fang Meng'ao salute him in that manner, Fang had already left the room. Zeng ruminated some more on the salutation and then something came to him: his personal charisma must be on the rise. He straightened out the military uniform he was wearing and left as well.

———

Wang Puchen's office in the secret military-controlled prison in Xishan reeked of cigarette smoke. A mahjong board was on the table. It looked as though he'd just finished a game. A glass of wine sat in front of Ma Hanshan. There was also a bowl of rice, and a larger bowl containing boiled duck and caterpillar fungus, the latter believed to be a cure for tuberculosis, coughing and other ailments. The food was, considering the time, a late-night snack. Half of it had been devoured. Wang Puchen went to sit down next to Ma Hanshan, while Fang Meng'ao stood near the door, smiling at the scene. Ma had gained weight since the last time he'd seen him. His hair and face had grown whiter, too. When he noticed Fang, he stood and smiled in reply.

"The food in front of you is more important. Finish it first and then we'll talk."

"Puchen's been kind to me. There's caterpillar fungus in the duck soup. It was meant for him, to help with his coughing, but he gave it to me instead... to give me energy so I could stay up all night playing cards. I think I'm done, though. Puchen, call in your men to take it away."

"Ah, Mr Ma, Captain Fang is here to collect you. You're to go with him. I'll get someone to tidy up, don't worry about it."

"Oh, OK." Ma Hanshan was suddenly lost for words. He simply walked over to stand in front of Fang Meng'ao.

"You don't want to know where we're going?"

Ma Hanshan smiled. "Whichever way I look at it, I imagine I'll soon be dead. What's the point of asking where that'll happen? Captain Fang, let me say I think very highly of you. I deserve a bullet, payback for the one I gave Old Cui. That's what'd make me happy for sure."

"How about seven to nine rifles, would that be enough?"

"Yeah, sure. One bullet would be enough. The old bugger wasted far more in his lifetime."

Fang Meng'ao's face drew tight. "Who's this old bugger?"

"No one, nothing you need to worry about. Captain Fang, I've had my fair share of women. They ended up running away, or I did, but I've got a son out of it. Such a shame he's like his old man, always out and about getting up to mischief. You're a good man, Captain Fang. If you're so inclined, I'd like you to help me look after him."

"No one's come to execute you. You're not going to die, so you can take care of him yourself." Fang Meng'ao looked at Wang Puchen. "The rations are to be distributed early tomorrow morning. Time is of the essence. I'm taking Director Ma there now. Send his things along afterwards."

"Oh no, not that!" It was as though Ma Hanshan had waited for this all along. He put his hands up towards Wang Puchen, his palms facing out like he was trying to stop what was happening. Then he plumped his rather large posterior on the chair. A moment later, he raised his head to look at Fang Meng'ao. "Captain Fang, you heard what I just said. Whatever way I look at things, my death is certain. If you put me in front of a firing squad, I'll go without any protest. But if you're here to get me to stand in for them and distribute rations, please tell them I've committed suicide. Please."

Wang Puchen lowered his face.

Fang Meng'ao, however, seemed to enjoy the energy Ma put into his protestations and laughed heartily. "So, you're not willing to be the scapegoat, huh?"

"You're fucking right. Excuse my language. Captain Fang, in the barracks, these last few days, did Zeng Keda not tell you…"

"Tell me what?"

"Shit, you really don't know, do you? Then listen, brother, I've got some advice for you. Those rations, I can't have anything to do with them. Nor should you. If it still needs doing, get Zeng Keda to handle it… or Xu Tieying, Chen Jicheng or Xu Huidong. They can take care of it."

Fang Meng'ao shot a glance at Wang Puchen, who showed the same surprise he did. He turned back to Ma Hanshan.

"What I'm going to tell you has nothing to do with Wang Puchen. Puchen, what you're about to hear, well, don't take it any further. You won't find anything, even if you do."

Wang had recovered a sense of calm. "I won't investigate. Please, Mr Ma, go ahead."

"I have a few of the latest figures here. We're in the thirty-seventh year of the Republic of China, it's the twelfth of August. Three hours ago, well, it was the day before, the eleventh, midnight. Compared with the figures for the end of July, that's eleven days ago, the rate of inflation in the cities in Kuomintang areas has risen ninety per cent. If we were to look more closely at things, then we could say that food prices have increased 2.5 million times over what was being paid before the start of the War of Resistance. And, over the last eleven days, prices have jumped 3.9 million times. There's more, too. The cost of housing at the end of last month rose four hundred and fifty thousand times. Over the last eleven days, it's jumped seven hundred and seventy thousand times. Clothes, hats, shoes, even pants and socks, everything has gone up multiple times. And at no faster rate than in the last eleven days. The numbers can't even be counted. Captain Fang, these numbers I've told you, you should understand what they mean."

Fang Meng'ao was stunned by the figures, his expression grave. His eyes darted back and forth between Ma Hanshan and Wang Puchen.

Wang was the first to speak: "Oh, OK, Mr Ma, can... can you tell me one thing? Who gave you these numbers?"

Ma Hanshan laughed. "Puchen. Did you think those men wanting to play cards with me knew what position I held? Haha, they only thought I still had American money in my pockets. I used to give them some US dollars, nearly every day, in fact. You know, spending money to buy whatever they wanted, they just had to use the Republic's legal tender."

"If nothing else, it seems you *were* the right man for the job." It was hard to disguise the disdain in Fang Meng'ao's voice.

"The hell I was. I knew the old bugger's daughter fled, though, and that his disgraceful son didn't care a whit. We can't go arguing about their legacy, though. Captain Fang, you've not been dirtied by any of this, your hands are clean, so listen to my advice. Rely on the Americans to handle it, it'll only take them a few days. Besides, there're more than enough thieving eyes focused on that American aid. The plan is to give rations to the students and their teachers tomorrow. But what about the rest of the city's residents? You don't need to remember your father's enmity. He's got a plan for sure. He'll talk to the Americans. Now, quickly, get out of here."

Fang Meng'ao looked at this man in front of him and couldn't help but feel something wholly strange. There was pity there, too, perhaps more pity than anything else, but there was nothing to say, at least not for the moment. Finally, he had a question: "Tell me, Mr Ma, at the time, why didn't you send your son to school?"

It was Ma Hanshan's turn to be surprised. Then he smiled bitterly. "Not everyone was victorious when Japan was defeated. I was put in charge of my own Peking committee. I was a director, had gold and silver passing through my hands daily. There were lots of women, sluts. They took me to the cleaners, and when I was out of cash, they ran. My son... ha... last year I gave him money to go to Hong Kong to study. Two months later he was back. He'd blown through every cent and didn't even attend a single class. And yet he still came looking for money. Had some girl that went to Peking University. Bah! I found out later the money was for a presidential suite he'd rented at a hotel across from the university's main gate. A party place it was, every day, loud, raucous, whores coming and going, drugs, too. In March, I publicly disowned him, had it published in the papers, mostly because I was due to become director of the civilian commission in April. I'm shameless, I admit it. I know there's an image the party-state wants to maintain. I shouldn't hold anything back, should make everything clear. Captain Fang... have I been clear?"

"Clear, yes, you have. We should go."

"You still want me to come with you?"

"Forget everything that came before. Just think of the students who'll be waiting for their rations tomorrow as your children."

"My... my children." The shock was clear in his voice. "And how did I end up with so many?"

"You only need to help them. They're your kids."

"I... I will!" Ma Hanshan stood up abruptly. "Captain Fang, one day, I'll ask you to remind me to help that no-good son of mine." With these words, he rushed towards the door. Fang Meng'ao didn't hurry after him, however. Instead, he turned to Wang Puchen.

"You go on ahead, Captain Fang, let me handle Secretary Sun. I'll escort him to the police station myself."

"I'll ask for your help with something else, too."

"Please. I'll do whatever I can."

"Send a few men you trust to look for Ma Hanshan's son. When they find him, send him to Nanking, get him clean."

"Of course. It won't be a problem," said Fang, extending his hand. "Let me first show you out."

"OK." They walked out together, both taking big steps.

Standing in the inner courtyard of the prison, near the gate that led outside, Wang Puchen waved to Fang Meng'ao. He watched Fang and Ma as they boarded the jeep and left. Wang turned and walked towards a wing of cells that lay to his left. Four members of his staff followed not far behind. Suddenly, Wang pulled to a stop. "Who spent the last couple of days playing cards with Ma Hanshan?"

The man in charge of the group answered: "Two were assigned each day. They took turns based on whose shift it was."

"And I suppose these were the same men who went into the city to buy stuff for Ma?"

"I would imagine that's the case, yes sir."

"And no one seemed to bother anything about this... that they were going back and forth to the city?" Wang Puchen had turned to face the man.

"You'll need to ask the warden, sir. Shall I fetch him, sir?"

"No, don't bother. Wait here."

Wang Puchen walked off towards the main building. As he reached the large steel gate that swung in and out, he paused for a moment and was nearly overwhelmed by where he was. A deep, long corridor coiled its way into the prison beyond. About fifty metres above the corridor hung what seemed to resemble greenish, fifteen-watt bulbs. He couldn't be sure how many there were, but the hallway was certainly dimly lit. The left wall was constructed entirely of granite bricks. The right was an iron-wrought fence of the type commonly used in prisons. Wang was standing, looking. He refrained from grabbing a cigarette. He wasn't coughing. His face was focused on the large glass window that overlooked the prison. It was the guard room and he wanted very much to peer inside. What he saw, however, only made his blood boil. He could make out the form of one guard snoring away in a small metal bed. Another guard was asleep at a table. Their clear dereliction of duty infuriated him, especially when he walked into the room and they remained completely unaware of his presence, dead asleep.

His anger increased tenfold a few seconds later when he noticed the man sleeping at the table clutching several American banknotes in his hand. Wang turned his attention to the guard asleep in the bed and saw the same US dollars stuffed into his pockets. There was no question these were the two men who'd been playing cards with the recently departed Ma Hanshan. They'd won, too. That much was obvious. He supposed that's why they were now fast asleep: their games had worn them out. Lazy bastards! Instead of being on duty, they were sleeping!

Wang didn't want to look at them any more. He diverted his attention to the keys that were hanging on the wall and walked over to them. Taking them in his hands, he left the sleeping guards to themselves. With the keys, he released the lock that bound the great steel gate together, and then placed both hands against it to push it open. The door yielded easily, making hardly a sound. Slowly, he entered the long corridor. Still, the guards slept. Wang moved further in and stopped in front of a single-person jail cell. A pair of eyes on the other side of the bars looked out at him. Without a word, Wang opened the cell and gestured to the man inside. The figure stood. It was Secretary Sun. As quietly as Wang had opened the door, Sun departed his cell. They walked out past the guards, neither of whom had stirred. Wang inserted the key back into the gate and locked it. Sun stared after him as he re-entered the guard room and replaced the keys. Their eyes met then, but they didn't say anything. Each man simply shook their head. Then they left together.

Entering his private office in Xishen prison, Wang Puchen gestured for Sun Chaozhong to sit. Large telecommunication equipment lay on one of the tables. Secretary Sun remained standing. Wang Puchen made no further sign for him to sit, and instead he reached for the direct line to Nanking and spoke forcefully into the receiver: "Line two, I need to speak to Comrade Jianfeng."

Standing to one side, Sun's hands moved subconsciously and patted at his legs. He straightened his posture and stood more rigidly than before. His eyes were fixed on the telephone in Wang's hand.

"Affirmative. Fang Meng'ao has already departed with Ma Hanshan in his custody. Comrade Chaozhong is still here... Affirmative." He pulled the receiver away from his ear and spoke to Secretary Sun: "Comrade Jianfeng would like a word."

Sun took hold of the telephone with both hands. He was noticeably unsettled. "I'm here, Sun Chaozhong... sir."

Finally, Wang had time to smoke. He reached for a cigarette and moved off to one side.

Sun Chaozhong's true allegiance lay with the Iron and Blood Congress. But he'd been ordered to infiltrate the Kuomintang's Communications Bureau. There his task had been to become a key player and influencer. No one other than Chiang Ching-kuo and the inner circle of the Iron and Blood Congress knew his true identity and purpose. Wang Puchen was one of these men.

Wang Puchen walked over to a small electric fan that sat on the floor. He turned it on so that the sound of its spinning blades would conceal the words now being spoken over the phone.

Sun Chaozhong had killed Cui Zhongshi. The order had come from Comrade Jianfeng himself; it had been his top-secret contingency plan. Part of that plan was to have Xu Tieying be the fall guy. Unfortunately for Sun, however, that part didn't quite work out. As a result, he'd been arrested. If it weren't for Wang protecting him in the prison, even though the two men never really spoke, who knows what might have happened. They both held true to the Iron and Blood Congress's discipline, which explained why Wang had turned on the fan. The conversation between Comrade Jianfeng and Sun Chaozhong was their business and their business alone.

"Affirmative. Comrade Jianfeng, you needn't be concerned. I understand." Sun's voice was clear and remarkably calm.

Wang Puchen faced the wall. Besides the cigarette being placed between his lips to draw in the nicotine, and then subsequently removed for him to exhale, he didn't move. He was simply waiting for them to finish.

"Affirmative." Sun clapped his legs together and waited. A moment later, when he heard the phone being hung up on the other end, he did the same. He turned around. "Comrade Puchen."

Wang, however, did not respond. He hadn't heard his name being called by Sun Chaozhong.

"Comrade Puchen!"

This time he did hear. He walked over to the communications equipment, stubbed out the cigarette and discarded the butt in the ashtray that lay on the table. "There's a vehicle outside waiting for us. I'll escort you back to police headquarters."

"Comrade Jianfeng has issued orders. To ensure the smooth implementation of the currency reform plans, suspected Communists must be closely monitored. From tomorrow, you'll be responsible for Peking station. Police HQ will be mine."

Wang Puchen listened calmly to the instructions.

"Let's go."

Wang Puchen understood there'd been no such orders, but he didn't say a word. Together, they walked out of the room. A few steps beyond, the colour of Wang's face changed.

Three men had quietly come to stand outside his private office.

Two of them were the formerly sleeping guards, the other was their immediate superior, the head jailer. All three looked terrified, anxiously waiting, it seemed, to see Secretary Sun emerge from the room. Once he did, they all relaxed, sighing in unison. "It's good you're here, sir," one of the three men said.

"Oh, it's good, is it?" Wang Puchen stared at the man who'd spoken, his eyes filled with a look he'd never shown before, a look to strike fear in any man.

"Sir, according to regulations, they'll be punished immediately. Their infraction will go into their permanent files."

It had been his order. He'd instructed men to play cards with Ma Hanshan. But he never once thought the guards would squirrel themselves into this setup and exploit it for their own ends, in which they would use Ma Hanshan's American currency to make purchases of sought-after items outside of the prison and thereby allow Ma to work out the extreme price fluctuations the country was now facing. It was hard for him to accept that the arrangements he had made himself had all gone awry. What made matters worse was that he was unsure how to rectify things. At first, he'd wondered if he could turn a blind eye and not investigate what was going on. But now these three men had rushed into something they shouldn't have, they'd put their nose in where it didn't belong, they'd seen him here with Secretary Sun. What a fucking mess!

Wang, however, bit his tongue and kept all of this to himself. Gesturing to Sun, the two men walked away.

The lead jailer's heart sank and words failed him. He signalled to the other men, and together they left, too.

Outside in the courtyard, two vehicles and men from four action teams were quietly waiting. As soon as the man in charge saw Wang Puchen leave the building with Secretary Sun, he opened the back door to the car and waited for them to draw close.

"Secretary Sun, here's your seat." Wang Puchen gestured for Sun to sit. Once inside, the man who'd opened the door climbed in. "You're not to leave yet," Wang continued, standing next to the vehicle. To the other men who had been waiting, Wang now gave instructions: "You see those three over there? Throw them in the cell just vacated by Secretary Sun. They're not to communicate with anyone, and no one is to come in contact with them."

Turning their attention to the three guards, they knew they'd run out of luck. They were momentarily distracted, however. They hadn't expected Wang would choose to deal with them in this manner. Throwing them into a prison cell couldn't really be considered disciplinary action, more a housecleaning exercise, a taking out of the rubbish. Several of the other men looked at each other in dismay as well, dazed and unsure of what to do.

"Now, dammit!" Wang Puchen's voice reverberated in the air. He said nothing further, but opened the front door of the car and positioned himself in the driver's seat. The ignition turned and the car started.

"Sir!" the lead jailer yelled after Wang, a clear sense of terror in his voice. Before he could do anything, two sets of hands fell on him and he was led away by two of the men who had been waiting next to the vehicles. The other guards were still and unmoving.

Wang Puchen stepped on the accelerator, shifting gears quickly. A brief moment later and the vehicle flew through the courtyard and away from the prison.

CHAPTER 3

Inside the Peking Police headquarters, Xu Tieying was already standing. Chen Jicheng remained seated at his desk. Both men were waiting to hear that word "report", but all they could hear from out in the hallway was Wang Puchen's interminable coughing. The sound seemed only to sour the mood in the room, forcing them to wait until he stopped. Finally, Wang's voice carried out: "Report."

Xu Tieying stood on tiptoes, ready to bound towards the door to welcome Wang, but just as he was about to do so, he realised Chen Jicheng had not called out the requisite "enter". He held his spot and looked over at Chen. Chen's eyebrows were uneven, one higher than the other. He was old, too, and displayed that quality of impatience so often seen in more senior men. He returned Xu's gaze steadfastly, then, after some more time had passed, gestured to him to tell Wang to come in. Xu nodded his assent and pulled the office door open. There was genuine emotion on his face, a somewhat rare occurrence. Secretary Sun was standing in the doorway, his face appearing as though he were still in prison. Wang Puchen stood behind him. Seeing the compassionate look on Xu's face, Sun straightened his posture and saluted. "Director!"

It was not customary for men in their positions to clasp hands and pat each other on the shoulders, so Xu used a gentle tone to console Sun: "Please come in."

"Ye... yes." Sun entered first, followed closely by Wang Puchen.

Somewhat unexpectedly, Chen Jicheng raised himself from his chair. After all, he thought to himself, this man who now stood in front of him had been arrested because he'd battled and lost against him. In such circumstances, he would at least adhere to the code of conduct taught to soldiers of the Whampoa Military Academy. "Tell me, have you suffered any beatings? Are you hungry? Why didn't they clean you up before coming? Surely a shower should've been in order?"

The questions, such as they were, couldn't help but cause embarrassment for both Wang Puchen and Xu Tieying. If he'd been beaten, then Wang would have been responsible. As for getting him something to eat, letting him bathe, there really hadn't been any time; more urgent troop matters took precedent, naturally. Wang and Xu shared knowing, if awkward, glances.

With a thin smile on his lips, Xu was the next to speak: "Our gratitude, Commander, for your concern. Of course, he was with Puchen, so certainly not abused in any fashion."

Xu's words had the desired effect, for Chen Jicheng realised that while he'd only meant to comfort Sun, he'd also overlooked the true reality of his incarceration. With a wave of his hand, Chen returned to his chair, acknowledging that things were as they should be.

"What's more," Xu continued, "there wasn't time for him to wash properly. After all, the assignment of responsibilities takes precedence, don't they?"

"You're correct, yes. Let's begin."

The two newcomers sat down and Xu returned to the sofa where he'd been sitting before. His attention on Chen Jicheng, he asked if he should speak first.

"Go ahead," was the brief reply.

"From the intelligence we've gathered, numerous universities across Peking have been infiltrated with Communist agents who are, in turn, stirring up trouble. Tomorrow, we've learnt, they are planning to get the students to refuse to accept the rations we've arranged to be delivered. At the front of this are members of the China Democratic League, which, as we well know, has been corrupted by Communist influence and is now little more than an offshoot of the CPC, certainly no longer a 'third way' proponent. At any rate, they managed to get more than a hundred professors to sign a petition stating their refusal to receive the rations. Such being the case, I don't think we should proceed with distribution tomorrow. These agitators are just looking to embarrass the party-state and make us lose face. We shouldn't oblige them. In fact, we should make arrangements, put people in place, as it were, to watch how things unfold and then make arrests. That said, we should at all costs avoid apprehending supporters of the Democratic League and instead focus our attention on arresting known Communists, and any student engaging in violence."

Wang Puchen listened, nodding when expected.

"What's with this nodding of your head?" The impatience in Chen Jicheng's voice was clear. "Have you made sure your staff at Peking station are ready? Have you handed out the list of names identifying known Communist agents? Are your men keeping an eye on them?"

"We've already got one fish in the net, namely Yan Chunming, from Yenching. He's more or less confined to the library. Oh, and most student reps are congregating there as well. Should we just go and arrest them now?"

"And what would be the point of that? No, tomorrow would be better. With him there, the bigger fish will be forced into exposing themselves, including Liang Jinglun whom we had once already but had to release. Once things blow up, then we'll nab them all."

"Understood. I'll go and make the arrangements."

It was Chen Jicheng's turn to question Wang Puchen: "Make what arrangements? I tell you what, you get on the phone now, call Peking station and get your men to come here. Then we'll have everyone in the same place for tomorrow – the special investigations team, the Fourth Corps Special Service battalion, your men, everyone. Xu, you plan how we'll carry out the action tomorrow."

Chen didn't wait for Xu to speak, however. Instead, he reached for the phone and barked into the receiver: "Get the Fourth Corps battalion here! And one more thing. I want five bowls of noodles delivered. Now!"

It seemed to be fated that the night of 11 August 1948 would be tumultuous. It was a night that stretched into the wee hours of the following morning, thus spanning two days. According to the Chinese calendar, it was the Double Seventh Festival, the only night the weaver girl could meet her lover the cow herder. The sky above the grassy lawn near the Yenching library was so bereft of clouds that the Milky Way itself could be seen. The moon, only half visible, shone what light it could, but the masses on that night never really noticed how its illumination both aided the tidal wave of humanity and obscured it.

Student reps from Peking University arrived. So too did students from Tsinghua and Peking Normal. Liang Jinglun welcomed all of them, shaking hands one after the other, sharing quiet words as well.

Just over half way through 1948, there wasn't really anyone apart from Liang Jinglun who knew just how complicated the student movements were. History turns on points like these. The Nationalists were loath to have the students protest; they hoped to avoid the surge in civil disobedience it would signify. Oddly enough, the CPC was in agreement, since they too hoped to avoid another wave of student protests. But at this moment, neither of the parties could control events. The organisation that could was the pan-university student federation; their members were the only ones who could influence the outcome of that evening. Its charter did not overtly support the Communist cause, nor did it resolutely oppose the current Kuomintang administration. Instead, their support was for the constitution and the rights it granted the Chinese people, to fight for their livelihoods, to fight for democracy. Because of this, the only person who could truly lead the federation and count on their support had to be a member of the China Democratic League and a staunch advocate for democracy. The Communists had their secret agents within the federation, so too did the Nationalists. This resulted in the complicated situation where there were a large number of so-called "progressive youth", but also a small minority of supposedly "reactionary students".

Since this was the case, since there were Communists, Nationalists and self-styled democratic professors all vying for influence within the student federation, the only possible choice was Liang Jinglun, however regrettable that may have been.

"The position of the Peking Students' Union is clear. We stand with the democratic professors who signed the petition. We thus refuse to accept American food aid."

Following these words, Liang Jinglun muttered to himself, then turned to address the other student reps: "And the position of Tsinghua?"

"We refuse to go to the Kuomintang-designated location. Should they decide to transport the rations to our university, however, we cannot prevent those students who are willing to accept the rations from actually receiving them."

"And Peking Normal, what's your position?"

"Our decision is much the same as Tsinghua's student rep just said. But we would like to add that we support rations being given to refugee students from the northeast. But there is a precondition that must be met – those students who've been arrested must be released and their student status must be recognised."

Liang Jinglun muttered again under his breath, his eyes focused on the empty sky above. He didn't see the majestic brilliance of the Milky Way, however. His eyes were instead trained on the lonely half moon and the light emanating from it.

"Mr Liang." The student rep from Peking University awoke him from his stupor. "Yenching University was set up with American money and academic and administrative support. Since we're in agreement to decline American aid, it should go without saying that we need the support of Yenching. We must present a united front."

Liang scanned the assembled students. "Yes, a united front is necessary. As for how to achieve that, give me half an hour, please, to think things over."

The rep from Peking University nodded and pulled out a pocket watch to check the time. The reps for the other two universities did the same. Certain of the time, the students looked at each other and nodded in agreement. The Peking rep spoke: "It's nearly four. We'll wait till half four. Then we expect your decision."

Liang Jinglun beckoned to several students who were standing some distance away. Three of them came over. "Two of you accompany the three reps to the small reading room so that they can rest."

"No, that won't be necessary," said the Peking rep. "We'll wait here."

"Well, that's entirely up to you." Turning to the two students he'd asked to escort the reps to the reading room, Liang continued: "You must ensure their safety, understood?"

"Please don't worry Mr Liang, we understand."

"You come with me," was all he said to the other student he'd called over.

Together, Liang and the student walked up onto the stone steps of the Yenching library. Fixing his eyes on the boy, Liang's voice was low: "I want you to report to Comrade Keda what you've heard here tonight. You must do this now."

"Sir." The student from the Chiang Kai-shek Student Society mimicked the volume of Liang's voice.

Liang said nothing further before walking into the library. The student stood still for a moment, his back to the door. Then, as though he were on patrol, he walked off towards the corridor that lay to the left.

Inside the rare books collection room, Yan Chunming was seated at the table he'd been at so often before, piles and piles of volumes surrounding him. Liang Jinglun was seated opposite, at the desk he'd used frequently in the past when writing reports. He relayed the positions of the three universities to Yan Chunming and now sat quietly, watching the other man for his reaction. The thick spectacles perched on Yan's nose seemed to emit a protective shield.

"What do you hope I can do?" Yan asked in a level tone.

"The party's instructions are clear. They hope there will be no needless sacrifice. Comrade Chunming, please report these developments higher up the chain of command."

"You replaced me, didn't you? Do you mean to tell me they haven't told you how to communicate with the higher-ups?" Yan

Chunming already knew well that neither Zhang Yueyin nor Comrade Liu would have told him how to reach them. It was difficult for him to press the issue, but his question was in no way unreasonable.

Yan's question hit the nail on the head. Liang, himself, had had misgivings about this central aspect of the new responsibility he'd been given in light of Yan's actions. He hoped, however, that there were good reasons for this oversight. "You do know, yes, the decision for me to take over your responsibilities was made by our superiors? They considered it an emergency situation, and it's only temporary you know. It also proves something, namely that the higher-ups still have faith in you." Liang now directed his attention to the telephone on the table.

Yan Chunming dialled the number several times but there was no answer. The line had been disconnected, deliberately, no doubt. Yan looked at Liang. It was not the time to ask this, he thought, but then, when would it be? "Tell me, Comrade Liang Jinglun, do you really believe the party still trusts me?"

"Dial it. I'll make the report."

Yan was silent for a spell, seemingly confused by what Liang had said. Finally, he answered: "I'll try." He dialled.

Liang felt it best to avert his eyes. He didn't want to see the number Yan was dialling. Once he was finished, he passed the receiver to Liang. He held it up to his ear and was surprised to hear the phone making a connection. His surprise quickly turned to disappointment, however. A recorded female operator's voice sounded through the phone: "The number you have dialled is in arrears. It will soon be disconnected. The number you have dialled is in arrears. It will soon be dis…"

Liang returned the phone to its base. He made no effort to hide his disappointment. "It seems we have little choice but to wait for our superiors to get in touch with us. The only problem is the student reps are outside waiting for us to tell them our ideas… on… on Comrade Chunming. It seems we'll have to make the decision ourselves."

"Right now, you're in charge. So long as you still trust me, you decide. I'll talk about what to do."

Yan Chunming's cautiousness, his rigour, it all conformed to the party's organisational procedures and command regulations. There was no longer any need, he felt, to continue to doubt Chunming, to probe further into his political loyalties. "In that case, let us follow the spirit of Comrade Peng Zhen's Sixth of July Instructions and make our decision."

"Yes, let's proceed."

"I'll go and make arrangements with those students whom I already know and trust to make use of the federation to carry out the work that needs to be done across all of the universities. You do the same. We'll tell the student reps that tomorrow, when the rations are to be distributed, they must refrain from antagonising the Kuomintang and thus avoid unnecessary sacrifice. Our crack forces must remain concealed. Once the rations have been received, we'll await further orders on deployment to the liberated areas."

"I agree with what you've laid out here, but there's no way I can implement it."

"Eh?" Liang Jinglun stared hard at Yan Chunming.

"I've already been suspended and I'm under investigation. I'm not supposed to have contact with any active operatives. I can't violate party regulations again."

Liang Jinglun tried to understand his compatriot, his fellow party member, but was yet again prevented from doing so by Yan Chunming. He thought some more about Yan's words, then replied: "It's me who has neglected party discipline. It's like this, Comrade Chunming. At present, I'm the only one who knows about your suspension and the investigation that's due to take place. Our fellow comrades still consider you to be a leader. That's why you need to be out there tomorrow when the rations are to be distributed. We'll go together. You can still take charge of tomorrow. On this point, you shouldn't disagree, right?"

"And you should know, too, that the punishment I'm due is because my intention was to remain here and assist you in maintaining control of the situation."

Liang Jinglun stood and extended his hand in a sincere gesture of comradeship. Yan Chunming reciprocated and they clasped each other's hands tightly. "Comrade Chunming, it doesn't matter what happens tomorrow, nor what dangers may arise. It doesn't matter what authorities in the party believe either. You and me, we'll stand side by side and fight this together."

"Thank you, comrade, for being willing to still fight alongside me."

Yan Chunming's attitude confirmed beyond a doubt that the instructions given in the letter from the General Academic Committee were correct. There was no reason for Liang to doubt it. A feeling rose up in his heart, a feeling he couldn't describe. Subconsciously, he grasped Yan's hand a little tighter. "I won't forget. You introduced me to the party. I'm forever in your debt."

Despite the thickness of his glasses, Liang Jinglun could see the tears at the corners of Yan's eyes. The only thing he couldn't see was the emotion welling up in Yan's heart.

Yan Chunming had endured an enormous ordeal. He couldn't hold back. "Watch your back. Stay safe."

"I will." Liang Jinglun released his grip and averted his eyes away from Yan Chunming. Then he turned to leave.

Yan Chunming saw him to the door and watched as he walked away, slowly disappearing until he could see him no more. Then he shut the door, bolted it and raced over to the bookcase. He scanned the spines of various titles until he located the one he was looking for. His eyes drew close to the cover, *Whampoa Military Academy Textbook*. He flipped through the pages, but he didn't need to use his eyes. He pulled the book closer to his face, and there it was, as plain as the nose on his face, the image of Old Liu's pistol! He inspected the image, and even though he was very short-sighted, there was a flash than flickered across his face. He pushed his face closer to the page. He walked over to the table, the book still absorbing all of his attention.

He placed the book on the table. He'd committed the image to memory. Again he lifted the glasses to their usual place. He pulled out a set of keys and opened the bottom drawer of his desk. From inside he lifted out another set of keys, his reserve set, and walked over to the metal strongbox. His movements were fast, hurried. The key clicked in the lock, the pin dropped and he pulled open the safe. Again, he held Old Liu's pistol in his hand, the same one he'd identified in the book.

He began to follow the steps in the book, his hands ready to grasp the smooth grip. Then he stopped. His mind was working things over. His fingers moved over the small button, he pushed and the magazine fell out. A smile crossed his face and he stared. The magazine was filled with bronze-coloured bullets. He returned to his chair like a child with a new toy and busily began popping the bullets out of the magazine. There were six in total, and he now laid them all out, carefully, in order, more precise than even his books. He stared at them for what seemed like forever, admiring their shape, their colour. He turned his attention back to the magazine, making sure there were no bullets remaining inside. Then he reloaded it.

Yan stood again, holding the empty pistol in his hands, passing it back and forth between them. He searched for a target, something to aim at. He scanned the room for more minutes than he could remember, and then he smiled. Clumsily, he held the gun in the air, pointing it directly at the bulb Old Liu had replaced.

In the woods that ran alongside the path between the Jingchun Botanical Gardens and Yenching University, the half moon in the sky shone almost singularly on the tarred electrical and telephone poles, illuminating the man shimming up: Old Liu. A valise was slung over his shoulder, an electrician's blade was held in his hand. In fast, precise movements, Old Liu sliced off the protective rubber of the line to expose the wires underneath. Then, just as quickly, he pulled out two clamps to grip the wire. With his free hand, he gestured towards the ground. There, among the trees, were several well-armed soldiers of the East China Field Army all on high alert.

Below, Zhang Yueyin clasped a telephone in his hand and held the receiver close to his ear. A long, continuous dial tone emanated from it; the phone was working. Zhang signalled for Liu to shimmy back down.

It took Old Liu only a few seconds to slither back down the pole. Once on the ground, he walked over to Zhang Yueyin and took hold of the telephone himself. Zhang shook the receiver in the air to emphasise that it worked. The soft voice of the switchboard operator, a woman's voice, could be heard: "Where would you like me to connect you to?"

"This is Yenching University Building Six. I want Building Two, the library office."

"Just a second." The operator began to make the connection. Zhang Yueyin listened gravely, while Liu held on to the telephone base.

———

Beyond the thick glasses, Yan Chunming aimed the pistol. Through the front sight, he could see clearly the light bulb Liu had changed. With his right index finger, he tried to pull back on the trigger but failed. He then placed both index fingers around it and squeezed. The gun sounded faster than Yan Chunming could smile. At the same moment, the sharp ring of the telephone surprised him, causing him to jump. He turned to look at the device on the table and moved towards it. But before answering, he pulled open the drawer and replaced the pistol inside. He swept the bullets he'd left on the table into the drawer as well. Pushing it closed, he picked up the telephone. "Yenching University Library, may I ask who's speaking?"

Old Liu's eyes widened. Zhang Yueyin was calm. "Professor Yan... Director Yan?"

Zhang Yueyin's voice reverberated in Yan Chunming's ears nearly as loud as spring thunder echoes in the sky. For a brief moment, he was overwhelmed with emotions before he was finally able to collect himself. "Yes, this is Yan Chunming. And who might you be?"

"Professor Zhang, from the philosophy department, my apologies for bothering you so late in the evening, but I have a request. Tomorrow, my class will be completing their research into Xiong Shili's *A New Treatise on Vijñaptimātra*, and, well, they've continually asked if I could invite you to give them a special lecture. Specifically, they'd like you to elaborate on Xiong's key precepts that original reality and the material world are one, that the heart and matter are likewise one, as well as his formulations concerning energy and matter and the heavens and man... all his points, basically, on the meaning of life and the worth of man. You must come. Please."

Old Liu's eyes had glazed over listening to the telephone conversation. He hadn't understood a word Zhang had spoken, nor what Yan Chunming had offered by way of a reply. For that brief moment, he'd been mesmerised by what these two much more intellectual comrades had blathered on about. As he stared at Zhang Yueyin, he began to feel as though the moon above brought into view a shimmering halo above his head. And at the same time, he imagined that same halo must be hovering about Yan's head, too, as he sat in the rare books collection room in the library.

"Will you be going to get the rations tomorrow?" Zhang Yueyin's words brought Old Liu back to reality and to the conversation he was listening to. He noticed, too, that Zhang had been cut off. No doubt Yan was again refusing to allow the party to rescue him. He was being insubordinate. Liu clenched his hand in anger, then he stared at Zhang.

Zhang Yueyin extended a hand and gestured for him to calm down. "Then we'll send men to the distribution site. They'll wait for things to finish and then bring you here."

Yan Chunming's answer was apparently brief, and he seemed to have hung up even more quickly. Zhang Yueyin grudgingly hung up as well and then looked at Old Liu.

"I don't think he's afraid of sacrificing himself. In truth, I don't think I've ever seen anyone keener to do so... Chief Zhang." Liu's words seemed to stoke the seriousness in Zhang Yueyin's face. "It's too late to request instructions from command. Make the call, please. Permit me to implement emergency measures."

"What emergency measures?"

"They were put together in secret by myself and Comrade Liuyun. They can only be resorted to in the direst circumstances. I'll see to it. You just get yourself to Mao'er Hutong and make the report to Comrade Liuyun. I'm sure he'll then give you the specific details."

Zhang Yueyin finally realised he was only second in command, that there were secrets he didn't know anything about. "And Comrade Liuyun... he'll be in agreement with this?"

"This is the responsibility of the Labour Ministry. The order must be obeyed, there is no choice in the matter. He'll agree."

"But won't it be dangerous?"

"What kind of contingency plans don't come with an element of danger? So yes, it will be dangerous, but it's all to prevent an even more dangerous situation from emerging."

Resigned to the fact he had no choice, Zhang Yueyin agreed to go and make the report to Comrade Liuyun. Liu clapped his hands, and the armed men quickly gathered round. His voice was low: "Each of you, I want you to shadow him, follow Chief Zhang's orders to the letter, and make sure he's safe."

"Sir, yes sir!"

By himself, Old Liu walked over to a nearby tree and took hold of a bicycle that had been propped up against it. He hoisted himself onto the saddle, his feet onto the pedals, and then speeded away, regardless of whether there was a path or not.

"How's it you're only coming here now?" Zeng Keda had gone to the rear garden of his home to receive Fang Meng'ao and Ma Hanshan.

The two men quickly fell into step with Zeng Keda before Fang answered: "I've accompanied him all the way here, but first we had to return to his home. There was something important he had to get, something he needs to give to Mr Chiang."

"And pray tell what is it? And who're you planning to give it to?" Zeng halted his steps. Ma Hanshan had a scroll rolled up under his arm. "Let's go inside first, then I'll explain."

The half moon in the sky along with the street lamps gave sufficient light for them to see the vague furrowing of Zeng's brow, but he quickened his pace nonetheless. "Fine, fine. We're here to cooperate, we don't want a repeat of actions taken south of the river."

Fang Meng'ao thought to laugh, but Ma Hanshan's voice cut him off: "Inspector Zeng, I don't believe that reference does right by Mr Chiang."

Zeng Keda slowed a little, but he did not stop. Nor did he respond to Ma's remark. Besides, they'd already arrived.

Once inside, Zeng Keda said to Fang Meng'ao: "Captain Fang, please take a seat." Then he joined him, afterwards looking at Ma Hanshan who remained standing, the scroll still wedged underneath his arm. "Captain Fang's told me about the men you've worked with. Tell me, who are they?"

"Yes... past associations, they're all working now in various departments. It's rare for them to make transfers, but they all still listen to me."

Zeng Keda looked at Fang Meng'ao.

"That should come in handy when we have to deal with them." Fang's tone was matter-of-fact.

"Crooks mixed in with honest folk. We don't want to complicate things for Comrade Jianfeng," Zeng added.

"I'm sure Mr Chiang will be overjoyed," Ma Hanshan interjected and before Zeng Keda could pull a face, he unrolled the scroll he'd been carrying and continued: "Would you mind removing that cup."

"Pardon me?" Zeng was noticeably annoyed, but Fang complied and picked up the cup that had been sitting on the tea table, placing it carefully on the end table next to the sofa.

Ma used the cuff of his shift to wipe away the drops of spilt tea that remained on the table. Once dry, he laid the scroll out on top of it.

Zeng looked doubtfully at the unfurled scroll and the words that were written upon it. Slowly, however, his eyes began to brighten. His interest grew even more when he saw the inscription at the bottom: "Xiangxiang... Zeng Disheng!" The words had been written by none other than the Qing dynasty statesman Zeng Guofan, Disheng being his style name. Subconsciously, Zeng Keda drew closer to the scroll, enthralled by the words inscribed upon it: "Rely on heaven to illuminate seas and flowers, but only one's heart knows whence waters flow from the tallest mountains."

"Are these words really written by Zeng Guofan himself?" Zeng's mood towards Ma Hanshan had clearly changed.

"Of course they are." Ma Hanshan knelt. "It was confiscated from the house of Wang Kemin in the thirty-fifth year of the Republic. That traitor... the bastard had been hoarding Zeng's work for ages. I had a confidant get Wang Shixiang to appraise it.

He verified it to be the work of Zeng Guofan. It had been given to the Xiang Military. He wrote it himself on this scroll. Its meaning is that we're all just mountains and rivers, that we must all be of one mind, loyal to one ruling household, and that we shouldn't covet noble titles and fame."

Again subconsciously, Zeng Keda moved closer. He seemed to have forgotten everything else, having become so mesmerised by the words.

Ma Hanshan was crouched alongside him, his voice sounding unusually pleasant: "It took quite a lot of effort to get this treasure. There were numerous bumps along the road. Chief Chen had sent men to get it, so did Bureau Chief Dai. They both wanted to give it to the committee head. At the time I thought their reasons were self-serving, they were just trying to toady up to the boss, as it were, and as a result, they lost sight of themselves. I mean, who were they, after all? The committee head belonged to the court, and they sure as hell weren't no Zeng Guofan. This scroll is fit for only one person, only Chiang Ching-kuo is worthy of it."

Zeng Keda turned his attention away from the calligraphy and back to Ma Hanshan. He didn't seem like the man who'd just come to his home moments ago. Zeng's tone softened: "You'd... if I take your meaning, you'd like me to present this to Mr Chiang. Is that right?"

Ma cut him off before he could say anything further: "But I can't put it like that. I mean, I'm nobody, worse than that, really. If I were to gift it to him, if it came in my name, how could Mr Chiang accept it? I spoke to Captain Fang about this. We agreed it'd be better to say that it had been seized from my house when it had been searched, and then turned over to you. Inspector Zeng, if you could return to Nanking and then wait for the best opportunity to quietly place this scroll on his desk, that would be best. There's no need to say anything about it... words are just not enough."

Zeng stood up slowly and focused on Fang Meng'ao.

"Let's discuss the plans for the distribution of rations tomorrow."

"Yes." There was no longer hesitation in Zeng's voice. Carefully, he took hold of the scroll and rolled it up, placing it gently on his desk. Then he turned to Ma Hanshan and said: "We shouldn't keep you."

"Ah... yes."

"Wang!" Zeng shouted to his aide-de-camp, who, seconds later, appeared at the door. "Have men assigned to Director Ma. They're to accompany him to meet with his associates. Then they're all to head to the distribution site."

"Sir. Understood."

Since his arrival in Peking, this was the first time he took the initiative and extended his hand to shake Ma Hanshan's. Ma responded quickly and the two men shook.

"Men all make mistakes, that's for certain. The key is whether or not they try to make amends. Director Ma, if you work well with Captain Fang here, if you work well with us, then you'll never need to run from men like Chen Jicheng again. I promise you, too, there'll be no military tribunal for you."

Ma Hanshan was not as excited as Zeng Keda might have imagined. "What you've just said is enough for me, Inspector Zeng. I'm a wretch, a bastard. I don't know anything else, but I can see what type of man is willing to give everything to the party-state and what kind of man has a heart blacker than mine. Captain Fang has already spoken to me about this. In general, it's true, my heart hasn't always dealt with students in the best manner possible. But tomorrow I will deal with Chen Jicheng, Xu Tieying and their ilk. I just want you to see that..."

"All right. Now, Captain Fang and I have other matters to discuss. You go first and take up your position."

Ma Hanshan released his grip, nodded in Fang Meng'ao's direction and left the room with Zeng's personal assistant.

Zeng closed the door after their departure and look solemnly at Fang. "This has all come rather suddenly. We must talk things over, hmm?" Fang Meng'ao cocked his ear to listen attentively. "Comrade Liang Jinglun, it seems, has suddenly received instructions from the CPC Peking General Academic Committee. They've put him in charge of coordinating things for tomorrow... with the rations. But the reasoning is strange. Apparently, the person responsible for overseeing things at Yenching has decided not to follow the instructions of his superiors and so Liang Jinglun has been put in his place. The whole situation has already been reported to Comrade Jianfeng, but we don't know if this is some kind of elaborate test of Liang or not, or if they're sacrificing him at the hands of Chen Jicheng and Xu Tieying…"

"Does the CPC know his true identity?"

"There's no intelligence to that effect. But there is someone else who *does* know his identity. And that's your… your father."

Fang Meng'ao had already learned this bit of intelligence in his discussion with Xie Peidong. The fact that Zeng Keda now divulged this information as well couldn't have been without reason, Fang thought to himself. "Tell me. How do you think my father came by this info?"

"Well, it ought to have been you." Fang Meng'ao was silent, unable to offer a rejoinder. He simply listened. "Comrade Jianfeng used you as the exception to the rule. It was a risky move because of your continued association with Cui Zhongshi, a known Communist. The man who first suspected Cui was, in fact, your father. Afterwards, once Cui Zhongshi was killed by Xu Tieying and his cronies, your dad was worried the Communists had recruited you to their cause, which is why he suspected Liang Jinglun. Of course, his suspicions of you were proved to be unfounded. He certainly doesn't suspect you've joined the CPC, but somehow your father has learned – by what channel I don't know – that Comrade Liang is a true believer. He's a Communist."

"OK. Suppose he does know. What now?"

"He Qicang will have the answer to that. John Leighton Stuart would too, I imagine. I know for certain that Liang Jinglun has lost He Qicang's confidence. As a result, there's no way to get those 'peacocks' to fly southeast. Comrade Jianfeng's analysed the situation. Your dad has arranged to meet Liang Jinglun today, alone. It's hoped that we can speak to him, too. In order for us to do this, Comrade Jianfeng has already contacted the various departments involved in the ration distribution tomorrow and has instructed them to delay the action until ten in the morning. This is also to let me go and see your father, to talk with him about these things. At the same time, however, I wanted to solicit your opinion on these matters."

"I… I don't have any opinion."

"That's settled then." Zeng Keda stood and checked the time on the wall clock, before adding: "It's nearly five o'clock. We've got a fierce battle ahead of us tomorrow. Let's tackle it on separate fronts."

Zeng Keda made all haste to Fang Buting's residence. Xie Peidong was standing at the foot of the stairs just inside to greet him. "Inspector Zeng, Mr Fang is in his office waiting for you."

The last time Zeng had visited, he'd been entertained in the drawing room. Now, on this occasion, looking at the long flight of stairs leading up to the first floor, to the large open door that led into Fang Buting's office, the man he'd come to see was nowhere in sight; he hadn't even done Zeng the courtesy of standing at the door. His heart quickened and he knew this time their conversation would be much more difficult. Then, something suddenly came to him. Xie Peidong ought to be able to shed some light on his boss's mood, so he turned and spoke to him as politely as he could: "Ah, Manager Xie. I imagine with all of this going on, what with the distribution of rations, you've had no time to rest. You have my sympathies. It's hard, I'm sure."

"You're too polite, Inspector Zeng. You've so looked after our Meng'ao. If there's anything you need, just let me know."

Zeng Keda rarely showed such warmth to anyone. He forgot, too, the decorum of age, and simply patted Xie Peidong on the shoulder. "Ah, thank you, Mr Xie. Please lead the way."

Xie Peidong leaned slightly and then began to ascend the stairs. Zeng followed close behind. At the same moment, the large grandfather clock in the drawing chimed. It was 5 pm on 12 August.

Outside the headquarters of the Peking Police, the bugle horn blared sharply over the loudspeaker, shattering the bright calm of the air. It was a call to assemble. Within seconds, there was a bustle of activity. The regimental commander of the gendarmerie signalled to his troops to line up in formation. Their helmets, rifles, leather belts and boots created a formidable display. The Special Forces battalion commander ordered his Fourth Corps into formation as well, their caps, pointed like the bow of a vast navy vessel, stuck into the air, their carbine rifles gleamed and their leather boots shone. Fang Mengwei arranged the Peking Police officers, truncheons at their sides. After these divisions had filed in, a single intelligence officer was led out by the officer in charge of the forces now gathered outside the police headquarters. Having arranged themselves in position so efficiently, they were a sight to behold. Each platoon commander directed his attention to the main doors. Only Fang Mengwei noticed the crows that had taken to the air in fright at the sound of the horn.

Xu Tieying, Wang Puchen and Secretary Sun were all standing near the door leading out of Chen Jicheng's office in the police headquarters. They were all waiting for him to depart first. Then, just as he was about to do so, the telephone rang and Chen reached for the receiver. A second later, his face grew noticeably dark. "Who made the changes? Why bump it to ten o'clock?" Xu, Wang and Sun all stared at him. They didn't know who was on the other end of the line. They only saw frustration grow on Chen's face. His voice became flustered: "If you're going to interfere in things like this, there'll be violence in Peking for sure! I need confirmation… immediately." The three men still had no idea what was going on. All they saw was the momentary look of confusion wash over Chen, and then he hung up. "Fuck!" was all he said before sitting back down.

Xu Tieying was the first to speak: "Chief Chen. Who… who was on the phone?"

"The Ministry of Defence."

"Did they get the orders from the president's office? Did they request them directly from the president?"

"The president is flying to Shenyang. We wait… till ten o'clock. Then we'll make the arrests and kill who we have to, just as planned."

"That's five hours away," Wang Puchen interjected. "The troops are all in formation outside."

"And they're to stay there, too. Just as they are. See to it that the depot is open and that they're given tins of canned food. Biscuits, too."

Fang Buting's office faced the sun, opening out onto a balcony that could be enjoyed on warm, sunny days. The tea was already steeped and waiting. Fang Buting had prepared it himself. The purple sand teapot and the three cups that went with it had been a gift from Chiang Ching-kuo. The tea paraphernalia seemed to encourage Zeng Keda to sit still and upright. It seemed to have the same effect on Xie Peidong. He didn't extend his hand to take one of the cups, either. Neither man did. They simply sat in front of the table and waited, watching Fang Buting and the tea as it continued to steep. Finally, Fang moved, lifting the hot water container to pour over the teacups, thus ensuring they were scalding hot. He then replaced the hot water container on the table and proceeded to pour the tea, one cup, two, three. It was high-quality tea, the best. This was first evident by the golden yet crystal clear hue of the liquid in their cups. The fragrance that reached their noses a second later confirmed the excellence of the tea.

Fang picked up one of the cups and handed it to Zeng Keda. He did the same for Xie Peidong. Both men received their cups with two hands and then waited for Fang Buting to take hold of his own cup. Unlike them, Fang used only one hand. But he didn't bring the cup to his lips. Rather, he poured its contents into the tea tray that lay next to the pot. Zeng Keda had been prepared for this and so he wasn't surprised by Fang Buting's actions. Subconsciously, however, he looked at Xie Peidong. His honesty, his thoughtfulness and deference to his superior were clear in his voice. Xie spoke softly: "Governor Fang..."

Fang did not look at them. His hand clutched the teapot, his eyes focused on his empty cup, before he tilted the pot and the last drops of tea poured out, drip, drip, dripping from the spout. There was an exact amount, just enough to fill the cup. He didn't lift it from the table, however. He just left it. Xie Peidong understood his boss wanted to speak, so he took the initiative and replaced his own cup on the table. Zeng watched the scene unfold and understood. He, too, laid his cup back on the table.

Fang now turned to Zeng Keda. "Today, I've only one thing to ask. Please, Inspector Zeng, tell me straight."

"Please ask your question, Mr Fang."

"Mr Chiang sent me four teacups. Could you tell me why you said there were three?"

This time, Zeng Keda was surprised. He hadn't expected such a question, and what's worse, he had no idea how to respond.

"Mr Fan Dasheng makes teaware. He's very precise, some might say too precise. But four teapots must mean there are four teacups, six teapots, six cups, you understand? This pot here can steep four cups, exactly four. How can there be three then? Inspector Zeng, if you lie when you give gifts, how can I trust anything you say?"

Zeng Keda stood up, abruptly; he felt he had no other option.

Fang Buting reached out his hand, his palm open. He waved for Zeng to sit back down. "I'm just asking. There's no need for an explanation. Peidong, go ahead, say what wants to be said. I shall just sit here and listen."

From the main gates of the barracks all along the outside wall, the young soldiers stood to attention, ready and prepared for any eventuality. Their mission was clear: provide defence and ensure the safe dispersal of food rations. Beside the main gate, the battalion commander was personally standing guard. Then, in a loud voice that echoed, he shouted for the gates to be opened and for his men to salute. A short while later, Fang Meng'ao's jeep appeared, followed by a convoy of civilian trucks. On top of each truck were men armed with rifles and iron batons.

Fang Meng'ao's jeep screeched to a stop. The young battalion commander could now see clearly who had arrived. He saw, too, who was sitting next to Captain Fang. The commander let his hand fall and walked over to the driver's side of the jeep. His voice was low: "Captain Fang, what's... what's he doing here? Who are the men in the trucks behind you?"

Fang Meng'ao answered from inside the vehicle: "This has been arranged by Inspector Zeng. Chief Ma is cooperating with us. The men in the trucks are here to assist you in maintaining order. We're all in this together, Commander, a united front."

"Sir, but who's in charge of these men? How are we to act in unison?"

"Chief Ma's in charge. In total, there're a hundred and fifty men in those three trucks. They're all wearing armbands to distinguish them. Each truck has a man in charge, too. Units one, two, three, just as there are trucks one, two, three. Tell your brothers-in-arms here that their mission remains more or less the same. They're to accompany Chief Ma to the distribution site and assist in maintaining order. To do that, you'll set up a perimeter to keep out those who would stir up trouble. If things get out of hand, your men will respond in conjunction with these men."

The young commander's brow furrowed. "Can we rely on them?" His eyes turned to Ma Hanshan as he asked the question.

"Captain Fang." It was Ma's turn to speak. "You go on in. I'll stay with Commander Li here at the gates. Will that be all right?"

"Yes, all right. Cooperate well."

Ma Hanshan alighted from the vehicle and Fang shifted into first gear and drove further into the barracks.

"Come on, all of you. Inside!" Ma's voice was loud, clear.

The trucks rumbled in, each following the one in front. Crooks mixed with honest folk. There was no denying it, the men in the trucks were a motley crew. There were those wearing Western-style hats, others revealing shaved heads; some wore suits, others wore Dr Sun Yat-sen-style jackets. There were even some sporting rattan hats and worker clothes. A few were empty-handed, but with pistols clearly hanging from their waists. There were also men with no visible guns on their person. But that didn't mean they were unarmed. Instead, they carried long pieces of rebar or steel rods to be used as clubs.

The young battalion commander looked over the gathered men. Thick, dark eyebrows adorned most of the faces. As the last truck pulled in, a number of the men aboard it greeted the soldiers with waves… of steel rods and rebar. One man even smirked, and that was Old Liu himself!

"So, Inspector Zeng, do you believe it was the Communists who gave Mr Fang this bit of information?" Xie Peidong wasn't looking at Zeng Keda, although his question was directed at him. Nor was he looking in the direction of Fang Buting whose attention was focused on the scene beyond the balcony window. He was just asking.

"I never believed that."

"Then, Inspector Zeng, where do you think the information came from?"

"It doesn't matter where it came from, that's not important. I just want to know why, why at this particular time you were looking for Liang Jinglun. And why you said he was one of us."

Xie Peidong had to turn his gaze towards Fang Buting. He hoped his boss would follow the cue and answer, or at least give him an inkling of how he ought to respond. Fang, however, remained motionless, his eyes fixed on the window. Xie had to answer: "Inspector Zeng. Truthfully, is Liang Jinglun one of you?"

Zeng thought to himself for the briefest of moments. It was time to lay all the cards on the table. Then they could negotiate. "Yes, he is."

Turning to Fang Buting, Xie addressed his boss. "Sir, Inspector Zeng has confirmed it. It's time for you to speak."

Fang turned round, but he didn't say anything, at least not straight away. Instead, he picked up his teacup and looked at Zeng Keda. "Please, drink." Zeng complied. Fang then looked at Xie Peidong and told him to do the same. All three now sipped at their teacups. Finally, Fang Buting spoke once more: "You two continue." He replaced his tea onto the table.

"Mr Fang, the difficulties the Peking branch has faced have been your burden to bear for far too long. You've suffered these grievances for too long as well. You shouldn't keep all of this to yourself, not now. If you don't speak, well, there's no way for me to put it into words either."

Zeng Keda jumped in: "What Mr Xie has just said is exactly right. The time has come. Mr Chiang has given me instructions to that effect. Whatever difficulties you've faced, whatever grievances you may have, please tell me now. This is the only way he can help resolve them... something he'll try and do for certain."

Tentatively, Fang Buting met Zeng's gaze. "Inspector, can you provide me with an answer to the question I first asked you?"

"And what question would that be?"

"Why are there three teacups?"

Zeng Keda's face turned a shade red, and for a brief spell he was embarrassed. Then he stood up. "I must first apologise to you, Mr Fang. When I return, I shall have to submit to Mr Chiang my own self-criticism. He did indeed gift you four teacups. In my carelessness, I accidentally broke one."

"Then how have these three cups come to represent three fathers and their three sons?"

Zeng's face turned scarlet. "It's... it's just my... an impromptu display."

"So there was no underlying meaning?"

"No, none whatsoever."

"Good." Fang Buting's mood changed, softened dramatically. He stood, extended a hand and encouraged Zeng to sit once more. Zeng returned to his seat, but even though he tried to sit upright, it felt unnatural, fake. Fang Buting turned to Xie Peidong, and said: "Bring some paper and something for Inspector Zeng to write with."

Xie hurried over to the desk and grabbed some official letter-headed paper and two sharpened pencils. Returning to where Zeng was sitting, he placed the items next to the tea table.

"Since it was Mr Chiang Ching-kuo who sent you here, please record what I'm about to say. It's best to write things down exactly as I say them. Don't add any of your own words, and don't try to interpret anything. Do you agree, Inspector Zeng?"

Zeng was the picture of seriousness. He didn't speak. He just picked up the pencil and waited for Fang to begin.

Fang's tone was sonorous and resounding, then gradually took on a higher pitch: "In the seventeenth year of the Republic, I, Fang Buting, was in America. Although this period happened to coincide with an economic recession, as a professor at Yale University, compared with other Chinese and most average Americans, life was all right. Your own TV Soong – Paul, I believe, was his Christian name – wrote me and an associate a letter, asking me to return to China. The country, he said, was in dire straits, and educated people had a responsibility to do something about it. He spoke of plans to establish a central bank and financial system. This was to revive the nation's economy. He had great hopes."

Sweat was forming on Zeng Keda's forehead as he raced to get every word down on the page. Finally, he had no choice but to interrupt the monologue and ask that Fang speak a little slower. Then he finished the last few sentences before signalling Fang to continue.

Once certain Zeng had caught up, Fang began again: "I gave up my Western-style home and garden, my high pay and status, and returned to China with my wife, my two sons and daughter. I made no requests to the government, not for anything. I simply devoted my energies to growing the financial strength of Mr Chiang's government. Regarding how much money was made, go and consult the files in the Central Bank. It's all there, every penny. As for the salary the government gave me, there are records for that, too. Before the Battle of Shanghai began in August thirty-seven, the government was desperate for me to empty the gold and silver in the central reserves, the foreign currency, too, and see it transported inland. They even wanted me to enlist the ships belonging to Lu Zuofu's Min Sung Industrial Company to aid in the movement of funds. No one believes me, but to carry out this enormous task, I abandoned my wife and children in Shanghai. What happened after August, well, you all know that. A bomb, dropped by the Japanese, killed my wife and daughter. It took two years before I could get my youngest son to Chongqing. As for my oldest boy, you've sent him to me to seek retribution."

Zeng Keda stopped writing and lifted his head. He soon realised Fang Buting was not soliciting a response from him. The best thing to do was to resume recording his statement, to get it over with.

"My younger son has never forgotten his older brother. From time to time he's asked one of my subordinates if he could go and see him, to bring him a little something. That's... that's brotherly affection, nothing more, but it didn't stop you from beginning to compile a file on suspected Communist sympathisers. Now, Cui Zhongshi is dead, for reasons I can't be sure of, and Liang Jinglun plays at being a Communist... all as a ruse for my idiot son. Inspector Zeng, you just asked me why I've been looking for Liang Jinglun, why I've sought to reveal his identity. Well, I want to ask you something instead, and I'd be grateful if you could help me in relaying this question to Mr Chiang: how is a father supposed to look at his son once he's been accused of being a Communist, accused of murder, of committing other crimes? All the while knowing full well that these accusations are, in essence, a death sentence. Am I supposed to not worry, to not make enquiries? If Mr Chiang isn't able to answer me, then I guess I'll just have to write another letter and have an assistant deliver it directly to Mr Chiang Kai-shek. He's the president of the Republic after all, and Ching-kuo's father. I'll ask him to teach me, what would he do if he were in the same situation as me? What should I do?"

Once Fang Buting made mention of Chiang Ching-kuo, Zeng Keda had already stopped transcribing what he was saying. Now with this break, he had to interject: "Mr Fang, will you allow me the opportunity to explain?" He then looked in the direction of Xie Peidong, hoping the other man would excuse himself.

Xie began to lift himself out of his chair.

Before he could make to leave, however, Fang Buting saw his intention and cut him off, his voice stern and unforgiving: "You're his uncle, a man of my age! If you're not concerned with what the younger generation is doing, does that mean you're leaving it to others to get involved?"

Xie lowered himself back into his chair.

Fang Buting turned once more to Zeng Keda. "Inspector Zeng, was it Mr Chiang who asked you to come and see me? Did he entrust you with this mission, such as it is, or are you here representing yourself?"

Zeng hesitated, a little stunned by the question. "I'm here on behalf of Mr Chiang."

"Then there's no need for an explanation," Fang Buting retorted. "What I'm telling you now, it's my opinion on events, my take on what's happened. It's what I want you to give to Mr Chiang. If you write down everything I tell you, then our conversation will be over."

Zeng picked up the pencil once more and said: "Understood.

Please continue, Mr Fang." With great effort, he tried to recall the last few words uttered by the branch governor and then added those to the paper. The calmness of a few moments ago had been replaced by an astringent, harsh feeling that made writing more challenging than it had ever been before.

The sky was already quite bright. The gate to the inspection team's barracks was wide open. Fang Meng'ao and the pilots under his command were inside. Only the younger troops and those men Ma Hanshan had brought were in the courtyard tidying up. Three trucks, an eclectic mix of criminals and supposedly honest people. It was painfully obvious they'd all taken three very different paths to get here. One unit, one formation, standing erect, each unit with its own commander positioned at the front of his troops.

The two section chiefs, Li and Wang, were banging drums, their minds on thoughts of what had transpired before. When Chief Ma had been arrested, they felt as though they were a wounded pack, shorn of its leader, a body without a head. They had felt betrayed. Now, Ma Hanshan had returned, but all they felt was guilt once more. They kept their mouths shut, however, and simply stood there, behind Ma and the battalion commander, watching him, wondering how he was going to manage all of this. It was best if they forgot them.

But Ma Hanshan didn't. He wouldn't. He might not have turned his face to look at them, but he knew they were there. He lifted his arm and gestured for the two of them to come forward. Li and Wang looked at each other, hoping that Ma hadn't called out to them. They remained where they were. Ma didn't shout, he didn't utter a further sound, but Li and Wang soon realised that more than one hundred men were staring at them. There was little they could do, and yet they didn't want to acknowledge they'd been summoned.

Wang leaned close to Li. "Did he call to us?"

Li, as was his habit, couldn't resist the opportunity to bully Wang, even just a little. "What the shit are you talking about? Are you playing at being a deaf-mute again!" And with that, Li straightened his posture and calmed his face, and walked to where Ma Hanshan was standing, coming to halt beside the chief. Again he tormented his fellow section chief: "Are you waiting for Chief Ma to invite you a second time?"

Wang hesitated a moment more before finally rushing over to stand next to Ma Hanshan.

"It must have been hard for you two when I was gone, hmm?" There was a surprising note of amiability in Ma's voice. Li and Wang remained silent, unable to respond. All they could do was look at each other. Ma continued: "I'm afraid, however, that I've more hardship to give you. Is the food for the men ready?"

Wang didn't dare reply. Li, who was a little shrewder than his fellow section chief, whispered in a low voice: "Chief Ma, should we give the men American money or Chinese... and how much to each? I'd say instruct Section Chief Wang to fetch them immediately."

Finally, Ma Hanshan let his eyes fall on the man. "Which one can you eat, huh, American money or Chinese? Will hungry soldiers be able to fight?"

The plan had been to prepare a grand meal for all one hundred-plus men, but as of this morning, no suitable place in the barracks could be identified, so the question was where? Where best to feed the men? Li and Wang were dumbstruck.

To their surprise, Ma Hanshan did not curse them. "Get on the phone right away. Tell warehouse three to load up a truck of canned food and biscuits and get them over here post haste."

Li had been seconded by the Social Affairs Bureau, his position here was temporary. Listening to Ma's instructions, he was truly at a loss as to what to do. He turned to Wang.

Speaking as quietly as Li had done before, Wang turned to Ma Hanshan: "Chief, you're in charge of warehouse three. You're the only one with the key."

"Just ring that Zhou fellow and relay my orders. Break the locks if necessary. Just get that bloody truck over here now." Ma's voice contained a slight note of annoyance.

Wang finally grasped the situation. "Sir, yes sir. Understood sir." And he strode off towards the guard room adjacent to the main gate.

With two hands, Zeng Keda handed the paper to Fang Buting. "Please, have a look. Check if it's accurate."

Fang Buting held his hand up to refuse and then turned to his assistant manager. "Peidong, your eyes are better than mine. You look it over."

Xie obliged his boss and scanned through what Zeng had written. "Exact to the word, sir. Inspector Zeng, the character you've written for Yale University is incorrect. It doesn't have the character for 'grain' in it. Rather, it's the same one used to transliterate 'Jesus' into Chinese." He handed the paper back.

Zeng took hold of the record once more. "I'll correct that now."

"It's not necessary," Fang Buting interceded and then laughed a little. "But let me say, seeing you being so sincere, Inspector Zeng, well, I think it's only right that I show the same. Please continue to take down my words."

Zeng complied once again.

"Currency reform and the issuing of new money is, to be frank, a last-ditch and probably futile effort. That said, given the current situation, not proceeding with currency reform is tantamount to simply waiting around to die, even if such reform won't really change anything. Twenty years ago, I, Fang Buting, chose to aid this government. I am not changing that decision now. What other people get up to are things that I cannot control or be worried about. I am ready and willing to cooperate with the activities taking place in Peking and Tianjin, I still have the ability to transfer my personal resources. I would request that our American friends provide greater assistance."

Zeng Keda was writing with growing vim and vigour.

"I have only one request. I would ask that Mr Chiang send my son, Fang Meng'ao, to the US, preferably before the implementation of the currency reform plans."

Zeng recorded this last sentence but then paused to look at Fang Buting. "This... issue you mention here, Mr Chiang has already given orders on. May I relay these to you now before we continue?"

"Please do."

"Fang Meng'ao is our most outstanding and capable soldier. His combat ability is without peer and among the people he has become quite the figure. It's hoped that in the three-month run-up to the implementation of currency reforms, the most difficult and challenging period of the whole scheme, I should add, well, it's hoped that he can remain in Peking in order to take charge of the situation. After those three months, I am certain special arrangements will be made to post Captain Fang to our American Embassy as a military attaché. Mr Chiang's orders must and will be obeyed. Please, Mr Fang, I would ask, on his behalf, that you trust and understand the need to have Captain Fang here for the time being."

Fang Buting couldn't help but be startled. Words failed him. He needed time, time to consider what Zeng had told him. He directed his eyes to the ceiling, and then to Xie Peidong. Xie could only stare back in response. Finally, he turned to Inspector Zeng. "Three months?"

"Yes, three months. This comes straight from Mr Chiang."

Fang turned again towards Xie. "Ah, that boy, held in such high esteem isn't he? I suppose he can manage those three months. He's coped with much more, hasn't he?" Fang Buting paused and Xie Peidong nodded his head in agreement. "I don't suppose I can haggle over this with Mr Chiang. Then… then I have another, smaller request to make. And you, Inspector Zeng, are just the man to help me with it."

Zeng once more lifted himself up from his chair. "Please tell me. I'm at your service."

"When it comes to these children, let me say it's not my two boys, Meng'ao and Mengwei, that I love most dearly, it's my younger sister's daughter, Mulan. Your man, Liang Jinglun, has… has brought her close to him. She's by his side now. I'm unable to say for certain, but I fear dearly for her well-being, for her life itself. Inspector Zeng, I would ask you to get in touch with Liang Jinglun and instruct him that he must, with great haste, get her to leave. He must sever his connection to her. I don't care how he does this, although constructing some logical reason would be best, but he has to get her to depart the university, to leave the student federation. Afterwards, I'll arrange for her to be flown to Hong Kong, and then on to France."

"I'll handle this immediately, Mr Fang. I'll make arrangements for her to fly within the week."

Fang Buting extended his hand to shake on the matter. Zeng Keda was not prepared for this show of affection. He stared a moment at the older man's hands and noticed the liver spots, the age. A wave of emotion welled up in him, and he reached out with both hands to clasp Fang Buting's.

"I've heard, Inspector Zeng, that every month you send money to your parents. You're a good son. Please, give my best to your mother and father."

"I don't know if that's entirely true, Mr Fang, but I will certainly pass on your greetings."

"Peidong, get the rations ready for immediate distribution. If things aren't done exactly to plan, there'll be student protests for sure. Please see Inspector Zeng off as well."

Xie Peidong escorted Zeng Keda to the main door and to his waiting car. Before letting Zeng climb into the vehicle, however, he reached out and took hold of the other man's hand. "In front of Mr Fang, well, let's just say it's not my place to speak openly, but there are a few things I'd like to talk to you about now, in private, if you will." Zeng's impression of Xie Peidong had been quite favourable, and so he now encouraged him to go ahead and say what was on his mind. "It's about my daughter, Mulan. You must, under no circumstances, heed Mr Fang's directions with regard to her. Do not instruct Professor Liang to have her expelled as a member of the student federation."

"Why? I've already made the promise to Mr Fang."

"There are tens of thousands of students in the Peking Student Federation. Expelling just her, well, Professor Liang would have no sensible reason to do so. She'd know, too. Mulan would figure it out immediately... that... that we intervened, we'd meddled. You can't, this is not the way to do it. If possible, just ask Professor Liang to distance himself from her. To stop her from participating in the federation's activities, that would be best."

"I understand. It won't be a problem." Zeng relaxed his hand, hoping Xie would do the same. He did not. Instead, he tightened his grip, if only slightly.

"Inspector, regardless of family, children are still just children. I heard from Mengwei that the various forces in Peking are all united in purpose today. I don't think that bodes well for the students. Inspector Zeng, you've been sent by the Ministry of Defence. You must do your utmost to see that the students are protected."

Zeng's impression of Xie Peidong was even more favourable than before. His voice became even more affectionate. "Mr Chiang has already said this, because of the corruption that has wormed its way into all levels of government, because this has resulted in us losing the support of the people. Our goal in coming to Peking has been to win back their hearts. Captain Fang and I will do everything possible to ensure the safety of the students. Mr Xie, if you trust us, I would ask that in the days ahead, should the opportunity arise, you put in a further good word with Mr Fang about what we are doing, that you show support for me and Meng'ao, and aid us in carrying out the job Mr Chiang has tasked us with."

Xie nodded his head and released Zeng's hand. Gesturing to the waiting car, he urged Zeng to climb aboard; time was not to be wasted. Before leaving the house, however, Zeng saluted Xie Peidong. Xie cupped one hand in the other and bowed. Zeng turned, got into the waiting vehicle and left.

A large, canopy-covered truck rumbled into the barracks assembly ground. The door to its rear truck bed was hanging open, exposing the cases of tinned food and biscuits inside. Adhering to expected norms, Section Chief Wang climbed up into the back of the truck and began to pass the contents out to Section Chief Li who was waiting to receive them. Ma Hanshan stood nearby, a crowbar in his hand. As the cases were laid on the ground, he began to pry them open. Inside the cases were tins upon tins of American foodstuffs, even including canned pork and beef. The young battalion commander stood to one side and looked somewhat enviously at the tinned food being unloaded. Men from all three contingents did much the same.

After crowbarring open ten cases, Ma Hanshan reached in and

lifted out a can of pork, then a can of beef. Holding them almost reverentially, he passed them on to the barracks commander and called to Li: "Commander Li, come here and give them a try. It'll boost your morale, that's for sure." The young battalion leader received the tins Ma handed to him, but he was not able to react, or respond for that matter. He simply watched as Ma Hanshan shouted to the men in charge of the three units: "Come on now boys, come over and help! You carry, I'll distribute." Each obeyed as though they were familiar with following Ma Hanshan's instructions. No words were exchanged. Each man took two cases, one filled with pork, the other with beef. Ma Hanshan walked closely behind and then up to the first man standing. Again with two hands, he lifted a tin of beef and a tin of pork out of the case. "It's hard work, I know. Here, take this, and when you're done, come back for two more."

Guo Jinyang called Fang Meng'ao out to the main gate to see Ma Hanshan handing out the tins of food. He swallowed and then laughed. "Captain, I searched those warehouses I don't know how many times. How's it I never discovered such... such toys to play with?"

Fang Meng'ao laughed as well. "The stuff Ma Hanshan squirrelled away, well, if it had been easy to find, I'm sure he wouldn't have been the man to have hidden it. What's the matter, your mouth starting to drool?"

Chen Changwu came out to join them. "Captain, working with these... men to carry out orders, aren't we doing a disservice to our own men?"

"So you think there are no men like them in the armed forces? You're worried about losing face? Wait a moment, when Ma Hanshan comes to give you a tin or two, make sure you refuse to accept it."

Several other troops in their contingent shouted in unison: "But we have to accept them!"

"Listen and listen good. Today we need to rely on these men to help us deal with Chen Jicheng, Xu Tieying and their cohort. They have their own ways of handling these kinds of things, so don't interfere. Understood?"

"Sir, yes sir!"

Fang Meng'ao turned around and walked back inside.

A pair of eyes followed Fang Meng'ao back into the building. They belonged to none other than Liu Chuwu. At the same time as he stared after Fang Meng'ao, Ma Hanshan arrived at the front of his contingent, still handing out the canned food, first to the man in charge, and then to the rest of the men. Old Liu was second in line. As before, Ma Hanshan repeated his by now familiar refrain: "It's hard, I know…" but he paused as his eyes fell on Old Liu's pair of hands, then his face. He'd not expected to see these eyes.

"This man here," said Ma, turning to the lieutenant, "tell me, what battles has he fought?"

"You've got a good sense about you. This man here has fought with the National Revolutionary Army. In an encounter with the Japanese, his whole platoon was wiped out… everyone except for him. He pulled himself out of the pile of dead soldiers, wounded but still alive. He wasn't willing to fight in the army any more, so he made his way to Peking. A number of our factories and warehouses wanted to hire him as a foreman, but he refused. He'd only take on odd jobs and stuff. The brothers of the Green Gang all follow him."

Ma Hanshan slapped Liu's shoulder heartily. "Good man, then, eh! Are you armed?"

"I've not held a gun since then."

Ma turned to the lieutenant. "See that he's given a Mauser. You mess up, say Xu Tieying gave it to you. What do you reckon?"

"Who's Xu Tieying?"

"The new chief of the Peking Police. Wait a bit and I'll point him out to you."

Old Liu directed his eyes to his battalion commander.

"Things… things won't get that bad, will they?" There was a note of uncertainty in the commander's voice.

"Taking down a rotten, no-good piece of shit police chief is no big deal. I've told you already, we've got the Investigative Department of the Ministry of Defence behind us, the princeling, Chiang Ching-kuo's own faction. When the time comes, whoever we need to take down, we'll take down. If you do right, they'll give you a medal for sure!"

"And you, fifth brother," the troop commander asked, "are you up to it?"

"I say we follow what Chief Ma here says."

"Excellent. Once things are finished, if you want to leave, that's fine. I'll give you ten thousand US dollars and you can be on your way. The gun… you give to him." He continued handing out tins of pork and beef.

CHAPTER 4

Zeng Keda was at home, the telephone receiver held up to his ear. "Thank you, Comrade Jianfeng, for your encouragement." It was clear by his choice of words that he'd received full support from his superior, but on this occasion, there was really no joy in his voice. He folded the paper on which he'd recorded Fang Buting's statement and slid it into his pocket. The clock on the wall read twenty-five minutes past eight. "An hour and thirty-five minutes to go before the rations are to be distributed. There are two other issues I would like to discuss, two more personal issues that have been on my mind. I wonder, Comrade Jianfeng, if I may take a few more minutes of your time. I'd like to give a full report."

"Are they that important, then?"

"Well, problems of this nature generally strike to the core. To me, they are important."

The line was silent for a moment or two. "All right, go ahead."

"Last month, on your behalf, I presented Fang Buting with the gift you had prepared, the teapot and cups made by Mr Fan Dasheng. I wanted to tell you that… I accidentally broke one of the cups."

"And how is this important?"

"Two points make this admission important. One, I didn't immediately report to you that I'd broken one of the cups. Two, when I gave the gift to Fang Buting, I… I lied. I told him your reason for giving three cups was to serve as a... the three cups... ah... they represented him and his two sons."

There was silence on both ends of the line, but only for a few seconds. Finally, Comrade Jianfeng responded to what Zeng Keda told him. The tone of his voice made apparent the seriousness of what he was saying, but the words themselves were quite contrary to what Zeng had expected. "You do know the organisation has already ruled on this matter. Between comrades, the simple 'you' can be used. Just now, I counted four times, you used the more formal pronoun when speaking to me. I trust you'll correct this."

Zeng Keda comprehended the meaning behind the words almost immediately. Then he laughed. "Yes... Comrade Jianfeng."

"Speaking of the issue you just mentioned," said the amiable voice on the other end of the receiver, "did Fang Buting expose your falsehood, and did it bring about any reticence on his part?"

"Yes, Comrade Jianfeng, it did."

"Then how did you explain it?"

"I came clean. I told him you'd sent four cups but that I had broken one, and that my story was just that, a story I made up on the spot to cover my own mistake."

"Which is what he just told me now."

"Yes, Comrade Jianfeng."

"All right then. What was the second thing you wanted to speak to me about?"

"Ma Hanshan has a gift for you. According to party regulations and general discipline, however, under no circumstances am I to accept any gift from him, certainly not any gift intended for you." Zeng Keda paused.

"Continue."

"Yes, continue... Well, once I learned the meaning behind his gift, I accepted it. Now, however, I'm worried I overstepped my bounds and wounded the image of the party... and you, too. I feel I've erred yet again. At first, I thought to give you the gift in secret once I returned to Nanking, and wait for you to ask me about it. I would then explain that we had confiscated it from his home after he was arrested. But after this recent episode with Fang Buting and the teapot, well, I've taken another look at the gift and... and I'm shocked."

"Tell me, what kind of gift would cause you to feel like this?"

Zeng Keda's eyes moved to the desk and the scroll that had been unfurled carefully, respectfully upon it. Two paperweights held it down, although he couldn't say where the paperweights had come from. There was no mistaking Zeng Guofan's handwriting. With great effort, Zeng tried to remain calm and composed. "It's a scroll, calligraphy... written by Zeng Guofan after the suppression of the Taiping Rebellion, a couplet given to the Xiang Army."

The phone went quiet. Zeng could feel and hear the sound of his own breathing. He stood a little straighter.

"Is it... are they *those* lines, *that* couplet?" There was awe in Chiang Ching-kuo's voice.

"Yes, Comrade Jianfeng. Ma Hanshan told us, too, that he already had Wang Shixiang verify the authenticity of the scroll. The handwriting is Zeng Guofan's." His words hung between them, causing him to hold his breath.

Chiang Ching-kuo's tone was resounding. "Check the flight schedules for the next available plane to Nanking, today or tomorrow, then give the scroll to an appropriate person, someone you can trust. Tell them to make haste in coming here. This gift needs to be given to the president as soon as possible."

"Yes..."

Never before, Zeng thought, had a voice over the telephone been so clear. "Comrade Keda, in response to the two issues you raised, I shall quote two sayings that are mutually reinforcing: 'All men err. They should not dread correcting their mistakes.' That's the first one. The second is: 'Should we see a man of worth, we should think of emulating them. Even though we may never attain such a level, we should not cease to strive to reach it.' This past month and more, and especially today, your way of thinking has improved enormously. I extend to you my greatest respect, Comrade Keda." Zeng had no idea how to respond. Fortunately for him, no response was expected. Chiang Ching-kuo simply paused for a moment for the words to sink in, and then carried on talking. "Head to where the rations are being distributed. Wang Puchen is waiting for you at Xizhimen. There is something he wishes to discuss with you."

"Yes, Comrade Jianfeng." The instructions had allowed him to regain his composure. At the same time, however, he felt that something wasn't quite right. "Comrade Jianfeng, may I ask… has the Intelligence Bureau set this up?"

"No, it has nothing to do with them. Let me hang up, and you get going."

"Understood." As soon as he said the word, he heard the click of the other end being hung up.

———

Zeng Keda's small jeep passed Yenching and Tsinghua on his way to Xizhimen. Close behind was a slightly larger jeep driven by his personal guard; another young officer tasked with ensuring Zeng's safety. About a kilometre beyond the gate, Zeng spied Wang Puchen standing tall beside his vehicle enjoying a cigarette.

"That looked like the Peking station master, Wang Puchen." Zeng's assistant clearly did not know the facts of what was going on. All he did was direct his attention to his superior in the passenger seat.

"Stop the car," ordered Zeng Keda.

"Yes sir." His voice was sharp like that of a loudspeaker; loud enough to signal to the jeep following behind to pull to a stop beside them. Conscious of maintaining an appropriate distance from its charge, the medium-sized jeep slowed down and stopped. One of its occupants alighted and walked straight over to the sentinel manning the roadblock.

Zeng Keda stepped down from his vehicle as well, before waving to the young soldiers behind. "Climb back into the jeep." There was no way to tell if Zeng's voice carried, no way to know if they heard him or not, but it didn't seem to matter, they understood his meaning and quickly climbed back into their jeep. Wang Puchen, who seemed to have been loitering quite contentedly like some crane in a marsh, now floated over.

"Your men?" Zeng's eyes were trained on Wang.

"They're already in position. They filed out along with the police from HQ." Wang Puchen's answer was immediate; he had no intention of allowing Zeng to ask further questions. He then turned towards Zeng's aide-de-camp and handed his keys over to him. "You drive my vehicle, I'll drive this one."

Wang waited for instructions on what to do. "Fine," was the only answer Zeng provided, so he did as he was told and took the keys, then walked over to Wang Puchen's jeep.

"Comrade Keda," said Wang Puchen, "please get in."

A look of bewilderment in his eyes, Zeng hesitated, staring at Wang Puchen, wondering what was going on. The other man smiled briefly, then averted his eyes to look at his own feet. In that instant, Zeng Keda realised what he was drawing his attention to. Wang Puchen was wearing a pair of black cloth shoes, footwear that was oh so familiar.

The Nanking Ministry of Defence, the Officer Training Corp flashed across his mind like a slap to the face! The dressing room assaulted his mind as well! Zeng Keda imagined two rows of neatly arranged hangers; civilian clothes without military rank hung upon them, while below were pairs upon pairs of black cloth shoes, arranged just as orderly as the clothes.

The black shoes moved, the Nanking Ministry of Defence, the Officer Training Corps, they both disappeared. Only the road that ran along Xizhimen remained before him. Zeng Keda raised his head abruptly. Wang Puchen had already walked over to the jeep and opened the door. Zeng did the same, manoeuvring to the passenger side and opening that door. They both sat down and Wang honked the horn for Zeng's assistant to get underway. Wang Puchen shifted gears and followed, but at a much more leisurely pace.

For the first time today, Zeng Keda appreciated how tall Wang Puchen was, so tall, in fact, that he had no desire to look at him all. Instead, Zeng focused on the rearview mirror and the vehicle that was behind them. He would wait, Zeng thought, for Wang Puchen to speak first.

"When the Nanking Whampoa Middle School held their establishment assembly, I was in Peking. I couldn't attend." Wang Puchen's eyes were focused on the road ahead, but he continued to speak: "The oath I made was to Comrade Jianfeng and what he stands for: 'For the revolutionary cause of the Three Principles of the People, I pledge unending loyalty to the vice-chancellor, now and forever.'" His oath recited, Wang extended his right hand.

Zeng stared at the hand that had been extended, its long and narrow fingers. He couldn't say why, but he felt uneasy. He understood, however, that there was nothing else he could do but take Wang's hand in his and repeat the latter refrain from Wang's oath: "I pledge unending loyalty to the vice-chancellor, now and forever."

Wang Puchen relaxed his grip, finally pulling away and replacing his hand on the steering wheel. He continued his monologue: "I know today's operations are related to the currency reform measures, and to the efforts being made to suppress unrest and save the nation. They're also meant to strengthen the cause against corruption, and against communism, too. Comrade Jianfeng tasked you and your department with pacifying public sentiment in Peking. He ordered me to arrest Communists. But the CPC is no longer encouraging and supporting the student protests, nor have they any plans to instigate labour unrest. In fact, they've all gone to ground. According to Comrade Jianfeng's analysis, they're biding their time, planning, scheming, getting ready for their final assault. It's because of this that we can't wait. We must act. We need to make arrests, and not just of anyone, but important figures, those directly responsible for arming the Communists in Peking... most especially Liu Chuwu, who's known by the designation 'Grandpa Five'. You ought to have received the intelligence on this last night, but the known Communist Yan Chunming is, apparently, no longer following the arrangements laid out by the CPC. In fact, he suddenly and without warning returned to Yenching University. In all likelihood, his actions have seriously jeopardised their plans. In order to contain the mess he's caused, there's a strong likelihood that Liu Chuwu will show himself today. Comrade Jianfeng's orders remain the same: you are to ensure that Captain Fang's distribution of rations passes without incident, and do your utmost to see that the students are not given any reason to turn this into a protest. I must locate and apprehend Liu Chuwu."

———

The convoy of trucks carrying their motley crews, criminals and decent people all together, drove past Yenching University, past Tsinghua, too. At the head was Fang Meng'ao's jeep. The young pilots under him were in a jeep just behind him. Ma Hanshan's three old, ten-wheeled trucks, each filled with rations and men of questionable backgrounds, brought up the rear.

There were only two people seated in Fang Meng'ao's jeep. For some time now, he had driven his own vehicle and had had no need for a driver. The man sitting next to him was Ma Hanshan. "Tell me," said Fang, "that man, the one you just gave a gun to, I know, I know… you didn't think anyone saw? Well, I did… but tell me, did you also give him a cheque or something like that? Who is he? What're you up to?"

Ma Hanshan remained silent, unable to answer.

Fang slammed down hard on the brake and Ma Hanshan lurched forward. Then he pushed on the accelerator, yanking Ma back into his seat. He was waiting for Ma to respond.

Ma smiled and then sighed. "Captain Fang, you don't want to ask these questions. But let me remind you, you promised to look after my son."

"Just what the hell are you getting at?"

"Come now, you've sat in on military court-martials, you know one is waiting for me. The less you know the better."

"But… but I was there. Inspector Zeng assured you, that if you cooperate, you won't face military justice."

"I'd like to call you… 'my boy'. Would that be all right?"

Fang Meng'ao hesitated a moment. "You can call me whatever you like."

"All right then, my boy, let me tell you something. Believe who you wish, but under no circumstances should you believe anything the Kuomintang says. I've been mixed up with them for years and years, and I'm still here, and that's because I've never once put faith in what they've said."

"Aren't you a member of the Kuomintang?"

"And so… don't take what I'm saying as true. But let me say this, I gave that guy a gun so that he could take out Xu Tieying. Do you believe me?"

Fang Meng'ao thought for a moment and then smiled. "Yeah, I do."

It was Ma's turn to smile. "Today's a good day. Someone believes the words coming out of my mouth."

The smile remained on Fang's face. "Don't cause trouble, just cooperate, I'll protect you." Ma Hanshan said nothing. Fang Meng'ao directed his attention to the road in front and let his words hang in the air. Out of the corner of his eye, however, he saw Ma Hanshan lean back into the seat and close his eyes.

"Don't say any more," said Ma. "Let me catch a few winks."

When he glanced at him again, Fang saw that Ma Hanshan was really asleep. His face never looked calmer. Fang Meng'ao's heart was tormented, awash with mixed feelings. He reduced speed, treating the car as some makeshift cradle with a baby fast asleep inside it. The vehicles following to the rear did the same.

The reduction in speed had its effect on the men in the trucks behind, at least the last one where the fifty men packed into the back had quite clearly been given orders to stay in a crouched position until they reached their destination. Now, however, several of them were standing up and training their eyes on the road ahead.

That was until their leader shouted: "Get back down, you scum!" The men quickly did as they were told. The commander was in the middle of the truck bed. Old Liu crouched facing him. It was at this moment that he remembered there was something he had thought to ask Lu Chuwu, but it had slipped his mind when the truck engine started and they hurriedly got going. Now, however, his question returned: "Chuwu, brother, tell me, you must have a death wish. Are you really going to go through with it? Are you going to kill Xu Tieying?"

Multiple sets of eyes fixed on Old Liu, who only smiled in response.

"Is your family that poorly off?" Again the eyes looked at him, and again Liu only smiled. The lieutenant sighed. "You know, generally speaking, Chief Ma has been decent to the men, but I know, too, that his whole family was brought down… he's broke. I worry for you, Chuwu. I reckon that cheque's not worth the paper it's printed on."

"I've looked at it closely," Liu finally responded. "The cheque comes from Citibank in Tianjin. It's got a 'one' written at the front, and then a whole bunch of zeros after it." Liu pulled the cheque out of his pocket and gave it to the commander to see. His eyes lit up when he saw it himself. Several more faces crowded in, all eager to see for themselves. Then more questions.

"How many zeros?"

"Is it real?"

"It's not Chinese currency, is it?"

"It's from Citibank. Of course it's US dollars!"

As the men crowded in, it became more and more difficult for the commander to continue crouching. Finally, he shouted: "Shit, give us a hand, will you! Help me up." Several hands reached out and helped lift him to his feet.

"How much is it?"

"Is it ten thousand?"

Once more the commander shouted: "Shit, are you all trying to rob a bank! Can you shut the hell up?" The truck went quiet, but the men continued to stare. "It's ten grand, US dollars. The branch of Citibank in Tianjin will cash it."

"That could get you to Hong Kong," blurted out one man wearing a tattered Western-style blazer.

"How about I give it to you," shouted the commander, "to get you the fuck out of here!"

Several men turned to look at the man in the old blazer. He swallowed hard and remained silent, not saying another word.

The commander turned back to Liu Chuwu. "Hey, brother. If this money is to save your family, I'll send it for you. If it's not, then give it back to Chief Ma. It's not worth selling your life for it."

With these words, the commander passed the cheque back, but Old Liu wouldn't accept it. He didn't say anything, didn't try to explain, just smiled as he had before. Those men crouched closest listened and stared; those squatting further away, out of earshot, just focused on the cheque.

Someone else offered his opinion: "You can't *want* to have that money, and if you do, well, your life is done for."

"He's not wrong, Brother Liu. There's no special bond between you and Chief Ma. You can't do what he's asking you to do." Another of the men offered their take.

The truck was quiet. Their words hung in the air as though everyone heard them.

"I'll fucking do it!" shouted another man, this one wearing tattered workmen's clothes. "And when I'm done, I'll just eat a bullet myself... so long as the money is sent to my family in Hohhot."

Cutting him off, the commander shouted: "No one's going to do it!" He scanned the faces of his men. "We're here to assist in the distribution of rations, that's it. If one of you goes ahead and does what Ma wants, you'll drag the rest of us down into it too." He turned to Liu Chuwu. "Brother, give me the gun, the cheque as well. I'll return them to Chief Ma once things are finished."

"Can I say something?" Liu's voice was loud and resounding. Everyone stared. "We can divide the ten grand, that'd be two hundred each, a decent amount."

The truck erupted into fevered conversations, men talking rapidly over each other, no one getting the chance to complete what it was they were saying. The cacophony continued until the commander stood up and spoke over everyone else: "For fuck's sake, can we give everyone the chance to finish saying what they're saying?"

As his words quieted the raucous men, the truck swayed and he lost his balance. Just as he was about to topple over, Old Liu reached out and steadied him. "Brother, carry on. Say what you need to, but tell us standing up. We'll make sure you don't fall."

Liu Chuwu took to his feet. The men around focused their eyes on him, their hands supported him. "Let me tell you, Chief Ma didn't tell us to assassinate any one person. This money is for us to protect members of the Defence Department and their investigative team. We just have to shield them, keep them safe, make sure nothing happens to them. This is what they want us to do, that's our responsibility. The money is here for us to divvy up."

Everyone on board the truck grew even more excited, and to a man, they all stared at Liu Chuwu. As for Liu, his eyes were on the commander, who now yanked at Old Liu's hand. "Pull me up." Liu obliged and held tight to the man's hand, supporting him firmly about the arms. "How many targets, and who are they?"

"Three." Liu Chuwu spoke surely. "I don't really know them personally, only that they're all affiliated with Yenching University. Two are professors, one's named Liang Jinglun, the other is Yan Chunming. The third one is a student, a girl. Her name's Xie Mulan."

"This means the Americans are in the background." The commander's eyes once again scanned the men under his watch. "Well, this is a job I think we're quite ready to accept. What do you say, men? No division of work, we just need to make sure we identify the right people. When the time comes, we'll use the distraction to get them into the clear. Then tomorrow we'll head off to Tianjin to collect our money and divvy it up the day after that!"

According to the available records, in 1946 Yenching University received an investment of thirty thousand yuan to purchase land and expand the university's campus. But they were only able to level the ground and set up the work sheds when civil war broke out. Naturally, work was halted and the site was left deserted for two years. It was therefore an excellent spot to use for the distribution of rations to all of Peking's institutes of higher education.

The row of work sheds lining the eastern side, where the building foundations would have been laid, served well to store the rations, although there was only room enough for the bags of flour. The rice was therefore piled just outside. Each bag of rice weighed a hundred kilos. The way they had been piled created a square-shaped platform or dais in the middle, the rice rising up around like some well-constructed bunker. As a result, here was an ideal spot to speak, and an even safer spot from which to sit and oversee the distribution of rations.

One mid-August day, at nine o'clock in the morning, the sun was already high enough in the sky to make things uncomfortably hot. It was difficult to say how many students were actually gathered in the clearing, all sitting, for the most part, very quietly. Student reps from each university were there along with several teachers. The rations were directly in front of them, but not a single student touched them. Nor did any student call out a shout of protest. They just sat as if in deep contemplation. In the parlance of Peking's residents, the way the students were behaving was yet another type of "troubled student". What would happen after this quiet meditation? No one, alas, had the answer to that question.

Behind the makeshift rice bag bunker, a number of other people were also sitting in supposed meditation. One person, in particular, stood out, a man sent by the civilian authority.

To the left of the rice bags sat Section Chief Li, his position mostly concealed from onlookers. To the right, Section Chief Wang, again nearly hidden from any wandering eyes. They'd spent most of the night supervising the workers as they unloaded the rations. They were tired and with one foot in the grave, at least according to them. By morning, the workers had all departed, but the members of the Defence Department's investigative team had not yet arrived, nor had Chief Ma. It was quite remarkable for so many people to be there in complete silence.

Most accepted their fate, like Section Chief Wang, who simply leaned against a rice bag and slept. Others, like Section Chief Li, couldn't sleep. All he could do was stare into the distance, eyes trained on the road that led towards the clearing.

Then, from somewhere far off, the sound of a vehicle came rumbling through the air. Section Chief Li's eyes grew alert. A second later, almost everyone else heard the same rumbling sound.

It seemed as though the students gathered in the clearing, all of them silently sitting in meditation, heard the noise, too. Unlike Section Chief Li, however, they remained as they were, seated and unmoving. Then, a single student shifted and began to raise herself up, her eyes looking in the direction of the first row of seated students. It was Xie Mulan. But within seconds, a fellow student reached out and prevented her from further movement. His eyes told her to stay where she was.

Liang Jinglun was in the first row. Sitting beside him were the lead student reps from Peking University, Tsinghua and Peking Normal. Behind him were a mix of students from the Chiang Kai-shek Student Society. And like everyone else, Liang had heard the sound of the trucks arriving. He'd turned his head, if only slightly, trying to get a better look.

Yan Chunming was also seated among the crowd of students, encircled as it were for his own protection. The morning sun shone down upon them, fierce and hot, reflecting dazzlingly upon the thick spectacles perched on his nose.

Liang Jinglun could not see Yan's response to what was happening. But he did edge himself closer to the head rep for the Peking University student federation. Liang now met the student's eyes, trying to get his attention. The student seemed to understand his meaning and signalled he would listen.

The rumbling sounds of the trucks that had seemed to be growing closer went suddenly silent.

On the road leading to where the rations were to be distributed, a scrabble of peasants had barred the convoy's passage. But that wasn't entirely true. The peasants hadn't actually blocked the road. Rather, it was once the vehicles had stopped and troops from the Military Police, the Fourth Corps Special Forces, as well as the Peking Police leapt down and melted into the sorghum fields that ran along both sides of the road, they were essentially waylaid by the peasants they encountered amid the tall stalks of sorghum.

The city was suffering from famine. There was fighting nearly everywhere outside it. Protesting students were causing their own fair share of chaos, too. And there in the midst of it all, fairly close to Yenching and Tsinghua universities, the epicentre of student activities, two hundred-plus peasants were trying to eke out a living by tilling the unforgiving land. For centuries, the month of August meant the sorghum would have taken on its familiar yellowish hue and would soon be ready for harvest. Men with supposedly greater aspirations might wish to turn heaven on its head, but for the farmers clinging to what little they had, August was a struggle to ensure their sorghum survived the next couple of months. Thus it was that they were out weeding the fields when scores of soldiers tromped in among them, frightening them half to death. The farmers had had dealings with Yenching and Tsinghua, and they knew a novel, supposedly constitutional government had been put into place. They were aware, too, that they could file grievances with the government, which was the main reason they now swarmed around the convoy searching to find the largest vehicle. They assumed, correctly, they would find the man in charge. And they did, in the form of Xu Tieying.

A peasant, one who had seen far too many seasons to still be out on the land, stepped forward and used the language of the city to accost Xu: "We don't owe the government any grain, or any of our harvest. So what gives you the right to come stomping in here destroying our fields?"

Xu didn't respond straight away. Instead, he craned his head to scan the area, saw the sorghum fields stretch on to come up near the row of work sheds, and then finally spoke: "Not a bad spot. Not a bad spot at all." Secretary Sun and the commander of the Special Forces voiced their agreement.

"Sir!" said the old farmer with a growing sense of urgency. "Your soldiers have ruined our crop. Where shall we seek compensation?" A few younger peasants, strapping lads, walked up to stand behind the older man, their eyes focused on Xu Tieying.

"Stop right there!" the Special Forces commander intoned threateningly. The farmers halted their steps but kept their eyes on the men in the jeep. The commander returned their gaze with equal force, preparing at the same time to frighten them away.

Xu reached up his hand and gestured for the soldier to stand down. Then he turned to Fang Mengwei who seemed to be waiting a few steps away. "Deputy Fang, come here a second." Fang's face betrayed no emotion whatsoever; he simply obeyed the command. Xu continued: "How much of their fields are destroyed? When we're done, you make an estimate of the damage and arrange for the government to compensate them accordingly."

Again, Fang Mengwei's face was stoic, unfeeling and cold. He walked over to the old farmer. "Uncle, I'm the deputy chief of the Peking Police. My family name's Fang. Our men have trampled your fields. Afterwards, make your way to police headquarters, tell them you're looking for me, and I'll settle things then. A potentially dangerous operation is about to take place. I would advise you and the rest of the villagers to vacate the area immediately."

"I… we'll need some note to that effect." The old man's voice was firm, resolute.

"And how the hell am I supposed to do that here and now!" The anger had risen quickly in Fang Mengwei. "You don't trust me? How's about I leave my gun here with you, huh!" He lifted his pistol out of its holster and held it out to the other man. The old man was stunned. So, too, were Xu Tieying, Secretary Sun and the Special Forces commander. All of them trained their eyes on Fang Mengwei.

"How…" the old farmer stuttered, "how can I dare to take it?" His tone then softened: "We'll… we'll take your word for it."

Fang Mengwei matched the older man's tone. He seemed to realise this was not the right individual to take out his anger on. He re-holstered his gun. "I've given you my word. Now please, you must leave. Quickly."

"Sir," said the old man, now becoming troublesome, "may I ask your name… I mean, your full name?"

Fang Mengwei sighed testily, but reached into his pocket and pulled out a fountain pen. "Give me your hand."

The farmer hesitated for a moment, then stretched out his old, wrinkled and callused hand. Fang Mengwei took hold of it and on his palm wrote his name. At the same time, another vehicle seemed to be drawing close. Xu and the rest of his entourage looked in the direction of the sound. Fang Mengwei did the same. A second later he knew it was his older brother. He turned back to the farmer. "Now go, quickly."

This time the man did as he was told, followed by the younger farmers. He grumbled as he walked away, however, complaining that he wouldn't be able to wash his hand for several days at least.

Xu Tieying's complexion changed abruptly. He imagined seeing Ma Hanshan fast asleep in the passenger seat of Fang Meng'ao's jeep.

Xu Tieying turned his attention to Wang Puchen, who had been sitting next to him smoking cigarette after cigarette. "How's it Ma Hanshan has been released?" he asked. "What the hell is going on?"

"The Ministry of Defence made a call. Captain Fang showed up in person to collect him. You didn't know?"

"The Ministry of Defence!" Xu's face went a shade of blue.

"Which Defence Ministry... that special clique tasked with making advanced preparation!" He paused for a moment, then shifted his attention to Secretary Sun. "So, the Intelligence Office has its secrets, and now you're keeping secrets from me, too?"

"Chief Xu," Wang Puchen interjected, "what we're doing is highly risky. It was necessary to have Ma Hanshan released first, then Secretary Sun could be." Xu Tieying's anger had been misplaced. He'd blamed the wrong person. He knew this, too, so all he could do was turn away.

―――――

Fang Meng'ao was navigating his jeep closer to where Xu Tieying's had halted and then pulled to a sudden stop. The jolt woke Ma Hanshan from his slumber. His eyes opened wide to the stern-looking face of Xu Tieying. Still somewhat drowsy, a smiling Ma turned to Fang Meng'ao and asked: "So, you wanted me to see him first, eh?"

Fang returned the smile. "You must allow him to save some face at least."

"I only fear he doesn't care." With those words, Ma Hanshan sat up, pushed the jeep door open and jumped down.

―――――

"What's the matter?" Ma Hanshan purposefully put on a look of surprise as he surveyed either side of the road and the troops in the sorghum fields. Then he turned to Wang Puchen. "The military have standing orders, don't they? They're not supposed to cause trouble for local farmers, certainly not destroy their fields. What you've allowed to happen here... it's unethical. The Civil Affairs Bureau, well, we won't be cleaning up your shit. There'll be no compensation coming from us."

Wang Puchen knew to whom Ma Hanshan was directing these words, but he also knew he had to keep quiet. He understood, too, that he had to keep calm.

Xu Tieying did not feel such reservations, however. "Mr Wang! This man was arrested on the direct orders of the Ministry of

Defence. How has he been released? I want to see that order with my own eyes."

"There's no reason for him to see it," Ma Hanshan answered deliberately in Wang's place and then stared in the direction of Xu Tieying. "Mr Xu, Brother Tieying, would you like to know why I'm here now, what I'm up to?"

Xu met Ma's gaze, but his focus wavered for there in the jeep was Fang Meng'ao, a slight smile clearly visible across his face. His mind then drifted off to thoughts of the past, his time spent involved with the Civil Affairs Bureau. He swallowed hard and then turned his whole body towards the sorghum fields and the soldiers standing there.

Ma Hanshan, however, would not let him go that easily. He walked up to Xu Tieying, determined to carry on their conversation. "You might not want to hear this, but I'll tell you just the same: hunger breeds discontentment. Your wife and children, your whole family are eating well... and safely in Taipei. They don't give a rat's arse about the common folk, about whether they live or die. We're here to see that they get food. You're here to make arrests, and to ruin these poor farmers' crops. I used to lack morals. That's why every woman I ever had left me, it's why I don't see my son, either. You ought to learn from the past. But you're choosing not to learn from my mistakes."

"And Zeng Keda?" Xu's voice was loud, his question not for Ma Hanshan, but for Wang Puchen. "You're all in it together, the Intelligence Department... Tell me, the orders you're following, which Defence Ministry officer gave them?"

Wang had just pulled out a new cigarette, but he hadn't yet lit it. His face betrayed his discomfort. "Inspector Zeng's returned to the city. Director Xu, I'm afraid I've got no answer for you. If you're intent on asking it, however, then I would suggest you telephone Chief Mao directly, or Mr Chiang Ching-kuo."

"Now that's the response expected of someone in your position, Mr Wang!" Ma Hanshan was sincere in his praise of Wang Puchen. So much so, he walked over to the other man and patted him on the shoulder. Ma then strolled back to Fang Meng'ao's jeep and opened the door. Before climbing in, however, he had one last parting shot for Xu Tieying: "It's best you steer clear, don't interfere. If you do –

if you cause trouble – well then, I imagine Nanking will set up a special court just to deal with you!"

Before Ma Hanshan had finished shouting, Fang Meng'ao was driving away, a grand smile on his face. His entourage of fellow pilots followed closely behind. After them came the trucks carrying the rations, three big ten-wheelers, each with men shouting and brandishing their iron pipes and batons at Xu Tieying and the men he'd brought with him.

Xu was left facing the sorghum fields, his mind seemingly lost in thought until finally, he shouted out for Secretary Sun. Sun walked over, but before he got close, Xu was barking orders: "That man, he needs to be taken care of. I want him gone… dead."

"Director… you… you can't give that order. You can't let yourself become the object of ridicule because of a…"

"Then you take care of it personally." Xu's eyes burned into Secretary Sun. "See that he's sent to Nanking. Make up any story you want. Understand?"

Sun could only look at his boss. Words failed him.

―――

"It's time!" Section Chief Li's voice echoed out from just behind the bunker. "Everyone up! Sleep when you get back home!"

In truth, everyone had long since woken up as one of the members of the civilian committee had seen Ma Hanshan and Fang Meng'ao walking towards them. As a result, they were all now standing, ready to greet the men, and the rations they had brought.

"Why's everyone standing? Sit, please!" Ma Hanshan's voice was eerily similar to a yamen official in days gone by shouting at the crowds. Fang Meng'ao had emerged from just beyond the bunker and now stood in front of the teachers and students, all of whom were still seated on the ground. His first action was to salute them. The twenty or so pilots who had walked up behind him followed suit, each holding their right hand up to salute.

Liang Jinglun's eyes then crashed into Fang Meng'ao's. Xie Mulan's face was filled with conflicting and confused emotions. She was excited and nervous at the same time to see Captain Fang, if only from a distance, and Liang Jinglun who had been sitting in the front row. The dense mass of students and teachers stared at Fang Meng'ao and the soldiers behind him. No one uttered a word.

At that moment, out of the three trucks that had entered the area, a hundred and more men jumped down. They were wearing all manner of clothes and seemed nothing but a motley crew thrown together on a whim. They looked woefully out of place. Some carried iron pipes, others steel batons, while still others were armed with pistols holstered around their waists. The teachers and students remained steadfast, none of them talking.

Fang Meng'ao strolled over to the platform created in the centre of the bags of rations, saluted once more, and then stood to attention. Ten of his men marched over to the left side of the dais and copied their commander. The other ten to Fang's right did the same.

"Brothers and sisters. I know this has been hard. My sympathies!" Ma Hanshan followed up in the rear, bowed, waved and then crouched down in front of the gathered mass.

"It's not been that difficult." The voice was weak and seemingly lacked any conviction. It came from the left, from the civilian representatives that were there.

Ma Hanshan turned towards the speaker. "Section Chief Li. Come here."

Li began to lift himself up, and as he did so, he turned to Section Chief Wang and waved.

Both Li and Wang had been there for some time, so when Captain Fang and his men had arrived, all they could do was look at the dozen or so young pilots in their uniforms; each so proper looking, each of them saluting. It was quite the sight. So much so that Section Chief Wang had no idea that Comrade Li was signalling for him to stand up. Fortunately, Guo Jinyang, who was standing nearby Section Chief Wang, saw what was happening and leaned in close. "Hey, he's calling to you."

Wang began to straighten his body and finally saw Section Chief Li frantically waving at him to stand up. He quickened his pace and navigated out from around the centre, making his way hastily towards the platform where Ma Hanshan and Captain Fang were.

Seeing Section Chief Wang breathing somewhat raggedly, Ma Hanshan gestured towards the vehicle he'd come in and the men milling about it. "You three, come here, too." Each of the group leaders scampered forward, including one Liu Chuwu.

Ma continued his oratory: "We're here today to distribute rations. Captain Fang and his men are to supervise, the civilian reps will oversee the list of names and who gets what. In other words, which university has how many students, how many bags of rations, etc. We can't afford to make any mistakes. As for the actual heavy lifting, my men and I will handle that. Bag by bag we'll pass the rations out. Afterwards, we'll arrange for them to be delivered to your respective campuses. Is all that clear?" Li, Wang and the three team leaders all shouted in the affirmative. Ma continued: "There's one more thing – and this is important – I want no violence whatsoever, nor any cursing. Understood?"

"Understood."

"Tell me, then. What do you understand?"

The five men looked at each other, slightly dismayed and unsure of how to answer.

"I'm referring to the students whom we're here to give rations to." Ma's face surveyed the area behind the workers' sheds. "If you feel the need to fight, swear and crack heads, then head on back to the sorghum fields and mess with that lot."

"Understood." This time, however, only the three team leaders from the trucks answered. Ma Hanshan had little hope of seeing any courage within Li and Wang. Instead, he just looked them over, somewhat dismissively, before saying to all of them to get to their specific tasks.

"Sure thing."

The rest of Li and Wang's gendarmerie followed them into the work sheds, leaving only the twenty young pilots standing on either side of the makeshift bunker. Staring at the bags of rice piled around, Ma Hanshan straightened up, brushed off his clothes and walked over to Fang Meng'ao. "Captain Fang, it's my turn, I guess. Will you escort me or am I allowed to go by myself?"

Fang Meng'ao kept his focus on what was in front of him. "Go ahead on your own."

"Alrighty!" His answer was deliberately loud as he scrambled up the pile of ration bags. Once on top, alone and by himself, Ma Hanshan announced: "Gentlemen, classmates!" His voice was at top volume. He paused a moment as if he was waiting for stones or other objects to be flung at him. But after seconds passed and nothing was thrown in his direction, he realised he would not be so assailed. The only response he did receive was the same stoic silence the students and teachers had shown since the beginning.

Ma Hanshan was moved by the response and expressed as much. "Thank you, thank you. Gentlemen, fellow students. First, I'd like to admit that what I'm about to say, I say without any real qualifications to back it up. But it is from the heart, nonetheless. So, if you'll permit, I will begin."

Silence.

Ma Hanshan cleared his throat. "In the inaugural year of the Republic, our prime minister, Dr Sun Yat-sen, promulgated the first interim presidential decree. In that decree, one key clause abolished kowtowing. Because of this, today, here and now, I cannot kowtow before you. So, I guess three bows will have to suffice!" He went quiet and then did as he promised, bowing three times deeply to his audience. He didn't wait for any reaction or response. It was as though he were alone in some valley performing his own soliloquy.

"Perhaps you know this, perhaps you do not, but up until a few days ago, I was in prison, incarcerated in Xishan, arrested on the direct orders of the Ministry of Defence. Why was I held? Because I was deputy director for the municipal authorities in Peking, I was responsible for managing the distribution of rations to two million people, fifteen pounds per month per person. But I made mistakes. Not everyone got the rations they were entitled to. As a director of civil affairs in Peking, I saw numerous reports daily, from the thirteenth of April when the civilian committee was established until today, the twelfth of August, more than two hundred people starved to death in Peking each day. On some of those days, the number was as high as six hundred. Over the next hundred and twenty days, how many more will die? I won't dare to guess. For each death I deserve a bullet, one bullet for each death. I fear, though, that it'll take a truckload to bring these bullets here." At this point, Ma Hanshan stopped. He was waiting for a response from the students. Something. Anything. All so that he could go on speaking as he had, violating taboos on what could be said and what shouldn't.

But the crowd said nothing. Silence remained. It was apparent, then, that Liang Jinglun and Yan Chunming had done their work, and done it well.

Still, Ma Hanshan waited. And still, no reaction was forthcoming. An awkward silence began to well up between them.

Seated in the front row, Liang Jinglun directed his eyes to Fang Meng'ao.

Fang remained standing where he had been, his eyes not making contact with anyone. He simply stared blankly in front of him.

Ever so slightly, Liang Jinglun tilted his head in the direction of Yan Chunming who was sitting some distance behind and to the right. As his eyes fell on Yan, he saw the sun reflected brightly off his thick glasses. He turned his head back and leaned over a little closer to the student representative from Peking University. "Ask him why has he stopped speaking."

"Why have you stopped?" The student's tone was loud, with a hint of aggression to it.

"Tell me," replied Ma Hanshan, meeting the student's eyes. "Are you the student rep for Peking University?"

"Yes, I am." He stood up. "You keen to arrest me, is that it?"

"Please, please..." Ma Hanshan watched as the student squatted again on the ground. Then he scanned the crowd, a seriousness on his face that had not been there before. "His question was a good one. Just beyond the work sheds there, in the sorghum fields, men are hiding, and their intention is to arrest the lot of you!"

Out behind the work sheds, deep within the sorghum field, the commander of the Fourth Corps Special Forces was the first to react, cursing in a low voice that Ma's words were tantamount to treason. He then turned to search for Xu Tieying, but all he could see was the vague outline of his troops lying in ambush among the stalks of sorghum. Xu Tieying was nowhere to be seen.

But he wasn't far away. His position and presumed status wouldn't allow him to hide in the farmer's crop, however. Instead, he was sitting on a mound of earth next to the field, waiting to signal his troops into action. He, too, had heard Ma Hanshan's claim, and now focused his attention on Wang Puchen and Fang Mengwei, both of whom were seated nearby. "Did you hear what he said?"

Wang nodded, while Fang stayed still, impassive.

While they watched each other, Ma Hanshan's voice echoed out over the field again. "On the fifth of July, the Peking Consultative Assembly passed a resolution... an apology to your fellow students from the northeast. A crowd encircled Speaker Xu's home. In the aftermath, quite a large number of students were wounded, and others were arrested. Nanking dispatched an official investigative team to look into what happened. But today, the men who brought those soldiers – the ones who want to make sweeping arrests – they are members of that investigative team. They were put in charge of the Peking Police after the fifth of July. The man in charge is Xu Tieying!"

"Arrest that man... now!" Xu was on his feet in seconds, his eyes hard on Wang Puchen and Fang Mengwei. The two men rose to stand as well.

"But," Wang began, "he was officially assigned this task, to distribute the rations. If we move to apprehend him, it's sure to draw a response from Captain Fang, likely a violent one."

Xu looked towards the sorghum. "Bring me the bloody radio transmitter!" Within a matter of minutes, a young soldier, no more than a porter, appeared with the transmitter strapped to his back. "Get me Deputy Commander-in-Chief Chen."

"Hello! Hello! This is the Investigative Department. Connect me to Deputy Commander-in-Chief Chen!"

In front of the sorghum fields, to the right of the clearing where the students and teachers had gathered, another transmitter-receiver was being set up. Seated beside was none other than Zeng Keda and his aide-de-camp Wang. Zeng's battalion commander Li had set up a perimeter not quite two hundred metres away from Xu and his men.

Zeng's voice was low: "Have you got the channel yet?" Wang nodded, his hand twisted the knobs, but Zeng forced him to stop. "Don't transmit for now." He cocked his ear to hear more of what Ma Hanshan was saying. Wang loosened his grip on the radio transmitter.

The reactions among the students and teachers to Ma Hanshan's monologue ranged from shock and amazement to resentment and anger. Needless to say, his words were riling them up, adding fuel to an already burning fire. Ma knew, too, that it wasn't only the authorities in Peking that were watching him, those in Nanking were paying close attention to what was happening as well. For a lifetime, he'd fought with Lieutenant General Dai Li in the campaigns aimed at unifying the nation. With Dai Li, he'd earned a reputation for fighting for the underdog, of understanding the difference between right and wrong. After the war against Japan was won, he'd been put in charge of identifying the traitors to China in Peking, and seeing that justice was properly levied. Quite a few benefitted from the confiscation of property once held by these Japanese sympathisers and collaborators. No one really knew the ins and outs of what he was up to, nor did anyone dare to ask. Most were too afraid of being implicated in his campaign to root out traitors, even if they were innocent. Once American aid arrived, the authorities reassigned him, this time to serve as the chief of the Civil Affairs Bureau. This past year he'd doubled up on duties, serving as the day-to-day deputy director for the civilian committee. Essentially, he'd been stealing food right from out of people's mouths. That's how his comeuppance had finally arrived. The investigative team dispatched by the Ministry of Defence had set their sights squarely on him, but no one ratted him out behind his back. Ultimately he met Fang Meng'ao, whom he made promise to look after his wayward son. And here he was today, handing out rations to poor students. If he could, at the same time, infuriate that coward Xu Tieying who was hiding out in the fields nearby, well, if he were shot in the back because of what he was saying, he wouldn't consider it anything but a good death.

"Fight against corruption!"

"Fight against hunger!"

"Oppose the civil war!"

The assembled students and their teachers erupted into a cacophony of shouting.

Wang Puchen and Fang Mengwei had already moved men from the sorghum fields in the direction of the roaring crowd. Secretary Sun was standing next to Xu Tieying, the latter having called him over. Xu was clutching the radio transmitter, waiting impatiently for a resolution to the current situation to present itself.

The transmitter burst into life. Chen Jicheng's voice bellowed out of it. Xu had his resolution. "Shoot them on sight!"

"Understood." He replaced the radio receiver and turned to Sun. "See to it."

"Director, Deputy Commander-in-Chief Chen wouldn't give that order. Shouldn't you maybe request instructions directly from Chief Ye?"

"Shoot the scum. Is that order not clear enough?"

"Understood, sir." Sun pulled out his pistol and trudged off towards the still-roaring crowd.

In the field on the opposite side, Zeng Keda's face was drenched with sweat, his eyes fixed on the radio transmitter that sat in front of his assistant. He, too, was waiting for a transmission. Finally, the machine buzzed and whirred; the message had come.

"There's no time to translate it," he said, the urgency in his voice unmistakable. "Just tell me what it says."

Wang's face was similarly drenched with sweat. He examined the coded text; he knew his business well. Then he began to relay the message: Instructed Captain Fang to protect Ma Hanshan <break> Soldiers to protect Captain Fang <break> Ma Hanshan to be escorted to Nanking asap <break> Chiang Ching-kuo <end>

"Commander Li!" Within seconds, Li had run up to Zeng Keda, who communicated the orders immediately. "Inform Captain Fang he must protect Ma Hanshan. You and your men must ensure Captain Fang's safety."

"Sir, yes sir!" Commander Li saluted, turned and then, accompanied by his men, ran out of the sorghum fields.

There was no need for them to inform Fang Meng'ao of what he was to do. He'd already climbed up on the improvised dais and was shouting for his own men to join him. "All of you, now, we must protect Ma Hanshan!"

The pilots standing to the left and right reacted immediately, all of them scrambling up to create a barrier to the rear and to each side of Ma Hanshan and Fang Meng'ao. Their backs were to the two men in the centre; they were ready for any provocation.

Captain Fang now addressed the crowd: "Gentlemen, students. We're in the same boat as you. I feel as you do, the same pain. To be known and recognised as a world power, a top four country, and yet to rely on aid from another nation to feed our own people, can only be because our nation's poverty has worsened. We've regressed as a country. As for what our government is doing, Ma Hanshan has already mentioned some of this, so I don't need to repeat it. Right now, American aid is… is right here, at my feet. Look for yourselves, you can see the words 'Made in USA'. It's perhaps true that my own feelings run even deeper than yours. I joined the Air Force in 1939. I was with the American Flying Tigers. We fought the Japanese together, Americans and Chinese. Two years ago, retired American soldiers aided us again, but the US government was unwilling to supply us with arms and other resources. Not until the Japanese launched their sneak attack on the Pearl River delta, not until the Pacific War fully exploded did the Americans become our true partner in arms, not until then did they provide us with aid. I remember the first time I saw that banner, 'Made in USA'. My brothers in arms, I, all of us, we cried." At this point, Fang paused.

Fang lifted his head towards the sun, and his eyes sparkled under its warm rays. The crowd that had only recently been shouting in protest and anger, was now exceptionally quiet.

Fang Meng'ao swallowed the bitter taste that had welled up in his mouth. He lowered his eyes and continued: "And now we have American aid once again, in my heart I don't want to accept it. What's more, I really don't know if we should distribute it. These words come to mind, told to me by our venerable Tsinghua University professor Liang Jinglun: 'Strong youth, then strong country!' So, all in all, should we hand out this food? If we do, will you, our country's youth, be able to repay it twice over, say, five to ten years?

If you think you can, then we'll start handing it out. And, thinking of the fifteen thousand refugee students from the northeast, well, then we should distribute this aid. I want to make a promise to all of you, a pledge, for all the food aid that is given out, I personally will write the IOU to the committee in charge of US aid to China and sign my name to it. When things improve, we'll repay it together. If you're in agreement, then all I'll ask is that the leaders of the various student federations sign the letter with me. We're not, today, merely accepting American aid, we're borrowing food. And anything a person borrows, they must give back!"

Again there was only silence. Then one person began to clap. It was Liang Jinglun. The tempo of his claps was slow but extraordinarily loud, forceful. Soon, the student reps took up the beat and began clapping, too. Like a great wave or gust of air, the clapping began in the first row and then in seconds swamped each row behind. Finally, the entire clearing reverberated with clapping hands.

Xie Mulan clapped the hardest.

Sensing the mood of the crowd, several students behind Liang Jinglun, each of them from the Chiang Kai-shek Student Society, now began to shout in addition to their clapping. "Accept the food aid! Accept the food aid!" It required only seconds for the other students to take up the chant, so enraptured had they all become by Fang Meng'ao's speech.

In response to the emotion he'd stirred in the young students, Fang Meng'ao could only call to his men, could only give them this order: "Attention!" And they, to a man, saluted the chanting and clapping students.

Ma Hanshan looked back and forth between Fang Meng'ao and the crowd, his face beaming.

Section Chiefs Li and Wang, both of whom had been ducking for cover near the work sheds, now stepped forward, along with their gendarmes, each feeling, perhaps for the first time, that they were truly government officials, bearers of office, men with real responsibility. The hundred-plus men who'd come on the three trucks were similarly swept up by the emotion running through the clearing, soon clapping as loudly and in rhythm with everyone else.

Even Old Liu, standing to one side, was clapping, although his eyes were fixed on Liang Jinglun and Yan Chunming.

For his part Yan clapped, if a little less vigorously than everyone else. But he did not join the chorus shouting to accept the aid. Liu Chuwu noticed this and leaned closer to a few of the men standing near him. "That man over there, with those thick glasses, the one not shouting out the slogan like everyone else, that's Professor Yan."

Men to the right and the left responded: "Understood."

"The man in the front row, in the middle, the one who clapped first, that's Professor Liang."

"Gotcha." This time, more men replied.

"And in the last row over there, the girl, the one shouting louder than the rest…"

"Understood."

"Pass it on. They're the three you must rescue." The men did as they were instructed.

―――――

Xu Tieying and the young radioman walked out from the sorghum field. Sun, gun in hand, was standing to attention. "You can put that gun away. I have another task. What Ma Hanshan and Fang Meng'ao just said, you heard them. I want you to relay it, first to Chief Ye, then to Deputy Commander-in-Chief Chen, and finally to Chen Jicheng. Request they inform the president."

The request was unsurprising. Secretary Sun had heard what the men had said, and he was, after all, skilled with both the sword and the pen. He holstered his pistol and dug a pen out of his pocket. From another pocket he pulled out a notepad, knelt down beside the sorghum crop and began writing as quickly as he could.

―――――

In the other field, Zeng Keda and his assistant were transmitting messages of their own: Jiao Zhongqing performed well <break> Liu Lanzhi gave his tacit cooperation <break> Situation under control <break> Keda

His aide-de-camp clicked in the last words, then turned to Zeng Keda. "Sent."

Zeng lifted the binoculars up to his face. The place they'd chosen was excellent; it was slightly raised and thus provided a vantage point from where to scan the fields of sorghum and the clearing beyond. If he tilted his head a little, he could even see the dais Fang Meng'ao was standing upon. A little further and he could make out both Liang Jinglun and Yan Chunming.

"We've received a response." The machine sounded and Wang held the receiver up to his ear. His face soon betrayed the startling content of the message. With one hand holding the receiver, his other raced to write down the coded text. As before, he relayed it as soon as the transmission had finished.

Zeng Keda walked over to his assistant. He watched the other man's hand scribble across the page. When it came to a stop, he was quick to ask if that was all. Wang answered in the affirmative, and like before, Zeng simply asked him to read it directly. There was no need to translate it: Report to me Jiao Zhongqing's exact words <break> Pay close attention to CPC movements <break> Report immediately on Xu Tieying's reaction <break> Jianfeng

Zeng was now similarly startled by what the message said. He looked at his assistant and asked: "Do you remember what Fang Meng'ao just said?"

Wang hooked the headphones around his neck and looked at his superior. His eyes were blank. "Inspector, I've had these headphones on the whole time…"

Zeng waved his hand. "Take note." The pen was already in Wang's hand, the paper on his lap. He waited for Zeng to begin. Zeng closed his eyes and used all his mental faculties to recall the words he'd just heard Fang Meng'ao deliver to the student crowd. "Gentlemen, students. I feel as you do, the same pain. No, that doesn't sound right, let's start again. My heart feels the same pain…"

Wang erased the previous line and resumed his recording of Zeng's words.

At that exact moment, Commander Li raced up. "Here to report, sir. They've begun distributing the food aid…"

"And this is worth reporting?" said Zeng. "Go, carry out your orders."

"Sir, there's more. Wang Puchen has information he says must be reported to you."

Zeng Keda finally stood up, devoting all of his attention to Commander Li and the supposed information he possessed.

"A report's just been received from the Peking Union Medical College Hospital. Zhu Ziqing of Tsinghua University has died. Students and teachers are protesting across the city. News of his death is no doubt on its way here."

At first, Zeng Keda barely reacted to the information. Then his face took on a grave complexion. "They're rioting... because Zhu Ziqing is dead?"

"That's what Wang Puchen said. It's likely the CPC are egging them on. They're saying he died of starvation."

"Oh no, no, no... that's not good at all!" Zeng's mood had changed, and so too had the look on his face. "This is liable to escalate into something far worse. Quick, communicate with Wang Puchen. He must keep an eye on Xu Tieying. If things deteriorate here, he must make sure no shots are fired. He has to wait for orders from Nanking!"

"Sir!" Commander Li spun on his heels and tore off through the sorghum field.

Zeng turned to his assistant. "Another transmission, now!"

He Qicang's telephone rang almost violently. He Xiaoyu left her father's study, skipped down the stairs and grabbed hold of the receiver. She lifted it to her ear, but never had the chance to even say "hello". The person on the other end was speaking fervently. A few seconds later, Xiaoyu's complexion changed. She tried to compose herself, then spoke into the phone to the person hurriedly speaking English to her. "Please wait a minute. I'll get Vice-Chancellor He." She placed the phone gently on the nearby teapoy and returned upstairs to get her father.

In his study on the first floor, He Qicang was reclining in his chair when he watched Xiaoyu come in.

She tried to portray a mood of calm. "The American Mission in Peking is on the telephone. Please can you come to answer it?"

He Qicang accepted her outstretched arm and lifted himself out of his chair. "The US Mission has rung me? What did they say?"

Still supporting him, they walked towards the door to his study and the steps that led downstairs. "Mr Zhu... has died in hospital."

He stopped. "Mr Zhu? Which one?"

"Zhu Ziqing." Xiaoyu's voice was low, seemingly reverential.

He Qicang was stunned but quickly regained his senses. "Didn't they say he was improving?"

"I don't know, but you don't want to worry, just answer the phone." They continued walking towards the drawing room, but now He Qicang's footsteps appeared much heavier. Xiaoyu exerted herself more to support him. "Slowly, slowly. There's no rush."

He Qicang entered the drawing room and deposited himself on the sofa. Xiaoyu held the telephone receiver up to his ear. "Use Chinese, please," he instructed the man on the other end.

Obliging in rather flowing Chinese, the person from the American Mission said: "These anti-American activities do nothing but strain relations and jeopardise the delivery of US aid to China. At present, only the teachers and students at Yenching University are in a position to help ease the growing tension. Please, Mr He, you must convene a pan-university committee meeting, or at least do something to stabilise the mood of faculty and students at Yenching."

"Tell me, why are you not reporting this situation to Ambassador Stuart?"

"We already have, sir. He was the one who told me to reach out to you."

He Qicang was silent for a few moments, then continued: "Please tell Ambassador Stuart, get him to inform the Nanking government straight away. If a new student movement starts in Peking, the authorities must not be allowed to fire on them, nor make any efforts to suppress them. Otherwise, well, I'll be out there marching with them!" He turned to Xiaoyu and instructed her to hang up. His daughter did as she was told. He Qicang slowly lifted himself up. "Take me out to where they're distributing the food aid."

"But... you... you can't go there."

He'd never looked at this daughter with such conviction before. But there was nothing to say, he just stared at her. A moment later, he clutched his cane and made towards the main door. He Xiaoyu thought to race over to her father, to help him, even though she didn't think he should go. But she paused before taking a second step in his direction, and instead grabbed the telephone. "School Office... yes... Vice-Chancellor He wishes to go to the designated food aid distribution area. Please send a car immediately to Yannan Garden!"

The acknowledgement was quick; a car was on its way. He Qicang had already gone through the door. Xiaoyu looked ardently at her father's back, and then dialled another number. Her call was answered almost immediately. "Assistant Manager Xie? Hello... Have you heard the news that Zhu Ziqing has passed? Yes... you have. My father received a call from the American Mission... he's just left now to go to where the aid is to be handed out... I don't know what else to say... I don't have time, he's already left. Can you think of how best to handle this? I must go." And with that, she returned the receiver to its base and chased after her father as quickly as she could.

When news of Zhu Ziqing's death finally reached the clearing where the food aid was being distributed, everything was halted. Section Chiefs Li and Wang, as well as their men, returned to behind the bunker. Fang Meng'ao and his men were stunned and unsure of what to do. The students and teachers, everyone in the clearing, just stood there, looking at each other. A moment later, quite a few began to recite out loud Zhu's *A Lotus Pond by Moonlight*:

> *These past few days I've felt rather uneasy,*
>   *But then,*
>   *On this night,*
>   *Sitting in the courtyard breathing in the crisp evening air,*
>   *My thoughts turned to the lotus pond I pass by every day.*
>   *I began to wonder what it might look like under moonlight,*
>   *How it must appear entirely different...*

On the road that passed by the work sheds, military boots ran on ahead of Xu Tieying. The bayonets fixed to their rifles flashed azure in front of his eyes. Xu's face was emotionless, but his eyes sparkled with excitement.

The poise Wang Puchen had possessed in the days running up to this had disappeared. He leaned close to one of his men from the Intelligence Department. "Keep a close eye on Yan Chunming. If anyone comes near him, besides his students, you arrest them immediately."

"Sir, yes sir." The agent hurried after the rest of the troops.

A great number of students had gathered around Yan Chunming and Liang Jinglun. Their voices were reciting in unison to Zhu Ziqing's words:

...Upon the surface of the winding, crooked lotus pond,
    The foliage of the nearby fields swirled about in complicated patterns...

Troops from the investigative team tramped into the clearing, to the left of most of the students and teachers. Still, they continued their recital:

...Then the leaves began to rise above the water's surface,
    Knitting together like the twirling hem of a girl's skirt as she gracefully danced...

The Fourth Corps Special Forces arrived and took up position at the rear of the clearing. The crowd intoned on:

...There, in between the layers of leaves,
    Fragments of feather stitched together to form pale and pallid flowers,
    Some, slim and graceful,
    Opened their petals to the moon, others were more bashful...

The police troops under the command of Fang Mengwei

claimed their space to the right of the crowd. Their recitation did not stop:

> ...*They were like brilliant pearls,*
>   *Like stars glistening in a jade-coloured sky,*
>   *Like a beautiful woman just emerging from a bath...*

Teardrops formed in the corners of Mulan's eyes. The girls standing alongside her all had tears in their eyes.

Ma Hanshan, his face dark, had climbed down from the impromptu platform to stand among his men. His eyes searched until they found Old Liu: "Brother, where's Xu Tieying?"

"I've not seen him."

Ma Hanshan spat invective, then began to scan in all directions. The chanting continued:

> ... *A fine, thin blue mist floated inches above the lotus pond,*
>   *The leaves and flowers appeared to be bathed in milk,*
>   *Like some dream wrapped tightly with a fine, muslin gauze...*

Ma Hanshan fixed his gaze on Old Liu. "I don't wish to embarrass you, or make things difficult, but I need your gun."

Liu Chuwu hesitated, then withdrew his pistol and gave it to him. He did the same with the cheque.

Ma Hanshan accepted only the gun, which he held tightly. "The money's yours to divvy up." He stomped off in the direction of the sorghum fields without once looking back at his men.

On the side of the road that led to the sheds, Wang Puchen stood, his eyes closed, a cigarette dangling from his mouth and his ears trained on the chorus of voices emanating from the clearing.

> ...*Shrubs growing in a thicket just above the water's surface cast motley shadows across the pond,*
>   *The steep edges tower like ghostly spectres...*

"Go and tell Secretary Sun," said Wang Puchen to the soldier standing next to him. "Ma Hanshan intends to kill Xu Tieying."

The soldier was taken aback by the information but then saw Ma Hanshan storming towards the field, a gun in his hand. He called out his acknowledgement of Wang's instructions and like the wind disappeared through the sorghum.

Wang turned to the man standing on the opposite side, this one an operational team leader. "That Communist who goes by the handle Red Flag Number Five, he's here. He's one of the men Ma Hanshan brought with him. Be on alert!"

"Understood, sir."

Numerous sets of eyes scanned the area around the trucks, looking at faces, trying to identify the man in question. At the ad hoc distribution sites set up for Tsinghua and Yenching universities, Old Liu seemed to sense that the Peking authorities were sweeping the area. He thus moved towards where Yan Chunming was standing.

Yan's glasses continued to reflect the sunlight. The assembled students and teachers kept up their homage to the dead Zhu Ziqing:

> ...My mind abruptly turned to the age-old custom popular in Jiangnan,
> That of picking lotuses,
> A tradition whose origin remains unclear,
> But a favourite pastime during the Six Dynasties...

Old Liu turned to a fellow worker. "Hand me your club." The man complied, and Liu took hold of it. It was the same kind of wrought iron rod he'd used the night before to pry open the library window. Carelessly, he raised it above his head, allowing it to flicker in the sunlight.

The crowd droned on, Yan Chunming included:

> ...Thus it was that people in those days amused themselves.
> A terribly fascinating spectacle.
> Pity then,
> That it's been so long for us to enjoy such a...

The sound of the unrehearsed eulogy ebbed, at least to Yan's ears. Something, someone, had stolen his attention; the man's appearance had woken him from the memorialisation. He'd seen Old Liu, and he knew, too, that on this occasion, he would have to respond. He turned to face him.

Yan shook his head.

Old Liu lowered the steel club.

———

Under the bright sunlight, Wang Puchen's eyes resembled those of a cat in the middle of the night: small, fine, slit-shaped pupils that belied their ability to see. He was talking with his men. "Yan Chunming is putting out feelers. His men are searching the crowd." Wang's men were doing more or less the same, except their eyes were all trained on Yan Chunming.

Yan removed his spectacles, pulled out a handkerchief and wiped the sweat from his forehead. It was time to rejoin the chorus, time for the final line of the spontaneous dirge:

> ...Pondering these thoughts,
> *I suddenly raised my head and realised I had returned to my front door;*
> *I pushed it open gently, quietly.*
> *There was no sound in the room.*
> *My wife had long since retired for the night.*

The clearing returned to being deathly quiet. No one was speaking. They were all deep in thought, observing a moment of silent tribute to Zhu Ziqing. Yan once more placed his glasses on his nose. He then tucked his right hand into his jacket to feel for the gun he carried to his breast. Without saying anything, he made his way to the ad hoc podium occupied now by only Captain Fang.

Standing among a group of men loitering near the trucks, Old Liu's complexion changed dramatically. As did Liang Jinglun's once he saw Yan Chunming begin to walk forward. Fang Meng'ao witnessed his approach, too, but he remained silent.

Yan stood beside the bags of food aid and directed his attention to Fang Meng'ao. "Captain Fang, I'm a professor at Yenching University. There are some words I'd like to share with the students, and my fellow teachers. I would ask that you keep me safe while I do so." With great effort, he clambered up over the rations. A helping hand from Fang and he was on top.

In the adjacent field, Zeng Keda's face blanched. Not a single bead of sweat appeared on his brow. "That's it, things are out of control!" He lifted his binoculars once more. "The CPC is about to speak…"

"Shall I report this right away to Comrade Jianfeng?" Zeng's assistant had remained seated next to the transmitter, his hand upon the dials.

"It's too late even if you did…" Before he could finish his thought, the sound of a gun being fired echoed through the air. "Make a report. Now!" Zeng Keda marched purposefully out of the sorghum field and in the direction of the gunshot. At the same time, he instructed one of his men to call for Commander Li.

As the echo reverberated, Xu's men lifted their rifles into the air, each one taking aim at the teachers and students in the clearing.

"Now… to arms. Protect the students!" Fang's command to his Air Force men was quick and precise. The pilots flew into action. Weapons drawn, they stepped into the crowd to fulfil their orders.

Captain Fang unholstered his own gun and took aim at the soldiers targeting the students. "Put those weapons down!" he shouted. "Now dammit, all of you, put them down!"

Another voice then carried, echoing and reinforcing Fang's words: "Put them down!" The voice belonged to his brother. The police heeded their commander's instructions and holstered their guns.

Fang Meng'ao now focused his attention on the military gendarmes and their lieutenant.

"Weapons down." The gendarmes complied.

By now, only the Fourth Corps Special Forces soldiers had their weapons raised, the teachers and students still in their sights. Fang Meng'ao lifted his pistol and trained it on their commander. Their eyes met, and for a moment it was as though he was going to accept Fang's challenge. But the moment passed, despite the anger and animosity he felt. "All of you, lower your weapons."

Fang Meng'ao turned to Chen Wuchang. "Find out who fired that shot. If they try to fire again without authorisation, arrest them."

"Sir!" Chen's reply was quick, his reaction quicker. Without another word, he raced over to the rear of the work sheds where the sound of the shot had seemingly come from.

Returning his attention to Yan Chunming, Fang Meng'ao urged him to climb down. Now wasn't the time for speeches.

"But what I wish to say is important… vital. I ask again that you make sure I'm safe."

Fang Meng'ao glimpsed the look in Liang Jinglun's eyes, but it was hard to get a read on what he was thinking. Did he want Yan to speak, or did he prefer that he kept quiet? Fang's brow knitted together, and he turned to see where Chen Changwu had run.

Chen Changwu raced towards the sorghum field, but what he saw was not what he expected. There was Secretary Sun, blood gushing from his shoulder, a military gendarmerie busy trying to bandage the wound. Two other gendarmes had wrestled Ma Hanshan to the ground and pinned him there. Still, Ma managed to yell out: "Xu Tieying, you bastard. If I can't kill you, then I'll at least report you to Nanking!"

"Shut him up!" Xu Tieying shouted to his men, before turning to Sun. "Did the bullet catch the bone?"

His wound not yet fully bandaged, Secretary Sun was using his left hand and his teeth to help the gendarme finish his work. "I don't know, but it doesn't matter."

"Can you still shoot yourself?"

Momentarily stunned by Xu's question, Sun took a second to gather his thoughts. "The director knows, I can shoot with my left hand just as well."

"Ah, such loyalty to the nation!" Xu's praise was effusive. "I shall report this to Nanking post-haste… and see that you're promoted to the rank of lieutenant colonel and deputy chief."

"That's not necessary, Director."

Xu turned around and caught sight of Chen Changwu standing

not far off. He looked beyond him to the sheds and smiled sardonically. "Do you fear Fang Meng'ao?"

"Director," Sun replied, "our party's never been afraid of anyone."

"That's right! Right indeed!" Xu raised his tone deliberately as though he was keen for Chen Changwu to hear. "His gun was loaded… his target in his sights. That Communist was up on stage, about to incite a riot… and he fired!"

"Yes exactly!"

CHAPTER 5

Chen Changwu was quick to report back to Fang Meng'ao, dexterously leaping up onto the dais where Fang had remained throughout the commotion.

"He... what? He actually fired!" Yan Chunming was beside him still, but that didn't stop him from looking towards the workshed to the rear.

Inside the shed, the bags of US food aid that had been piled up formed a sort of crossroads passage. Secretary Sun was standing in the middle as though all of this was planned. His eyes were fixed on Fang Meng'ao, who now turned and returned the stare.

Resolutely, Fang spun round once more and edged a little closer to Yan Chunming. "Go ahead, Professor. I'll make sure you're safe." Fang shifted his stance, placing his own broad shoulders and back directly behind Yan, shielding him, as it were, from any potential attack.

"Thank you." Yan faced the crowd. "Fellow students..." He'd meant for his voice to be loud, clear, forceful and sure, but instead, it was hoarse and rough. Fortunately, the students and teachers seemed to be interested in what he had to say, so they fell quiet, content to wait for him to speak. Yan Chunming could feel the sweat roll down the bridge of his nose, then round his nostrils and onto his top lip. He reached into his jacket for his handkerchief, but his hand fell only on the pistol he had concealed. Realising it was still there, however, calmed his nerves. He reached beyond it to take hold of the handkerchief. Pulling it out, he wiped his face and recommenced his speech, his voice as strong and as resonant as he initially intended it to be. "Fellow students! Just now, we recited Zhu Ziqing's *A Lotus Pond by Moonlight*. I experienced a strange sensation, a feeling as though this was the first time I had read Zhu's essay. But in truth we knew each other, we were fast friends, both of us having been at the National Southwestern Associated University during the war against Japan. At least, I thought I understood him well. Today, however, I discovered something. Quite often, when we're with our fellows, or reading a text... well, it's like two old hoary-headed men who become friends, or like knowing something by heart. It's not really necessary that we fully understand each other... or the words." He began to choke up at this point. Sweat rolled down his face, mixed with tears. He had to reach for his handkerchief again, remove his spectacles and wipe his face.

The crowd watched and grew even more silent. Liang Jinglun, still standing among everyone else, felt his face to be wet as well. Sweat? Tears? Perhaps both. He watched Yan and Fang intently, refusing to turn away, incapable of doing so even if he wanted to. He was filled with an incomparable sense of anticipation about what would happen next.

Secretary Sun continued to stand where he was, his gun gripped tight in his left hand. He, too, was sweating profusely. And his mind raced: Comrade Jianfeng had instructed him to accompany Wang Puchen to carry out clandestine arrests of Communist agents. But Xu Tieying had ordered him to go alone, choosing not to use the military gendarmerie he had at his disposal since he'd sent him and only him to take down Yan Chunming. To kill him. The question was why? After all, whether he pulled the trigger or not, the party-state was already in a mess.

"Xu's told you to murder him... Yan Chunming. He's ordered you to kill him, hasn't he?" The sudden sound of Zeng Keda's voice tore him from his troubled contemplation.

"Xu..." Sun refrained from turning round to look at the other man, but his tone betrayed his surprise. "Xu's over there, just beyond the work sheds." His voice was low, troubled.

"Wang Puchen called him away." Sun turned to meet Zeng's stare. Zeng continued: "There haven't been any orders from Comrade Jianfeng. No one's supposed to open fire."

"Xu Tieying has already requested instructions from Ye Xiufeng... the Bureau of Investigation wants to kill Communists. There's no reason not to carry out those orders..."

"And the Bureau is where Comrade Jianfeng is..." Zeng realised as soon as he said these words that his tone was perhaps too grave, overly serious, and so he softened it a little. "Give me the gun. If Xu asks anything about it, I'll handle it."

Sun lowered his head, his grip loosened, and Zeng Keda took hold of the pistol. In the silence between them, both men heard again Yan Chunming's speech to the gathered students and teachers. They looked towards the dais.

"Not long ago," said Yan, his voice still firm, "Mr Zhu's son came looking for me, a loan receipt in his hand. Mr Zhu had written it, and at the same time, he'd sent several rare volumes from the Song and Ming dynasties. These were to be collateral for the loan. He wanted to borrow a month's salary, some forty thousand US dollars." He paused and placed his dampened handkerchief back inside his breast pocket. Unbeknownst to him, his movement drew Liang Jinglun's attention to the slight bulge underneath his coat. The shape was unmistakable. Yan Chunming was carrying a gun – that gun!

The beads of sweat on Liang Jinglun's face no longer dripped. Not for a second had he entertained the idea that Yan could have opened that lockbox, could have taken out that gun, could have brought it here of all places. He'd been keeping so many secrets for so long, it was perhaps inevitable that he would overlook something: Yan's office had two sets of keys! That was the how. The question now, Liang thought, was why the hell had he brought it? Was he intending to go up against the CPC's mouthpiece, the General Academic Committee... or was his intended target the Iron and Blood Congress? He just couldn't be sure.

The sweat that had settled on Liang's face now began to drip again. Over beside the trucks, another pair of eyes narrowed and focused on Yan Chunming. These eyes were equally as stunned as

Liang's had been, for Old Liu realised as well that Yan had brought that gun with him.

"Dammit, dammit, dammit!" Liu Chuwu cursed under his breath.

"What… what will we do? Are we still to try and save him or…" Some of Liu's men had seen it, too, for they all stared at him, wondering what they should do. Liu, however, ignored them all, so fixed were his eyes on Yan Chunming.

"…and I thought to myself," Yan's story continued, "how could a professor making forty thousand dayang a month ask to borrow forty thousand US dollars from me? You all know this, I'm sure. Yenching University pays its salaries in American currency. What's more, the government in Nanking had already stopped using its dayang currency, switching to a newer legal tender. Mr Zhu was receiving fifteen million *fabi* a month, but spending all of that on food only gave him and his family enough to eat for ten days. For the rest of the month, they had to rely on American food aid. But you know, Mr Zhu refused it. He didn't want American handouts. That day, the day I brought him the loan, I asked him whether he was doing this because the CPC had told him to. His reply was that he was a free man, it was his choice, but at the same time, he was a Chinese, and so many of his compatriots were starving. If he and his family were to start taking American charity, well, that would, he felt, degrade his entire nation, his people. His choice had nothing to do with being a Communist, nor anything to do with the CPC… or any other political party for that matter!"

Yan Chunming's words had riled up the students once more, but this time different slogans were being shouted, and different calls to arms reverberated through the air.

"Fight against hunger!"

"Fight against persecution!"

"Long live Zhu Ziqing!"

"Reject American food aid!"

More subconsciously than anything else, the Special Forces troops to the left, as well as the military police to the rear, raised their weapons.

Yan Chunming lifted his left hand into the sky, gesturing for the audience to calm itself. Liang Jinglun followed Yan's lead by raising his hands, signalling for the students and teachers to settle down.

Fang Meng'ao directed his attention to the soldiers who'd raised their rifles. "Down, put them down! Let him finish what he's saying!" Without verbally acknowledging the order, the men lowered their weapons.

The clearing was silent again, the explosiveness of the chanting of only a few minutes before had ceased.

Yan Chunming leaned back and felt Fang Meng'ao's closeness. "My gratitude, captain, for your... protection, but I wonder if you would mind now taking a step back." Fang backed up a little, resuming his previous position.

Yan readied himself to continue, then cocked his head towards the work sheds, determined to speak loud enough so that everyone could hear. "As you can all see, the Kuomintang has sent its agents. There, over there, lurking behind those sheds. I'd like to ask them something. I hope they can hear me... you sent so many soldiers here to encircle a crowd of unarmed and defenceless students and teachers. I'd like to know, what are you really here for? Is it to assist in distributing rations or to make arrests? You always have a reason, right, but so long as you continue to act in such perverse ways, the people will protest and the charges made against you by the CPC will be legitimate. You heard, I'm sure, you heard me tell everyone what Mr Zhu said. He had no connection, no affiliation with the CPC. I hope this news will make you reconsider his death. The moral indignation of the students and the people should not be viewed simply as the result of some Communist plot. I tell you, if all the students and teachers here were Communists, do you think you'd still be here holding those guns!"

"Suppressing revolt and saving the nation is the order signed into effect by the president himself!" The ferocity by which Chen Jicheng's voice echoed through the transmitter stunned Xu Tieying, pounding his eardrums like a grenade going off. Instinctively, he pulled the receiver away from his ear, holding it to his chest instead. Unfortunately, this did little to reduce the volume of

Chen's invective. "That bloody Communist is up there spieling off his nonsense and still you've not fired? I want him dead, I tell you, right there, now. Yan Chunming is to be shot dead, nothing less. As for the rest, apprehend them, all of them! And if they resist, kill them!"

"Sir," said Xu Tieying, his voice wavering a little, "I would advise that Deputy Commander-in-Chief Chen come here personally and take charge."

"Shoot, dammit! Make those arrests! I'm on my way!"

Xu handed the transmitter-receiver back to his assistant and walked towards the work sheds. The military police moved immediately to open a path, the stalks of sorghum parted by the Thompson submachine guns they held. Xu Tieying appeared as though he were at the bow of a ship cutting through the waves. The sound of Yan Chunming's speech grew closer; the sorghum lay parted in front of Xu like the Red Sea.

―――

The sun beamed and Yan Chunming, his thick-rimmed glasses still perched precariously on his nose, turned once more to the mass of students and teachers in the clearing. His demeanour displayed his sincerity. He felt like a devoted teacher talking to his equally dedicated charges. "We all admire and deeply respect Zhu Ziqing and his courageous spirit, but to truly understand him, we ought to read and reflect upon the words he wrote that summed up his admiration for life, his yearning for simplicity. The essay we just now recited, *A Lotus Pond by Moonlight*, I can't help but think it reads like a violin piece. At the same time, we shouldn't forget his essay *The Sight of Father's Back*. How could we, after all, it's such a poignant piece and worthy of great admiration. Fellow students, I need to say this: not only was Mr Zhu your teacher, he was also your father, a father to all of us. And such a teacher, such a father, well, you must know he hoped for the best for you, for us. Eight years we fought the Japanese, and we've paid for it dearly. We've seen more than our fair share of death and destruction, and now the Civil War... already three years. Ah, our sorrowful, grieved and grieving China, its day will come, our country will be renewed. But whether or not that New China will be prosperous, I hope that will come down to all of you."

At this precise moment, Fang Meng'ao manoeuvred once more behind Yan Chunming, shielding his back. He spoke over the other man's shoulder: "Mr Yan, you've spoken well, but it's time to finish." Ever alert, Fang Meng'ao had spied out of the corner of his eye Xu Tieying walking purposefully towards them.

Yan, too, seemed to sense the impending danger. "Not all members of the Kuomintang are reactionaries, Captain Fang. Thank you for protecting me. Please do the same now for the students, for the other teachers." He reached into his breast pocket. Fang Meng'ao took hold of his free arm and prepared to help him down from the dais.

"Gun! Arrest him!" The alarm came from inside the bunker. A shadow flashed past Fang Meng'ao's men. A second later and Wang Puchen had scaled the platform. Another second later, a shadowy figure flickered past Wang's men and bounded up on top of the dais.

It was Liu Chuwu. His movements were quick, his words just as fast: "Captain, I'm here with a situation report."

Wang Puchen was to the right, Old Liu to the left. In a matter of seconds, they were both standing in the centre of the makeshift stage.

Liu was a step quicker and before anyone else could react, he leaned into Yan Chunming and pushed him off the platform. When he spun round to look at the other two men, he had Yan Chunming's gun in his hand.

Old Liu's movements were impressive, nearly as fast as a thunderbolt crashing through the sky. Wang Puchen, a step slower, now climbed onto the stage. His gun was held tightly in both hands, the barrel pointed straight at Old Liu. "You're a Communist agent, we all know that. Lower your weapon, now!"

Liu Chuwu looked at Wang Puchen, but also beyond him. It was Fang Meng'ao whom he wanted to address: "Captain Fang, I'm one of Ma's men. He's been arrested... by them. The whole operation to distribute food aid is unravelling, Captain Fang. Please, you must do something." While speaking, he brandished the firearm he'd taken from Yan Chunming.

Inadvertently or not, Old Liu seemed very much to be threatening the captain! Most of the onlookers were stunned by what they were seeing, unable to do anything at all. To make matters worse, Fang Meng'ao did not even know who Liu Chuwu was, nor did he realise that at this moment he'd sprung into action to try to save Yan Chunming, as well as his own identity.

Fang dodged, then grabbed at the weapon Liu was holding. The older man, with a strength that surprised Fang Meng'ao, would not let go. Fang's hand closed over the barrel of the pistol. They each pulled. Finally, the gun fell from both their hands and landed on the stage.

By this time, the soldiers to the left and right, and to the rear, had all raised their rifles. Each one had Old Liu in its sights.

"Don't fire, we must take him alive!" Wang Puchen shouted at the men as he, too, jumped up onto the platform.

The sound of gunfire echoed throughout the clearing.

Wang Puchen froze for a moment, before twisting his head in the direction of where the shot had come from.

Another bang rang out.

Fang Meng'ao opened his eyes wide and let his hand slowly loosen.

The chest of the man in front of him turned a bright red as his blood soaked through his clothes. His hand still clenched his gun, but he was already falling down. Fang turned his head, and his eyes fell on the figure who had emerged from behind the work sheds.

There was a gun in Zeng Keda's hand. Several military police were also holding firearms. But they were all staring at Xu Tieying.

Xu let the muzzle of his gun drop, then handed it to Secretary Sun. "Get that Communist bastard down off the stage! Arrest Yan Chunming! There are other Communist agents here. Don't let any of them get away!"

His orders given, Xu Tieying headed back towards the sorghum fields. At the same time, Fang Meng'ao, Wang Puchen and Zeng Keda all stared after him as he walked away. Xu did not deign to even acknowledge them.

———

The clearing was pure pandemonium. Liang Jinglun waved at a student standing nearby, beckoning him closer. "Protect Professor Yan, and make your way towards the back."

The student did as he was told and put his arm around Yan Chunming to support him. Yan, however, resisted. "My glasses! I need my glasses!" Moments before, when Liu Chuwu had somewhat roughly pushed him off the stage, he'd lost his spectacles. In turn, all he had heard was the gunshot. He'd not seen Old Liu fall.

Liang Jinglun responded to Yan's plea: "Go, you must go. The man who just saved you has been shot!"

The words exploded in Yan's mind and he froze, unable to move. Liang implored the student who'd put his arm around Yan: "Go now. Take him to… to wherever Vice-Chancellor He is!"

The crowd of students and teachers collided and jostled into one another, but some linked arms to form a spontaneous human wall. They weren't sure, however, whom they should protect, so they simply yelled out for calm, and for the students to make their way back to their respective campuses.

The Special Forces raised their weapons into the air and fired. The military police followed their lead and shot into the sky as well.

At the rear of the mass of humanity, He Qicang was noticeably stirred by the scene he was witnessing. "No shooting!" he shouted. "Stop!" Unfortunately, his voice failed to carry. Only his daughter, Xie Mulan, and the student charged with looking after him heard his entreaty for calm.

He Xiaoyu held on to her father's arm, but her eyes were on the stage in front. Tears stained her face. The image of the military police roughly lifting the corpse of Liu Chuwu off the platform and transporting it back behind the sheds ingrained itself in her mind.

Xie Mulan, whose face was drenched with sweat, stood on the tips of her toes, frantically trying to see Liang Jinglun at the front of the crowd. It was then she spied a small number of students escorting Yan Chunming their way. They were pushing through the mass of people as best they could. Mulan turned towards He Xiaoyu and said: "Get Uncle He out of here… now. I'll try to save anyone I can!" With that, she rushed into the jostling crowd, pushing her way through in the direction of Liang Jinglun.

Back on the platform, Fang Meng'ao had drawn his weapon. His personal guard, the twenty pilots he'd brought with him, had done the same and were now standing beside him on the stage. Fang called to his men: "Chen Changwu! Shao Yuangang!"

"Here sir!"

"One of you take aim at the commander of the Special Forces, the other at the man in charge of the investigative team. If either of them dares to shoot, take him down!"

"Under no circumstances are you to discharge your weapons!" Zeng Keda said, bounding up onto the dais and leaning in close to Fang Meng'ao. "The man Xu's just killed, he was a Communist agent, one of their leaders. If clashes ensue, you'll all face a formal court martial!"

Fang Meng'ao gave Zeng a cold look and repeated his order: "Take aim!"

Chen's contingent, ten men, took aim at the commander of the Special Forces. Shao's ten men followed suit, lining up the commander of the investigative team. All twenty yelled in unison: "Lower your weapons!"

The Special Forces, along with the men in the investigative team, responded by targeting Fang and his pilot guard.

Through the sights of his pistol, Fang Meng'ao could see clearly the spot right between his eyes. One squeeze of the trigger and the Special Forces commander would be dead. Amid the chaos, the noise, the shouting, Fang Meng'ao yelled at top voice: "Fang Mengwei!"

"Tell your men to lower their weapons. Tell them to surrender them!" Fang Mengwei's voice cut through the hubbub as his brother's had.

"Stand down, all of you!" Zeng Keda shouted before shooting three rounds into the sky. "Everyone, all of you, lower your damn weapons! Anyone – and I mean every single one of you – fire and it means your own court martial!"

Zeng's voice, its ferocity, had the desired effect. It rippled through the men aiming at each other. Weapons were lowered, although neither side uttered a word.

"Wang Puchen!"

"Here!"

Zeng Keda scanned the crowd, searching for where the answer had come from. Failing to find him, Zeng continued with his orders. "Xu Tieying... get him and bring him here. I want him to order his troops to stand down!"

Liu Chuwu's body had been carried out into the sorghum field, his chest a gaping wound, his clothes matted and stained in blood. Wang Puchen was crouched nearby, Xu Tieying standing just beyond. Military gendarmes and other soldiers surrounded them.

Wang stood and pulled out a cigarette. "This was the man... this Communist agent. He's the one Chiang Ching-kuo wanted arrested. Red Flag Number Five, that was his codename. Director Xu, you'll have to explain these gunshot wounds to Chiefs Chiang and Mao."

"I'll report to them. Deputy Commander-in-Chief Chen can then report to the president."

Wang threw the cigarette and matches he'd just taken out of his pocket. "Fine. Inspector Zeng is waiting for us. Let's go." Wang reached out and took hold of Xu's arm, pulling him back in the direction of the recent raucous. Before he had the opportunity to resist or struggle free, Xu felt his arm go numb; in fact, he ceased to feel anything at all. Wang Puchen's finger, long, slender, almost delicate, now seemed to be like wrought iron nails driven into Xu Tieying's arm. As he escorted Xu, Wang yelled out for the men to implement phase two of their plan: Yan Chunming had to be arrested.

Fang Buting was seated in his study, his eyes gazing out past through the window that separated the balcony from his room. The sky was empty, but still Fang stared at the nothingness. Xie Peidong was behind him, expecting a phone call that just wouldn't come. His mind was occupied, his face was white. He stood in front of Fang's desk, his eyes as blank and empty as the sky outside.

Zhang Yueyin, still in the Jingchun Botanical Gardens, was speaking on the telephone, striving to contain his racing emotions. "It's confirmed, shot three times. By all accounts, he was shot trying to save Professor Yan. We can't lose anyone else. Please, Mr Fang, telephone the vice-president, call Li Zongren. Ask him to dispatch troops. The situation needs to be contained. At present, you and Vice-Chancellor He are the only ones who can stop further bloodshed."

He replaced the phone on its stand. Small teardrops formed at the corners of his eyes.

Fang Buting had been listening to Xie Peidong on the telephone.

"Who called? Isn't he dead?"

"It was the Peking Police HQ. He was at the site where the food aid was going to be distributed. Xie Peidong opened fire. Meng'ao and Mengwei, they're both in danger…"

Fang Buting stood up abruptly. "Mulan and Xiaoyu? Aren't they there, too?"

"Yes, they are… and so is Vice-Chancellor He."

"Get me Li Yuqing!" Fang Buting's voice failed him, and he stomped over to his desk. The same rumbling train of thought that raced through Zhang Yueyin's mind now carried off Fang Buting as well.

"Vice-President Li… is he the one to call?"

"Yes. Do it quickly!"

Xie Peidong grabbed the telephone and dialled the number.

Cheng Xiaoyun had heard the tone of Fang Buting's voice and it had caused her to worry as well. She stood in the doorway to the study, anxiously watching Fang Buting. Normally, Cheng Xiaoyun was not permitted to even stand in the doorway to Fang's study, but on this day, she broke that rule, even though she didn't dare to actually step inside. Fang saw her standing there, and shook his head desolately, but he didn't tell her to leave. Nor did he invite her in.

The phone rang.

"Yes," said Xie Peidong. "Li Yuqing? I'm calling on behalf of the Peking branch governor of the Central Bank. An emergency has arisen. Fang Buting would like to speak to you. Please wait a moment." Xie handed the receiver to Fang.

Not a single bag of food aid had been distributed. The students, the student reps, the teachers, they all remained in the clearing, unable to depart. Phase two had been implemented. Secret arrests were being made. The soldiers had surrounded them. The military police, along with the Special Forces troops, were following orders to apprehend Yan Chunming. As for those who shielded him, they were to be arrested, too. To that effect, the exit routes out of the clearing were sealed.

Fang Mengwei instructed the Peking Police not to make any arrests. They weren't to intervene or interfere with the actions being carried out by the other troops, either. Their task was simply to stand where they were and ensure that no one got by them. The young soldiers who had accompanied Zeng Keda were to continue providing him protection. They were also ordered to protect Fang Meng'ao. To carry out these instructions, Commander Li directed three teams to take up positions around the stage. His remaining men moved to stand tight to the work sheds, facing the sorghum fields beyond.

These deployments left the four most unlikely characters together on the platform: Zeng Keda, Xu Tieying, Wang Puchen and Fang Meng'ao.

The twenty pilots under Fang's command brought up the rear.

Yan Chunming had delivered his speech. Old Liu had been shot dead. The plans Zeng Keda and Wang Puchen had made were utterly destroyed. Now, four pairs of eyes stared out at the clearing. The group of students who had surrounded Yan in order to protect him were there in the middle of it all. The scariest sight of all was Liang Jinglun and Xie Mulan standing alongside him.

Time seemed to stop and the scene transformed into a silent

movie. Everything and everyone took on shades of grey, black and white:

Zeng Keda's face was empty and blank.

Xu Tieying's carried an ominous glint in his eye.

Wang Puchen's attention skewed to the left.

Fang Meng'ao stared up at the sky.

The students and teachers in the clearing were silent, yet determination showed on their faces.

To the rear, He Qicang was full of rage. His daughter was striving to hold him back.

He Qicang's black and white visage then burst into colour, his question was accusatory and sudden: "Who the hell's in charge here?"

The stage that had likewise seemed to be frozen in time now returned to the present. All four men turned to look at He Qicang, but not one of them could respond to his cutting reproach.

"Out of my way! Let me pass!" He Qicang pushed his way through the crowd.

"Dad… no. Don't!" He Xiaoyu attempted to get him to stop. "There's no point. There's no use in you going forward."

The men who had accompanied him from the university's administration office manoeuvred closer to him as well, seemingly intent on stopping him. On this occasion, however, He Qicang's own frailty did not prevent him from wrestling free of his daughter and navigating into the mass of people. Once the students saw the determination on his face, they began to give way. Then a small group of military police suddenly appeared. They formed a line and lifted their rifles up towards He Qicang, blocking his path.

Up on the stage, Fang Meng'ao's pistol flashed in the sun. A second later and it was pointed at Xu Tieying's temple. "Tell them to let him pass!"

Xu, however, seemed undisturbed. "Hold him there, but don't hurt him!"

The human wall the military police had constructed and the black, glistening barrels of their guns thwarted He Qicang's advance.

Fang Meng'ao began to squeeze slowly on the trigger.

Zeng Keda stretched out his hand and gently pulled Fang

Meng'ao's gun away from Xu's head. "If you shoot, you'll only put He's life in danger... and everyone else's. Don't."

Stiffly, rigidly, Fang Meng'ao allowed his arm to drop.

Somewhere in the clearing, a number of student voices began to echo in song, a stirring, unmistakable tune: "Unity is strength..."

More voices joined in: "Unity is strength..."

Soon, all of the students were singing:

Unity is strength,
   This power is iron,
   This force is steel.
   Harder than iron, stronger than steel.

A number of the teachers clearly did not know the words, so when the students began, they were at a loss as to what to do. But as the singing continued, they were able to join in:

Fire upon fascism,
   Let all undemocratic systems die.
   Towards the sun,
   Towards freedom,
   Towards a New China, emit a radiant glow.
   Unity is strength...

The singing continued, the words repeated again and again. The students moved together, one body forming a protective circle around Yan Chunming, Liang Jinglun and Xie Mulan. Further to the rear, the students formed their own protective shell around He Qicang and his daughter, preventing any effort by the military police from getting a clean shot at them. Standing next to him, He Xiaoyu had been transfixed by the muzzles of the guns pointed at them. Now, however, she turned to look at her father. His mouth was moving. He, too, was singing. In seconds, tears streamed down her face. She held on to her father even tighter than before and began to sing as well.

Suddenly, the ringing sound of gunfire echoed across the field and drowned out the students' singing. It had come from the road that led between the clearing and the sorghum fields. A moment later and a large convoy of vehicles came into view. It was hard to work out how many trucks had come, even harder to tell how many troops, all of them military police, and all of them firing their rifles into the sky.

Chen Jicheng had arrived.

The sorghum stalks were being trampled down one after the other. In among them, Zeng Keda was covered in sweat. And like a pig rushing after fresh feed, he lurched frantically towards the transmitter. Behind him, in the clearing, gunshots echoed out. The whole area was in chaos as arrests were made. Zeng did his utmost to calm his nerves, and then shouted at his assistant: "Get me Comrade Jiangfeng... now!"

The assistant obliged, quickly spinning knobs and clicking buttons. He then passed the microphone to Zeng Keda: Chen Jicheng's come <break> It's a mess <break> Liang Jinglun's been arrested <break> Captain Fang is surrounded <break> The whole place's gone to hell <break> Everything's out of control <break> Zeng Keda.

The message recorded and sent, the radio went silent, and Zeng's assistant stared at his superior, while Zeng's eyes remained trained on the transmitter. As for the gunfire and the sounds of people being arrested, they no longer registered in his ears. Zeng's mind was blank, the world in front of him had vanished. All he could do was hold on to the receiver and wait for a reply, for instructions... for anything.

As though in freakish response to Zeng Keda's state of mind, the radio whirred, a response from Nanking had come!

Zeng's aide-de-camp copied down the message furiously, his hand racing over the notepad. To Zeng's eyes, however, he was writing too slowly. Then, suddenly, he stopped writing and stood up, the coded transmission in his hand. He translated it: Conflict to be avoided <break> Captain Fang to withdraw <break> Immediate attendance at general headquarters required <break> Jianfeng. Before his assistant had finished, Zeng had already spun around and set off frenetically into the sorghum field.

That an emergency planning meeting had been hastily convened in Peking on how to deal with the situation in the north boded ill; for certain, all parties involved would have their daggers ready. As for the meeting room itself, it was arranged as expected. A raised stage was positioned at the rear of the room on which the men who presided over the meeting would sit. There was a podium, also, and adjacent to it three high-backed chairs. Outside the meeting room, the marching feet of soldiers could be heard, and then shouted command for the troops to queue up in strict formation. Security for all such meetings was now the remit of the Peking military police. Thus it was that Chen Jicheng took the lead.

Xu Tieying followed in immediately after, but before he could step inside, the gendarme halted his advance. "Sir, your weapon sir. You must hand it over."

Xu obeyed without protest and surrendered his pistol before walking inside. Wang Puchen came next. He didn't show any regard to the gendarme. He simply pulled out his weapon as though he were taking out a cigarette and handed it over; his stride never altered. Next to enter were Zeng Keda and Fang Meng'ao.

The guard appeared nervous facing these two men, but he still repeated his instructions: "Sirs…" Zeng Keda displayed his own worry then, but not for himself. Rather, his concern was for Captain Fang and how he would react. He turned his head to look at his companion as he pulled out his gun and handed it over. Then he stood and waited for Fang Meng'ao to do the same. Fang unholstered his pistol, and in that moment, Zeng grew even more anxious, fearful that something could still yet happen. He held the weapon towards the guard, but then pointed it towards the ceiling and squeezed the trigger. The gunshot echoed, rumbling throughout the entire meeting hall.

Beyond where the meeting was to be held, a Buick belonging to Li Zongren had just pulled up. He Xiaoyu, who was helping her father out of the vehicle, blanched at the sound of the gunfire. So, too, did her father. In the car immediately behind them, Fang Buting and Xie Peidong had just alighted and begun to walk over towards He Qicang and his daughter when they froze as well, shocked by what they had heard.

Chen Jicheng looked in the direction of the shot, astonishment washed over his face. Xu Tieying and Wang Puchen were equally drawn by the sound, both of them as surprised as Chen. Zeng Keda felt lightheaded and shut his eyes, unable to move, do or say anything. The gendarmes were pointing the muzzles of their guns at Fang Meng'ao. Gunfire sounded again. In that moment, it seemed as though all of the tireless efforts made by Comrade Jianfeng had unravelled.

"That's the first shot!"

It was Fang Meng'ao's voice, Zeng was certain. And with it, he pried open his terror-shut eyes. That's when he saw Fang fire five more shots into the ceiling. Six bullet holes could be seen above them.

He Xiaoyu and Xie Peidong were not permitted into the meeting, so they remained outside, under a nearby tree and fairly close to the cars in which they had arrived. Their anxious eyes, however, followed the footsteps of the two older men walking inside. Fang Buting was now supporting He Qicang. Surprisingly, their pace was rather quick. Two other men strode confidently in after Fang and He. One was Li Zongren's aide-de-camp, Li Yuqing, the other was Fu Zuoyi's secretary, Wang Kejun.

The commander of the gendarmerie and his four subordinates still held their pistols at Fang Meng'ao, presumably awaiting orders from Chen Jicheng. Chen, however, said nothing. He simply stood at the podium, his hostile eyes fixed on Fang Meng'ao.

Slowly, deliberately, Fang lowered his firearm and replaced it in its holster. "I've emptied my gun, all six shots. Do you still wish me to hand it over?" He didn't wait for a reply; instead, he walked into the hall, found a seat in the back row and sat down.

Chen Jicheng now shifted his gaze onto Zeng Keda, the rage still barely concealed. Zeng hadn't moved, nor showed any indication of doing so. He just returned Chen's stare, silent, unmoving.

"Please, Inspector Zeng," said Chen, "will you immediately report to Chief Ching-kuo and ask for instruction on what to do with this... this fellow here!" He gestured towards Fang Meng'ao.

"Should I report during the meeting, or should we depart and then file it?"

"Fine. No reporting of anything right now. Let's begin. Once we're done, I'll report his actions myself." Chen's tone revealed clearly the anger that was boiling up within him. He walked over to the raised platform on which the three chairs had been placed and seated himself in the middle.

Fang Meng'ao had already taken a seat in the back. Now, he directed his eyes to the front and Chen Jicheng. But his gaze was not focused on the other man's face. Instead, he looked past Chen's, focusing on the hat he was wearing.

As for the other three men in attendance, they slowly began to regain their composure, even though the echo of Fang's gunfire still rang in their ears. They knew the meeting had to begin and so they found seats in the back as well to sit.

"Attention!" The gendarme commander standing in the doorway shattered whatever stillness remained.

Chen Jicheng's face grew crestfallen. He'd asked for Li Yuqing and Wang Kejun to co-chair the meeting with him, so why had He Qicang and Fang Buting showed up, too?

Li Yuqing entered first and scanned the room. Discovering quickly that everyone who should have been in attendance was actually there, he turned to Mr He and Mr Fang, his voice almost gentle: "Please, gentlemen, take up seats in the front."

Neither He Qicang nor Fang Buting responded to Li. Both men were transfixed by Fang Meng'ao seated in the back. Fang slowly stood up once he saw their faces. Even more slowly, he walked over to them. He didn't say anything. His actions were enough to confirm that he was all right, that he wasn't hurt. He Qicang nodded in response, then squinted at Fang Buting, who was still

163

grasping his arm. Fang Buting met the elder man's gaze and then realised that he himself was the one about to lose control. He loosened his grip and let go of He Qicang. He clasped his own sweaty hands together in an effort to restore his equilibrium.

"Let's go." He Qicang tapped his cane on the floor, beckoning Fang Buting to follow him to their seats. For Fang, this had been the closest he'd been to his son in ten years. Needless to say, emotions swirled inside him.

The two section chiefs, Li Qingyu and Wang Kejun, followed the two older men. Zeng Keda, Wang Puchen and even Xu Tieying stood up as they did. Behind them, the gendarmes closed the doors.

Outside the meeting, white marble steps led to the main door. On each side stood the military police. He Xiaoyu, still standing under the tree near where they had parked, watched Xie Peidong edge his way towards the building.

Before he even reached the steps, one of the guards yelled out for him to halt. Xie pulled out a name card to show the young gendarme, and to his surprise, the young man could actually read it. He flipped it over in his hand a moment before returning it. "Assistant manager for the Central Bank here in Peking, huh?" Xie nodded. "Over there," he said, gesturing in the direction of He Xiaoyu. "Stand under the tree like that young woman is. Wait for your boss over there."

Xie Peidong remained where he was, instead offering his official attaché case, with both hands, to the guard. "It's our manager's bag. If you won't let me in, please be so kind as to take this to him."

The young man thought the matter over for a moment, then decided he should do as Xie requested. He reached to take hold of the attaché case, but Xie Peidong chose not to loosen his grip. That's when he noticed the American money, ten dollars, Xie was holding underneath. Their eyes met. In a low voice, Xie Peidong made his enquiry: "The gunshots we just heard. Tell me, was anyone hurt?"

The guard pulled on the bag once more, taking it and the cash in his hand. "The man who fired… he was… he just emptied his pistol into the ceiling. No one was hurt. You can relax and wait over there." Again, he gestured towards He Xiaoyu.

"My gratitude." Xie Peidong didn't say anything further. He simply turned around and walked back towards He Xiaoyu, all the while looking at her intently.

The guard climbed the white marble steps. They could hear him knock softly on the door. Suddenly, Xie Peidong spun his head around to stare at the imposing iron gates that sheltered Xishan secret military prison. The doors swung open and a jeep from the Intelligence Bureau rushed forward, followed closely by a ten-wheeled truck and a contingent of military police, all armed and seemingly ready for anything. Lights flashed and sirens wailed. Close behind came a prisoner transport.

It was a standard American-style prisoner transport. Two rows of seats, the prisoner and his escort sitting next to each other. This was convenient insofar as it supposedly ensured the proper behaviour of the detainee, as well as offering the semblance of respecting the rights of the accused. The Americans, after all, assisted in drafting the Republic's constitution. Seated between two military gendarmes was Yan Chunming, his hands sporting iron manacles. Behind him was Liang Jinglun, similarly cuffed. Beside one of the guards was Ouyang, a student from the Chiang Kai-shek Student Society. His hands were not shackled. Seated next to a different guard was yet another student from the society, this one a so-called "special operative". His hands were not handcuffed. To the right sat the lead student reps from each of the universities in Peking. First, there was the representative from Peking University, followed by the one from Tsinghua and then Peking Normal. None of them had their hands in manacles.

In the last row sat Xie Mulan. She'd been arrested on the assumption she was the student leader of the Yenching University student federation. When she looked at the others in the vehicle, she felt a thrill of excitement run through her. It was only when her eyes fell on Liang Jinglun that she felt a profound sense of loss and frustration. Liang kept his eyes shut. His face looked pallid and almost sickly. Not once on the entire journey here had he tried to rally collective spirits, even just with a look of his eyes.

The vehicle heaved and then came to a stop.

"All of you, off!"

Xie Mulan tried to stand and rush forward so she could be near Liang Jinglun, could try to look into his face. Unfortunately, just as she made the attempt, the bright summer sun radiated in through the rear window, blinding everyone in the vehicle.

At the emergency meeting, He Qicang and Fang Buting refused to sit down, choosing to stand instead. Li Qingyu and Wang Kejun had little choice but to follow suit. The other men in the room, Fang Meng'ao, Zeng Keda, Wang Puchen and even Xu Tieying did likewise, each standing where they were. Only Chen Jicheng was up on the platform, feeling rather awkward. He remained motionless, his eyes cold.

Li Yuqing glanced in Chen Jicheng's direction but didn't seem to pay him much mind. He turned to He Qicang. "Mr He, you're a consultant to the national government. How would you advise us now in this situation? Please tell us."

"I'm no consultant to the government." As He Qicang spoke, he became increasingly excited: "I'm vice-chancellor at Yenching University. You've arrested my students, and my teachers. Now you ask me for advice?"

Li Yuqing averted his eyes from Chen Jicheng, and he turned to Wang Kejun. "Did the order to make arrests come from Commander-in-Chief Fu?"

Wang Kejun's answer was evasive: "I... I can't say. I don't know if he gave the order or not. If Deputy Commander-in-Chief Chen reported to Fu, then he should know."

Li Yuqing had ceased to pursue the issue. Instead, he reached into his attaché case and pulled out an official government document. "Here are the instructions from Vice-President Li."

All eyes turned towards Li Yuqing and the document he held in his hand. After a suitable pause to emphasise the importance of what he was holding, Li Yuqing borrowed Li Zongren's Guangxi accent and began to read out the orders:

Commander-in-Chief Fu Zuoyi, Deputy Commander-in-Chief Chen Jicheng: As you know, I have been selected as vice-president of the Republic. Moreover, I've come to Peking to assume direct responsibility over the Pingjin area, both with regard to the military and the civilian government. So tell me, why have you turned a deaf ear to the orders I issued regarding northern China? Why have you not provided an explanation for your actions? Why has no report been filed? Do you consider the constitution on which the Republic has been founded to be no more than waste paper? Or is it that you believe I serve in name only and thus there's no reason to follow my orders? If this is truly the case, then I should promptly resign from parliament. I trust you understand this announcement.

Li Zongren, 37th Year of the Republic, 12 August

Beside the iron gates to Xishan prison, two rows of men lined up, one the military police, the other members of the Intelligence Bureau. Between them was a path that led directly to the prisoner cells.

Xie Mulan was the first to alight from the transport, but she was the last to walk down the path. Liang Jinglun and Yan Chunming were thrust to the front of the line and escorted towards the cells. Behind them were the many arrested students. Xie Mulan brought up the rear, walking alongside the student rep from Peking Normal.

Suddenly, two great pops rang out. Surprised, the soldiers and escorts stopped moving. Everyone turned to look. Again, great popping sounds echoed in the air.

Fang Mengwei reached out to one of the guards seemingly blocking his way. "Block me, will you? I'm deputy chief of the investigative team. I go where I wish to." And with that he moved forward, brushing aside the guard. The commanders of the Special Forces and the military police dared not obstruct his passage. They all stepped aside to let him pass.

Secretary Sun greeted him: "Deputy Chief Fang…"

Fang Mengwei halted and met Sun's eyes. "We're not screening the prisoners, not investigating their cases. We're just throwing them in jail… is that it?"

"To properly screen, we need to take testimonies and things need to be recorded. If they're not Communists, and we have proof to that effect, we can let them go. You understand this."

"Let me ask, then, what if you release them into my custody, on my authority, pending whatever investigation you need to carry out?"

"Who… who do you want released?"

It was a question Sun already knew the answer to, of that, Fang Mengwei was sure. For a moment he thought to walk away without saying a word, but he didn't. Instead, he angled his neck towards the sky, allowing the sun to sting his eyes. He'd seen Xie Mulan in the clearing. He watched as she went to help Liang Jinglun when things got out of hand, and then he'd seen her arrested by Chen Jicheng's military police, along with Liang and Yan Chunming. He saw her now, too, her eyes never straying far from Liang Jinglun. On the one hand, he was unsympathetic to her plight – why should he care – but as these thoughts ran through his mind, something else occurred to him. He remembered a poem he'd read often with his father, written by Gu Zhenguan during the Qing Dynasty. It was all about the poet's efforts to rescue his friend from certain death. One line in particular resonated in his mind: "One hopes the unicorn's horn will be saved in the end."

The merciless sun continued to shine down upon him, bringing glistening teardrops to his eyes.

Secretary Sun waited patiently for Fang Mengwei to utter Xie Mulan's name. As he watched Fang struggle with his inner thoughts, however, he realised everyone else was now waiting as well. The silence continued for what seemed to be an age. Finally, Sun could no longer refrain from speaking. Turning to look at the guards in front, he yelled: "Come on now, bring them forward!" The guard complied with his orders and marched his prisoner down the path. Sun then added: "Deputy Chief Fang wishes to personally question one of the prisoners. Call them forward."

"Sir." The guard looked at Fang Mengwei, waiting for him to name the prisoner.

Sun interjected: "You needn't ask him. There, in the middle, that female student from Yenching. Her name's Xie Mulan. Yes, that one."

"Understood." The guard made no further effort to ask Fang Mengwei for a name. He simply signalled to Xie Mulan's escort to bring her forward.

―――――

The large tree that stood outside where the meeting was taking place was, according to legend, planted by Zhu Di, the Yongle Emperor of the Ming Dynasty when he designated Peking the capital of the empire. Over hundreds of years, the tree had experienced numerous conflagrations. The nearby hall had been burnt and rebuilt several times. Even as Yuan Shih-kai assumed the presidency of the Republic, later to call himself emperor, the tree had stood as it always had, its gentle shade providing cover from the hot summer sun.

A contingent of military gendarmes stood not far away. Only Xie Peidong and He Xiaoyu sat underneath the tree on the stone steps that encircled it. The cicadas nestled in the tree above forgot they were there and erupted into cacophonic clamour.

"Comrade Liu… one of our senior leaders… killed just like that. Did any of the higher-ups know this was going to happen?" He Xiaoyu's voice was quiet, but it brought a halt to the chirping cicadas. A lonely silence enveloped them once more.

Xie Peidong turned round to look at her. He Xiaoyu met his gaze, her eyes dry and free of tears. He didn't answer.

"If there's no… no suitable answer, forget I asked it."

"They knew… the higher-ups. They knew." His voice was low as he twisted and directed his eyes towards the guards standing outside the meeting.

The lieutenant in charge of the gendarmes returned his look unflinchingly.

He Xiaoyu looked at his back. "Mulan… and Yan Chunming… Liang Jinglun… so many comrades… students… all of them arrested. How is… what… what preparations have the party made to rescue them?"

Xie Peidong did not turn around this time. He only took her

hand and squeezed it gently. "Right now, you and me, we're the party."

Beyond the iron gate that separated Xishan prison from the outside world, Fang Mengwei called out to Secretary Sun that he didn't want him to leave, despite the other man's intentions to give them space. "You don't need to go, Secretary Sun. What I have to say to my cousin, it's fine for you to hear."

Sun halted a few steps away from Fang Mengwei and Xie Mulan. He scanned the crowd of guards and prisoners and then retorted: "Please, say what you need to say, but be quick about it."

Finally, Fang turned to Mulan. "Do you know him... Professor Yan... Yan Chunming?"

She avoided his gaze but responded: "He's director of Yenching library. Of course I know him."

"And Liang Jinglun, Professor Liang, he's your teacher, as well as Uncle He's assistant. Is that why the two of you tried to protect Yan Chunming, tried to help him flee?"

Xie Mulan hesitated. She needed to collect her thoughts before answering. "That's... that's right."

"Secretary Sun," said Fang Mengwei, shifting focus, "please come closer." Sun had really no other option than to comply. Once he approached, Fang Mengwei continued: "I'm finished. I've asked her what I wanted to and you heard her response. I'm going to take her now, into my custody. You shouldn't have any objection, no?"

"Of course not." Sun now turned to the lead guard. "Escort the rest of them in, then bring me the release papers."

"Sir, yes sir."

"No, there's no need," said Xie Mulan, interrupting the exchange. "If my teachers and fellow students are to be detained here, then I'm to be detained with them." Her eyes were on her escort, whom she now urged to move forward along with the rest of the guards and their detainees.

Sun turned to Fang Mengwei. "Deputy Chief..."

Fang did not reply. Instead, he marched off towards the main gate. As he walked away, he could hear Sun give the orders: "All of them, now, bring them inside."

"Sir, yes sir!" the guard shouted, before adding: "Separate the men and women!"

Finally, He Qicang and Fang Buting took their seats. In the back row, Zeng Keda, Wang Puchen, Xu Tieying and Fang Meng'ao did the same.

Li Yuqing and Wang Kejun, as well as Chen Jicheng, however, remained standing in front, all three of them near the stage. Li and Wang were both fixated on another document, this one given to them by Chen Jicheng. They were drawn to the three characters that identified the person who had written it – Chiang Kai-shek! Then, as they read the lines, an all-too-familiar voice rang in their ears: "While it's become perhaps common for many of my Whampoa classmates to forget the spirit of that school, to forget what it meant, I tell you now, those of you who have forgotten were never my students to begin with. I trust that this document will be read by Chen Jicheng, Li Yuqing and Wang Kejun…" Li and Wang stared at each other, then directed their attention back towards Chen Jicheng.

He met their gaze with an inquisitive look. Li hesitated a second, and then returned the document to him.

"Please sit," Chen said. "Everyone."

Li Yuqing took the chair to the left. Wang Kejun manoeuvred past the chair in the middle Chen was standing by and seated himself to the right. Neither man made a sound.

"Where should we begin?" Chen Jicheng seemed to be soliciting opinions instead of first offering his own. He placed the microphone in front of Li Yuqing, suggesting that he start.

The men seated all stared at Li. His embarrassment was hard to disguise. But nor did he try to keep it hidden. He moved his mouth to the appropriate distance in front of the microphone and began: "I've just now relayed to all of you the instructions given by Vice-President Li Zongren. Deputy Commander-in-Chief Chen has also shown us comments given by President Chiang himself. According to the Republic's constitution, the president is its first citizen, the head of state. If there is disagreement or conflicting opinions between the different branches of the government and/or with the military, then, according to our constitution, the president's point of view takes precedence. He is, after all, the supreme commander-in-chief. Please, Deputy Chen, relay the orders of our head of state."

Li picked up the microphone and gingerly passed it back to Chen Jicheng. All eyes fell on him. The other men in the meeting waited for him to stand. Once he did, they followed suit. All, except for Fang Meng'ao, who remained in his seat, eyes fixed on Li Yuqing. When he felt there was nothing more that Li would say, Fang stretched and reclined further in his chair. He even went so far as to close his eyes.

"Fang Meng'ao!" Chen's rage was as clear as day. His eyes were daggers. The other men in the room all turned their attention to Fang Meng'ao. Even He Qicang and Fang Buting, standing in the front row, couldn't help but look at the younger man.

"Here!" Fang Meng'ao's response seemed louder than Chen's voice through the microphone. He stood as abruptly as he spoke. Like the prototypical American soldier, he stood to attention, surpassing even the rigidity of the national honour guard. All manner of different expressions greeted Fang Meng'ao's performance. But only He Qicang shared his reaction. He turned to his companion Fang Buting and gave him a slight smile. Fang Buting smiled bitterly in return, then turned his head away from his son. In seconds, they were all seated again.

Chen boomed through the microphone: "Our country is now governed by a constitution."

As though on cue, Li Yuqing and Wang Kejun took the lead and stood once more. Xu Tieying, Zeng Keda and Wang Puchen did likewise. He Qicang and Fang Buting did not.

Chen Jicheng remained on stage, seated in the centre. He paused a few seconds more, deliberately so, then continued: "In the United States, in all countries governed by a constitution, it's the president who stands to speak and his audience remains seated. Henceforward, I hope the people will correct the bad habits acquired during the period of provisional rule. There's no need to stand and listen to the vice-president giving instructions."

Li Yuqing's head dropped as he sat back down. Wang Kejun also returned to his seat. Zeng, Xu and Wang did the same.

Chen Jicheng leaned closer into the microphone: "Fang Meng'ao! The way you stand to attention is impressive, most impressive, textbook, you could say. Please continued to stand, there's something I wish to tell you!"

"Sir, yes sir!" Fang Meng'ao maintained his performance, his eyes meeting Chen's with equal determination.

"Did you know the man you allowed to speak, one Yan Chunming, is a known Communist agent?" Chen's first question went for the jugular. And not just Fang Meng'ao's as his eyes scanned both He Qicang and Zeng Keda. The only reply was silence. Everyone seemed to be holding their breath. He Qicang now closed his eyes, his brow locked in a grimace. Zeng Keda remained in his chair, his back straight, unmoving. He had no idea how Fang could respond.

"May I ask a question in response, Deputy Commander-in-Chief Chen?" He didn't actually wait for consent before continuing: "Do you hope that I'll say I knew, or are you hoping I'll say that I didn't?"

At the sound of Fang's voice, He Qicang opened his eyes. But he did not direct them to the back of the room, instead squinting them towards Fang Buting. He made no attempt to hide the pleasure he felt in hearing Fang Meng'ao's question. Fang Buting, however, betrayed no emotion whatsoever, not even the bitter smile he'd shown him before.

Chen Jicheng scanned the room. His stare was determined, purposeful. He was looking for their reactions. Suddenly, he gripped the microphone tighter and focused on Zeng Keda. "Inspector Zeng, I'll reiterate the president's words. Fang Meng'ao is under your command. Tell me, do you wish me to question him here, out in the open, as it were, or would you rather I ask my questions in private?"

Zeng got to his feet slowly. "I must first ask a question of my own. Do the president's orders mean you should ask my department these questions, or that you ask Captain Fang himself? Please, Deputy Commander-in-Chief, let us see these orders. We'll obey them."

Of course, Chiang Kai-shek's orders did not include such specifics. Zeng knew this, and so did Chen Jicheng. However, they did not stop Chen from trying to use the president's words for his own purposes. As the saying goes, if you have a hold over the feudal overlord, you control his vassals, too. While the tactic worked with Li Yuqing and Wang Kejun, both students of the Whampoa Military Academy, it did not have the same effect on Zeng Keda and Fang Meng'ao.

"You wish to see the orders?" Chen held tight to the microphone. He was doing his utmost to control his growing anger. He shot a glance at Li and Wang. "You've both seen the orders. Do you believe Inspector Zeng has sufficient credentials to see them, too?"

Wang Kejun might have been the secretary-general for the north China planning group, but Chen Jicheng outranked him. He was deputy commander-in-chief, and it was not his place to say yes or no. All he could do was shake his head.

Li Yuqing was there to represent Li Zongren, this was true. But he had already indirectly offended Chen Jicheng when he read aloud the vice-president's orders and did not wish to further antagonise him. He thus turned to Zeng Keda. "The president's orders were given to us. I'm afraid you don't have the rank necessary to see them. Inspector Zeng, I would please ask that you respond to Deputy Chen's question. If you don't have an answer, or if the one you have is not something you wish to share at this moment, you may contact Chiang Ching-kuo and ask for instructions."

If the first few sentences Li spoke were enough to annoy Chen Jicheng, the latter ones made his face drop.

Zeng seized upon the opportunity. "Yes! That's exactly what I want to... need to do. Get me a telephone. I'll call Chief Chiang right away!"

"There's also a call I'd like to make," Xu Tieying interjected. "Please, Wang Puchen, come help me do so." He stood without waiting for a response. "The Communists we arrested should be interrogated immediately as well. After all, the more we wrangle over details here, the more opportunity we give them to concoct their own version of events."

"Then let's all make our phone calls!" Chen shouted into the microphone before slamming it hard down on the podium. The crack it made reverberated throughout the room. Chen's face drained of colour and he shouted once more: "We should never have had the meeting in the first place if we weren't going to finish it. See to it that Yan Chunming is interrogated, hold nothing back. Do the same for Liang Jinglun, too. I want confessions out of both of them. I know they're both Communists, but I want you to get them to say it themselves!"

Xu Tieying did not hesitate. He stood and made for the door, followed by Wang Puchen. Cool and composed, Zeng Keda also left his seat and walked out of the room.

Chen Jicheng, Li Yuqing and Wang Kejun stayed on stage. He Qicang and Fang Buting remained seated in front. To the back, Fang Meng'ao was still standing to attention. There was a brief lull in the action before He Qicang stood abruptly and departed, the clack of his cane echoing off the floor. Fang Buting stood shortly after, but he was unsure if he should follow He out of the room, or if he should stay. While mulling things over, his eyes fell upon his son.

"Vice-Chancellor He!" Li Yuqing's voice was unexpectedly loud. He Qicang stopped and turned around. Li reached into the attaché case on the nearby table and pulled out another document. He then leaned close to Chen Jicheng and whispered: "There are also several urgent dispatches from the Nanking National Assembly." Then he looked towards He Qicang. "Vice-Chancellor, Governor Fang, you were both specially requested to attend this meeting. There are still other important issues that we could like to solicit your opinions on…"

"You've just given orders to have my own professors interrogated. Do you think I can remain here and discuss anything with you?" He Qicang was looking at the documents given to Chen Jicheng by Li Yuqing.

Chen Jicheng failed to notice, however. His attention was drawn to the paper he was holding, the Kuomintang emblem prominently displayed, the urgency of the items clearly outlined:

> Presidential Decree No. 148: Urgent establishment of committee to manage the distribution of American Aid

Like He Qicang, Li Yuqing regarded Chen Jicheng. By the look on his face, he knew Chen had seen the list of names.

Director in charge: Weng Wenhao
   Deputy Directors: Wang Yunwu, Gu Weijun, Yu Hongjun, He Qicang

Chen Jichang couldn't tear his eyes away from that one name, He Qicang! When he saw whose name was designated as a committee member, the rest of the colour drained from his face.

Committee Members: Fang Buting...

Li Yuqing saw how the information contained in the document tormented Chen Jicheng. He turned to He Qicang. "Vice-Chancellor He, if those persons you wish to protect are not Communists, once our meeting is complete, we will certainly consider your views."

He Qicang did not answer but turned to Fang Buting. "You're an official employee of the government, you stay and discuss." Then he turned back to Li Yuqing. "Deputy Li, please pass on a message to Vice-President Li Zongren: I hereby declare that I am resigning from any and all consultancy roles I previously held with the government. After returning home, I shall inform Mr John Leighton Stuart of my resignation from Yenching University as well. After all, he's the man primarily responsible for the establishment of the university. He can take care of its teachers and students!" His declaration made, he walked out of the room.

"Vice-Chancellor!" Li Yuqing's voice was urgent, and he jumped down from the stage and chased after Hi Qicang. "Please, wait a moment!" At this point, Li turned to shout towards the main gate: "VIP on the way!"

The gate had remained open, so it took little time for the gendarme commander to appear. He saluted immediately.

"Report to Xu Tieying and Wang Puchen. The detainees are not to be interrogated, at least temporarily. They are to wait until we've come to a resolution." Li spoke his order quickly, imparting to his subordinate the importance of delivering them just as fast.

"Sir, yes sir!" The man saluted, turned and raced off to deliver the message.

Li Yuqing finally focused on He Qicang. His voice was low and gentle. "Please, Vice-Chancellor, come back and sit down."

Slowly, He relented and allowed the other man to turn him around. He glanced in the direction of the stage and saw Chen Jicheng. He was silent and standing, seemingly deep in thought. He asked Li Yuqing: "The orders you gave him certainly had quite the effect."

Li helped the older man back to his seat. "This meeting was called by the authorities in Nanking. None of us here can actually give any orders. All of them come from Nanking."

He Qicang permitted Li to direct him back to his chair. He avoided making eye contact with anyone. Then, suddenly, he raised his walking cane and pointed it at Fang Meng'ao. "It's a meeting. What the hell are you doing standing there like that? Sit down."

"Yes sir!" Fang Meng'ao kept up his performance, answering as a well-trained soldier, saluting, and then sitting down, straight and stiff.

He Qicang again acquiesced and moved with the assistance of Li Yuqing back to his chair.

Fang Buting reached out to help the older man sit, but He deftly pushed him away. "I'm no older than you. Let me tell you, if, at the end of this meeting, my teachers and students, and your niece... well... if they've not been released by then, my advice to you is to resign from your position at the bank. Together we'll return home, to our old hometown. We can take up teaching middle school. What do you say?"

"Yes, that's what we'll do. We could till the land, too. That would be just as good."

Beyond the main gates to the prison, the hallway stretched for about sixty metres. Individual cells were positioned on both sides. None of them was empty. Despite the numbers, however, the prison was quiet, almost strangely so. As a result, the hallway seemed to carry on into the distance, disappearing into the silence. Alongside the main gates, soldiers stood on guard. But not just those normally stationed at the prison. On this occasion, they were accompanied by the military gendarmerie, the men under Chen Jicheng's command. In the duty room to the right, Secretary Sun held a telephone to his ear. He said little, nothing more than an intermittent "eh", "yes" and "affirmative". Like the hallway beyond the gates, the room was quiet and still. A few seconds later, Sun hung up the phone and stepped back out to stand in front of the gates.

"The keys to the gate... give them to me."

The lieutenant in charge handed Secretary Sun the large key ring he had been carrying. Sun said nothing further. He was quiet, his actions careful, deliberate. He inserted the key and opened the gate. Then, just as careful, just as deliberate, he pushed the new detainees into the passageway. Once through, and with the keys still in his hand, Secretary Sun walked through the iron gate as well. He strode down the passageway that seemed to stretch into forever, unhurried. He said nothing.

Inside his cell, Liang Jinglun sat on a bed that was no more than a foot above the ground. He was silent, his eyes trained on Secretary Sun as he walked in. There was no greeting between the two men. Sun simply stepped in and squeezed, somewhat roughly, onto the bed next to him. Liang averted his eyes but said nothing. All he could do was wait.

"Out of the persons we've arrested," said Sun, his voice barely a whisper, "how many besides Yan Chunming know that you're a Communist agent?"

Liang hesitated a moment. "I don't understand your meaning."

"My meaning is this. Once we begin the interrogations, who's most likely to spill the beans and say that you're a Communist?" Liang Jinglun remained silent. Sun continued: "Comrade Jianfeng's orders are clear. The peacocks must fly southeast, nothing can get in the way of that. Furthermore, Jiao Zhongqing and Liu Lanzhi must be protected." At these words, Liang couldn't help but direct his full attention towards Secretary Sun. Sun, however, chose not to meet his gaze, there being more he had to say. "If one of the detainees clearly identifies you as a party member, Chen Jicheng and Xu Tieying will surely react and end up mucking everything up. As a result, the currency reform initiative will also end up being blocked... all because of you. So tell me – and I'm not giving you a choice here – which of the detainees knows your true identity?"

Liang Jinglun finally grasped what Secretary Sun meant. It was also clear that Sun was a member of the Iron and Blood Congress. Unfortunately, he felt no warmth at this realisation, only an unmerciful chill that seemed to swirl up from deep in the silence.

A moment passed and Sun said to Liang: "You're in a difficult spot, so am I. Right now, I've got one responsibility: implement Comrade Jianfeng's orders… and protect you."

"The best way to protect me is to make sure no one is interrogated," Liang replied. "If the interrogations have to happen, then see to it that only Yan Chunming is questioned. These past few days… well, to be frank, his behaviour has been atypical… I can't be sure if the Peking Labour Union has figured out my true identity or not. If they have, then there's really no other option. I can't be a part of the plan to fly those particular peacocks southeast."

"I think it's best if I go and speak to Yan Chunming immediately." Sun stood. "If the Communists in Peking suspect you, I'll be able to find that out based on Yan's reaction to my questioning. One more thing: is Xie Mulan… is she a Communist agent, too?"

"No."

"Then there's no need to worry. Now, about the contents of that letter you received last night, the one from the Communist-controlled academic committee. Tell me everything you can recall about it."

"All right." Liang Jinglun stood and began to recite what he could, his voice low. "It was addressed to me specifically. It started with… yes, I remember, it said Comrade Yan Chunming has blatantly disobeyed organisational orders. He's returned to the university on his own accord… he's armed."

Secretary Sun feigned to stare at the wall as though each and every word Liang Jinglun had just spoken was imprinted upon it.

———

"Fine!" Once more Chen Jicheng grabbed the microphone, his voice echoing: "Let's discuss matters, let's get things straight. Once we do, we'll report to Nanking and decide who to release and who not!"

Zeng Keda, Wang Puchen and Xu Tieying had returned and taken up their seats again. Chen's venomous eyes enveloped them, and he continued: "First, why the hell did you allow that Communist to take the stage? And how did that Communist bastard, Old Liu… Liu Chuwu… how the hell did he get himself placed in one of the teams charged with distributing the food aid? And don't throw all of it at Ma Hanshan's feet. He couldn't have done this on his own. Who was pulling the strings? I want to know all of it!" Silence was the only response he received. Finally, he turned to Zeng Keda. "Did you make your phone call?"

"Yes… I did."

"And? What did Chief Ching-kuo have to say?"

"He said he'd call me back in half an hour."

"Well then, in the meantime you can answer the questions I ask. Start with Yan Chunming, Yenching University's Communist ringleader."

Yan Chunming was seated on his bed in a cell that was more or less a carbon copy of the one Liang Jinglun found himself in. A man had come into his cell, was standing almost on top of him, but Yan Chunming could not make him out. His spectacles had been shattered, and without them, he was effectively blind, able to see faint outlines and not much else.

"Your superiors ordered you to retreat into the so-called liberated areas. Why did you disobey that order and return to the university?" The man who asked this question spoke in a low voice, as he had done before. But to Yan, it was a stranger's voice, someone whom he did not know. As for the question, it was straight to the point.

Yan prevaricated: "I… I don't understand."

Sun persisted: "Yesterday evening, Liu Chuwu, your comrade, did his utmost to get you to leave. Do you understand this statement?"

Yan Chunming ambled closer to where the voice was coming from. He was trying his best to make out the image of the man who had come into his cell, who had begun to ask him these questions.

"Please, sit." Secretary Sun's voice remained low, but the seriousness of his tone was clear. "Even if you could see me, you don't know me." Yan Chunming returned to sit on his bed. Sun continued: "Comrade Liu gave his life for you. Tell me, how many more will have to do the same, how many more will have to sacrifice everything to make up for your error… for your mistake?"

Yan's response was cold, unfeeling: "I don't understand your meaning…"

"Well, in that case, let me tell you a few more things. Let's see if you get it then." Sun went quiet as he recalled what Liang Jinglun had told him. Once he was sure, he began: "Comrade Yan Chunming has blatantly disobeyed organisational orders. He's returned to the university on his own accord… and he's armed. Does any of this ring a bell? How about the stuff about self-serving martyrdom? Violation of the spirit of Comrade Peng Zhen's Sixth of July directives… no? What about Liang Jinglun being ordered to assume your duties at Yenching… for him to settle things down, avoid unnecessary sacrifice? Do you understand now? The order for you to hand over the weapon you took… the bit about Liang being instructed to show you the letter on which all of this was written and for him to control your activities… as well as keep you safe. Surely you now grasp what I'm trying to tell you?"

The prison cell was deathly quiet, except for the sound of Yan Chunming's racing heartbeat. Yan's hesitation did not last long: "I accept whatever punishment you deem appropriate."

Sun crouched down. He wanted to look squarely into the other man's face. "You still want to talk about punishment. Isn't it rather too late for that?"

"Then why have you come?"

"I want to discuss your point of view on these orders."

"Point of… I don't have one, I can only obey."

"Obey who? Obey the academic committee that gave those orders? Or obey Liang Jinglun?" Sun's voice had quickened. He'd deliberately omitted calling him "comrade".

Yan Chunming went silent again. He shifted his gaze, blind though he was, and exposed the confusion he now felt. It was the party that had told him of Liang Jinglun's true identity, his allegiance to the Iron and Blood Congress, that's why he didn't hesitate to return to the university. He wanted to correct his mistake, grooming Liang for party membership. He shouldn't have tried to do that. Did this man here in front of him… did he know all of this, was he a party member? Or was he a member of the Iron and Blood Congress, just like Liang Jinglun? Whatever the case might be, Yan thought to himself, he couldn't reveal that the party was aware of Liang Jinglun's true loyalties… even if this man was a comrade. Yan was certain that this bit of information had to be kept secret. Yan knew, however, that he was being tested. It had already begun. The question for him now was how to respond. The pace of his delivery was slow: "I'm in charge of things at Yenching. Just because I am in danger doesn't mean I can renounce my position and disregard the safety of fellow comrades, including Liang Jinglun. How the organisation looks at me… I know that already. I'm nothing but small fry."

"So you've never once suspected the veracity of this letter?" Sun was keen not to give Yan Chunming a chance to catch his breath.

"Subordinates obey their superiors, party members trust the party. Suspicions are forbidden."

Sun had one last question: "So you do not doubt Liang Jinglun?"

Feigning surprise, Yan Chunming answered with a question of his own: "Does the party doubt him?"

Sun rose to his feet, slowly, carefully. "I hope you'll be able to withstand the ordeal that is to come."

Yan Chunming stared after the hazy image of the man who'd just interrogated him. Once he knew he was gone, he lay back on his bed and gave himself over to his thoughts.

Ma Hanshan had no recollection of when he'd been escorted into the meeting. All he knew was that he was standing in front of a stage and that his hands were shackled. In defiance, he kept his eyes closed, refusing to look at anyone.

Chen Jicheng looked him up and down, and then turned to Fang Meng'ao. The other men in attendance refrained from looking at Ma Hanshan, everyone except Fang, who couldn't focus on anything else.

Once more, Chen Jicheng's voice boomed through the microphone and he redirected his eyes to the man in chains in front of him. "Ma Hanshan!" Ma opened his eyes to meet Chen's glare. Chen continued: "You know what you should say. So go ahead and say it!"

"What, what I should say?" It was now Ma's turn to scan his audience. He took a moment to respond, pretending to mull things over. Finally, he spoke: "Well, there's too much I should say, isn't there? At least by my reckoning. How's about Deputy Commander Chen? Why don't you point me in the right direction, eh?"

"Liu Chuwu!" Chen's voice was absent of any of the mirth shown by Ma. "Did you enlist this man, or did someone else send him to you? Do you need any further reminders?"

"Who's Liu Chuwu?" Ma Hanshan was being honest since he didn't recognise the name. That said, it took only a moment for him to appreciate that, whoever this man might be, it was highly likely he'd been intimately involved in what he had been up to. A few seconds later, an image of the only man it could be flashed through his mind: Old Liu! Yes, Ma thought, it had to be him. Of course, he couldn't let his interrogators in on this realisation, so he dissembled some more: "My apologies. I can't think of who that is. I don't suppose you could give me any further details…"

Chen Jicheng laughed coldly, then turned to Xu Tieying. "Chief Xu, you ask him."

Xu stood. "You enlisted him, you gave him a gun, you told him to murder me. Are you still going to say you don't know who we're talking about?"

"Ahhh, that man, yes, I know him." Ma's tone was matter-of-fact. "I got an assistant of mine to reach out to members of the Green Gang. He was one of them, I believe. I gave him ten thousand US dollars, asked him to… to cut out a cancer in the body of the party-state. He and his men agreed, at first, but then they didn't follow through. So I figured I had to try to do it myself. Xu Tieying, do you find all of this amusing or something?"

Xu did his best to portray an image of calm. He smiled and directed his attention to Wang Puchen. "Mr Wang, Ma Hanshan here says that this man was a member of the Green Gang. Should we enlighten him on this matter?"

Like Xu before him, Wang stood before speaking. "This man, Liu Chuwu, was a known Communist agent and member of the Peking Labour Union. He was particularly skilled at procuring arms and instigating riots... a provocateur, you could say, going by the codename Red Flag Number Five. Mr Ma, you're no doubt keenly aware of the orders regarding the need to suppress all forms of rebellion and to safeguard the nation. For you to become associated with this kind of man, well, you're the only one who can explain it."

Somewhat unexpectedly, Ma Hanshan was silent, but he did appear to the others in attendance as someone stricken by fear and panic. A moment later, he responded: "Motherfucker. Goddammit, no choice but to admire the fucker."

"And..." Xu Tieying interjected.

"In April, when I received word from the civilian authorities, I spoke to this Liu Chuwu. He said this year that that word 'Red', that it was a crime, that it signalled nothing but impending bloodshed and disaster. I'm afraid there's no getting beyond that particular pit..."

"Liu Chuwu?" Xu questioned.

"More like Iron Mouth Liu from *Dream of the Red Chamber*. Out there, on the street, telling fortunes for a dollar. You ought to call this meeting to a close and go out and get your fortunes read."

"Deputy Commander Chen," said Xu Tieying, turning to his superior, "I would request Ma Hanshan be transferred to the investigative team for continued interrogation. He's admitted to his Communist sympathies."

"I second that!" Ma Hanshan held his chained hands in the air and shouted in agreement. He looked at Xu Tieying with nothing but disdain. "Xu, you know what, I'd still like to kill you, just as you'd like to see me dead. How did we get to this point? The interrogation's over. Whatever there is to do with me and this Liu Chuwu, whoever he was, I understand what I'm facing."

Wang Puchen now jumped in: "Liu Chuwu barged up onto that stage with the intent to kill Captain Fang, but Chief Xu fired first before he could enact his murderous plan."

Wang Puchen's statement stunned Ma Hanshan, forcing him to take a moment before he could add: "Well, fuck me! I thought I'd got a man to help me remove a cancerous tumour, and now I hear I almost got Captain Fang killed. Well, the dead can't testify can they, nor can they defend themselves. You say I was in cahoots with that Communist, then so be it."

"What about Yan Chunming and Liang Jinglun?" Xu Tieying barked. "What connection did they have to Liu Chuwu?"

"Let's go!" said He Qicang, rising abruptly from his chair. "Mr Fang, it's time for us to leave." Fang Buting lifted himself from his chair without hesitation.

"Gentlemen, please!" Li Yuqing had seen He Qicang's reaction to the questioning. Now, he stood up and turned to Chen Jicheng. "The instructions from Nanking were to discuss the allocation of American aid. Ma Hanshan and his purported Communist sympathies can be discussed at a later meeting, can't they?"

Chen stood as well. "The vice-chancellor and the governor of the Central Bank are here to discuss the release of... certain detainees. If we don't, then they have said they won't cooperate with us in weighing up our options regarding the distribution of American aid. But, gentlemen, I would like to ask something: don't you want to get to the bottom of all this? Don't you want things to be clear?"

"The only thing we should do is submit our resignations," Fang Buting answered, before turning to He Qicang. "We've seen our fair share of years, haven't we? Now we've seen members of our family arrested. Then... these people drag us in here as what... witnesses to their interrogation. And yet they still say they want to discuss how best to allocate foreign aid? Brother, I advised you already, you don't want to get involved in any of that currency reform stuff. But you didn't listen to me. I bet you understand now, though, don't you?"

"Hey!" He Qicang returned Fang's look. "You sold half your life to the Central Bank... to them. Now you want to tell me where I erred?"

An argument ensued, leaving everyone else in a daze by the unexpected turn of events.

"Come on, let's not argue." Fang Buting extended his hand. "We've never fought before, and I don't want to start now. Let's go."

"Shut that door!" Li Yuqing's voice echoed throughout the

room. To those inside, however, his order seemed unnecessary; the door was, after all, already closed. At least it was for the moment, for as though on cue the commander of the military police pushed it open, shouting as he did: "Sir, yes sir!" He then spun on his heel and barked orders to his men to lock all doors from the outside.

"What the devil are you up to?" asked He Qicang. "Do you mean to confine us?"

"Captain Fang!" said Li Yuqing, ignoring the older man's question. "Please come forward and sit with our two distinguished gentlemen."

At the same time, a look of hope and expectation flashed in Zeng Keda's eyes. Fang Meng'ao did as he was requested and joined his father and He Qicang in the front of the room.

Li Yuqing turned back to the soldier. "Bring the phone!"

The soldier hesitated, surprised by the request. "Sir, the wire… it isn't long enough."

"Then make it long enough!"

"Yes sir!" With that, the soldier left, unsure of whether or not he could actually carry out the instruction.

Fang Meng'ao was standing beside the two older men, both of whom now stared at him, a look of concern on their faces. There was no way they could even try to leave now.

Li Yuqing looked to Zeng Keda. "Inspector Zeng, didn't you say Chief Ching-kuo was to call back in half an hour?"

Standing, he glanced at his watch. "That's correct. It should be any minute now."

Li Yuqing paid no further heed to Chen Jicheng, or to Wang Kejun. "Let's take a brief rest. When Chief Ching-kuo's phone call comes, we'll start again."

CHAPTER 6

Secretary Sun, with the prison executive officer following, walked towards Wang Puchen's office, coming to a halt just outside the door. The executive officer looked on nervously, then spoke: "Sir... aside from our commander, Mr Wang, no one else is allowed to enter."

Sun pulled some keys out of his pocket. "You see these? Your commander gave them to me. Get yourself to the end of the corridor. No one's allowed to approach." Sun offered no further explanation. He turned to the door, inserted a key and opened it. The officer was equal parts surprised and doubtful, but all he did was stand in the doorway. Sun stepped halfway in, then shot the officer a stern look. "You're not to say anything to anyone about what I'm doing in here. Only Mr Wang – and you, of course – know I'm here."

"Sir." This, at least, was something the officer could believe. He didn't say anything further, but turned and walked to the end of the corridor as Sun had instructed.

Sun stepped inside, gently locking the heavy door behind him.

Seconds later, he was on the telephone, filing his report: "Yan Chunming seems to be unaware of any suspicions the CPC might have concerning Liang Jinglun's identity. There are five detainees in total who believe Liang Jinglun is a Communist Party member. Two of them are students at our Chiang Kai-shek Student Society.

The three others are also students whose loyalty is to the CPC. Comrade Liang does not want them tortured."

"Then they won't be." Comrade Jianfeng's voice echoed down the telephone. "Except for Yan Chunming, I want you to allow Vice-Chancellor He to lobby successfully for the release of Liang Jinglun and the students arrested today… on bail of course."

"Understood, Comrade Jianfeng. That is, well, I do have one worry. If Wang Puchen makes arrangements for their release, that will certainly trigger fierce resistance on the part of Xu Tieying… and Chen Jicheng especially."

"You worry about things unnecessarily. Remember, you serve as a facilitator, a communicator. You are, after all, Xu Tieying's secretary."

"Yes. Understood."

A long extension cord was found, and the telephone was brought into the meeting room and placed on the table. Finally, it rang. Wang Kejun could not answer it, his rank forbade such initiative. Chen Jicheng and Li Yuqing looked at each other, neither one sure who should pick up the receiver.

"You get it," said Li Yuqing.

Chen Jicheng, who did not really wish to answer it even though he was chairing the meeting, resigned himself to the fact he had to. He reached over and picked up the phone, holding it close to his ear. No one else could hear what was being said, but to Chen, the voice on the other end was crystal clear: "Jicheng?" His composure changed, his legs clapped together: "Yes, Vice-Chancellor."

Those words prompted everyone in the meeting room to stare at Chen Jicheng.

The voice on the phone answered: "I'm no vice-chancellor. I'm the president of the Republic." Chen Jicheng's eyes went blank. After a short pause, the voice again spoke: "So…"

"Sir… yes, Mr President. It's me, Chen Jicheng."

"Do you know what's on the table in front of me?"

Chen hesitated a moment. "No sir. If you would… sir… please tell me."

"There's nothing to tell. The commands I've given you in northern China, the orders I asked you to follow, the plans I wanted to see completed… you've not done any of it. And yet you still think I will protect you. You're to leave Peking today. You're ordered to return to Nanking. Tomorrow, I will telegraph the orders confirming your dismissal." Click.

Chen let the phone down from his ear, but he didn't replace it. His mind was racing. From his first days at the Whampoa Academy, this hand that now clasped the receiver had held so many guns. He thought, in that moment, that it held one now. Instinctively, he made to holster the phone as though it was a pistol.

Li Yuqing rose quickly and grabbed the phone, intending to speak to the man on the other end: "Sir, it's me, Li Yuqing. Mr President…" But all he heard was the dial tone. Li stared at Chen.

"The president has ordered me to return to Nanking immediately." While Chen had begun to regain his senses, his hoarseness belied the significance of that order. "You all continue with the meeting." He said nothing else. Nor did he give anyone the opportunity to ask questions. He simply walked down off the stage and straight towards the exit.

Zeng Keda was unable to conceal his knowing reaction to this turn of events. Wang Puchen, on the other hand, pretended to have no reaction whatsoever. As for Xu Tieying, he reacted most explicitly, standing up at nearly the same time as Chen Jicheng departed the stage, his eyes following Chen intently as he began to disappear through the doorway.

But then, Chen stopped and turned around. His eyes met those of his closest confidant, before announcing: "You come, too." He didn't say anything else. He merely left.

Xu said nothing more about rank. He just did as he was told, quickly walking down off the stage, passing Li Yuqing and Wang Kejun, apparently determined to march in the same direction as his superior, Chen Jicheng.

———

The guards beyond the door saluted as the men walked by. He Xiaoyu's eyes flashed and she stood up without really realising why.

Xie Peidong also lifted himself up from the stone steps that circled the aged tree they'd been sitting under.

The first man to leave was He Qicang, walking as slowly and as carefully appropriate for a man of his age. The men who followed behind him had little choice but to match his pace. Fang Buting came second, then Li Yuqing and Wang Kejun. Once these four men left, Zeng Keda and Fang Meng'ao appeared. Finally, Wang Puchen and Xu Tieying brought up the rear.

On seeing her father make to descend the stairs, He Xiaoyu thought to race towards him. Xie Peidong, however, held her back. "Wait."

In seconds, the Buick belonging to Li Zongren rushed to a stop near the foot of the steps. Wang Kejun's American-style jeep pulled up behind the Buick. Fang Buting's driver thought to do the same, but Xie Peidong stopped him as well, shaking his head to signal to the driver that the car was to remain where it was, near the tree where they had been sitting.

He Qicang and Fang Buting alighted from the car. Next were Li Yuqing and Wang Kejun. The doors to their vehicles opened immediately for them.

Li spoke to his assistant: "The vice-chancellor and the governor of the Central Bank will ride in my car. I'll accompany General-Secretary Wang in his jeep."

"Yes sir." The aide directed his hand towards He Qicang, gesturing for him to climb in. He, however, rejected the gesture and instead turned to look at Li Yuqing.

Li understood the meaning of He Qicang's look straight away. He leaned back towards Xu Tieying and Wang Puchen, and said: "Release the detainees."

"Understood," said Wang. At the same time, he motioned for them to board the vehicles.

Xu Tieying's visage was expressionless as he turned towards the main gate, and walked off. A moment later, Wang Puchen trailed after him.

He Qicang's voice was markedly softer than it had been. "Please, if you will, Section Chief Li, could you give me a few minutes? I would first like to speak a moment to my family who've spent all of this time waiting."

"Certainly."

He Qicang winked at Fang Buting, and the two men walked off towards the tree. There, Xie Peidong and He Xiaoyu watched them closely as they strolled over.

He looked at his daughter before turning to Xie Peidong. "Mr Xie, could you please escort Xiaoyu home? Could you also tell Mr Fang's wife that once our meeting is over I shall join them for dinner?"

Xie Peidong wasn't entirely sure if he understood the full meaning of what the older man had asked him to do, but he did not seek clarification. He merely acknowledged the request and told him it would be done.

"Oh, just a minute, before you go..." and he turned around in the direction of the steps. "You, come here." He'd motioned to Fang Meng'ao.

Fang barely reacted to being summoned. At least not until Zeng Keda leaned close and told him He Qicang had called out. Then, as though awoken from some stupor, Fang Meng'ao dashed over towards them.

"Do you fancy a glass of wine?" He Qicang's eyes looked closely at the younger man.

"Sorry sir, not today. I'm not much in the mood."

"Nonsense!" He turned to Xie Peidong and asked: "What wine do I have at home, hmm, something good I trust?"

"There are still several bottles of Lafite, I believe."

"Open two and let them breathe a while." With that, and holding his cane in his hand, He Qicang strode off in the direction of the Buick.

Fang Buting glanced at his son. "You tell them, all right." Then he departed, too.

Fang Meng'ao met his uncle's eyes, as well as Xiaoyu's. "Nanking's formed a new committee to manage the proper distribution of American aid. Ambassador Stuart proposed who should make up this committee. Uncle He agreed to serve as deputy director, and Dad's agreed to be on the committee. The detainees are to be released, Wang and Xu are seeing to it. Uncle He will be over to our place tonight. I imagine he wants to share a meal with Mulan."

Three Communist agents looked at each other, but none of them knew, in that moment, what to say to the other.

Over nearer the building, He and Fang were seated in the Buick. Just behind them in the jeep were Li Yuqing and Wang Kejun.

Three sets of eyes watched as the two vehicles exited through the main gate.

"They're off to another meeting. Zeng Keda and I have to attend as well." Fang Meng'ao said nothing further. He turned and strode over to the jeep that was waiting for him and Zeng.

Xie Peidong looked at He Xiaoyu, whose eyes were directed at the back of Fang Meng'ao. "Come on," he said. "Let's go."

Wang Puchen's car pulled in through the gates at Xishen prison. Xu Tieying followed close behind. They'd called ahead and so Secretary Sun, the prison executive officer, as well as the commanders of the military police and Special Forces were all there to greet them. Wang stepped out of his vehicle and then waited for Xu to do the same. Together, they walked over to their less-than-enthusiastic welcoming committee.

"The list of detainees," Wang said to his executive officer, who complied immediately, pulling several sheets of paper out of his jacket. Wang scanned it before continuing: "We're to release them. We'll do so in batches. How exactly, you'll have to wait for," and he motioned towards Xu Tieying, "*our* orders."

Surprisingly, none of the four men reacted to what Wang had said. Or rather, they tried their best not to do so.

Wang turned to Xu Tieying. "Let's get to it then. We've a lot to discuss." He stuck out his hand and gestured Xu to accompany him inside.

Wang Puchen's bedroom was sparsely furnished, but everything was in its place. To one side, tight to the wall, was a simple wooden bed. Across from it was a basic desk, made of the same white wood. Beside the desk was a rudimentary bookshelf. Also white.

In the middle of the room, there was a Chinese rosewood mahjong table, as well as four matching chairs. The very sight of it clashed with the other pieces of furniture.

Upon stepping into the room, Xu Tieying scanned its contents and then moved to sit on the left-hand side of the mahjong table. Wang Puchen sat facing him.

Tapping on the table, Xu asked: "Chinese rosewood?"

Wang smiled a little. "That's right."

"Before... recent events, this is where Ma Hanshan was living, yes?"

"When he was in charge here, this was his room, yes. You haven't looked at the list of detainees." And with that, he placed the sheets of paper in front of Xu and deftly opened a small drawer under the mahjong table and removed a pair of reading glasses. He placed these on top of the paper.

Xu knew immediately that these glasses were the ones worn by Ma Hanshan when he played mahjong, but he accepted them calmly, unperturbed. The names were bunched together and difficult to read, especially without the glasses. Xu scanned them quickly, then looked up at Wang Puchen. "You're really something, I must say. I doubt there's many around as skilled as you."

"I'm not sure how to take that, Chief Xu. Surely you're being too critical."

For the first time this day, Xu Tieying allowed himself to smile. But he wouldn't give him anything more, he wouldn't respond with actual words. He let the smile stay for a brief moment more and then tilted his head back down towards the list. He read through the first page quickly, the second page even faster. When he got to the last, he slowed his pace as though the page was filled with the most serious offenders, and fixed his attention on one particular name: Liang Jinglun! He removed the reading glasses, placing them purposely atop Liang's name. He lifted his face again and stared at Wang Puchen. "I have a list of names, too. I've thought about it for days. Today, I think I'll let you see it." He opened the button on his jacket pocket and pulled out his own sheets of paper.

"Chief Xu, if this is something I shouldn't see, then it's best you don't show me." Wang held up his hand to refuse, but Xu Tieying persisted and placed the pages on the table. Wang's eyes were drawn immediately to it. The blue letterhead marked its providence, the Kuomintang Communication Bureau, the stamp on the right indicating its top-secret classification. The colour drained from Wang's face. His eyes lingered on the title: "Report on measures to be taken to ensure the safety of Comrade Chiang Ching-kuo", then on the name of the person who wrote the document, Director-General Chen Lifu. Further essential details were outlined below, and then two groups of names. Wang could not hide his astonishment at what was written beside one group of names: "Persons most threatening to Comrade Chiang Ching-kuo".

Xu Tieying looked at the other man, keen to see how he would react once he read the names listed.

Wang read the list. Involuntarily, his right hand pulled out a cigarette while his left took out a box of matches. Wang struck a match and in that moment of light, the fire illuminated one name: Liang Jinglun!

He lit his cigarette and drew back on it deeply, extinguishing the match in the process. He didn't exhale, however. There was no cloud of smoke to blanket the room. The next name on the list was clear: Fang Meng'ao! These two men, placed under the category of most threatening to Chiang Ching-kuo, were the only two names there. Wang continued to run his eyes over the document. The second group of names bore the opposite classification to the first: "Persons most useful to Comrade Chiang Ching-kuo". The name that followed was one clearly known to him, for it was his own. He knew Xu was watching him closely, he knew the reaction he had to show, one of appreciation at being shown the document, despite his initial reluctance.

Xu Tieying gave him a restrained smile in return, then his eyes too scanned the document, suggesting Wang Puchen continue. Wang understood and redirected his gaze. His surprise grew, for the next name on the list of persons useful to Chiang Ching-kuo was Sun Chaozhong.

"All good." Xu reached out and lifted the sheets of paper from the table. "Light a match for me, will you?"

Wang Puchen stood, struck a match and handed it to Xu Tieying.

Xu received the match carefully, and then put it to the paper.

Two pairs of eyes watched as the flames devoured the document, mesmerised by the bluish hue of the conflagration.

Xu Tieying waited for the fire to reach up to his thumb, then released it gently so that the ashes could float to the floor. "Let's sit."

Wang said nothing, but sat. The two men looked at each other.

"I know the questions you have," said Xu Tieying. "First, you'd like to know why I'm still using Secretary Sun. Second, you want to know why I showed you the document. Well, let me tell you straight, these are Chief Chen's orders. My use of Sun is necessary because, as you've seen, he is considered to be of use to Comrade Ching-kuo. I use him, although I pretend not to know Comrade Ching-kuo considers him thus. During this afternoon's meeting when we separated to make our phone calls, I called Chief Chen. He told me to show you the document… for the party-state, and for the protection of Chiang Ching-kuo's plans. Comrade Puchen, your cigarette is going to burn your hand…"

"No matter." Wang Puchen squeezed his fingers, killing the flame. "What does Chief Chen want of me? What does he want me to do?"

"There's nothing he wants you to do, nothing whatsoever, in fact." Xu put all his cards on the table. "Quite a few of the younger members of the Iron and Blood Congress have ended up being… problems for Mr Chiang. Zeng Keda is inconsequential. But Liang Jinglun, well, he's wrapped up with the Americans and with the CPC, wrapped far too tightly. To get him out of this falls on me. I have to take care of things. That's why I keep Secretary Sun around. He reports each step to Comrade Chiang-kuo. It has nothing to do with you. Remember this, the report… you never saw it. Not even Comrade Ching-kuo knows about it. And we intend to keep it that way. If there's one thing we want from you, it's for you not to lose Comrade Ching-kuo's trust."

"May I ask another question?"

"Please."

"Has the president seen that report?"

"If the president hadn't, do you think I'd let you see it?"

"I… I understand."

Secretary Sun, the prison executive officer, and the commanders of both the military police contingent and the Special Forces all stared at Xu Tieying and Wang Puchen as they re-emerged from the latter's office. Wang held the list of names in his hand and signalled for everyone to come over. The three men acknowledged the orders by nodding and then marched towards them.

Wang drew attention to the papers he was holding. "Based on this list, we're to release certain persons. For those holding Peking residency, get a vehicle to bring them back to their respective universities. As for those from elsewhere, put a mark by their names and then arrange transportation to the train station. They're to purchase tickets and return home. If they don't have the money for their own tickets, then you step in and buy them. In short, they're to go home, wherever that may be."

The three men set about their task, giving orders to their subordinates where needed.

While Wang had been talking, Secretary Sun also moved over next to Xu Tieying. Once Wang had finished delegating, Sun leaned towards Xu. "Director, not one of them is to be interrogated… all of them are being released?"

Xu, at last, acknowledged Sun's presence. "The Americans got involved, and Nanking has set up a committee to manage the distribution of US aid. Ambassador Stuart is leading things, He Qicang is deputy director of it. The condition for this to happen was that the detainees be released." He stopped for a moment, wondering how best to continue. "Where are Yan Chunming and Liang Jinglun?" he finally asked.

"Yan's in cell one, Liang's in three."

"Let's go and look in on them." Xu hadn't finished before he had already begun to walk in the direction of the cells.

Sun hastily walked after him. "Shall we signal for Warden Wang to accompany us?"

"These are Deputy Commander-in-Chief Chen's orders. We don't need to involve him."

Secretary Sun said nothing further, leading the way to where Yan and Chun had been detained. Xu stared at the man just in front of him and saw the seeming youthfulness of his pace. A feeling of tired desolation welled up inside.

"This wall was built later, no?" They'd reached the rear courtyard of the prison, where they could see the unending stretch of the Western Hills beyond the walls of the prison.

A prison guard who escorted them was the first to reply: "Sir, yes sir. Warden Ma Hanshan had it rebuilt."

Xu shifted his gaze away from the towering walls and back to the courtyard. His eyes fell on the Chinese crab apple trees that, by the looks of them, hadn't been pruned in years. They'd grown wild and unruly, looking nothing like how they were often depicted in paintings. Xu then spied a small pavilion in the middle of the prison grounds and walked over to it. He spoke to no one in particular: "This is where Cui Zhongshi was executed, yes?" The same guard, who'd followed after him, replied in the affirmative. Xu sat down on the ground. "Choosing such a spot to kill a man… your former warden was certainly a wet blanket, wasn't he?" The guard had no idea how to respond, and so he didn't, at least not before Xu spoke again. "Tell Secretary Sun to bring Yan Chunming here."

"Yes sir."

A long corridor stretched between the inmates' cells and the rear courtyard. Those being escorted to the back of the prison had to first step through an iron gate, turn left and then walk between high stone walls that formed a sort of channel leading them to what appeared to be daylight at the end, although those walking through could never be sure. The tunnel-like corridor opened to the courtyard, and as Sun ushered Yan Chunming down the passageway to what lay ahead, he made a deliberate effort to rush. At one point, Sun even leaned in towards the other man and whispered that they'd met, that they'd chatted before. Yan recognised the voice immediately. He'd spoken to this man in his cell; he was the one who had read back to him the letter written by the academic committee concerning his recent actions. Yan hesitated for a moment, then finally responded. "Please, tell me. Who are you?"

"Let me ask you something. Have we met before?"

"No, we don't know each other."

"That's as it should be. Tell me my identity. My family name's Sun. I'm Xu Tieying's private secretary."

They reached the end of the corridor. Beyond it was the courtyard and the high walls of the prison. Past them lay the Western Hills. But for Yan Chunming, all that was in front of him, the mass of grey that must have been the walls, the green tips just above, none of it mattered, for he couldn't escape the feeling that the book of his life was about to come to an end. He'd reached the last page.

"You ask him. Be sure to make a record of everything, too," Xu Tieying casually called to his secretary on entering the courtyard with Yan Chunming. He barely looked at them, however, instead focusing his attention on the mountains beyond the walls. Inside the pavilion, there was a small stone table and four stone benches.

Sun acknowledged Xu's instructions.

Xu was already seated on one of the benches. Now he turned his back to the wall and focused on them. Sun directed Yan Chunming to one of the other stone stools. "Sit. Then we can talk." Yan Chunming did as he was told without saying a word. Sun took the stool opposite him and pulled out a notepad and a pen. "Yenching University has stepped in and has arranged for your release on bail." As he spoke, Sun recorded his own words in the notepad he held on his lap.

Yan Chunming remained silent, listening only.

Xu Tieying appeared to be doing the same.

"We've confirmed beyond doubt the identity of the man who saved you. He was a Communist, a fairly important one, too, in the Peking Labour Union. His name was Liu Chuwu. You should understand what it means for us to say this, yes?" As Sun spoke, he lowered his head to make sure he got each word in his notepad.

Words rang in Yan's ears, but not the ones Sun had just said. Instead, his mind was transported to the words he heard previously in his cell: "Comrade Liu had done his utmost the night before to get you to leave. You can't say you didn't understand what he meant…"

Sun lifted his head once more. Xu Tieying and Yan Chunming had gone back to looking at the mountains. Everything was quiet. There was no sound, not birds chirping in the great mountains that stretched into the distance, nor even the rustling of the wind.

Secretary Sun held his breath and lowered his head again. He wrote a line of characters and as he did, he continued talking. "Because of this, we cannot release you. Vice-Chancellor He cannot save you. Nor can Ambassador Stuart, Comrade Communist Yan."

Yan Chunming slowly turned his head away from the Western Hills. "I've never counted on anyone to save me."

Xu Tieying let his gaze fall on the two men, shifting back and forth between Yan Chunming and Sun Chaozhong. Sun completed transcribing Yan Chunming's response, and then focused his attention on Xu Tieying, awaiting instructions. Xu's eyes were vacant, however. Sun had little option but to continue: "We're the only ones who can save you... on the precondition, of course, that you identify every other Communist among those who were arrested along with you."

Yan Chunming stood slowly. "Must I?"

Again, Secretary Sun raised his head. First, he glanced at Yan Chunming, then at his superior's back. There was no response. Xu Tieying didn't move, he seemed enraptured by the mountains to the west. Sun had no choice but to record Yan's reply and continue: "We can, naturally, keep this secret. No one else needs to know."

"No secrets are forever. I'm the only Communist, the only one you've arrested."

Sun chose not to look up again. "Do you think we can believe you, accept this as the truth?"

"Don't record that," said Xu Tieying, interrupting the interrogation. "Get him to sign the record."

"Understood."

It was rare for Secretary Sun to conceal so naturally the astonishment his heart felt, but he did as he was instructed and handed the record to Yan Chunming. "Sign it."

Yan Chunming accept the notepad, held it close to his eyes, took a few moments to read over everything that had been written, and then responded: "Give me a pen."

Sun obliged.

Once more Yan held the notepad close to his face. Without his glasses, this was the only way he could see what was on the paper. He found where he needed to sign, and then wrote accordingly: "Comrade Communist Yan Chunming!"

Xu Tieying reached out and took hold of the notepad. He tore the confession out of it and passed it back to Sun. "Bring out the other Communist agents from Yenching University."

"Sir," said Sun, "the... the other Communist agents, sir?"

Yan Chunming was similarly surprised and looked in the direction of Xu Tieying as well. Unfortunately, his poor eyes would allow him to see little more than a hazy, grey expanse in front of him.

Sun sought clarification: "Chief, which Communist agents do you mean?"

It was as though Xu Tieying's pockets were filled to overflowing with papers. He tucked Yan Chunming's confession inside his jacket and pulled out a different sheet. "They're all listed here."

Sun was immediately taken aback by the first name written on the sheet: Liang Jinglun. He was unsure about the remaining names. Some looked familiar, others less so. That was until he reached the last name on the list: Xie Mulan! He could no longer mask his hesitation. He walked over to Xu Tieying, pointed to the last name on the list, and spoke to Xu in no more than a whisper: "Chief Xu, perhaps it's best not to call this name?"

Xu did not deign to follow Sun's hand. "All of them. Call them all."

The sunlight shining through Liang Jinglun's prison cell fell exactly onto the list of names Sun held in his hand. Liang looked at it in disgust. "This isn't for arresting Communists," he snarled, "nor is it to beat me down. It's all about bringing the currency reforms to a halt!" He threw the papers back at Sun. "Talk to Comrade Jianfeng... now! Tell him what's happening."

"Xi Tieying has already set things in motion. I don't have time to report."

"And Zeng Keda? Am I the only soldier fighting in Peking for the Iron and Blood Congress!"

"Comrade Liang Jinglun," said Sun, his voice low, but urgent. "Zeng Keda is in a meeting as we speak, along with He Qicang and Fang Buting. Once I escort you to stand in front of Xu, tell him… no… ask him if you can speak to Wang Puchen. Ask him to contact Zeng Keda, and that He and Fang make haste to get over here and protect Xie Mulan. Involving the CPC, reporting to Comrade Jianfeng… that's far too troublesome for him."

Wang Puchen watched as the two vehicles get ready to depart the prison, one the military escort, the other containing the recent student detainees. In his ear, he could hear a guard giving his report, but he wasn't really paying any attention to what was being said. Slowly, as he had done so many times before, he reached into his jacket and pulled out his cigarettes and matches. Then, suddenly, a name spoken by the guard made him spin around. "Who?" he asked.

"Xie Mulan."

Wang threw his matches to the ground and took out the list of names. He scanned it quickly but he already knew: her name wasn't on it! He raised his head and looked at the vehicles being boarded. "Wait!" he yelled. "Someone's missing, there's one more. Halt. You can't leave yet!"

An alert guard heard his superior and hurried off to the front driver's cab to relay the orders: "You're to standby… the orders come from Warden Wang."

Bringing the guard along with him, Wang Puchen stormed off into the prison.

In the year-plus since he'd been assigned to the prison by the Peking Intelligence Bureau, Wang Puchen had always enjoyed walking by himself in the rear courtyard. As he entered it on this day, however, he felt strange, as though he'd never been to this part of the prison before. Xu Tieying was still seated on his stool. The mountains reached up on the other side of the high walls were quiet, no birdsong, no wind. In the past, Wang had wandered about the grounds, almost carefree. Then, after a while, he'd stroll into the pavilion and sit. This time he couldn't. Xu's eyes greeted him almost immediately. Wang met them but didn't speak.

Xu took the initiative: "Did Secretary Sun call you here?"

"No, it was Liang Jinglun. He's being difficult. He's protesting…"

"Protesting what?" Xu's question was quick, sharp.

"Director Xu." Wang Puchen used his formal title and then took a seat next to him in the pavilion. "As you know, an emergency committee is being established today to deal with the issue of American aid. It's clear this is designed to appease the Americans who have been pressuring the Nanking government. Ambassador Stuart has named He Qicang to be on the committee, to be its deputy director… and for Fang Buting to be a committee member."

Changing topics, Wang continued: "Exposing Liang Jinglun's true identity in front of Xie Mulan, if she doesn't submit to being interrogated is one thing, but it won't matter if you kill her or incarcerate her, neither Fang nor He will let it go. The potential for this to disrupt current plans is far too great. Director Xu, I ask you to reconsider your current dangerous actions."

"You know what? It's as though I'd forgotten these connections." Xu Tieying squinted and looked intently at Wang Puchen. "Chief Chen once told me that if things got overly complicated that I should listen to you. Tell me, how do you think we should proceed?"

"I've just told you."

"Release Xie Mulan?"

"Request the central authorities to at least consider my point of view."

"All right. But everything has to be done by the book. Release procedures must be followed."

"We all know Xie Mulan's no Communist. There aren't, therefore, any procedures to speak of."

"But Liang Jinglun is, and I think you would agree that he is currently grooming Xie Mulan for the same. And because of this, Liang Jinglun should come clean and reveal to Xie Mulan his allegiance to the Iron and Blood Congress. Speaking the truth, as it were, won't change her mind. She'll still go with him. Then we can release her."

Wang Puchen lost any remaining calm he might have felt. "Director Xu, I understand there is a need for party discipline. I only thought to propose that the party consider what I've said. After all, the release of students today was on the direct orders of the president. Now, to drag Xie Mulan into all of this, it's bound to cause alarm among our American allies. I would therefore request that the current situation be reported to the president…"

"The Republic of China is not mistress to the Americans! Nor is the president required to check first with the Americans before dealing with internal matters." Xu Tieying had abruptly lifted himself from his stool. "Let me remind you of something. The president, first and foremost, is the leader of the party. He's our representative. Right now, our chairman is listening to Chief Chen make his report on everything that's happened. And you're requesting what? That we make yet another report to him?"

Wang Puchen was stunned. "Eh, not… I mean… not even for Liang Jinglun?"

"You still think this is just all about one man, one Liang Jinglun?" Xu Tieying chose to reveal everything. "Over the past year, diplomatic relations between us and the Americans have deteriorated, become strained. One of the reasons for this is that there have been certain people in the party who have actively and deliberately tarnished its image… for reasons, immoral and corrupt, that only they can attest to. One such example is Liang Jinglun. He's taken advantage of his connections to He Qicang and Ambassador Stuart to spread falsehoods about the party. But, at the end of the day, is he really trying to see that Comrade Jianfeng's currency reforms are implemented, or to see that his own Communist agenda is advanced? Mr Wang, you remember the report I showed you? You're both members of the Iron and Blood Congress. The party has faith in you, rest assured. But the same can't be said about Liang Jinglun. To borrow an analogy Liang himself has used before, we have to ask ourselves, has he joined up with Cao Cao's rebels or is his loyalty still to the Han? You don't know, and nor do we. That's why we've gone as far as to get him to join up with Fang Meng'ao, whom we suspect is a diehard Communist if ever there was one. It's a risky tactic for sure, but it is the one Comrade Jianfeng has chosen to employ. As for the rest of you, well, you can ingratiate yourselves to whomever, but we in the centre must devote ourselves fully to the party-state. We have no other choice."

Wang Puchen shifted his eyes to the mountains as though he suddenly understood why no birds dared to sing.

"Enough," said Xu, glancing at his watch. "Careful consideration will have to be given to all of Chief Ching-kuo's work. One last chance can be afforded Liang Jinglun. We'll give him thirty minutes to win over Xie Mulan. After that, we'll reveal his true identity to those few Communists we've detained. As for Xie Mulan and whether or not he can win her over, and how that will impact on the Fang and He households, well, to be frank, that's down to you, Mr Wang. Either as an intelligence agent or as a member of the Iron and Blood Congress, I imagine you should know what to do."

Wang Puchen said nothing further, for there was nothing to say. Slowly he rose from his seat and sauntered out of the courtyard. His departure was not at all like his arrival. His feet were now heavy, his footsteps seemed to echo. Xu Tieying squinted after him, trying, it seemed, to discern the meaning behind Wang Puchen's ostensibly sullen gait. In truth, Wang Puchen's mind was empty, or rather filled with entirely different thoughts. Indeed, he wondered more about what he would have to do to frighten the birds beyond the wall into taking to the air. Would the usual clamorous bang do the trick? Would that get rid of the ringing in his ears...

The Western Hills remained silent and still.

———

In the sitting room of Fang Buting's home, China's "golden voice" rang out... or at least a fair approximation of it.

The floating, scattered clouds,
The bright moon shines on the people as they arrive

Fang Mengwei stood in the doorway, his eyes fixed on the kitchen.

Today is the happiest reunion...

The words were sung in Shanghainese. He could notice the particular cadence and tenor. But today was different. Cheng Xiaoyun's voice was faint and distant, seemingly more unreal than real. Beside her, He Xiaoyu thrust the large salad fork into the vegetables. She'd been singing along, too, but now she had stopped.

Cheng Xiaoyun turned away from the bread oven and looked at the younger woman. "Why aren't you singing any more?"

"Sister, why does it feel like you're singing something from *Dream of the Red Chamber*?"

"Really?"

"Y... yes. I don't know why."

"My mind must have wandered." Cheng Xiaoyun smiled apologetically. "Tonight's our reunion dinner, but I can't sing *Dream of the Red Chamber*. Come on, let's start again."

> *The floating, scattered clouds,*
> *The bright moon shines on the people as they arrive*

Fang Mengwei again heard the singing coming from the kitchen, but he was back on to them now; he'd already taken the steps up to his father's study. The door was open and he could see his uncle tidying up; he could see, also, that his uncle was listening to the singing coming from below.

> *Today is the happiest reunion...*

As Fang Mengwei's shadow reached into the room, Xie Peidong lifted his head. Their eyes met and for a moment neither man said anything. Finally, Xie spoke: "Mulan's not come with you?"

Ignoring his uncle's question, Fang Mengwei responded in a voice that was indifferent, detached: "Find me some of Uncle Cui's letters, ones he wrote himself. If there aren't any, tell me what was in them."

Xie Peidong was surprised by Fang's question and averted his eyes from the younger man's stare. He turned around and opened one of the nearby cabinets. "Your Uncle He made an appearance. The authorities in Nanking telephoned. Everyone arrested today is to be released, if they haven't been already. A meeting took place, too. Your father's coming with your uncle here to have dinner." Xie Peidong picked through the letters and then looked at Fang Mengwei, expecting a response. When none was forthcoming, all Xie could hear was the voices floating up from downstairs.

This soft wind blows upon the beautiful flowers...

A moment passed and Xie found his voice. "It's not so easy to get Vice-Chancellor He to come here, you know. You're auntie's teaching Xiaoyu how to sing. It's a song Zhou Xuan made famous, you know. She's hoping it'll be pleasing for your father and his guest tonight." Fang Mengwei still said nothing; he merely extended his arm to take hold of the papers Xie was holding. Xie, however, didn't hand them over immediately. "Why do you want your Uncle Cui's letters? What can they possibly be good for?"

"Uncle Cui has children, two of them. It's only natural for them to still be thinking of their father. It's been ages… I thought I should write a letter."

Fang's reply astonished Xie Peidong, and for what seemed like far too long he was silent. At last, he gathered his wits enough to respond. "When you're in the US… no doubt it'll take quite a bit of time for any letter to reach them… now, if what you write in the letters doesn't resemble the words Uncle Cui would use, well, you're liable to make his wife worry… and become suspicious."

Fang Mengwei grabbed the letters. "American planes travel back and forth daily. I'm sure she knows what's going on. She probably knows more than anyone else. Uncle Cui should have said something before now." And with that, he turned and began to leave his father's study. In the doorway, however, he stopped. Again the sounds from the kitchen filtered up through the house.

Full of warmth and affection between the people...

"Uncle Xie, can you go downstairs and speak to them? Today's not a day for singing." He didn't explain any further but continued out of the room.

Fang Mengwei went straight to his own room and laid the letters on the desk. His eyes hovered over the three characters for his uncle's name. On a clean sheet of paper, Fang wrote the last character of his uncle's name with a Parker pen: "stone". His eyes then returned to his uncle's letters in search of another character, the word for "prince", or "king". He also found the character for "white". He repeated these two characters on the clean sheet, writing them just above the character for "stone" to make the compound figure *"bi"* meaning "green jade". Once again he began looking through his uncle's letters, searching. Finally, he composed the phrase he wanted, an address to Cui Zhongshi's wife. A droplet fell on the page, a single teardrop at first, then more.

Fang Mengwei stood up abruptly, wiped his eyes, turned and walked over to the window.

In the rear courtyard of the prison, a single cry was heard. Another one quickly followed. To the untrained ear, it sounded like birdsong. However, the whistle that had echoed through the air was not uttered by any bird, but by Xie Mulan. Great pity it was there were no birds in the mountains to respond.

She was exhausted, her body seemingly spent of all energy. She turned and let her eyes fall on the empty, barren courtyard, then allowed them to work their way along the ground to the passageway that led from it. Standing there, she saw the silhouette of a figure dressed in a long gown, a cheongsam it seemed. Her heart jumped like a frightened deer and she spun around once more to face the mountains on the other side of the towering walls. She considered practising her birdcall, but her throat was dry, her breath uneven. Xie Mulan bit her lower lip. She thought she could hear the distance between herself and the figure in the corridor. A gradual sense of calm came over her.

Liang Jinglun walked slowly into the courtyard holding the hem of his traditional gown in his hand. He lacked the same measure of composure and grace he usually seemed to possess. Again a crisp, clear bird's whistle echoed. Liang Jinglun let go of his hem to stop and listen. Mountains ranged outside the prison walls. Inside there could be no birds to sing. Xie Mulan had whistled. Liang Jinglun closed his eyes. Two more calls, then silence.

Liang's eyes remained closed, lost to a deep sense of melancholy. His lips, however, smiled, if only at the corners. He would wait for Xie Mulan to come. "How strange, it's as though there isn't a single bird around." Her voice was already next to him. He opened his eyes and met hers; they were like two sparkling pools of water. He had to look away. He didn't want her to see the longing in his eyes, the depths of the emotions he felt. He would have to say something, however. But what? His response was utterly banal: "Like people, I suppose. Maybe they're out scrounging for food."

"That reminds me of a famous saying…"

"Whose?"

"Socrates."

All he could do was look at her. Words failed him.

Xie Mulan's eyes flashed before she recited the saying: "Thou should eat to live, not live to eat." Liang Jinglun remained quiet. Xie Mulan focused on his face and discovered his slight smile had disappeared. "I didn't say it for me, you know. It… it was for you." Her voice had become hurried as she tried to explain. "For faith, trust, belief in the dream… the ideal. That's why we live!"

"What faith, what belief?" Liang Jinglun's voice was without feeling, cold and detached. He stared past her and out towards the mountains to the west.

Xie Mulan failed to see the vacant look in his eyes, or chose not to see it. She whispered in reply: "The fight… for the cause of Communism. Until death if necessary!"

"I'm no Communist."

There was no means by which she could grasp and appreciate the desolation in his voice. She only scanned the scene around them. "I understand."

Liang Jinglun still stared past her, purposefully, deliberately. He just couldn't bear to meet her eyes. "Understand what?"

Xie Mulan moved a little closer. "That we're in the lion's den, a secret facility run by the Kuomintang."

Liang Jinglun reached out and clasped her hand. Xie Mulan raised her head to look at him. From this angle, his face resembled the figure of a Rodin sculpture.

———

Fang Mengwei returned the pen to the table and stood up.

Cheng Xiaoyun, who had been standing quietly in the doorway, now spoke, her tone soft and gentle: "You don't feel like joining us for dinner?"

"Save some of the bread rolls for me. Then send them to Uncle Cui's children."

"I've already done that. They just need another ten minutes in the oven."

"Thank you, Auntie Cheng." Fang Mengwei sat back down, picked up the pen and buried his face in the papers once more. It was clear he had nothing further to say and that he wanted her to leave.

Cheng Xiaoyun, however, stayed in the doorway a little longer. "Uncle has asked me to tell you something. The letter... whenever Uncle Cui wrote to his family... his letters were always short. Writing a long one will..."

"You all know that I'm lying, lying to a widow and her orphan kids!" He dropped the pen abruptly and spun his head round to stare at Cheng Xiaoyun. "This whole family lies to itself every day, it lies to everyone. Auntie, you're lying to yourself right now. You do it daily. You lie to Dad too. Do you think the lies aren't all the same?"

Cheng Xiaoyun was quiet. All she could do was look at him, teardrops forming in her eyes.

Fang Mengwei regretted his outburst. He was motionless for a while, but then opened a drawer in the desk and swept the papers into it. "You're... what you said... you're right. I shouldn't try to write such a letter. I shouldn't have said what I just did either."

"In this home, there aren't any shoulds or should nots. I would just like to tell you something. Since I've been with your dad, I've never lied to myself, and I have certainly never lied to him. I realise it's hard. Every heart in the house is troubled, but there is some good here, too. We don't... we can't lie to each other. Me and your dad, you and your older brother, your uncle and Mulan as well. In this, we're all the same."

Fang Mengwei was quiet for a moment, letting what she said sink in. When he did speak, it no longer contained the anger it had before. His voice was calm and soft. "You're right..."

"If you don't feel like having dinner with Mulan, then why don't you head over to Uncle Cui's house? The bread will be ready any minute now. You can take them some."

Cheng Xiaoyun turned to leave but was stopped by the younger man. "Auntie!"

"When you go back downstairs," said Fang Mengwei, "don't try to teach any more of that song to Xiaoyu. You're the only one who can sing it as it should be. We all love hearing you."

"I sing it better than your mum did?"

"Yeah, you do."

Fang Mengwei kept his head low, but he knew, he could feel it. Cheng Xiaoyun smiled, if just a little. He'd waited eleven years for that.

———

Out of the thirty minutes Xu Tieying had been given, only a few remained. Liang Jinglun *had* to discuss things with Xie Mulan; time was running short. They were both sitting on the stone stools in the courtyard, Liang Jinglun's gaze fixed on Mulan. Her mind raced. She remembered several times before when he had looked at her like he was now, and as before, she couldn't return his stare; not for more than a few seconds at most.

Liang Jinglun's heart was torn, but there were things he had to say. "Can you answer something for me?"

"OK," she responded quickly, allowing her eyes to meet his for just a moment.

"Why is it that each time I wish to look into your face, you turn your eyes away?" This was not the question he originally had in mind. Nor did he understand why he had asked it. He was somewhat surprised Xie Mulan provided him with an answer, or at least a question of her own.

"Is that a poem by the Crescent Moon Society?" Once more she lifted her head. Her cheeks were already flush. Unlike before, however, she didn't avoid his gaze this time.

She felt as though the poetry radiated in her eyes; this was met by the poetry in Liang Jinglun's; the entire courtyard was enveloped in poetry.

Liang Jinglun felt helpless. It was now his turn to look away. He laughed bitterly under his breath and gazed towards the wall and the mountains behind. "At this time, in this place, how can there be poetry here?"

"But we just recited poetry, Mr Zhu Ziqing's. We sang in memory of him!" Xie Mulan's words were quick, hurried.

Liang Jinglun didn't know how to respond. While he sat on the stool, trying to gather his thoughts, Xie Mulan began to recite another verse. Her voice was tender, but the emotions she felt were profound:

In the trembling rays of the morning sun, two small birds frolic and play, hopping back and forth;
　They have nothing to discuss, they simply chirp and squeak, a wondrous clamour of birdsong;
　Short tweets echoed in between smiles;
　In that laughter there was freedom, although neither bird noticed.

Whether it was because the prison was so eerily quiet, or that Xie Mulan's voice grew louder and louder no one could be sure, but her recitation filled the entire courtyard, emanating out to the mountains and sky beyond, even into the corridor that snaked its way back to the cells.

"What the hell are you doing? Reciting poetry?" Xu Tieying's eyes scanned the area, first the passageway, then Wang Puchen, and finally Secretary Sun. Sun trained his ears on the sound that gradually grew up around them:

To us poor bystanders, it was as though they were saying,
　"We live, so we must jump, we must sing; life itself brings us joy,
　And there is no one anywhere who can take that away."

He'd heard the words clearly and turned to Xu Tieying: "It's Xie Mulan's poem, the one she just recited. Zhu Ziqing's the author. It's titled 'Small Birds'."

Xu Tieying appreciated Sun Chaozhong's knowledge in these matters and merely nodded his head before slowly adjusting his gaze to fall on Wang Puchen.

Wang Puchen resisted acknowledging the smug look on Xu Tieying's face. He knew Xu was toying around with this member of the Iron and Blood Congress and was very satisfied with his own seeming cleverness. But Wang would not recognise it; he looked at his watch instead. "There are still twelve minutes to go."

"Then by all means let them continue for another twelve minutes. Oh, and yes, bring Yan Chunming and those other Communist dogs out here. Let them all listen."

Liang Jinglun stood up abruptly.

Xie Mulan's recital came to a sudden end. She looked admiringly at the long gown Liang was wearing and saw it flutter as though an unexpected breeze had swept through the rear courtyard, through the pavilion and on down the corridor to the cells.

Liang walked to the mouth of the corridor and shouted back into the yard: "Come on all of you degenerate Kuomintang scum. You're all eager to join the funeral procession for Dr Sun Yat-sen's Three Principles of the People, aren't you? Well, come on then. Get yourselves over here!"

Xie Mulan sprung to her feet and rushed over to where Liang Jinglun was standing. His words and display of indignation had fired her up.

Liang's roar had reverberated throughout the courtyard and down through the corridor and the prison, assaulting the ears of everyone. Xu, Wang and Sun all stared in his direction. Yan Chunming, as well as four other men, all of whom had their names listed as being suspected Communists, looked on in similar fashion.

Xu was the first to speak: "Guards!"

Within seconds, the sound of military boots clapping on the stone floors of the prison could be heard.

"Director Xu!" Despite the urgency in his tone, despite the clear note of resistance, Wang Puchen's voice was low and somewhat feeble: "As the warden, I'm responsible for reporting everything that goes on here to the Ministry of Defence."

The guards had already marched into the courtyard and now stood to attention, awaiting orders from their superior.

Xu threw a look in Wang Puchen's direction. "Defence Ministry... which branch, huh? The Intelligence Bureau or some other department?"

"The Intelligence Bureau... those responsible for executing criminals. I must ask for instructions from Chief Mao."

"Asking Chief Ching-kuo would be just as good." Xu looked away from him and towards the military police. "Get everyone back to their cells... now!"

But there was no need. Yan Chunming had already guided the suspected Communists into the corridor and back through the iron door that led to their cells. Xu's guards had only to escort them the remainder of the way. Once the courtyard was cleared, Xu spoke to his secretary: "Let's go."

"Yes sir." Sun didn't have the opportunity to exchange a knowing glance with Wang Puchen. He could do nothing else but follow Xu along, charged, as he was, with his protection. Seething with anger, Wang Puchen strode off in the direction of the prison cells.

———

The office was dark; Wang hadn't turned on the lights. A match burst into flame, illuminating Wang's face and the emergency telephone that sat on his desk. He moved the match close and lit the cigarette perched on his bottom lip. His eyes were consumed by the phone, the direct line to Comrade Jianfeng. The match died. The only light that remained was the burning tobacco. He took a drag and then squeezed the cigarette between his fingers. Deftly, he placed it on the edge of the ashtray that sat next to the telephone. Wang struck another match, lit another smoke. In the weak glow of the burning match, his eyes fell on the adjacent table and the phone that lay there. The cigarette in the ashtray wavered and went out. Wang flicked the match onto the floor and reached purposefully out for the other telephone. He dragged in on his cigarette, inhaling as much of the smoke into his lungs as he could, using the burning glow at the tip to allow him to see the number he wanted to dial.

The line rang three times and then connected. "Mao Renfeng. Is that you, Puchen?"

The cigarette dimmed and Wang replied: "Yes, it's me. There's something urgent I need to report."

"Go ahead."

Again, Wang Puchen pulled in deeply on the cigarette. The flame, although weak, illuminated the phone. "Director Xu of the Communications Bureau intends to execute, right here in my own prison, men connected directly to Chief Ching-kuo. He's told me these are the orders given by Chief Chen Jicheng. It seems we're stuck in the middle of an internal struggle between two factions in the party. I've telephoned to ask for instructions on how to deal with this… problem."

The other end of the line remained silent.

Wang Puchen tossed his cigarette to one side; he'd already finished it. Lodging the phone between his chin and shoulder, he reached for another match and struck it. Again the phone was bathed in light, feeble though it may have been in the dark of the room.

Sound echoed through the receiver. It was still Mao Renfeng's voice, but it seemed as though he was speaking to someone much closer and not into the phone at all. "What's wrong with the telephone today? There's no sound whatsoever. Get someone to look into this immediately."

Wang's face could be seen in the light of the match. Although the thought of this possible reaction had occurred to him, the despair that now swallowed his face made it abundantly clear that this was not what he had hoped for.

The match went out. There in the darkness, the only sound was the humming dial tone in Wang Puchen's ear.

Dusk was the best time of day in the prison. The setting sun would fall upon the trees in the prison grounds and transform them into an exquisite oil painting. Yan Chunming was sitting in the courtyard, his back against the wall and the Western Hills on the other side. He, too, looked like part of the composition. Liang Jinglun, Xie Mulan and the other four named Communists were standing in a row in the pavilion facing him. The military police, as ordered by

Secretary Sun, were positioned on both sides of the corridor leading back into the prison. They were quiet, unmoving. They were also maintaining a specific distance from the centre of the grounds, a certain distance away from the people standing in the pavilion.

Xu Tieying strode into Yan Chunming's painting, a cruel smile on his face. "Here, now, in front of these people, please repeat your confession. Tell them your identity."

Yan Chunming still had no glasses, but he knew who these "people" were, he knew Liang Jinglun, Xie Mulan and the four other comrades were standing in front of him. He didn't hesitate: "I am a Communist, a loyal member of the CPC."

"And what were you tasked with undertaking? What was your role?"

"I was responsible for Communist activities at Yenching University. I was branch secretary for the party's agents."

Xu had taken the most ideal position in the courtyard. With the sun shining on the back of his head and straight into the pavilion, he could clearly see the reactions of Liang Jinglun and the others he'd gathered there; no response, no matter how slight, would escape him. His eyes focused first on Liang.

At the same moment, Xie Mulan edged a little closer to Liang, lifting her head to look at him. Liang Jinglun, however, directed his gaze towards the mountains.

Xu continued his attack on Yan Chunming: "Now let me ask you, is Professor Liang Jinglun of Yenching University's Economics Department a member of this branch of the CPC?"

Yan Chunming's response was clear, sure: "No, he is not."

"Professor Liang, he says you're *not* a party member." Xu's voice had increased in pitch as he called towards Liang Jinglun.

Hearing his name called, Liang Jinglun shifted his eyes away from the mountains and onto Xu Tieying's face. He did not try to hide the contempt he held for the man.

Xie Mulan stared into Liang's face. His eyes were like the moon hidden behind faint clouds; they sparkled and awed. Xie Mulan became entranced. Like a foolish girl unable to look away, all she wanted to do was to fall into his eyes.

In that moment, Xu's many years of experience proved their

usefulness. He kept his focus on Liang Jinglun, but at the same time, enveloped Xie Mulan in the unspoken conversation. He smiled knowingly, slyly. "Tell us your true identity then, Professor Liang."

Liang Jinglun appeared to be already well prepared for this moment. His resentment shattered the cloudy screen that had covered his eyes. He met Xu Tieying's stare. He was neither too slow nor too fast, the pitch of his voice was somewhat high when he finally spoke: "For forty years I have devoted myself to the cause of the people's revolution with but one purpose in mind: the elevation of China to a position of freedom and equality among the nations."

Several of the students in attendance, those with Communist loyalties, directed their attention towards Liang Jinglun and saw the somewhat vacant look in his eyes.

Liang Jinglun droned on at the same pace: "Over these forty-plus years of experience, I have come to appreciate the great need for this purpose to be fulfilled…"

Xie Mulan soon added her excited voice to Liang's: "To reach this goal we must arouse not only our people, but all peoples of the world to unite in the mutual struggle for freedom and equality."

With Xie Mulan joining him in his recitation of Dr Sun Yat-sen, Liang Jinglun lowered his voice and soon brought it to a halt.

It was Xu Tieying who spoke next, urging them on, a surprising smile on his face. "Go ahead… continue."

Deep in Liang Jinglun's heart, his desire to resist whatever Xu Tieying might say or do prohibited him from continuing. "Xu Tieying, according to the constitution of the Republic of China, all citizens have the right to be treated equally. You just now asked me where my allegiance lies, what my identity is. I'd like to ask the same question to you. Please, are you a member of the Kuomintang or not?"

Despite the pointed nature of the question, Xu presented the image of someone entirely unperturbed. "Of course I am."

"What post do you hold in the Kuomintang?"

The smirk on Xu's face faded.

"You are national director of communications, responsible for liaising with party members across the country. Isn't that right?"

Xu Tieying kept his silence, declining to answer.

Liang Jinglun's voice grew sterner. "According to the party's constitution, and the regulations of your own communications department, all Kuomintang members, regardless of where they might be, are to join in unison and recite together 'Dr Sun Yat-sen's Last Will and Testament' whenever they hear it being spoken. Considering your position and rank, why did you just now not follow your own party's rules?"

Xu Tieying's face turned a slight shade of blue.

Liang Jinglun persisted: "If you wish to continue with the recital, we can do so together! Yes?"

Secretary Sun's attention was fully on Xu Tieying, because in that moment Xu had directed his focus onto his secretary. The look on Sun's face, however, caused the bile to rise up in Xu's throat. In that instant, he loathed his confidant and hated his expressionless demeanour. He was like the epitome of the party's constitution, and Xu despised him!

"I gather you heard all of that?" Xu's question was directed to Yan Chunming.

But Yan's face only further enraged him. For a man who usually displayed few emotions, Yan Chunming was now smiling as though he was the victor.

"Sun Chaozhong!" Xu's shout resounded across the prison grounds.

"Here, sir." Sun walked closer over towards his superior.

Xu Tieying reached into his pocket and pulled out an identification card. The Kuomintang insignia was clear, white star on a blue background. "This here is the true identity card for the fake Communist Liang Jinglun. Take it. Show it to those students!"

Sun strived to maintain his calm. He accepted the card, subconsciously turning it over in his hand. Liang Jinglun's photograph was unmistakable, even if it had been taken some time ago, and showed a younger man. A steel clamp, gripped tightly to the lower right-hand corner of the card, held it together. More astonishing still were the details under the photo. Name: Liang Fusheng. Affiliation: Kuomintang Party member. Date of membership: Twenty-ninth year of the Republic. Recruiter: Chiang Ching-kuo! Issuing Authority: National Communications Bureau of the Kuomintang.

"Show it!" Xu's voice was noticeably sterner, more enraged.

Secretary Sun remained calm. He walked towards the pavilion where the students stood, Liang Jinglun's supposed identification card in his hand. He ignored Liang, choosing instead to direct his words only to the students: "Queue up. Make sure to maintain a suitable distance between yourselves."

The students looked towards Liang Jinglun. So, too, did Xie Mulan.

Liang's eyes were directed to the open sky above. When he spoke, his voice seemed to emanate from some far-off place: "There's nothing you can't look at. You'll have to discern things for yourselves."

Sun flipped over the cover of the identification card.

The four students, including the two double agents from the Chiang Kai-shek Student Society, looked at the card in shock and bewilderment.

"You're despicable! You've botched it all up, too!" Xie Mulan moved to grab Liang Jinglun's arm. Her eyes scanned the four young students, then shifted to Xu Tieying. "You... you're the head of the Communications Bureau. *You* make these identification cards. I'm sure it wouldn't be difficult for you to make fake ones. Ah, but you got clumsy. Tell me, does anyone believe any of this?"

Xu Tieying smiled again, even more maliciously than before. He paid no attention to Xie Mulan, but spoke to Sun Chaozhong: "They've seen it... hand it back." Sun obeyed. "Oh, let Yan Chunming have a look, why don't you." Again, Sun obeyed. He walked over to Yan Chunming and passed him the card. Yan was quiet, unruffled and seemingly uninterested, but he had to accept it nonetheless. Xu spoke again: "You already knew, didn't you?"

"Knew what?"

"You knew, and so did the Peking Labour Union. Your party knew he was a double agent. Why are you still pretending otherwise? What's the point?"

"Double... double what? Please, tell us what his first identity is supposed to be."

"A member of the CPC branch at Yenching University. Isn't that right?"

Yan Chunming didn't look at anything in particular, nor could anyone really discern what was going on in his mind. Then, suddenly, he appeared to direct his attention towards Xu Tieying. "Are you the party branch secretary at Yenching University, or am I?"

"You are, naturally." Xu's response was quick, and then he paused. When he spoke again, his voice was clearly at a higher pitch. "You're not only the branch secretary for the CPC at Yenching but also the man responsible for grooming Liang Jinglun, for initiating him into the party in the first place. Just now you denied he was a member. There can be only two possibilities for this denial. One, you didn't know about his allegiance to the Kuomintang. As branch secretary, as the man who groomed him, you don't want to give him up... you've invested too much into him. Pity, then, that this possibility invalidates your current attitude to these proceedings. You've just heard Liang Jinglun recite Dr Sun Yat-sen's *Last Will and Testament*, quite fervently I might add, so he has, in fact, already revealed his true identity. But still you protect him. That leads, it can only lead, to the second possibility: you and the party already knew his true identity, but pretended you didn't. Yesterday, you abruptly returned to Yenching University. Earlier today Liu Chuwu, a rather high-ranking agent involved in labour activities in Peking, did not hesitate to put himself in danger... he died because of it. But tell me, can we really believe that you would do the same to protect these students? There can be only one reason for you to do so and that is there's an even greater struggle happening behind the scenes, happening behind Liang Jinglun's very back!" At this point, Xu paused again and let his eyes fall on the students. "So, would you like to know who these people are?"

Two of the four students, the two who were committed to the cause, were silent, shocked by what Xu had seemingly reasoned out. As for the other two, the ones who were playing at being Communist agents but were in fact members of the Chiang Kai-shek Student Society, they were equalled stunned and unable to answer.

For Xie Mulan, Xu's words had caused her face to blanch. She held on even tighter to Liang Jinglun's arm. A sudden ringing began in her ears, drowning out most other sounds. The ring grew into a buzz and then a roar.

"You all saw it. We showed it to you. There, clearly marked on Liang Jinglun's Kuomintang identification card. You know who recruited him, none other than Chiang Ching-kuo himself." Xu Tieying's voice had swallowed the Western Hills, resounding throughout the air, drowning out every other sound imaginable.

All sets of eyes in the courtyard fell on Liang Jinglun, who remained standing tall and erect. He appeared as though he had not heard a single word Xu had said. Moments passed, and then he sprung into action. Xie Mulan's body had grown soft, her grip on his armed had failed and she was falling. In quick movements he took hold of her, supported her and saved her from crashing onto the hard ground.

Wang Puchen clapped his hands and finally turned on the desk lamp in his office. Then he picked up the second telephone, and it connected almost immediately. "Secretary Wang, yes, it's Wang Puchen... I don't care where Comrade Jianfeng is, you must reach him. There's something vital I must report."

His voice had been hurried, his tone urgent. Now he waited for his secretary to reply. But the other end of the telephone was quiet. It was as though the person who'd picked it up was waiting for Wang Puchen to say something more.

"I've finished... Secretary Wang? Please say something."

"It's me."

Wang knew the accent immediately. Fenghua... Zhejiang... it was Comrade Jianfeng! Surprise nearly overcame him. He was standing and didn't even realise it. It took all his effort to rein in the flood of emotions. In that moment of silence, Wang heard the sigh echo through the receiver, its volume unexpectedly high, exasperated. To Wang's ears, the sigh was akin to an enveloping wave of sound. But as quickly as it had come, it now receded and Comrade Jianfeng's voice returned to normal, more or less, as Wang Puchen was sure he could detect a note of anger just beneath the surface.

"Comrade Puchen, I've just come back from a meeting. I know the broad strokes of what has happened, but give me your side of things now."

"Ah, yes..." Wang attempted to sound calm. "Xu Tieying arrested several students suspected of being Communists. Well, we know two of them are… and he's revealed to them Liang Jinglun's true identity as a member of the Iron and Blood Congress. Aside from the two students who are in fact members of the Chiang Kai-shek Student Society, he's chosen not to release the others. What's most incomprehensible is that he's lumped Xie Mulan in with the students he won't free. It's abundantly clear she's no Communist, and that she's a member of Mr Fang's household. She's also only nineteen years old…"

"Why didn't you stop him, prevent all of this? Why didn't you report?" Comrade Jianfeng interjected, the furiousness in his voice unmistakable.

Wang Puchen chose to stay quiet. It wasn't that he was trying to think of some excuse, rather, the brief respite was meant to demonstrate how difficult it was to be clear on what he had to say next. "Yes, Comrade Jianfeng. Comrade Sun Chaozhong had relayed to me the urgency of these matters, and I did go to speak to Xu Tieying, but he informed me his orders had come from the top… that the director-general of the party, Chief Chen, and… yourself… knew about everything… that you were, at that moment, discussing the situation at hand. I telephoned Chief Mao, but unfortunately, there was a problem with the… with the connection."

Wang Puchen stopped. The other end was silent.

But the silence could not last. Finally, Wang Puchen spoke, his voice soft: "Comrade Jianfeng…"

"Tell me your opinion on all of this." There was no emotion in Comrade Jianfeng's tone, only a cold detachment, something Wang Puchen had never heard before.

Wang squirmed a little. He wasn't wholly inclined to reveal his point of view, but he had been asked to… ordered to… by his superior, by Comrade Jianfeng. He had little choice. "To my mind, Xie Mulan knew Liang Jinglun's true identity, but even though she might have accepted this, she wasn't about to… that is, she couldn't say it out loud, at least not then. That being the case, and considering her somewhat emotional character, her general attitude, I don't think it possible she could conceal her true thoughts from the rest of the Fang family, nor could she conceal them from the Communist agents in the Labour Union in Peking. The most challenging thing for us is that, on the one hand, we can't release her, but neither can we keep her detained. If Fang Buting, Fang Meng'ao, his younger brother Fang Mengwei... even He Qicang... if any one of them found out, they'd surely get involved and then we'd have to release her no matter what. It's a fait accompli. Xie Mulan has to live. Comrade Liang Jinglun must depart Peking. The plan to send our peacocks south will have to be abandoned, and... and finally, the currency reforms will have to be postponed."

"You've covered everything, analysed everything." A distinct sense of loathing emerged in Jianfeng's tone. "But you've not told me your point of view!"

Wang was backed into a corner. "Comrade Jianfeng, Xie Mulan... along with the Communist students... they need to be executed. The key will be how to deal properly with the inevitable aftermath. Most important, the Fang family cannot suspect anything, we can't let them have any doubts about our involvement. Nor can we let the CPC get wind of what we've done... or rather what we will do. In their hands, that information would be dangerous."

Once more, Wang Puchen was treated to silence, even if he knew himself that he had passed through the worst of it.

"Make it happen."

Wang Puchen was left holding the receiver close to his ear. He had heard the click of the phone being hung up on the other end. With his free hand he robotically pulled a pack of cigarettes from his jacket; a box of matches, too. He placed them on the table. Normally, no matter how many plans he had to consider, no matter how many problems, a smoke would help him through, resolve his problems. But today was different. Would a cigarette aid him in thinking of how to deal with the inevitable repercussions of what he had to do? Finally, Wang replaced the receiver and focused on the cigarettes. For the first time in ages, he didn't feel like smoking.

―――

Near the wall separating the prison from the Western Hills behind it, Yan Chunming was still seated in his oil painting. But there were more people than before. Two were the committed Communist students; two were from the Chiang Kai-shek Student Society.

Liang Jinglun remained where he had been, in the pavilion, but he wasn't standing as before. Rather, his back was against one of the wooden beams, his rump on the ground, and Xie Mulan was in his arms. Oblivious to the people around them, they sat as though they were alone on an island. Mulan's eyes were open, but they seemed lifeless, her face was as white as bleached paper.

Xu Tieying, who had been standing nearby watching the scene unfold, finally interrupted them: "Should I call for the prison doctor?" The look Liang Jinglun gave him was unfamiliar, something he'd never seen before in the man. Xu averted his eyes in the direction of the guards and his secretary. "Sun!" At being called, Sun Chaozhong turned, but he did not walk over to his superior; he just looked at the other man. Xu didn't seem bothered, he simply spoke: "Give me your take on this. Should we call for the prison doctor to come and take a look at her?"

"Chief, I don't think it's that serious. There's no need."

"Fine. Get two men to come over here and assist." Xu Tieying finished his order and began to walk away. He said nothing further but continued on through the passageway and down the corridor away from the courtyard.

Sun signalled two guards to come over to the pavilion, where they stopped to look at Liang Jinglun and Xie Mulan on the ground. He didn't issue orders. Liang Jinglun couldn't be sure how long they had stood there, but finally he noticed their presence. He didn't say anything to them, however. He merely lifted Xie Mulan up from his lap and held her even closer than before. Then he walked over to the wall. As he did, the hem of his long gown once more fluttered in a breeze no one could feel.

―――――

"So, so much, why? Whatever for?" Ye Biyu took hold of the items Fang Mengwei had brought.

His hand free, Fang lifted his uncle's children: Boqin in his left arm, Pingyang in his right. Together they walked into the garden and sat beneath one of the larger trees, one child on his left leg, the other on the right.

"Aunt Cui, don't bring all the stuff inside," he called out to Ye

Biyu before she disappeared into the kitchen. "In the food tin, there's freshly baked bread. Take out a couple and give one each to the children."

Smiling, Ye Biyu called: "But it's soon time for dinner. I'll give them the bread then." Her eyes fell on the children, and she could see their outstretched hands eagerly anticipating the treat Fang Mengwei mentioned.

Watching, Fang Mengwei felt a pang of hurt in his heart, but he couldn't let the children see it. He had to put on a brave face. "What do you think? Should you have the treats now or with dinner?"

They responded in near unison: "Whatever Mum says."

Fang Mengwei laughed. "Well, let's not listen to her today, hmm. Aunt Cui, bring them over."

Ye Biyu relented without much protest and brought the treats to the children.

"Take our four containers," Fang Mengwei reminded her.

Ye Biyu found the containers, opened their lids and saw the golden-coloured treats inside. "They're so big. Just have half of one now." Ye Biyu's words weren't open for discussion, she simply split the treats in half and gave each of her children a half. "Deputy Chief Fang, you sit first. I'll fetch some tea."

The children had been raised well. They both leaned against Fang Mengwei while they ate, making sure he didn't see them stuff the bread treats into their mouths.

The wind picked up and the leaves above their heads rustled. Fang Mengwei stared into the branches and caught sight of a bird taking flight. It was quick, its movements abrupt. As it flew past, he could see a small piece of bread in its beak. Fang's eyes followed the creature, watched it soar towards his uncle's house and then land on a windowsill. He knew the room to which the glass opened had once been his uncle's study. A shadow seemed to cross the closed window and Fang Mengwei looked on in disbelief – Uncle Cui! He stared more intently, but all he could see was the bird in front of the window, its head tilted upwards as it swallowed the bread it had stolen. Fang closed his eyes and his mind took him back to that spot, to that moment when the gunshot rang out, when it ended his uncle's life.

Fang's eyes grew damp.

CHAPTER 7

Rifles, military police and fixed eyes all confronted Secretary Sun. Sun, however, kept his eyes closed. He was wearing a cap, the peak of which hung low and shaded much of his face. But he was nonetheless enjoying the warmth of the setting sun.

On the inside of the high prison walls, in the middle of the courtyard, Liang Jinglun stood with Xie Mulan held tight in his arms. How could anyone fire their rifle!

Finally, Secretary Sun opened his eyes. But he didn't direct his attention towards the people lined up beneath the wall. Rather, he reached for the pistol he had at his waist. He had to use his left arm to do this, however, for his right had been wounded earlier by Ma Hanshan. At the same moment, the military police pulled their weapons as well.

"Wait!" Yan Chunming shouted.

At last, Sun Chaozhong turned to look at the detainees.

Yan Chunming was now standing beside Liang Jinglun. Instead of speaking to Sun, however, he leaned in to converse with his fellow prisoner: "It doesn't matter if you believe me or not. What I say now represents the personal integrity of a committed party member."

Liang Jinglun said nothing in reply; he simply listened.

"I speak for myself," said Yan Chunming in a firm, confident voice, "and for those closest to me. I have never once suspected that you, Liang Jinglun, were a member of the Kuomintang. What's more, right now, I also don't believe it."

A flash of hope crossed Liang Jinglun's face and he turned to Yan Chunming. An instant later, he directed his attention to Secretary Sun, hoping the other man would also see the same glimmer of hope, however weak and frail it might be.

Yan's voice surrounded him then, harkening him back like a rushing tide. "Don't place any hope in these people, they have nothing but blood on their hands. They murdered Li Gongpu, killed Wen Yiduo, Zhu Ziqing died today… none of them were Communists. But that didn't matter. Sima Qian said it best: 'Though death befalls all men…'"

His movement, as quick as a startled rabbit, Sun Chaozhong's gun cracked.

The bullet tore through Yan Chunming's forehead in an instant; he fell back against the wall, then crumpled to the ground like a pile of dry wood. A second shot resounded and Liang Jinglun's hands went heavy. The bullet had bored into Xie Mulan's chest. Blood gushed forth, soon drenching her clothes. The gendarmerie fired. A great chorus of gunfire exploded against the prison walls, then over them and into the mountains beyond.

Up until that point, the mountains had been eerily quiet, strangely still. Now they erupted as birds took flight, their calls splitting the sky, their wings blocking out the sun and bathing everyone in darkness. The ground went dark, too, a deep scarlet hue.

The great number of birds that took to the sky, the clamour of noise they created, reverberated throughout the prison, reaching even the ears of Xu Tieying. He'd been standing, for too long in his mind, in the open prison grounds just inside the main gate, on the opposite side of the facility. But even there the sun was shadowed by the birds.

"Are there always so many birds about?" His question was for Wang Puchen.

"I've never seen such a number before."

"I agree with your proposal concerning the imminent aftermath of what we've done here," Xu muttered more to himself than to

Wang. "I shall write a detailed report for the central authorities. Comrade Wang, this won't be easy for you, you know…"

Wang ignored this last point and instead called out to the gendarme standing next to one of the transport vehicles: "Get a jeep here now. One with a canopy."

"Sir, yes sir!" The young lieutenant's voice was loud and cut through the air. He rushed off just as vigorously as he had replied.

Turning back to Xu, Wang informed him of the next step: "I'll take my leave. Mr Fang deserves a telephone call."

Xu nodded. "My sympathies to you for having to make that call."

Wang Puchen smiled bitterly and walked off in the direction of his office.

———

"Xiaoyun, Xiaoyun!" He Qicang had just stepped in through the doorway. Fang Buting and Fang Meng'ao were right behind him. As they walked in through the door, they glanced at each other and exchanged a knowing smile. Their hearts, for perhaps the first time, were in sync, and this was reflected in their smiles. Neither father nor son wanted to be the first to let this go.

"Eh!" Cheng Xiaoyun's response came from deeper inside the house, but her voice made He Qicang smile a smile of his own. He didn't go beyond the door, however. He waited instead so that she could come and properly greet him. The other two men waited behind him.

Finally, Fang Buting grew tired of waiting. "What's going on? Why hasn't she come?"

He Qicang cocked his head in his friend's direction. "I imagine that's because she's in the kitchen. She's got to remove her apron first and wash her hands. That needs time, doesn't it?"

Fang Buting shook his hand. "Hey now… she's a graduate of St John's University. How do you know I'd marry a woman like that!"

"I just do." He Qicang stared a moment at his friend, and then glanced at his son.

Fang Meng'ao was standing stiff and erect, as though he were at attention. Upon seeing He Qicang glance at him, he understood immediately. He removed his large-brimmed service cap and placed it under his left arm.

"Vice-Chancellor He," Cheng Xiaoyun said. "What are... what are you all doing here?"

Upon seeing her, He Qicang could not hold back his delight, or the happiness she created by her mere presence. He recited from Du Fu: "'My flowered path has never been swept for guests.'" He paused for a moment. "What's the next line?"

Cheng Xiaoyun's face blushed, and she grew a little annoyed; she was the only person who could get away with this with He Qicang. "I don't know," she said huffily, "just come in."

"If you don't answer, how can I come in?"

"Why so sour, Mr Vice-Chancellor sir?" And with that, she went over to him and took hold of his arm. "'But now a gentlemen guest opens my old battered gate.' Come in, please."

He Qicang laughed heartily, but where it had come from, none of them could say. Cheng Xiaoyun no longer hesitated; her hand was still around his arm, and she led him into the sitting room.

He Xiaoyu was standing in the sitting room, along with Xie Peidong who had just come down from upstairs. He Qicang looked at the room searchingly. Fang Buting's eyes were filled with questions for Cheng Xiaoyun. Fang Meng'ao only stared at He Xiaoyu.

"Where's Mulan?" asked He Qicang. "Has Fang Mengwei gone to get her?"

"Mengwei is... busy with something else. Mulan should be here any minute."

"And what does 'any minute' mean?" Fang Buting had grown noticeably unhappy, his eyes shifting back and forth between Cheng Xiaoyun and Xie Peidong. "Xishan prison is quite far. What could be so important for Mengwei that he couldn't go and get her?"

Xie Peidong tried to answer, but he wasn't really sure what to say. "We could instruct Young Li to take a car and meet her on the way."

"I'll go," Fang Meng'ao offered.

"No one's going anywhere." He Qicang's spirits had clearly dampened from just a few moments ago. Anger now rose in his voice. "Call Li Yuqing, call him immediately. Tell him I want his own men, someone, to drive her home... now!"

"Yes sir. I'll call him this instant." Xie Peidong began to walk away, but stopped. "Sirs... do you want me to enquire about Professor Liang? Do you wish him here as well?"

"And why would we want him here? He's got so many students to think about." He Qicang stumbled a moment as though the anger he was feeling had sapped his strength. Ever alert, Cheng Xiaoyun was quick to lead him over to the sofa so that he could sit.

"Understood." Xie Peidong turned, left the room and ascended the stairs to Fang's study.

"We're all famished," Fang Buting said to Cheng Xiaoyun. "Bring some tea and pastries, will you?"

"You go, Xiaoyu." He Qicang reclined on the sofa as though he was in his own home. "And you, too, Meng'ao. Go and help."

There was meaning behind He Qicang's words.

He Xiaoyu, however, only looked on in embarrassment, her eyes focused on Cheng Xiaoyun. But Xiaoyun avoided her stare, instead directing her attention to Fang Meng'ao. Fang said nothing. He simply walked into the kitchen.

Cheng Xiaoyun finally turned to He Xiaoyu and smiled. "What can I do? Your father loves me terribly... he wants me here next to him. Go on, do as he says."

Xiaoyu obeyed and followed Fang Meng'ao into the other room.

Fang Buting watched the scene unfold without betraying any emotion. In truth, he had no idea what he should be feeling, or how to react.

"I'm right, yes?" Cheng Xiaoyun smiled and looked at He Qicang, all in an effort to extricate her husband from his awkwardness.

"The person who should love you terribly, as you say, is him." He Qicang now purposefully tried to alleviate Fang Buting's embarrassment. "I want you to sit next to me because I'd like to hear you sing... not in the style of Cheng Yanqiu, though. That's too heart-wrenching for today. Sing like Zhang Junqiu..."

"How about *Return of the Phoenix*?" Cheng Xiaoyun's suggestion was not random; there was a hidden meaning behind her choice, something Xiaoyun was trying to bring to attention.

He Qicang was incapable of resisting Cheng Xiaoyu. He simply closed his eyes and told her that anything was fine. Cheng Xiaoyun stood and clasped her hands in front of her breast.

Suddenly, the telephone upstairs in Fang's study rang. Fang Buting turned abruptly in the direction of the sound.

He Qicang opened his eyes lazily. "That ruins everything."

There would be no singing now.

———

Xie Peidong's hand was on the telephone, but he refrained from picking it up. His eyes were drawn to a small group of pigeons that had perched on the balcony. The clang of the phone had not disturbed them. They merely stared in through the glass at Xie. A deep sense of foreboding rose in him. Finally, he lifted the receiver. "Peking branch, may I ask who's calling?"

The call was from the prison.

"Mr Xie? My name's Wang Puchen." Wang's voice was neither rushed, nor slow, but there was a hint of deep concern. "Excellent, you're the person I need to speak to. Sir, may I ask if your precious daughter Xie Mulan has arrived yet?"

Xie Peidong did not answer immediately. He paused for a moment, then responded with his own question: "They're all with you, there, Mr Warden, sir. What is the meaning of your question?"

"The situation is like this. There were quite a few people released today, on the orders of Nanking. Because it's the summer holidays, the students are not being allowed to return to their university campuses. Those from Peking were told to go home, and those from outside the city were escorted to the train station where they have been put on trains taking them to their respective hometowns. I've just received a report, however… and… and I'm sorry to tell you this, but, it seems your daughter may have been on one of the vehicles taking students to the train station."

The pigeons out on the balcony cooed as though they wished to crash through the glass and into the room. They were an ill omen, or so it seemed.

"What the hell are you talking about? What do you mean she may have ended up heading to the train station? Mr Wang, you were there at the meeting, and so were two members of the Fang family. And now you've rung us up, you wish to speak to Mr Fang... for surely that's why you've called, isn't it!"

"To be frank, it doesn't matter who answered the phone. What's important is the news I've just given you. Your daughter got on *that* truck. Apparently, she was swayed by the other students to accompany them to the so-called 'liberated' areas. I've already ordered troops to pursue the convoy, the general focus is routes leading to Fangshan. Right now, I've only one request, and that's that I'd like you to come here. Once she's found, you can bring her home yourself. Before that happens, I would advise you not to share this information. You don't want to cause anyone to panic. It's not, after all, the best of times..."

"Bring it over here." Cheng Xiaoyun watched He Xiaoyu carrying the silver tray towards the dinner table. "We're all family here, there're no strangers."

He Xiaoyu walked over to the sofa and placed the basket of bread in the middle of the tea table. The tea was brought out next, a cup for each of them. There was also a serving bowl and ladle that were brought to sit in front of He Qicang.

"Something just for me?" He looked at Cheng Xiaoyun and she nodded in reply. "Oh, I must try to guess what it is."

Everyone else had little choice but to wait for He Qicang to make his guesses. At the same time, they sneaked glances at the stairs that led to the first floor.

"Oh, I've not had this in years." He Qicang appeared to have surmised what it was and sighed contentedly. "Black sesame congee. Xiaoyun, am I right?"

"Right first time. You're no fun at all." Cheng Xiaoyun smiled sweetly as she said this, and then picked up a small dish. With her free hand, she lifted the lid to the larger serving bowl and handed it to He Qicang.

A serving bowl, a small ladle, congee that was neither too thin nor to thick; only at a child's birthday south of the river would one receive such treatment.

He Qicang was so deeply moved by the fact she had made the congee for him that he couldn't yet look away. "Ah, Cheng Xiaoyun, why do you spoil me as though I were your child?"

"Do you believe you're that filial? It's not hot. Go ahead and eat."

He Qicang pretended no longer and began to ladle up the warm black sesame porridge.

The door to the study above them opened very gingerly and Xie Peidong left.

"Who rang?" Fang Buting asked before Xie Peidong even left the first-floor landing.

Xie smiled. "It was the prison, where they're releasing the detainees. I'm going to take Young Li with me to go and collect them."

"Didn't I ask you to telephone Li Yuqing to get him to provide an escort?" He Qicang asked.

Xie finished his descent of the stairs and smiled again. "I didn't get the chance to ring him. Just as I reached for the phone, it rang. They're our children. It makes sense for us to go and get them. Please, Vice-Chancellor He, you can relax and eat. Cheng Xiaoyun's made a lovely meal. You don't need to wait for us. Just save us a little. We'll be back before you know it."

Cheng Xiaoyun stood up.

He Xiaoyu had already walked over to the clothes stand and had Xie's straw hat in her hand. Her eyes met his in a knowing glance.

"Thank you, dear." The look in his eyes was much the same as it had been before, calm and collected. At the same moment as he took hold of his hat, his free hand shot out to the nearby cupboard to grab a folding fan. Turning to Cheng Xiaoyun, he had some final words before his departure: "Get busy, all right? Make sure you entertain the vice-chancellor well." With those words, Xie turned to face He Qicang. He bowed low, nodded his head and walked slowly, purposefully, out.

He Xiaoyu found herself back in the kitchen. Fang Meng'ao was still there, but the terrifying look he had in his eyes shocked Xiaoyu. She'd seen it once before, next to the Yongding River. It was when he told her about what had happened to Uncle Cui. And now she saw it again, she couldn't help but feel worried. Her voice was quiet, but she had to ask: "Is... something wrong?"

Fang Meng'ao didn't turn to look at her. His attention was drawn to what was happening outside the window. He'd seen Xie Peidong walk past and he knew it boded ill. "Uncle won't be back with Mulan…"

He Xiaoyu's face changed. "Why?"

"The phone call… it was Wang Puchen."

"What! Did you hear what they were talking about?"

Xie Peidong had disappeared from Fang Meng'ao's line of sight, and Fang abruptly turned around. "Mulan isn't on her way home. I… I must go."

"You can't." He Xiaoyu reached out and pulled on his arm.

Fang Meng'ao never imagined she might like this, that she'd take hold of his arm and pull, if only lightly, on his short sleeve. If he wanted to get away, it would've been easy to do so, but he couldn't. He didn't want to, it seemed. The only thing he could do was gaze at her.

She released his hand gently. "I just gave Uncle his straw hat. His eyes were clear and determined. He said we should all wait for them here."

Fang knitted his brow. When he spoke, his voice was low and contained a sense of desolation. "Do you know, when Uncle Cui was arrested, no one called for me to come then either…"

"Do you think…" He Xiaoyu was startled by his admission and what it might mean. She thought for a moment, then continued coldly: "They can't. We all know, Mulan's just a student. This situation… it's nothing like what happened with Uncle Cui. What's more… Dad… he was there, the students were being released. How could anything have happened to Mulan?"

Fang Meng'ao's eyes appeared blank, empty.

"Am I wrong? Did my words make no sense?"

"I only hope my intuition, my gut feeling, is wrong. Everything you said makes sense."

He Xiaoyu's heart raced and pounded in her ears. "I… I don't understand."

"When I was young, I had no intuition whatsoever. I only ever listened to Mum. Later, when I still lacked insight into how things are, I listened to you. Do you understand?"

He Xiaoyu couldn't see it, but she felt her face flush red hot.

The sun was setting when Zeng Keda's vehicle raced down Fuxingmen Inner Street. Unfortunately for Zeng, however, the gate was closing just as he arrived. He was covered in sweat, still wearing a long-sleeved garment despite it being summer. He lifted the collar of his shirt and looked at his watch. It had just turned five o'clock.

Zeng's assistant brought the jeep to a stop as close as possible to the closed gate. He leapt out and bade welcome to the captain on guard: "Have you seen the Ministry of Defence's transport come through?"

The captain saluted before answering: "As per orders, the gate was closed at seventeen hundred hours."

Zeng's aide-de-camp turned to look at his superior still seated in the jeep.

"Ask him," Zeng called out, "whether or not a car bearing the mark of the Peking branch of the Central Bank has passed through."

Wang put the question to the guard.

"No sir. No such vehicle has passed through here."

"Tell him orders have changed. The jeep I'm in, as well as the aforementioned vehicle bearing the Peking branch's crest, will be coming through here today. Consequently, the gate is not to be shut."

"Did you hear the inspector?" Zeng shifted his position to stand beside the captain. "Open the gate."

"Sir, yes sir. But... ah... that is... I must inform my superiors, ask for instructions."

A gunshot rang out, ending their conversation.

Zeng Keda was holding his pistol. He'd already got out of the jeep and had walked over to the railing. He kicked it once as he passed, and then strode confidently into the guard station just inside the city gate. For the men to see a major-general march in, gun still in his hand, their stunned reaction was to be expected. An instant later, they all hurriedly saluted.

Zeng holstered his weapon upon seeing them, and returned their salute; military protocol had to be observed, after all. What he did next, however, could only be considered bizarre to the junior soldiers. Without giving orders, without asking for assistance, Zeng spun on his heel and walked over to the gate. He placed his hands on the rather thick, heavy iron bar used to seal the gate and began to lift it up.

"Inspector!" his assistant called out, similarly shocked by his superior's actions.

The assistant called out again, this time to the guards. "The gate's still not open!"

The captain of the guard responded by shouting to his men: "Open the gate!"

Several guards rushed forwards, but as soon as they laid eyes on Zeng Keda now holding the iron bar just above the mounting irons, they shouted: "Clear away!"

The large iron bar clanged loudly as it hit the ground.

Zeng turned and began to walk back to the jeep. He called to his assistant as he did so: "Back in the jeep."

"Open the gate, clear the roadblock!" Zeng's aide-de-camp hollered to the men and then hurried after his boss. When he got to the vehicle, he saw Zeng Keda in the driver's seat. "Inspector…"

"Get in." Zeng Keda didn't deign to look at the younger man, who had little choice but to obey. He walked around the rear of the jeep and climbed into the passenger's side. Before he was seated safely, Zeng Keda was stepping on the accelerator and switching gears. The vehicle raced through the gate.

The roadblock cleared, and the gate opened, but no one in the jeep seemed to care. With a whoosh they were on the other side, where there happened to be a single parking space. The jeep sped towards Xizhimen, leaving the guards and the gate well behind them. Zeng's assistant regained a measure of composure, which is when he noticed the palms of his hands were drenched with sweat.

Underneath several tall white poplar trees that lined Fuxingmen Outer Expressway, a vehicle, that particular vehicle, was stopped. A tall man was standing next to it, smoking.

Zeng Keda did not reduce his speed; he was in rush to get to Wang Puchen.

"Ah…" Zeng's assistant's voice trailed off before he said anything further. They'd arrived and now Zeng slammed on the brakes, bringing the jeep to a sudden stop. In fact, he'd hit the brakes so hard that the vehicle fishtailed and spun, nearly crushing Wang Puchen as he smoked his cigarette. Despite the near miss, Wang never moved. The only thing he did do was flick his cigarette away, not out of fear, but because he'd finished it and only the butt remained.

Zeng stayed seated behind the wheel, his eyes focused on Wang Puchen. When he saw no change in Wang's composure, Zeng's anger only increased. "What the hell is going on?"

Wang Puchen ignored the question and directed his attention to Zeng's assistant: "It's best if you get into my vehicle…"

"Tell me, now. What's going on?"

Wang had never seen Zeng Keda so irate and figured he'd best respond. "Nanking's orders were to remove from Peking all students whose homes were elsewhere, which, let me tell you, is quite a number… so many that we haven't got enough men to see the task done. As a result – and we only discovered this after the fact – Xie Mulan was in among these students and presumably on her way to Fangshan…"

"You… you… you're disgraceful. That's what this is, absolutely disgraceful!" Zeng spat the words. "Do you know what'll happen when she doesn't show up at home?"

"I've got men out looking for her now. We're pulling out all of the stops to locate her."

Zeng Keda was boiling over with anger, but there was little he could do. He looked up at the poplar trees. "How the hell am I going to explain this to Comrade Jianfeng…"

"Her father's already on the way. Together, we're sure to find her and bring her back. My advice is to leave Comrade Jianfeng out of it. You don't need to report anything, at least not for the time being."

"Inspector," his assistant called, "another vehicle's come, an Austin. That should be Mr Xie."

Zeng Keda turned around. In the distance, a car could be seen, gradually getting bigger as it drew closer. Zeng shifted in his seat once again and faced Wang Puchen. "Issue orders on behalf of the Ministry of Defence. Inform all military personnel along the roads that they're to detain any and all students they encounter."

"Fine."

When the Austin pulled closer, Zeng climbed down from the jeep. When it stopped, he was the first to approach it. In the passenger seat, he saw Xie Peidong. Zeng's look was apologetic as he opened the car door: "Mr Xie…"

As he stepped down, Xie Peidong stumbled a little. It was clear he had lost his usual capable, affable demeanour.

Zeng reached out to help him. "You don't need to worry. We've already issued the necessary orders. Everyone's on the lookout for her. We'll find her in no time."

Xie nodded in appreciation, then directed his attention towards Wang Puchen.

"Rest assured," Wang said, "we'll bring her back. Come, Mr Xie, let's get going."

Xu Tieying and Secretary Sun escorted Liang Jinglun to Wang Puchen's office.

Xu pulled some keys out of his pocket and handed them to Sun. "I won't be going in with you, but you tell him, it's the number 'two' telephone. Get him to speak directly to Chief Ching-kuo… but don't leave him alone."

Sun accepted the keys but hesitated. "Sir, is it… appropriate for me to go in?"

"No, it's not, it's not appropriate for anyone to enter. Just stay in the doorway and watch him. But don't listen to what's being said over the phone. That should be all right."

Sun looked at his superior, wondering if he had any hidden intention, but Xu Tieying had already begun to walk back down the corridor. The only thing he could do was put the key in the lock and open the door. Strangely, however, he struggled at even this simple task, fumbling the key. It was only just a short time ago that he fired his pistol with such precision, but now he couldn't even open a door.

Standing next to him, Liang Jinglun didn't seem to notice Sun's difficulty. He'd lost his usual demeanour and it was clear he was having trouble keeping his composure. In a word, he looked a mess. His words matched his appearance, for he spoke only one sentence: "Give my report to Comrade Jianfeng. Ask to be disciplined."

As Liang Jinglun repeated his sentence, Sun found the keyhole and slowly pushed open the heavy metal door.

Sun picked up the phone and held it to his ear. "Is this Secretary Sun? Yes… excellent." He then turned and handed the receiver to Liang Jinglun. "Comrade Jianfeng wishes to speak to you…"

"Put the phone down there." Sun complied and laid the receiver gently on the table. Liang did not make any move to pick it up. He simply looked at the other man and spat two words: "Get out." Sun left as quickly as he could and pulled the door shut behind him.

The heavy door was closed, but a seemingly heavier telephone lay in front of him. Liang Jinglun grasped it in two hands and slowly brought it close to his ear. The imagined strain was nearly unbearable.

"I know everything, Comrade Liang Jinglun." The words coming from the other end of the phone were crisp, almost cold. Liang Jinglun had no words to offer by way of reply. He felt it hard to swallow. His silence made Chiang Ching-kuo wonder if he was actually listening at all. "Comrade, you do hear me…"

Tears rolled down his cheeks. He did his best to hide the sound of his crying. The other end of the phone was silent now, too. Jianfeng knew; he understood. Once he regained a measure of control, once he had suppressed the tears, Liang Jinglun tried to respond in a normal voice: "Comrade Jianfeng, are you… are you doing well?"

The phone was silent again, this time for longer. Finally, Chiang Ching-kuo spoke, his tone much changed from just a few seconds before. He was no longer trying to conceal his own sense of distress. "No, no I'm not doing all that well. I've been in meetings all morning and all afternoon. Comrade Liang Jinglun, I've not protected you well… not at all. Please forgive me."

Zeng Keda's jeep headed down the highway in the direction of Fangshan. The small flag bearing the emblem of the Ministry of Defence flapped violently in the breeze. Xie Peidong's Austin came next, followed by Wang Puchen's vehicle that was being driven by Zeng's assistant. They hurtled past any and all other vehicles on the road, forcing several to pull over on the side guard rails.

Zeng Keda's foot never left the accelerator; his eyes were glued to the road in front of him. Wang Puchen sat silently next to him. For quite a long time, neither one spoke.

Finally, it was Zeng who shattered the quiet: "Tell me, Comrade Liang Jinglun, where is he right now?" His foot eased up on the pedal.

"He's with Yan Chunming, busy recording their confessions." Wang Puchen's tone increased. "We're trying to ascertain if the CPC really does suspect him of being a double agent. That's the first order of business. Second, well, so long as Yan Chunming doesn't confess and confirm he's a Communist, then everything will be in order. We'd have done our due diligence and they'll be released."

"And what about Xu Tieying? Where's he?"

"He's with the investigative team, the police, too. They're seeing to the discharge of the students. They should be leaving by now I would think."

"If what's happened to Xie Mulan had anything to do with Xu Tieying, if this is some trap he's put into motion, I'll be in Nanking tomorrow to report him. I… I hope you'll be with me. The Intelligence Bureau will need to investigate all of this thoroughly."

"Agreed. But we'll have to request instructions from Comrade Jianfeng first and then discuss what to do."

Zeng Keda looked him over for a minute and then pushed on the accelerator again.

"Fusheng…" The name that came through the phone reverberated like distant thunder crashing against mountains just over the horizon. Liang Jinglun's hair stood on end and he shuddered. The words that followed echoed still like thunder: "Do you remember your trip to America… and what I told you then? The quote from Su Shi of the Song Dynasty?"

"I… I remember."

"Today, I'm going to quote them again, in the hope that they'll serve to encourage you." There was a marked change in the tenor of his voice as he began his recitation: "'For brave men in this world, they do not fear death should it suddenly approach, nor do they become angered without reason. While their ambition may be great, it is also far, far away.' Fusheng, to my mind, you're the great Zhang Liang from the Han Dynasty, one of its three heroes. Comrades Zeng Keda, Wang Puchen and Sun Chaozhong, and a great many others, they're no more than field generals…"

"Comrade Jianfeng…"

"Let me finish." His voice, which had seemed somewhat distant, now sounded very close. "There's something else I've not told you, should have told you… the first time I saw your name on that register, I immediately thought of someone else with an equally impressive name: Tan Sitong, one of the so-called Six Gentlemen Martyrs of the failed reforms of 1898. This is perhaps the main reason why I suddenly sought you out. I remember when we first met, you were terribly surprised, so unexpected was the meeting. I was greatly pleased. You were everything your name suggested you were. Fusheng, you've borne this name well in the past, you bear it well now, and you will continue to do so into the future."

"Comrade Jianfeng…" Liang Jinglun once again swallowed his tears, but his voice was full of emotion. "Tan Sitong said it: 'The changes a country faces invariably involves bloodshed.' Fusheng knows, it doesn't matter if it were Kung of Soong or the two Chens. If blood needs to flow, then let it start with me!"

"You don't need to bleed to see these changes happen. In truth, you can't." The passion in Jianfeng's voice had clearly intensified. "If blood is needed, let it be shed by those corrupt officials. I've already declared to the central leadership committee of the party that it's vital that we do away with the old *fabi* currency and issue the new one. If blood must flow like a river to make this happen, then let it flow!"

"I understand."

"What happened today shouldn't have happened. I've already issued orders for Wang Puchen to properly deal with the aftermath. The president has made his own enquiries as well. Chen received orders, too. He's to make sure Xu Tieying shoulders his share of the responsibility for dealing with what happens next. The currency reforms must go ahead, you must be protected, and at the same time, all of this must be kept secret. Even Zeng Keda and Fang

Meng'ao must be kept in the dark. Once you leave where you are, your main struggle will be with yourself… and with those you'll have to face."

When he finally exited Wang Puchen's office, Liang Jinglun noticed how the weather had changed. The sky was dark. Rain pounded against the windows of the prison, fast and hard as though they were bullets fired from a gun. It was impossible to see outside, the windows transformed into white, watery sheets.

"It's raining." Secretary Sun had been waiting outside and now greeted Liang Jinglun with a frivolous, meaningless comment.

Liang seemed to be a different person. His demeanour was nothing like it had been before. "It's raining?"

Liang said nothing further. He merely walked on past the other man as though his presence was of little or no significance to him.

"Professor Liang!" Sun shouted and then raced after him.

Liang Jinglun had already walked outside and into the pouring rain.

It didn't matter if they used their windscreen wipers or not, the three vehicles had been waylaid under the Marco Polo Bridge by the raging heavens. Zeng Keda was spellbound by the torrents of rain that seemed to envelop the world around him.

"I would suggest," Wang Puchen began, speaking loudly over the hammering rain, "that we tell Mr Xie to return home first."

Zen, woke from his stupor and looked at Wang. "If your daughter was missing, would you go home?"

"But he's of no use here. It's getting dark, and we're not all that far from the front line. The Communist-held areas are just a little distance away. His only choice is to rely on us to search for her. And besides, He Qicang, Fang Buting and his captain son are all at home waiting for news. If we allow Mr Xie to remain, you know they'll get increasingly worked up. And you know what that means.

They're liable to ring Nanking and get Comrade Jianfeng involved as well."

Zeng Keda closed his eyes as he mulled this over.

Wang took his silence as consent and opened the door to the jeep. He climbed out into the violent downpour and, with great difficulty, made his way to the rear car.

Xie Peidong, seated in the Austin, had his eyes closed, too. But he was not asleep, and nor was he resting. His body was erect and alert, and while his eyes may have been shut, Xie seemed to have trained his ears on every sound that could be heard amid the ferocious storm.

"Dad..."

Xie's eyelids moved, but he didn't dare to open them. He concentrated all his efforts on the sound he heard, desperate to hear the voice again, hoping beyond hope that it wasn't just an illusion, a trick of the mind.

"Dad..."

His eyes were open faster than the sound dissipated into the storm. It was her, just beyond the car window... his daughter, Xie Mulan!

Xie Peidong reached out for the door handle, turned it and pushed the door. His actions were cautious and fearful. He didn't want the car door to swing open and crash into his daughter. In the darkness, he extended his hand to take the one proffered by Xie Mulan. But the elation he felt disappeared nearly as soon as he grasped the waiting hand. His face transformed for the appendage he held felt more like an old rat than the gentle touch of his daughter. He released his grip.

There, in the rain, soaked to the bone, Wang Puchen stuck his head into the Austin.

―――

The lights in Fang Buting's sitting room were all on. Outside, the rain continued to fall in powerful sheets, its darkness swallowing the last rays of the setting sun, bringing a premature end to the twilight. They were all seated at the dining table, but no one had removed the cover from the dishes. The knives and forks remained in place, untouched, tidy. At the head of the table, He Qicang sat, unmoving. His eyes were distant, his mind somewhere else, focused on the rain and the wind, it seemed. Fang Buting was seated to the immediate right of He Qicang, and across from him was his son Fang Meng'ao. His eyes, however, were concentrated on the scene that lay beyond, on the rain and how it seemed at times ready to smash through the glass and pounce on them all, his son before anyone else. Cheng Xiaoyun sat next to Fang Buting, her hand holding his beneath the table, her eyes trained on He Xiaoyu sitting opposite.

"Dad," said He Xiaoyu, standing up, "shouldn't we send Meng'ao to go and collect them?"

All eyes at the table turned towards He Qicang.

"No, we'll wait for them here… all of us." He Qicang avoided his daughter's eyes.

"How about I make a telephone call and see if I can get any news of the search?" Fang Meng'ao directed his attention to the head of the table.

"Telephone who?" said He Qicang. "Besides, what's the use? How would anyone know?"

He Xiaoyu felt a wave of emotion wash over her like the rain outside. She thought to stand again and challenge what her father said, but Fang Meng'ao reached out his hand under the table and held her back.

"Let me go!" Her shout echoed through the room.

Three sets of eyes fell on Fang Meng'ao. Never before had he felt such embarrassment. There was little he could do but release her hand.

He Xiaoyu stood up again. "All of you can stay here and do nothing but wait. I'm going out after them!"

"You dare!" He Qicang stood to confront his daughter's seeming impertinence. The tone of his voice was unfamiliar. No one had ever heard him speak in this manner.

"Now, now, Mr He, there's no need for such fury." Cheng Xiaoyun pushed her chair away from the table and hurriedly moved over towards He Qicang. She manoeuvred one arm under his to support him. The other went to his back in a consoling gesture. "How can you speak to your daughter like this?"

Tears were streaming down He Xiaoyu's face. She spun around and left the table. All eyes in the room followed her. She didn't exit, however, but went over to the steps that led upstairs from the dining room. Cheng Xiaoyun didn't know whether to continue to soothe He Qicang's anger, or chase after his daughter and try to console her.

Fang Buting looked at his son. "Go on…"

Never before had Fang Meng'ao so readily obeyed his father. Without a word, he stood up and walked swiftly after her.

As soon as he pushed open the door to Xie Mulan's room, Fang Meng'ao felt a chill run up the back of his neck. Time stopped for him. He saw the movie poster she had tacked to the wall, Rhett Butler holding Scarlett O'Hara.

Fang Meng'ao stepped further into the room and closed the door gently behind him. He walked over to her desk and stood behind He Xiaoyu. "When did she put this poster up?"

It was clear she was still crying, unable, or unwilling to answer. Fang Meng'ao didn't press the issue. He merely waited until she was ready to respond.

Suddenly, she stood up and turned to look at him, her face stained with tears. "Has your intuition… your gut feeling… has it ever been wrong?"

Fear crossed his face. He stood there, quiet, lost in thought.

He Xiaoyu moved closer and wrapped her arms around his waist, laying her head on his chest. "Tell me… tell me it has…"

Fang Meng'ao allowed himself to put his arms tightly around He Xiaoyu, his voice a soft, gentle whisper in her ear: "Don't trust in intuition, there's no such thing. Now tell me, when did she put that poster up? Did she say anything to you when she did?"

He Xiaoyu pressed her head closer to his chest. "I… I don't know. I just know she bought more than one *Gone with the Wind* poster, but that this was her favourite. She told me it was her hope, her dream, I suppose… that should she join the revolution and die… that she die like this."

Fang Meng'ao's embrace tightened. "Do you know if she shared these thoughts with Professor Liang?"

Again his intuition!

He Xiaoyu trembled in his arms, then suddenly lifted her head and pushed away. "Go now. Go and find Liang Jinglun. If you find him, you'll find Mulan. Go!"

Fang Meng'ao remained glued to where he was. He Xiaoyu shoved him, but to no effect.

"There's no use..." Fang Meng'ao shifted his gaze to the window and the rain that continued to hammer against it.

"What do you mean?"

"There's nothing I can do. Listen to me. The only thing we can do is stay here and wait."

He Xiaoyu grabbed his lapel. "Tell me, what do you know? What're you afraid of?"

Fang Meng'ao's voice seemed off, a little strange: "I don't know anything. As for what I'm afraid of, I've been afraid for a while. It's just now... I feel there's nothing we can do for them. I can't think of anything. My mind's a blank..."

He Xiaoyu only stared at him.

"Don't... don't press me to try and save them... save anyone. On the day the Japanese launched their full attack on Shanghai, on that day I went to rescue my mum... and... and I saw a bomb land next to her. I also tried to save my sister... fighter planes followed me. I felt their machine guns fire right over me. I saw them tear into her flesh during the War of Resistance. Everyone I tried to save ended up dead, all of them. Do you know why I didn't try to rescue Uncle Cui? I... I just couldn't. I had to beg Dad to go, but he failed. All because of me. I had asked him to try..."

He Xiaoyu watched on in surprise as Fang Meng'ao slowly lowered himself to the floor. "Xiaoyu, listen to me. I can't go. Uncle Xie can perhaps succeed in bringing her home..." His words trailed off and he let his head fall between his hands.

He Xiaoyu leant forward and took his face in her hands, pulling him close to her, allowing him to feel the beat of her heart. "We'll stay. No one will go. We'll wait for them to return."

―――

On the road back to Fang Buting's residence, they both remarked on the unrelenting nature of the wind and rain. But then, the weather improved. Xie Peidong's vehicle shifted into gear as Young

Li got them going again. But just as soon as they began, the car came to a sudden stop. Xie, sitting in the back, opened his eyes when he heard the horn sound.

Li turned around to look at Xie. "There's a rickshaw in the road," and he honked again.

The rickshaw driver, draped in rain gear, came ambling up. Li opened the window of the Austin just a crack so that he could hear the man. "There're trees blocking the road further up. The storm knocked them down. Two electrical poles have toppled over, too. You can't get through!" Li did not respond and so the older man continued: "Is that Mr Xie in the back there? I know you. If you're in a rush, climb into my rickshaw. You won't get wet and your home's just two hutongs away. I can get you there quick."

Xie Peidong looked at the man and a glimmer of recognition dawned. He turned to his driver and said: "Get my umbrella."

Three rickshaws snaked their way through the small alleyways of the hutong. The first tromped through the rain. The rickshaw in the middle had stopped under an eave. The third one maintained a discreet distance behind, the rickshaw driver walking slowly, apparently in an effort to shield the one in the middle.

The driver of the middle rickshaw pulled open the curtain and pushed his head in to look at his passenger. "Mr Xie, someone's waiting for you. You'd better climb down."

"Who is it?"

"You've no need to ask." The driver's tone had suddenly grown hoarse. "We're all Comrade Liu's men."

Xie Peidong grabbed the curtain and pulled it the rest of the way back. An umbrella was waiting to shield him from the rain.

In an undisclosed location, in a courtyard house that was fully enclosed, the man holding tight to Xie Peidong's hand was none other than Comrade Liuyun. The other hand was hot in his, he could feel it almost burning his skin, and at the same time, he could sense how icy cold his own hand was. No words were exchanged. Liuyun simply held tight. Seconds passed, then minutes. Xie Peidong could feel himself being led. Seconds later, he was standing beside a table. Things finally became clear, and Xie could see Zhang Yueyin standing just a few steps away.

Liuyun released his hand and placed his own on the table in

front of them. "Mr Xie, please sit. We have things to discuss." Xie did as instructed without uttering a sound. Liuyun sat at the head and then looked towards Zhang Yueyin. "Sit."

Zhang moved to the other side of the table and sat. Extending his hands across the surface, he was the first to speak: "Mr Xie…"

Xie Peidong stood and offered his hand. Zhang took it robotically, and Xie realised the other man's hand seemed as icy as his own.

Liuyun's eyelids drooped while he waited for the two of them to exchange pleasantries. Neither Zhang Yueyin nor Xie Peidong would dare look at the other, however. Nor did they shake hands for long. Seconds later, they both returned to their seats.

Liuyun now spoke: "I've received a most urgent communiqué, contingency plans in fact. That's why I've made contact as quickly and abruptly as I have. I fear, however, I'm too late…"

Zhang Yueyin stood again. "I request once more that the party deal with…"

"Don't worry, they'll pay, there'll be punishment coming," said Liuyun, his voice heavy and ominous. "Just be glad it's not come round to you yet!" Zhang Yueyin sat back down without saying anything more. Liuyun continued: "There's nothing we can do for Comrade Yan Chunming. He returned to the university on his own accord, against our instructions. The same goes for Comrade Liu Chuwu. He did the same. As a result of their actions, in the span of a day, we've lost two… indispensable comrades."

Liuyun's words exploded in Xie Peidong's mind. "Comrade Chunming is… is…"

Liuyun nodded his head.

"When?"

Liuyun's eyes fell. "At four this afternoon… in Xishan prison."

"Xishan prison…" The name fell like a hammer on Xie Peidong's chest. His heart skipped a beat and then began to race, pounding in his ears. He didn't have the courage to ask anything more.

Suddenly, the thump of his heart turned into a knock on the door.

Just as suddenly, Liuyun stared at Zhang. "It's the comrade with the ginger soup. Go and fetch it will you?"

Zhang Yueyin had no wish to hurry, nor did he dare to be too slow. He stood up and walked over to the door. Opening it just enough, he accepted the tray that the unnamed comrade had brought and closed the door once again. Returning to the table, he spoke to Xie Peidong: "Mr Xie, please have some."

His years of service to the party became clear at that moment. He took hold of the offered soup with two hands and placed it carefully on the table in front of him. Before eating, however, he looked at Liuyun. "Comrade, whatever has happened, whatever the outcomes may yet be, we have to face them. Please… speak."

Liuyun's expression was grave: "Two comrade students from Yenching University and… and Comrade Xie Mulan."

Xie Peidong and Liuyun stood up abruptly. Zhang Yueyin was only a few seconds behind.

Liuyun shot a pointed glance at Zhang Yueyin, who understood his meaning immediately. Zhang moved closer to Xie Peidong, his hands ready to catch him.

Although Xie, on his own accord, returned slowly to his chair, Zhang Yueyin did not move to assist him, choosing instead to stand calmly behind.

Liuyun remained on his feet. The words he had to say hung around his neck: "Comrade Xie Mulan had the strongest and most intense desire to join the party. Zhang Yueyin and I were just speaking of this before you arrived. Arrangements will be made, in the name of the Peking Labour Union. She's to be posthumously recognised as a party member…"

Both Liuyun and Zhang Yueyin reached out and took hold of Xie Peidong. Xie, however, did not at first move. When he finally did, Zhang took the initiative and extended his free hand to support him.

Xie pushed them off. He didn't want their assistance. Zhang and Liuyun exchanged glances and then relented. The two men stared at Xie Peidong, who now took hold of the bowl of ginger soup and brought it close to his lips.

"Careful, it's very hot, Mr Xie." Zhang's concern was honest, but he didn't dare to try to actually stop him.

Xie Peidong's hands quivered a little and the bowl listed. A second later and Xie collapsed, his face landing in the scalding soup.

Xie's left hand held the rim of the bowl. With the sleeve of his right arm, he wiped the soup off his face, the tears, too. He'd been burned, his skin red, his eyes redder. Xie looked at Liuyun. "How... how could they have? The gall..."

"They've already done it," Liuyun sighed. "To be frank, we never expected they would do... do what they have done. We know Chiang Ching-kuo and Wang Yunwu are committed to reining in inflation. That's why they've pushed for the currency reforms as vigorously as they have. We've also determined that large amounts of gold, silver and foreign cash reserves – more than half of the country's holdings – are being controlled by the Kung and Soong families. In addition to this, we also know the Kuomintang's own holdings are in the hands of a few select members. But who could have known they'd be willing to act as they've done... to be so brutal! Nor did we think that the assistance Liang Jinglun gave to He Qicang yesterday in writing all of this down would wind up in the hands of Ambassador Stuart and that Nanking would respond by establishing this so-called committee for the correct management of American aid. It certainly demonstrates the Kuomintang's insistence on seeing the currency reforms happen. Today, in Xishan prison, Xu Tieying exposed Liang Jinglun's true identity to Mulan and our comrade students. This was Xu's... and his allies... counterattack on those who support the reforms. Exposing Liang Jinglun, sacrificing Mulan and the others, it was all to attack Chiang Ching-kuo, to wound him... and to judge how we will respond. Our error is that we forgot Chairman Mao's teachings. All reactionaries will inevitably destroy themselves, they'll crush their own feet when trying to manoeuvre a stone. Mulan... Comrades Liu and Yan... they shouldn't have been sacrificed like this!"

"So why the hell did Zeng Keda and Wang Puchen go out with me to look for her?" Again, there was a tremble in his voice. "Are they that oblivious? Do they not know their own party is tearing itself apart?"

There was an emotional pointedness to his question, one that did not escape Liuyun. "Wang Puchen knew," he said, sitting down slowly, "but Zeng Keda didn't... still doesn't I should think. Then, this afternoon actually, just after Xu Tieying exposed Liang Jinglun's real identity, open conflict emerged between Chiang Ching-kuo and

Chen Lifu. A compromise was reached. They are to pretend to protect Liang Jinglun, to create the façade that he's still a valued member. To see this through, they actually released a group of student detainees in the buffer zone between our forces and theirs. And none of those students knew that the place they were let go... the buffer zone... is filled with landmines. So, so many students!"

Xie Peidong could control his emotions no longer. Tears flowed freely.

Liuyun's eyes were moist as well. "To make matters worse, because the area these students were released in has been so heavily mined, and because so many have fallen victim, the whole area is littered with shrapnel and... and body parts... but none worth burying. This farce of a release allows them to say the students, including Mulan, have all fled to our liberated zones, but there's no way to prove this, nor really where they've gone. I must stress, however, that the source of this information has to be protected, which means we have to pretend we know nothing. Mr Xie... I... I have to tell you, this whole affair... everything that's happened... well, it's taken an even greater toll on Vice-Chairman Zhou."

"Then, well, why have you told me all of this?"

"Because, as Vice-Chairman Zhou has said, no one can take your place. The central authorities must have faith in you."

Xie Peidong placed both hands on the table again and used them to lift himself up. "Comrade Liuyun, please, tell me my instructions."

Liuyun looked searchingly at Xie. "Only that you pretend to believe that Mulan and the other students have made it to the liberated zone and that your belief satisfies the Fang family, as well as He Qicang. They, too, have to believe Mulan is alive. We have to make sure the Kuomintang thinks it has fooled you... and them... that they've successfully concealed the truth of what has actually happened."

"I better get going, then. Everyone is waiting for me."

Liuyun stood up and walked over to Xie Peidong. As he did, he shot a look at Zhang Yueyin, signalling him to open the door. Then he put his arm around Xie and assisted him to the exit. "Mr Xie, one last thing, under no circumstances whatsoever is Comrade

Fang Meng'ao to learn the truth. The importance of this is, well, it's something you understand better than us, I'm sure."

"Yes, I do."

Liuyun paused as they reached the door. The courtyard looked as though it had been freshly washed. Stars were in the sky above. None of them could say when exactly the hours of violent rainfall had stopped.

By evening, security around the Fang household was at the same level as that generally reserved for the most important and highest-ranking members of the Peking authorities. Fang Meng'ao's jeep, as well as the slightly larger vehicle belonging to his young military guardsmen, was stationed at the entrance to the street. The men stood erect, vigilant. When they saw Xie Peidong come into view, his gait slow and deliberate, they saluted immediately.

He walked past without saying anything, and was surprised to see Li Zongren's private car; evidently, a retinue had come with He Qicang. Alongside the vehicle, another high-ranking imperial guard stood to attention. When he realised the man walking towards him was Xie Peidong, he saluted in the same manner as the previous soldier had.

A car passed and then the gate was quiet. Xie took a step forward but stopped, startled by what he saw. There, just beyond the gate, his driver, Young Li, was standing entirely alone. Xie moved closer and asked: "When did you return?"

"Sir... well, not long after you left. The road was cleared and I was able to get through."

"And the car?"

"I asked the guards as soon as I pulled up if you had returned. They told me you hadn't, so I parked the car in the garage."

"What did Governor Fang say?"

"I didn't go in sir. I've been out here waiting for you."

The tone in Xie Peidong's voice relaxed. He looked admiringly at Li and then stepped across the threshold and into the courtyard. As he did, however, a wave of dizziness flowed over him.

Li reached out his hand and supported the older man. "Mr Xie, allow me to accompany you, please."

Xie nodded. "Once you're finished here, make sure you contact the financial affairs office. Tell them I've ordered your salary to be paid, beginning this month, in American dollars."

"Sir... oh thank you Mr Xie, thank you!" His excitement was unmistakable as he forgot the usual rules regarding a driver's expected behaviour; it was not his place to ask questions or to pass on things he might have overheard. But he leaned close to Xie Peidong nevertheless and whispered in his ear: "Sir, I heard the guards speaking... Professor Liang's here."

Xie stopped and slowly turned to face his driver. "Let go."

Li's face changed. He complied immediately with the order.

Xie Peidong collected himself, his face once more revealing his typical detached, dignified manner. He moved to step inside but paused for a moment and directed his attention to his young driver. "Remember this. You say one more word, and you can pack your bags and leave tomorrow."

Xie Peidong walked into the drawing room and was met with more staring, expectant eyes than he had ever seen before. Such was their intensity that he had difficulty maintaining his composure. He laughed tiredly. "Gosh, did it ever rain!" The room remained quiet, the eyes unblinking. Since no one offered a rejoinder, Xie continued: "You've not finished dinner yet?"

"Mulan?" Fang Buting's question was blunt, direct. It was what all of them wanted to ask.

Xie Peidong looked in the direction of his boss, doing his best to present an image of calm. "First, let's eat. There's much to tell..."

"Put away that serene exterior!" Fang Buting pounded his fists on the table. "I've been waiting patiently for you long enough... we all have. We all want to know. It's not for you to now make up your mind about what to tell us. You must tell us, me, the vice-chancellor, all of us. What's happened? Where the devil is Mulan?"

"And just what have you been enduring for far too long?" Xie Peidong pulled out a chair from the table and sat down heavily. "At the bank, here in this house, when have I ever done anything without first consulting you? She's *my* daughter. I wanted her to stay home but *you* let her go out. Right now, I have no idea where she is. And yet *you* pressure *me* with such questions!"

Stunned looks appeared on everyone around the dining table. It did not occur to any of them that the bow that had been pulled so taut while they had waited for news would be snapped so completely by Fang Buting and Xie Peidong. Underneath the table, Fang Buting's hands trembled. Cheng Xiaoyun knew he had been hurt by Xie's rebuttal, but she couldn't look at him. All she could do was squeeze his hand reassuringly. The look on his face, however, was terrifying to the man sitting opposite. Liang Jinglun knew, and so did everyone else, that Fang Buting's outburst was not directed at Xie Peidong, even though Xie had been the target just the same.

The tension and embarrassment in the air fell on the shoulders of He Qicang, who had, until now, remained silent. His head trembled a little as he looked at Liang Jinglun. "Jinglun, you were arrested along with her. You don't need to repeat what you just said. Just tell us what you think. Where has Mulan gone?"

Liang Jinglun stood up slowly.

Beneath the table one hand took hold of another: He Xiaoyu had reached out to Fang Meng'ao, only to have Fang grasp hers first. Everyone was on tenterhooks, waiting for Liang Jinglun to speak.

"I... I don't know where she's gone. At the same time, however, I certainly don't believe she's run off with those other students and left Peking."

"Who told you she'd left the city?" After Xie Peidong had rebuked Fang Buting, he'd sat with his eyes closed. Even when he asked the question, he chose not to look at Liang Jinglun. The dinner guests could all see, however, the wetness around his eyes.

"Xu Tieying's secretary, Sun Chaozhong. He told me." Liang Jinglun's answer was direct as could be. "They knew Mulan, or rather knew her family connections. They knew, too, that if she didn't make it home, there'd be no small amount of trouble. Now tell me, how could they fail to see her going off with students *not* from Peking? Mr Xie, Governor Fang, I suggest you contact Li Zongren and Fu Zuoyi directly. Their involvement is necessary if we're to find Mulan and bring her home."

He Qicang slowly shifted his attention to Fang Buting, whose face was vacant, lost. Fang, in turn, looked at Xie Peidong. Finally, he spoke, his voice hoarse and husky: "How about opening your eyes, please?" Xie obliged, but it was clear he was in no rush. Fang continued: "You must now tell us everything. Who called you out, where did you go and where is Mulan?"

"Let's eat first." Again Xie Peidong answered as he had before.

"What the hell is going on?" Fang Buting was suddenly on his feet. Cheng Xiaoyun had been unable to hold him back.

"Mr Xie…" Supporting himself with the table, He Qicang lifted himself from his chair.

Fang Meng'ao, He Xiaoyu and Cheng Xiaoyun did likewise, however reluctantly.

Xie Peidong matched their actions and stood.

"Tell us, right now, what's happened," He Qicang's pleaded. "When I see Li Zongren and Fu Zuoyi, that's the only way I'll be able to say anything useful."

Xie Peidong couldn't meet his stare head on, but he did answer: "You don't need to involve them. Mulan went off with those students… in the direction of Fangshan."

"Are Zeng Keda and Wang Puchen still out looking for her?" Fang Meng'ao interjected.

It was simple and straightforward enough, but it set He Xiaoyu's heart aflutter. She knew the meaning behind his words, she knew what his intuition had told him.

Xie Peidong had not looked at Fang Meng'ao, had chosen to avoid making eye contact. Now, however, he had little choice, and so slowly turned in his direction.

Fang Meng'ao continued: "There are so many sentries along the roads. A quick phone call ought to have been enough to see that they were held. But you're telling me an inspector from the Ministry of Defence, as well as the Intelligence Bureau's lead agent, were out looking for her with you! Uncle… what can I say? Do you believe it's true… that she's left with them? If you trust in that, then I guess we must too, yes?"

This was what Xie Peidong had been waiting for, these words. All eyes focused on him once again, anxiously awaiting his response. After a moment's pause, Xie found his voice: "Nanking's orders were explicit. Those students from outside Peking were to leave the city upon their release. Not even Wang Puchen had the power to intervene, which is why he called for Zeng Keda to assist him. They worried, too, that we wouldn't believe them, which is why they called for me. After all, she's my daughter."

It was now time for Fang Meng'ao to close his eyes. "And... and what, your small car couldn't catch up with the larger one?"

"But it was all a waste... the rain... the downpour chased us all the way. We called ahead, but the rain hadn't hit them. When we got Fangshan, the transport was empty. The students had already crossed the line of defence between us and..."

Xie Peidong's visage, the tone of his voice, and especially his description of the rain... they all shivered as though a cold winter wind suddenly swirled about them.

Fang Meng'ao's heart skipped a beat, and he turned to face Liang Jinglun. "Professor Liang, are you willing to travel to the so-called liberated area and bring Mulan home?"

"If you're willing to come with me, Captain Fang, let's leave immediately for Fangshan."

"Don't be absurd, none of you is going!" This was the first time Fang Buting had ever acted, at least in front of his son, in the dignified manner expected of a father. But the moment passed almost as quickly as it had come, replaced by Fang Meng'ao's characteristic opposition to his father. Fang Buting's face looked desolate and bleak. "Peidong, there's no need to look. Sooner or later our children will no longer side with the Kuomintang. Their allegiances will lie with the Communists. There's nothing you can do, nothing I can do..."

"Buting..." He Qicang extended his hand.

Fang Buting took it in his own, his complexion changed precipitously. "Get me a car. Take me to Yenching University Hospital."

He Qicang's entire body went limp and he began to fall to the floor. Fang Meng'ao reacted first and sprung to catch the older man.

"Dad!" He Xiaoyu rushed forward as well, but Fang Meng'ao already had her father in his arms. "Out of the way!"

Fang Meng'ao carefully lifted Xiaoyu's father and made for the sitting room door. While Liang Jinglun was startled by this turn of events, frozen to the floor, He Xiaoyu manoeuvred forward and pushed the door open for him. Liang Jinglun remained behind, stunned and unable to say or do anything.

Fang Meng'ao departed the drawing room, He Xiaoyu hot on his heels.

In that moment, at least to Liang Jinglun's eyes, another figure appeared right behind Xiaoyu. It was none other than Xie Mulan! He knew his eyes were playing tricks on him, they had to be, he thought, and within seconds of the illusion manifesting itself, it proved its illusory composition by dissipating just as quickly. Liang Jinglun blinked, the doorway empty. Then, his senses restored, Liang Jinglun rushed after them.

"Uncle!" Xie Peidong had remained standing, but now Cheng Xiaoyun's exclamation woke him from his stupor. He turned around.

Fang Buting shook off Cheng Xiaoyun's hand and started to walk around the table, his gait awkward and stumbling. Xie Peidong pulled him back.

In truth, Fang Buting was wholly unable to walk any further, regardless of whether or not Xie Peidong held him back. He stood there, his eyes trained on the doorway. Cheng Xiaoyun moved to offer support and saw how tightly he clasped Xie Peidong's hand. "Peidong, can you... can you ring Zeng Keda for me?" His voice was weak, frail and seemingly defeated.

Xie Peidong looked at his superior, then at Cheng Xiaoyun.

"Come," Fang Buting began. "Xiaoyun should be with us when we face the difficulties ahead. There's no avoiding them. Make the phone call, and ask for Zeng Keda to come here."

"Sir, what's the use of asking for Inspector Zeng?"

"Use his hotline... I want to speak with their superior directly. I want to speak to Chiang Ching-kuo, he's the only one who can really tell us where Mulan is. And one more thing, I want him transferred!" Xie Peidong was silent, so Fang Buting continued: "Don't hesitate, listen to what I say, ring him now." Xie Peidong had little choice but to comply.

"Xiaoyun..."

Cheng Xiaoyun squeezed his arm. "Governor."

"Is Mengwei still at Cui Zhongshi's?"

"I'm not sure."

"Then take a car and go and see. At the moment, I know Meng'ao won't cause any trouble, but Mengwei may. Find him, speak to him, tell him not to go looking for Xu Tieying, or for Wang Puchen, and especially not Liang Jinglun. You're perhaps the only person he'll actually listen to."

"I'll leave immediately." A tear rolled down her cheek and fell to the floor.

———

Fang Meng'ao handled the vehicle smoothly. In the passenger seat, Liang Jinglun felt as though time had stopped. In the rear seats, He Xiaoyu cradled her father's head, her ear focused on his frail and failing voice.

His condition had seemingly stabilised a little. "Let's go home…"

"Dad…"

"Just ring for the campus doctor."

He Xiaoyu lifted her head and spoke to Fang Meng'ao: "We don't need to go to the hospital. Dad just wants to go home. We can call the campus doctor to come and see him."

Liang Jinglun spun around. "Mr He, it's still best for us to take you to the hospital."

He Qicang only closed his eyes and repeated his request: "I want to go home."

Fang Meng'ao didn't wait for He Xiaoyu to relay her father's plea. He simply shifted gears, turned the wheel and headed off down a different street, presumably back to Yenching University.

Liang Jinglun turned his head again. Fang Meng'ao's voice sounded far off, as though it were being carried on the wind. "You don't need to say anything else."

The car lights flashed brilliantly, but Liang Jinglun could not escape the feeling that everywhere was shrouded in unending darkness.

———

The lights of a small jeep reflected off the narrow walls of the hutong, creating a spotlight effect that shone brightly upon Cheng

Xiaoyun. She was standing in the eastern-central part of the city, searching for Fang Mengwei.

Then, in the glare of the lights, she could hear a voice shout: "Young Li!" It was Fang Mengwei.

Poor Li had already endured quite a day. He'd been dragged too far into things at the Fang residence. He'd been humiliated and threatened. And now again, it seemed more was about to befall him. When he heard the shout, there was nothing he could do but frantically answer it: "Second Master Fang…"

"Fetch her over here. Now!"

Cheng Xiaoyun spoke at almost the same moment: "Young Li, take my car and go!"

The young man was frozen to the spot, unsure of what to do, unsure of whom to obey.

Cheng Xiaoyun was unrelenting. "Take my car, now. That comes from the mouth of the bank governor. Get in and go!"

"Ye… yes ma'am." Li had no option but to leave right away. Seconds later he was racing down the small alleyway, out of the hutong, and over to the car that Cheng Xioayun had arrived in.

Fang Mengwei pushed his foot down on the jeep's accelerator, and the engine roared. "Out of my way!"

Cheng Xiaoyun refused to budge.

The jeep lurched forward.

Suddenly, it was as though Fang Mengwei could see the dimples on Cheng Xiaoyun's face. This woman who could have been his older sister, his auntie…

The tyres screeched and the jeep came to a halt just before it would have crashed into her. "Auntie!" Fang Mengwei shouted again, then pushed open the jeep door and bounded down. Cheng Xiaoyun remained where she was, defiant, unmoving. Fang Mengwei grabbed her by the hand and was startled by how ice cold it was. He looked hard into her face. There were no longer any dimples, if there ever had been. All he saw was complete and utter shock. "Auntie," he said, his voice hoarse, "give me your hand. Will you dare?"

Slowly she came to, her eyes fixed on his. "Where to?"

"The police station. I mean to speak with Xu Tieying!"

"But… but your dad said you're not to have anything to do with Liang Jinglun… or Wang Puchen… or Xu Tieying."

"Can't we choose to ignore him, just this once?" There was an urgency in his face she'd not seen before.

"But what's the point? Why go and look for Xu Tieying?"

"There is no point. I just want you and me to do it."

"Let's go." Cheng Xiaoyun tracked back along the vehicle lights and to the passenger side. A second later, she was seated and waiting for Fang Mengwei to put the jeep in gear.

Tears formed but he wiped them away hurriedly. Then he turned and followed her to the jeep.

CHAPTER 8

Xu Tieying was sitting in his office with Fang Mengwei. "Deputy Fang, how could you bring a lady to such a place?" Xu had already surmised that men from the Fang family would come – Fang Buting, Fang Mengwei, really just about anybody, except, of course, for Cheng Xiaoyun.

"This place? Well, what is this place, hmm?" Fang Mengwei's eyes were intense, his stare pointed. "Auntie, you tell him. You've been pretty much everywhere."

"I've paid visits to HH Kung, TV Soong, Liu Kung-yun, and more."

Xu Tieying had to direct his attention to her. "Madam Fang, I know your associates, the important persons you've met, but all of those visits were government-related and had more to do with family... and children."

"But Chief Xu, your family's in Taipei." Cheng Xiaoyun now took on the airs of someone of great importance. "If I have the opportunity to one day visit the island, I would be honoured to meet your wife."

"Are you going to keep her standing, Chief Xu, or will you offer us a seat?" Fang Mengwei jostled forward, pouncing upon Xu's moment of indecision. Xu, in turn, allowed the other man to push his way in, subconsciously standing to one side so that Cheng

Xiaoyun could enter his office. She strode between them and straight to the sofa.

"Secretary Sun!" Xu Tieying called out towards the conference room down the corridor. Within seconds, Sun Chaozhong appeared. Xu delivered his instructions: "Get a car ready. I will be escorting Madam Fang to it momentarily."

"Of course. I'll see to it right away."

Before Secretary Sun could depart, however, Fang Mengwei manoeuvred in front of him. "Your timing is excellent. Bring us some tea."

Sun took a half step back. "Deputy Fang, while you're here, please listen to the chief."

Fang Mengwei looked the other man over. He saw the bandage still wrapped around his right hand. Instinctively, Fang shifted his own hand to his pocket, slowly so as not to cause alarm. "You're wounded, I see, so I shan't pick on you. Still, and despite your unwillingness to fetch the tea, there is something I'd like to ask you. Let's walk together." As he spoke, Fang Mengwei reached out and grabbed hold of Sun Chaozhong's wrist, giving it a painful twist.

Secretary Sun was unprepared for the pain that shot up his arm and could do little but allow Fang Mengwei to begin to lead him out of the room.

"Just what the hell are you playing at, Fang Mengwei?" Xu Tieying yelled in response and moved towards them.

Quickly, Fang Mengwei pulled his right hand out of his pocket, grasping his pistol. He turned and pointed it straight at Xu Tieying. "Sit the hell down! You have accounts to settle. You'll do that here with Madam Fang, I'm going to do the same out here with your secretary." As he spoke, he applied more pressure to Sun Chaozhong's wrist. "I've got my gun pointed right at your boss. I suggest you don't try anything."

Sun offered no physical resistance, but he did try to speak. "Deputy Fang…"

"Shut up, I've not asked you any questions yet," said Fang Mengwei, turning to look at Xu Tieying, the pistol still pointed between his eyes. "Chief Xu, there are quite a few people who'd like to see you dead. I only hope that it's not right now." Fang Mengwei's hand twitched. His index finger began to squeeze down on the trigger. In that moment, time seemed to slow and come to a stop.

Xu Tieying shifted. The terror that was on his face turned into a profound sense of loneliness and isolation. He seemed to forget the gun still directed at him. He walked over to his desk and lifted the lid from the teacup. He added leaves, then hot water from the nearby flask, and finally carried it over to Cheng Xiaoyun. With the tea placed carefully on the table in front of her, Xu Tieying lowered himself onto the sofa. At the same time, he looked in the direction of Fang Mengwei and Sun Chaozhong.

Sun's face was still the picture of devotion.

"Go with him," Xu said, "talk things over."

"Chief…"

"Go!"

"Fi… fine." This was perhaps the first time his secretary didn't answer with a "yes".

Cheng Xiaoyun now interjected: "Mengwei, leave the gun here."

Fang Mengwei focused on Xu Tieying: "Chief Xu, would you rather I leave the pistol here?"

"That's entirely up to you."

Fang Mengwei now looked at Sun. "Did you hear? Being anyone else's dog is much greater than being his bitch." He placed the weapon on Xu Tieying's desk.

"You know my hand is smarting. Help me unholster my own gun."

Fang Mengwei's response was quick: "I think I'd rather you keep it." And with that, the two men walked out of the office, one with his wrist still twisted behind his back.

"Chief Shan!" Fang Mengwei shouted as he appeared in the doorway to the conference room.

Just outside, Deputy Chief Shan, along with several other men, had presumably been waiting for an extended period of time, none of them daring to knock or to leave. The only option he seemed to have was to wait and listen to whatever it was that was going on. As he did, the anxiousness on his face grew more and more pronounced. Then, when he finally saw Fang Mengwei appear, still holding Sun Chaozhong's arm behind his back, Shan knew the situation was far from ideal. In fact, his mind was racing with thoughts of how best to avoid getting involved. Unfortunately, Fang Mengwei's address killed any hope of that. Too late to hide, Shan could only reply: "Ah, Chief Fang..."

Fang Mengwei didn't allow him to say anything further before inviting him in.

At first, to Shan's mind at least, there was nothing obviously sinister about Fang Mengwei's tone. This did not, however, stop Deputy Shan from hesitating. To be frank, he couldn't be sure if he was being drawn into a trap, but when he felt the men behind him push him forward, he knew there was nothing he could do but let himself be guided in.

Once inside, Fang Mengwei wasted little time in getting to the point: "I want to ask you something. That day I escorted Deputy Director Cui and his family to the train station, where exactly were you, and why were you avoiding me? Were you waiting for me to depart before arresting my uncle?"

Deputy Chief Shan was stunned by the question and its directness.

Fang Mengwei continued: "Was it Xu Tieying who gave you the order, or was it Secretary Sun here who relayed it?"

"Chief Fang..."

"Be honest. I'm not out for you... yet."

But Deputy Shan was unwilling to open his mouth. He looked at Secretary Sun, who, in turn, looked back at him, hoping, it seemed, for Shan to say something. Perhaps anything.

Finally, Sun answered Fang's question: "It was me. I relayed the instructions."

Fang Mengwei, his eyes still on Deputy Shan, spoke matter-of-factly: "My questions are done. You may step out."

Deputy Shan turned to go, but as he did he noticed the men who'd brought him still standing in the doorway, essentially blocking his exit. His eyes betrayed the look of a traitor, while his voice was bitter as he cursed at them: "Does it make you laugh to see your boss brought down? You've all been treated well by this place. How's it that you've let the dogs have your hearts! You bastards still won't get out of the way!"

"I didn't actually say you could leave. I want you to stay at the door. You're all to be my future witnesses."

"Sir, yes sir!" the men answered quickly, uniformly. It was difficult to know why they seemed to harbour such ill intentions. Deputy Shan was at a loss, forced to acquiesce and stay where he was.

There were four tables in the conference room, positioned to make a square with space in the middle. Fang Mengwei walked further inside, pushing aside chairs and one of the tables with his foot. He was still holding Sun Chaozhong's arm behind his back, and together they walked into the middle. Fang then turned and again shifted the table with his foot, this time back to its original place.

At the door, Deputy Shan's eyes grew wide as he watched. So did the eyes of the other soldiers standing just behind him.

Finally, Fang Mengwei released Sun's arm. His right hand returned to his pocket and he stared at Secretary Sun. "Examining your file, I've seen that we both trained as part of the Three Principles of the People Youth League. We also received certain specialised advanced studies, notably with regard to the capture and interrogation of enemy agents and traitors. Your right hand has been wounded, but I won't use that to my advantage. We'll fight using a single hand each. If you win, I won't ask you another question. If you lose, you'll answer every question I ask." The rules in place, Fang Mengwei shouted to the men at the door: "Tell me, does this all sound fair to you lads?"

"Fai…" Deputy Shan shot them a look that caused their voices to die in mid-air.

Sun Chaozhong spoke into their silence: "It's true. We've received the same training, but a subordinate can't strike a superior. You can hit me, Deputy Chief Fang, but I cannot raise a hand to you."

Fang Mengwei flung off his cap and tore off the rank insignia on his shoulders. "Now I'm not your superior. I'm just me, Fang Mengwei, and I've come to settle accounts with you. First, how the hell did you secretly order Deputy Shan to arrest my uncle, and then how did you get Ma Hanshan to murder him? Second, where the hell is my cousin, where's Mulan? I'm giving you the opportunity to pay up. You can do that by beating me. If you choose not to settle, then I'm going to poke out your eyes, one for each account. And make damn sure you never murder anyone else again!"

As his words fell, Fang Mengwei lurched forward, his fingers driving straight for Sun Chaozhong's left eye.

Sun reacted instinctively, twisting his head and using his uninjured left hand to parry the blow.

At the door, Deputy Shan flinched and stumbled violently backwards as though Fang's hand had struck his own eye. If not for the two guards behind, he would have crumpled to the floor. As it was, they grabbed him, perhaps a little too forcefully, and prevented him from falling. Shan whispered to both of them: "Quickly, call for help!"

"You're not to call anyone!" Fang Mengwei's voice rang loudly in their ears, even as his hand grappled, deflected, struck and evaded Sun Chaozhong's.

The sounds of their battle filtered out through the door, reaching the ears of Xu Tieying in his office. Cheng Xiaoyun heard them, too. Xu cocked his ear to hear better, then turned to Xiaoyun. "Is that how the Fang family household indulges its children?"

"It's not indulgence. It's how we've taught them to bear what life throws at them."

"To bear? Bear what?"

"Pain and hope. We bear it with them."

"Are you trying to preach to me? Madam Fang, you're not in some missionary school now. This isn't St John's University. Nor do they have such a class in St John's, do they Madam Fang?"

"Let me say this. I'm here with Fang Mengwei to bear the pain together. You're smart enough to figure this out, Chief Xu. You understand, I didn't just come here with him today. That gun, just now, you can't hide away from it by pretending to make tea."

"Do you and your family plan on raising the stakes, is that it?" Cheng Xiaoyun's words had hit their mark, noticeably wounding Xu Tieying.

"That all depends on whether you're willing to confess, to show remorse for what you've done."

Xu Tieying finally lost control and rose to his feet. "This is the party-state! Don't go peddling that remorse crap with me! I'll tell you this, you either go get Fang Mengwei and leave, or you wait for me to arrest him!"

Cheng Xiaoyun shouted back: "You forget I'm right here, which means you won't be arresting him!"

Xu Tieying marched towards the door. Just as he reached it, he heard a loud thud. He didn't see what had happened, but he knew one of the battling men had crashed violently onto the floor.

Xu paused and turned to look at Cheng Xiaoyun. "Madam Fang, you're not worried it's your poor Fang Mengwei who's been thrown to the floor are you?"

"Chief Xu, you still don't understand, do you? It's you that's on the floor."

Just as Xu Tieying opened the door, a hand shot forward and grabbed hold of his collar. It was Fang Mengwei.

"Wha... what the devil are you..." The hand squeezed tighter and Xu was unable to utter a sound. All he could do was let himself be dragged out of his own office.

———

Secretary Sun was slumped against the wall in the conference room, his injuries unknown. Fang Mengwei stormed in seconds later, hauling Xu Tieying along with him. Although his throat was being held tightly, preventing him from saying anything, he was able to size up the situation. For Xu Tieying this was rather important, for it allowed him to see Deputy Shan and the other soldiers standing, surprisingly, at the door, even if none of them was moving.

Sensing what Xu had in mind, Fang Mengwei leaned close. "I suppose you're imagining calling for them to arrest me." Fang released his hold on Xu's throat. "Go ahead, give the order."

His ability to speak now restored, Xu Tieying turned to Deputy Shan. "What? Do I really need to call for investigators to tell you what's going on?"

Deputy Shan's face was weighed down with bitterness. None of the men behind him said a word, and nor did they acknowledge Xu Tieying's supposed command.

As he looked at them with growing rage, however, two additional figures standing a little further back became clear. One was Zeng Keda, the other was Fang Buting. Xu had never felt such humiliation before. He'd been dragged into the conference room as if he were no better than some mangy beast, and these men had seen it. Xu Tieying fumed. His embarrassment, at least to his mind, was complete, for neither man thought the scene they'd witnessed was even worth a smile.

Zeng Keda's face was cold, like hardened steel. His eyes focused on the window on the far side of the conference room. Fang Buting's attention lay with Xu's office and the person still inside. Cheng Xiaoyun was standing in the doorway, her eyes trained on Fang Buting.

"I've come here today to settle things, once and for all. Do not hope that someone will intervene and save you the embarrassment!" Fang Mengwei tightened his grip on Xu's collar once more. "Where is my cousin? Where's Mulan? Either you tell me, or I'll make sure your secretary does!"

Sun Chaozhong's voice was eerily calm. "The Intelligence Bureau has the report. You can go and ask Wang Puchen for the specifics."

"Don't push this off onto someone else, dammit!" Fang Mengwei directed his entire focus onto Secretary Sun. "When I went to get my cousin, to see that she was safe, I found you… you had the guarantee in your hand. Who knows more about what's happened than you? You're the one I wanted in the first place. At the same time, I know that if Xu Tieying didn't give you the order, then you wouldn't have the balls to do anything… which also means my cousin wouldn't be missing. And what… now you want me to go and find Wang Puchen?"

Sun Chaozhong laughed bitterly. "Do you really want to know who gave the order?"

All eyes fell on Sun.

Sun continued: "Then I suggest you ask Nanking."

"Ask Nanking!" cried Zeng Keda, who now strode into the

conference room to stand in front of Fang Mengwei. "Release him. Let's not lose your head."

To perhaps everyone's surprise, Fang Mengwei followed Zeng Keda's advice.

Zeng now turned and looked at Cheng Xiaoyun. "Madam, Deputy Fang and I must discuss matters related to Mulan's disappearance. Would you be so kind as to accompany Mr Fang home?"

Cheng Xiaoyun walked towards the door, but before exiting she paused. "Mengwei!"

Fang Mengwei's eyes never left her, but when she tossed him his pistol, his eyes purposefully followed it into his hand.

"Return the gun to the Ministry of Defence, find Mulan, and then the two of you are off to France." Cheng Xiaoyun's voice was matter-of-fact.

A billowy glaze drifted over Fang Mengwei's face.

Deputy Shan and the other men at the door stepped aside as Cheng Xiaoyun approached them. Seconds later, she was next to Fang Buting and both were leaving.

When Young Li saw both Fang Buting and Cheng Xiaoyun exit the building, he flashed the lights of the car and drove over to greet them. The pair stood on the steps waiting, hands clasped tightly. Neither said a word; they only looked towards the eastern sky. It was near the end of the seventh month of the lunar calendar, and the moon was high in the sky, half of it visible. The grounds of the police station were quiet and still. Indeed, it seemed as though the entire city had chosen not to make a sound.

"Do you think Vice-Chancellor He can try to work things out?" Cheng Xiaoyun's voice was timid, hesitant.

"Let's go home. The campus doctor will have a look at me, and you'll see there's nothing wrong."

"It's come to me already, you know. If he can do... something... perhaps we can take a walk to go and see him."

"We can also walk home."

"You're... you're not angry with me?"

"A stepmother who takes her stepson to cause trouble with the police? My dear, you're a Fang if ever there was one."

"Then let's walk home." Still holding his hand, Cheng Xiaoyun guided him down the steps. "Go slow. We'll give Uncle some more time."

"Yes, that sounds best." Fang Buting appreciated Cheng Xiaoyun's ability to think of others and to understand what was best for them. "My younger sister's husband is much stronger than I… he's never cried in front of anyone…"

"You don't need to get out of the car," Cheng Xiaoyun shouted to Li. "Stay here and wait for the younger master. We're going to walk."

"Ma'am, take care on the road home." Li remained in the car, his eyes watching as the two of them walked away from the police station. For some unknown reason, he cried.

Chief Shan and the men standing next to him had been called into the conference room and were now standing in a row against the wall. Xu Tieying, Zeng Keda and Fang Mengwei were still standing inside the rectangularly arranged tables. Sun Chaozhong was slumped against the wall.

"Repeat once more what you've just said," said Zeng, without any emotion in his voice. "Chief Shan, go ahead."

"Yes sir. The official date, thirty-seventh year of the Republic, twelfth of August, evening. Chief Xu Tieying convened a meeting involving Deputy Chief Fang Mengwei and Secretary Sun Chaozhong. Matters related to the release of student detainees, and the subsequent aftermath, were discussed. Report filed by Shan Fuming."

Zeng Keda squinted at Xu Tieying. "Chief Xu, any objections?"

Xu was disinclined to meet Zeng Keda's stare. There was a gloom that hung over his face, and all he wished to look at was the blackness outside the window.

Zeng turned to Shan Fuming once more. "Go and make the official record. Whosoever says anything to conflict with the official log will wind up in Xishan prison, I guarantee that now!"

"Sir, yes sir."

The guards who had been lined up alongside Chief Shan now exited the room.

Chief Shan remained where he was, and looked at Xu Tieying. "Sir… do… ah… that is, are there any instructions, sir?"

Xu finally took his eyes off the window. "You're following the inspector's orders now, aren't you? Why ask me?"

"Chief…"

"Go on, get out of my sight!"

Turning on his heel, anger in his face, Shan Fuming left without another word.

Zeng now focused on Fang Mengwei. "Deputy Fang, I must speak alone with Chief Xu. I represent Nanking in these matters and will subsequently inform the Fang family. It goes without saying that what has just transpired between you, a deputy chief, and your superior, cannot happen again. Men might not care for their reputation, but the party-state certainly does."

Fang Mengwei had never seen Zeng Keda act with such assertiveness, such righteousness. His reply was noticeably subdued: "May I be permitted to ask this… person… further questions?"

Zeng Keda's eyes narrowed and he looked in the direction of Secretary Sun. "There's no need. You'll get nothing useful out of him."

Xu Tieying shot a glance towards Sun Chaozhong, but only saw his closed eyes, his face expressionless. A sense of loss welled up in Xu Tieying. Could it be, he thought, that Zeng Keda is unaware of Sun Chaozhong's affiliation? Is he in the dark about Sun being a member of the Iron and Blood Congress? If that was the case, Xu's train of thought continued, then the strictness by which the faction operates is even more terrifying than he imagined. Xu began to worry that perhaps the National Communication Bureau was really his true adversary and that perhaps he was the first person to be brought down by them.

Zeng Keda woke him from his meditations. "Chief Xu, let's go into your office to speak more."

This time, Xu seemed to understand the true extent of Zeng Keda's pitiable nature. "Yes, let's talk." Xu said nothing further but walked towards his office.

Zeng turned to Fang Mengwei once more. "Go home. Keep your father company. You don't want to make him more worried than he already is." Zeng followed Xu Tieying out of the room.

A feeling of calm seemed to wash over Fang Mengwei and he

turned to face Sun Chaozhong, whose body was still bent against the wall. Fang extended a hand. "Get up."

Sun did not accept the proffered hand. He stood up on his own and looked very much like someone who wished desperately not to be hurt again.

A look flashed across Fang Mengwei's face. "You're letting me go first, are you?" "Inspector Zeng's correct, there's no point in setting yourself against me. It's not worth it."

The door to Xu Tieying's office was pushed closed from the inside. Zeng strode into the office and sat down. Xu Tieying did the same. They had a shared experience of working together in Nanking, which had carried over to Peking, but now they were pitted against each other in what seemed to be close-quarters combat. Neither man spoke. They just sat, appearing to size each other up, deciding upon how to attack. Xu Tieying discovered that Zeng Keda's eyes were more trained on the clock on the wall than on him, but he couldn't let Zeng in on this. He had to force himself not to follow the other man's line of sight. The short hand of the clock was on nine, the long hand on thirty.

The telephone started to ring, the direct line to Nanking. Zeng spoke first: "That's Chief Ye calling, for sure. Say what you must. There's no need for me to excuse myself. Go on, answer it."

Xu Tieying stood up and adjusted his jacket. He walked over to the table and picked up the receiver. "Chief Ye... hello. Xu Tieying speaking."

The voice on the other end was exceedingly polite, cultured, but barely audible beyond the receiver. "What I'm saying to you now is in code of the highest level. Understand?"

"Yes," Xu Tieying replied without saying anything more. He knew he needed to listen. Voicing his own opinion or concerns to the person on the phone was out of the question. Nothing other than "yes" or "no" would be accepted.

Ye Xiufeng continued: "In a moment, someone else will be speaking to you, but you mustn't let Zeng Keda know this. Refer to him with my title, Chief Ye, understood?"

"Yes, Chief Ye."

The line went silent for a moment, and then another voice spoke. "Director Xu, this is Chiang Ching-kuo."

At the sound of this voice, Xu Tieying's training came in hand for he was able to maintain the same expression on his face, despite his astonishment at who was addressing him. "Yes, Chief Ye."

Chiang Ching-kuo continued: "Your department has drafted a list of individuals closest to me. It contains those considered to be assets, as well as those considered to be threats. I gather you're all greatly concerned about my well-being…"

"Yes… Chief Ye."

"I asked your Chief Ye here if you were the one who compiled the list, if it was Chen Jicheng who gave you the names in the first place, if you then handed it to the director-general who in turn passed it on to me. I'd like to give you some additional information about this list, some info for your department as well. Would that be all right?"

"Yes, Chief Ye."

"There is only one party for the Republic, one government, one leader. All of its departments, offices and ministries, yours included, they belong to this party, this government, this leader. There are no single individuals who are assets for me, nor individuals who are threats. I trust that there'll be no such lists like this in the future, yes, nor that such lists will be used. And I can't stress this enough, to pursue vendettas against other members of this party, this government, for instance, say, against Comrade Liang Jinglun, or, say, against those men close to you like Comrade Sun Chaozhong… do I make myself clear?"

"Yes."

"Now, let's speak about Xie Mulan. This matter has already caused great difficulties for the things we've planned. Your Chief Ye has already accepted his responsibility for what's happened, and he's vowed to provide a self-criticism to the chairman of the party. The key is what happens next. Those who know the truth, that is, you, Wang Puchen, Sun Chaozhong and Liang Jinglun, you just all be on the same page, yes. The story must be the same. Now I know that Zeng Keda is there along with you. Once we're finished on the phone, you must explain to him that because Xie Mulan's continued presence in Peking would prove troublesome for the work Liang Jinglun and Fang Meng'ao must complete, namely the implementation of the currency reforms, it was necessary to arrange her transportation into the so-called 'liberated zones'. Tell him Chief Ye formulated the idea, with my total agreement."

"Yes."

"Finally, there's one more thing I need to say, and I want to say this in front of Chief Ye, one last bit of information you must hear. I don't want anything like what happened today to happen again. You're not to disrupt the Ministry of Defence's work in any way, nor try to thwart the plans for currency reform. Understood?"

"Yes." Xu had barely made the promise when he heard the receiver on the other end click. But it didn't stop him from finishing: "...Chief Ye."

Xu Tieying hung up the phone and turned his attention to Zeng Keda. Before speaking, however, he walked over to the table and prepared some tea. Once ready, he carried the cup over to Zeng and with two hands placed it on the tea table in front of the sofa. "Inspector Zeng, may I ask for your opinion on something?"

"Of course."

"In Peking, whatever happens, whatever transpires, all of it ends up at my doorstep, you would agree, but it's not worth palming these things off to Chief Ye, is it?"

"Have I ever made a direct telephone call to your Chief Ye?"

Xu Tieying smiled and looked at the clock on the wall. "My, it's nearly ten o'clock. Let's talk about Xie Mulan."

Fang Meng'ao stood in the doorway to the sitting room, his eyes focused on his wristwatch. The desk clock not far away chimed, once, twice, three times. In rhythm with the clock, Fang Meng'ao walked towards the stairs to the right. When he arrived at the door to Xie Mulan's room, he whispered the word "uncle". He couldn't, he wouldn't push the door open. He could hear noise from inside and knew it was Xie Peidong. His uncle, however, didn't answer. Fang Meng'ao leaned against the wall, silent, waiting. Finally, the door opened and Xie Peidong walked out. He closed the door behind him and heard Fang Meng'ao address him once more.

Xie Peidong's answer was quick: "Let's go and sit amid the

bamboo for a while." Xie never looked at him. He simply carried on and made his way down to the ground floor.

Xie was sitting alone on the stone stool. Fang Meng'ao stood beside him. Xie spoke first: "Mengwei and your stepmum paid a visit to Xu Tieying. Your father and Zeng Keda went after them. They know Mulan won't be returning, but still they went for… answers… went to find out where she was."

"Which liberated zone has she gone to? Have you heard any news?"

Xie Peidong turned towards Fang Meng'ao. "There are many students heading to the liberated zones daily. If it isn't the party arranging this, then surely they're all being investigated and screened. Mulan's my daughter. If there was news, I'm sure to be the first person they tell."

Fang Meng'ao stared intently at his uncle. "I don't know. Right now, should I call you 'Uncle' or should I refer to you as my superior?"

"It doesn't matter how you refer to me. Anything and everything is all right."

"Whatever I call you, will you tell me the truth?"

Xie Peidong did his best to remain calm. "Of course I will."

"Then tell me, has Mulan really gone to one of the liberated zones?" Fang Meng'ao's stare was unrelenting.

"I already told you, told everyone, Zeng Keda and Wang Puchen didn't appear to be lying."

"Then it's you that's lying."

"And why would I be doing that?" Xie's voice had taken on a severe tone.

"Because you have to, I should think. Before Uncle Cui died he too swore he wasn't a Communist, but it was the two of you who groomed me. Tell me, it was all to get your hands on several aeroplanes, wasn't it? You met with members of the labour union this evening. What did they say?"

"These questions, they're because Young Li returned in the car before me… because I arrived later?"

"Can you just answer me?"

Xie rose slowly. "Let's both go and speak to them directly." With those words, he walked out of the bamboo grove.

For a man who feared very little, Fang Meng'ao was alarmed by the scene now in front of him. From behind the wallboards in his father's office, Xie Peidong had pulled out a small radio and was now sitting at his father's desk, in his father's swivel chair! At the same moment, he realised the door behind him was still open and thought it best to close it. Before he could do so, however, Xie called out.

"Leave it open," said Xie, holding on to the radio earpiece. "This radio is used to communicate between the Central Banks' Peking branch and its HQ in Nanking. When it comes to the issue of me lying, well, I guess you should say I've duped your father, too." Xie began to fiddle with the radio knobs and dials. It was clear to Fang Meng'ao that this was not the first time he'd used the machine. Staring at the man who was his uncle, Fang could not help but feel he was both someone he knew well and someone who was a complete stranger.

Suddenly, Xie's hands stopped. It was evident he'd successfully located the intended radio channel and now he waited for a response. As he did so, his eyes drifted once more to the hole behind the wallboards. His back remained to the wide-open door. He was calm, at ease.

Fang Meng'ao was entranced by the figure his uncle cut. Quietly, however, he turned and moved softly to shut the door to his father's office. When he turned back towards his uncle, he saw him busily copying down the message he was receiving, his hand transcribing the information with a speed only possible by means of repeated practice.

Although the radio receiver was looped over his uncle's head, Fang Meng'ao felt as though he could hear the clicks of whatever code they were using being relayed. He remained standing near the now closed door, transfixed by what he was seeing.

Finally, Xie Peidong put down the pen and removed the headphones. Seconds later, he had returned the radio to its hiding place and replaced the wallboards over it. He spun around in the swivel chair and placed the coded transmission on the desk in front of him.

"Come see." Xie did not look up but rather began to decipher the message.

Fang Meng'ao refrained from moving closer. He watched as his uncle decoded the transmission. He was mesmerised by the scene.

His uncle's hand stopped, but still, Fang Meng'ao remained where he was, focused on his uncle's reaction to the message sent. Xie Peidong kept his head low. At that very moment, just as he put the pen down and looked at the words on the page, Liuyun appeared behind him. "Mr Xie," said Liuyun. "You cannot, under any circumstances, allow Fang Meng'ao to learn the truth, the importance of this fact you yourself know better than I…"

At last, Xie lifted his face. There was a slight smile on his lips, but his eyes were moist. He looked at Fang Meng'ao and pushed the paper over towards him. Fang walked closer, his eyes bright and focused on the transmission his uncle had decoded.

On top of the page was the original checked pattern, four lines in total. Below, Xie had written his translation:

Ten thousand miles she rode to war, crossing mountain passes as though on the wings of a bird. Do not read. Follow the peacock flying southeast!

The first line was from the *Ballad of Mulan*. He knew it immediately, he'd learned the poem as a boy and could still recite it word for word. He used it, too, to amuse his cousin. The reason for such a message, he thought, was obvious: it was telling him that Mulan had escaped to the liberated zones. Still, Fang was puzzled. The vagueness of the message was so concise that he wondered whether it was truly sent by the labour union or had his uncle simply made the whole thing up?

Fang Meng'ao stared at the message for what seemed like ages, until finally he picked it up and looked towards his uncle. "This is wrong, Uncle. Please tell me, what does 'four-six-eight-one' mean?"

"It's code for 'small bird'." Xie Peidong stood but refused to meet his stare. Instead, he turned and walked towards the balcony, halting just in front of the French doors.

Fang Meng'ao gazed at his uncle's back, the paper still in his hand, his mind racing. Should he pursue the issue? Should he ask more questions? Challenge his uncle?

All of a sudden, there was movement in the courtyard below. Someone had opened the main gate.

Fang Meng'ao kept his eyes trained on his uncle's back, watching for any reaction. "Are Dad and my stepmother back?"

"Yes," Xie Peidong responded, but he didn't turn around. "Do you wish to show them the decoded message?"

As though in a trance, Fang Meng'ao reached into his pocket and pulled out his lighter. Seconds later the page was no more and he was walking towards the door. As he opened it, a light breeze greeted him. He couldn't help but feel how fitting the breeze was as it seemed to carry away his questions, just as it lifted the ashes of the paper and carried them out through the French doors. Fang Meng'ao didn't dare to turn around to look at his uncle. He left his father's office and walked down the stairs to greet them.

"Meng'ao is home?" It was only fitting that Cheng Xiaoyun's question would be greeted by Fang Meng'ao's enquiring look when she opened the door to the sitting room. Coming down the steps just behind him, she also saw Xie Peidong and immediately resumed her role as madam of the house. "You've not eaten yet, have you? I'll go and warm something up."

"Auntie." Fang Meng'ao's voice caused her to halt, but his gaze switched towards his father. "Dad, do you know it's been more than ten years since I've eaten the bread you used to cook for us? Would you mind making some today?"

Fang Buting was surprised by his son's request, and unable to respond.

"Don't you think Auntie Cheng's been put through enough today... spending that time at the police station, making enquiries into Mulan's whereabouts, dealing with Xu Tieying. Surely it's been a trying day for her, yes?"

Cheng Xiaoyun was stunned into silence by his words.

Fang Buting turned to his wife. "Meng'ao is certainly effusive in his praise for you. It's been more than ten years, that's true. I should do as he says. I think I'll prepare the food for tonight." He didn't wait for her response but walked into the kitchen.

Cheng Xiaoyun made to follow him but Fang Meng'ao halted once more. "No, you don't need to, Auntie."

She turned to look at him. "But he doesn't know where everything is... nor where it goes."

"I would disagree with that assessment," Fang Buting shot back playfully as he disappeared into the kitchen.

Xie Peidong had descended the stairs and was now standing next to them. He offered no input in the conversation.

"Auntie, making dinner, making music… I'm nowhere near as good as Dad. But I'd like to play something for you if that's all right. Would you let me?"

Cheng Xiaoyun glanced at Xie Peidong. His face was absent of any significant reaction. She smile and looked at her stepson. "I should like that a great deal, yes."

Fang Meng'ao seated himself in front of the piano and lifted the cover. "Auntie, you must have learnt *Ave Maria* while at St John's. Tell me, was it Charles Gounod's version?"

"Yes, it was. But the Chinese translation didn't really match the original."

"That doesn't matter. I'll try. Shall we sing together?" His fingers fell on the keys before he had finished speaking.

Cheng Xiaoyun was surprised as the music emanated from the piano. Fang Meng'ao seemed so much like his father! The first note sounded, then the second and third, and Fang Meng'ao no longer resembled his father. Fang Buting played like a spring breeze, or a stream of running water, gentle, soft. His son, however, played like a rushing river, powerful and vast. She couldn't contend with such thoughts. The prelude was over and she had to sing:

Dear Lord, you suffered for our sins

Her voice was distinctly nervous on the first syllable, but with the second it grew clearer and passion showed through. Fang Meng'ao was moved. Xie Peidong, focused on the darkness of the night beyond the window, seemed to be similarly affected. Fang Meng'ao joined her in song. Then, from some unknown place, the sound of a violin echoed in chorus with them:

You bore chains for us
   Dear Lord, you carried our burden and pain

In the kitchen, Fang Buting trembled, his eyes staring blankly out the window as though he were mesmerised by the garden beyond. On this day, he thought, all heaven and Earth had conspired to cause man to cry, whether by song or music, or both:

In front of your altar, dear Virgin Mary, we kneel

Tears began to roll down Fang Buting's face and he shuddered even more than before. Then, out in the courtyard, he saw the solitary figure of Xie Peidong.

With your gentle hands

The words and the music accompanied Xie Peidong into the bamboo grove.

Dear Lord, please wipe our tears dry

Fang Buting closed his eyes, but it didn't stop the tears from falling.

When we are faced with our greatest suffering

The singing stopped abruptly, as did the sound of the piano. Fang Buting kept his tear-filled eyes closed.

Fang Meng'ao rose slowly to his feet, unable to conceal the tears in his eyes. He looked at Cheng Xiaoyun. Her face was even wetter, so she tried to avoid his stare and instead gazed towards the door. Fang Meng'ao followed her line of sight, unaware of just when exactly the door to the sitting room had been opened. He glanced towards the stairs. His uncle was gone. Without hesitating further, Fang Meng'ao bounded towards the door.

"Meng'ao!" Her shout died on the air. But it was enough to cause him to stop. Cheng Xiaoyun walked up close to stand behind him. "Tell me, do you know whether or not something else entirely has befallen Mulan?"

"Nothing else." Fang Meng'ao turned around, his tone soft. "Auntie Cheng, Mulan's gone to the liberated zones. It's where she should be. As for Uncle Xie and my father, they're both old and frail, they rely on you. Especially now." Fang Meng'ao left the room.

"But your father's making bread for you, just as you asked. Where are you going?"

"Tell him thanks, but I've no time. I need to see Uncle He." And with that, he disappeared into the night.

———

He Qicang was sitting alone in his office, his eyes closed, an empty IV bottle on his desk. He Xiaoyu skilfully removed the needle from her father's arm and used a cotton swab to press down on the small dab of blood that had formed on his skin. Liang Jinglun walked over and took hold of the pole that was used to hang the IV while it drained into the needle tube. He grabbed the IV and began to walk out of the room.

"Give that to Xiaoyu." He Qicang's voice was weak, tired.

Liang Jinglun stood at the door but turned to look back at the older man.

He Qicang now directed his eyes to his daughter. "Go downstairs. There's some rice. Make me a bowl of congee, will you."

"Eh, yes." Xiaoyu lifted the cotton swab and gave it to her father. She strode over to the door and took the empty IV container from Liang Jinglun, then left and headed towards the kitchen.

"Close the door." He Qicang's voice seemed somewhat stronger.

Liang Jinglun asked himself whether he should comply, and then closed the door softly. As he had done so many times before, he picked up the stool and placed it in front of the chair He Qicang was reclined in. But he didn't sit, at least not right away. He had to wait, first, for He Qicang to offer it to him.

"It's too close. Move the stool a little farther away."

Liang Jinglun was surprised by the older man's words and paused. He looked at the vice-chancellor and was even more surprised for He Qicang was focused on the window and the scene outside. The stool was rather heavy, and he was disinclined to move it again, but then felt he really didn't have much of a choice. He shifted it to about a metre away and then heard the old man speak again: "Right there is fine."

When he sat down, Liang Jinglun couldn't escape the feeling that he was sitting rather far away.

"You're what, thirty-three years old?"

"That's right, sir."

He Qicang now looked at him and observed: "This past year, especially the last month or so, your hair's gone quite white. You've noticed, haven't you?"

"Yes, I have."

"Heh… have a look at my own. It's all white isn't it?"

"It is, sir."

He Qicang sat upright. "Let me ask you about an idiom, the one about hair going white. You know it, yes?"

Liang Jinglun trembled. "Mr…"

"Answer me!"

"Vice-Chancellor, there are things I haven't told you, that's true. But now you've asked, I can tell you everything if…"

"Everything?"

"Yes. Did you know I never knew my father, never had a brother, either? But later on, I found a father… you. I also found a man kind enough, concerned enough to be a brother to me."

He Qicang narrowed his eyes and stared at him.

"This man… was Chiang Ching-kuo."

"You're… you're one of his men?"

Liang Jinglun was stumped. How could he answer this question? A moment passed, then another. Finally, he nodded.

"And you're a Communist, too?"

This time Liang Jinglun shook his head.

"Answer me fully. I need to hear you say it."

"I'm not."

"Then why is it that each and every student protest has something to do with you? Why have the Kuomintang wanted to arrest you… more than once, I'll add?"

"Because I attended the student federation meetings. You know this, the federation was first organised by both students and teachers… from all of Peking's universities."

He Qicang had a few further questions, but by the time they were answered, he believed Liang Jinglun and his tone had become markedly softer. "Move your stool a little closer." Liang Jinglun picked up the stool, placing it alongside He Qicang's chair. But he kept his head slightly low, choosing not to look fully into the other man's eyes. He Qicang continued: "When did you first come to know Chiang Ching-kuo?"

"Not long after graduating high school."

"So before you met me?"

"The War of Resistance had just begun, I went to enlist. Apparently, he'd read something I wrote, an essay on rebuilding the economy after the war. That's when we met, and we talked. For a long time, he told me not to enlist, not to go to the frontlines, but to sit the exam to get into Yenching University. Mr Weng Wenhao wrote you that reference for me, the one you read, but it was Chiang Ching-kuo who asked him to write it."

He Qicang remained silent, digesting what Liang Jinglun was telling him. Finally, he spoke: "Later, when you went to Harvard, he helped, didn't he?"

"Yes. He wrote me a reference letter. And more. At that time, getting to Hong Kong and then on to America wasn't the easiest thing to do… it still isn't… but it was Chiang Ching-kuo who made the arrangements for me."

"What's that idiom, the kindness of recognising someone's worth and seeing they're rewarded for it?"

"Although Chiang Ching-kuo listens to his father on all matters, he is, however, in great disagreement with him over the involvement of the Soong and Kung families in the Republic's economy. He believes that if their monopolies are not reformed, if they're allowed to control and dominate the country's finances, then the Republic of China will never be a true, modern nation-state. In order to bring about this needed change, Mr Ching-kuo knows you need real economic scholars and specialists who can push through the necessary reforms."

"These scholars, specialists, do they really exist?"

"In his mind, Mr He, you're one of the men he needs."

"So this is why, once you received your PhD in the US, you were called back to teach at Yenching, to be my assistant… all to advance his economic reform agenda!"

"He knows it was TV Soong who did what he could to impede these reforms… that he's the man primarily responsible for the financial chaos the country is in. That's why he accused him of official misconduct and tried to have him removed, then the historian Fu Ssu-nien made an appearance. But the really monkey wrench in the works were the articles you and several other scholars published in those American journals..."

He Qicang's eyes flickered and he looked over at the window, trying to gather his thoughts. Liang Jinglun held his breath and waited patiently. "I've one more thing to ask you," said He Qicang, "and I need an honest answer."

Liang Jinglun did not say anything. He simply nodded as though he knew already the question He Qicang was going to ask him.

"Mulan's situation, her release, this was all arranged by Chiang Ching-kuo, yes?" Liang Jinglun remained silent, a look of desolation on his face. He Qicang continued: "Because of you, or because of Fang Meng'ao?"

"Because of me. Mulan... she wouldn't let go of her belief that I was a Communist."

He Qicang sighed long and hard. "You won't dare to love Xiaoyu, nor to love Mulan. Is your whole life to be given over to Chiang Ching-kuo?"

"I haven't given myself to anyone." This was the first time he'd ever contradicted something Vice-Chancellor He had said. "You know this, sir, those of us who studied overseas and then returned, we didn't do it for ourselves, nor did we do it for some political or government party."

Liang Jinglun could see clearly that his heartfelt words had touched upon He Qicang's own strong emotions.

"You're right." He Qicang slowly shifted his body in the chair and reclined once again. "You know the American government bound generations of us to them through the Boxer Indemnity... bound us up and threw us into the back of their car. From the last years of the Qing through to the Republic and up until now, we've had to rely on them more and more. Our returned students, those who studied in the US, now they're the supposed elite of the country, but they're only tools used to further our reliance on the Americans. Ah, why did the government name me an economic consultant for the country? Why did Chiang Ching-kuo go through so much trouble to place you by my side? They think little of my importance, think little of yours, too. It's my relationship with Ambassador Stuart and his American backers, that's what's important to them. Without American assistance, this government of ours won't last much longer. They shouted about currency reform for far too long now, so why hasn't even the Central Bank gone ahead and printed new notes? They all reference the two billion in bonds offered by the US in 1945. It's why they've kept at you to keep pressuring me to write up the proposal for currency reform... and to give it to Ambassador Stuart, this is how they thought they could win over American support for the plan, which would also allow the US to honour its wartime pledge to compensate China for its losses... to agree to use the two billion in bonds as the new currency. But then the Civil War happened, and the corruption... endemic, systematic. All that the Americans have agreed to is the issuing of the bonds, but there's no cash to support them. And to add to the mess, the two billion in bonds is far and away from what's needed to maintain market liquidity. The results have been predictable enough. The military has been brought in to help control the economy, the use of gold has been prohibited, silver and foreign currencies, too, all to force everyone in the country to use whatever gold and silver they have to purchase this new currency! And if the flow of goods in the market dries up, then things will get further out of hand, first with the new currency, and if that goes, then all that gold and silver the people gathered up to buy the new money, it'll be no more than waste paper, barely fit for use in the loo. If all of this really comes to pass, then we'll all be the tiger's accomplice, we'll have done nothing to stop the evil deeds of other men! In fact, we'll have actually helped them! Oh, I don't want to think more about this. Would you like to know why I've spent my limited free time over the last few days consulting the *Spring and Autumn Annals*?"

"As Mencius says, 'those who praise me cite the *Spring and Autumn Annals* to do so, those who censure refer to the same!' Such is often the case with books so old and so well known."

He Qicang sat up straight again. "If I'm to be condemned by history, then let it be so! Come on, before the sun rises, help me finish these papers."

"Mr He..."

"Go!"

"Yes sir." Liang Jinglun stood up, teardrops filling the corners of his eyes. He walked over to the desk and the English typewriter that lay on it.

He Qicang continued to stare at the ceiling. The room was soon filled with a slightly colloquial Wu-accented English. Liang Jinglun's fingers fell on the typewriter keys, one after the other. Neat rows of English words and sentences spewed forth, the ink of the machine dark upon the white page. A moment later, the title came into view: "On the relationship between the current currency reform initiative and the signing of the joint US-Sino compensation agreement". Just as he reached for the carriage return bar to jump to the next line, however, a light flashed and swept across the window. Someone seemed to be downstairs. Liang Jinglun paused.

"Is that Meng'ao's car?"

"I believe so."

A second later, they could hear the sound of a jeep pulling up.

"Should we continue?"

"He's come looking for Xiaoyu." He Qicang appeared flustered at this unexpected turn of events. "Yes, let's continue. Finish typing what I just told you and let me have a look at it." He Qicang closed his eyes again, seemingly lost in thought.

"Yes sir." Liang Jinglun' fingers fell heavy on the keys.

———

He Xiaoyu had already opened the door to the sitting room and was quietly waiting for Fang Meng'ao. "Did you speak to Uncle Xie?"

He didn't respond to her question. He only stood in the doorway listening to the sound echoing from upstairs. It was clear someone was at the typewriter. He turned to He Xiaoyu and asked: "How's your father?"

"I gave him an IV, and then he asked me to make him some congee. I imagine the two of them are typing up his report to the committee handling the question of American aid. You haven't answered my question. Did you see Uncle Xie?"

"Can you come with me for a moment? I can't answer you here."

He Xiaoyu lowered her voice, but the tension in it was clear. "At this hour?"

"Go up and tell your dad. You'll be back by twelve o'clock."

"And how am I going to tell him that?"

"Is that Meng'ao?" He Qicang was standing at the top of the landing.

He Xiaoyu started, surprised by her father's voice.

Because the clicking of the keyboard upstairs could still be heard, Fang Meng'ao was similarly surprised. He had no idea when or for how long He Qicang had been standing at the top of the stairs. Embarrassment stained his voice: "Uncle He…"

"You're still all worked up about Mulan?"

"Yes I am, Father," his daughter replied.

"Don't bother with the congee. Turn off the stove and the both of you go." He turned around and walked slowly back into his office.

He Xiaoyu went into the kitchen and turned off the stove. Fang Meng'ao waited in the doorway. He was focused on He Qicang's back as it disappeared beyond the landing of the stairs. He realised again, and perhaps even more strongly than ever before, how old his father's generation had become. They could no longer take care of their children, no longer protect them from the vagaries of this world. Nor could they any longer assume full responsibility for the future of China.

Outside the door that led to the Youth Aviation Brigade barracks, Chen Changwu was standing guard. When he saw his commander's jeep drive up and stop, then saw the man climb down and walk around the front of the vehicle, the moment he thought to walk over and properly greet him, his feet wouldn't obey. All he could do was open his eyes wide at what he saw. His commander opened the passenger side door and gestured to He Xiaoyu inside.

"Why have we come here?" Xiaoyu's question was quick as she scanned the barracks, the gates and Chen Changwu.

His mouth agape, Chen turned his head hurriedly when he realised her eyes had fallen on him. He Xiaoyu then returned her stare to Fang Meng'ao and discovered again the look he'd had on his face earlier in the day in Mulan's room. Her chest tightened. "Tell me what's going on. You didn't say a word on the ride over here."

"Let's go inside. Then we can talk."

There was little else she could do or say, so she climbed down from the jeep.

As they drew near, Chen Changwu could no longer pretend he hadn't noticed them. He saluted. "Commander, Miss He."

He Xiaoyu bowed politely in response.

"The men… they're all asleep?"

"Yes sir, all asleep."

"Get them up. I want them out of bed and in uniform right away."

"Yes sir." Chen Changwu spun around and marched into the barracks to wake the men.

Fang Meng'ao guided He Xiaoyu into the barracks, there to be greeted first by his men.

"Attention!" Chen Changwu had already roused the soldiers, many of whom had by now put on their summer uniforms and were ready for their commander's arrival. Nineteen men, each one decked out in aviator attire, standing erect at the foot of their beds, now saluted. "Greetings, Miss He!" they said in unison.

He Xiaoyu couldn't help but feel somewhat embarrassed at the display.

"Hands down men." Fang Meng'ao looked at the pilots under his command and his eyes softened. "I have news to relay. The students arrested have now all been released." Gratified by the information, the soldiers shouted their acknowledgement. Fang Meng'ao continued: "The probability is high, however, that further action by us will be needed. I'd like you all outside where you're to wait for orders."

"Yes sir!" The troops formed into two lines and marched outside.

The two of them walked into Fang Meng'ao's office. A light from the other side of the window shone into the room, along with the moon that was still high in the night sky. It fell softly over both of them like a gentle water spray, and they sat down without at first saying a word. The barracks they were in once held an entire military garrison, but now the only men still stationed here were Fang's pilots and one security platoon. As a result, the practice fields were open and generally free of men. In the grass that lay beyond, crickets could be heard, the echo of their song reverberating in the evening air.

"'As crickets chirp, one after the other; Mulan stands at the doorway weaving.'" Fang Meng'ao was staring through the window as he cited the first lines of the *Ballad of Mulan*, then he stopped for a moment before speaking again. "Mulan's situation… Uncle Xie made enquiries. He received a telegram response, too."

He Xiaoyu's eyes grew round. "And what did it say?"

"Two lines from the *Ballad of Mulan*." Again he paused.

He Xiaoyu hesitated as well. This was something she had to reflect upon before asking anything further. Finally, a thought flashed in her mind and she questioned Fang Meng'ao excitedly: "Tell me, were these the lines: 'Ten thousand miles she rode to war, crossing mountain passes as though on the wings of a bird'?"

"Yes, but how…"

"Then she's safe, she's gone to the liberated zone!" He Xiaoyu raised herself from the chair abruptly.

Fang Meng'ao had no reaction whatsoever. His eyes remained on the window, a look of dejection covering his face.

He Xiaoyu's complexion slowly changed. "Is there more news?"

"No, nothing. Those were the only two lines." He paused for a second. "You don't think they're… too vague?"

He Xiaoyu thought it over. "Perhaps that's due to necessity. Clandestine communications have to be in code, after all."

Fang Meng'ao shook his head. "But I can't help but feel I'm being kept in the dark by the party, and by Uncle Xie. It's not that I believe they're lying, they wouldn't, but I don't think they're telling me the whole truth."

"Why would they both try to conceal things from you? Do you still think…"

"This has nothing to do with intuition." Fang Meng'ao stood up and walked over to He Xiaoyu. He reached out his hand and took hold of hers. "The telegram, the one Uncle Xie received, it also quoted another poem…"

He Xiaoyu squeezed his hand. "What poem?"

"Another one written during the Northern and Southern dynasties…"

"*The Peacock Flies Southeast?*"

"Yes."

"What line?"

"No line, just a reference to the title."

He Xiaoyu could tell there was something else Fang Meng'ao wanted to tell her, so she steeled her heart and asked: "What does it mean?"

"Promise me, after I tell you, that you'll be able to bear whatever happens."

"I promise."

Fang Meng'ao looked deeply into her eyes and paused before speaking: "The reference to the poem… that poem… about peacocks flying southeast, it refers to a top-secret plan formulated by Chiang Ching-kuo himself." He Xiaoyu's eyes opened wide. Fang Meng'ao watched her reaction, but had more to say: "The two people involved in implementing this plan, both are connected to you." He Xiaoyu held her breath. "One is me. My code name is Jiao Zhongqing."

He Xiaoyu was stunned by the admission and could hold her tongue no longer. "Does Uncle Xie know? Does the party know?"

"Yes, they know. The other person is code-named Liu Lanzhi. The party knows who that is, too, but they've feigned ignorance of the operative's identity. Remember, you just promised me, when I tell you this person's name you have to be ready, have to accept it." His words hung in the air and she seemed to know who it was already. A chill ran down her spine and she shifted a little closer to Fang Meng'ao. He welcomed her into his arms and held her tight. "It's… Liang Jinglun."

Small beads of sweat rested on Liang Jinglun's forehead, despite the fact that both the window and the door to He Qicang's office were open and an evening breeze was blowing through. His fingers moved over the typewriter keys likes waves rolling over a beach. In the reclining chair, He Qicang had been lulled to sleep by the clicking of the keys, a thin blanket shielding him from the draught. The paper spooled out by the machine was covered with lines of English text:

> Severe currency inflation is pushing the turbulent tide of Communism ever further! Systemic corruption is catalysing inflation and exacerbating things! The American government must be called upon to honour its wartime pledge to aid China and push forward the desperately needed currency reforms.

The beads of sweat on his forehead were coagulating and growing denser. His fingers typed faster and faster.

Fang Meng'ao did little to console He Xiaoyu, whose tears had already soaked his chest. "I can't help but think that what's happened to Mulan is all because of Liang Jinglun!"

At these words, however, she stopped crying and grabbed the front of his clothes. "When did you… when did everybody know? And why's the party pretending not to?"

"Who in the party are you talking about? Uncle Cui is already dead, and the only other members of his cell that I know of are you and Uncle Xie."

The cloud of confusion lifted a little and He Xiaoyu slowly released her hand from Fang Meng'ao's grip. "What else did you and Uncle Xie talk about?"

"Nothing, other than that Mulan has gone to the liberated zone. I know it has something to do with the planned currency reforms. The Central Bank, along with the Kuomintang in Nanking, is beginning phase two. There's no way Uncle Xie can combat this on his own, nor can the other operatives in Peking. I know for sure that what's happened with Mulan is connected to Liang Jinglun, and me. It's also clear that it involves the currency reform plans and this so-called 'peacock flying southeast'. I think, right now, anything is possible, anything could happen. But at the same time, there's nothing I can do. I have to keep playing dumb, pretending I know nothing."

Listening to his words, seeing the pain on his face, his sense of helplessness, his self-recrimination... she finally realised, felt, what it meant to be him. Her head on his chest, she marvelled at how so much had happened over the last month, so much jumbled together in a chaotic, topsy-turvy mess:

A speeding jeep rushed up and then suddenly braked, spinning 180° in front of her and Mulan!

Appearing in the sitting room of his father's home holding Mulan across his chest!

Lifting her out of the Yongding River, his eyes the colour of a golden blue sky!

Earlier this morning, standing on the sacks of food aid facing an uncountable number of people, ear-splitting gunshots ringing out...

Too much, far too much... She couldn't think about it all again, didn't want to. She held him tighter. "Tell me, what do wish for me to do?"

Fang Meng'ao reciprocated her embrace. "But will you even listen to..."

She pressed her head even more strongly to his chest. "I will..."

"Then find a reason to get out of Peking, to get away from me and Liang Jinglun. I'll let Uncle Xie know."

He Xiaoyu lifted her head and stared into Fang Meng'ao's eyes. "Where do you want me to go?"

"To the liberated zones, or Hong Kong, anywhere but here. Uncle Xie can get the party to make the arrangements."

"They won't do it. And I can't just leave."

Fang Meng'ao pulled her off his chest and held her by both arms. "In what's to come, I know you'll be in the greatest danger. You understand, don't you?"

"There's more danger for you... and for Uncle Xie. And yet, you're asking me to leave, but you're going to stay?"

"I... I'm a man. We're both men, do you understand?"

"Do you mean to tell me the Communist Party differentiates between men and women?"

Fang Meng'ao released her arms. "For me here, right now, I'll always see men and women as different! I… I have to work with Liang Jinglun from here on. Can you? They've hidden things from me, kept me in the dark. Now it's my turn. This is a battle to the death. How can I ask you to join me in it?"

"If you're here, then so am I. If you don't believe me, then let's go to see Liang Jinglun right now. Do you think I can't? Just watch me!"

Fang Meng'ao felt his blood surge. He could think of nothing to say, so he turned abruptly and walked with great strides towards the door, leaving He Xiaoyu behind.

He Xiaoyu made no effort to follow him. She stood, her mind lost in thought.

―――

A loud, resonant bugle call woke the night. It was Fang Meng'ao. Standing just outside the barracks, his lips pushed the air through the horn, calling the men to assemble. Soon, the sound of running boots could be heard.

The bugle had also called He Xiaoyu out of his office. She stood in stunned silence, her eyes focused on Fang Meng'ao. Again he blew the bugle.

The footsteps stopped. Fang stopped. His men had formed up in front of the barracks, waiting for instructions.

He Xiaoyu hurried over to him, then saw Fang's men, all twenty of them, in neat, tidy array, their eyes all trained on their commander. She moved up behind him. "What are you planning to do?"

"I'm going to Xishan prison, to the police station, to the so-called Northern Command. I'm going to get Mulan. If they don't bring her out, then I'll arrest anyone and everyone I see. Are you going to leave or not?"

He Xiaoyu bit her lip, unable to answer.

Again in military pose, Fang Meng'ao marched off.

Twenty pairs of eyes watched Fang Meng'ao, not one blinking. Over near the barracks gate, the young security troops had also been called out by the bugle. They, too, queued up. Fang Meng'ao stood in front of them, his gaze meeting theirs. He wondered to himself if he really could give the orders.

Then, out of the blue, the men's attention shifted to something... someone behind him. It was He Xiaoyu, who was striding out of the barracks doors, past the men and out of the main gate. Fang Meng'ao was staggered and unable to react. A feeling of desolation buffeted him where he stood.

She was already outside the main gate when she heard the bugle call sound again. While she didn't recognise the sound for what it actually meant, she knew it didn't have the same vigorous energy of the first few blasts. All she felt was the deep sense of anguish it conveyed.

The men dispersed in silence, each of them quietly returning to their barracks and presumably their beds. Chen Changwu was the last to leave the grounds. He stopped when he noticed Fang Meng'ao glued to his spot. "Commander..."

Fang turned towards his subordinate and smiled remorsefully, then handed him the bugle. "It's nothing. To bed, all of you. It's late." He turned and walked to his jeep.

Liang Jinglun allowed himself to look out through the window, but he didn't dare let his fingers stop. They continued to tap, tap, tap at the typewriter keys. He had seen Fang Meng'ao's jeep, but not its lights, for he hadn't turned these on it seemed. Nor did Liang note the speed, for Fang seemed to be driving ever so slowly. Nor did he hear the rumble of its engine, for this appeared to be no more than a gentle hum. Liang kept typing but shifted his gaze to He Qicang who was, rather surprisingly, still napping peacefully in the chair. Liang closed his eyes but continued to type.

Outside his father's home, Fang Meng'ao parked the jeep. On this occasion, He Xiaoyu opened her own door and stepped down. Fang Meng'ao, however, remained seated in front of the steering wheel, not moving a muscle.

Then, all of a sudden, He Xiaoyu appeared at the driver's side. Her hand lifted the lever and pulled his door open. Her voice was low and serious: "You came and fetched me in the first place. Aren't you at least supposed to see me to the door?"

"And what would be the point of that?"

He Xiaoyu glanced up towards her father's office on the first floor. Fang Meng'ao's eyes followed. The light was weak, but the clicking of the typewriter keys continued.

He Xiaoyu looked back at Fang Meng'ao. "Come in and help me say what needs to be said. Help me get my father to agree to my engagement to… Liang Jinglun."

Fang Meng'ao couldn't hide his surprise, but nor could he say anything, for He Xiaoyu had already walked inside. He followed her, leaving the jeep door open and lonely in the night.

The door to He Qicang's office was also wide open. Liang Jinglun was still busy at the typewriter, his fingers running over the keys at a remarkable speed. When he heard their footsteps approach, he lifted his head. He was surprised to see He Xiaoyu already standing in the doorway. They both stared at each other. The cadence of the typewriter keys clicking and clacking resounded about them. Gradually, Liang shifted his gaze to the reclining He Qicang. He Xiaoyu did the same. He was still fast asleep or at least appeared that way. They turned back to each other.

This time, Liang's eyes held a question. He Xiaoyu seemed to know what it was, for her eyes responded in the affirmative. She urged him to get up and come out so they could speak without waking her father. Liang's gaze returned to the keys, his tempo gradually decreasing until he finally stopped. He stood up from the desk and his robes fluttered, lifted by the light breeze.

He Xiaoyu stepped to one side and Liang Jinglun walked out of the office before stopping just beyond the door. He Xiaoyu continued to watch him, scanning his face for… what? She couldn't say. Finally, she strode over to the stairs and down to the ground floor, Liang Jinglun following quietly after.

He Qicang, still reclining in his chair, slowly opened his eyes. It was as though he could see the wind blowing in through the window, swirling about, and then exiting the room.

In the sitting room below, He Xiaoyu's eyes fell on Fang Meng'ao, who had been standing there since they returned. From the way he was standing, from the look on his face, Fang Meng'ao could see that Liang felt empty, as though a great void had claimed his heart.

He Xiaoyu walked over to stand in front of Fang.

He Xiaoyu spoke first: "Meng'ao has tried to find out more about Mulan's situation. He's also got some things he'd like to ask you, Mr Liang. Perhaps it's best you go to Liang's room so that you can speak more openly?" Two pairs of eyes turned towards the stairs. He Xiaoyu continued: "Dad should be up by now. I better make him something to eat, some congee I think." She began to walk towards the kitchen before she'd finished speaking. Seconds later they could hear her getting the stove ready to be lit, first lifting out the honeycomb-shaped coal briquettes and then lighting them. Afterwards, she reached for the pot used for making rice porridge. Then she called to the two men still in the sitting room: "I forgot to mention something, Mr Liang. Meng'ao and I were just out… chatting. He's proposed to me."

Liang Jinglun leaned against the wall of his room and managed a subtle smile. "Congratulations and best wishes are in order." He extended his hand to Fang Meng'ao.

"Congratulations? Best wishes?" Fang did not accept his hand, but instead pulled out a desk chair and sat down. "Best wishes that Mulan isn't here?"

Liang Jinglun strolled over to the desk and sat down as well. "After being arrested and packaged off to Xishan, I was the last one to be released."

"You were last… and what? Mulan was sent off to the liberated zone?"

Liang Jinglun remained silent for a moment and looked towards the window. "Whether or not Mulan's gone to one of the liberated zones, I think it's best to get Inspector Zeng to radio Nanking tomorrow. Perhaps then we might know for sure…"

"Why do you say 'tomorrow'? Why don't we go and speak to him now?"

"Yes, why not now, let's go. I'll come with you. Since we're in this mess, I think you need to tell both Mr He and his daughter that I'm a member of the Iron and Blood Congress… that you and I, that we're working together to implement Chiang Ching-kuo's plans... to see the peacocks fly southeast. I won't deny it."

"It doesn't matter a wit if you're a member of the Iron and Blood Congress. And as for your true identity, whether or when you tell them is your business, not mine. Execute his plans, get the peacocks to fly southeast. I never formally agreed to that. I'm only asking you about Mulan. That's all I want to know. And you're doing what? Trying to involve... implicate... even more people?"

"These people you refer to, they don't include me. My loyalties lie with the Iron and Blood Congress, but they're the ones who come to me. I'm not in a position to do the same... like today. And the people involved, those who know our identities, we were both kept in the dark. I give my approval, but you won't do it. So I guess I won't either."

"You won't support the currency reforms?" Fang Meng'ao's face dripped with anger and surprise. "Then what the hell were you typing all that... that shit for?"

"If you really want to know – I mean really, really – then I'll tell you."

Fang Meng'ao gazed towards the window.

"In 1941, when the Pacific War first erupted and the US entered World War II, our people not only committed everything to halt the advance of the Japanese, we also joined with the other Allied nations and participated in campaigns in Burma and India. Because of the price we paid, the sacrifices we made, the Americans pledged to provide us with wartime financial compensation. When victory over Japan was achieved in 1945, the US government should have fulfilled its pledge to us. But, in truth, most of their aid, their money, has gone to the rebuilding of Japan... which is what's led to the rise of anti-American activities. The currency inflation we've experienced has made it almost impossible for our people to get by. It's due in large part to the Civil War, and the corruption throughout nearly all levels of the Kuomintang. But these two things can't be the reason why our people are starving by the thousands. Our cities are being hollowed at the same time as the Americans provide us with food aid. It just doesn't make sense. Today, when you were up on that makeshift stage and I was down below, why did so many teachers and students, all of them with empty stomachs, why did they refuse what the Americans offered? It was then that word came to us that Zhu Ziqing had died. He'd starved to death because he had refused US food aid. They grieved at the news and grew increasingly resentful, rightfully so. You felt it too, and so did I. And let me tell you, upstairs, Mr He felt it as well! The letter we just wrote, it's for Ambassador Stuart. It asks for him to urge the Americans to uphold their wartime commitment to us, to give us the money they promised in 1945! But think about it. So what if they do? What if they provide us with that compensation, what then? Corruption is rife, inflation is out of control, and the people... the people... they're the ones who are suffering. This is why I want to see the currency reforms happen. It's why I'm helping to make them happen. Mr He and I, we're both academics. Our speciality is economics. We understand, too, if we bring in those vested interests within the Kuomintang – if they get involved – then it's most likely the reforms will never come to pass. They'll be stalled before they ever get the chance to change things. And then we'll all end up drinking poison to quench our thirst. But I know this, if the reforms aren't implemented, the only outcome will be more starving people, more dead people on the streets. 'Those who praise me cite the *Spring and Autumn Annals* to do so, those who censure refer to the same.' You need to get to the heart of the matter. Who am I? What am I doing? That's all I can give you answers to."

Both men stood up slowly.

Fang Meng'ao, his voice heavy, spoke: "There's one more thing I'd like to ask." Liang Jinglun looked at him, waiting to hear his question. After a pause, Fang put it to him: "So, where do your loyalties lie... with the Kuomintang or the CPC?"

Liang Jinglun smiled bitterly. "I'm a professor of Economics at Yenching University."

In a great flurry of motion, He Xiaoyu lowered herself onto the sofa in her father's sitting room. She heard faint steps out in the courtyard, the sound soft and gentle, but echoing in her ears. She didn't dare turn towards the door but kept her head low and in her arms, her eyes closed. She had no idea when the light in her father's study had been turned off. Nor was she aware of the pair of eyes staring down through the window at the courtyard, dimly lit by the streetlights. He Qicang was standing, watching the lonely figure of Liang Jinglun.

Liang was completely unaware.

He Xiaoyu continued to listen to the footsteps, but she didn't hear them come up the stairs. Instead, they remained in the courtyard. She turned around but lacked the courage to get up and see who it was, even to go to the window. Then, suddenly, she heard another set of feet. These she recognised as belonging to Fang Meng'ao.

He Qicang's face seemed dazed, his eyes fixed on Liang Jinglun. Liang paced back and forth before he walked out through the gate. He didn't get very far, however, before he stopped and turned around. At first glance, he appeared to be looking in towards the sitting room… or perhaps up at He Qicang looking down at him. Out of the blue, Fang Meng'ao's figure appeared at the gate.

In the sitting room, He Xiaoyu stood up and went over to the door. She stepped out into the courtyard, gazing first at Fang Meng'ao and then at Liang Jinglun. Fang Meng'ao returned her stare before shifting his attention to Liang Jinglun.

He Xiaoyu's voice was low, loud enough for only the three of them to hear: "You're both leaving?"

"Tell your father, I'm going back to the bookstore," Liang Jinglun answered. "I need a few hours of sleep. I'll be back early tomorrow morning."

He Xiaoyu turned back to Fang Meng'ao, who stood stoically. He volunteered no response.

Liang Jinglun smiled. "According to custom, it's only proper for Meng'ao to tell He Xiaoyu's father that he's proposed marriage." He didn't give them a chance to respond, but spun around and left, the smile still on his face.

He Xiaoyu's eyes followed him out, watching as his robes rippled in the breeze that blew beneath the Chinese parasol trees in the southern section of the Yenching campus. Then she turned to Fang Meng'ao. "What did he say?"

Fang's eyes were similarly focused on Liang Jinglun's departure, on the small alleyway that seemed to disappear into the night. "I'd like to go for a stroll."

The courtyard had emptied before his eyes. Slowly, he turned away from the window. He didn't flick on the lights, however, but walked cautiously over to the book cabinet to get a candle and a box of matches. The candle flickered into life. Before long, its wax dribbled down the stem and onto the desk near the typewriter. He Qicang stuck the base of the candle into the still-molten wax, making sure it would not topple over. He stretched his fingers and began to type. Again, page after page spewed out of the machine, line after line of English:

> It is recommended that currency reforms be implemented before the 20th of this month. During said reforms, it is advised that all hostilities cease and that peace negotiations begin.

CHAPTER 9

One o'clock in the morning on 19 August 1948. In the offices of the *Central Daily News* in Nanking, the printing presses hummed and spun rapidly, their noise deafening. Ream after ream of the daily paper churned out, their titles purposefully provocative:

Measures to be implemented to deal with current financial and economic troubles
  Measures concerning the issuance of new currency notes
  Measures concerning public ownership of gold, silver and foreign currency
  Measures concerning the registration and administration of foreign exchange assets deposited by nationals of the Republic of China
  Measures taken to strengthen national financial and economic regulations

On the previous day, after intense debate, the national government announced the following currency reforms: all banking transactions in the Kuomintang-free areas to be frozen, all currency circulation to cease. The two billion in wartime aid pledged by the American government in 1945 will in future serve as the only legal tender; this new tender, named *jinyuanquan*, has a US dollar value of $0.25; the exchange rate for the older *fabi* currency is set at 1:3,000,000; all gold, silver and foreign currency can be exchanged for *jinyuanquan*, but only for a limited time; no other currency, not even precious metals, is to be used as legal tender. Violators will be prosecuted to the fullest extent of the law.

It was a quarter past three in the morning. Xie Peidong, seated at the desk in Fang Buting's study, was wearing radio headphones, and his hand was busily transcribing an urgent telegram. Fang Buting stood beside him, his eyes mesmerised by the numbers Xie was writing down. Once the first telegram was transcribed, he passed it on to Fang Buting, who then sat on the opposite side of the table to decode the message. Numbers transformed into words, line after line...

Measures to be implemented to deal with current financial...

Xie Peidong listened and began to take down the second telegram. Fang Buting was still busily deciphering the first telegram, even though the second one was coming in.

Zeng Keda didn't possess the same orderly nervousness as Fang Buting, nor the same calmness. He was sitting in his aide's room, located in the mansion belonging to Gu Weijun. He couldn't decode the telegram; all he could do was stand beside his assistant and watch him transcribe number after number, his forehead damp with sweat. As soon as the first message was complete, Zeng shouted at his aide: "Decode. Now!" Not daring to remove the headphones from over his ears, his assistant answered that there were still four more transmissions to come. Zeng Keda grabbed the paper in response and scrutinised the series of numbers. His voice grew even more urgent: "What's the subject of the first one?"

Wang felt trapped between a rock and a hard place. On the one hand, he had to listen and record the messages still being transmitted by Nanking; on the other, he felt obliged to answer his commander. Finally, he relented to the more immediate demand

and looked at Inspector Zeng. "The first telegram has to do with the urgent measures to be adopted to contend with the financial and economic troubles."

Zeng Keda, still holding the telegram, paced back and forth between the table and the window. Then he stopped and felt a great wave of apprehension roll over him. He looked outside and saw a large, round moon above. A moment later he walked purposefully over to the wall opposite. He moved close to the calendar that was hanging there and inspected the parallel reckonings of time, the solar and the lunar. He was shocked by what he saw: 19 August, according to the Gregorian calendar. That same date, however, determined by the moon, was the fifteenth day of the seventh month: the Ghost Festival. Zeng closed his eyes and muttered under his breath: "Why now? Why today? Why choose this damnable day to announce this?"

―――

Xie Peidong had removed the headphones and was at the table, busily decoding the messages. Fang Buting was seated nearby, carefully poring over those transmissions he'd already completed. The clock downstairs chimed, one, two, three. It was three in the morning and they'd been at this nearly the entire night.

Fang Buting looked at his assistant manager. "How many more?"

Xie did not answer immediately. Instead, he completed the last five characters he was working on, and then stood up. "Finished." He gave the telegram to Fang Buting.

At the same moment as he took hold of the transmission, a knock came at the door to his office, and Cheng Xiaoyun called out: "You two should eat something, don't you think?"

Xie Peidong was already standing, but Fang Buting raised himself from his chair. "I'll get it."

He walked over to the door and opened it. Outside, Cheng Xiaoyun was holding a serving tray, upon which were two bowls of congee and two steamed loaves of bread. He looked at Xiaoyun holding the food. "It's all going to be announced in a couple of hours. There's nothing to conceal. Come on in."

Cheng Xiaoyun accepted the invitation and walked over to the table that faced the balcony outside. She put the tray down and turned to leave. "Eat first, OK?"

Despite her sincere desire to leave the study as quickly as possible, Fang Buting called out to stop her. "There's something I'd like to talk to you about. Peidong, come over, let's all eat together."

Xie Peidong walked over to the table and sat down again. Cheng Xiaoyun did the same. Xie had sat purposively in front of his favourite bowl.

Fang looked at Cheng. "In less than a month, we'll have been together for ten years. I remember how hurried our departure from Shanghai was. Our gold and silver, our valuables, all of it was with Meng'ao and Mengwei. I remember the bombs going off, too, and then there was nothing left behind. Afterwards, we had eight years of war, eight years fighting the Japanese. And during all that time, I never once gave you anything. And now, these past couple of years, I've only purchased for you some small bits of gold and silver jewellery. I know it's not much, but how much do you suppose?"

"Eh? Not a lot, I guess…"

"Ah this country, this Republic, I can't even give my wife what she deserves." Fang Buting turned to Xie Peidong. "Go ahead. Tell her."

"Once the sun comes up, the planned currency reforms will be announced. According to the new regulations, all gold and silver, foreign cash, too, it will all have to be exchanged for the new *jinyuanquan*. No exceptions, especially given the president's position. He'll have to lead by example."

"I understand," said Cheng Xiaoyun. "I'll get everything ready, everything out before the sun comes up. Don't worry." There was nothing else for her to say, nothing that could change what had to happen, and so Cheng left the two men alone in the office.

The bowls of congee and steamed bread remained on the tray. Neither man moved. Xie Peidong noticed Fang Buting looking towards the window, noticed, too, the teardrops in his eyes. He didn't say anything, however. Xie simply stood up and began to walk back to the desk.

"It's the fifteenth day of the seventh month, you know,

according to the lunar calendar." Fang Buting's voice made Xie pause. "There's nothing else but… but… it's come to me that, well, Meng'ao and his brother – on this day of all days – we should try to pay our respects to their grandma, to their mother. I remember, too, there's a gold bracelet there belonging to their grandmother. One was given to their mum, the other to Mulan's mum. I suppose, well, Mulan's gone now, she doesn't need it. We might as well take it back…"

A tidal wave of grief washed over Xie Peidong as he listened to Fang speaking. His heart felt tortured, but there was nothing he could say. He turned away from Fang Buting and sat down at the desk again. The telegrams had to be sorted. A moment passed and finally, he spoke: "Understood."

———

Zeng Keda had returned home. There was an urgent telephone call to make. His finger spun the rotary dial, the line rang, but no one answered. He clicked the phone and hung up, annoyed. Then he dialled a different number. This time, the other end answered almost immediately.

"Ministry of Defence, Department for Economic Investigations. May I ask who is calling?"

"Inspector Zeng. Is this Commander Li?"

"Yes, Inspector."

"And Captain Fang, is he there? I called the number for his office but no one answered."

"Sir… I can report… that is, Captain Fang has just left, sir."

"At this hour? Where's he gone?"

"He didn't say, sir. Nor did any of us dare ask him."

"Well, Commander, you're to tell him to return my call as soon as he gets back."

"Yes sir."

Zeng Keda hung up without saying another word and began to dial another number. This one also answered immediately. Zeng spoke first: "Professor Liang?"

"Yes, that's me."

"I'm Professor Zeng from Tsinghua University. My apologies

for telephoning you so late, but there's something urgent – an article – that I'd like your assistance with."

It was the night of the Ghost Festival, and a full moon was shining. The gravel on the road into the city from Yenching University sparkled and reflected the moonlight, creating the impression of a night stream twisting its way through Peking. The trees that lined both sides of the road stood erect like the masts of a flotilla of ships. Three bicycles tracked along the road as though sailing on water. Riding the first bike was a young plainclothes soldier. Liang Jinglun rode on the second. Taking up the rear was another plainclothes officer.

Further up the road, the faint outline of a jeep could be seen.

The feet on the bicycles pumped, increasing their speed.

A young man in a pilot's uniform stepped down from the jeep.

The bicycles pulled up and stopped. The two soldiers alighted quickly and flipped down the bicycle kickstands. One of them walked over to Liang Jinglun and took hold of the bicycle he had been riding.

Liang walked towards the jeep and the young officer in military attire saluted and then opened the door to the rear seats of the jeep. "Please, sir, climb in. The uniform is on the seat."

"It's been a long day for you, I bet." Liang Jinglun lifted his robes and climbed inside.

Driving by only the moon's light, the jeep raced down the road, shaking and bouncing as though it were a ship at sea.

The one jeep became two, the flat land they were driving on changed into an incline, and in front of them loomed the Western Hills. When the road came to an end, the jeeps stopped. The door to the first one opened and Fang Meng'ao appeared. Fang Mengwei stepped out of the second vehicle holding a basket. He walked over to his older brother.

Fang Meng'ao looked towards the dark, quiet mountains. "Will we be able to find Uncle Cui's memorial in this?"

Fang Mengwei had already walked past his brother. "We will."

Staring at his younger brother's back in the moonlight, Fang

Meng'ao paused for a moment, and then followed. Despite the pressure he felt in the circumstances, his footsteps were calm and steady.

Young Li was surprisingly strong. The chest he carried over his shoulder was heavy; the one he held in his hand perhaps more so. And yet he carried them from the bedroom upstairs down to the sitting room. Cheng Xiaoyun, holding a small jewellery box, could only stand at the top of the steps and look on in admiration at the young man.

Once he reached the ground floor, Li stopped and turned to look back up the stairs. "Ma'am, where shall I put these?"

"Right where you are will be fine."

Li shifted his weight and placed the two chests down gently on the sitting room floor.

Cheng Xiaoyun called out to him again: "Go and get the car, will you?"

"Yes ma'am."

Cheng Xiaoyun was about to walk down the stairs when the door to her husband's study opened and Fang Buting emerged. They were standing at opposite ends of the landing, one on the eastern side of the house, the other on the western side. Fang Buting smiled apologetically, then walked towards the stairs. Cheng Xiaoyun remained where she was, holding the jewellery box, her eyes trained on her husband as he descended.

Once in the sitting room, he stopped in front of the two large chests Young Li had just brought down from upstairs. He turned his head and looked up at Cheng Xiaoyun. She smiled, somewhat bitterly, but did not move. Fang Buting pulled out a set of keys from his pocket, found the keyhole and opened one of the chests. He lifted the lid and stacks of Benjamin Franklin notes stared back at him. Fang hesitated, then reached in and picked up one stack, ten thousand US dollars. Beneath it, he could see layers of the old *dayang* currency. He replaced the dollars in the trunk but left the lid open. Then he fished in his pocket for another set of keys to open the even heavier container. This one was filled with hundreds of gold bars. He left both boxes open and walked into the dining room. He grabbed the nearest chair and sat down quietly.

Finally, Cheng Xiaoyun descended the stairs. She went straight to the dining room and placed her box of jewellery on top of it. She had already unlocked it and now opened it up for her husband to see. Fang Buting refused to look at it. His eyes were instead focused on her. Slowly, he reached out his right hand, and Cheng Xiaoyun extended her left. They clasped. Fang Buting shook her hand gently, but almost as soon as he started, he stopped.

Cheng Xiaoyun stared at her husband's hand. His finger was atop her wedding ring.

Fang Buting could not bear to look at her. He lifted his head and shouted: "Uncle!"

Cheng Xiaoyun closed her eyes. Tears rolled down her face.

Xie Peidong appeared in the doorway to the office, a small bundle in his hands. He walked towards her bedroom, then turned and strode down the stairs. He placed the bundle on the table and opened it: a single half-inch stack of American money, a gold necklace and ring, and the gold bracelet given to Mulan by Fang Meng'ao's grandmother.

Fang Buting watched the other man closely, his eyes tearful. "As assistant manager of our Peking branch, these have been your only belongings. But besides me, if you were to tell anyone else, they wouldn't believe you. But these… items… they wouldn't be enough to pay for Mulan to study overseas, or to marry. I also made preparations for her, but now all of it, it's gone. And even if I did still wish to give her this inheritance, well, no one in the liberated zones really needs them, do they?"

Xie Peidong's choice of words made it clear he wished desperately to avoid this topic. "Mr Governor, the currency reforms are to be announced as soon as the sun rises, but exchanging these precious metals, the gold and silver, that'll take days at least. Is it really necessary for us to hand it all in right away?"

"Are we being called employees of the Central Bank? Are we to gouge out dearest possessions, give them up? But tell me, if we don't take the lead, will anyone else do it, will those wealthier individuals choose to exchange their belongings for the new currency? Ah, I just don't know what, but I do know one thing. Before we set about making the exchange, there's somewhere you need to go first."

"And where is that?"

"To the offices of the *World Daily*. I want you to ask their chief editor for help. We need them to publish this in the first edition, in the interests of getting everyone on board with the launch of the currency reforms, that we, you and I, the governor of the Peking branch of the Central Bank, and his assistant manager, that we've already gathered up our personal belongings, our gold and silver, our foreign cash, all of it. Even my wife's wedding ring and your daughter's bracelet…"

Xie Peidong glanced at Cheng Xiaoyun. To his surprise, he saw her remove her wedding ring and place it gently in among the items Xie had brought downstairs in his bundle.

"Buting… this is too much."

Fang Buting didn't hear him, or pretended not to. He merely turned and walked back up the stairs. The clock in the sitting room chimed. It was four in the morning.

On the road to the *World Daily* offices, the same road he'd taken when the rain poured and the way had been blocked, Young Li, his driver, slammed on the brakes.

From the back seat, Xie called out in surprise: "What the… what is it?"

"There's a rickshaw in the road. It's the driver, the man who took you home last time."

Xie Peidong leaned forward and looked out of the window. The car lights illuminated the early morning road, and he could see two rickshaws in the middle of the street. Two more were parked on the side. One of the rickshaw drivers was staring back at the car, a smile on his face. It was indeed the same man who'd transported him before, Liuyun, and his companion, Zhang Yueyin. Xie immediately began to think of the best excuse to get Young Li to leave, but before he could say anything, Liuyun had already strolled confidently over to the vehicle.

There was no hesitation in his movements. Liuyun simply

reached out and opened the door, then climbed in alongside Xie Peidong. He didn't hesitate to speak, either: "Mr Xie. My boss over there, Mr Zhang, is in possession of a rather urgent remittance that he needs cashed as soon as possible, at the break of day, if truth be told. I can lead the way. It will delay no more than half an hour."

Li looked back at Xie Peidong. Xie met his gaze and replied: "Let's go. We'll follow his directions."

"You see that hutong up there on the left? You need to turn sharp into there."

Young Li shifted the car into first gear and edged a few metres ahead. He then turned, as instructed, and entered the narrow hutong on the left.

In the same four-walled compound as before, in the same room in which he'd spoken to Liuyun, Xie Peidong now saw only Zhang Yueyin. As before, Zhang extended both hands and clasped Xie's before speaking: "Mr Xie, I know you're pressed for time. Our chat won't take long, I assure you." He guided Xie to the table. "Have the Kuomintang currency reforms been announced yet?"

"They will be soon, when the sun comes up. There are five directives in total, each with its own specific details, far too many for me to report on everything. I'll summarise, that's best I think."

"The higher-ups have not requested you to report," Zhang Yueyin interjected, gesturing for Xie Peidong to sit. "Please…"

Xie understood immediately. The file concerning the Kuomintang currency reforms was no doubt already on the desk of Chairman Mao and Vice-Chair Zhou. His heart and mind were filled with a swirl of thoughts and emotions. He tried his utmost to remain calm, to wait patiently for the impending thunder from the nearby mountains to roll over Peking.

Zhang Yueyin was similarly excited, doing his best to keep his own emotions in check. "Comrade Liuyun has relayed orders from Vice-Chair Zhou. The Kuomintang's currency reforms, their timing, their motive is clear. According to the party, the plans are an unprecedented assault on the average citizen, a boldface attempt to plunder every last coin and bit of wealth they possess. They're trying to swim against the tide of history by using the current economic difficulties – collapse, really – as an excuse. And as a means to prepare for the final battle against us. The central authorities believe, however, that this plot will only advance the timeframe and expedite our ultimate victory."

"So what have you and your men been tasked with? What are my responsibilities?"

"Our orders are not to get involved. From this day forward, we're not to meddle in anything that is going on, not the currency reform plans for the Pingjin area, nor the plans to send the peacocks southeast, as they call it, that Comrade Fang Meng'ao and the Kuomintang are arranging. All of us, including the north China agents too, we're to stay out of everything. That is, except for you. You're to wait for the most opportune time and then take charge."

Xie Peidong stood up, shocked by what Zhang said. "I'm to take charge of what, exactly?"

"Yes, you." Zhang Yueyin joined him on his feet. "According to the judgment of the central command, whether we intervene or not, the Kuomintang's currency reforms will last at best two months, no more. Vice-Chair Zhou's orders are thus for you to do what you can to advance the reforms in the Pingjin area, to make them of the greatest use to us. To do this, you will of course need to use your position at the Peking branch of the Central Bank, and your relationship with He Qicang, just as Chiang Ching-kuo seized the opportunity to make use of Fang Meng'ao and his position. We must do the same. We need to obtain goods and supplies for *our* efforts. That way, when the day comes and the new *jinyuanquan* becomes worthless – and believe me, that day will come – *we'll* have the food that the people in Peking and Tianjin will need."

"Are we to ensure that the citizens have food to eat, or that Fu Zuoyi's army has food?"

Xie's question caused Zhang Yueyin to become solemn. "That's a good question, you know. Chairman Mao's instructions apply here: 'Everyone eats!'"

Xie Peidong suddenly realised the enormity of what Zhang Yueyin had just said, the implication coming from it. It was as though a great roar had been let loose, a roar to shake the heavens. "Am I... am I to understand that Chairman Mao, and Vice-Chair

Zhou, that their orders are for us to take advantage of the Kuomintang's currency reforms to… to ensure the supply lines for Fu Zuoyi's armed forces, to make sure they're secure in the Pingjin area?"

Zhang Yueyin's solemnity of a moment ago was now replaced by a certain reverence. "We've not received those specific orders, but other orders issued by the chairman perhaps answer that question of yours." Xie Peidong's face could not hide his surprise. Zhang Yueyin continued: "A family grows old together, far more valuable than any treasure!" Xie Peidong remained stunned while Zhang continued speaking: "This was the chairman's assessment of you, Mr Xie. The central command is well aware of your importance, they rely heavily on you. Comrade Liuyun instructed me to tell you something: the Kuomintang, Xu Tieying's department, they've been investigating you for some time now, all on the sly. They've been looking into your connection… your relationship to Comrade Cui Zhongshi. Xu believes you're keeping Cui's personal papers safe, which is why we'll not contact you again after today. Nor will any other agents. All communication between us has to cease. What you're being tasked with, the responsibility being put on your shoulders, it's hugely important to the cause. It's also terribly difficult for you. As for Comrades Fang Meng'ao and He Xiaoyu, you're to be responsible for them now, too. Keep them safe, and yourself as well!"

Zhang Yueyin extended both hands again to shake Xie Peidong's. With that handshake, Xie couldn't help but feel that so much had been thrust upon him. So much indeed.

In the Peking area, Xishan was the first place to feel the warmth of the morning sun. The fine line of light cresting over the eastern horizon illuminated the narrow trail that snaked its way down the mountains. It illuminated, too, the Air Force uniforms worn by Fang Meng'ao and his younger brother Mengwei. They'd spent the evening amid the mountains and trees, tending to their uncle's burial mound. Their parked jeeps appeared much larger against the backdrop of the mountains than they had the night before. Neither man had seen the soldiers arrive: one a platoon from the Peking Police headquarters, the other a detachment of military police.

The two brothers came to an abrupt stop. Fang Meng'ao surveyed the scene, the soldiers and their two convoy trucks. He spoke over his shoulder to Mengwei: "They're here for us. That much is clear."

Fang Mengwei did not reply.

"Do you have any idea why? Do you think something's happened?"

"I don't think I want to know, to be honest."

"I'd say it has to do with the currency reforms." Fang Meng'ao stared into the distance. At the same time, he shifted to stand next to his brother and placed a hand on his shoulder. "Our family… me, our dad, Uncle Xie, too. We're all mixed up in this, you know that. But I want to tell you something, and I don't want you to forget it: don't let yourself get mixed in it. It's too late for the three of us, but you, you need to stay out of this. You need to take care of Auntie Cheng. and Uncle Cui's widow. It's up to you. You've got to get them out of here." Fang Meng'ao patted his brother's shoulder and then walked down towards the waiting soldiers.

Fang Mengwei stood there looking on sorrowfully as his brother climbed into his jeep and started the engine. He watched as the jeep turn around. Then he saw one group of soldiers race over to their transport vehicle. A few minutes later, the mountains and everything beyond them were bathed in light. Fang Mengwei remained standing, seemingly waiting for the sun.

"Chief!" It was his deputy, Shan. He had run part way up the trail, unable to wait for Fang Mengwei to descend on his own. His voice was urgent: "It's an emergency, sir. Director Xu is waiting for you."

"How did you men know I was up here?"

Shan finally walked up to stand next to his superior, his face displaying his continued loyalty. "It's the middle of the seventh month. I know of your affection for Deputy Director Cui, you and your brother's. I know there was no need for words between you either. Your hearts told you to come here."

"Thank you. Tell the men the same." Fang Mengwei didn't wait for his subordinate to find sure footing before he started down the path. "Tell me, what's the mission?"

Deputy Shan could only follow quickly behind. "Urgent orders came down at two this morning. We've been given a special task of the greatest import. I've heard that when the sun comes up, the currency reforms are to be announced."

"What's that got to do with the military, or with the police for that matter? Has money been stolen?" Fang Mengwei had increased his pace and was now bounding down the mountain.

"No, of course not." Shan tried with difficulty to match his superior's gait. "Our mission is to escort Ma Hanshan to Nanking, first thing in the morning, where he's to go in front of a special tribunal. According to Director Xu, Deputy Cui was murdered by Ma Hanshan. You're to lead the escort because Director Xu wants you to be on the jury that deliberates on Ma's fate, even though death will really be the ultimate outcome. The explanation given to your father is that this will give you the chance to have your revenge."

Fang Mengwei stopped abruptly. "This is what Xu Tieying told you?"

Before Shan realised, he was too late and bumped into his superior's back. He nodded his head in response to Fang Mengwei's question, before adding: "Well, perhaps not in those specific words. But that seemed to be the meaning of what he said."

"Then I'll trouble you to tell Xu Tieying that I want nothing to do with this. You can see to it yourself, without me." Fang Mengwei continued down the mountain path, his pace even quicker than before.

Shan chased after him. "Chief Fang, Ma Hanshan is to be escorted by the military police and you're its lead investigator. I don't have the authority to…"

Fang Mengwei had already reached his jeep, had thrown his hat inside and climbed in himself. He punched the horn of the jeep, signalling for the men to stand aside. Seconds later, he raced past them. The soldiers turned their heads and watched him speed away.

―――

In the conference room of the police station, the radio rang out: "This is Police Detachment Number Three calling Secretary Sun!"

Sun's eyes fell on the personal radio on the table. Again, the speaker crackled and he heard the same sentence ring out. Sun reached out and took hold of the radio. He pressed the "speak" button and held the device close to his mouth. "This is Sun Chaozhong. Go ahead, Deputy Chief Shan."

"I report that Chief Fang has refused the mission! Please inform Director Xu. Over."

Sun again pressed the "speak" button. "Wait a moment. You'll deliver this report to Director Xu personally. Over." With the personal radio in his hand, Sun left the conference room and walked to Xu Tieying's office. He knocked quietly on the door and waited for a response.

"Enter."

Sun opened the door and walked in. Xu Tieying was neatly dressed in his police uniform.

"Director, Deputy Shan has radioed in with a report. I thought it best he give it to you personally." He handed the radio to Xu Tieying.

"This is Xu Tieying. Go ahead. Over."

Xu lifted his hand off the "speak" button and Shan's voice blared out of the speaker: "Director Xu, I report that Deputy Fang refuses to follow your orders. Our location is the base of the Western Hills. We await your command. Over."

"You're to wait for me at Xishan prison. Over." Xu Tieying said nothing further, but passed the radio back to Sun Chaozhong and told him to turn it off.

Sun did as instructed, then moved to get Xu's bag ready. Xu, however, had beaten him to the punch and had already gathered the papers and documents he needed. Before Sun had a second to say anything, Xu Tieying was walking through the door. There was nothing to do but follow him out and close the door behind them.

Two jeeps were parked just inside the police station compound. One belonged to Xu Tieying, a smallish, canopy-covered vehicle. The other was a little larger and with a matching canopy of its own. The garrison commander stood alongside the vehicles, directing his men first to attention and then to board the second jeep; they followed his orders without delay. Seconds later, Secretary Sun and Xu Tieying descended the stairs and walked over to the smaller jeep. Sun lifted the handle of the rear right door and opened it. Then he placed his hand on the frame and waited for Xu Tieying.

"I'm going to sit in front," said Xu Tieying, ignoring the open door and standing beside the driver's side. Leaning forward, he spoke to the driver: "Get out. Ride with the other men."

"Yes sir." The driver pushed open the door and did as instructed.

Sun seemed to realise the meaning behind Xu's decision and quickly stepped forward, assuming Xu wanted him to drive. His commander, however, would not give way.

A smile crossed Xu's face. "You've been my right-hand man for such a long time, yet you haven't seen me drive, have you?"

Sun paused, unsure of what to do. Xu did not, however, hesitate. He passed the attaché case to his secretary and said: "Get in on the passenger side, I'll drive today."

Sun quickly regained his senses and had already pulled open the driver's door. Xu Tieying climbed into the jeep and glanced at Sun. He smiled again. Sun closed the door and walked hurriedly around the front of the jeep to the passenger's side. The vehicle came alive, and within seconds Xu had manoeuvred it through the main gate. The guards, shocked by who they saw driving, all saluted nonetheless. Xu Tieying kept his left hand on the wheel. With his right, he saluted in response. Subconsciously, Sun gripped the attaché case and stared at Xu Tieying. "You're quite skilled behind the wheel, Director, but you must still pay attention to safety."

"And you as well." He replaced his right hand on the steering wheel. "We must both pay attention to our safety."

The jeep navigated down the road. Xu drove neither too fast, nor too slow.

When Fang Meng'ao walked into Zeng Keda's drawing room, only Liang Jinglun was present, sitting in an armchair, dressed in the military attire of a simple enlisted man. As their eyes met, Liang raised himself from his seat. Fang looked him over, then focused his attention on the tea table in front of him and the wide-brimmed military hat and sunglasses that lay there. Before either thought to say anything to the other, Zeng Keda walked in holding a telegram in his hand.

"Ah, everyone's here. Excellent. Please, be seated." Zeng gestured for both men to sit.

Fang did not hesitate. He walked over to an armchair that leaned against the wall and lowered himself into it. Liang Jinglun remained standing, awaiting Zeng Keda to move past him and to the long sofa. Once he sat, Liang returned to his own armchair.

It was clear to the two of them that Zeng Keda was trying with difficulty to contain his excitement and seemingly bursting emotions. "Finally, at long last, the currency reforms are to be announced. Comrade Jianfeng has entrusted me to convey to you, Comrade Liang Jinglun, that the letter you helped Vice-Chancellor He compose, the one sent to Ambassador Stuart, is quite excellent. The president has seen it, too, and concurs. Furthermore, it has served its purpose in moving things forward, and, equally important, it has preserved the dignity of the nation in front of the Americans. Comrade Jianfeng has said you're both the backbones of the people and worthy of the highest respect."

Fang Meng'ao glanced in the direction of Liang Jinglun. Liang's face betrayed no reaction. He wasn't pleased by the comment, nor did he feel smug. His voice was low when he spoke. "We're both scholars of the economy. We only did our job."

Zeng Keda smiled and passed the telegram he had been holding over for the two men to see. "That paper contains all the details concerning the announcement of the currency reforms. Time is of the essence. Please note the main points. Nanking has an important mission for us."

"The meeting was recorded. Open the case. It's the document on top." They were already in sight of Xizhimen. Xu had been navigating Peking's streets for the better part of ten minutes before speaking.

Sun opened the attaché case and pulled out the transcription of the meeting. He remained silent. According to regulations, he wasn't supposed to ask if he could look at the document or not, and it was obvious he couldn't pass it to Xu Tieying. He just sat there waiting. Xu Tieying had decided to lay everything on the table.

With his eyes still facing forward, Xu continued: "Have a look. Whatever I've seen, you can see, too."

There was nothing for Sun to do but open the file folder. And although he had steeled his heart for what he might see, he was greatly surprised by the heading on the page: Central Command, Kuomintang, Implementation Committee.

The contents that followed were even more astonishing:

Record of Special Standing Committee meeting
  Host: Zhu Jiahua
  Attendee: President Chiang Kai-shek
  Standing Committee: Dai Jitao, Chen Guofu, Zhang Qun, Zhang Lisheng, Chiang Ching-kuo...

Sun dared not look any further. He closed the file and spoke to Xu: "Director, this is a... a top-secret document. It's not for my eyes."

"In a few hours, the currency reforms will be announced and implemented. The party-state is on the precipice between life and death. There's nothing really that you shouldn't see. This all comes down to the responsibilities of the party-state, your precious Chiang Ching-kuo. Go ahead, read it. Once you do, there'll be no need for me to conceal anything from you."

Sun closed his eyes, bit his lower lip and opened the file folder again.

Liang Jinglun skimmed through the first article concerning the currency reforms; Fang Meng'ao thumbed through the pages, only paying attention to the main points. Zeng Keda watched the hands of the clock on the wall. The short hand was approaching six.

Finally, Zeng could wait no longer. "Let me explain our mission. The country has been divided into specific areas. Shanghai, Tianjin and Guangzhou constitute three economic areas. Shanghai is naturally the centre and most important engine of economic growth, hence, Comrade Jianfeng will oversee it directly. Next is Tianjin, the second most important economic area. This jurisdiction includes Hebei, Peking and all regions in northern China, which is also where the Communists have their base of operations, and their areas of greatest influence, namely Tsinghua, Yenching and Nankai universities. It's from these places that they instigate student protests. The safeguarding of goods and supplies needed by the people in these areas is paramount, especially in Peking. How well we do this will directly correlate to the success or failure of the currency reforms. There are also the soldiers, the fifty thousand-plus stationed at the Northern Command. Their supply lines need to remain open... after all, they're vital to our efforts to restrict Communist activities in the north, to say nothing of their importance when it comes time to launch the final offensive against the CPC. Those lines have to be protected at all costs. Nanking has determined that Vice-Premier Zhang Lisheng will oversee these matters, with his main seat based in Tianjin. The three of us will provide assistance to VP Chang in Peking. Our main priority will be the implementation of the currency reforms in the city itself. Two important points must be noted, for they are equally difficult. One, we are to continue our investigations into corruption in the Pingjin area, and ensure that any attempts to stockpile goods destined for the market are stopped. Two, we're to spare no effort in making sure that American aid reaches Pingjin. There are additional orders that Comrade Jianfeng has also given, and these relate to the core mission of sending the peacocks southeast."

Zeng paused and looked at the clock on the wall, before turning his focus on Liang Jinglun. "Comrade Jianfeng has made special note, too, for you, Comrade Liang, and that has to do with the economy, particularly with regard to financial matters. Both Captain Fang and I need further study in this... area. Thus you've been tasked with bringing us up to speed."

Liang stood up slowly. "Allow me to explain in simple terms..."

―――

"Finished?" They were now getting fairly close to Xishan prison.

"Yes, I have."

"Did you see Chiang Ching-kuo's signature?"

"I did."

Xu Tieying continued. "The reason I point this out to you is that there are only a select few individuals who can use his name in this manner, to use anti-corruption slogans to disrupt and throw the party-state into chaos. Tell me, has corruption infiltrated the entire party apparatus and government, too? Of course it has, and it's true the perpetrators must be weeded out and punished. But at the same time, we cannot allow this to be used as a tool by certain persons, to topple the party-state. Chiang Ching-kuo established the Iron and Blood Congress. There are some who believe he set up this internal organisation as a means to replace the older generation within the party and advance his own power and prestige. But it's never occurred to these people that the director-general would have consulted with the central command of the party before establishing such an organisation. He never would have been allowed to create it if he hadn't.

"What's more, this faction doesn't have a monopoly on rooting out corruption. It's long been a key mission of the central command. It's just that national policy has forever been focused on national unity and the suppression of disruptive elements! Now, you've just read the report of the Standing Committee. The main and most arduous task of the currency reforms is the halting of Communist advances. The party has put me in charge of its implementation in Peking. Would you like to know who they've selected to assist me?"

Sun directed his eyes towards the Western Hills. "It's best you tell me, Director, instead of me trying to make guesses."

"Two people: Wang Puchen... and you."

Even though Sun had already surmised what Xu Tieying was going to say, to actually hear the words still surprised him.

Xu sighed. "From now on, you no longer need to conceal your identity as a member of the Iron and Blood Congress, nor do I need to pretend any longer that I don't know. You executed Cui Zhongshi, you dealt with Yan Chunming and Xie Mulan, you've passed both tests, you've confirmed your anti-Communist credentials. The party has affirmed it. That's why I've broken regulations and told you to read the Standing Committee's report. I want you to understand, Chiang Ching-kuo *is* the Standing Committee. They've made the decision, and thus Ching-kuo will see to its implementation... at any cost. If you still have misgivings, tell me them now, I will need to inform the party immediately."

Sun Chaozhong could feel that the jeep had entered into the Western Hills, for their shadows had already enveloped them. He glanced at Xu and answered: "I obey party orders."

———

"Please, a moment..." Zeng Keda interrupted Liang Jinglun to write down the words he had been saying. The page in front of him was densely packed, characters almost merging into one another. His pen formed the words for cloth yardage, then he sketched a thick rod and below it wrote the words for financial leverage. Once done, he turned again to Liang Jinglun and asked: "How do yards of cloth factor into financial leverage? Could you explain?"

"Unlike the US and other advanced industrial economies in the West, China lags far behind. Its economy is still based on agriculture. From the average citizen to a university professor, our standard of living is determined by the clothes we wear, the food we eat. That food is what China's farmers produce. After the harvest, they bring what they've grown to sell in the city markets. The primary currency of that exchange is cloth yardage. Hence, the amount of cloth a farmer can receive for the produce he brings to market constitutes the financial value."

"Aha, then that's the main point! Now I understand." Zeng Keda put his pen down on the table and turned towards Fang Meng'ao. "Captain Fang, do you have any questions?"

"No, I'm just listening."

Zeng Keda leaned forward and picked up a ledger of names that lay on the tea table. "'Financial leverage', it's all in here!" The ledger was a complicated set of information. The first column listed the name of the company or firm, the second detailed the range and scope of each company's business, and the third column was for property assets, although this was blank. The fourth and fifth columns, which had also not been filled in, had headings for shareholder identities and the current tax situation.

Zeng held the ledger and shook it. "This ledger is the financial leverage we need over the companies and manufacturers based in the Pingjin area, who, according to Professor Liang, control and manipulate the economy, presumably for their own benefit. Most have their head offices in Tianjin, but they have branches and accounts in Peking. More than a year ago, all of these enterprises operated under the wing of either HH Kung's family, or the Soong's. But what's even more hateful is that just before HH Kung and TV Soong were removed from their posts, the former from the Ministry of Finance, the latter from his position as president of the Executive Yuan, they changed the names of the shareholders and linked each and every one of them the Central Command of the party, to all levels of the party in fact! Now, the circulation of gold, silver and foreign currencies in the market has been prohibited. Moreover, all hoarded goods are ordered to be brought to market and sold at controlled prices and in the new legal tender, the *jinyuanquan*. Behind closed doors, these men were the first to oppose the new regulations, for not only do they jeopardise the fortunes of the Kung and Soong families, they also leave exposed other members of the central command and the party. Hence their opposition as well. But let me tell you both, if we don't risk aggravating them, the currency reforms in the Pingjin area will fail before they even begin." Zeng looked back and forth between Liang Jinglun and Fang Meng'ao.

Captain Fang responded first: "But how do we proceed? Should we investigate the accounts of their Peking branches, should I go and arrest them?"

Zeng Keda shook his head. "We've looked into those accounts for more than a month. We know what they've done, they've already washed them through the Central Bank in Nanking. The Peking accounts are clean. There's no way to dig out anything of use now. Out of the two people who knew the inner workings of all of this, one is dead, namely Cui Zhongshi. The other one is alive though, and we know who that is, Ma Hanshan. If we truly want to proceed with an investigation, if we hope to have any success, we will need his assistance."

Zeng reached out for the last document that lay on the table. "The Executive Yuan's subcommittee in charge of economic affairs has already ratified our request. Ma Hanshan, who was responsible for the Tianjin economic area, has agreed to cooperate, and I will oversee the investigation personally."

Fang Meng'ao smiled. "But will Xu Tieying and his supporters listen to the Executive Yuan?"

"The Executive Yuan's subcommittee is the highest authority concerning the currency reforms." Zeng Keda stood up abruptly. "I'm going to Xishan prison to get Ma Hanshan. Captain Fang, Comrade Liang Jinglun, your mission is to see immediately to the peacocks flying southeast. Specifically, Captain Fang, you're ordered to see to the reinstatement of your aviation unit. Three Curtiss C-46 transport aircraft are already at Nanyuan airbase waiting for you to assume command. Your task today is to cooperate with the Peking branch of the Central Bank and to see to the secure transportation of the new *jinyuanquan* to Tianjin. Afterwards, you must assist the committee in charge of distributing American aid to the Hebei and Pingjin areas. Comrade Jianfeng stressed the need for you, especially, to cooperate closely with Mr Fang – your father – in this endeavour. As for you, Comrade Liang, you're to assist He Qicang in exhorting Ambassador Stuart to use his powers of persuasion with the American government to get them to increase their aid. In the month before the currency reforms come into full effect, we must ensure there is at least six months' supply of foodstuffs for the citizens of Peking and Tianjin. The supplies, too, for the fifty-thousand-strong army in the north is also of paramount importance."

Zeng Keda was clearly impassioned by the tasks at hand. In one hand he picked up his military hat, the other he extended towards Fang Meng'ao. As he did so, however, the telephone rang. Zeng was obliged to answer it: "Yes, it's me. Please go ahead Warden Wang." Zeng listened as Wang Puchen explained why he had called, but what he said could not be overheard by the other two men. All they saw was a changed expression come over Zeng Keda's face. "Already late by half an hour! That's on me, my failure. But in that half hour, you allowed Ma Hanshan to be taken. You'll have to explain this to the Executive Yuan!"

Zeng Keda slammed down the phone and turned to Fang Meng'ao. "You hit the nail on the head, Captain Fang. Xu Tieying hasn't listened to the Executive Yuan, he's taken Ma Hanshan into his custody and together they've set off for Nanking." He reached out and took hold of their hands, shaking both at the same time. "The party-state is on the edge, the peoples' welfare is facing calamity, we've had one revolution already, now a Civil War. Everything from here on depends on us acting in good faith together!"

Zeng Keda placed the cap on his head and strode out of the drawing room. He called out to his assistant: "Wang!" Moments later, Zeng's footsteps could be heard descending the steps and out into the garden.

Fang Meng'ao and Liang Jinglun were left alone together. Neither spoke. Fang directed his attention towards the wide-brimmed military hat and the thick-rimmed sunglasses on the table. "Do you remember what I asked you that night? You've not answered me, you know."

"If I did, would you believe me?"

"Go ahead."

"You don't want to think of me as a Nationalist, nor as a Communist. All of China's five hundred and forty million people, everyone, we're all still trapped in this torture. In the future, it won't matter who won or who lost, neither side can let our people suffer any longer, to starve and be beset by crippling poverty. It's intolerable." His words finished, Liang Jinglun reached out and picked up his hat. "As for your family – your father, Xiaoyu and those students who were guilty of nothing – my conscience wouldn't allow me to do anything else but protect them. Please, you must believe!"

Liang put on the hat and sunglasses. Then he did something he'd never done before to Fang Meng'ao: he saluted. He didn't wait for the standard response, however, but spun on his heel and departed.

As Fang watched him leave, he noticed a ray of sunshine etch its way across his back. A second later and Liang Jinglun was gone. Standing alone, Fang saluted to the open door and marched away as well.

The gendarmerie under the command of the investigative services stood at high alert in the grounds of the secret prison, their helmets and carbine rifles at the ready. Wang Puchen appeared from the main doors of the central building to greet Xu Tieying and his secretary, Sun Chaozhong, both of whom were standing not too far from the soldiers. They stared at Wang as he walked over to them.

"I've received instructions from the Intelligence Bureau, orders for us to cooperate with the party. Please wait a while, Director Xu. I'll fetch Ma Hanshan immediately."

"This must be tiresome, Mr Wang. I do apologise."

Wang Puchen turned in the direction of the cells and walked off.

Xu Tieying glanced at Sun Chaozhong, but was startled by what he saw. Not once before had he seen such a look of total emptiness on his loyal servant's face. He felt compelled to speak: "What's with you? Do you suspect Wang Puchen of... betrayal? Something else?"

"I apologise, Director, but I do not know what you are referring to."

"Are you wondering how the party views him? What the central command's take on him is?"

Sun looked at his superior but did not answer.

"Wang Puchen joined the party in the twenty-fifth year of the Republic. When the Republic turned thirty-eight, he became a member of the Iron and Blood Congress. He's loyally carried out party missions and done his utmost to assist both Chiang Ching-kuo and the central authorities in their efforts to maintain party unity. Do you think there's something you should learn from him?"

Finally, he grasped Wang Puchen's true identity and allegiance! At almost the same moment, he couldn't help but feel that the halo that had supposedly surrounded the activities and aims of the Iron and Blood Congress had been dimmed by shadow, swallowed even by a creeping darkness. He remained silent for a moment before answering in the affirmative; there were things he could learn from Wang Puchen.

"Then learn well," was all Xu offered as a response.

Wang did not bring anyone with him. The only thing he carried was a clean set of clothes, which he held underneath his arm. He walked up to the main door that led into the cells and unlocked it. Before entering, however, he picked up a rather large container of water that lay next to the door and then marched towards cell number one.

Ma Hanshan was sitting crossed-legged on his small prison bed, his eyes closed in meditation. Considering his current internment, Ma's complexion was surprisingly good. A book lay next to him on the bed; evidently, it was what he was reading to keep his mind busy.

Wang Puchen placed the water container on the floor, and then did the same for the clean clothes, placing them softly on the bed without disturbing him.

Ma Hanshan spoke first: "Zeng Guofan carried out three tasks every day." Ma's words suggested he was aware of his impending departure from his prison cell, but still he kept his eyes closed, and explained: "His first task was to write in his diary. The second, he had to play a game of Go. Finally, he would meditate in silence, seated for at least four hours, what the neo-Confucianists called *jingzuo*. Wang Puchen, I've greatly enjoyed your copy of Zeng Guofan's diary. I've been reading it daily myself. Why didn't you lend it to me earlier?" At last, Ma opened his eyes.

Although Wang Puchen was used to Ma Hanshan's affected mannerisms, and although he did his best to conceal his true emotions, he couldn't help but feel a pinprick to his heart. "My dear former warden, if you like the book that much, it's yours to keep."

"Oh my, excellent. Yes, excellent. Thank you so much." Ma Hanshan was well practised in *qigong*, particularly the Quanzhen School, and now stood up from the bed, stretching his hands high above his head as though he were reaching for heaven. In quick, deft movements he removed his prison attire and stood naked in front of Wang Puchen. A second later he walked to the basin filled with water that Wang had brought. "After we get to Nanking, I imagine we'll try to root out those unsavoury actors, those whom we can't be sure what they're up to, but we reckon it's nothing good. Ha, we'll make use of Zeng Guofan's stratagems to find them out and then record their confessions. Then, once the president reads them, I'm sure he'll see fit to appoint me as a researcher in

Academia Sinica. Puchen, tell me, do you not think there's a possibility of that happening?"

Wang Puchen walked over to the door, giving Ma Hanshan space to get ready. His heart, however, was empty. "Take your time to wash, Mr Ma. Cleanliness is valued highly across the armed forces."

Wang stepped out past the door, but Ma Hanshan called to make him halt: "Puchen!"

Wang turned around slowly.

There was little sense of urgency in Ma Hanshan's voice: "Your book..." He paused and picked up a nearby cloth, rinsed it and washed his face. When finished, he thrust it back into the basin, soaked it through, wrung it out and then proceeded to wash his body. "It's yours, take it."

Wang Puchen stared at Ma.

Ma continued: "You know, there's no medicine available that can save this party-state. Zeng Guofan said it thus: in this world, there are only one or two gentlemen who can be relied upon. Struggling over split hairs is futile. And I tell you something else, the only place you're going to find those one or two gentlemen is, well, in your Iron and Blood Congress..."

"I'm sorry, Mr Ma, I don't understand." Wang could not hide his astonishment. How did Ma know about the Iron and Blood Congress? And even more important, how did he know he was a member of it?

"Whether you understand or not isn't really the issue. It's certainly not all that pressing." Ma Hanshan began to scrub his back with the towel. "I wish to give you something, a contribution as it were, in your book. These past few days, I've written some stuff down, just notes... details on all of the black accounts I know of, all of the underhanded, dirty deals I and many others were involved in. Give it to Chiang Ching-kuo. It's enough to ensure the provisions for everyone in Peking for six months at least... and salaries for the fifty thousand troops in the north, too."

Wang Puchen walked over to the bed and took hold of the diary of Zeng Guofan. He thumbed through the pages. The light was not especially good in the cell, but he could see Ma Hanshan's notes, words pressed tightly together, almost on top of each other. He scanned the book for a moment longer, shut it and then walked over to stand next to Ma Hanshan. "Mr Ma, you know that Xu Tieying and his clique have, with great urgency, made arrangements to get you to Nanking. They want you to explain, talk about everything you know. At the same time, Inspector Zeng is on his way here. He's racing against time, you know, he wants to get to you before they take you away. He wants you to assist him in his investigations. The only one who's properly positioned to save you, the only one who has the power, is Chiang Ching-kuo. Remember this, what you've written down in this book, don't tell anyone else. I shall try to think of some way to get it to him, to Chiang Ching-kuo."

Ma Hanshan stopped washing, looked at Wang Puchen, and sighed. "Chiang Ching-kuo certainly knows how to choose his confidants! There are things I didn't intend to say, and if I say them now there's no guarantee they'll be of any benefit. But would you like to hear nonetheless?"

"Please go ahead, Mr Ma."

"Did you know, last year, when they were deciding upon who to replace me with, you weren't their first choice? There were quite a few who jostled for the position. Ultimately, after much debate, one of the old guard from the United Army was chosen. The VP was going to sign the order to confirm it, too. Do you know why you ended up being selected?"

Wang Puchen could only stare at Ma Hanshan. Words failed him.

Ma answered his own question: "I have a great amount of respect for your Chiang Ching-kuo, you know. He was the one who called me personally to recommend you. And you know what I did? I paid him off with fifty gold bars and he excused himself from consideration."

Wang Puchen could not hide the surprise on his face.

Ma continued: "Ah, the older generation are so easily blinded by money. The fifty bars was all it took. And now today I'm adding to what I've done by giving you these accounts. You know, sooner or later, Mao Renfeng's position next to Chiang Ching-kuo will be yours. Listen to me, take that book and hide it well, and let the rest of them make trouble. You don't need to try to save me. Just make sure you don't get wrapped up in what's going on."

It had been some time since Wang Puchen had felt his heart in so much turmoil. There were things he wanted to say, but when he saw Ma Hanshan return to washing himself, he remained silent. Seconds later, he was standing outside the prison cell, patiently waiting for Ma Hanshan to finish.

"Attention!"

Where the bonnet and the front windscreen met, Zeng Keda had placed a small Ministry of Defence flag. In the larger canopy-covered jeep that followed behind him, the soldiers were in standard military uniforms, although each one bore a particular armband, red with white lettering, signalling their unique authority over the economy. The soldiers stationed at Xishan prison saluted as the two jeeps drove through the main gate. Zeng Keda was at the wheel of his own jeep and purposefully drove past the saluting gendarmerie. When he came up close to where Xu Tieying was waiting, he slammed the brakes and halted his vehicle.

Xu Tieying watched as Zeng Keda bounded out of the jeep. He smiled and began to walk over to the other man.

Zeng Keda, however, paid him no mind but instead focused on the prison guards standing a little farther away. "And where is your commander, Warden Wang?"

The lieutenant in charge of the guardsmen ran over, saluted and answered: "Inspector Zeng, report sir, Warden Wang is now preparing the prisoner, Ma Hanshan."

"Go tell him to expedite matters. I've arrived."

The lieutenant glanced at Xu Tieying.

"Now, Lieutenant, you don't need to look at him!"

He answered with a tentative "yes" but couldn't help but shoot another look at Xu Tieying. He hesitated to leave, then decided he would.

All eyes fell on the door that led towards the cells, for there stood Ma Hanshan and his escort, Wang Puchen.

Ma's face was washed, his hair combed. He was wearing a glistening white Zhongshan jacket, which enhanced his look further. It was suddenly apparent: Ma Hanshan cleaned up very well, very well indeed.

Wang Puchen was standing behind him, his hand on Ma's shoulder. He leaned forward a little to whisper: "Mr Ma." Ma Hanshan halted his steps. Wang continued: "I'm sure you can see the situation in front of you. Allow me to lead." He didn't wait for a response but began to walk over towards the men, all of whom seemed to be waiting for them.

Ma Hanshan watched Wang Puchen's back as he walked. He allowed his eyes to scan the scene. Then he smiled. They were all members of the national armed forces, but they had formed up into two different square-shaped formations. To the left were the military police, their armbands emblazoned with the words denoting such. Xu Tieying stood in front of them. On the right was a contingent of young soldiers, the left arms all bearing armbands as well, these coloured red and white: stewards of the economy. Zeng Keda stood among them.

Ma Hanshan felt disinclined to pay them much attention. Instead, he turned his head and looked at the Western Hills that lay beyond the prison walls.

Wang Puchen strode up to stand between the two battalions.

Zeng Keda walked over to greet him. He pulled orders out of his jacket and handed them to Wang Puchen. "Here are the transfer papers."

Wang received the document, scanned the contents, and then replied: "Should these be shown to Director Xu as well?"

"Yes, certainly. Signal for him to come over."

Wang Puchen looked towards Xu Tieying. "Director Xu!"

Xu Tieying nodded and walked over, slowly.

"Director Xu, these orders come directly from the Executive Yuan subcommittee for the economy. Please look them over."

Xu Tieying reached out his hand and received the document. He read it over carefully, deliberately. When he had finished, he turned to look at Zeng Keda. "It seems we have very little choice but to cooperate and follow the orders given by the Executive Yuan. But I, too, have my own document. I believe you need to see this, Inspector Zeng."

"If your papers contradict the orders I carry from the Executive Yuan, then I don't need to see them."

"And if the director-general has signed them, if Chiang Ching-kuo has signed them… what then, will you not look at them?"

Zeng Keda could not conceal his surprise.

Xu continued: "Here, it's top secret, a record of what was discussed by the party's Standing Committee. Warden Wang, if you could find a more private place, I suggest you read the documents together."

Moments later, the three men entered Wang Puchen's office. The mahjong table that had been there when Ma Hanshan had been staying in the room had since been removed and the room was spartan as it had been before: one bed, one desk, a bookcase and a single chair.

"Please have a seat, Inspector Zeng." Xu Tieying gestured to the only chair, then walked to the bed and sat upon it.

Zeng, however, remained standing. "The document?"

Xu Tieying did not repeat his suggestion. He only took out the papers and passed them to Wang Puchen, who was standing closest. Wang accepted them and then gave them immediately to Zeng Keda. Zeng Keda did his best to remain calm, but his facial expression betrayed the growing disquiet he was beginning to feel.

The blue lettering on top was most striking:

Kuomintang Central Executive Committee
    Contents: Record of Special Standing Committee meeting
    Host: Zhu Jiahua
    Attendee: President Chiang Kai-shek
    Standing Committee: Dai Jitao, Chen Guofu, Zhang Qun, Zhang Lisheng, Chiang Ching-kuo…

On the very day the currency reforms were announced, the Executive Yuan and the Standing Committee, both organs of the Kuomintang, issued two sets of distinctly different and contradictory orders, both with Chiang Ching-kuo's signature on them. The resistance, the reactionary elements, whatever they were, were far greater than Zeng Keda could have imagined.

Zeng collected himself. He couldn't show the others his doubt.

He turned to Wang Puchen and said: "Let me use your telephone. I need to contact the Ministry of Defence. I must report to Chiang Ching-kuo."

Xu Tieying stood up and grabbed the document. "Comrade Chiang Ching-kuo is a member of the Kuomintang, but he is not your chief! The resolution of the Standing Committee is the highest order here. Are you trying to get Chiang Ching-kuo to disregard them? The currency reforms are the party's efforts to maintain the stability of the nation. Suppressing revolt and saving the country are the prime objectives of the party-state! The criminal Ma Hanshan colluded with the known Communist Cui Zhongshi when he was working in the Peking branch of the Central Bank. Together, they tampered with numerous accounts. His apprehension for these crimes also exposed the connections they had to the ringleader of communist activities in Peking, namely the scoundrel Liu Chuwu, as well as Yan Chunming who was responsible for instigating student protests. Inspector Zeng, did you report all of this to the Executive Yuan? You've both seen the resolution decided upon by the Standing Committee, and yet you're still trying to oppose them. You're a member of the Iron and Blood Congress... tell me, just what the hell are you playing at? Are you trying to drag Comrade Chiang Ching-kuo into your little game... is that it?"

Zeng Keda's face blanched. He stood there, flabbergasted by Xu's words, but unable to say anything.

Xu took advantage of his astonishment and continued: "For the past month and more, you mistakenly thought I'd been sent by the Communications Bureau to disrupt and impede efforts to implement the currency reforms, but I had no way to communicate to you the error of your assumption. Now, you've seen both documents, and I don't feel like saying anything more about them. I only wish that we can arrive at... at some unity of thought. After all, without the economic base, there is no superstructure that can be built upon it. And that superstructure, of course, is the Kuomintang! The currency reforms are hugely important for the economy. If there is no unity of thought within the party, then how can it be successfully implemented? Since the thirty-first year of the Republic, there has been a certain group within the party that has attempted to use three youth leagues to supplant the old guard, to replace the premier and the president, to take away from them the party they established. And the result? The three youth leagues are no more, they've been dissolved to safeguard the position and unity of the party. But yet there is still a coterie of individuals with their manipulative fingers all over the decisions supposedly made by Chiang Ching-kuo. They're still trying to usurp power and take over the party. But these people... heh, heh... they've forgotten one key element, the most fundamental thing. Comrade Ching-kuo is a man who puts party unity above everything else! He's the epitome of loyalty to the Kuomintang! The subcommittee formed by the Executive Yuan, the one they've apparently tried to put in charge of economic affairs, this is only a recent development. And they've got so much on their plate, their fingers into everything... and they've issued orders for you to take custody of Ma Hanshan. The question is why? For what purpose? I'll tell you. They're using the anticorruption campaign to tear apart the party! You've seen the document pertaining to the Standing Committee's special meeting. It made clear that the currency reforms must not endanger the party's ownership over its assets, for without those assets and the funds they generate, there would be no party to speak of. And if there was no party to govern and maintain the economy, where would that leave the country? Warden Wang, do you believe that Ma Hanshan should be given over to Inspector Zeng, put in his custody and remain in Peking, or should the orders of the Standing Committee be followed... should Ma be brought to Nanking?"

Wang Puchen glanced at Zeng Keda.

With Xu's document hanging over his head, Zeng had little choice but to endure this apparent masterclass on the party. All he could do was bite his lip and listen, but he could feel the resentment growing in his heart. "Are you finished, Director Xu? If you have, I would like to ask for guidance on one particular issue."

"Let's not talk about guidance. If you have any questions to raise, you're free to report to the central authorities."

"And just who would these central authorities be?" There was an unmistakable sternness in Zeng Keda's voice. "Will my investigative teams even be allowed to pursue violators of the new economic regulations? All such violators would only need to have some connection to the Kuomintang to get off the hook, yes?"

"If anyone were to do that, to tarnish the name of the party for their own selfish interests, then you would have my full support in confiscating their property and assets... and in executing them on the spot."

"But who would know whether the party banner they brandish is real or not?"

"Since any such cases would involve party assets, and since I will remain in Peking, naturally, I will be the judge. If you are in disagreement with this, then you're free to request verification."

"Am I correct in assuming, then, that whatever accounts we look into in Tianjin, and whatever we discover in the accounts held by the Peking branch of the Central Bank, we're to turn all of them over to you... and then, what, wait for your judgment?"

"No, you needn't give any of that to me, I should think it's best to give them to the Communists in the Peking Labour Union."

Zeng Keda shot a glance at Wang Puchen and laughed. "Ah, so now you consider me a Communist, is that it? Mr Wang, tell me, what does the Intelligence Bureau say to that?"

Wang Puchen had to answer: "I don't think the Communication Bureau is trying to imply that, nor do I think this was what Director Xu meant."

Zeng Keda spun his head to stare at Xu Tieying once more. "Is that true? If it is, well then, what do you mean?"

"I think you should answer this question, or rather, I would like to ask, the man you rely on and value so highly, a certain Fang Meng'ao, tell me, is he a Communist agent or isn't he?"

There was no easy answer to this question, so all Zeng Keda could do was stare at him.

Xu took advantage of Zeng's inability to answer and shouted: "On the sixth of July in the Nanking Special Criminal Court, I represented the Communication Bureau and defended Fang Meng'ao. I pointed out there was no hard evidence to prove he was a Communist. You, Inspector Zeng, you represented your department and claimed for certain that he had Communist sympathies, that he was, in fact, working to further their interests. But then there was the phone call. And what happened next, you remember, our positions were reversed. Chiang Ching-kuo suddenly reinstated Fang Meng'ao, promoted him, in truth, to captain of the economic investigative team based in Peking and working under the Ministry of Defence. At the time, you didn't understand Chiang's intention, and I must say, nor did we. Now, to safeguard Comrade Ching-kuo's own position, and, perhaps even more importantly, to ensure the director-general was not embarrassed, the Standing Committee dispatched me to Peking. My mission has been to seek out heretofore unrecognised dangers to the party and to determine, once and for all, whether or not Fang Meng'ao has been working for the Communists. After a series of surreptitious investigations, we began to suspect Cui Zhongshi... and to believe that *he* was a Communist agent. What's more, we also figured it was Cui who served as Fang Meng'ao's contact, or handler, or both. But then, right at that moment, and entirely unexpected, your agent – yes, I know of Sun Chaozhong's allegiance to the Iron and Blood Congress – murdered Cui Zhongshi. His death cut off the only line of investigation we had that could have proved Fang Meng'ao's loyalty to the CPC. Nevertheless, things have sort of worked out, for you also sent an agent to play the part of a Communist, to try to tease out of Fang Meng'ao where his true allegiances lay. Of course, our investigation into Fang's links with the CPC ended. But what's been of greater disappointment to the party is, well, the Intelligence Bureau in Peking!"

Xu stopped his monologue and shot a glance at Wang Puchen, looking for any reaction on his face. When none was immediately evident, he continued: "Mr Wang, a few days prior, the central command of the party gave the order to have Xie Mulan executed. At the time, however, you were disinclined to carry it out. I thought you would have understood why the party gave this order, but still you resisted. But something's come to me since. As the key organisation set up to combat the advances of the CPC, well, I would like to ask a question: does the Intelligence Bureau really not understand the order, or is all of this just a ruse?"

It never occurred to Wang Puchen that Xu Tieying would bring up the issue of Xie Mulan's death, and would use it to put him off balance. He was resentful of Xu's tactic, but did his best to remain calm: "In our efforts to save the nation, the Intelligence Bureau has never been remiss in its duties, nor has it ever been lenient towards its enemies. I therefore cannot fathom the reason why Director Xu has chosen this baseless means to attack and criticise the work I've done. Tell me, Director Xu, where does this suspicion come from? Is it your own personal belief, or the belief of your superiors?"

"Aha! So the battle between spy agencies can finally come to an end!" Xu's voice dripped with venom. "Your department's main adversary has been the CPC-controlled Labour Union in Peking, but has it ever once occurred to you that besides Yan Chunming, and that known Communist Liu Chuwu who was killed on the spot instead of arrested and brought to Xishan prison, that there are even deeper-placed agents working for the CPC inside the Peking branch of the Central Bank?"

Finally, Zeng Keda heard the clue he had been waiting for. That night, in the torrential rain, Wang Puchen had accompanied Xie Peidong in searching for Xie Mulan... of course! That was it! It was all so clear to him. A great expanse of whiteness opened up in front of him, but Zeng could not make out if it was that night of pouring rain, or the blankness that seemed to now swallow his thoughts. But then, just as suddenly as it had come, the empty space of his mind was filled anew with thoughts of what this all meant. His face grew ashen, and he stared at the two men. He had to be patient, he had to let them finish their conversation. He had to know!

Everything, the whole world itself, seemed to dance in Xu Tieying's eyes, but at the same time, he seemed not to notice Zeng Keda, hadn't seen him from the beginning, so lost he was in the rhythm of this verbal confrontation. His voice was even growing louder than before: "Cui Zhongshi was a Communist. How was he permitted to remain in his post at the Peking branch for so long? We'd already targeted him, we knew who he was, so why did Fang Buting waste so very much to protect him? Did you not connect the dots, did you not even see them? To allow such a man to remain in such an important position, to let him see the financial workings of the party-state, most especially the imminent currency reform initiative, how could it not be harmful to our interests!"

Wang Puchen was in no position to answer Xu Tieying's challenge, so sinister were the implications of his question. But nor could he look at Zeng Keda. Instead, he reached into his pocket and pulled out his cigarettes.

Zeng Keda was about to burst. It took all his willpower to

restrain his mounting anger. He stared at Xu Tieying. "So, there's a Communist agent inside the bank?"

Xu Tieying shifted his attention to Zeng Keda, but he didn't answer.

Zeng continued: "Is it Fang Buting or Xie Peidong?"

"Who do you think it is?"

Zeng Keda snarled. "This is all your conjecture. Why the hell do you want me to answer? If there is a Communist agent in the bank, why haven't you arrested him?"

"Sooner or later we will arrest the traitor!" Xu's voice became sterner. "Both our agencies, mine and Mr Wang's, have strict procedures and plans in place to apprehend Communist spies, but you have constantly interfered with these plans. Inspector Zeng is now doing the same!"

"Xie Mulan was a Communist? You murdered her in the name of apprehending Communist agents?" Zeng Keda could no longer control his growing anger. "And you've interfered with our economic reforms, you executed Xie Mulan, and then lied about… you told us she'd gone to the so-called liberated zones. We, me and her father I mean, we spent hours searching for her. Do you mean to tell me this is how your capture Communists!" Zeng ceased speaking, but his anger boiled. When his eyes fell on Wang Puchen, he couldn't control himself. "Answer, dammit!" he shouted.

Wang Puchen felt the most intense emotions. He was conflicted. Everything he and the Iron and Blood Congress had fought for had become muddied and unclear. Faced now with Xu Tieying's apparent subterfuge, Zeng Keda's anger, he found it difficult to respond: "Should I report on all of this? If so, to whom would I report… to the Intelligence Bureau or to Chiang Ching-kuo himself? Director Xu has already revealed the details of what happened to Xie Mulan, that she was executed. Should we tell him, tell Inspector Zeng, the reason why?"

"I know the reason already!" Zeng shouted. "It's all tied up with those bloody accounts held in the Peking branch, the graft perpetrated by men supposedly serving the country! And among them there are men seeking to divvy up party assets, notably the shares held by Hou Juntang, about twenty per cent, I believe. And should anyone get in his way, they're to be done away with. I know the inside details, too, I know why Ma Hanshan's to be escorted to Nanking. And I know who's in charge of those accounts: Xie Peidong. Which is why his Xie Mulan was murdered. They are, or were in the case of his daughter, Communist agents. Surprising and unexpected though this may be, Xu Tieying, you know full well that the final, decisive battle against the Communists will be launched by us, not you! You can take Ma Hanshan, and you can keep killing anyone who gets between you and those shares. But I and my investigative teams across the economic area surrounding Tianjin will be watching you. I'll also be launching investigations into those people connected to your precious party assets! At the same time, I use the power granted me by the Executive Yuan to warn you in no uncertain terms, that if any of your actions, your conduct, whatever, if any of it impedes the implementation of the currency reforms, you'll be the first person I arrest!" Finished, Zeng marched purposefully out of the room.

It was now time for Xu Tieying's face to turn pale.

There was no longer any need for Wang Puchen to conceal his dissatisfaction: "Director Xu, should we implement the Standing Committee's decision? Will you take Ma Hanshan to Nanking?"

"Do you still need to question their decision before seeing it done?" Xu appreciated the fact he had put all his cards on the table. There was no turning back, it was now up to the Iron and Blood Congress to make the next move. He looked hard at Wang. "The central authorities will continue to evaluate your assessment of the situation. Comrade Wang, there's still the matter of my secretary, Sun Chaozhong. All I will say is that I hope you'll both remain of benefit to Comrade Chiang Ching-kuo and his plans." With those words, Xu straightened his jacket, turned and left Wang Puchen's office.

Wang watched Xu depart and reflected that the man had always made him uneasy. He reached into his pocket as he had done so many times before, apparently to get a smoke. But on this occasion, he didn't. Instead, he pulled out Zeng Guofan's diary, the one Ma Hanshan had filled with notes. He flipped through the pages, then stopped, mesmerised by Ma's handwriting: "Shanghai Cotton Mill. Ten thousand rolls of cotton yarn, party assets..."

Wang Puchen shut the book quickly. His office was blanketed in darkness as though it were night. His slender fingers were upon the telephone; he was busily dialling numbers. The only light came from the desk lamp, tinged green by its lampshade.

The click, click of the rotary dial travelled through the telephone wires, beyond the walls of Wang Puchen's office and into the air above. Soon it raced over the mountains and plains, arriving at its destination: Shanghai! Then the speed of sound plummeted, the Shanghai Bund came into view, then Jiujiang Road and the offices of the Central Bank. On the third floor, a telephone rang.

Wang Puchen held the telephone receiver tight to his ear. He could hear the sounds of the bank, the hustle and bustle of finance in the distance, then a voice: "Yes, we've established a presence in the Central Bank. Comrade Jianfeng is making preparations to convene a high-level meeting. Time is of the essence."

"Secretary Wang," said Wang Puchen, "if it's possible, please ask Comrade Jianfeng to give me five minutes."

"Impossible." By the sound of his voice, it seemed as though Secretary Wang desperately wanted to hang up: "This is the first meeting. Du Yuesheng, Liu Hongsheng, Rong Erren… they're all here. Comrade Jianfeng, it's Comrade Wang Puchen calling."

Wang Puchen felt a shiver go up his spine. In his mind, he could see the chaotic scene being played out at the Central Bank in Shanghai. He could see the figure of Comrade Jianfeng rush out from the middle of the chaos, his breath tight.

"Comrade Puchen?" Chiang Ching-kuo took hold of the phone.

Wang Puchen was both excited and calm: "Yes, it's me, Comrade Jianfeng. I know I shouldn't be taking your time at a moment like this, disrupting your important…"

"Just get on with it. Report."

Wang Puchen spoke quickly: "The Executive Yuan's subcommittee on economic affairs, its orders were to hand Ma Hanshan over to Inspector Zeng, but Xu Tieying had orders, or rather the record of a meeting held by the Standing Committee that stipulated Ma Hanshan be put into his custody and brought to Nanking. Needless to say, Inspector Zeng was quite worked up by this seemingly contradictory situation. A heated argument ensued, during which Xu Tieying revealed highly confidential information. He informed Inspector Zeng of the order to execute Xie Mulan. He also put forth, threw it out there, really, an entirely unexpected explanation for her death, namely, that Xie Peidong, her father, is a Communist agent. Because of this turn of events, I fear the Peking branch of the Central Bank will soon be thrown into chaos, which will jeopardise the plans involving our peacocks flying southeast. I thus have two questions. One, do you still wish to have Fang Buting involved in implementing the currency reforms? Two, is it wise to allow Fang Meng'ao to take command of the transport aircraft? The currency reform initiatives have already encountered serious obstacles, but if it's dragged into the anti-Communist campaign, we can't directly oppose…"

"In your judgment, is Xie Peidong a Communist agent?" said Chiang Ching-kuo.

"At present, I don't think I can make that call, I must investigate the matter…"

"I can give you two minutes. Make sure you remember what I'm about to say." Comrade Jianfeng's voice was crystal clear: "You will not carry out an investigation. It doesn't matter if Xie Peidong is a CPC agent or not. If he is a Communist, then I truly hope they involve themselves in the currency reforms and try to thwart them. If they do, they'll surely lose the support of the people and that will work in our favour. If he's not a Communist, then he'll be at Fang Buting's side, assisting him in all matters related to the successful implementation of the reforms. These reform efforts we're pushing, they're not only for the benefit of the economy, they're also a political movement. Their aim is to save the masses, to turn the tide, regardless of whether it's the CPC or the corrupt elements in our own party. I don't fear their attempts to obstruct my plans, I only fear they won't appear, that they won't oppose what I'm trying to do. 'With one hand I'm determined to resist the Communists, with the other I root out corruption.' This is no simple battle, it's not just a matter of making arrests, it's about striving for popular sentiment, winning the hearts and minds of the people. Let Xu and his men bounce and hop about, let the Communists rile people up, let them recruit new adherents. Fang Buting is the man for the job, he must be involved in issuing the new legal tender. The three Curtiss C-46s must also be put under Fang Meng'ao's command. I must go, my meeting needs to begin. What I plan to say in it will be published tomorrow in the party press, domestically and internationally. Regardless of the machinations of the Communists, the corrupt figures in the Kuomintang, including Xu Tieying's Central Committee Clique, my speech is a declaration, a manifesto. I hope you'll all understand well my intent."

"Yes, Comrade Jianfeng. I understand."

The receiver on the other end clicked.

CHAPTER 10

Control Tower.
    Runway.
C-46 aircraft.
Security fence.
Beyond the fence, helmets, rifles, guards.
Inside the fence, the same.
Within ten steps of the runway, channels had been dug for additional protection.

In the northern China warzone, Nanyuan airbase was the most heavily fortified and guarded centre of operations. When Fu Zuoyi left for Nanking, Tianjin and the areas around Hohhot, it was from Nanyuan that he left and returned to. The airbase was also used by Li Zongren when he flew back and forth between Nanking and Peking. Even Chiang Kai-shek used the airbase to fly between Nanking, Peking and Shenyang. Hence, its security was paramount and set to his exacting precision. The guards on both sides of the fence were all vetted personally by the president. The fortifications were built to his specifications. It was thus logical to use Nanyuan to transport the new *jinyuanquan* currency.

The rows of guards parted when they saw two familiar vehicles arrive. Their urgency was clearly visible by the speed at which they drove. In the first jeep sat Fang Meng'ao. Immediately behind him was the young contingent of pilots; for all intents and purposes, his personal guard. Coming hot on their heels, however, was a third vehicle, a British-made Austin bearing the mark of the Peking branch of the Central Bank. Fang's jeep stopped first. Then the jeep carrying the young pilots pulled up beside him. Finally, the Austin stopped.

In the back seat sat Fang Buting and his assistant manager, Xie Peidong. Both men looked out towards the heavily guarded airbase. It was the first time either of them had seen Fang Meng'ao dressed in his Air Force fatigues. As he stepped down from his jeep, they noticed his pilot's helmet wedged underneath his arm. He was standing to attention. Moments later, the twenty young pilots under his immediate command filed out of their jeep and hurriedly formed up behind their captain. Both Fang Buting and Xie Peidong, still seated in the back of the Austin, watched on in amazement and no small amount of pride.

Xie Peidong smiled at Fang Buting. "Mr Governor, you're finally getting the opportunity to fly with your son. Are you at all afraid?" Xie had rarely smiled this past year, and even though he did so now, the smile hid a multitude of pain and hurt. It was more for his companion than anything else, an attempt to lighten the mood, if only a little.

Fang lifted his hand slowly. "Do you know, I've never flown before. I haven't dared to try. Look, my hand is covered in sweat."

Xie turned to their driver, Young Li. "Quick, bring the governor's towel."

"Yes sir." Li obliged immediately, as he had done so often before.

Xie softened his tone and looked at Fang Buting. "If they're letting Meng'ao take command of these planes, letting him fly, then at least that means they no longer suspect him of being a Communist agent. If only Chiang Ching-kuo would honour his commitment, his promise, that when the time's right, both Meng'ao and Mengwei will be allowed to leave China."

"Peidong, the family has no savings left. If they leave, if the younger generation departs us, who'll look after us in our old age?"

"We can always beg for food. And in any case, I've been by your side for ten-plus years."

Li's reappearance cut him off. The young man had returned with the towel. "Mr Governor, here…"

Xie glanced at the window. "Look, Meng'ao is coming to fetch you."

Fang Buting turned his face in the direction Xie Peidong indicated and saw his son walking towards them. He pressed the towel to his face, wiping away the sweat.

By the time Fang Buting had finished and Xie had taken the towel from him, Fang Meng'ao was standing beside the Austin. "Dad, if you will…"

"Yes, certainly." Fang Buting waited for his son to open the door and then stepped out.

Xie Peidong climbed out from the same side.

The airport sprawled out beneath them, just as the sky expanded outwards above them. Fang Buting scanned the enormity of the scene. "How long's the flight between Peking and Tianjin?"

"With me at the controls, fifteen minutes or so." There was a confidence in Fang Meng'ao's voice.

Xie Peidong walked up alongside them and said: "Meng'ao, you're father's never flown before. He's rather terrified of the prospect, truth be told. Be sure to take it easy."

Fang Meng'ao glanced at his uncle. "Don't worry, Uncle Xie. After the first time, you're never afraid again."

"You better get yourself to the treasury to make the appropriate preparations," said Fang Buting. "It took us thirty minutes to get here. It'll take you that long or more to get back, but it should only take us an hour at most to pack the new *jinyuanquan*. Time can't be wasted."

"There's no rush, I've got time. Besides, I've never seen an aeroplane up this close. I want to see you both off."

"In that case Uncle, if you will, please review the troops as we depart!" Fang Meng'ao, dressed in his fatigues, saluted and then passed on the info to his men.

Xie Peidong nodded, his eyes flashing with excitement.

Fang Meng'ao guided his father to the aircraft. The sun had risen fully in the sky and now shimmered down upon them, reflecting off the metal of the aeroplane. Xie put his hand over his eyes to shield them from the glare.

They reached the plane and Fang Meng'ao helped his father up the steps and into the belly of the aircraft. Several of his men climbed aboard right after. The remaining men split into two groups, each boarding one of the two other planes. Soon, their engines began to rumble, the huge propellers began to spin. Moments later, Fang Meng'ao's C-46 was moving towards the runway. The aeroplane accelerated and soon its nose lifted off the ground. The C-46 was soon airborne. Xie lowered his hand and tilted his head upwards. A magnificent sight!

Over the roar of the aircraft, Xie Peidong heard Zhang Yueyin's parting words: "Vice-Chair Zhou's orders are for you to do what you can to advance the reforms in the Pingjin area, to make them of the greatest use to us. To do this, you will of course need to use your position at the Peking branch of the Central Bank, and your relationship with He Qicang. Just as Chiang Ching-kuo seized the opportunity to make use of Fang Meng'ao and his position, we must do the same. We need to obtain goods and supplies for *our* efforts. That way, when the day comes and the new *jinyuanquan* becomes worthless, and believe me, that day will come, *we'll* have the food that the people in Peking and Tianjin will need."

The sun began to blind him. By now, Fang Meng'ao's aeroplane was no more than a speck of silver in the sky. The second and third C-46s were not far behind. Xie turned and saw that Li had already opened the door to the Austin. The guard vehicles escorted them off the airbase.

―――――

The sound of running boots echoed clearly. Two contingents of men, all of them wearing armbands identifying them as Zeng's men, came marching towards the main gate that opened into Gu Weijun's residence. There, they formed two lines. Each had a pistol at his waist. They stood to attention, their figures straight, erect.

Zeng Keda's jeep rolled up, followed closely by his lieutenant's slightly larger vehicle. Behind it was a ten-wheeled convoy truck. Zeng's vehicle slowed enough for him to jump out, and then it drove away. His lieutenant's jeep pulled to a stop beside him.

Zeng signalled to two soldiers standing guard at the gate. "You two, yes, come here. Your assistance will be needed."

"Yes sir." The two young men rushed over, then around to the back of the jeep.

Zeng Keda followed them, his face expressionless, but still polite. "Sirs, if you will…"

Two people climbed down first from the rear of the jeep. The two young soldiers extended their hands to assist them. The first one was dressed impeccably in a Western-style suit. The second wore gold-rimmed glasses. The treatment they were being given indicated clearly their status, but they appeared sombre nevertheless.

"Please, this way." Zeng Keda didn't say anything more. He merely turned around and walked towards the main gate.

The two soldiers repeated their commander's words: "Please, this way."

In total, eight persons were escorted into Gu Weijun's residence by the two young guards, each face as sombre as the rest. Once inside, the heavy metal gates were pushed closed.

———

The doors to the treasury of the Peking branch of the Central Bank slowly shut. The immense gate was the only wheeled door in all of Peking. A track had been cut into the cement floor beneath it, and the heavy gate would, bit by bit, move from right to left until it reached its frame. Then the smallest of small cracks would be sealed tight. An electrified net would then come alive, further cutting off the treasury from the world outside.

There were soldiers here as well. And like the great gate, they were the only soldiers of their kind in Peking. Trained and tasked exclusively with the protection of the treasury, the lieutenant in charge of the guardsmen now formed the men. He'd seen the Austin approaching and knew who was inside.

"Attention!" Despite the apparent seriousness of the situation, the lieutenant's tone lacked a little energy and purpose. The salute by the men was equally dispirited.

Xie's driver stepped out and opened the door for him. Xie emerged and nodded towards the soldiers. As uninterested as they had raised their hands in the first place, they now lowered them.

Xie spoke to Li: "The task at hand is of grave importance.

Distribute the items in the back of the car to them." And he pointed towards the guardsmen.

As soon as the soldiers heard these words, however, their eyes seemed to brighten. They all stared in the direction of the Austin.

Xie Peidong strode towards the gate, and the lieutenant hurried over beside him. Xie spoke: "Open the gate."

"Yes sir!" This time, there was unexpected vigour in his voice. The lieutenant turned and walked to the guard room. There, he picked up the special key and inserted it into the lock. At the other end of the gate, Xie Peidong lifted out his own special key and inserted it into the locking mechanism closest to him. Their eyes met, and they turned the keys simultaneously. The guard shouted: "Gate opening!" Two other guards now rushed forward, one on each side. Together, they pushed to swing the gate open.

Xie removed his key from the lock and then turned to the lieutenant. "I've brought something for all of you to eat. See to it that it's distributed among the men."

"Yes sir!"

Xie walked into the treasury vault. Before they enjoyed the food Xie had brought, the two guards repositioned themselves on the other side of the gate and pushed it closed.

The lieutenant turned around to face his men but discovered they were no longer in formation. While he had been busy with opening the vault door, his men had broken rank and crowded around the Austin, watching as Young Li lifted out boxes from the boot. "Attention!" he shouted. The men complied immediately. The lieutenant continued: "About face! March! Hup to, hup to." Seconds later, the men were back in formation, but their eyes were still trained on Li and the Austin.

The lieutenant now walked over to the vehicle to stand next to Li. They both smiled at each other. The lieutenant then glanced at the boot. His eyes lit up, and he gulped. "Standing guard over the treasury, I won't lie, we're starving. Tell me, brother, we should be thanking Mr Xie by the looks of this. What's in there?"

"Each box contains soda crackers and two cans of cured beef."

Li had spoken loud enough that the men standing to attention couldn't help but hear. To a man, they all stared in his direction, their eyes apparently as ravenous as their stomachs!

Li continued: "Come on, let's give them out as quickly as we can." Li passed the box he was holding to the lieutenant, and then reached into the boot for more. The lieutenant did not know whence his strength came, but it took him only seconds to tear open the box. Inside were English-branded soda crackers and a beautiful girl's face on the package encouraging them to enjoy!

The second steel door protecting the treasury's vault lay about a dozen steps down from the main gate. Once Xie Peidong walked through, it, too, was closed from the inside. There were lights in the ceiling to illuminate his path down the next corridor, but about two metres before he arrived at the third door, he stopped. There was a small office to the side, bathed in darkness. Xie noticed the light switch on the wall beside the door. He reached out to flick it, but then paused. A moment later, he let his hand fall, and instead borrowed the light from the corridor to look into the small room. Deep in the shadows, he could see a strongbox up against the far wall. His eyes scanned the nearby desk, then stopped abruptly on the chair just behind it. Xie closed his eyes, as a low voice carried out of the room: "Mr Xie..."

He trembled. The hairs on the back of his neck rose up; the voice was that of Cui Zhongshi!

A dead man alive?

Xie was transported back to 4 July 1948. The same office. "Mr Xie," said Cui Zhongshi, placing a stack of ledgers on the desk in front of them. "Everyone in the Kuomintang, from the inner circle of the party, to the government and even the military, they're all greedy, venal and corrupt. Now the Peking Senate is using the excuse of financial challenges to drive more than ten thousand refugee students out of the city. I recommend we send their dirty books to our superiors, and then publish them in the newspapers for all to see!"

Xie's eyes were not on Cui Zhongshi, but on the stack of ledgers on the table. "Put them away."

Cui Zhongshi chose not to look at Xie Peidong either but rather directed his attention above.

Swiftly and suddenly, Xie grabbed the ledgers and strode over to the strongbox just behind the desk. "Open it!"

Cui Zhongshi stood up, dug in his pocket for the key and placed it in Xie's waiting hand. "I demand to be allowed to leave Peking for the liberated areas. I can take up work in the banks there." As he spoke, he stormed towards the door, not waiting for a response.

Xie called after him, his voice a shout: "Fang Meng'ao's been arrested, did you know?"

Cui Zhongshi couldn't help but quake in the doorway. He turned around and said: "When? Why?"

"First, put the ledgers away."

Cui Zhongshi walked towards the strongbox and to where Xie Peidong was standing. He reached out for the keys in Xie's hand, his own trembling as he did so. Seconds later, the safe was open.

Xie placed the ledgers in Cui's hands. "Comrade Liuyun has given orders. You must go at once to Nanking to rescue Fang Meng'ao! There's a plane this afternoon at four, departing from the northern airbase. Take ten thousand US dollars with you, as well as the twenty per cent shares belonging to Hou Juntang, and get yourself to Nanking. Once there, find Xu Tieying."

Cui Zhongshi placed the ledgers in the strongbox.

Xie's eyes were still closed, but he reached out his hand once more and found the switch. The room burst into light and the exhaust fan in the corner also came to life. Xie opened his eyes wide, scanning the room, the empty chair. He walked inside and around behind the desk. He extended his hand and opened the drawer. The keys were there, untouched. He picked them up, opened the strongbox and lifted out the stack of ledgers.

Xie sat down and looked into the first ledger: "Shanghai Cotton Mill, ten thousand rolls of cotton yarn, party assets…"

The words Cui Zhongshi had written were exact in every way

to what Ma Hanshan had written down inside Zeng Guofan's diary. He shut the ledger with a great slap.

―――

Gu Weijun's residence had been used before for meetings. The room was at the rear of the compound and had served Koo's five-man groups on several occasions before. The table, covered in white cloth, now had eight glasses laid on top of it. Each was filled with plain boiled water. Sitting around the table were eight impressively dressed heads of industry and finance, Peking's bigwigs. Lying beside the glasses were printed copies of the terms of the currency reforms.

There seemed to be a silent agreement among the attendees. They all kept their mouths firmly shut. No one said a word, nor did they look at the document in front of them.

Zeng Keda finally stood up. He walked behind the seated figures, ultimately stopping at the person around the table who seemed to be carrying the most weight. "Why aren't you reading the file?"

The man did not reply. Instead, he reached into his pocket and pulled out a pack of cigarettes. He laid these on the table and then searched for his matches. Finding them, he lifted one out and struck it. Several of the other men seated around the table followed suit.

"The place we're in is dedicated to the father of our nation!" said Zeng Keda, slapping at the cigarette hanging from the lip of the man in front of him. "There are words on the wall. Haven't you seen them?"

Never before had a man in his position been treated so humiliatingly. He guffawed and stood up right away. "Mr Zeng, we've had meetings with Fu Zuoyi, Li Zongren has treated us to dinner. Who the hell do you think you are to treat us with such disrespect? Who gave you the authority to hold us here like this, to order us to read this bit of paper on the table? The nerve!"

The seven other men all rose from their seats.

Zeng Keda laughed and walked to stand under the image of Dr Sun Yat-sen, the father of the nation. "There's no need for me to tell you who I am. I'll say just one thing. In Shanghai, at this very moment, our very own Mr Chiang Ching-kuo is holding a meeting of his own. He's called Big-Eared Du to attend, you know, Mr Dou Yu-seng. Liu Hongsheng is there as well, along with Rong Erren. They're all there to examine this document." At this point, Zeng paused, before slamming his fist on the table. "The orders come from the Executive Yuan, from their subcommittee charged with handling the economy. They're the ones who've asked you to read this document. I must say I'm surprised you're choosing not to. The nerve indeed!"

Each man seemed stunned and unable to say a word.

Zeng shouted towards the door: "Commander Li!"

"Here sir!" It took only seconds for Commander Li to appear in the doorway.

"Call in eight more men. I want one by each of these gentlemen here. They're to assist as needed!"

"Yes sir!" Li glanced behind him and shouted to his men: "You men, I need eight of you!"

Eight soldiers marched into the room, each manoeuvring to stand beside the men of industry and finance. They barked forcefully: "Be seated please!"

The businessmen, however, remained standing. Seven faces turned towards their ringleader.

"Help them to their seats, men!" It was now Commander Li's turn to bark orders.

The soldiers complied, each putting hands on the shoulders of Peking's business elite. Up close, they could all see the armband each soldier wore, which seemed sufficient for the men all returned to their chairs needing no further assistance.

"Now read the file in front of you!" Zeng Keda's voice bounced off the walls. Once he saw them obey, he walked out of the room to permit them the necessary time.

The lieutenant of the treasury guard walked over towards Young Li, who was still standing near the Austin. The other guards were all enjoying the soda crackers and cured beef. The lieutenant looked at Li. "Brother, will you have some?" He proffered his open box.

Young Li smiled and scanned the yard outside the treasury. The men were in various states of gorging themselves on the food he'd brought. Their rifles were holstered on their waists, their hands occupied with the crackers and beef. There was little thought given to decorum or manners. After all, it wasn't a fine meal they were enjoying. Most had already devoured the crackers, and all that could really be heard was the munching of their jaws.

Li smiled again and accepted the food offered by the lieutenant. He spoke to him in a low voice, seeming conscious of not wanting to disturb the men: "There're still two boxes of crackers in the car, and four cans of cured beef, I think. Mr Xie's told me these are especially for you. When it's more convenient, I'll let you have them."

The lieutenant's eyes sparkled. "That's… that's too much. How about I take half and leave the rest for you?"

"Mr Xie's told me already. Once the new legal tender enters the economy, a great number of goods and supplies will be delivered to Peking, and because of the price controls that will be in place, you and your men won't have to worry about going hungry again."

"Thanks for passing on this bit of news," said the lieutenant. "How much will you be able to buy with one *jinyuanquan*?"

"I'm not too sure about that, to be honest. All I know is that one yuan of the new currency will be worth three hundred thousand of the old one. One yuan will get you two feet, eight inches of fine blue Shilin cloth. If you spend it on food, I imagine a single yuan will get you a jin each of meat and flour."

"How will our salaries be converted?"

"Ten yuan a month for you, six per month for your men."

"Give me a second to work that out." After calculating the numbers in his mind, the lieutenant's eyes opened wide when he realised just what the new salary would get him. "That's twenty-eight feet of yarn, thirty-three jin of flour, a little more than thirteen jin of meat. You've got to be joking, haven't you?"

Li smiled ear to ear. "I'm just a driver. Why would I dare try to pull your leg? I was just at Nanyuan airbase. I saw off the bank governor. I heard him going over these numbers in the back of the car with Mr Xie. There's a rule I have to follow, you know, and that's that whatever I overhear, I'm not supposed to say anything. But I've told you, I trust you. Don't let me down."

"Of course I won't!" It was the lieutenant's turn to smile from ear to ear. "When I get my first monthly salary – in the new currency – I'll treat you…"

Before he could promise more, the guard siren sounded. The lieutenant put the crackers and cured beef to one side and drew his pistol. He shouted to his men: "I need four of you over here now!" Before he had finished barking his command, he started marching towards the gate.

Four men, weapons drawn, rushed after him.

The metal gate was five inches thick. Level with an average man's height was an iron-barred window about five inches square. The lieutenant lifted the bolt and pulled back the cover so that he could see who had come.

Xu Tieying stood outside, the look in his eyes full of purpose. "Chief of the Peking Police," he announced, handing his ID card to the lieutenant through the barred window.

The lieutenant accepted the ID but didn't really pay it much attention. Instead, he turned round to look towards Young Li. "Come here a second, if you will." Li did as requested. Once closer, the lieutenant asked in a low voice: "The chief of police… his name's Xie, yeah?"

"I think so. That sounds right."

The lieutenant handed the ID back through the window. "Let me see your orders from the bank governor."

"I have special orders to be here. I'm to meet Mr Xie. Please let him know I've arrived."

"I'll still need to see orders from the bank governor." The lieutenant's tone made it clear he was unwilling to diverge from protocol.

"Tell Mr Xie to come here. He knows me."

"Mr Xie is presently occupied… in the treasury." The lieutenant didn't feel further explanation was needed, so he moved to shut the window.

Xie Tieying suddenly saw Xie Peidong's driver standing just behind the lieutenant and shouted out to him: "Li! Hey!"

Li had little choice but to draw closer to the window. "Ah, Chief Xu…"

Xu Tieying smiled. "A large amount of the new currency is to be transported here, today, and then put in storage. We're here to assist in this operation, to strengthen the protection detail to make sure nothing goes wrong. Please, would you go and get Mr Xie to come here?"

"Bank regulations stipulate you have to remain here, please, Chief Xu. Wait outside while I ring the bell and see if Mr Xie hears it."

"Ah, apologies for the trouble then. But thank you."

———

After passing through the second door, Xu Tieying slowed his pace to look around the treasury to see how well the actual one corresponded with his imagination. Although he was fifteen metres below ground, Xu couldn't help but feel the hallway to be incredibly spacious. It was, to his mind, at least five metres wide. The ceiling had to be a good three metres above him. And there were yet thirty metres to go down the corridor to reach the final door. Xu Tieying didn't verbalise any of this. He remained quiet beside Xie Peidong, simply following along after him. When they arrived at the last and thickest door, he asked: "So, is this the place that safeguards the food and supplies needed for all of Peking's residents, for its citizens, its government officials, teachers, everybody? It also protects the military supplies for several tens of thousands of soldiers… all of that is in here, yes?"

Xie Peidong paused but didn't respond.

Xu continued: "The gates… only you and Mr Fang are allowed through. Is that right?"

"Yes, that's correct," Xie reluctantly answered.

"And what about Cui Zhongshi? Was he permitted inside?"

"Yes, he was."

"And the transport of gold?"

"The guards outside are responsible for logistics."

"Oh." Xu stepped back from the gate a little and peered into the adjacent office. "I suppose you know TV Soong has organised his own tax-enforcement force. The Ministry of Defence is not bothered, nor is the Ministry of Internal Affairs. I just learnt of this today."

Xie Peidong remained silent.

"Let's go in for a while, OK?" He didn't wait, but walked into the office and plopped down in a chair in front of the desk as though he were in charge and not the other way round. "Come in, let's sit and talk."

Xie Peidong followed reluctantly. "Chief Xu, please get up."

"I beg your pardon?"

"That's the president's chair. It's for his use only. The rest of us simply stand when we're in here."

Xu Tieying remained seated, and instead scanned the contents of the office, especially the strongbox next to the far wall. His eyes lingered on it for a moment, and then he resumed his inspection, soon realising there was only one chair. "Is that some sort of treasury regulation?"

"Yes, as a matter of fact, it is. The regulations stipulated by the Central Bank in Nanking – regulations that every branch is required to follow – state that in the treasury office there's only to be one chair, reserved for the bank or branch governor. They're the ones in charge of the treasury and thus the only ones permitted to sit. As for why such a regulation exists, I can't tell you."

Xu Tieying chuckled a little under his breath, but he did stand up. "Perhaps it's to ensure people don't linger too long?"

"I can see, Chief Xu, that you understand."

"I shall be brief, then. I have just three questions."

Xie Peidong looked at the other man, waiting for him to begin.

"The first question is, who recommended Cui Zhongshi to serve as deputy director of the Peking treasury? Who checked his credentials and background, and who signed off on the appointment?"

"Such appointments, and the checks made into the candidates' backgrounds, everything and anything, it's all carried out by the Central Bank offices in Nanking. They're the ones who make the final decision. If the government wants to investigate the appointment, it's best to ask the bank's chairman, Yu Hongjun, or perhaps the former chairman Liu Kung-yun."

"But I'm here asking you." Xu reached into his pocket and drew out an official letter. He paused a moment and then placed it on the desk. "This letter here has your Liu Kung-yun's signature and stamp, Mr Xie. You've recently seen this. Would you like to have another, closer look at it?"

The paper had the Kuomintang seal stamped into the centre. The heading was in the familiar blue colour, written in regular script: "Kuomintang Central Executive Committee".

The words that followed were in the Song script:

> I, Yu Hongjun, chairman of the Central Bank of the Republic of China, hereby appoint the chief of Peking Police, Xu Tieying, as special investigator charged with investigating actions taken by the Peking branch of the Central Bank.

Below these lines, Chen Lifu, in his own accomplished calligraphic hand, had signed his name as witness. Immediately following were lines requesting Peking bank officials to cooperate and assist in Xu's investigation, signed, once more in beautiful handwriting, by Yu Hongjun.

"That's your chairman's signature, is it not?" Xu Tieying's stare bore into Xie Peidong.

"As you said, I've already seen the letter." Xie kept his calm, meeting Xu's look with an equal amount of confidence.

Xu glanced back at the chair. "So, do you think it's all right if I sit and ask my questions?"

"Yes. But you must get Chairman Yu to ratify these orders."

Xu locked eyes with Xie Peidong and then smiled. "Hmm, in that case I won't sit. Please, answer the questions I just asked."

"I can tell you what I know." Xie Peidong paused to collect his thoughts. "Cui Zhongshi, male, thirty-nine years of age. Graduated in the twenty-sixth year of the Republic from the National Central University, a degree in finance, passed the Central Bank's admission examination, eventually promoted to deputy section chief, then section chief. In the thirty-fifth year of the Republic, on the recommendation of the manager Fang Buting of the Peking branch of the Central Bank to former chairman Liu Kung-yun, Cui Zhongshi received appointment to the post of deputy director of the Peking treasury."

"Absolutely correct, yes, excellent. You didn't miss anything. I have a question, however: why did Mr Fang Buting think so highly of Cui Zhongshi?"

"I suggest you ask Governor Fang that question."

"I intend to. In the meantime, I'll ask you something else. When did you first meet and get to know Mr Cui Zhongshi?"

"Chief Xu, when you say get to know him, do you mean in a work-related way or in some other capacity?"

"That's a very good question. In truth, I have an interest in both. Please, Mr Xie, you might as well go ahead and tell me everything about your relationship with Mr Cui."

"I first got to know Mr Cui in a work capacity shortly after the war. It was when Mr Fang and I left Chongqing and returned to the bank offices in Shanghai. Cui Zhongshi worked with us at that time. As for how else I knew him, well, that was when we were still in Chongqing. We were both working for the bank in the same building – not on the same accounts, mind you – but I did frequently bump into him in the hallways and such."

"And that was it? Just in the hallways, nothing more?"

Xie Peidong smiled. "I'm sorry, Chief Xu. Is there something you don't understand about frequently meeting in hallways?"

It was Xu's turn to smile in response. "There are times I understand what that means, and there are other times I don't, truth be told. In the party, what you describe as 'frequently bumping into somebody' contains some ambiguity. On the one hand, if you bump into them and strike up a chat, well, we would consider that more a formal face-to-face encounter, a meeting, if you will. On the other hand, your 'bumping into somebody' only refers to an exchange of 'hellos', say, to a passing acquaintance. Then that's entirely different, yes? So you see, there is some ambiguity in what you say."

Xie continued to smile. "I'm not a party member, I'm afraid, so I don't quite see the ambiguity, as you call it. What I mean by 'bumping into' is just that, nothing planned, a simple hello, maybe, between two people who happen to work in the same building, nothing more than that."

"In that case, may I ask for some additional details? During your time in Chongqing, did you and Mr Cui ever 'bump into' each other outside of work, say, for instance, at a café or a bar?" Xu

Tieying hesitated for a moment, but he didn't wait for Xie to answer before he continued: "For example at Hongyancun number thirteen, or perhaps Zengjiayan number fifty? The first is on Dr Sun Yat-sen Road, number two sixty-three, I believe, the latter on Minsheng Road, number two zero eight. Did you ever meet at either of these places?"

Xie Peidong thought things over for a moment, then replied: "Chief Xu, do you mean the residence of Zhou Enlai, the place where he launched recruitment activities with the Eight Route Army during the war? Or are you referring to the offices of the Communist-controlled *Xinhua Daily?*"

Young Li pulled open the iron-barred window softly and looked out. Secretary Sun was standing erect just beyond the gate. On both sides behind him were military police, each one helmeted and armed with a rifle. Li shut the window just as carefully and walked back to the Austin, gesturing as he did towards the lieutenant in charge of the treasury guards. Seconds later, they were standing next to each other.

In a soft voice, Li said: "I need to get to the airbase to receive the bank governor."

The lieutenant glanced at the rear of the car. "Then take out the stuff in the boot and leave it here. It'll be all right."

Li, however, couldn't disguise his growing anxiety: "That's not what I'm talking about. The man who just came in, the chief of the Peking police, well, he and our Mr Xie don't get on well at all. There's trouble brewing, which makes it all the more imperative that I get to the airport. I have to report this to Governor Fang."

"That's excellent!" said the lieutenant, his eyes narrowing. "I'll march right in and arrest him now!"

"You… you can't. He's got written orders from Chairman Yu. Just help me with something, will you?"

"Sure, tell me."

"His men are waiting outside, and I don't think they'll let me past. I hope you can help with that."

"We're still in charge here, aren't we? I'll make sure you get through." The lieutenant spun round and looked at his men. "Put down your food, boys, and grab your guns. There's work to do!"

―――――

As expected, when the treasury gate was opened, the rifles of the military police were there to greet them. Secretary Sun was standing tall in the middle of the road, his eyes trained on the Austin as it manoeuvred forward.

The lieutenant and six men marched out alongside the car. He shouted at the top of his lungs: "Do you men plan on robbing the treasury!" Then he narrowed his eyes and stared at Sun. "Out of the way!"

Sun Chaozhong did not flinch or move an inch.

A shot was fired. The bullet from the lieutenant's pistol swirled through the air in the direction of Sun Chaozhong. It seemed to be headed straight for the blue and white star on his service cap. A second later and Sun's cap flew violently into the air, taking strands of his hair with it. The lieutenant was a magnificent shot.

The military police released the locks on their rifles and prepared to return fire.

"No! You're not to fire," Secretary Sun shouted, while aiming his own pistol at the lieutenant. "Lower your weapons!"

His men did as they were told, and soon their rifles were all pointing at the ground. Sun looked at the lieutenant once more and then moved out of the middle of the road.

Young Li pushed the accelerator and the Austin came to life. A second later he put it in gear and drove hurriedly past Sun Chaozhong and the rest of his military police.

―――――

Military police had also been dispatched to Nanyuan airbase. On arrival, they were similarly greeted by two contingents of guards under the employ of the Peking branch of the Central Bank. They were on protection detail and in a square formation. In between them were two armoured cars. Fang Mengwei was positioned at the front of the formation, a black cloth umbrella in his hand.

It was the fifteenth day of the seventh month, according to the lunar calendar. The sun burned high in the cloudless sky. It had not yet reached its apogee, as it was still before noon, but already the wide open airbase was scorching. Suddenly, the sound of an aircraft could be heard and all eyes turned to the sky. At first there was only one, then before long two more appeared. They grew larger and larger as they approached the airbase, the three C-46s captained by Fang Meng'ao.

Fang Mengwei opened his umbrella.

The first Curtiss C-46 touched down and rolled across the runway. The other two, however, remained in the air, circling and waiting for the green light to begin their approach.

As soon as the first C-46 came to a stop, the ground support walked up to the aircraft with the steps necessary for the flight crew to disembark. The two armoured cars drove up next. Fang Mengwei's eyes shone when he saw his brother and father appear, the younger man helping the older one down from the plane. He ran over to greet them, and to extend the umbrella so that his father would be spared the full force of the sun.

Still behind the wheel, Young Li didn't get very far from the treasury before his way was blocked. It was near the offices of the *World Journal* when he came upon a crowd of young people overflowing the street. And even though he leaned hard on the Austin's horn to try to get them to move, they paid it little attention and made virtually no effort to leave the street.

He knew things across the country were in turmoil. He knew, too, that in such cases, time seemed to drag and almost come to a full stop. In the unified areas, in cities such as Peking, people were starving and had really only two options: to endure, muddle through as best as possible, and leave things to fate; or to be out in the streets looking for any opportunity, to see and feel which way the wind was blowing, and then let it take them to wherever. The newspapers were one such source wherein people sought to find a window to the future, to any future so long as it didn't mean starving in the streets. The newspaper began to be seen as a font of hope. Now, normally, they would be printed by six in the morning. On this day, however, when Li drove up and ran into the newsboys still waiting for their daily papers, it was already well past ten.

In front of the barred iron doors that separated the newsboys from the offices beyond, a notice had been posted explaining the delay. Whether or not they paid any attention to it, however, was debatable. Such is often the case when popular sentiment flows like water and peoples' movements come and go like smoke in the air. As for the notice, it made clear there was important news for the day: "Breaking news to be announced. The paper will be out later today. Please watch this space!"

Outside the car was pandemonium. Inside, Li's face was drenched with sweat. He needed to get through but realised there was little chance of that. He considered putting the car in reverse and backing away, but he was already too late for that as the people had swarmed around the Austin. He could hear chants bellowed in the air:

"Are we talking about total war?"

"Are the Kuomintang and the CPC going to sit down and talk?"

"I heard that Truman and Stalin are both in Nanking and that they've invited Mao Zedong to negotiate peace."

"Surely that'd be a trap for him. Mao Zedong won't go, will he?"

Li's head buzzed, the voices swarmed, he had to get away. Leaning hard on the horn, he shifted the Austin into reverse and began to push against the people.

"Hey, this car, it's from the bank. Ask him, he ought to know!" The shout rang out like a giant bell, calling the people to arms, and making them push back at the car. In moments, he was surrounded. Li shut his eyes and buried his head in his hands. Slumped forward against the steering wheel, he felt he had no other choice but to let things fall to fate.

Suddenly, he heard sirens roar nearby. They grew louder and louder. Li lifted his head from his arms to see what was happening. Although the road was blocked with people, he managed to see the blaring lights of the sirens on the armoured cars.

The crowd shifted and then Li saw the vehicles on which the sirens were placed. His eyes gleamed.

A jeep at the front of the convoy also came into view, and Li could see the man seated in front of the wheel: Fang Meng'ao had returned. Sitting next to him was his father, the bank governor. Li's face lit up even more. He then noticed a second jeep, which bore a striking resemblance to Fang Mengwei's. Behind them were additional police vehicles. Evidently, they were tasked with protecting the armoured cars. Li strained to see more, but couldn't.

He switched off the Austin's engine, stepped out of the car, locked the door and squeezed into the crowd.

———

"Mr Xie, your answer aligns perfectly with what our investigation has turned up." Xu Tieying and Xie Peidong were still in the treasury office, but Xie could not be certain from where, or even when, Xu Tieying had pulled out a notebook filled to the brim with seemingly every detail related to their current discussion. Indeed, Xie could see barely any blank space on the pages Xu now consulted. Just as suddenly as the notebook appeared, however, Xu shut it and returned it to his pocket. He looked at Xie again and said: "In Chongqing, you say you never once attended any Communist-led meetings or participated in their activities, and that the same is true for Cui Zhongshi as well. Such being the case, it becomes rather easy for me to infer that Cui Zhongshi's superior – his handler if you will – was already in the employ of the Central Bank! After the war, it's clear this man made arrangements for Cui Zhongshi to be promoted and ultimately sent to Peking. I'm sure he arranged for him to be given the post here at the treasury, too. That's how Cui came to know about the hidden accounts, and also how he made it possible for huge sums of money to be redirected to the Communist-fronted Great Wall Company in Hong Kong. He didn't need to ask anyone to make it happen, he could do it all himself! Mr Xie, you've just said that Cui was promoted on the basis of a recommendation from Mr Fang Buting, and that Liu Kung-yun signed off on the appointment, thus sending him to Peking and making him deputy director of the treasury. Now, are you trying to suggest that

Cui's superior was in fact not Mr Liu Kung-yun, but rather the governor of the Peking branch, Mr Fang Buting?"

"There's no question here, Cui Zhongshi was a bank employee. Thus Mr Liu, the former chairman of the bank, was, at one time, his superior, and thereafter, once he arrived in Peking, Mr Fang was, of course, his boss. It could be no other way, surely."

"This is an interesting prevarication you're engaging in, Mr Xie, wouldn't you say?" Xu Tieying smiled, but there was no warmth in it. His eyes were unrelenting. "One month ago, Cui Zhongshi handled a large money transfer, sending a huge sum to the CPC, and you, Mr Xie, were able to persuade your branch governor to move other funds around to compensate our own party's assets. Didn't you think that at that time you would be exposed?"

"I am not prevaricating." Xie Peidong returned Xu's glare, his face calm and collected. "Chief Xu, you've gone on so much, said so much, let's get to the heart of the matter. Are you trying to say that I was his handler, that I'm a CPC agent that's infiltrated the bank and used my position to fund the CPC?"

"My hope is that you'll come clean, yes."

Xie Peidong glanced at his watch. "The new currency will be here any minute. The announcement pertaining to its distribution across the nation will be given just before noon. Chief Xu, if you suspect me of being a Communist, if you wish to continue this line of your investigation, I suggest choosing another time to do so, and another place. Wouldn't you agree?"

Xu Tieying laughed. "Of course, another place will be necessary, but we don't need to choose another time. It's now past ten. To ensure that the currency reforms announcement takes place at noon, to guarantee it comes off without a hitch, I think it best for you to let me see Cui Zhongshi's ledgers. We can then go over them together."

"I am more than willing to accompany you, Chief Xu, but at the moment, I am afraid that is not possible. What, then, do you suggest we do?"

"I'm sorry but I don't follow your meaning. Why can't you leave?"

"I have keys only for the inner two gates. The main gate into the treasury must be opened by the guards. The problem is, however, urgent orders were given last night that in the time leading up to the delivery of the new currency, anyone who is already inside the treasury must remain inside until delivery is complete."

"So you have to wait until Fang Buting arrives?" For the first time in their conversation, Xu Tieying let slip the malevolence he was feeling. "You still think someone's coming to save you!"

"If I was waiting for someone to rescue me, would I have allowed you to come in?" There was a sternness in Xie Peidong's voice now as well. "I am the assistant manager of the Peking branch, the central offices in Nanking have not removed me from my position. Hence, I *am* protected. If that changes, if I'm dismissed, then you can see fit to dispatch military police to arrest me. But surely you won't need to handle such a thing yourself?"

"That's right, I wouldn't need to come myself, would I?" Xu moved a little closer to Xie. "You've buried yourself so deep, haven't you? Even the arrest of your daughter didn't bring you in from the cold. Are you sure there would be no need for me to handle things personally?"

"What did you just say?" Xie Peidong's complexion changed. "Could you say that again?"

"It was clear enough already. Why repeat myself?"

"Wang Puchen and Zeng Keda both told me my daughter's gone to the liberated zones. Are you trying to say she's not, that you have her?"

Xu Tieying stared at Xie for what seemed like forever. Finally, he answered: "What do you think?"

"I think, whether you tried to or not, you've let me go. I, however, will not do the same for you. You've got four children in Taipei, yes, but I have only the one daughter! This morning, do you know what I did in support of the currency reforms? I… I gave the only thing I had kept to give to her, my one precious possession, a gold bracelet. I gave it up, as the reforms dictated. And you, what about you? All you're doing is whatever you can to hoard a little more cash, to steal away a bit more money, ostensibly for them. If you've something to say, then save it for the special court in Nanking. This is not the place for it. Please, get out. The corridor is quite long. Go for a walk while we wait. Just get out of this office."

"Xie Peidong!" said Xu Tieying, grabbing the manacles he'd had around his waist. "I'm here to arrest Communist agents. There are no fortunate holes by which you can escape my net, even if you might be Zhou Enlai's own student! You've seen Chen's orders, and Yu's, your own bank chairman. Do you still think this can end up in the special court in Nanking?" Before he had finished speaking, Xu had moved with lightning speed to clamp one of the manacles around Xie's left wrist.

It took only seconds for Xu Tieying's face to transform, for Xie Peidong had deftly spun around, grabbed the other end of the handcuffs, and clamped them down onto Xu Tieying's right hand.

Xu did his best to remain in control, and with his free hand he reached for his pistol. Unholstering it quickly, he pointed the barrel straight at Xie Peidong's forehead. "Open the door, we'll exit together!"

Xie smiled. "According to bank regulations, anyone caught trespassing is to be immediately arrested, and immediately shot! Chief Xu, go ahead. You might as well shoot." Xie didn't say anything further. Instead, he lowered himself down into the chair, striking a pose that couldn't help but make a person think of an immovable mountain.

Xu Tieying began to realise he'd chosen the wrong place to confront this adversary. He bit his lower lip and holstered his weapon. Then he held up the key to signal he would release the cuffs. Xie, however, grabbed the keys dangling from Xu's hand before he could unlock the manacles, and threw them into the nearby mechanical fan. The sound of the keys making contact with the metal propellers of the fan rang throughout the office.

By the time Xu turned to look at him, Xie was already waiting for his glance. He spoke first: "Let's wait for your Chief Chen, or perhaps Chairman Yu. They can release us from these cuffs."

Unexpectedly, the armoured car convoy stopped outside the *World Journal* offices. Fang Mengwei stepped out of his jeep and moved to the centre of the street. The Peking police officers he brought with him formed a circle around him, ensuring the crowd could not get too close. Guards from the Peking branch of the Central Bank formed up around the armoured cars. The looks on their faces showed clearly the seriousness of their responsibility. Only Fang Meng'ao's twenty pilots remained in their transport vehicle. Their eyes scanned the scene in each direction. They watched as more and more people began to show up.

In the back of Fang Meng'ao's jeep, Young Li relayed to them everything that had happened. His lips had drained of colour. His mouth had grown parched. Fang Meng'ao stared towards the front. Out of the corner of his eye, he could see his father doing the same. He had never seen such an iron look on his father's face before.

"Understood," said Fang Buting. "Go back to the Austin and wait for me there."

"Yes, Mr Governor." Li opened the rear door and climbed down from the jeep.

Father and son continued to stare ahead. It was as though they both wanted to look at each other, but neither could actually do it.

Fang Buting recited a favourite line from a Yuan Dynasty poem, which seemed to encapsulate his sense of desolation at this turn of events: "'I turned my heart to the brilliance of the moon, but the moon only shone into the dreary gully.'"

Finally, Fang Meng'ao turned to face his father.

His father spoke first, however: "That year, when I heard the terrible news of your mother's death, and your younger sister's too, I didn't sleep for days. I drowned with regret. Why, I kept thinking, did we return from the US? Why didn't we stay there? But we'd already returned, and this land, this China, it is the home of our ancestors. And it was enduring such pain, such torment, if we'd stayed in America, we'd be just as tortured. It would have been equally unbearable, I'm sure."

They at last came together.

Fang Buting continued: "This past... what... a little more than a month? Do you know I've met your mother in my dreams almost every night since you've been in Peking? She's told me you're in danger and that I have to protect you and keep you safe. Let me ask you something, that is, if you'll let me..."

"Please."

"Did you know Cui Zhongshi was a Communist agent?"

Seeing the kindliness in his father's eyes, Fang Meng'ao knew he couldn't lie, but nor could he tell the truth. He hesitated for a moment, and then spoke: "This question, the day before he was taken, I asked him the same question."

"And what did he say?"

"He told me, he said he wasn't a Communist."

"Then that should be it. That should be enough!" Fang Buting demonstrated a new vigour. "Cui Zhongshi was a Communist. Xu Tieying and those supporting him are using this knowledge to their advantage to beat us down. And I know why, they're trying to get money out of us. But there's something they've forgotten. Mr Chen Bulei's daughter and her husband are both Communists. They're daring to attack me? Their party assets – ah, who's kidding who, their private, personal assets, nothing really to do with the Kuomintang – and what? Xu Tieying's using this moment to claim your uncle is a Communist, too! Whoever may or may not be a CPC agent, I can't say, but to say Peidong is... I've known him twenty years. Are they trying to say I'm blind!"

Fang Meng'ao could see the ire and emotion in his father's face. The blood surged up within him like a geyser surging to the surface. He reached out and took hold of one of his father's trembling hands.

Fang Buting continued: "Mulan disappeared, what, a few days ago now. They told us she's gone to the liberated zones, but I've... I've had a premonition about this. They're using it as an excuse to get at your uncle, to cause a fuss. I never thought, however, that they'd put their plan in motion at this crucial moment in the nation's history. It's as though, on the one hand, they want the two of us to throw our lives away in trying to see the reforms come to fruition, and on the other, they want to barge down the doors of our home and arrest us as Communists. Meng'ao, I've been head of the family for a lifetime now, but I've only overseen it being wrenched apart, its death and destruction. Today, I'll take my last act as head. Do you want to hear what I have in mind?"

"I do."

"Let's leave all of the new currency here in the street, just abandon it. I'll go to Xishan prison and wait for your uncle. I'll let myself be buried alongside this infernal government. If you can, take Mengwei and your stepmum, and that plane you were just flying, and get away. To where it doesn't matter, wherever you want, just go!"

Fang Meng'ao's looked at his father through his tears. "Dad, since we were little, you always taught us to memorise certain poems. I've got two lines I'd like to recite for you now."

Fang Buting watched his son expectantly.

Fang Meng'ao began: "'Old Ruan Ji was not bothered by failing to be recognised. He always went out with a smile on his face, and the lofty quality of a gurgling river.'"

Tears streamed down Fang Buting's face and he rushed to wipe them away. He smiled at his son. "These lines, they're wonderful, excellent... Yes, yes, your father understands!" He pushed at the door of the vehicle, determined to get out.

Fang Meng'ao acted lightning fast and was already standing by his father's door, waiting to help him out. At the same time, he called to his younger brother. Seconds later, Mengwei was standing next to the pair of them.

"You don't need to bring the soldiers with you," Fang Meng'ao said. "Dad needs to be brought to Xishan prison. He'll tell you why."

Fang Mengwei was both astonished by what his brother said, and increasingly angry: "What... why? What are the two of you up to?"

"Let's go. I'll explain everything as we walk to the car." And with that, Fang Buting began to move in the direction of the parked Austin.

Fang Mengwei hurried after him, abandoning the military police under his command. Assisting his father took precedence, that he knew.

Minutes later, they were in the Austin and Young Li was revving the engine. He was a skilled driver, there was no disputing that. He cut the wheel hard to the right, brushing past the detachment of men, and turned the car around in the middle of the street.

Fang Meng'ao watched them depart, and once he was sure they were gone, he yelled to his personal guard, the twenty young pilots still waiting patiently in their vehicle. "Men, it's time to roll out!" He climbed back into his own jeep, turned the ignition, blared the horn and made a sharp, 180-degree turn. Seconds later, he passed his men and shouted: "Let's go!" His men followed suit and soon the two jeeps were racing back the way they had come.

The armoured truck guards could no longer see the bank governor. The military police could no longer see their commander. The people crowded around, growing thicker and thicker. The two vehicles, full of brand new *jinyuanquan*, had been abandoned by the men charged with their care!

Two armoured cars, isolated, discarded, were like two tired tortoises surrounded by hungry and starving mayflies.

No one was sure when Zeng Keda had returned to the meeting room in Gu Weijun's residence, nor when he had seated himself under the image of Dr Sun Yat-sen. He looked at the last business leader who appeared to have just finished digesting the document, and said: "You've all read it?"

None of the eight men answered.

Zeng stood up and gathered together the stack of papers. He then signalled to the young soldiers who were still standing behind the businessmen. "One per person, hand them out."

The soldiers acted in unison, regular, determined. Each man took hold of one set of documents, and then each one returned to their original positions, placing the paper in front of the men they were ostensibly serving as escorts for.

Zeng intoned: "According to these five articles, you can see them here in front of you, you're required to list all of your companies' assets, your holdings of gold and silver, foreign currency, everything must be filled in on the paper in front of you. And don't tell me you don't know, or that you need to leave to consult with your financial officers. I'll accept an approximate number, and be able to tell whether or not you're trying to conceal anything. Worry not, we'll investigate everything fully."

"Inspector Zeng," one of the eight men said, rising to his feet. "We've all read the document you gave us. We understand we have until the thirtieth of August to declare all of our assets and to exchange them for the new currency. Could you please remind us of today's date?"

Zeng Keda smiled. "Today is the nineteenth."

Again the same businessman spoke: "Well then, who has given you the authority to request these details today?"

The remaining seven businessmen now displayed their own

reactions. Some leaned back against their chairs, others crossed their arms. It was clear that not a single man intended to fill in the details Zeng had demanded.

Zeng Keda put away his smile. "That's an excellent question. Why do I want this information today? The answer is quite simple." His tone strengthened. "Because I know if I let you leave, if I give you but a single day, you'll all make arrangements to have your personal assets written over to the party! I won't give you that time. Start with the last column and fill in the names of your shareholders, the times. Use whatever form you need to complete the information. Write. Now!"

At exactly the same moment, the telephone over on the tea table rang.

Zeng Keda scanned the faces of the eight men, and then the eight soldiers standing behind them. "Give them pens." He rose from his chair and walked over to answer the phone.

The soldiers obeyed, each one reaching into their uniform pockets and pulling out a pen.

"You've reached the Ministry of Defence's Investigative Division. You're speaking to Zeng Keda." The receiver was close to his ear, and now the other men in the room could see that he was listening to the person on the other end. As he did, his complexion changed. "Where are you right now?" The answer came, although no one in the room could hear it. Zeng continued: "You're standing guard around the armoured cars? I'll send a platoon immediately. If even a single bill of the new currency is lost, you'll all face the firing squad!" He slammed the phone down and marched out of the room.

Commander Li appeared to be waiting for him.

"Have the men file in. You need to get yourselves to the offices of the *World Journal* straight away. You're charged with making sure the *jinyuanquan* reach the Peking treasury!"

"Yes sir!" He saluted quickly, spun around and walked away.

Zeng stepped back towards the meeting room and then abruptly stopped in the doorway. He looked in at the eight young soldiers. "Keep watch. Make sure they fill in the details I want. Not one of them is allowed to leave."

"Yes sir!" they answered in accord.

Zeng Keda did not linger. He turned and marched off.

The sun that shone down upon the main entrance to Yenching University's library seemed especially warm, the shade from the nearby trees especially welcome, the grass especially green. Because of the deportation of students a week earlier, the archway-like gate was nearly deserted, with only a few students milling about, each one quiet and nervous.

Among the small number of students, one was the Peking University student representative. Another was the rep from Tsinghua University. The Peking Normal rep was there as well. They'd all been there on 12 August when they'd been arrested and then released. Liang Jinglun's frequent student companion, Ouyang, was in front of the library, too, as were a few other student union representatives. So while their numbers may have been small, their importance was not.

A few of the students noticed him first. Their eyes turned in the direction of the trees, the shade and the path that led out beneath them. At some time or other, Liang Jinglun had changed out of his military fatigues and back into his long, scholarly robe. He was on his familiar bicycle, emerging out of the shadows like a figure out of some well-known story.

But no one moved to greet him. The students remained standing about near the library archway. It wasn't until Liang had passed through the archway to draw closer to the library itself that a number of the students took a few steps towards him.

Liang jumped nimbly down from the bicycle. Ouyang was there to take hold of the handlebars, and, at the same time, shoot a look at his teacher, then at the Peking student representative.

"How many of you have come?" Liang Jinglun scanned the small crowd, finally letting his eyes settle on the student rep from Peking University.

"Whoever we were able to send word to – Peking, Tsinghua, Peking Normal – I reckon there's two hundred of us or more, all members of the city-wide students union."

"Let's go in then."

"Mr Liang!" The student's voice was perhaps louder than he had intended, but it had the desired effect of stopping Liang. The student lowered his tone: "Please, let's go this way."

Liang hesitated for a moment, and then followed the student leader back towards the trees and the shade that still covered the path.

The Peking student rep explained: "Not long ago, a student appeared and handed me a letter addressed to you..." As he spoke, he pulled the letter out from his pocket and handed it to Liang Jinglun. He didn't say anything else as he turned and walked away.

Liang inspected the letter and his heart skipped a beat. There was not a single word written on the envelope. He tried hard to remain calm, to keep up appearances. He tore at the side and pulled out the letter inside. The handwriting was one he well recognised:

> Professor Liang,
> I fear there are big changes to come to the current political situation. You must look after yourself, take care of your students, too. We do not want any needless sacrifice, not again. Yenching University is your responsibility.

The letter was unsigned, but Liang knew who had written it; there was no need for a signature. He stared hard at the paper he held in his hand. Felt it under his fingers. It seemed to be thicker, unusually so. He looked at it more intently, and then he could see it, there, apparently, between the lines. It was the letter he had received before, in the same place he was standing now. The letter that had outlined Yan Chunming's transgressions, his supposed desire for martyrdom, his appropriation of the gun... as well as Liang's orders to avoid unnecessary bloodshed, and to keep Yan Chunming safe. He could see it all as plain as day.

The handwriting was exactly the same, down to the last stroke!

Liang Jinglun closed his eyes and breathed in deeply. He had no way of knowing for certain if the CPC suspected him of being a double agent, but there was no turning back now even if he could. He pocketed the letter and walked back over to the students.

"Mr Liang!"

It took only for his name to be shouted for all the students, two hundred or more, to turn their eyes towards him. They had been pretending to be absorbed in reading, but in truth, they'd all been waiting for his arrival. Liang quickened his pace; his long gown fluttered. Once he got close enough, he looked throughout the crowd for a familiar face, for He Xiaoyu. Unfortunately, he could not see her.

"You've all been waiting for a while, I imagine." His demeanour had lightened; he was trying his best to leave thoughts of the letter behind him. Seconds later, he was standing in the centre of the student body, looking at the expectant faces. "Every newspaper in the city has delayed publication today, which is a clear indicator something's afoot… I believe today we'll witness the Nanking government announce to the public its currency reform initiative."

Reactions were immediate:

"The conspiracy's revealed!"

"We must demonstrate against this!"

"We must resist, show them we won't give in!"

Liang raised his hands to try to quell the uproar. "Fellow students!"

It took a moment, but gradually the students quieted.

―――

He Qicang was listening to the morning radio broadcast: "According to the official government communiqués, the meeting in Lushan between Mr Chiang Kai-shek, president of the Republic of China, and Mr John Leighton Stuart, ambassador in charge of the American Mission in China, has concluded…"

He hadn't listened to the radio in ages; in fact, it had been packed away for some time. But today, he'd brought it downstairs into the sitting room and had placed it on the table near the sofa so he could listen to it in greater comfort. Indeed, he looked half asleep, quiet, his eyes closed, the radio droning on: "…the president and the ambassador returned to the capital yesterday evening onboard a special chartered flight."

The water on top of the stove bubbled.

He Xiaoyu spooned some powdered milk into a glass, and carefully poured the hot water into it. She stirred the mixture and carried it into the sitting room for her father. His eyes were still tightly closed, and she was unsure of whether or not to disturb him.

The radio report continued. The female announcer had a soft, distinctive southern accent to her Mandarin: "The special tribunal convened in Nanking began hearing public cases yesterday into suspected Communist and bandit activities aimed at destabilising the safety and security of the nation…"

He Xiaoyu stood next to the sofa and her reclining father, her ears trained on the radio broadcast: "More than four hundred students in total have been charged with sedition and with supporting Communist activities. This includes a hundred and forty-seven in Nanking, two hundred and fifty-plus in Peking…"

He Qicang reached over and turned the radio off.

He Xiaoyu looked at her father. The glass of warm milk was still on the tray. "Dad, there's no need to get angry. You haven't had breakfast yet in any case."

He Qicang reached for the milk.

"It's still too hot." She placed the tray on the table. "Wait for it to cool a bit before you drink it."

He Xiaoyu sat down beside her father. He Qicang took her hand in his and spoke softly: "This government… eh… with famine everywhere, does it want to enact currency reform, or does it want to fight the Communists… or arrest and investigate students? I don't know, I really don't. Is there any point in me helping them? Is it worth it or not? Tell me, is there another student meeting today?"

"I think, yes, at the library."

"Will Liang Jinglun be there?"

"I don't know. He should be."

"I hope there won't be a fuss. You'll only lose in the end, and you're all still children."

"We're not causing a fuss, we're resisting."

He Qicang sighed. "And what's the point of this resisting? Turn on the radio again, will you, they're announcing the currency reforms today."

"Sure." He Xiaoyu stood up and walked over to the radio on the table. Before she could turn it on, however, the telephone rang. She looked at her father, whose eyes told her to bring the phone to him.

"Yes, this is he, go ahead."

He Qicang sat upright. "Say again, I didn't hear you clearly. Who's gone to Xishan prison?"

He Xiaoyu stared, her eyes growing wide at the snippets of the conversation she heard. She could see the effect it was having on her father. His head trembled, and so, too, did his hand holding the receiver. She sat down next to him again and used her arm to support He Qicang.

Using what strength he had to remain calm, He Qicang listened until the man on the other end was finished. Then he spoke: "I understand, thank you." He wanted to hang the telephone up but his hand no longer seemed to obey his command.

He Xiaoyu saw his discomfort and reached out to assist. "Dad, give it to me. And try not to get angry. There's no use getting anxious. Just tell me slowly, what's happened?"

He Qicang looked at the face of his daughter, and saw the growing panic in her eyes. He knew he had to get a hold of himself: "Your uncle, Uncle Fang, because of the... the pressure put upon him, because of everything that's going on, he's decided to turn himself in. He's gone to Xishan prison."

"What? How?" There was worry in her voice. "Why, what for?"

"Today, this morning, Xu Tieying – that Kuomintang bastard – at the same time as the currency reforms were to be announced, he showed up at the bank to... to interrogate your Uncle Xie."

"Which, which Uncle Xie?" He Xiaoyu's face drained of all colour.

"You know who, Mulan's father of course. It's ridiculous! Totally and utterly absurd!" He Qicang slapped his hands against the sofa and lifted himself up. "Prepare some clothes, a towel... and my toothbrush."

There were tears in He Xiaoyu's eyes. She gripped her father's arm. "Dad, you're in no state to. You can't, no you really can't. That's right, there's Fang Meng'ao. Yes, Fang Meng'ao. I'll telephone him. Let's first ask him..."

"No, don't. There's no point anyway. He's in the air."

CHAPTER 11

"Captain Fang! Captain Fang!" The control tower was in uproar. The air traffic controller was on his feet, staring out through the window, his hand grasping the headphones and speakers. He was shouting with great urgency: "You've no permission to depart. Disengage and bring your aeroplane to a halt! Shut down immediately! You're not permitted onto the runway! Respond, please! Respond!" Everyone in the control tower was on their feet, gaping out of the window, stunned by what they were witnessing.

The C-46 showed no sign of obeying the commands it had been given. Rather, its engine rumbled and it edged quicker out onto the runway.

The air traffic controller's face grew wet with sweat. He yelled into the microphone: "A bomber's due to land in five minutes! You're ordered to vacate the runway immediately! Right now! Respond please!" He put the headphones to one side, exasperated by what was happening, and yet at a loss as to what to do.

Finally, the microphone crackled in response: "We've urgent orders to depart. Order the bomber to hold. I repeat, order the bomber to hold. They must delay landing."

From the window of the control tower, the airbase personnel could see the C-46 had stopped taxiing. Its vast wingspan shaded the entire runway.

The air traffic controller spoke with even more urgency: "What urgent orders? We've not received any here in the tower. You're in violation of military orders. Captain Fang, please execute the orders you've been given. Taxi your aeroplane off the runway now. Respond!"

The microphone bristled again, this time with the faint sound of Chen Changwu's voice: "This is Number Two, I repeat, this is Number Two, second in command. Urgent orders have been received, giving us permission to lift off. My team's commander is in the rear jeep. Please relay this to him. I repeat, please relay this to him."

The air traffic controller finally took notice of the jeep racing down the taxiway adjacent to the runway. He narrowed his eyes and realised he hadn't been speaking to Captain Fang aboard the aircraft, for Captain Fang was the man behind the wheel of the jeep!

In the back seats were the eight captains of industry and finance in the Pingjin area. They were being held at gunpoint by Guo Jinyang and another of Fang Meng'ao's men. To a man, their faces were pale and much like the colour of the yellow earth.

The jeep swerved onto the runway and there in front of it was the C-46. Fang Meng'ao slammed on the brakes, bringing the vehicle to an abrupt stop. The eight men in the back were thrust hard against the front seats. The cargo hold door creaked and began to open, the entrance growing larger and larger in front of them. Fang Meng'ao was anxiously waiting for the ramp to fully open.

The airbase loudspeaker echoed with the air traffic controller's voice: "Captain Fang, Captain Fang, you're in serious breach of military and Air Force regulations. We're closing the runway and invoking emergency orders!"

Seconds later, Chen Changwu's voice came over the same loudspeaker: "We are a special Air Force detachment. We have the authority to execute emergency orders when we see fit! Direct any questions you have to Central Command! I repeat, order the bomber to delay landing. If you have questions, contact Central Command!"

The air traffic controller was dazed and unsure of what to do. Outside, the aircraft's cargo bay door had opened fully and he could see Fang Meng'ao manoeuvre the jeep onboard the plane. He shouted to no one in particular: "Get me Central Command! Now!"

"Yes sir!" Another of the tower officers reached for the telephone: "This is Nanyuan airbase control tower. The situation's urgent. Connect me right now to the Nanking Air Force Central Command! I repeat, the situation is urgent. I must speak to the Central Command in Nanking."

"Sir!" shouted the officer sitting in front of the radar panel. On the glass board on the desk in front of him, he'd traced the route of the incoming aircraft. "Sir, the bomber is already beginning its descent. They've started their approach!"

The air traffic controller responded: "Order the bomber to abort! They're to circle the airbase and await further instructions!"

"Affirmative sir!" The radar specialist picked up the microphone and hurriedly relayed the orders.

Outside, the jeep had already been swallowed by the C-46. The plane's ramp was slowly being retracted.

―――

They could hear the sound outside. The university car had arrived. He Qicang grasped his walking stick and raised himself up from the chair. He glanced at his daughter, then allowed his eyes to drift towards the stairs. "I should like to bring some books, too, I think. Run upstairs and get my *Spring and Autumn Annals*. Pick up the *Collected Tang Poems*, too, both volumes. Your Uncle Fang is fond of them."

His old, yellowed leather suitcase was still open, several sets of clothing visible. He Xiaoyu wiped away the tears that had settled on her cheeks. "Dad, if you're going to go through with this... you... you can't take the university's car."

He Qicang looked at her intently. "And why not?"

"If you show up in the university's car, they'll think you're there at the behest of Ambassador Stuart, that you're trying to pressure them."

He Qicang stamped his cane on the floor. "I wouldn't want him to lose face. Ring the chancellor of Tsinghua for me, Mr Mei, ask to borrow their car."

"How many more people do you intend to disturb with this…"

"Then I'll walk, dammit!" His growing impatience was clear.

"Dad!" He Xiaoyu's cry made him stop. "The Kuomintang government is apprehending everyone and anyone. You should make them send a car for you."

He Qicang thought the matter over and then turned to face his daughter. "Dial the Mobile Barracks in Peking and ask for Li Yuqing. The number is there above the telephone."

He Xiaoyu walked over to the telephone to do as her father requested.

———

"Yes, affirmative! Set up roadblocks immediately, prevent them from taking off! Understood?" The air traffic controller repeated his orders into the receiver and then turned to the other officers in the tower. "You heard, those are the orders from Central Command. We're to block the runway and stop Captain Fang from taking off. We can't let him leave…" He paused in mid-sentence. He was looking at the other officers, but most of them were directing their attention to what was happening outside.

The C-46 was soaring into the sky!

———

He Qicang spoke into the telephone, his voice low, but his tone serious: "At the drop of a hat, you're liable to make your complaints known to the Americans, to file suit even. But what is it, does this government not care anything for face? You presume I'm the same! I refuse to say anything further to Ambassador Stuart. I don't even want to see him. I'll give you half an hour, and if you don't send a car to convey me to Xishan prison, then I'll board a plane and fly to Nanking and be incarcerated there!"

Xe Xiaoyu was seated next to her father, her hand on his arm to support him. She couldn't hear what the person on the other end of the phone was saying, but she could tell her father's ire was increasing.

"The name of the Air Force Command's secretary general is

Soong Mei-ling, the commander's name is Zhou Zhirou... How the hell do I know where Fang Meng'ao has flown to?"

He Xiaoyu reached out and took hold of her father's arm holding the telephone. Her voice was soft and gentle: "Dad, if Fang Meng'ao's plane's not returned, there's no point in your going to Xishan. You can't save Uncle Fang no matter what you do. Nor can you save Uncle Xie."

He Xiaoyu's words had had their desired effect. He Qicang seemed to realise the situation had changed. He looked at his daughter and could see the image of Fang Meng'ao in her eyes. He sighed long and hard, and then removed her hand from his arm. He pulled the receiver close again, his voice noticeably calmer than before. "The currency reforms need to be announced immediately, within half an hour or an hour... that's not of importance to me. But let me say, at a time like this, you need to keep close those who are of greatest benefit to you. Pressuring Mr Fang to turn himself in... forcing his son to... to appropriate an aeroplane in a futile effort to save his father. These are not the actions that... it shouldn't be like this. Please, you must relay this to Vice-President Li. He needs to step in and question what's going on. If he does, then I can cooperate. I'll give you an hour to get back to me."

He Qicang reached out to replace the phone and felt his remaining strength disappear. The phone clattered onto the table before He Xiaoyu could catch it. She picked it up and put it back on its base. As she did, she heard the faint sound of Li Yuqing's voice droning on: "Vice-Chancellor He, hello... Mr He, please don't worry. You must relax. We'll see to things immediately..." She hung up the phone and looked at her aged father.

"Li Yuqing is probably going to head to the airbase right away. Ring Xishan prison for me. I want to know how your Uncle Fang's doing. Is he all right?"

He Xiaoyu took hold of the receiver again, her finger moving towards the rotary dial. Her father stopped her, however.

"There... there's no point in making that call." He Qicang shut his eyes and leaned back into the sofa, mumbling: "Neither son nor father seems to want to live. I'm dead, I'm dying. Should I lump all of this on my daughter? Does she need to keep on fussing about them?"

"Dad." He Xiaoyu squeezed her father's hand tightly but didn't know what to say.

———

Fang Buting's Austin was parked outside the main gate to Xishan prison, but he remained inside, waiting to be greeted. Wang Puchen did this in person, even opening the door for the bank governor, and then holding it for the older man to climb out.

Fang Buting, however, stayed where he was, ignoring the open door and speaking to his driver and younger son Fang Mengwei instead: "Is that the sound of an aeroplane?"

Fang Mengwei craned his neck and peered into the sky.

Wang Puchen did the same while standing next to the Austin.

The C-46 loomed large in the sky, larger than any aeroplane they had seen before. It seemed to be flying rather low to the ground, despite the Western Hills nearby. As a result, its metallic body cast a dark shadow over the ground, stretching into the prison yard.

"It's my brother's plane all right."

Fang Buting lifted himself out of the car. Wang Puchen reached out to assist, but Fang brushed it away and looked searchingly to the sky instead.

The C-46 swooped past and then rapidly turned to circle the area, tilting its wing lower so that the craft could rotate around. It passed over them again. Fang Buting was mesmerised by the scene, conscious, too, that his eldest boy was relaying his best regards.

Moments later and it was gone, disappeared from the sky. Still, Fang Buting kept his eyes on the sky.

"Dad…" Fang Mengwei walked to his father, removed his cap and tried to place it on top of the older man's head. The brilliance of the sun was sharp and merciless. "Dad, it's gone."

"I know, Son." And he waved his hands in the air as though saying farewell.

Fang Mengwei replaced the cap on his own head.

This was the first time Fang Buting had ever been to Xishan prison. He took a moment to take it all in: the mountains in the background, the high, imposing walls, the few birds perched upon the barbed wire that ran across the top. Then he turned to Mengwei and said: "It's best you go home. Ask your stepmum to prepare clean clothes for me. Young Li can bring them when they're ready." Fang Buting stayed focused on the birds all the while.

They'd discussed the situation on the way to the prison, but seeing his father's demeanour, Fang Mengwei couldn't wholly control the emotions he was feeling. "Dad, I'll stay here with you, all right…"

"No you won't!" Fang Buting turned to stare at him. "You're no Communist, after all. Get back in the car and go!"

Fang Mengwei closed his eyes dejectedly and returned to the Austin.

Even though Wang Puchen had received a phone call telling him of Fang Buting's imminent arrival, he did not know the specifics. Now, looking upon the scene before him, he knew he couldn't stay quiet. There was more going on that he had to know about. He thus reached out a hand and grabbed hold of the car door. "Deputy Fang… what Communist? What's your father talking about? Why's he here… what's he up to?"

"You've arrested everybody else, surely you've interrogated them all. Aren't things clear to you already?"

"Deputy Fang!" Wang Puchen's voice couldn't conceal his growing anxiety. "What interrogation? Interrogate who? What the devil are you talking about?"

Fang Mengwei could see the tension on Wang's face and realised it wasn't fake. "Mr Wang – all of this – it's got nothing to do with you. If you'd like to help, then I'll ask you to have a clean cell prepared, one with a bed."

"But I've not received any orders. Whom should I make cell arrangements for?"

"This is where you lock up the Communist agents, isn't it?" The loudness, the sharpness of Fang Buting's voice caused Wang Puchen to turn. Fang continued: "Communist agents have infiltrated the Peking branch of the Central Bank. Me, I'm the one. The cell's for me." Fang didn't wait for a reply before he started to walk slowly into the prison.

Wang Puchen was still clutching the top of the car door, but shouted to his prison guards standing not far away: "Block his way!" The guards marched over, then up to Fang Buting as though they were going to greet him as an honoured guest. They had no idea how they could stop him, besides physically laying hands on him, and so that was exactly what the commander of the guards did. He tried, also, to plead with Fang Buting, to ask him to stop.

"Get your hands off me," was the only response he received. Fang Buting did not even deign to look at him.

The commander looked plaintively back at Wang Puchen, but he didn't dare release the older man from his grip.

Fang Buting lowered his voice: "Are you the ones who arrested Cui Zhongshi? I bet you are. You probably arrested Xie Mulan, too, yes?"

The guard had not expected such a question, but it did stir his memory like a slap to the face. His eyes darkened.

Fang Buting could feel the fury rising up in him. "Just what the hell are you? It's come time for my arrest, but not yours! Humph!"

"Mr Fang!" Wang Puchen had no choice but to rush over.

Fang Mengwei, who had yet to leave, pushed open the car door and ran towards his father as well. "Dad! Dad!"

Wang Puchen maintained a respectful distance but blocked Fang Buting's way nonetheless: "I'm in charge here, which means everything is my responsibility. If you want someone to be punished, then report me to the Intelligence Bureau... or the Ministry of Defence."

Fang Buting narrowed his gaze, his eyes focused on Wang Puchen. "The election was held in April, wasn't it? It supposedly represented our democratic constitutionalism, yes? Hogwash! Bullshit, all of it! You've got this secret prison here, your special operatives, Intelligence Bureau... hah! Communications Department... hah! I tell you, I'm a Communist agent, I'm here to turn myself in. If you won't dare to interrogate me, then get Xu Tieying here, he'll bloody well do it, I'm sure! I'll wait right here for him to come! Mengwei, get him out of my way."

Fang Mengwei looked at Wang Puchen. "It's nothing to do with you. Make the arrangements I asked you to."

"Even if a crime has been committed – by whom I don't know – today's the launch of the currency reforms. And I'm greeted at my prison by the Peking branch governor. How come you're all forcing me into ringing Nanking to request instructions? Are you trying to add to my problems?"

Fang Mengwei turned to his father: "Dad…"

"I'm turning myself in, admitting my crime. You still need to ask for instructions?" Fang Buting's voice was still angry.

"Dad, he has his duty to fulfil… let him make the call."

Wang Puchen did not hesitate any longer. He turned to the guard and said: "Go, get some chairs and bring them here!"

"Yes, yes, yes! We tracked the airplane's flight path, hence our report!" The officer in charge in the Nanyuan tower had just hung up another urgent call from Central Command. When he turned around, his face was drenched in sweat. But all he saw waiting for him was another officer holding yet another telephone for him to answer.

"Who's calling?" he asked as he walked over to the phone.

"It's the northern command base."

He took hold of the receiver and held it to his ear. A few sentences later and it was easy to see his increasing fretfulness: "The CPC has no aircraft of its own. Well, that's not entirely true, they do have some of ours. Fire what cannon? Low flying, low flying, so? Can we force it down? Report to Commander-in-Chief Fu, the airplane is under the control of the detachment tasked with aiding the implementation of the currency reforms. They're under the authority of the Executive Yuan subcommittee. Any problems, ask them directly… ask the Air Force Central Command!"

He slammed down the telephone and marched over to where flight routes were displayed. He leaned in close to inspect the glass board. "What's going on?"

The radar officer replied: "The plane, after passing over the Western Hills, has turned back towards Peking. It's flying lower over the city."

At last, the armoured cars arrived at the Peking treasury. Unfortunately for Zeng Keda and the young soldiers he had tasked with taking charge of the armoured vehicles, the iron gates of the treasury remained shut. The Executive Yuan's special economic detachment, along with the military police under Xu Tieying's command, were all now standing outside the main gate. Together, their eyes trained on Inspector Zeng and Secretary Sun.

Zeng Keda's voice was sombre and cold: "So, what's your position in the party now? What role are you playing?"

Sun Chaozhong's tone was equally sombre and cold. "My brief has remained the same, will always be the same."

"And the traitor within?"

"I'm willing to accept any investigation into my activities the party wishes to carry out."

"From the beginning, you've cooperated with Xu Tieying to disrupt the currency reform initiative. Do you still mistakenly believe there'll be any investigation?"

"If Comrade Jianfeng has given the order, you can execute me now."

"If I had orders…"

A low-altitude roar punctured their discussion. Zeng and Sun, as well as both contingents of men under their commands, all felt a shadow wash over them. They seemed to raise their faces in unison, each pair of eyes drawn to the C-46 flying across the azure sky. The sun gleamed off its metallic body, bringing into clear relief the plane's colours.

In the blink of an eye, however, the C-46 was gone.

"If that plane does not return, you and I, the two of us, will have no choice but to execute Xu Tieying, and then take our own lives, too!"

"For everything, we must follow Comrade Jianfeng's orders."

"Don't mention him again!" Zeng Keda shouted. "You still think to drag him into this bloody mess?"

"Attention!" Both groups of soldiers saluted, their stances, to a man, stiff and erect.

Wang Kejun's car had arrived at the treasury, followed by a jeep. Zeng Keda closed his eyes for a moment and then walked over to the vehicle to greet his superior. He saluted as the other soldiers had.

"You don't need to say anything." Wang Kejun did not return the salute. Instead, he turned to his aide. "Call for the radio operator. I need a wire connected immediately."

"Yes sir. Operator, you're needed!"

The radio operator climbed down from the jeep, carrying his radio equipment with him: a roll of wire that was as large as one of the jeep's tyres, a utility pole on which to string up the electrical line and the saw-tooth metal claws used for climbing – a great array of tools.

Finally, Wang Kejun looked at Zeng Keda. "We must speak to the treasury guards inside. Nanking has ordered it. Hence the need to string this wire."

"Yes." Zeng Keda could feel the bile in his stomach rush to the back of his mouth. He wanted to turn away, but just as he intended to do so, an alarm rang and shattered the uneasy calm.

Secretary Sun had strode over to the treasury gate and slammed the palm of his hand over the power switch to the electric bell.

"Attention!"

The air control tower officers rushed to queue up and salute. The duty officer accompanied Li Yuqing, as well as other ranking members from the Peking garrison. Their pace was quick, their footsteps hurried.

"Get them on the radio. I want to speak to the aeroplane." Li Yuqing demonstrated his familiarity with control tower protocol and walked over to the main radio table.

The duty officer barked: "Radio the C-46. Now!"

"Yes sir." The junior officer picked up the headphones, twisted the dials and spoke into the microphone: "This in Nanyuan airbase calling Captain Fang, respond please. I repeat, this is Nanyuan airbase calling Captain Fang, respond please."

But there was no response. The junior officer looked back in the direction of his commander.

"Keep calling them, dammit!"

The younger soldier did as he was told.

Li Yuqing strode over to the radar display and demanded: "Where is the aeroplane now?"

The officer tasked with operating the radar traced the flight path of the C-46 with his water marker, and was startled but what he saw. "Sir… the plane… it's heading southwest, sir! It's currently over Fuping County in Hubei!"

Li Yuqing's composure evaporated: "Communist territory… does Fuping have an airbase? A runway?"

The duty officer responded: "According to reports, no sir, it doesn't have an airbase. In the past, there was a rudimentary airstrip in Shijiazhuang."

"This is serious. Pay attention. Is the plane heading in the direction of Shijiazhuang?"

"Yes sir." The radar operator was drenched in sweat, his eyes focused keenly on the radar display.

On the other side of the tower control room, the radio operator had stopped trying to reach Fang Meng'ao. Li Yuqing noticed the silence and shouted: "What the devil are you doing? No one told you to stop!"

The duty officer yelled: "Keep radioing him. Do it!"

"Captain Fang, respond please! Radioing Captain Fang, come in please. This is Nanyuan airbase, I repeat, this is Nanyuan airbase. Please respond. Respond please."

The only response was static.

Li Yuqing's gaze fell on the telephone and his brow wrinkled. He walked over and picked up the receiver. "Connect me to Yenching University, Vice-Chancellor He Qicang. No, wait. Don't!" Li slammed the phone back down on its base, turned and stormed back over to the radar display. "Where are they now?"

"Sir, they're still above Fuping, circling."

The anti-aircraft defences were on high alert. Above the skies of Fuping, a C-46 circled. Soldiers of the People's Liberation Army were standing in the yard, holding weapons, their eyes trained upwards. Several radio and telegraph operators were seated in front of their machines, but they had all stopped sending and receiving messages; except for one operator who was busily transcribing a coded report, number after number after number. Liuyun stood behind him, observing what the soldier was writing.

"I'm finished." The operator laid down his pen.

Liuyun snatched at the paper, walked over to another soldier seated at the middle of the table and handed him the paper. "Decode it. No mistakes, understand."

The soldier was an especially proficient cryptographer. On most occasions, he had no need to consult the coded manuals they were given. Before long, below each of the numbers, he had written their corresponding words. Liuyun's eyes scanned the lines of text:

Xu Tieying has burst into the Peking treasury to personally interrogate Xie Peidong <break> Fang Meng'ao has appropriated a C-46 transport plane <break>

A PLA soldier ran up, looked for Liuyun and then rushed over: "Report, sir, the aircraft is not a bomber, sir, it's a Kuomintang transport plane. It remains circling above us, sir."

"I know." Liuyun kept his eyes on the transmission as the cryptographer continued his work.

"Yes sir." The PLA soldier quietly excused himself.

The cryptographer finished and handed the paper to Liuyun. To the men seated in front of the radios, Liuyun appeared to be concentrating on reading the transmission, but in truth he was deep in thought, contemplating the significance of the information he had been sent. A blanket of silence hung over everyone. Outside, the plane circled, the sound of its engine vaguely audible to the men in front of the equipment.

Suddenly, Liuyun marched over to the radio operator who had received the message and ordered: "Take a message. Vice-Chair Zhou needs to be informed."

The operator took hold of the microphone and flipped the dials. Liuyun dictated his message. Within seconds, his coded text was transformed into sound waves that shot rapidly through the air.

The Nanyuan airbase control tower continued to call the aeroplane: "Captain Fang! Captain Fang! Come in, please! Deputy Chief Li Yuqing demands you make contact. Please respond. Please respond."

"Please wait a moment, Vice-Chancellor." Li Yuqing pulled the telephone receiver away from his ear and leaned in the direction of the radio officer. "Discontinue." Still with the phone held away from his ear, Li turned to the duty officer, and asked: "Can this phone be connected to the radio?"

The duty officer looked to his subordinate. "Well, can it be connected?"

"Sir, Commander-in-Chief Fu has a hotline…"

"Can you dial that number and connect it to his telephone?" asked Li Yuqing.

"Yes sir!"

Li Yuqing finally returned his attention to He Qicang. "Vice-Chancellor, we can connect your call to the tower radio. Will you please use it to try to contact Captain Fang? Please don't hang up."

Li Yuqing turned back to the radio operator. "Connect immediately!"

"Yes sir!"

The officer took hold of the telephone receiver, pulled over a telephone line and placed it beside the radio equipment. He then linked both lines to the central radio control box. Turning to Li Yuqing, he said: "Sir, the lines are connected. You can go ahead, sir."

Li spoke to He Qicang: "Vice-Chancellor, if you will…"

The officer removed the headphones and handed them to Li Yuqing: "Sir…"

Li understood and accepted the headphones, placing them over his ears. "Turn on the speaker."

The soldier did as instructed and Li began to speak into the microphone: "The lines have been connected, Mr He. Please proceed in calling Captain Fang. Vice-Chancellor He, do you hear me? Mr He…"

"I'm not deaf, you know." He Qicang's voice echoed over the headphones. "Can you stop yelling?"

Li Yuqing was left stunned but quickly recouped his composure. "Excellent. Can you call Captain Fang, please?"

The eyes of nearly everyone in the control tower turned towards Li Yuqing. They could hear a voice over the speakers, but not that of an old man, rather that of a young woman! Some of the soldiers exchanged puzzled glances. Others just stared, almost unblinking. They all listened to He Xiaoyu's voice: "Meng'ao… my dad… he'd like to say a few words. Please respond." The eyes remained trained on the radio equipment. One second passed. Then two, then three.

"Uncle He, I'm here."

Li Yuqing's eyes brightened. The soldiers' eyes widened.

He Qicang's voice could now be heard over the speakers: "So, you're just going on a trip, are you, some free and easy wandering as Chuang Chou suggests? Fang Meng'ao, you've got skills, a great number of them, but I've got something to say, something you need to hear and learn from."

"I dare not, Uncle, but go ahead."

"I'll start with a quotation: 'A man seeking revenge does not go so far as to smash the sword of his enemy; a man, no matter how hot-tempered, does not rail at the tile that happens to fall on him.' Do you recognise it? Do you understand its meaning?"

There was silence for a while until finally, Fang Meng'ao answered: "Yes, Uncle He, I understand."

"Understand what!" He Qicang's voice was noticeably more agitated. "What are you doing with that blasted aeroplane then? Are you planning to crash it into the mountain? And your father, what's he hoping to achieve by running off to Xishan prison? Just what the hell are you two up to?"

Again there was silence.

Finally, Fang Meng'ao spoke once more: "Uncle He, what's going on has nothing to do with you. Please don't try to get involved."

"Then why have you proposed to He Xiaoyu?" There was anger in He Qicang's voice now. "That year, when your father abandoned your mother and left for Chongqing, it's the same as what you're doing now. Tell me, what kind of morality are you and your father trying to show?"

Li Yuqing relaxed his tense face, his eyes widened and his lower lip dropped. He seemed to be at a loss listening to this most unexpected of exchanges. Several of the officers in the control tower couldn't help but chuckle, perhaps somewhat embarrassingly.

Suddenly, the speaker sounded again: "This is Captain Fang. May I speak with Deputy Li?"

All faces turned towards Li Yuqing. He took a moment to collect his thoughts and regain his composure. The radio operator woke him from his contemplation: "Sir, Captain Fang wishes to speak to you."

Li Yuqing spoke hesitantly into the microphone: "Captain Fang? This is Li Yuqing. Please go ahead."

Again, Fang's voice could be heard over the speaker: "Deputy Li, using your position of authority, sir, can you bring Ma Hanshan to the control tower? I need to speak with him."

Li Yuqing was startled by the request: "That'll take some doing." He gestured to his assistant who had come with him. "Where exactly is Ma Hanshan? Find out immediately!"

"Sir," said the duty officer, "I know where he is."

"And where is he?"

"He's being held here at the airbase, sir. A plane for Nanking has been arranged for this afternoon."

Li turned back to his assistant. "Use my name, my order. Get Ma Hanshan over here now!"

The Central Bank was key for the government, it propped it up. The treasury was key for the bank, its reserves kept it functioning. Despite the seriousness of the situation, however, even Wang Kejun knew it would be impossible for him to exceed his authority. The treasury's gate stood wide open, and the lieutenant in charge stood facing Wang Kejun. They both watched as two radio operators, guarded closely by two treasury guards, made the final connections. Then the men came running over, and said: "Sir, the lines are connected."

Another officer came up to them with a radio receiver. He placed it in front of Wang Kejun, who lifted the microphone and spoke: "I want the Nanking Central Exchange. Yes, operator, I'm calling from the Peking Branch Treasury. Urgent matters need to be discussed with Nanking. Please make the connection immediately."

Zeng Keda stared at Wang Kejun. Sun Chaozhong stared at him as well.

A sudden look of gloom appeared on Wang Kejun's face. "I was instructed to have the lines connected, but now that they are, I realise I've not been informed of which department I am to speak to... What? Still in a meeting? How long has it been going on?"

Zeng Keda could hold his tongue no longer and had to interject: "See if a connection can be made with the Executive Yuan's special subcommittee tasked with overseeing the economic reforms."

Wang Kejun narrowed his eyes and looked at Zeng Keda, and then spoke into the receiver: "Understood. I'll remain here and wait."

Zeng Keda was still staring at Wang Kejun.

Wang Kejun's complexion betrayed his displeasure. "If the two of you still feel as though you haven't yet caused enough trouble, then by all means continue, but make sure you answer the radio when the call comes through. I'll be off."

"General Secretary Wang, the currency reforms are to be announced at any minute. Can you please contact the Nanking Central Exchange and tell them..."

"The president is, at the moment, admonishing his subordinates. Will you tell the Central Exchange to interrupt him so that he can take your call?"

Zeng Keda closed his eyes, unable, or unwilling to respond.

A deep sense of regret and sorrow could be seen in Li Yuqing's eyes. Things seemed far more complicated than he had expected. The weather did little to help, for it was intensely hot. When his eyes fell on Ma Hanshan, dressed in a grey Zhongshan suit, his back straight and rigid, Li wondered only more about what to do. Two military police served as escorts but almost appeared to be more his subordinates than his guards. The men smiled and extended their hands towards Li Yuqing, and for a brief moment, Li mistakenly thought they wanted to shake hands. Then he lowered his gaze and saw the manacles just underneath the cuffs of Ma Hanshan's pristine jacket. Li shifted his focus back to the two guards behind him. "Remove the shackles."

"Nah, don't bother." Ma Hanshan walked over to the radio table himself and sat down in a chair beside it. "Headphones!"

Li Yuqing responded, although not directly to Ma Hanshan. "Do as he says."

The radio dispatcher placed the headphones over Ma Hanshan's ears.

"Move them a little further back." Ma Hanshan squinted at the man. "My hair…"

The dispatcher glanced at Ma Hanshan's distinct hairstyle, and then carefully complied with his instructions.

Ma Hanshan stared out of the window and observed: "Hell, there's not a cloud in the sky. Beautiful weather we're having, hmm." His words, spoken into the microphone, did not seem quite appropriate to the situation at hand.

Li Yuqing furrowed his brow.

"Chief Ma?" It was Fang Meng'ao's voice.

Li Yuqing's brow relaxed.

"Yes, go ahead Captain Fang. It's me."

"Have you seen the orders from the Executive Yuan's subcommittee?"

"Yes, I have."

"Why didn't you stay and coordinate the investigation into the accounts?"

Ma Hanshan laughed. "Captain Fang, do you still have faith in the Executive Yuan? They're not much more than a bloody temple, and the Standing Committee is in control there. The party wants me dead by midnight. They're not going to drag it out any longer than that. Captain Fang, I know you're an honourable and upright fellow. But trying to save my worthless soul, well, you've got better things to do, let me tell you. Now, turn that bloody plane around and get back here."

"It's clear what you're trying to say. Right now, everyone in Peking can hear what we're saying, Nanking too. You know those dirty accounts you've spoken about. Well, because of them, no one will dare have you killed… Whenever I get to Nanking, I'll come to see you, all right. We'll have a drink of wine and a laugh, too."

"Whether they kill me or not, I don't really care. Captain Fang, those rotten ledgers, nobody's going to be able to control what happens. You're a fine lad, you know, easy-going, carefree. Maybe you're up there now, flying a bloody aeroplane. I reckon having a glass of wine's even better, you know. Ah, don't bother with it any more. Land the plane. Perhaps we'll have the chance to see each other again..."

"I understand." Fang Meng'ao's voice had grown more noticeably excited. "You know, I'm not just trying to save you. I'm trying to save all of us! Xu Tieying arrested you first, all to get his hands on those damn ledgers. He's at the treasury now trying to arrest my Uncle Xie. He's saying Uncle Xie's a Communist agent, and me too. Do you understand what I'm saying?"

"I'm a Communist, so is Xie Peidong. It's all fucking bullshit!" Ma Hanshan was now clearly agitated. "Xu Tieying murdered Cui Zhongshi and for what, twenty fucking per cent, that's all. He said he was a Communist, that was cause enough. Then afterwards he said he wasn't a Communist. How's he not claimed that TV Soong and HH Kung aren't Communists, too? I understand, I understand well, Captain Fang. By all means ask your questions, ask whatever you want. Our brothers will make good use of advanced American equipment to tell the whole bloody world. Tomorrow in the *New York Times*, in *The Times*, too, in England. We'll be the lead fucken story!"

Yuqing was now nervous, his body stooped a little. "Mr Ma, you must pay attention to the image of the party-state!"

"You're afraid of what I might say, hmm? Then I'll leave."

Fang Meng'ao's voice crackled over the speaker again: "Chief Ma... got questions from my guests. The men on board, they've apparently got things they want to ask."

Ma Hanshan could guess whose questions they were. "I know who you're talking about. Their names are on those dirty ledgers, yeah?"

Once more, Fang Meng'ao's voice could be heard by everyone in the tower. "Yes... eight men... names all there. They've been instructed to fill out certain forms, but they've refused thus far, saying their supposed companies are all registered in Shanghai, and that Peking and Tianjin have no authority to make them declare anything." Fang Meng'ao went silent for a second and then spoke again: "I've turned on the wide-speaker. Go ahead and ask Chief Ma your questions. Ask him if Peking and Tianjin have the authority to compel you to fill in the declaration."

"Excellent!" Ma Hanshan's voice grew louder: "Captain Fang, if I may, I've a question to ask first. Afterwards, if they're still unwilling to fill in those forms, then I suggest you toss them from the plane. Let's see who'll show up to collect their pulped corpses!"

"Chief Ma, please proceed with your question."

"All right then, let me get started. Now, you eight dirty fucking corporate bastards, let me ask you, when the Citizens' Food Allocation was set up in April of this year, whose hands were all over the accounts, who supposedly managed the distribution of food and supplies to Peking's and Tianjin's millions of people? Hmm… not a peep. I'll continue then. Much of the government's money was given to you, yes, and what about food and supplies, were you provided with that, too? Still no reply. So you've argued your companies are all registered in Shanghai. Hah, it's all dirty money, laundered through your accounts in the Central Bank. All your activities supposedly run under the banner of helping the people, and yet they were left to starve and die. Even the distribution of food aid was impeded, which forced the students to rebel. Nanking sent a team of investigators, but they didn't touch you fellas. Instead… hah… I was made the scapegoat. But still you're all blathering on about having fifty-one per cent of your bigwig companies' shares in Shanghai! The president announced the currency reforms today. This means all money, and I mean every cent, every coin across the nation, all of it is to be collected and returned to the National Treasury. And what are you fuckers still doing? Wagging your chins about your so-called enterprises in Shanghai! Hah! Mr Chiang Ching-kuo's in Shanghai right now, Captain Fang, you don't need to bother talking to them. Just fly them to Shanghai, let Mr Chiang interrogate them himself, he'll get to the bottom of it, he'll find out whether this fifty-one per cent is personally owned or if they belong to these… what… dummy corporations! I guess that's what they can be called. Hah!"

Ma Hanshan was fuming with rage, his throat shouted raw. He lifted the manacles and shook them in the direction of Li Yuqing.

Li couldn't help but feel an unexpected measure of admiration for Ma, even if he didn't want to show it. He looked at the man, then turned and spoke quietly to a subordinate: "Get some water for him, will you?"

Seconds later and the duty officer handed him a small enamel cup. Ma Hanshan accepted it readily but took his time drinking the warm water inside.

Captain Fang's voice echoed again: "They've all filled in the forms, declaring the fifty-one per cent as personal shares. Chief Ma, do you have any other questions to ask?"

"Opening a new factory, starting a new business, it's not easy. But this knife will cause them all enough pain. They have to protect what they have to I suppose." Ma Hanshan finished his water. His throat properly moistened, the tone of his voice changed: "After all, those twenty per cent of shares were yours in the first place, yeah? So why did you let some bastards in the military, in the government, too, why did you let them blackmail you, then smuggle what was yours? The sixth of July... that's when they executed Hou Juntang. The lot of you know this. So again, I ask you. Why did you let some prick keep hold of those shares? Just because Xu Tieying says they're party assets doesn't make it so, does it? Captain Fang, make sure they put this additional twenty per cent down as their own personal property. Nanking's heard every word I've said, and who knows, the Americans are probably listening in. And what's Xu Tieying getting up to right now? He's pulling out the old Communist card, saying the stocks are party assets. Ah, he'll get his comeuppance any day now. All of it will be exposed. That's why he wants me dead, he wants to shut me up. Hah. I'll see him jump off the building first!"

"Understood, Chief Ma!" Fang Meng'ao's voice was crystal clear.

―――

The telephone in the treasury office rang sharply. Both men were shackled to each other, however, so neither moved. They just looked at the phone. Finally, Xu Tieying spoke: "You're afraid to answer, aren't you?"

"The telephone is closer to your free hand."

Xu slowly reached out and lifted the receiver. "Peking branch, treasury office. Speak please."

"Who the hell told you to go to the treasury?" Ye Xiufeng's reprimand pounded against his ear.

Xu Tieying did his best to maintain composure: "Yes, Chief, the orders to interrogate Xie Peidong came from Commander-in-Chief Chen, sir. The Central Bank chairman, Mr Yu, also signed off on the…"

"Chief Chen gave the order?" Ye Xiufeng's voice betrayed his growing anger and irritation. "Do you know Fang Meng'ao is in the air? He's been speaking to Ma Hanshan, who's in the Nanyuan control tower. He's made public, he named names, the phoney companies. He's claiming the Communications Department – your department – expropriated Hon Juntang's twenty per cent. Do you know anything about this? This is the first day of the reforms, and what have you been doing? You haven't escorted Ma Hanshan to Nanking. Instead, you show up at the Peking treasury, and for what? To give them the rope to hang you with! There's more, too. Fang Buting, of his own volition, has turned himself in at Xishan prison. He Qicang's been raging. He says he's coming to Nanking to be incarcerated. This, all of this shit, it's forced the president into convening an emergency meeting. You damn fool… did you know?"

Escorting Ma to Nanking, coming here to the treasury to interrogate Xie Peidong, the two fronts of their attack had been so well planned. The only thing Xu had not thought about was Fang Meng'ao communicating with the control tower… speaking to Ma Hanshan… revealing to everyone the situation around Hou Juntang's shares. Xu couldn't figure out if he'd been brought down by the CPC, or if it had been the inner circle of his own Kuomintang that had sunk him. He was silent as these thoughts ran through his head. His only recourse, he felt, was to try by any means to redeem the attack plan. There was little else he could do. At last, he responded: "Chief, the currency reform is a presidential policy announcement, and on the very first day of it, Communists in Peking have sought to manipulate and thwart the initiative.

Chief Ye, you and Commander Chen should discuss the pros and cons of this situation with the president…"

"Explains what pros and cons?" said Ye Xiufeng. "What the hell are you getting at? Would *you* like to hear the president go over the pros and cons?"

"Chief Ye, if… if you could just pass…" Xu Tieying closed his eyes.

In Ye Xiufeng's voice could be heard both his Jiangsu 'officialese' tone, along with a Zhejiang Fenghua accent: "I'll quote you something: 'Your department has shown little concern for the affairs of the party. The only thing you're concerned about is his money. You have stuck your hands in so much, and still it seems to be not enough. You have even involved yourself in the activities of the Executive Yuan's economic subcommittee. I, the president of the Republic of China, call you here to appear in front of…' That's the president explaining things to me! You, Xu Tieying, all you've done is taken a great big shit in Peking. You've turned it all to shit, an arse far larger than I can wipe, I'll tell you that. And what, you want to get Chen involved? Ask him to wipe your arse, too!"

Xu Tieying kept his eyes closed and held his breath. Moments passed, but then he seemed to feel a gush of air blow across his face and his breathing began to even. "I understand. Chief, party assets can no longer be protected. The arrest of CPC agents is no longer possible. Sir, I request to be relieved from…"

"Before you step down, wipe that oversized arse of yours!" There was greater venom in Ye Xiufeng's voice: "First, you have to make sure we have no shares in any of those eight blasted companies. Second, the emergency meeting will pass the following resolution: Captain Fang Meng'ao has violated military law and thus he's to be arrested immediately!" Xu could hear the phone being slammed down, leaving him with nothing but a dial tone.

The phone was still in his hand when the treasury's electric bell pierced the silence between him and Xie Peidong. Xie's eyes looked empty, however, as though he had not heard a word of the telephone conversation. After all, he thought, if the treasury bell had been ringing like it was, there was no way he could have heard Ye Xiefeng's voice. Xu waited for the bell to stop, then smiled, if only slightly. "Mr Xie, you... you win. The investigation is over. Do you fancy hearing the reason why?"

Xie stood up slowly. "I've never experienced such... combat before. Where there's a winner and loser... I don't think I care therefore to hear the reason why I've won."

"I'll tell you anyway. Someone else's taking the fall for you. Would you like to know who?" Xie Peidong stared at Xu, but he did not respond. So Xu continued: "Fang Meng'ao has violated military law. He took that plane without permission, and he threatened the party-state with blackmail. A special military tribunal is to be called. But this time I won't be able to speak in his defence."

The information cut deep. Xie's heart skipped a beat. He responded softly with a question: "If I gave you... a hundred thousand US dollars, would you be willing to represent him?"

The rage on Xu Tieying's face was plainly visible, but still he smiled. "The CPC certainly has money, doesn't it? Mao and Zhou live in caves and wear simple clothes, but with a wave of their hand and... and what... money from our Central Bank ends up in Hong Kong, and then in the hands of so-called democrats. They can also divert funds to various Kuomintang departments, all with the wave of a hand. Did I give you any sense that I would agree to your proposal? Besides, the market situation has, shall we say, changed. If you want me to help you save Fang Meng'ao this time, it'll cost you a hundred thousand at least. Do you have that kind of cash?"

"You're not that avaricious a man are you, Director Xu? That tape recording of Hou Juntang agreeing to take a hundred thousand was enough to get him the death verdict in court. Are you worried I might have a tape recorder in the locked strongbox over there?"

"Xie Peidong!" Xu Tieying could no longer hold his anger: "You know the name of my predecessor. You know the entire apparatus of government has got its eyes trained on you right now! For the rest of my life, there's nothing else I want to be doing. I'm just waiting to serve as public prosecutor. The first time will be when we drag Fang Meng'ao in front of the special tribunal. The second time will be for you. Your precious Zhou Enlai could bring a mountain of gold, but it won't do you any good!"

"Whether or not Zhou has a mountain of gold, I'm afraid I don't know. The only thing I do know is that my life would hardly be worth it. I lost my wife when I was young, I've only got my daughter. She's my everything. A few days ago, she was arrested by you lot. Then I was told she was released but sent to the liberated zones. But you just said her life, her death, too, is in the palm of your hands. If there is still a court in this ruined Republic, if there is any law to speak of, I'd go and find the best solicitor I could to get him to turn my daughter back over to me. Xu Tieying, I hope you have something to say to that."

Xu suddenly lifted his pistol from its holster.

The treasury's electric bell rang again sharply.

Xu Tieying's gun sounded! The decibels of sound in the office went well beyond the extreme, so much so that for a moment at least, neither man could hear anything.

In the silence, the two men stared at each other.

In the silence, the shackles holding the men together had shattered.

In the silence, Xie Peidong's back left the office and made its way to the steel door.

In the silence, Xu Tieying reholstered his weapon and followed Xie out of the room.

The air traffic control tower at Nanyuan airbase was similarly quiet. All eyes were transfixed by the scene outside the window. The C-46 had finally landed. Its rear cargo door was open, and the jeep that had recently been swallowed by it was now being spit back out. Li Yuqing watched Fang Meng'ao, who was again behind the steering wheel. He saw, too, the eight businessmen seated in the back, as well as the two young pilots serving as guards. Fang's remaining eighteen men hastened down the cargo ramp after the jeep.

Li turned to the duty officer. "Dial Central Air Force Command."

"Sir, yes sir." The officer quickly spun the rotary dial.

Li turned back to the window and saw Fang Meng'ao's men form into two neat lines. He knew they were waiting for him.

"Deputy Li!" There was a clear change in the sound of the duty officer's voice.

Li Yuqing turned in his direction and saw the man gripping the telephone receiver, his eyes wide and focused on him. Li walked over towards the younger man, his own eyes asking for some kind of clarification. There was a look of seeming terror on the duty officer's face. Without saying anything, he handed the telephone to Li, then swiftly moved away to stand to attention.

"Is this Li Yuqing?"

The Fenghua accent of the man speaking on the other end brought Li Yuqing to his senses and he felt his legs stiffen to attention. "Yes, Vice-Chancellor, it's me!"

"I'm no longer your vice-chancellor now, am I? I should think that Whampoa would not dare to have a student such as you either!"

Li Yuqing's complexion changed.

The voice on the phone continued: "Was it Vice-President Li who instructed you to go to Nanyuan, or did you go on your own initiative?"

In a certain way, Li felt as though he was back in Whampoa, but this helped him to calm his nerves and respond more confidently: "Yes, Mr President, to answer your question, I made the decision to come here myself."

After a short silence, the voice spoke again: "Explain the reason."

"Yes, Mr President. One of my subordinates received a telephone call from the vice-chancellor of Yenching University, Mr He Qicang. That's when I learned that Fang Meng'ao had taken to the air without proper authorisation. I also learned he'd cut off all communication with the tower and ground crew. This was of course a serious matter, and since you, Mr President, sent me to handle things in Peking, I thought it best to get myself over to the airbase as quick as possible and make sure that Fang brought the aircraft back. Right now, I can confirm that the plane has landed safely. Captain Fang and his men are outside standing to attention, awaiting orders."

"The plane is back on the ground, you say. Then the party-state has lost face, for sure. Who made you bring Ma Hanshan into the tower?"

Sensing his predicament, Li Yuqing made no further effort to justify his actions: "That was a dereliction of duty on the part of a subordinate, sir. I take full responsibility for his actions, sir, and am willing to accept whatever punishment you deem necessary, Mr President."

Li's answer seemed fitting, a review would happen accordingly. The tone of Chiang Kai-shek's voice relaxed: "We can speak about that later. To more immediate matters, it's been determined that Fang Meng'ao violated military law. How best to handle this?"

Li Yuqing paused for a moment, but he knew he couldn't leave the president waiting for long. "Mr President, sir, Fang Meng'ao and the men under his immediate command, sir, that was arranged by the Ministry of Defence. Fang himself was appointed by Chief Chiang Ching-kuo."

"You will not bring his name into this!" There was renewed sternness in the president's tone: "I asked how best you think *you* should handle this."

"We'll follow any and all orders you give, Mr President, sir."

"Then arrest him now. And escort him to the Peking Police headquarters!"

The sound of the shackles clamping down on Fang Meng'ao's wrists echoed across Nanyuan airbase. Li Yuqing carried out the order personally, then patted Fang lightly before turning round. "Bring Ma Hanshan out here, too."

Standing nearby, Fang Meng'ao's twenty pilots, his personal guard, as it were, looked on in silence, their faces heavy and hard. Positioned on the other side of the taxiing lane, the military police, three divisions, watched them keenly.

Some distance away, Ma Hanshan appeared, escorted carefully by Deputy Shan, who had been unable to extricate himself from all of this unpleasant business.

Fang Meng'ao laughed. Ma Hanshan did the same and then hurried his pace in the direction of Fang.

Deputy Shan did his duty, as he had always done. Once Ma had quickened his pace, they followed suit, determined not to allow the older man to get too far in front of them.

As it turned out, Li Yuqing was standing in the most appropriate spot for it allowed Ma Hanshan to simply pass by, but yet permitted Li to stare at Deputy Shan.

Shan hurriedly drew to a stop and saluted. "Report, Deputy Commander Li, as ordered sir. Ma Hanshan has been escorted here, so awaiting new orders, sir!"

"You wait there." Li Yuqing gestured to the spot where Shan was standing.

For a moment, Shan looked puzzled, but then quickly comprehended the instructions: "Sir!" Shan glued his feet to the ground but directed his attention elsewhere.

The twenty pilots and the contingent of military police were equally quiet, aware of what was expected of them. Their eyes remained forward; not a single soldier looked towards Fang Meng'ao nor towards Ma Hanshan.

Fang offered Ma his hand to shake. But Ma had already seen the shackles on Fang's wrists and was deliberately avoiding looking at his hands. He spoke without offering his own: "Captain Fang, I know you're a clean fellow, you don't want to shake my hand."

Fang looked him up and down, his hair parted to one side, his figure straight and erect in his Zhongshan suit. He smiled. "I would say, today, you're a much cleaner fellow than me." He kept his hand extended in midair.

Slowly, Ma Hanshan relented and extended his own.

When they clasped, Fang leaned a little closer and spoke softly: "The matter with your son... I've already taken care of it. He's in hospital in Nanking, a facility for wounded servicemen. He's being looked after for drug addiction. When the time's right, arrangements will be made for him to visit you."

Hands still tight together, Ma Hanshan sighed. "I won't say thank you. This son of mine has only incurred debts. Besides, he won't want to see me, nor do I wish to really see him. You don't need to make any arrangements." Fang Meng'ao's smile hardened, and Ma Hanshan continued: "Captain Fang, please don't misunderstand me. You and your father, you've got a good relationship there. Me and my son, we don't. I've done far too many awful things in my time, and not enough good. I know that once I get to Nanking... well... a bullet is waiting for me there, and then that will be it. So in the end... good, bad... it doesn't matter. All I have to ask of you is that you help me see it through, help me finish things." Fang Meng'ao bent his ear to listen. Ma went on: "Captain Fang, tell me, have you visited Deputy Director Cui's tombstone, just outside Xishan prison?"

"I've been there, yes."

"Ah, excellent." Ma Hanshan moved a little closer, and lowered his voice to not much more than a whisper: "Fifty steps or so up the mountainside from Cui's tombstone, you'll find a forgotten embankment. It's old, but there is the bottom half of a stone marker dug into the ground. Carved into it is the year in which it was placed, 'thirty-seventh year of the Kangxi Emperor's reign'. Underneath are buried a dozen or so gold bricks. They're all that's left of my family's savings. The government's currency reforms... they'll be dead in the water within two months. Afterwards, the government will be in such disarray it won't be able to bother with who lives and who dies. Captain Fang, my request is this: when you think the time's ready, when it's safe, dig up those gold bars and give them to Cui's widow. They should be enough to see her children through to adulthood..."

Fang's eyes hardened.

Ma Hanshan had already released his hand and had begun to turn around. "I should be off!"

Deputy Shan glanced at Li Yuqing. Li nodded his head in response, and Shan, along with his military police, shifted and walked towards them.

For one last time, Ma Hanshan looked at Fang Meng'ao. "Brother, Xu Tieying has lumped us together. He won't let you go, nor will the central members of the party. Don't say a word, nothing... at least not until they drag you in front of that special tribunal. Make sure your dad is also there, Vice-Chancellor He. You'll need them. The best that can happen is you'll be dishonourably discharged from the military. If you are, then get the hell out of China, go overseas. Chiang Ching-kuo is not one you want to mess with. And it's better to avoid antagonising the CPC, too." Ma turned away from Fang and then ran by himself towards the waiting aircraft. Deputy Shan, along with his men, hurried after him.

Li Yuqing walked over, but Fang Meng'ao spoke first: "Where are you taking me?"

Li smiled bitterly. "You broke military rules. There's only one place I can bring you, police headquarters. Surely you understand."

Fang Meng'ao returned his smile, and then glanced at his pilot comrades. "And them?"

"They're to return to their barracks. Those are the arrangements made by Inspector Zeng. Would you like to say hello to him?"

"No, there's no need." Fang Meng'ao began to walk in the direction of Li Yuqing's waiting vehicle. Li hesitated a moment, then followed after him.

Li's driver and personal aide-de-camp opened the rear door. Fang Meng'ao drew closer. He wanted to worm into the back seat, disappear, but he stopped before doing so. There was something else he had to do first. He turned and looked at his men, his pilots, his comrades. They all saluted in unison. Fang's hands were still shackled so he couldn't return the gesture. All he could do was smile at them and then board the waiting car.

The radio in He Qicang's sitting room echoed again with the sound of a woman reporter: "This is the Central Broadcast Station, I repeat, the Central Broadcast Station. At the same time as President Chiang Kai-shek announced the emergency economic measures, the Executive Yuan announced the method by which the new currency will be issued…"

"It's all so absurd! Ridiculous nonsense! Madness!" He Qicang's rage boiled over. He grabbed for the telephone and slapped the sofa three times with his free hand. He Xiaoyu and Liang Jinglun were standing nearby, each holding their breath, looking on in concern at the old man.

The radio continued to announce concurrent measures associated with the currency reforms. "The people are to declare their foreign cash holdings, their property assets, everything. The government is to exercise greater financial control over the economy..."

"Turn it off! I don't want to hear anything else about this blasted currency." He Qicang's voice boomed throughout the sitting room.

Liang Jinglun acted quickly, flipping the dial and silencing the radio.

He Qicang spoke into the telephone: "Called me to show my face, wanted me to help convince Fang Meng'ao to land, which he's done, and then you... you go and arrest him. You're telling me, what bastard gave these orders!?"

Outside, Fang Buting stared at the door. He was poised to knock on it, but he couldn't decide if he wanted to or not. He let his hand fall and closed his eyes. In the distance, his Austin was stopped beside the road. Inside, he could hear He Qicang continue to rage: "Li Yuqing won't answer me. He won't dare. Then, dammit, connect me to Li Zongren!" For a moment, there was silence, then He shouted again: "Speaker! Say something. I want answers, dammit..."

The sitting room was quiet. Liang Jinglun and He Xiaoyu looked ahead. Neither said anything. He Qicang's anger had swept through the room like a tidal wave washes away small seaside communities. His eyes were filled with worry, irritation and confusion. He pulled the receiver away from his ear and just stared at it. Then he shook his head and brought it back close to the side of his face. His eyes darted in the direction of his daughter.

He Xiaoyu understood and walked over to him.

He Qicang was silent, his movements robotic. He passed her the phone but said nothing.

He Xiaoyu took the phone and lifted it to her ear. She listened for a moment, then spoke to her father: "Dad, there's no one there. The line's dead."

"What do you mean 'dead'?"

"I mean, the line's been cut, severed."

"But this phone, it's the university's. Yenching University's! They wouldn't dare." He Qicang stood up abruptly from the sofa, his eyes dark and foreboding.

"Dad!" He Xiaoyu threw the telephone to one side and reached to support her father. She was too later, however.

Fortunately, Liang Jinglun was not. She caught the sight of his robes fluttering out of the corner of her eye, his arms coming around her father to make sure he didn't crumple to the floor.

"Qicang..." Fang Buting had heard the commotion inside and now, almost violently, pushed open the sitting room door.

Liang Jinglun helped the older man return to his seat on the sofa. He Xiaoyu's eyes welled up with tears as she moved to cradle her father's head towards her chest.

"Don't move him!" Fang Buting's voice was excited but gentle, soft. He walked to his old friend and spoke again: "Let me..."

Liang Jinglun and He Xiaoyu stepped away.

Fang Buting reached out his hand and took hold of He Qicang's wrist. His grasp was firm but soft. Using three fingers he felt for the other man's pulse. His eyes were nearly closed, but his waist was straight, his back against the sofa. He looked like a monk in some sort of meditative trance. He Xiaoyu and Liang Jinglun both looked on anxiously.

Fang Buting's breathing eased and he placed He Qicang's hand on the sofa next to him. Then he turned to look at He Xiaoyu, his face consolatory. He shot a glance at Liang Jinglun as well, before seating himself next to He Qicang on the sofa.

Gradually, He's eyes opened. At first, he seemed to look at his daughter, then at Liang Jinglun. Slowly, He Qicang turned his head and was surprised to see Fang Buting sitting next to him.

"Try not to move, and don't be angry." Fang Buting extended his hand and placed it on his friend's.

He Qicang looked at Fang for what seemed like an age, then moved his hand out from under the other man's. "Why are you so concerned about me? Why would I be angry?"

"That's right, yes." Fang Buting retracted his hand and placed it on his own lap. "Anger is taking on other people's mistakes and punishing yourself."

"Eh!" He Qicang sighed and looked up at the ceiling. "Isn't it supposed to be young people that cause all kinds of trouble? What are we, nearly in our sixties? But you're doing the same. Your son took that plane... you tried to turn yourself in... wanted to be imprisoned. And for what? And now, well, Meng'ao's been arrested, my telephone line's been cut. How can we save him? Who should we look to for help?"

Fang Buting did not respond, but He Qicang kept his eyes on him. Fang's eyelids drooped. Suddenly, He Qicang realised Liang Jinglun and He Xiaoyu were standing in front of them. His eyes turned towards Liang, and just like that an idea occurred: this young man in front of him, still a student, was someone of great importance to Chiang Ching-kuo!

Liang Jinglun seemed to understand what was going through his mind. "Mr He, it's not worth it looking for them. You tell me who to find, and I'll do it."

There was an underlying meaning to Liang's words. He Qicang knew this. He appreciated the tacit agreement Liang was making. He understood, too, that they couldn't let anyone else in on it.

He Qicang refrained from looking at Fang Buting. He wouldn't look at his daughter, either. His eyes were trained only on Liang Jinglun. "What department does Fang Meng'ao belong to?"

"Before, it was the Ministry of Defence. Now with the currency reforms launched, I would think he's been attached to the office in Tianjin charged with managing the economic reforms."

"You go as my representative." He Qicang sat up straight. "Go and find that inspector, Zeng Keda. Get him to communicate with Chiang Ching-kuo. If the Kuomintang want to use people as weapons, then I'll head to Nanking to muzzle their guns myself. I hope, too, that Chiang Ching-kuo will pass this on to his father!"

Liang Jinglun shot a glance at Fang Buting, but his eyelids were still half closed as though he were lost deep in thought and not really hearing anything that was being said.

"Why glance at him?" The secretive look in He Qicang's eyes was simple and clear: Go!

"Yes, Mr He." But despite his words, Liang Jinglun still shifted his eyes back to Fang Buting. "Mr Fang, sir, may I borrow your car please?"

Fang Buting stared at the younger man. Liang's face was calm, unperturbed. Fang turned to He Qicang's daughter. "Xiaoyu, go with him, will you? Tell my driver, tell Li, he's to take Professor Liang wherever he needs to go. But first, return to my house and get my wife, your Auntie Cheng, ask her to go with you to see Meng'ao."

He Xiaoyu had already nodded her head, but at the same time she knew she had to get her father's assent. He spoke before she could: "Go on. Use my name, and do as he says."

Liang Jinglun was already walking out the door. When He Xiaoyu turned to follow after him, tears were in her eyes.

Fang Buting stood up and closed the door after them. He waited a moment until he heard the car engine start, and then turned back to his old friend. "How about we go upstairs to talk? Would you like me to help you up?"

He Qicang grabbed his cane and lifted himself up from the sofa. In his friend's eyes, he could see the many years they had lived, the many, many things they had gone through. "Yes, I could use a hand."

"Do you know who made this teapot? It was made in the twentieth year of the Republic by none other than Fan Dasheng. Did you know that?" Fang Buting put down the thermos, and then picked up the enamelled teapot and gave it to He Qicang. They were upstairs in He's study, a more comfortable room for them to talk.

He Qicang accepted the proffered teaware.

Fang pulled over a stool and sat down in front of He. "You know, not long ago someone also gave me one of Fan Dasheng's masterpieces... a teapot and three cups to go along with it."

"Who? And why three cups? What was the meaning behind that?"

"Chiang Ching-kuo. He'd got Zeng Keda to give the set to me. As for the three cups, apparently they were to represent me and my two boys."

"What a politician eh! A rather despicable trick! Did you accept the gift?"

"I didn't think to accept it, no, but my son was in their sphere... in the palm of their hands, really. And by the sounds of it, he was someone they considered quite important. I only realised after that he was, in essence, their hostage. I've often wondered who it was that put my name forward to be manager of the Peking branch. I've thought, too, about how I ended up having a friend like you, someone so able to hold their own against the Americans, to wrestle from them the aid they promised in the first place. But, you know, I don't think the people behind these... ah... let's just say I don't think they're short of money."

"Then isn't that all the more reason to get Meng'ao to stop what he's doing! Get him out of the country, that's what's best!" He Qicang sat up straight as he said these words. He looked, too, for a place to lay down the teapot.

Fang Buting extended his hand to take it from him, and for a moment, they held it together between them.

Fang Buting spoke first: "Brother, for that's how I think of you, do you want to know why I went to Xishan prison today? Why I asked Meng'ao to do what he did? You should understand, I had no other choice."

They were silent for a moment, each looking deeply into the other's eyes.

He Qicang spoke: "Did you have no other way? Are things that desperate?"

Fang Buting's grip tightened on the teapot. "I began to understand once I was at the bank. I imagine when you were named as an economic consultant for the government you understood too... the Kuomintang's assets had all been tunnelled out. The assets, the profits, all of it had been transferred out. The president and his son haven't been willing to give up. That's why they've launched these currency reforms, a last-ditch effort to breathe new life into the economy, but it's useless, it won't work. You know what's happened today? There's internal fighting at the highest levels of the Kuomintang. Meng'ao is just cannon fodder to them. Do you know I read the military's so-called rules of conduct? I've read their files on legal conduct, too. Meng'ao took that plane today, without authorisation, but he also returned it, without anything major happening. The harshest punishment he can receive, according to their own military rules, is six months detention and then a dishonourable discharge. So let him be detained for a few days, let them escort him to Nanking. You and I can make our appearance then. That might at least get a slight reduction in his sentence. He might even be discharged on the spot without serving any period of detention. Then, finally, he'll no longer be of any use to Chiang Ching-kuo. And, if you agree, he can leave the country with… with Xiaoyu."

He Qicang directed his eyes to the ceiling and let the words percolate in his mind. Then, suddenly, he stood up. "We need to make a phone call… now. We've got to tell Liang Jinglun to get back here!"

"But the line's been cut," Fang Buting reminded him gently. "Besides, we can still let him go and see them."

"No, you don't understand!" He Qicang walked over to the window, trembling as he did so: "I'll… I'll tell you when he gets back."

Fang Buting stared at the back of his scholar friend. A strange emotion welled up inside him and he felt as though he was still a child, that he'd not grown up, and that perhaps he never would. As he stared at his friend, he couldn't help but feel the same was true for him.

Liang Jinglun stopped the car on the road that ran behind Gu Weijun's residence and looked at He Xiaoyu. She returned his stare, and then shifted her gaze to the hutong and the sentry beyond. "Are you going to be able to get in?"

"I just need to explain things. I'm here on your father's behalf, which should be enough for them to let me pass."

"And if you can't explain things clearly?"

"Fang Meng'ao rescued me twice. If I can't explain things, if the worst comes to the worst, I imagine I'll be arrested a third time."

He Xiaoyu turned her face to the side window to hide the fact her eyes were growing wet. She heard Liang Jinglun speak to the driver: "You don't need to wait here for me. Take Miss He home."

"Sure."

Liang Jinglun climbed out of the vehicle, and Li shifted into first gear. As he began to drive off, He Xiaoyu spun her head around to look at Liang. An unexpected gust of wind blew through the hutong. Willow tree branches swayed, and Liang Jinglun's robes did the same.

The car wound its way down Zhang Zizhong Road. Li reached into the glove compartment and drew out a letter. Handing it to He Xiaoyu, he said: "Miss He, this is for you."

A little stunned, she took hold of the letter. There was no name on the envelope, no words at all. She glanced at Li behind the steering wheel but could see he was focused on navigating the car down the street. Xiaoyu tore open the envelope and pulled out the letter. She was greeted by two neatly written rows of characters, one running across the page, and one running down it:

> Look after your father, and look after yourself. Refrain from making enquiries, and refrain from trying to stage manage. The path is filled with twists and turns, but the future is bright.

"Where did this letter come from?" He Xiaoyu asked Li.

"At your place, the main gate. A student ran up and gave it to me. I was told to give it to you when you were alone."

She was moved by his explanation, but almost immediately felt a pang of disappointment. She didn't express this to Li, however. Instead, she returned her attention to the letter, let her eyes linger over it for a minute, and then placed it back inside its envelope. Finally, she put it in her pocket, as close to her skin as possible.

Suddenly, she noticed the speed of the car had picked up and she raised her head. "Have you seen Uncle Xie?"

"Who?"

"The bank's assistant manager, Mr Xie."

"I haven't seen him today. I don't expect to now. With the currency reforms being launched and the bank branch governor tied up with other affairs, everything's fallen on Mr Xie's shoulders."

He Xiaoyu didn't ask anything more. Instead, she directed her attention out of the window and the city beyond.

The green of the tree shaded the pond. The beauty of the scene, the trees, the pond, the cobblestone path lined with flowers that stretched its way through the Koo garden was marred by the soldiers and military police standing guard. Commander Li walked in front, Liang Jinglun close behind. In front of them, they could already see Zeng Keda's residence within the compound.

Commander Li stood to one side. As Liang Jinglun focused his eyes on him, he was surprised to see Secretary Sun standing in the middle of the path. Sun spoke before Liang had the chance to say anything: "You fight well, don't you?" He stepped closer and lowered his voice: "Comrade Liang, I'm afraid to say you're not permitted in… at least not at the moment."

"Step back from me." Liang Jinglun's voice was even lower than Sun's.

Sun Chaozhong backed up a step. He did not, however, step aside.

Liang Jinglun turned to Commander Li. "Give me your weapon."

"But Mr Liang…"

Liang Jinglun's tone was stern, forceful: "If I was in military attire, you'd be calling me 'colonel'. Now, give me your gun!"

He hesitated a moment more, and then complied, unholstering the pistol he carried about his waist and passing it to Liang Jinglun.

Liang lifted the barrel of the gun and pointed it at Sun Chaozhong. "Pull out your weapon."

"Comrade Liang Jinglun…"

Liang kept the gun pointing at Sun's face. "It's just like that day you held your pistol at me, isn't it?"

Sun still refused to reach for his gun.

"Then get the hell out of the way!" Liang Jinglun raised his hand towards the sky and fired. The shot rang out through the garden, but before the echo died, Liang had started to walk past Sun Chaozhong.

Commander Li was quick, his movements practised. Before Sun could respond, Li had already pulled him away. Another gunshot rang out. The soldiers, the military police, everyone stared in Liang Jinglun's direction, shock and amazement on their faces.

"Who fired?" Zeng Keda was the first of the men inside to emerge.

"Commander Li!" Liang Jinglun strode into view, calling to the other man behind without looking back to make sure he was there.

Li appeared seconds later.

"Here, take your weapon back." Liang Jinglun handed it to him and stepped inside.

Zeng Keda looked at Liang Jinglun, puzzled and confused.

Liang Jinglun did not pause, but spoke instead: "Where's Xu Tieying?" He walked into the room without waiting for an answer.

CHAPTER 12

Zeng Keda dashed into his own sitting room, but his eyes did fall not on Liang Jinglun's perturbed face. All he could see was the man's back as he stood towering over Xu Tieying. Xu was seated on the sofa, seemingly unaware of Liang's presence. His attention was occupied by the forms filled in by the eight businessmen. Zeng had heard no words exchanged. This was a confrontation between the two men, albeit a quiet one.

Zeng's eyes darted towards the bedroom that lay adjacent to the sitting room. The door was open, the curtains had been pulled back, and a dim, weak ray of light shone in. Liang Jinglun was the first to break the silence.

"I've a number of questions I'd like to ask Mr Xu here…"

Zeng turned his head quickly.

Liang's face was fixed on Xu's, as he said: "If he refuses to answer, I'll ask the police to respond."

"And what role are you playing now?" Xu Tieying finally acknowledged Liang's presence and looked up. "Are you Liang Fusheng, Kuomintang Party member, or are you Liang Jinglun, loyal CPC agent?"

"Either will do."

"Commander Li!" Zeng Keda shouted towards the door.

"Here sir!" Li said loudly from out in the corridor, just outside the sitting room.

"I want you and the other guards to withdraw. You're to stand guard outside the main gate."

"Sir, yes sir!"

Liang persisted: "May I go ahead with my questions?"

Zeng Keda again ignored Liang's apparent request. Instead, he moved past him, sat down at his desk and flipped through several more papers.

Xu Tieying focused on Liang Jinglun. "You know, you've not answered my question yet."

"No, I did." Liang Jinglun's voice was firm, confident. "You arrested Liang Fusheng once before. You also arrested Liang Jinglun. Which identity do you wish me to use?"

"Let's go for the Communist one."

"Fine, if it pleases you. Inspector Zeng, may I ask you to record our conversation?"

Xu glanced at Zeng Keda.

Zeng hesitated before picking up a pen. "Director Xu, should we both take notes?"

Xu Tieying had no means by which to extricate himself from this increasingly embarrassing situation. All he could do was reach for his own pen, as well as his notebook.

Liang began: "The first day of the currency reforms, you, Mr Xu, openly and without forewarning, showed up at the Peking treasury and intruded upon the activities then being carried out by its staff. I would like to ask, was it your plan to arrest Communist agents, or were you more interested in those shares, the twenty per cent held by your government department?"

Silence.

Recorded as such.

Liang continued: "If your department does indeed hold assets in the Pingjin area on behalf of the party, then I would request that Inspector Zeng make official note of this, and clearly indicate the legal source of these assets. If, Director Xu, your department denies holding these party assets in the Pingjin area, then please explain clearly why you burst into the treasury as you did and why you thought to disrupt their activities."

Again, only silence.

Again, recorded as such.

"Director Xu, are you refusing to answer?"

Silence.

Recorded.

"Then please answer my following questions, will you?"

Once more, silence.

Recorded.

Liang persisted: "In your final analysis, was Mr Cui Zhongshi, the former deputy director of the Peking treasury, a Communist agent? If so, why didn't your office not take your evidence and call for a special tribunal to preside over his case? If he wasn't a Communist, why was he executed in secret?"

Xu Tieying had already lain down his pen.

Zeng Keda continued: "Another question: is Xie Peidong a Communist? If he is, why haven't you convened a special trial? Why did you instead expose my true identity while we were being held at Xishan prison? Why execute his daughter? Did you not go to the treasury today to arrest a supposedly known Communist agent? Indeed, why has Xie Peidong been permitted to carry on in his post as assistant manager at the Peking branch? Why has he been left in charge of the currency reforms? There can be only one answer, I think. They possess proof of your department's illegal ownership of those shares... the twenty per cent! Am I right?"

"Inspector Zeng!" Xu Tieying finally reacted. "You just clearly indicated, the Ministry of Defence has never once investigated my department. The words this... man... is now spouting, do they represent his Kuomintang faction or that of the CPC?"

Zeng Keda laid his pen down on the desk, but he did not answer. Rather, he once more glanced towards the bedroom.

Xu continued: "If Inspector Zeng will not answer for his own party, it proves Liang Jinglun is representing CPC interests here." Xu Tieying refused to follow Zeng's line of sight. He sat down again and instead looked at Liang Jinglun: "You've asked quite a number of questions, haven't you? May I ask you one in return? Inspector Zeng, will you keep record please?"

As he spoke, Xu grabbed his pen and made notes: Thirty-seventh year of the Republic, 19 August; CPC Committee Member for Labour Activities in Peking, Liang Jinglun.

"Today, the government of the Republic of China formally

announced its currency reform initiative." Xu copied down every word as he said them. "What is the CPC doing? Surely, as an important agent active in Peking, you have received orders, yes? Have you reported these orders to your Kuomintang handlers? If not, then please do so now."

Liang Jinglun stared at Xu Tieying with nothing but contempt and loathing in his eyes. A moment passed and he turned slowly towards Zeng Keda. He was surprised to see Zeng recording every word. There was a chillness in his voice when he spoke: "Inspector Zeng, would you like me to answer?"

Zeng lifted his head. "If you've something to say, then say it."

"Then please continue to record everything that's said!" Liang's tone grew noticeably higher: "You both wish to know what the CPC is doing?"

The only sound that could be heard was the scratching of pens racing across the page.

Liang Jinglun looked out of the window. "In truth, you both already know. Up to today, the nineteenth of August in the thirty-seventh year of the Republic, the Kuomintang government has had no choice but to launch the currency reforms in its effort to combat the soaring inflationary pressures on the economy. At the same time, in northwest, northeast and northern China, as well as in the east, the CPC has already implemented land reform in all liberated zones. A hundred and thirty million poor farmers have been allocated their own pieces of land. They have thus become ardent supporters of the Communist cause. The regular CPC army's numbers have swelled to three million, plus an additional two million militiamen. These one hundred and thirty million farmers now provide all the logistical support an army would need. Take the PLA in the northeast as an example. Each soldier is given five hundred *jin* of rations a year. In some liberated areas, they receive double that amount. Last year, when famine hit northern China's liberated zones, the CPC mobilised peasants to combat the catastrophe. There had not been a more serious disaster for decades, but, do you know, not a single person starved. And what's more, the CPC guaranteed that both soldiers and peasants would receive three hundred *jin* in rations for the year…"

"It's a good story." Xu Tieying's face was ashen as he recorded

Liang's words. "But I have a suggestion. It seems to me at least… well… in that spiel you just gave us, mention of the CPC should be replaced with us."

"Then do so, dammit!" Liang Jinglun was growing distinctly irate. "'Equal rights to land, land to the tiller', that's what our first President, Dr Sun Yat-sen, said when he established his democracy alliance. It was his guiding principle. Hell, it was written into the Kuomintang's constitution when the alliance was reorganised into the Kuomintang! Over the past dozen years or so, in the unified areas under Kuomintang control, about two-thirds of all of rural China, ten per cent of the population owns ninety per cent of the land. And… and three hundred million peasants have nothing to eat! The cities are no better, where everything is owned by a tiny fraction, not more than one per cent. That's why tens of millions of urban residents have had to depend on American aid… just to get by! Over the course of last year, numbers in the Kuomintang military have dropped off a cliff – fewer than three million men now – and yet the party still couldn't feed them. Some detachments have even taken to stealing food at gunpoint. If the people of the country have no means to even put food in their mouths, they'll lose faith. Popular sentiment will turn. What will the Kuomintang do then?"

"Ah, another good story. Yes, excellent!" Xu Tieying finished transcribing Liang Jinglun's diatribe and then, subconsciously, he glanced towards the bedroom before continuing his response: "Liang Jinglun, you've just told us that the CPC, in their liberated zones, have implemented land reform. You've also brought up this initiative's connection to what our first president said about equal rights to land, and so on. I'd like to ask, do you consider Communism, and Dr Sun Yat-sen's Three Principles of the People, to be one and the same? Is that it? Could you explain?"

Liang Jinglun did not meet Xu Tieying's stare, but rather looked at Zeng Keda again. Once more to his surprise, Zeng's head was low, his hand busy writing down everything Xu Tieying said. The chillness in his voice now reached his heart. Liang waited for Zeng to finish and then spoke directly to him: "Comrade Zeng Keda, the question Director Xu's just asked, I would like your help in answering it. Will you assist?"

Zeng Keda raised his head and looked at Liang. But he did not answer one way or the other.

Liang continued: "Your family is from the south, yes? Jiangxi, I believe. Your parents and your older brother are still there, they're still farming. Do they understand what Communism is? And what about Sun's Three Principles of the People? Do they know what that is?"

Zeng Keda offered no support. He was silent, listening, his face expressionless. His pen remained on his desk.

After a pause, Liang kept going: "Then I'll explain..." He averted his eyes away from both men and continued: "China is the world's largest agricultural country. There're more than four hundred million engaged in farming of some kind. Ninety-nine per cent of them are illiterate. They have no idea, can't even comprehend what Communism is, nor Sun's Three Principles of the People. The only thing they understand is that if there is no land to till, then there is no food to fill their bellies. They only know to follow whomsoever says they can feed them! Dr Sun Yat-sen, our first president, the leader of the revolution over the Qing, he understood well the national conditions. That's why he coined his phrase, 'equal rights to land'. The Kuomintang has abandoned this principle, but the CPC hasn't, which is why they launched their land-reform initiatives in their liberated areas. It's how they're winning the hearts of the people. In the Kuomintang, it's only Comrade Chiang Ching-kuo who's seen this. In southern Jiangxi he tried to implement his own land reform, but all he did was receive your opposition. Your Central Committee Clique called him a Soviet, a Communist. Internal strife in the Kuomintang began in 1941. Your clique won, the Political Department won. The rich industrialists headed by the Kung and Soong families won. This is why ten per cent of the nation's people control ninety per cent of the land, why one per cent owns ninety per cent of the cities. And right now, all you're doing is trying to protect your own interests. You're desperate to maintain positions of privilege, which is why the Kuomintang is on the path to ruin and failure... to its own destruction!"

Liang Jinglun ended with a harrumph and then stayed quiet.

The sun stood high in the sky, its scorching heat baking the garden where not a single bird made a sound. There were no chirping insects, either, nor even a soft breeze. Inside, the soft sound of pen on paper was all that could be heard.

"Are you finished writing?" Liang Jinglun turned to look at both men. "If so, you're free to report everything I've said to your higher-ups. I don't care which name you use – Liang Fusheng, Liang Jinglun – it doesn't matter. What is important is that you release Fang Meng'ao immediately. At this moment, the governor of the Peking branch, Fang Meng'ao's father, is awaiting your response at Vice-Chancellor He's home. If he remains in custody, Mr Fang will have no choice but to make public what he knows about the illegal assets held by your department, Director Xu, which would most likely bring an immediate freeze to fifty million in US aid. And wouldn't that be something, eh? The currency reforms launched and aborted in the course of a single day! You've arrested me twice. Go ahead and make plans to arrest me a third time, just not right now. First, I must return and give Mrs Fang and He your answer."

Liang turned as though he were intending to leave. A wind had picked up outside and now blew in through the door, rustling the robes he was wearing. He took a single step, but then stopped. "Oh, there's one more thing. Please ring Vice-Chancellor He's residence straight away. This despicable turn of events has caused the Kuomintang to lose quite a bit of face!"

Before he moved again, Zeng Keda's voice boomed: "Wait right there!"

Liang was puzzled to see both men standing erect in the doorway of the adjacent bedroom. Then something occurred to him, something in the back of his mind, and before he knew it, he felt himself drawn to the room, too.

At that moment, a man, perhaps in his early fifties, appeared wearing a fine Zhongshan jacket. He looked reserved, but also good-natured. He nodded towards both Zeng Keda and Xu Tieying, then walked over to Liang Jinglun. "Comrade Liang I take it?"

Liang glanced at Zeng Keda.

Zeng spoke: "Let me introduce you. This is Mr Chen Fang. He works in the Presidential Palace, director of the fourth order."

Liang Jinglun suddenly realised that he'd been sold out,

betrayed! "Please, Director Chen, do you have any advice or comments for me?"

The man's eyes remained good-natured as he replied: "I don't dare, no, considering the amount of experience you have, Comrade Liang. Our meeting is purely by chance. I'm simply here in Peking because of orders received. There are a few matters I need to deal with. You understand, I'm sure."

"Nonetheless, please, if you've anything to add…"

"I overheard that both Vice-Chancellor He and Mr Fang Buting are awaiting an answer. This is rather important. With regards to the other things you discussed, could you please tell them that the party, including Director Xu's department of course, has no assets held in the Pingjin area, certainly not the supposed twenty per cent of shares once held by Hou Juntang. The currency reforms are linked to greater issues, namely the safety and security of the country. They have to succeed. Failure is not an option. As for the fifty million in US aid, nothing and no one will be allowed to bring about a halt in their disbursement. And the currency reforms, let's just say nothing will abort them, certainly not on the day of their launch. All of this you understand."

"I was involved in drafting the report in favour of currency reforms. Of course I understand."

"Excellent, yes, wonderful. I would be grateful if you could explain this to Mr He and Mr Fang."

"I… I'm allowed to leave?"

Chen Fang nodded.

"I'll arrange a car to take you back," said Zeng Keda.

"If I may borrow a bicycle, that would do." Liang Jinglun had already begun to move towards the door.

The three men left in the room – Zeng Keda, Xu Tieying and Chen Fang – all watched him depart.

Chen Fang strode over to Zeng Keda's desk. His hand went straight for the papers lying upon it. At the same time, he spoke, his voice soft and almost gentle: "Please, both of you, sit."

Zeng Keda and Xu Tieying remained standing.

Chen Fang put the papers back down again, then focused on Zeng Keda. "Inspector Zeng, you need to sign your name. You did transcribe it, after all."

Zeng Keda complied and walked over to the desk.

Chen Fang said nothing to him. He merely walked past him and picked up Xu Tieying's notebook that was lying on the tea table. Given the dimensions of the notebook, Chen flipped through the pages and then returned it to the small table. He looked at Xu and said: "You need to do the same. Your signature is required."

Xu Tieying lowered himself onto the chair next to the tea table and picked up his notebook. He wrote his name, his hand slow and deliberate.

Chen Fang remained standing and silent while they formalised the records. Zeng Keda finished first and then brought the report over to him. Seconds later, Xu Tieying stood and did the same, using both hands to pass his notebook to Chen Fang.

"Please, let's sit."

Once they were seated in chairs, Chen Fang moved to the sofa and made himself comfortable. Sitting alone on the three-person sofa, he appeared exceptionally cautious, if not modest. The tone of his voice was still soft and gentle: "Inspector Zeng, this Liang Jinglun... how does Mr Chiang see him? What's his assessment of his abilities?"

Zeng Keda thought for a moment before answering: "I would say he sees him as an uncommon talent."

Chen Fang folded the two reports and placed them in his pocket. "These records, they're to remain confidential. Neither of you is permitted to divulge to anyone the contents of this... exchange. I will hand them over to the president personally."

They answered in near unison: "Understood, sir."

Cheng Fang now turned to Xu Tieying, speaking as he had before to Zeng Keda: "As for the shares, the twenty per cent, what evidence is there of who owns them?" Xu Tieying was quiet. Chen Fang continued, his tone unchanged: "If you have something to say, then say it."

"My department has not taken a single cent from those shares. The forms filled in by those eight businessmen... it proves the shares are personally held."

"My question was whether or not anyone else had proof of who owns them. Liang Jinglun just mentioned the Peking branch, Mr Cui Zhongshi and Mr Xie Peidong. Why did you go to speak to them? Are there yet more potentially catastrophic outcomes to consider, such as the CPC coming into possession of such detailed account information? Are there other channels by which this could come back to haunt us?"

Xu Tieying closed his eyes. "There was one such file. It was in the hands of Cui Zhongshi. Now, Xie Peidong has it. Both of these men… it's highly likely they are Communist agents, although the former has already been taken care of."

"So there is the possibility that evidence exists?"

"I am currently investigating this, yes."

"Then I would suggest you do so urgently." Chen Fang rose from the sofa. "Xu Tieying."

Xu's eyes opened wide. Chen Fang had called him by only his name; he did not use his title.

Chen continued: "For the record, no members of the party's central working committee, nor staff in your department, no one in the Kuomintang as a whole has owned any shares in the enterprises operated by these eight businessmen in the Pingjin area. This is all just vicious rumour and hearsay. You must explain this clearly. As of today, you're relieved of your position and all of your duties in Peking. You're to return to Nanking immediately to face investigation." Xu Tieying stood up slowly and looked at the other man, but Chen paid him little attention. There was more he had to say: "An hour ago, I was at the Northern Command and received a telephone call directly from the president. Before you say anything about your dismissal, know that I am just the messenger; the orders come from him." Chen glanced at his watch. "Moreover, I should tell you that transportation has been arranged by Commander-in-Chief Fu. An aeroplane will fly you to the capital at five this afternoon. The time's tight, I know. Nonetheless, there are a few additional things I must discuss with Inspector Zeng. If you will, please go and wait by the back door. I'll be with you shortly and we'll return to Nanking together."

This outcome had occurred to Xu Tieying before, so he was not completely unprepared for it, but he hadn't thought it would be so decisive, so final. Xu spoke: "Director Chen, there are certain secret documents still in my office, as well as personal belongings for several people…"

"I've already seen to this," said Chen. "You needn't worry…"

"Ah, thank you, Director Chen." Xu had one last chance, he thought, one last opportunity to reveal what he knew. "There is… well, sir… I do have some extra information, most important. It has to do with safeguarding the nation and quelling dissent. May I have a minute or so to explain things to Inspector Zeng?"

Chen looked him over. "I suppose you may…"

Xu turned to Zeng Keda: "In Nanking, at the special tribunal on the sixth of July, your suspicions concerning Fang Meng'ao were correct. Afterwards, once you came to Peking, the suspicions you had concerning Cui Zhongshi were also correct. The CPC, Zhou Enlai in particular, they've been at it for ages. They've placed agents in nearly every department of the party-state, all to disrupt and hinder the operations of government. My department has been focused on finding out who these infiltrators are since the beginning. In essence, it's all we've done. It's been the basis of all of our secret investigations… but because identifying evidence is so damned difficult, when Fang Meng'ao was on trial, I had little choice but to defend him so that I could continue our investigations… find the proof I needed.

"I came to Peking not just because of questions concerning party assets. My key mission has been to ferret out Communist agents buried deep within the operational management of the Peking branch. There is no money for party expenses, or for military and government expenditures. Even the livelihood of the people, public education, everything relies upon the bank. But the accounts held by the Peking branch are in the hands of Communists. Cui Zhongshi is dead, true, but Xie Peidong is still there, and he's Zhou Enlai's man through and through, his most deeply placed chess piece… It will take much more than a day to dig him out, but sooner or later, this I know for a fact, he'll prove to be the greatest danger within, not just for the currency reforms, but for the entire northern campaign against the Communists. And then there's Liang Jinglun. He's not a true Communist believer, but nor is he on our side either. He just goes on and on about the prime minister, on and on about Mr Chiang Ching-kuo, but, if you've not noticed, he never mentions the president. This is the heart of the matter of the internal divide in the party, the wedge between kith and kin. But whenever possible he's used He Qicang and his connections to Ambassador Stuart to drive his own agenda... which is to oppose the president. As for Fang Meng'ao, there's only one thing I want to point out: under no circumstances should he be permitted to fly one of our planes into the liberated areas."

At this point, Xu Tieying stopped and held out his hand to Zeng Keda. Zeng, however, did not immediately reciprocate. Instead, he did his best to avoid Xu's eyes, first directing his attention to Chen Fang to see if accepting a handshake would be acceptable. When it appeared as though it was, Zeng turned to Xu Tieying and clasped the man's hand.

"Brothers may have cause to argue with each other, but when outside dangers present themselves, they know to come together!" Xu shook his hand vigorously and then turned to leave.

By the time Zeng Keda thought to look, Xu Tieying had already stepped out of the door.

"Inspector Zeng..." Chen Fang's voice was still quiet, still soft.

It took a moment for Zeng to gather his senses, but then he answered the other man's call: "Yes sir, I'm here."

"It's important to remember, Inspector Zeng, being resolute in combating corruption does not mean that one forgets to be resolute in combating Communism. There is actually nothing I need to pass on. I just have a question: how should we deal with Fang Meng'ao, and, furthermore, what is your take on the views espoused by this Liang Jinglun fellow?"

"Sir, I can only defer to your wisdom on this matter."

Zeng Keda was being effusive in showing his respect towards Chen Fang, but Chen could not be sure if he was doing so because he truly felt this way, or if he was simply trying to fawn on him and curry some sort of favour. With these thoughts in mind, Chen simply smiled and deflected: "I'm sorry, but I wouldn't dare to give instructions on this." As he spoke, he pulled out the notes Zeng and Xu had transcribed only moments ago. He looked them over, then passed Zeng the record he had written: "Report the conversation to Mr Chiang Ching-kuo. Let's get his instructions on how to proceed."

"Yes sir." Zeng accepted the papers with both hands.

Chen extended his hand.

Zeng pinched the pages between his fingers and then accepted Chen's with both hands: "My sincere appreciation for the confidence the president has shown in me, and for your concern as well, sir."

Chen Fang's hands were soft. "We're both from Jiangxi. There's no need to be so polite. Overcoming the difficulties we face together is our greatest challenge. We shouldn't add to them."

"Yes sir." Zeng Keda answered and at the same time ushered Chen Fang towards the door. There, he shouted for his assistant; after all, time was tight.

From the other side of the main corridor that ran through Zeng Keda's residence, a door opened upon the sound of Zeng's voice and his young assistant Wang stepped out, along with another young man wearing a Zhongshan jacket. This man hurried down the hallway in the direction of Chen Fang, lifting open the attaché case he carried and handing Chen a pair of sunglasses. In his free hand, he held a large black umbrella, which he now opened. Chen put the sunglasses on and walked out into the garden, the umbrella shielding him from the burning sun.

Zeng's assistant appeared quite astonished. His boss was not escorting his guest beyond the doorway, but neither was he turning round to go back inside. He was just standing in the door, seemingly unsure what to do. Wang waited for several minutes, hoping his superior would come to his senses, but finally, he could wait no longer. His tone was soft: "Inspector…"

"Eh?" at last, Zeng noticed his assistant.

"There's a phone call, sir, from Police HQ, they're saying that Madame Fang and Vice-Chancellor He's daughter are both at the station wanting to see Captain Fang. Without having Director Xu's approval, they've not dared to allow Captain Fang visitors. An argument with Deputy Fang has ensued…"

"Director Xu is director no longer." Zeng Keda glanced down the small path that snaked its way through the garden. "Go tell them that, without Nanking's approval, no one is allowed to see Captain Fang."

"Yes sir."

"Wait…" Zeng Keda's voice was louder than he intended, but it had the desired effect of causing Wang to stop. Zeng handed him the papers he was still carrying. "These notes… I want you to transmit them in code to Comrade Jianfeng… immediately!" Zeng spun around and went back inside. He closed and locked the door.

Zeng's assistant looked on for a second, then returned to his own room.

Liang Jinglun's legs pedalled hard and fast. He was on the small road that ran through the Yenching University campus in the direction of He Qicang's residence. Above him, the sun burned hot. There were no clouds, no people, only Liang Jinglun and his borrowed bicycle. He didn't even try to shade himself by riding closer to the trees that ran alongside the road. He had to get back as quickly as possible. His robes were drenched and pinched at his waist. It was only when he could finally see He Qicang's home that he reduced his speed.

Suddenly, an object flew past, landing a couple of metres in front of him, bouncing a little. Liang Jinglun clenched the handlebars and slammed hard on the bicycle brakes. He looked at the object on the road and realised it was a leather satchel containing electrical tools. Liang looked towards the sky and saw an engineer high up the street-side telephone pole. The man was in the process of releasing his safety harness, presumably so that he could climb down.

"Sorry mate!" The man nimbly scaled down just over half of the pole and then leapt backwards and onto the ground. He strode onto the road and picked up his equipment, paying little more attention to Liang Jinglun.

"Not easy, is it?" Liang offer a simple response, then started to pedal again.

"It's Professor Liang, isn't it?"

Liang Jinglun returned the man's stare and searched his memory for any recollection of him; unfortunately, there was none. The man was unsurprised by Liang Jinglun's failure to recognise him, but he most assuredly knew Liang Jinglun long before he began his current work as an electrician. He was Cui Zhongshi's underground contact at the train station.

With Liang appearing somewhat puzzled, the man spoke: "I heard that Vice-Chancellor He's telephone line had been cut. I'm here to make repairs. Are you heading there yourself, Professor Liang?"

"Yes, I am. Please, could you tell me who gave you the work order?"

The man cinched his tool bag together. "Professor Liang, who do you believe sent me?"

Liang could not answer, nor did he wish to try. Instead, he decided to ignore the man and carry on his way.

"Comrade Zhang Yueyin…"

The man's voice was soft, but when Liang Jinglun heard it, it sounded as loud as a temple bell! He turned around slowly. "What did you say?"

"Comrade Yan Chunming sacrificed himself. I'm here to continue his work. I was sent today to make contact with you." As he spoke, he put his hand into his leather bag and pulled out a letter to pass to Liang. "It's an introductory letter from our superiors. You're to read it, and then torch it."

Liang Jinglun did not accept it, so the man simply allowed it to fall to the ground at Liang's feet. The man then turned around and walked towards another electrical pole where he had rested his bicycle. He took hold of the bicycle and guided it back in Liang's direction. As he did so, he noticed that the letter was no longer lying on the ground and smiled. "Vice-Chancellor He requested the university to reconnect his telephone line. The office has arranged for someone to come this evening. I'd be grateful if you could let him know." With that, he climbed on his bicycle and pedalled faster than Liang would have expected. He never looked back. Nor did Liang bother to let his eyes follow him off. He only pushed his own bicycle the last few metres to He Qicang's home.

He Qicang was reclining in his familiar chair in his study. Fang Buting was seated near the window. They knew Liang Jinglun had returned, and they also knew he was downstairs in the sitting room. Soon, they heard his voice call up to them, telling them he was back.

"Come on up," He Qicang called out.

As they heard his footsteps on the stairs, Fang Buting stood up and walked back to sit near his old friend. A few seconds later, Liang appeared.

"Mr He and Mr Fang, I've met with Inspector Zeng."

According to manners, it was for He Qicang to invite Liang Jinglun into the room, but all he did was stare at the younger man in the doorway; Fang Buting did the same. Liang knew, too, that he couldn't just walk in on his own accord, and so he stood there quietly, waiting.

Minutes passed before finally, He Qicang broke the silence: "I started my learning early, you know. I was four, if I remember correctly, when I went to private school. That first day, my father, Xiaoyu's granddad, told me something I still remember to this day. He told me to be diligent, careful, but to keep things to myself. Naturally, I asked him why. His answer was that if I alone know something, then I shouldn't let on what I know to anyone else. If I and a friend knew something, we shouldn't let a third person in on it... you get the idea. At the time, I didn't really understand, but I did follow what he told me. It wasn't until many years later that I grasped the meaning of my father's advice: there is nothing in this world that innately causes trouble, it is people who have the penchant to create mountains out of molehills. I felt the need to tell you this now. Look at what's going on with Zeng Keda... with Meng'ao. You only need to speak to Mr Fang. There's nothing for me to say."

Liang Jinglun felt a pang of pain in his heart. He was disconsolate, but answered nonetheless: "Yes, I understand."

Fang Buting rose from his chair and said: "Let's go downstairs."

He Qicang remained in his recliner. "That would be best."

Zeng Keda paced the room until finally, the telephone rang. It only needed to ring once before Zeng picked up the receiver.

"Comrade Keda?" He heard, as expected, Chiang Ching-kuo's voice.

"Yes, it's me, Comrade Jianfeng."

"What's the meaning of the telegram you had sent to me? Who said those things?"

Zeng Keda held his tongue for several seconds, before saying: "Comrade Liang Jinglun. They are a record of his words."

"What record are you talking about? Who was there to transcribe?"

"I was there... and so was Xu Tieying."

"Why didn't you put a stop to him?"

"Comrade Jianfeng, I need to tell you, Mr Chen Fang paid me a visit."

"Which Mr Chen Fang?"

Zeng Keda had seldom heard astonishment in Comrade Jianfeng's voice, but it was unmistakable now. He answered carefully: "The Mr Chen Fang who works in the Presidential Palace." The silence was even longer this time. Zeng glanced at the wall clock and watched at least six or seven seconds pass by.

"Secretary Chen paid you a visit. Did you consider it an inconvenience to let me know this, or was it that you didn't have time to do so?"

"Secretary Chen just suddenly appeared without any advanced notice. There was no way to inform you. He also told me and Xu Tieying that he was here to relay presidential orders. Comrade Liang Jinglun showed up minutes after. He burst in, truth be told... all because of Fang Meng'ao's arrest. The guards proved unable to delay him. Secretary Chen didn't wish to see him at first and so he stepped into my adjacent bedroom to wait. Comrade Liang was terribly worked up about things, he wouldn't be calmed. We had little choice but to let him go on. Xu and I transcribed the... the conversation."

Again there was silence on both ends of the telephone. Finally, Chiang Ching-kuo spoke: "Did Secretary Chen take Xu's transcription?"

"Yes, he did."

"And what was Secretary Chen's point of view about this... this situation?"

"He didn't divulge his own thoughts. He only asked what you and I thought about Comrade Liang, how we measured his abilities." Zeng Keda paused, expecting Chiang to take up what he was saying, but when he didn't, the silence grew more terrifying than any he had experienced before. Ultimately, Zeng could not endure and had to continue: "I answered him. I told him you thought Comrade Liang was an uncommon talent." Still, there was only silence, so Zeng felt compelled to go on: "Secretary Chen replied with a single sentence. He told me to report the conversation with Comrade Liang to you... then to listen to your instructions."

The silence dragged on even longer. At last, Chiang Ching-kuo had a response: "I'm still in meetings here in Shanghai. In the shortest possible way, give me your thoughts on what Comrade Liang Jinglun has said. Tell me, also, what you think we should do with Fang Meng'ao. Be specific. I want suggestions."

Downstairs in the sitting room, Liang Jinglun's attitude was the epitome of the younger generation. He looked Fang Buting up and down intently, then said: "Mr Fang, speaking with you now, today, like this, I wonder if I might use a different form of address – if you'll permit me, of course."

"And what would that be?"

"I should like to call you 'Uncle Fang'."

"However you wish, my boy."

"Uncle Fang, what Mr He just said to me, upstairs in his study, can I understand it this way? That is, what I'm about to say to you today shouldn't be shared with anyone else? The same would apply to what you say to me, yes?"

"If you can understand what he said to you in that way, then yes, we can continue our discussion."

"Then let's begin. There are things I should tell you, need to tell you. There are also other things that I shouldn't and won't. This is not to keep things concealed from you, to hold things back, but rather because these other details, such as they are, are of no use to you. I hope you understand this."

"Go ahead."

"There is no money in the government treasury, nor does the average citizen have any. All of it is in the hands of a very small minority, and, what's more, they will, under no circumstances, sacrifice their own wealth and power to support the currency reforms. As a result, they're doomed to failure within a month, two at the most. This is clear to you, to me as well. Mr He understands this, too. You're wrapped up in this because you're the governor of the Peking branch. I'm wrapped up in this because I'm a member of Chiang's Youth League. Mr He is entangled in these matters because of his unique connection to Ambassador Stuart… his, shall we say, ability to get more American aid out of him. The one person who shouldn't be involved is Fang Meng'ao. He's not an economist, nor does he understand politics all that well. He shouldn't, therefore, be manipulated and used yet again."

Fang Buting looked at Liang Jinglun with renewed interest. "Manipulated and used by whom?"

"By the Kuomintang, and by the Communists."

"Could you be a little more specific?"

"I don't need to, as you should already know who I mean."

"Not necessarily. Please elaborate."

"Those who manipulated others in the Kuomintang don't need to be named. The same is true for those who manipulated the members of Chiang's Youth League, and Chiang Ching-kuo himself. As for the CPC, before it was Deputy Director Cui, now it's Mr Xie, your assistant manager."

Fang Buting rose abruptly from his chair and scanned the room as though he were looking for something. "Where's the water?" he asked.

"Let me get it."

"I've a few observations I'd like to mention."

Comrade Jianfeng's tone had rarely been so flat, forcing Zeng

Keda to do his utmost to rein in his growing frustration. "Yes please, Comrade Jianfeng. I await your instructions."

"They're not instructions, but observations."

"Yes, of course."

"For any and all occasions, whenever and wherever, no matter what is happening, the president's take on things is final. Perhaps I am in Shanghai to launch these currency reforms because the president doesn't wish to distract me. You're in Peking because perhaps that is what sets the president's mind most at ease. Secretary Chen's personal visit demonstrates the faith the president has in you..."

"Comrade Jianfeng!"

"Don't cut me off."

"Yes, of course..."

"Your suggestion, regardless of whether or not you have already mentioned it to Secretary Chen, I also agree. Fang Meng'ao violated military protocol and should be held accountable for his actions. A special Air Force tribunal should be called, and as for Liang Jinglun's views that there is a concerted effort to split the party, these should be properly investigated. If because of this Fang Buting decides not to assist us with the currency reforms, then he should immediately be removed from his post as governor of the Peking branch. Finally, if He Qicang decides to pass all of this along to the Americans and thus cause them to halt their aid, then fine. We'll go along without it..."

"But Comrade Jianfeng," said Zeng Keda, interrupting his superior once more, "this is not the meaning of my suggestion! The currency reforms are one thing, but there's also the matter of our other operation, the peacocks flying southeast..."

"Do not bring this up, dammit!" There was a certain finality to Chiang Ching-kuo's tone that would brook no additional argument. "Using the full force of the Defence Ministry's Investigative Division, I order you to put your suggestion down on paper and make a formal report. At nine this evening, you're to transmit this report to the Presidential Palace. Mark it as for Secretary Chen, and that he is to pass it on to the president to get his ruling on the matter!"

There was no further exchange between the men, only the sound of the telephone being slammed down onto its base. A dark expression enveloped Zeng Keda's face, but he was unable to pull the receiver away from his ear. All he could hear was the drone of the dial tone sounding in rhythm with the cicadas buzzing outside.

At last, he put the telephone down and walked towards the door. He paused another moment and then pushed it open. "Wang!"

"Yes sir!" Hurriedly, almost panicky, his assistant appeared in the door.

Zeng saw the look of desolation on his assistant's face and felt it mirrored his own. "Get a pen and paper. I need you to take down an urgent report." Zeng Keda turned around and went back to the chair he had been sitting in. He had to try to calm himself.

A few minutes later, Wang returned with the pen and paper ready to transcribe Zeng's report. He held his breath as he approached his superior, unsure of what reaction he would receive. Zeng tried to gather his thoughts, and then he spoke: "'The righteous and upright are greeted with death, while those who are corrupt and immoral achieve great fame...'"

Was this to be the report? Zeng's aide-de-camp was astonished. Was he to record these words? Should he not?

Zeng Keda turned away from the window to look at his assistant. "Do you know where that quotation comes from?"

Realisation came suddenly to Wang and he regretted his momentary indecision. He could not, however, allow Zeng to see that in his face. Instead, he took a second before answering: "I think I've heard it before. Is it from the *History of the Later Han*?"

"And who said it?"

"After this, I'll go and find out."

"There's no need. Just transcribe my report."

"I have only one question." Fang Buting was in the sitting room of He Qicang's home, his eyes trained fervently on Liang Jinglun. "If you answer honestly, Mr He and I will use our considerable influence to see you're sent overseas to the US."

Liang Jinglun met his stare with equal intensity. "Go ahead and ask."

"Is Mulan dead?"

"Yes, she is."

A cold shiver went up Fang Buting's back and he trembled a little. He could feel a lump growing in his throat but could say nothing. Tears began to appear in his eyes.

Liang Jinglun did not avert his eyes, he merely sat quietly, patiently waiting for Fang Buting to continue. His eyes remained dry.

Finally, Fang spoke, swallowing back his tears: "That evening of the twelfth... Mulan's father – you too, your search – it was all an act, wasn't it?"

"Yes, we were..."

Fang Buting pulled out a handkerchief and wiped his face. "Tell me, who murdered Mulan? Was it Chiang Ching-kuo, Chen Kuo-fu, Chen Lifu?"

"None of them would've given such an order. Xu Tieying is the person responsible. He gave the order."

"Xu Tieying, he's nothing, less than nothing." Fang Buting's anger was rising. "Tell me who's behind him!"

"There's no one specific. All I know is he has the backing of the Central Committee Clique."

"I'm going to call a press conference, for both domestic and international news outlets. Are you willing to be a witness?" Fang Buting's eyes flashed with renewed brilliance.

"I would, but I don't think Mr Xie will agree to..."

"Not for his own daughter!" Fang Buting cut himself off when he realised how loud his voice had been. He glanced towards the stairs, his expression growing sad once more. "Twenty years, he's been keeping me in the dark for twenty years. His daughter's dead and he's concealed that from me too. You and your lot, the bloody Kuomintang... the CPC, too... just what the hell are you all up to? What's going in your minds?"

Liang Jinglun did not know how to answer such a question, and so decided to say nothing.

Fang Buting appeared to grow dispirited again. When he looked at Liang Jinglun, there was a blankness to his face. "The... the Kuomintang, that man, Xu Tieying, why didn't he arrest Mulan's father?"

"He had no proof. No, that's not quite right, it's also because Mr Xie has proof of their own malfeasance."

Fang Buting thought this over for a moment. "Tell me, does Fang Meng'ao know his uncle's true identity?"

"I would think that he does."

"Is Peidong his superior in the CPC?"

"Both Xu's department and Chiang's Youth League believe this to be the case."

Fang Buting turned towards the window. "Then the only thing I can do is go straight to the source and ask him…"

"Ask who? Mr Xie or Meng'ao?"

"That's right, neither one will answer me truthfully, will they?" Fang Buting sighed and then directed his attention back to Liang Jinglun: "Today, you've been honest with me. Now, I'll be the same with you. Mr He and I have already discussed things. He's going to reach out to Ambassador Stuart and tell him all he knows. He's also going to ask Ambassador Stuart to speak directly with Chiang Kai-shek. We want Meng'ao to be discharged from the military. Then we're going to send him overseas. In your opinion, do you think Chiang Ching-kuo will try to interfere? Try to stop us?"

Liang Jinglun mulled over this revelation before answering: "Even if Chiang Ching-kuo does not try to stop you, there'll be others who will, which means you won't be able to send Meng'ao away."

"You mean his uncle?"

Liang Jinglun shook his head. "No, I mean Zhou Enlai!"

Fang Buting swayed, his eyes went wide with surprise.

Liang continued: "Mr Xie is a card-carrying Communist Party member. He has direct contact with Zhou Enlai. Meng'ao is a Communist, too, and under Zhou's orders, he's to be especially groomed. Chiang Ching-kuo has used Fang Meng'ao. On the surface it's been about winning you and Mr He over, to get you to support the currency reforms, but under the surface, it's been little more than an indirect struggle against Zhou and his influence over Meng'ao. If one of these men disagrees with your plan, Meng'ao will not be able to leave. Uncle Fang, everything will hinge on how you discuss things with Mr Xie."

Fang Buting raised himself from his seat. "That, I know. I hope that what we've discussed here today remains between the two of us. If you think you'd like to leave, Mr He and I will begin making arrangements for you to depart China."

"What we've discussed will not be shared." Liang stood up as well. "As for what I hope, there's really only one thing. I hope Xiaoyu and Meng'ao will be able to leave with me. Mr Fang, please believe me."

Fang Buting allowed his eyes to linger on Liang Jinglun, but he said nothing. A moment later, he walked over to the tea table and the telephone that lay upon it. At almost exactly the same time, the sound of a car engine reached them from somewhere just out past the garden gate. The unexpected noise caused Fang Buting to stop and direct his attention to the window. He knew it was his Austin returning. Moments later, Cheng Xiaoyun alighted from the car, followed by He Xiaoyu. Moments after that and Cheng Xiaoyu was pushing open the door that led into the sitting room, Xiaoyu close behind.

Both women were stunned when they saw Fang Buting and Liang Jinglun together in the sitting room. Fang Buting was the first to break the tension: "I was just about to make a call, and then thought you might be on the way home…"

"Home? Do you even have one?" Never before had Cheng Xiaoyun been quite so worked up. "You… you lost your home ten years ago. We've no idea where Mulan is. You were supposedly off to Xishan prison, your oldest – Meng'ao – he's been arrested. Home? I imagine the bloody bank's the only home you have!"

Fang Buting did not reply. Liang Jinglun diverted his attention to the floor.

He Xiaoyu, however, hurried up to try to soothe her rage: "Auntie…"

"And where's your father? Please ask him to come down."

"Excellent questions, excellent indeed!" He Qicang was already standing on the landing. "Go on, get him to answer."

As soon as she saw He Qicang, tears began to roll down Cheng Xiaoyun's face: "Vice-Chancellor He…"

"No crying, please." His tone made clear the sympathy he felt for Cheng Xiaoyun, the pain he felt on her behalf. "What's the point of crying? They don't recognise their own good fortune, so why cry for them? Go home, curse them, hit them. That would be the better response."

Cheng Xiaoyun stifled her tears. "You understand, don't you? Since coming to Peking, I lived on the outside. Then, last month I moved into that blasted place, but now… I don't want to go back, I'd rather stay here a few days, stay with Xiaoyu. If you'll allow…"

"I think that would be great. Yes." There was no hesitation in He Qicang's response. "Make him go home by himself, let him sample what it's like to live alone… to be alone." He Qicang said nothing further, and he turned around and walked back into his study.

"Xiaoyu, let's go upstairs." Cheng Xiaoyun moved towards the stairs, refusing to look at her husband.

"Uncle Fang…" Xiaoyu's voice was halting, unsure.

"I caused you enough trouble," said Fang Buting as he turned and headed for the door.

He Xiaoyu, at last, let her eyes fall on Liang Jinglun.

"I'll go with him," was all he said.

Fang Buting walked through the gate and into his garden. He went straight to the veranda and sat down underneath its eaves, his eyes scanning the emptiness of the scene, then gradually up towards the first floor of his Western-style home. It had been cloudy on the way home, and now there was a red tinge to the sky. The clouds were dense, heavy and hanging low. It was the middle of the seventh month of the lunar calendar. The monsoon season would soon begin.

"Mr Fang," said Li in a soft and low voice.

"What is it?" Fang replied.

Li hesitated at the gate, unsure of what to do or say.

"Spit it out. Speak."

"Your wife's not at home. Should I call Mrs Cai and Mrs Li to come? Someone needs to prepare your meal and tidy up."

"You don't need to right now. Tomorrow will be fine." Fang Buting turned and looked at Li, his face sincere, concerned. "Go to the bank. Whether he's finished or not, I want you to bring Mr Xie here."

"Yes sir."

Li went to pull the gate open but stopped when Fang Buting called out. "Do you know where my youngest boy is?"

"From what your wife said, I believe he's gone to the police station to look for Chief Xu."

"Understood. Go on now, to the bank."

"Sir…" Li stepped outside and latched the gate before departing.

A wind picked up and blew through the garden. Fang Buting held his hand up to judge where it was coming from; it was a western wind. Then he noticed the leaves on the bamboo trees. The wind had picked them up as well and furled them through the air before allowing them to spiral down to the ground. The breeze had such force it knocked over a bamboo broom leaning against the wall, throwing it on its side, and then pushing it across the garden grass. The sky grew darker and a flower drifted through his line of sight. Xie Peidong appeared at the other end of the garden, slowly sweeping the ground free of leaves. The wind increased in strength and continued to buffet the garden. It enveloped Xie Peidong, causing even the bamboo twigs of the broom to whirl. He shut his eyes and then opened them again. Xie was nowhere in sight. He'd never been there in the first place. The broom continued to roll across the ground. Fang Buting stood up and walked over to pick it up. The leaves swirled up around him, following the broom as it was thrust into the air. Pulled to the east with the gale, Fang Buting appeared to be sweeping the sky around him. The wind grew stronger and stronger until the bamboo leaves seemed to be whistling along with it. The sound grew sharper and sharper. He felt his grasp weaken, and he wondered if he should relent. Then he heard the sound of a ringing telephone, carried on the wind. He let go of the broom and walked towards the clanging bell.

―――

"Xu Tieying has been removed from his post and ordered to return to Nanking." Outside the window, the wind blew hard, the rain fell harder. Despite the ferocity of the weather, Fang Mengwei's voice on the other end of the telephone roared like thunder.

"Wait a minute," said Fang Buting, his voice trembling. He

placed the telephone on the table, stood up and walked over to the windows to make sure they were all shuttered tightly. Every light in the house was turned on, those on the ground floor in the sitting room, as well as those upstairs. Fang walked back to the table and lifted the receiver once more. "Who's the new chief?"

"Zeng Keda. A telegram came. We're to wait here in the station for him to come… everybody."

"I see. After he arrives, the situation with your brother, and your uncle, don't mention a word about them… or anything else for that matter. Don't telephone again either."

Their conversation over, Fang Buting pressed hard down on the telephone, waited for it to reset, and began to dial a new number straight away. "Director Xue? Yes, has Mr Xie left yet… Yes, yes, I sent Li to fetch him… Yes, we've things to go over this evening, Mr Xie and I… Yes, yes… You take charge of things there at the bank… understand, overtime is authorised, and required. According to directives from the Executive Yuan's economic subcommittee, all accounts are to be frozen by the twenty-first at the latest."

Fang Buting hung up the phone and was suddenly overwhelmed by a craving for something to eat and drink. He reached out for the enamelled teaware and swallowed back the final dregs still in the pot. As he did so, he noticed for the first time the note that had been left alongside the porcelain. The handwriting belonged to Cheng Xiaoyun: "I've already prepared your meal. The meat is on the stove, and the rice is warming in the oven."

Fang Buting replaced the teacup on the table and strode towards the kitchen, Xiaoyun's note in his hand. He walked only a few steps before stopping, his heart tight in his chest. The sweet aroma of braised pork smothered in plum sauce, something he had not smelled for ages, tickled his nose.

He lifted the lid and the smell of the pork grew more intense. The meat was stewing away, and Fang Buting was by himself. He grabbed a pair of chopsticks and grasped a piece of succulent meat. As it melted in his mouth, he reached into the pot again to seize another piece.

"I haven't eaten either, you know…"

Fang Buting spun around, surprised to see Xie Peidong standing in the doorway to the kitchen. Fang couldn't take his eyes off him, surprised at his presence, even though he had been the one who had instructed Li to bring him here. Xie Peidong, however, was mesmerised by the simmering pot on the stove. Fang Buting threw his chopsticks down onto the countertop and marched out of the kitchen.

Fang Buting was seated on the sofa, watching Xie Peidong fiddle with the pot on the stove. He was also somehow holding on to two bowls having already placed the chopsticks on the dining table. Moments later, with his bare hands, he carried the piping hot bowls to the table, and then went back for the rice. He seemed unbothered by the heat, unafraid that his hands would burn. One bowl was placed at the head of the table, the other in Xie's usual seat. Once ready, he called to Fang Buting: "Let's eat."

In response, Fang Buting only lifted the teaware and took two swigs from the bottle. He did not stand up, nor did he speak a single word.

Xie Peidong did not call for him to come to the table a second time. He only sat and polished off his own bowl in silence. He enjoyed the pieces of plum that had been cooked along with the pork, and went back for seconds, pouring some of the sweet broth into his bowl to finish off the remaining bits. He stirred everything a few times and then swallowed it down.

Fang Buting remained seated, staring at the figure of Xie Peidong enjoying the food by himself. But the longer he sat there, the more his mind began to race. He thought of Xie, his brother in-law, and wondered what kind of man he was. Xie's wife, his younger sister, was dead. Xie's daughter was dead, too, and yet, here he was, eating as though nothing seemed to trouble him. Fang marvelled at the man, but not in an especially admiring way, and wondered again what kind of man he was. A Communist, yes, but what kind of man was he?

After a couple more bowls of pork and rice, Xie Peidong returned his cutlery to the kitchen and tidied up. Fang Buting could hear him washing the dishes, the water pouring from the tap. He emerged a few minutes later and walked towards the sitting room where Fang was still seated. Before entering the room, he paused at the cabinet that was near the door and picked up the stack of thick files. Then he turned to Fang Buting and said: "These were to rescue me, I take it. That's why you went to Xishan prison, and it's why Meng'ao hijacked the plane. Li told me everything. Eat and then we can talk, yes?" Xie did not enter the sitting room, but turned around and went upstairs.

Fang Buting could only stare, at least for the first few seconds after hearing Xie's words, but then suddenly blurted out a question: "You're not afraid of Xu Tieying trying to arrest you again?"

Xie was already standing on the first step when he answered: "Xu Tieying has already been removed from his position. If I'm to be arrested, it won't be by him. Please, eat."

Fang Buting got up from the sofa, his eyes fixed on Xie Peidong's back. "Who told you that?"

"Don't you all suspect I'm a Communist agent? Given the present situation in the country, there's very little that can slip by the CPC's notice." Xie continued his way up the stairs.

On entering his study on the first floor, Fang Buting chose not to look at Xie Peidong. He also said nothing about the files on the desk. In fact, all he did was stroll over and lower himself into his comfortable chair positioned in front of the balcony window. The wail of the wind could no longer be heard, but still the rain poured. As he stared at the scene beyond the window, Xie Peidong walked over and sat down beside him.

Fang spoke first. "The twelfth of August. That day, the day you went looking for Mulan, it poured then, too." The sound of the rain echoed outside.

"Yes, it did."

"It was 1928, the first of November, that's when the Central Bank was established in Shanghai." Fang Buting paused, then turned towards Xie Peidong: "The fifth of November, that's when you came to find me. Mulan was in your arms. It was raining that day too if I remember correctly."

Xie Peidong shifted in the chair to look out of the window. "I believe you're right…"

"For twenty years we've been through thick and thin, haven't we? We've talked about virtually everything, discussed every matter, regardless of how big or how small. But you're saying very little now, aren't you?" Fang Buting rapped his hand on the desk.

"How would you like me to answer?"

Fang couldn't help but feel somewhat dejected by Xie's response. He looked his brother-in-law up and down and felt as he had when they had first met, that this man was nothing special, that he was someone of little or no interest. Fang looked back out of the window. "There's something I want to ask you, a single question, something I've never asked before, but today I have to. You must answer me truthfully."

"What's your question?"

"My younger sister... you know, her vision was incredibly wide. She looked outwards, never inwards. I remember writing her a letter when I was still in the US. I wanted to introduce her to a soon-to-be-returning student, but she wasn't interested in him at all, not one bit, so... Tell me, what made her so attracted to you? How did you win her over?"

"This question, can I not answer it?"

"Today, right now, you still want to conceal things from me!" Fang Buting pounded his hand on the desk.

"That's not my intention."

"Then answer me, dammit."

"How she looked at me, how she saw me, only she can answer that. Your question... I'd like to ask her." All of a sudden, the pitch of Xie's voice increased: "But she's been dead for twenty years now. She can't ever answer me, can she!"

Fang Buting swallowed the lump growing in his throat and for a moment all he could hear was the pouring rain outside. He wasn't sure how long the silence lasted before he could speak again: "Then let me ask you something direct. That year, did she join your precious CPC? I mean, you're a Communist. Why did you marry?"

Xie Peidong turned to Fang Buting. "Do you know, Xu Tieying wanted to know the answer to that question, so did the secret service. This morning, at the treasury, Xu Tieying kept pressing me. He even asked if I'd met Zhou Enlai when I was in Chongqing..."

The name drop made Fang Buting tremble, made him hold his breath, if just for a second. "How did you answer him?"

"We spent eight years in Chongqing. You know more about what happened there than he ever could. I never met Zhou Enlai. I'm not a Communist agent, nor was your younger sister. You shouldn't be asking *their* questions. I'll answer them." He stood up and walked over to the desk.

"Answer who? Aren't you the one who told me Xu Tieying's been removed?" Fang Buting returned to his first question.

"I know what you want to ask." Xie was now at the desk, his eyes on the files upon it. "Mengwei was the one who called. He was the one who told me Xu was sacked."

The lump in his throat returned and Fang found it difficult to breathe. His heart began to race as he started to hyperventilate.

Xie continued: "The acting director is Zeng Keda. I imagine he'll be the man responsible for investigating me now. I prepared two things in advance of this, and I'd like to show you them first." As he spoke, he picked up two pieces of paper from the desk.

Fang Buting stared at Xie Peidong for a while, then finally walked over to the desk.

Xie passed him a sheet of paper. "This is my formal, written resignation. Before they confirm whether or not I'm a Communist, I request permission to resign from my position as assistant manager of the Peking branch. This way I can more readily accept their investigation into me and my supposed activities. You need to sign it first."

Fang Buting took the letter and scanned its contents, then looked at Xie. "And the other piece of paper?"

"It's my signed complaint to be submitted to the special tribunal in Nanking."

Fang Buting couldn't hide his shock at this admission, nor could he take hold of the paper. All he could do was stare at Xie Peidong.

"On the twelfth of August, they arrested innocent students, including my daughter. On the same day, they released their detainees and Wang Puchen told me Mulan had been mistakenly sent to the liberated areas along with the other students not from Peking. But today, Xu Tieying informed me that Mulan is still being held by them. In response, while I was at the treasury with Xu Tieying, I told him, as a father, I would not let them get away with what they've been doing."

Fang Buting felt as though he'd been hit by some unknown force. His heart pounded in his chest and he grabbed at the second piece of paper Xie was holding. Fang's eyes grew blurry, however, and his head felt as though it were being buried under an enormous amount of sand. "Do you really think they're holding Mulan? Do you think she can be rescued?"

There was only quiet. Even the sound of the pouring rain was drowned out by the silence.

Fang continued: "And can you guarantee they won't bring you up on charges of being a Communist, that they won't bring the full weight of their special tribunal down on you?"

"I don't need to make any guarantee. There's no one who can confirm I'm a Communist."

Fang Buting passed the document back to Xie Peidong, but before Xie could accept it, Fang clenched it tightly. "Have you thought about whether or not the special tribunal will even accept your appeal? After all, you've told Xu what you plan to do. Naturally, he's reported this to his superiors, even if he's no longer in charge, and that means the secret service knows, too."

"Then everything will depend on whether they decide to prosecute Meng'ao or not."

They'd finally arrived at the heart of the matter between them.

There was greater nervousness in Fang's voice. "Do you think they'll prosecute him?"

Xie Peidong hesitated a moment before replying: "Meng'ao is your son."

"I hope they do prosecute him." Fang Buting looked hard at Xie Peidong, trying to gauge his reaction. "His crime is nothing more than the violation of military law. He can't be punished with anything greater than a dishonourable discharge, and to be frank, that's what I'm hoping for. That way I can more easily arrange to get him out of the country. There are only two people who would rather not see this outcome. One is Chiang Ching-kuo, and he still hopes to make use of my son for his own aims."

And the other person? Fang Buting deliberately paused at this point, again to test Xie Peidong's reaction. But Xie did not ask the question that hung in the air between them.

Fang continued: "As for the other person – and this is purely speculation – I think the other person is Zhou Enlai."

Xie Peidong's eyes were empty, void of any reaction, but Fang only stared even harder, looked ever deeper. Fang spoke: "There's more that could be said, but I don't think there's any need. I only hope that Chiang Ching-kuo and Zhou Enlai can be made aware of what I'm thinking. Meng'ao is really of no use to either of them. My hope is they'll let him go."

At exactly that moment, a flash of lightning lit up the sky, ripping past the French windows as though it were intent on tearing the room apart. Fang Buting and Xie Peidong waited for the next bolts to come, waited for the thunder to echo.

The thunder, however, was delayed.

There was a look of desolation on Xie Peidong's face as he reached for his resignation letter and returned it to his attaché case. "I would like to speculate on something, too. If I were truly a Communist, if I could speak directly with Mr Zhou Enlai, tell him what you have just told me... well, do you think I would tell him?"

"In public, in private, yes, I think you would ask him to let Meng'ao leave."

"Do you think he would listen?"

Fang Buting stood there, stunned by Xie's words.

"In public, in private, let Meng'ao leave..." Xie Peidong closed his case and wedged it under his arm. "Zeng Keda ought to be at the police station, no? I should get myself over there so I can hand him my resignation letter and my complaint for the court in Nanking. As for whether or not I'm a Communist, I'll ask them to launch their investigation immediately. I will, at the same time, pass on what you've just told me and ask that they inform Chiang Ching-kuo. Hopefully, that will see to Meng'ao being prosecuted straight away."

The sound of the rain intensified. Its echo seemed as though it were pounding upon Fang Buting's heart itself.

Fang reached out and clasped his hand on Xie's attaché case. "The rain's too heavy right now. Wait a bit before you go."

"You've forgotten. That day I went looking for Mulan it rained, too, more than it is now."

Fang Buting loosened his hand. "I'll call for Li."

Fang Buting went out onto the first-floor landing, his hand on the banister. "What the hell are you doing here? Who told you to enter?" His voice was loud and stern. Xie Peidong was standing beside him and now noticed Young Li walking towards them.

"Sir, Mr Fang..." Li could not hide his alarm at being discovered. "Madam wanted a fresh set of clothes. I'm supposed to bring them over to her this evening." He leaned over and picked up the suitcase that was next to the railing.

"Are you telling me you were just in the other room getting the clothes?" Fang Buting's voice was even sterner than before.

"Yes sir."

Fang Buting glanced back at Xie Peidong, then returned his stare towards Li, who was already walking in the direction of the stairs. "That's right, go!"

With the suitcase in hand, Li carefully descended the stairs. Xie Peidong followed shortly after.

Downstairs in the sitting room, Fang Buting's eyes held Li in his sights.

"Open the case."

"Yes sir." Li placed the suitcase flat and opened its lid. It contained what he said it did: Cheng Xiaoyun's clothing.

It wasn't wholly appropriate for a man of Fang Buting's status to browse through his wife's belongings, so he simply asked Li instead: "Tell me, you were there in the adjacent room the entire time, in my room, yes?"

Li nodded.

"You were terribly quiet going about your work. I suppose you heard everything we were discussing, hmm? Who sent you?"

"Mrs Cheng, your wife." Li's face bore no trace of guilt. "She telephoned... that is your wife, Mrs Cheng, she rang the guard station, and I answered. She told me where her clothes were and asked me to fetch them for her. If you do not believe me, sir, please call and ask your wife."

"Then why did you take the rear stairwell?" Fang Buting was unrelenting in his suspicions.

"Sir, I'm speaking the truth, your wife asked me. Please, Mr Fang, there's nothing to be alarmed about."

Fang Buting turned to Xie Peidong. "Dammit, who am I to trust in this blasted house?"

"If I may..." Xie Peidong had an answer even though Fang Buting wasn't really asking a question. "I would say that you should trust no one." Xie then turned to Li. "You're to take me to the police station. Then you can bring Mrs Cheng her clothes."

Xie Peidong didn't wait for a response. He merely walked towards the sitting room door. Young Li closed the suitcase and picked it up, but he didn't dare follow Xie out of the door.

On the porch, Xie grabbed an umbrella and spoke to no one in particular: "It's really pouring, isn't it? I doubt you could hear anything over the rain." Xie pushed the door open, released the umbrella's locking mechanism and lifted it above his head. The open door allowed for the wind to escape inside and swirl about the sitting room.

"Go on, go…" Fang would not look at Young Li.

"Yes sir." Li chased after Xie Peidong, grabbing his own umbrella before stepping out of the door. Seconds later, Fang could not see either one of them.

Fang Buting stood in the room alone watching the downpour outside. He then walked over to the telephone and realised he still hadn't made the call he had intended. He sat down on the sofa, alone and lost in his thoughts.

Xie Peidong sat in the back, while Li was behind the steering wheel. The rain continued its assault, buffeting the Austin from all sides, obscuring the world beyond the four doors of the car. Xie called out to Li in front: "In the future, no matter what it is, make sure you speak to Mr Fang before you do anything. He is, after all, your boss, and it is his house."

"Understood, sir."

Xie let his eyelids drop, seemingly overcome with fatigue, but then suddenly opened them wide and stared at Li again. "Have you gone the wrong way?"

"I heard the usual route was blocked, a fallen electrical pole."

Xie Peidong sat up straight. "And who told you that?" To Xie's surprise, Li did not answer. Xie asked another question: "How did Mrs Cheng telephone you and ask you to fetch her clothes?" Again, Li did not answer. Instead, he turned the Austin down a small side road and brought the car to a stop. Xie stared in disbelief. Before he could say anything else, the rear door of the Austin opened and someone climbed in. Seconds later, the door was closed and Li shifted into first gear. The car ambled forward and the man who had climbed in removed his Western-style hat; he extended his hand and greeted Xie Peidong: "Mr Xie!"

It was none other than Zhang Yueyin.

The door to the sitting room was opened from the inside, allowing for the violence of the raging storm to echo throughout He Qicang's home. He Xiaoyu stood in the doorway and yelled: "Director Fan!" Her voice was loud, but still she appeared rather weak. "It's pouring…"

Director Fan was out under the eaves of the veranda, an umbrella in his hand. He replied to Xiaoyu in an equally loud voice: "Mustn't delay, yes… Vice-Chancellor He is no doubt quite anxious. He's been waiting awhile, hasn't he?"

In the courtyard garden, two workers were lugging ladders despite the torrential rain. Underneath their raincoats, they carried He Qicang's new telephone line.

"Tell them to come inside. It's not fit to be out in this."

Liang Jinglun appeared and called out to the two workers: "At least come under the eaves like Director Fan."

The men seemed to understand the wisdom of their entreaties and did as suggested, finding a measure of respite from the rain underneath the eaves. As they approached, however, Liang Jinglun was startled to recognise one pair of eyes: they belonged to the man he'd seen earlier in the day.

The new telephone line not yet connected, Director Fan gave instructions to the workers: "You two, Master Wang, you carry the line inside. Your young assistant, Mr Liu, you make the connection outside."

"Quickly now!" He Xiaoyu stepped aside to let Director Fan and the older man in.

Director Fan stamped his feet, shook his umbrella free of excess rainwater and then walked inside. Master Wang followed closely behind, removing his wet raincoat and stamping his feet. He entered He Qicang's home carrying the ladder and the telephone line.

Liang Jinglun turned to He Xiaoyu and said: "You accompany them. I'll stay outside by the door to watch over things here. It's raining too hard to keep the door open."

He Xiaoyu did as Liang suggested and closed the door behind her.

The man referred to as Wang's assistant, Mr Liu, stayed outside with Liang Jinglun. His ladder remained over his shoulder, but he placed the wire on the veranda and extended his hand. "Comrade Liang Jinglun."

Liang clasped it and responded in kind: "Comrade Liu."

"I'm one of the survivors of the Shanghai massacre of Communists in April 1927!" Xie Peidong had never before spoken to Zhang Yueyin in such a furious manner. He cocked his head towards the car window and stared outside into the rain. "Before, only Deputy Chair Zhou knew my true identity. He was the only person trusted with it, but last year circumstances dictated that our paths would have to cross, and what's this, I realise now you secretly inserted someone to keep an eye on me. This young man driving Mr Fang's Austin has been keeping tabs on me, and you're here to what, speak to me about the complicated political games being played behind the scenes, that certain things have happened? Comrade Zhang, let me be clear, I have no means by which to keep Fang Meng'ao in Peking any longer, nor any means to stall whatever plans Chiang Ching-kuo has hatched, including his so-called 'peacocks flying southeast'. You must, please, you have to, for my sake, pass this along to Comrade Liuyun."

The onslaught of rain continued as the car lurched to a stop, flinging both Xie Peidong and Zhang Yueyin forwards to slam against the back of the front seat. Zhang Yueyin extended his arm to cushion Xie's impact, and at the same time glared at Young Li behind the wheel, scolding him harshly for how he was driving.

Li responded, the terror in his voice clearly audible: "My apologies, Chief Zhang, but a tree just crashed down into the roa…"

Zhang turned back to Xie Peidong, his arm still supporting him. "He'll be reassigned tomorrow, Mr Xie. You can arrange for your own driver."

Xie Peidong pushed away Zhang's arm, swatting at his hand as he did so. "I'm not a child, dammit. Nor is there anything wrong with being young. Fang Buting knows, my cover is blown. There's no way I can continue to keep things from him. I need to put everything on the table, show my hand to the Kuomintang. I need to make them interrogate Fang Meng'ao. That way, arrangements for him to leave China can be made. If you and your men continue to insist upon your interpretation of events, I'll have no option but to report everything to Deputy Chair Zhou."

Zhang Yueyin grew serious in response: "Mr Xie, your meaning is, if I understand things, is that, at present, you'll only see to Fang Buting's plans and that you can no longer implement those we wish to put in motion. Do I understand your meaning correctly?"

"Stop the car now!" Xie Peidong's voice echoed in its ferocity.

Carefully, Li shifted the car into a lower gear, bringing it to a stop.

Xie Peidong turned to Zhang Yueyin and said: "I am the assistant manager of the Peking branch of the Central Bank. When I see Zeng Keda, I can only relay to him the views held by the bank. Time is short, Comrade Zhang Yueyin. If you would, please get out."

"Mr Xie, the orders I was to pass along today have to do with the war to liberate our country from the clutches of the Kuomintang and their imperialist backers. I would ask you to be prudent, Mr Xie, and reconsider what you've just said."

"Don't worry. China will still be liberated, even if Fang Meng'ao and I are not present."

"Then there's nothing more I need to say." Zhang Yueyin pushed open the car door and climbed out without saying another word.

"His umbrella," Li shouted from the front seat and then hurriedly tried to grab it to give to him. The rain was still falling in sheets, and Zhang Yueyin had already disappeared into it.

"Let's go," said Xie Peidong, leaning back against the seat. "When we get to the police station, we'll tell them we had a slight accident, which is why we're delayed."

451

"Yes sir."

"Now, step on it!" Xie Peidong closed his eyes.

The pouring rain only served to bring into sharper relief the scene playing out at the police station where outside its main gates police officers, all wearing rain clothing, stood in rows as though waiting for something to happen. Fang Mengwei was there along with his men, an umbrella held above his head to shelter him from the deluge. Sun Chaozhong was standing nearby holding an even larger umbrella, shielding not only himself but also Zeng Keda who was decked out in a major-general's uniform. By the time the Austin finally arrived and pulled up in front of Fang Mengwei, they had already been waiting far too long.

Fang reached out to the rear door of the car, holding his umbrella above so that the car's occupant would not have to deal with the rain. Sun Chaozhong and Zeng Keda walked over to the Austin as well, Sun's umbrella still held aloft; it would add even more protection from the rain for Xie Peidong.

"Mr Xie," said Zeng Keda, "it's rather late. The rain's falling rather heavy, too…"

Half blocking Zeng Keda from moving closer, Fang Mengwei tapped on the glass. Li lowered the window, allowing Fang to ask his first question: "You left Mr He's house half an hour ago. Why did it take you so long to get here?"

"Sir… the rain… we had a small accident. That's what caused the delay."

"And yet you were still able to drive?"

"Yes sir, it was just a minor inconvenience, sir."

"You needn't wait for Mr Xie. Bring Madam Cheng her clothes."

"Yes sir."

Fang Mengwei helped Xie Peidong out of the vehicle and then guided him inside, leaving Zeng Keda behind standing next to the Austin. Sun glanced at Zeng, who met his eyes with a stare. Zeng lifted his hand to grab hold of the umbrella and said: "You should consult the rules regarding proper codes of conduct for the Youth League. Comrade Jianfeng carries his own umbrella, his own bag, too." Holding the umbrella, Zeng Keda walked towards the building by himself.

Sun Chaozhong remained standing in the rain. When he turned to look at the officers, each one of them still standing in their rows, he noticed they were all saluting Zeng Keda. With one hand still holding the umbrella, Zeng saluted in return and then strode into the building. Sun glanced back towards the Austin, but it had already vanished in the rain.

Zeng Keda was alone in his new office in the Peking Police station. Fang Mengwei had not come in, nor had Sun Chaozhong. Zeng was crouched down in front of an open cabinet looking for a suitable tea to drink. He picked up one container, then another and another, finally sighing somewhat ruefully. "Xu Tieying really had taste when it came to his tea. He's got Lu'an melon seed tea, yellow Junshan Yinzhen tea from Hunan, Wuyi's oolong Da Hong Pao, along with several other famous teas from across the country... Mr Xie, what would you like?"

"Water will be fine." Xie Peidong was seated on the sofa, apparently uninterested in Xu's tea collection.

"Ah, have some tea." Zeng picked one and turned to Xie. "How about some Lushan Yunwu... a taste of home?"

"Will you have some as well, Chief Zeng?"

"I'm no chief. This is just temporary. I'm only acting chief. If you would prefer I have some with you, then I shall."

"What about the New Life Movement? You mustn't break protocol."

Zeng Keda put the other containers back into the cabinet and stood up holding the Lushan Yunwu. He walked over to the desk, took two cups and placed tea leaves inside. He then reached for the thermos of hot water and poured it on the leaves. "Ah yes, the New Life Movement. You know, it's more an idea, the spirit, if you will, of how best to live in these times, how to interact with others, how to bring China into the future. Sharing tea with a guest is part of that, part of the Chinese spirit." Zeng walked over to the sofa carrying the two cups of steeping tea. "I imagine it's been ages since you've been back to Jiangxi, hasn't it Mr Xie?"

"Thank you." Xie accepted the tea, lifted the lid over the cup, blew on it a second and then brought it to his lips. "This is lovely, harvested from high up Mount Lushan, you know. I was there last year and had the same tea."

"You were there last year, Mr Xie?"

"Well, since it is the Republic's summer capital, the Central Bank has a villa there as well."

"Oh yes. It's a shame you've not been able to go this year." Zeng Keda had his own tea in his hand. "However, once the currency reforms come into full effect, once the final battle is waged with the CPC, I have faith that next year we'll be able to visit Lushan, perhaps together. I could host you at the Ministry of Defence's guest house, or you could have me over to the bank's villa, either would be fine. We could enjoy some freshly prepared tea."

"Yes, if only… it would be nice." Xie placed his teacup on the table and opened his attaché case. He pulled out a single sheet of paper. "It's my resignation, Inspector Zeng. Please look it over."

"What? What resignation?" Zeng Keda held on to his teacup and made no move towards accepting the paper Xie held in his outstretched hand.

Xie placed his letter on the table in front of Zeng and said: "Xu Tieying, his department, they suspect I'm a Communist agent. I, therefore, need to resign from the Peking branch of the Central Bank. It'll let you investigate more easily."

At these words, Zeng Keda placed his teacup on the paper and picked up Xie's resignation letter. He looked it over and returned it to the tabletop. "Xu told you he had evidence?"

Xie smiled a little. "I don't think he would let me see the evidence, would you?"

"I assume if there was no evidence, you would not be in such a hurry to resign, yes? The currency reforms may have been launched, but everything is in flux, mistakes are… inevitable. In the Tianjin economic area, Peking is the key. If you were to resign now, Mr Xie, don't you think you would only exacerbate the situation and cause more confusion?"

"Xu Tieying's been removed, Fang Meng'ao's been arrested and

I'm the cause, I know that. If you choose not to investigate me, won't *you* be causing more confusion?"

Zeng Keda mulled this over for a minute. Xu Tieying's words from earlier in the day echoed in his mind. "Cui Zhongshi is dead, true, but Xie Peidong is still there, and he's Zhou Enlai's man through and through, his most deeply placed chess piece. It will take much more than a day to dig him out, but sooner or later, this I know for a fact, he'll prove to be the greatest danger within, not just for the currency reforms, but for the entire northern campaign against the Communists."

Finally, Zeng spoke: "Let me ask you a few questions, Mr Xie. You answer if it's convenient. Your resignation, your request to be investigated, are you doing this of your own volition, or are you following the advice – the instructions – of Mr Fang?"

"My own volition, but Mr Fang agrees."

"I see. Then permit me to speculate. If I launch an investigation into you and your activities, if I turn up links to Cui Zhongshi and his supposed expropriation of tens of thousands of US dollars, which were, it's assumed, diverted to Hong Kong to support the Communist cause, tell me, Mr Xie, would you be able to explain all of this in detail?"

"No, I would not be able to."

"What if my investigation led me to certain accounts held at your bank? What if this led to the twenty per cent shares supposedly held by Xu's former department? Would you be able to explain?"

"No, again, I would not be able to."

Zeng Keda stood up. "Then my dear Mr Xie, if you can't explain either of these two things, why on earth would I launch an investigation into you and your activities?"

"But it's precisely because I cannot explain that I'm asking you to investigate."

"Ah, Mr Xie, how's it you put so much faith in us?"

It was Xie Peidong's turn to stand. "I thought this would be my last time to put faith in you. At the same time as I'm asking you to investigate, I would like to ask you something... and I hope you will be able to explain."

"And what, pray tell, is your question?"

"Seven days ago, on the twelfth of August, you accompanied me in searching for my daughter. Earlier today, Xu Tieying told me, however, that my daughter was not mistakenly sent to the liberated areas. Inspector Zeng, can you tell me, is Mulan alive or... dead?"

Zeng Keda hesitated. He had not expected this particular question, and could only respond with one of his own: "Is that what Xu Tieying told you?"

"Whether I'm a Communist or not, I hope you can launch your investigation as quickly as possible, and come to some resolution, give *me* some closure. If you determine I am a CPC agent, then do what you must to me, just don't harm my daughter. Only... only... you must not drag Fang Meng'ao into this as well. Get him dishonourably discharged, that's my request... his father too. The Republic is supposed to be based on the rule of law, and it's to the law that I make my appeal!" Xie paused and reached into his attaché case for his signed complaint. He passed it to Zeng Keda and waited for the other man's reaction.

Zeng Keda accepted the piece of paper and read it over, a serious, intense look on his face. There was absolute quiet in the office. Neither one was sure when the rain outside had stopped.

Finally, Zeng lifted his face to stare at Xie Peidong. "Do you really wish to have the special tribunal convene a trial on the actions of Captain Fang?"

"He was arrested on orders given by the Ministry of Defence and by the Air Force. Don't tell me you're not the ones who would put him on trial?"

"Mr Xie, these two letters, may I copy them? I can then return the originals to you tomorrow."

"Inspector Zeng, I'm fine if you arrest me right now."

"Let's not go overboard, shall we?" Zeng Keda took hold of the two sheets of paper. "I would like you to return and speak to Mr Fang. As for your requests, I'll pass these on to Nanking this evening. I'll have a response for you tomorrow."

CHAPTER 13

Both the sky and the earth below seemed to have been washed clean after the first monsoon onslaught. The moon now appeared in the sky, and, judging by its brightness, it would have been easy to mistake it for a huge glowing globe more suitable for late summer.

The officers remained outside in the garrison square waiting for orders. They had been standing in the downpour for ages and were thoroughly drenched. Now that the rain had stopped, some of the men removed their soaked rainwear. There was little else they could do; their new acting chief had not issued any directives. So they stood, erect and unmoving, waiting.

Until it was time to salute again.

Zeng Keda emerged from the main building, accompanying Xie Peidong. From a short distance away, Fang Mengwei's jeep approached, coming to a stop in front of them. On this occasion, Zeng Keda did not return the salute his men gave him. Instead, he walked with Xie, down the steps to stand next to the jeep. Fang Mengwei opened the rear door for Xie to climb in. They exchanged no handshakes, nor even a routine "goodbye". Zeng Keda merely stood beside the jeep, watching Xie Peidong as he seated himself in the back. Once inside, Fang Mengwei closed the door and walked round to the driver's side. Seconds later, he shifted the vehicle into first gear and left police headquarters.

Zeng Keda watched them for a moment and then turned around, finally noticing the officers standing to attention, their right hands seemingly stuck to their foreheads. Zeng looked down the line, impressed at their stamina until his eyes fell on Sun Chaozhong. He was soaked to the bone as were the rest of the men, but Zeng could see his salute was even more precise, more rigid than every other officer's.

"At ease," was all he said, and the men complied, grateful for the command, for any command. Zeng began to walk back towards the building, speaking as he did so: "It's been quite the past few days, hasn't it? The currency reforms launched, accounts frozen, stores shut, no business taking place whatsoever… each precinct put in charge of maintaining order. I asked the individual division commanders that for the next twenty-four hours you're to walk your beats."

"Sir, yes sir!"

Zeng Keda continued inside, saying nothing further.

He returned to his new office with Sun Chaozhong following closely behind. "Xu Tieying's on his way back to Nanking, but you're still here. Are these the arrangements put in place by Comrade Jianfeng?" Zeng began putting the tea and teacups away without really paying much attention to Sun.

"Not exactly, no. If Comrade Jianfeng had made the arrangements himself, surely he would have given the orders to you directly."

Zeng Keda looked up. "Strange, I've not received such orders. You don't suppose Comrade Jianfeng has forgotten about us?"

"With the currency reforms being launched and with everything else going on, he's got a lot on his plate. That we should understand."

"Understand?" Zeng Keda narrowed his eyes and looked at Sun for an extended moment. "Comrade Jianfeng has a single core plan, something I've understood since the beginning. Can you thus help me understand the current situation? I'm afraid I don't really grasp it."

"If it doesn't break protocol, please, Comrade Keda, could you be more specific?"

"All right then, I will. There's a poem, written during the

Northern and Southern dynasties period. Ah, what was its title again?"

"*An Old Poem Written for Jiao Zhongqing's Wife*," Sun Chaozhong responded surprisingly quickly.

"Yes, that's the one, that's the poem. Do you know it by heart?" Zeng Keda kept his eyes trained on the other man.

"I do," Sun replied, lowering his voice, "but I should begin with the preface since it dates the poem to the last years of the Han Dynasty when the mother of a minor official in Lujiang County, one Jiao Zhongqing, gets in between her son and the love of his life, Liu Lanzhi, essentially breaking up their relationship by sending her away."

Zeng was surprised by Sun's response. He hadn't expected Sun to know the poem by heart, let alone the preface. His expression betrayed the growing animosity he was beginning to feel.

Sun, however, seemed not to notice: "Things grew even more complicated when Lanzhi's family attempted to force her into a marriage she did not want. Indeed, she was so distraught that she threw herself into a nearby pond and drowned. Jiao Zhongqing later heard the news and proceeded to hang himself – from a tree in his own courtyard I should add. The preface acknowledges the fact that it's quite a painful story..."

"Yes, excellent. I must admit, you certainly have remembered it. Please continue."

"All right." Sun's tone grew even more serious than before. "Southeast the peacock flies, but every five *li* it hesitates in flight. At thirteen, she knew to weave plain silk. At fourteen, she learned to cut clothes..."

"Hello, central university exchange?" The director of University Housing Services was still at He Qicang's home, despite the lateness of the hour. He had little choice since he had to check to see if the new telephone line had been properly connected. He Qicang, his daughter and Cheng Xiaoyun were standing nearby, waiting expectantly to be reconnected.

A response came from the other end, and Director Fan replied:

"Yes, hello, this is Fan Yinong, director of Housing Services… Eh, I'm at Deputy He's home… That's correct, it's a new telephone line. We just finished installing it, yes… Connect us to Nanking, the home of our former vice-chancellor, now ambassador, Mr Stuart…"

"No! No! Not right now! It's not the right time!" He Qicang's voice was abrupt, loud.

"Sorry, don't connect… not now!" Director Fan shouted into the receiver in response to He Qicang's directive, his eyes trained on the older man, if somewhat confusingly.

"Pass me the phone."

"Please wait a moment," Fan said into the telephone, this time in a more level tone. "Vice-Chancellor He wishes to speak to you."

He Qicang accepted the phone and brought it close to his face. "Apologies for the trouble. I would like to speak to Mr Stuart this evening… Yes, that shouldn't be a problem, should it… Ah, excellent, thank you, and sorry for the trouble." He Qicang hung up the phone and turned to Director Fan. "Apologies to you as well, Mr Fan."

"No sir, it's no trouble at all. It had to be done."

"And the two workers? Ah, yes." He Qicang shifted his attention to his daughter. "Be a dear and see if there's anything we can give them to eat…"

"Ah, sir, there's no need for that," Fan Yinong interjected: "We give them extra for overtime. We'll be off. If there are any problems, don't hesitate to call for us."

"Xiaoyu, you and Jinglun see them to the door please."

"Of course."

"Vice-Chancellor, there's no need to see us to the door." Again, Director Fan deflected He Qicang's attempt at politeness before assiduously departing.

He Xiaoyu saw the man out.

The room was more or less empty, and He Qicang looked at the newly installed telephone line. As he did so, Cheng Xiaoyun walked up beside him. "It seems everything is falling on your shoulders, Mr He."

He Qicang turned slowly to face her. "Is that driver of yours still downstairs?"

"Yes, I asked him to fetch clothes for me."

"You still intend to stay here with us?" He Qicang smiled but there was a certain sadness to it. "I hope you and your husband aren't putting on some kind of performance. Go home and tell Fang Buting that I've never, not once, contacted Ambassador Stuart concerning personal matters. Ask him to wait for me. I'll pass on what I learn... when I learn it."

"Please Mr He..." Cheng Xiaoyun couldn't hide her emotions. Teardrops formed in her eyes.

"You see, you see, why so many tears? If you want to cry, go home and show them to your husband."

Cheng Xiaoyun swallowed her tears. "I'll never let him see me cry again."

Wang Puchen had no idea how long he had been waiting for Chiang Ching-kuo to telephone him. But all he could do was wait, wait for a phone call that just wouldn't seem to come. He'd filled two ashtrays on his desk, and still the telephone remained silent.

Then, finally, the clang of the phone shattered his reverie.

As though a bolt of lightning had struck him, he sat up straight in his chair, tossed away the cigarette he had been burning down in his fingers and reached for the receiver. "It's me, Comrade Jianfeng. I must report, Comrade Liang Jinglun has just telephoned me from the Foreign Languages Bookstore. The CPC branch in Peking has suddenly informed him he's to relocate to Hong Kong. At about the same time, Vice-Chancellor He has had a new telephone line installed. Apparently, it's a direct line to Ambassador Stuart. He's most likely speaking to the ambassador right now, requesting that he reach out to the president, probably to try to persuade him to agree to let Fang Meng'ao go, his daughter too, so that they can leave China and marry overseas. Additionally, at nine o'clock this evening, Xie Peidong paid a visit to the Peking Police station to speak to Zeng Keda. He passed along Fang Buting's views, his hope that Fang Meng'ao will shortly be discharged from the military, again to allow him to go abroad and get married. To my mind, this all stinks of CPC involvement. That much is clear.

It's their attempt, I'm sure, to thwart our peacocks from flying southeast…"

The instructions he received were incredibly concise.

Wang Puchen continued: "…since the twelfth of August, we've been monitoring all lines going into and out of the Peking branch. As of now, we've not discovered any suspicious transmissions, nor has anyone found any contact between Xie Peidong and persons of interest… Yes, we will continue to monitor everything."

Suddenly, the bell of the other telephone on Wang's table came to life. He looked at it sharply but continued to speak: "Yes, Comrade Jianfeng, I imagine that's Comrade Zeng Keda calling me… I understand. Answer it, listen to what he has to say and then report back to you."

"Comrade Puchen? Have you had any contact from Comrade Jianfeng?" As he expected, it was Zeng Keda who had telephoned him from the Peking Police headquarters.

Wang Puchen picked up the other telephone receiver and said: "All lines of communication with Shanghai have been cut off." Wang Puchen lit another cigarette. "Do you need me to get in touch with Chief Mao and ask for his help?"

On the other end of the line, Zeng Keda lifted his teacup and brought it to his lips, before discovering there was no tea left in it. "It's a matter concerning the Youth League. There's no need to drag the Secret Service into it. How is the situation with Fang Meng'ao going to be handled, and what about Liang Jinglun? Both matters are directly connected to the peacocks plan and whether or not it can be implemented. Unfortunately, I've not received any instructions from the Presidential Palace, nor can I get in touch with Comrade Jianfeng. I wonder if I should ask Director Chen Fang myself… to see if the president has issued any orders himself."

Wang Puchen deliberately held his tongue for a moment before speaking: "Certainly, if the president issued direct orders that would be ideal… If Comrade Jianfeng had questions, I would naturally help to explain… Excellent, yes. I'll hang up now."

Wang replaced the phone and stubbed out his cigarette. Then he lifted the other receiver that was simply left lying on its side and quickly explained: "Comrade Jianfeng, Comrade Zeng Keda is, as expected, quite anxious and seemingly unable to wait. He should be calling Director Chen Fang as we speak... Yes, I will remain here and await instructions."

———

"Director Chen, sir, are you well?" Zeng Keda was still seated in his acting chief's office in Peking, but he felt as though he was in Nanking, in the Presidential Palace itself. "Yes, still many things to deal with. I do apologise for disturbing you. I shouldn't be calling at this hour..."

"No need to be so polite." As before, Chen Fang's voice had the same melodious tenor, the same amicable tone. "I saw your report when I returned. I've passed it on to the president. What did Mr Chiang Ching-kuo think of it?"

"His only response was to wait for the president to decide."

"The Youth League doesn't have any concrete ideas on how to handle things?"

"This is why I'm telephoning you now. Xie Peidong came to see me this evening. He passed on Fang Buting's views. Mr Fang hopes his son will be punished according to military law. He wants Fang Meng'ao to be discharged from the service, even if that means dishonourably."

"Did you report this to Mr Chiang?"

"I tried many times, but I couldn't get through. If you ask me, Xie Peidong's request was entirely on behalf of Mr Fang. At the same time, however, I feel it's highly likely this is what the CPC wants as well. Director Chen, the urgency of this is why I've called. I think the president needs to be made aware, as soon as possible."

There was only silence on the other end.

"Director Chen, sir, Director Chen..." Zeng Keda spoke impatiently into the phone, his voice soft, pleading.

"Yes, I'm still listening." His voice remained friendly. "Let's think for a minute. If I were Mr Chiang Ching-kuo, what advice would you give me?"

It's said that some people are blessed with good fortune, but in truth, those who do receive it are quite likely to be in especially precarious circumstances. For good fortune does not easily come, and usually only for those who truly, desperately, need it.

Zeng Keda answered almost immediately: "This is what I would advise, sir. Fang Meng'ao's punishment should be decided upon by the Air Force and only by the Air Force. As for Liang Jinglun, he's already made his arguments concerning the currency reform. He's demonstrated clearly, too, his great dissatisfaction with the president. It's inadvisable to keep him on at Yenching University as he shouldn't be given further opportunities to have direct contact with the American interests there... I believe, yes, this is the advice I would give to Mr Chiang."

Again there was only silence, but on this occasion, Zeng Keda exercised his patience better than he had before and did not speak.

Finally, Chen Fang offered a response: "I've got five more minutes before I must see the president. Once I see him, I will pass along the position of the Youth League. If the president agrees with this position, what do you think we should do with Captain Fang's men?"

"To be honest, sir, Director, I have thought a little about this. The successful implementation of the currency reforms requires the transportation of a large number of goods in and out of Peking. The military in the north also needs to be constantly resupplied. My suggestion is to reassign Captain Fang's men to the Central Air Transport Corporation. The Youth League will be able to provide assistance in this matter as well."

"I must go. My advice to you is to contact Mr Chiang Ching-kuo and give him the advice you just gave me. If you can't get a line through, contact the Executive Yuan's economic subcommittee directly and tell them your ideas."

"Sir, thank you. Yes, you have my sincere gratitude!"

Zeng Keda hung up the phone and shouted towards the door: "Wang!"

"Coming, sir!"

Zeng Keda stood up and walked towards the exit, ready to speak to his assistant, but when he got near the doorway he spied Sun Chaozhong standing in the adjacent meeting room, presumably waiting for orders, for something. Before their eyes could meet, however, Zeng looked away and instead spoke to his aide-de-camp who was still a little distance down the hallway: "Afterwards, you're the only one authorised to be on duty here. Now, join me in my office, and make sure you close the door behind you."

Wang nodded his acknowledgement and continued towards his superior's office. When he saw Zeng step back inside, he moved towards the meeting room and called softly to Sun Chaozhong: "Secretary Sun, please. If you wouldn't mind, go outside and take up a chair in the duty room."

Sun Chaozhong left without saying a word.

Wang shut the door to the meeting room after Sun had exited, paused a moment and then followed after Zeng.

Over the course of the next couple of hours, Zeng Keda repeatedly had his assistant transcribe and then send telegrams to the Executive Yuan's economic subcommittee, which, given that the radio equipment sat on the table in Zeng's office, meant Wang spent the same amount of time seated in front of it. He, of course, said nothing. All he did was tap out whatever text Zeng wanted him to send, and then sit quietly waiting for a response that never came. Eventually, the tapping of his fingers on the telegram machine overtook the sound of the ticking clock on the wall, but still Wang said nothing, nor did they receive a reply.

Finally, Zeng glanced at the time and saw that it was just past eleven o'clock. He checked his wristwatch to make sure, and then spoke aloud to no one in particular: "The wall clock is about a minute slow…"

"Should I be off then, sir?" Wang stood up and slowly began to lift the headphones off his ears.

Before he could escape, however, the machine flashed and beeped.

"Take that down!" Zeng shouted.

Wang complied without hesitation and sat back down, pen in hand.

Zeng did his best to keep calm. He poured himself a glass of water, and then he poured another for his assistant, placing it on the table next to the radio. That's when he noticed the surprising brevity of the telegram. Indeed, Wang had already finished transcribing it.

Before deciphering the coded message, however, Wang stretched and stifled a yawn. It was getting late.

Zeng Keda stood over his shoulder, watching intently, waiting for the words to form on the page. Wang proceeded to complete his task.

At last, Zeng thought, a response from the Executive Yuan!

Before Wang could properly hand the completed message to his superior, Zeng had already snatched it away from him:

> The Air Force pilots dispatched to Peking are to be reassigned at 0300 hours to Tianjin to assist in the urgent transportation of goods <over>
> Zhang Lisheng <over>

Zeng Keda's eyes lit up. Zhang Lisheng was deputy premier of the Executive Yuan and inspector for Tianjin Economic Zone. The telegram instilled him with confidence in his recommendations. Zeng decided, too, that he would no longer wait around for Comrade Jianfeng's missive. Instead, he walked straight over to where he had hung his military cap and said to his assistant: "Reply to the Executive Yuan's telegram. I'm going straight to speak to Captain Fang's contingent of pilots to give them their new orders. Once you've finished your response, I want you to pass along to Comrade Jianfeng the instructions sent by the Executive Yuan!"

In the western quarter of Peking, the contingent of pilots waited. It was late. The lights of their barracks were all on, although they flickered like flitting fireflies. They had no captain, thus no orders. For men more accustomed to following orders, now they couldn't help but feel adrift, lost to an evening lunar haze, unsure of what the future held.

Zeng Keda killed the lights of his jeep as he pulled into the training square in front of the barracks. He parked the vehicle just outside the main building. Commander Li had watched him drive through the main gates of the compound and now came running up. He saluted once he drew near and reached out to open the door. Zeng climbed out, his eyes fixed on the darkened building. "What's your status? Is everything all right?"

Everything all right? Li swallowed the bile in his mouth and replied: "Sir, yes, everything's all right."

"And what does that mean exactly?" Zeng Keda walked towards the barracks doors.

Li followed quickly behind. "After leaving the airbase, we returned here. No one ate, no one said anything. Everyone just hit the sack."

Zeng Keda halted his steps. "No one ate? Are they on some kind of hunger strike? Protest?"

"Sir, I shouldn't think so…"

"And why is that?" Zeng Keda had turned around to stare at the man.

"To speak freely, sir, the sudden arrest of Captain Fang… Well, sir, in their hearts they understand."

"Hah! I didn't think the word 'understand' is in a soldier's dictionary!"

Commander Li had no response to such a statement.

Zeng turned away and softened his tone, at least a little: "Get the men up and into formation. They've been given new orders, an urgent task."

"Yes sir."

Watching the younger man walk into the barracks, Zeng Keda suddenly felt an indescribable sense of loneliness. He looked up into the sky and saw only the moon; the rest was a dark emptiness that appeared to stretch into oblivion. But despite the openness, he couldn't see Nanking. As he stood there entranced, he began to hear an old man's voice carry on the wind. A familiar cadence, it crept softly up around his ears to speak directly to him: "Is it the moon that's drawing near, or is it the ancient capital of Chang'an?" This was followed by the sound of young voices, tender and gentle: "The moon is near, the capital is far. The moon we can see, Chang'an we cannot…" A smile reached across Zeng's face, a smile he'd not had since he was a boy…

His trance was shattered when the tungsten floodlights burst upon his retinas, dissolving the moon and the night sky. Zeng Keda looked towards the barracks and saw Commander Li, as well as his own assistant, standing over two rows of beds. There appeared to be some sort of verbal excoriation taking place, but Zeng could not hear. All he did was stare into the still poorly lit barracks until he saw Commander Li walking towards him again. No one followed after him.

Zeng narrowed his eyes.

"Sir, none of them will speak, nor will they follow orders." Li was now standing outside the barracks door.

Zeng began to stride past the younger man. He heard him call out from behind "Ten hut!" and then race closer to speak more privately: "Sir, shall I bring men to rouse them, sir?"

"Under no circumstances is anyone else permitted inside!" Zeng's tone brooked no further discussion.

———

The lights inside the barracks were off. The only illumination came from the tungsten filaments outside. It was enough. Zeng did not enter much past the door. He only stood there, his eyes staring at the men. To the left, there was one row of military beds and ten reclining figures. To the right, there was the same. Zeng stood there for several seconds and then flipped the light switch. He walked over to the far end of the barracks, to where a door opened to Fang Meng'ao's personal room. He paused for a moment in the doorway to Fang's room and then turned on its light as well. With the barracks fully illuminated, Zeng Keda directed his attention to the pilots still in their beds. They were all facing Fang Meng'ao's room, so naturally, they were facing Zeng Keda. But not one opened his eyes.

"Chen Changwu!" Zeng shouted.

He knew they had heard him, he knew they were feigning sleep. But still they kept their eyes closed.

All except for Chen Changwu, who now climbed up out of his bed to stand in front of it: "I'm here, sir."

"I've a question for you," Zeng Keda began. "Tell me, which is closer, Nanking or the moon?"

"I couldn't say, sir."

"Are you familiar with the military code of conduct?"

"Yes sir, I am."

"Then recite to me Article Number Thirty-Two."

"Persons in the military or those subject to emergency measures who cause a delay in the transport of weapons, ammunition, rations, bedding, clothing or other such items, without sufficient cause, will face imprisonment for a maximum of three years. Those who impede or otherwise disrupt the operations of military aircraft will be subject to the death penalty or life imprisonment."

"Well done, yes. You recited it word for word!" Zeng Keda's voice was full of admiration when he delivered his subsequent orders: "The Kuomintang Youth League under the guidance of the Ministry of Defence hereby commands the Peking Air Force detachment to assemble and carry out the task of transporting goods!"

The entire room was silent.

Thump, thump. Zeng Keda could hear the beating of his heart as though it were a drum being carried on horseback in a military parade.

Finally, one person got to his feet. It was Guo Jinyang.

Then another, Shao Yuangang.

Then one by one the rest of the pilots climbed out of their beds. Zeng Keda's heartbeat began to slow. His eyes assumed a look of anticipation, and ultimately praise for the men seemingly rising up to do their duty.

But the look vanished as quickly as it had come. Not one of the men made any effort to form ranks and get ready.

Finally, Chen Changwu walked over to him. Another pilot did the same. Without making much noise, the entire detachment queued up behind Chen and marched over to stand in front of Zeng Keda.

Chen came to a halt directly in front of Zeng and stretched out both hands to hand him an official document. Zeng accepted it robotically, and then realised what it was: it was Chen's official military ID certificate! Before long, Zeng's hands were full with twenty military IDs!

Once they handed in their IDs, each officer returned to stand in front of their beds.

Twenty pairs of eyes stared at Zeng Keda, each pair glowing with a certain fierceness.

"So, you're all intending to resign your commissions, is that it?" Zeng Keda met their stares with equal ferocity. "That's it, isn't it? Come on and answer me, dammit!"

"Sir, yes sir!" Chen Changwu responded for the men.

"All right, all right. Recite for me, if you will, Article Ninety-Three, Paragraph Two of the military code of conduct."

Chen Changwu again replied for the men: "Persons in the military or those subject to emergency measures who, without sufficient cause, choose to resign their commission, or who fail in their duty, will face imprisonment for a maximum of five years."

"So tell me, are you all willing to stand in front of the military tribunal in Nanking and face punishment?"

"Sir, on the sixth of July each and every one of us was brought up on charges by the special tribunal, and all twenty of us were summarily dishonourably discharged from the military. Up to now, the military court has not reinstated us. Thus the military code of conduct does not apply, and we are not subject to its... justice."

"But what of the IDs you just gave me? Surely you're subject to the codes of conduct stipulated by the Youth League and the Ministry of Defence?" Zeng threw the certificates down onto the floor, their leather pockets slapping hard against the wood. "Go on," he shouted, "have a look at the seals printed on them!"

"No, sir, we won't. Give them to the special tribunal in Nanking. They can look at them!"

Guo Jinyang and Shao Yuangang already had suitcases in hand. They turned and marched towards the barracks door. They were followed by the rest of Captain Fang's former pilots. Soon, only Chen Changwu remained in the building with Zeng Keda. He, too, had picked up his own personal belongings, but before he departed he had a few last words for Zeng: "Escort us back to Nanking? Haul us up in front of the special tribunal? We'll see you there..." Then he turned and left.

Zeng Keda's face was ashen. He was standing in the sentry booth, his hand lingering over the telephone rotary dial. Finally, he hooked his finger into it and dialled.

The receiver echoed: "Sorry, this number cannot be connected. Sorry, this number cannot be connected. Sorry..."

Zeng Keda looped his finger around the rotary dial, shook the phone and then barked into the receiver: "I'm an inspector with the Ministry of Defence. Please connect me to Nanking, you hear. I need to reach Nanking!"

"Sorry, this number cannot..."

Frustrated, Zeng hung up, then picked up the phone again and dialled. The response this time was different: "You've reached the Northern Command switchboard. Please, how may I connect you?" Zeng Keda hesitated and did not answer. The voice repeated: "Please, how may I connect you?"

Zeng Keda summoned what faith he had left and replied: "Listen carefully. I am an inspector with the Ministry of Defence, I am also on special assignment with the Executive Yuan's economic subcommittee. I've been sent to Peking to manage affairs here. I ask you to connect me immediately to the investigations department in the Shanghai offices of the Central Bank. Do you understand?"

"I'm sorry sir, that number cannot be connected..."

Zeng Keda slammed the phone down in fury. He looked out through the window and shouted: "Commander Li!"

The sentry room door opened from the outside, but to Zeng's surprise, it was Wang Puchen standing in the doorway. Zeng looked at him for a moment and then suddenly seemed to realise something.

Wang spoke first: "The telephone line here has been disconnected. Come on, let's talk."

Zeng walked alongside Wang Puchen until they came to a somewhat secluded spot near the compound walls. Zeng had already shouted out orders for the floodlights to be turned off, and so now the two men stood in the dim light of the moon. Further along the wall, the twenty pilots once under Captain Fang's command stood silently like some old worn photo.

Wang looked in their direction and then turned back to Zeng

Keda. "Are you really getting things ready to send all twenty of them to Nanking to face trial?"

"I'd be interested to hear your take, if I'm being honest."

"I'm afraid I don't have any personal views on the matter. But would you like to hear Xu Tieying's?"

"He's more or less in the same boat as them isn't he? How can he even know what's going on here?"

"Yes, it's true he's in Nanking being investigated, but he did make one assertion to the central leadership of the Kuomintang, and that's that Fang Meng'ao is a Communist. That said, his appointment, as well as that of his men, was made by the Youth League, the orders signed by Mr Chiang Ching-kuo himself."

A look of astonishment and consternation spread across Zeng's face. "This is what the central leadership has told you?"

"No, this is not what the central leadership has told me. It's word for word what Xu said, and what, in turn, was reported to the president."

"And what was the president's reaction?"

Wang Puchen was quiet for a moment before answering: "The president listened in full to Director Chen Fang's report."

Again, Zeng was surprised by this detail. "And what did Director Chen report?"

"Do you know, you've not yet asked me why I've come to see you." Zeng was caught off guard by the question and remained silent. Wang noticed his response but didn't draw attention to it. "According to the code of conduct for the Secret Service, or, I suppose, for the Defence Ministry's Youth League, I shouldn't be here. In fact, it's strictly prohibited for me to even talk to you about any of this, but..."

"Comrade Jianfeng..."

"Did Director Chen speak to you?" Wang interjected. "Did he tell you he reported everything to Comrade Jianfeng, that he sought his instructions on everything?"

"Yes."

"Well, I have to pass on what the president has said, word for word." Wang Puchen paused in order to allow the weight of what he was about to say to sink in. "Don't talk to me about what the

Youth League is up to. My son's in charge of what they do. Go speak to him."

Zeng Keda slowly turned his head towards the dark sky, the lonely moon. He removed his wide-brimmed hat, and then spoke: "I'll go with you."

Zeng lowered his head and began to walk towards the barracks, but Wang called out to stop him and then moved closer. "Where are you going? As a comrade of long standing, I should first like to give you some advice. Would that be all right?"

Zeng Keda turned around. "Please…"

"You just gave orders to Captain Fang's former men, yes? You asked them if the moon was closer or if Nanking was. At the moment, the moon is right above us, so I'd like to ask you the same question: Which is closer, the moon or Nanking?"

Zeng felt a mixture of bafflement and shame. "If you're going to ask me that type of question, then I shan't answer. Whatever the party decides, however they wish to punish me, I will accept it. I'm prepared to obey."

"I'm not here representing the party, nor have they said they intend to discipline you. If you feel that this question is somehow disrespectful, then allow me to explain my point of view."

Zeng Keda could only look at him.

"There is an answer to this question, a very old answer in fact, which most people acknowledge as being correct. It goes that even if the moon were close, we wouldn't be able to walk to it. But no matter how far we might be from Chang'an, it's still a place we can reach. But you know what, using this analogy of distance, of what's far and what's near, well, to be frank, I don't think this answer makes sense. In truth, I think it's wrong. Let me explain. If you say that what is nearby is a place we can walk to, how is it then that during the eight years we spent resisting Japan, during the time they occupied the capital, we weren't able to go to Nanking? During that time, in our hearts and minds, there was only Chongqing. Once the war was won, well, let me ask you: are there still many people going to Chongqing? Now, as for the moon, it's different, fundamentally so. It doesn't matter where you are, or where you're going, the moon will always shine down upon you. Today, you and me, we're in Peking, and

Comrade Jianfeng is in Shanghai. Let me ask you, is Nanking shining upon us or is it Shanghai? The moon is close, always has been and always will be, to my mind. The same is true of Comrade Jianfeng."

"I... I agree."

"May I pass on his orders, then?"

"Please, Comrade Puchen, yes."

"The primary aim of Operation: Peacocks Flying Southeast is to ensure that the Northern Command and its five hundred thousand soldiers have sufficient supplies in arms and munitions and that their logistical requirements are met so that they can maintain their position in the north, and down into the central plains, and into Shandong. The key to the operation is the American aid, and the assistance of the Central Bank. This is the reason for using both Fang Meng'ao and Liang Jinglun. Responsibility for seeing this through has come to weigh on your shoulders, but on the first day of the reforms, you advise the Presidential Palace to bring Fang Meng'ao up on charges of insubordination and dereliction of duty, you also advised that Liang Jinglun be investigated. Needless to say, Comrade Jianfeng feels the time for such actions is wholly inappropriate. And so, quite naturally, he wants to know what you're up to, what your real thoughts are on all of this."

"Comrade Puchen, things must be much clearer to you, but let me ask, if Xie Peidong truly is a Communist, what then? If Fang Meng'ao is a Communist, what can we do? These two questions are plaguing my thoughts."

"The issue regarding Xie Peidong's political affiliation, you let me handle that. As for Fang Meng'ao, that's Comrade Jianfeng's responsibility. Allow me to reiterate Comrade Jianfeng's orders to you: always suspect those you employ of having ulterior aims, but that doesn't mean you don't use them. The key is to use them well. I hope that's something we both grasp."

Zeng Keda had learned not long ago that Wang Puchen was a member of the Iron and Blood Congress like himself, but he had thought of him as nothing more than a special operative, but now, listening to the man speak, he finally realised, he was, he had to be, Comrade Jianfeng's trusted confidant. Zeng looked at the man, careful to keep his feelings of regret for Wang's position buried deep. "At present, I've no means by which to speak to Comrade

Jianfeng. All I can do is ask that you please pass along to him my concerns."

Wang Puchen nodded.

Zeng continued: "Wang Yangming once said: 'It's easy to vanquish the thief hiding in the mountains, but much more challenging to vanquish the thief of the heart.' Right now, my chief responsibility is to destroy this thief of the heart. I need to review everything that's happened, reflect upon all of it."

"Excellent, well put, I will pass on all of this."

"There is, however, one urgent matter that must be dealt with immediately." As he spoke, Zeng Keda pulled out the telegram he'd received from Zhang Lisheng. Wang accepted it but didn't seem to pay it much notice. Zeng explained the message: "You can see who it's from, the Executive Yuan. At zero three hundred hours, they're supposed to transport the first consignment of goods. It's nearly zero two hundred hours, but they're refusing to do so. How should I handle this?"

Wang Puchen handed the telegram back to him and smiled. "Do you really think the Executive Yuan would give the Youth League a direct order?"

Zeng Keda still looked puzzled and doubtful.

"This order came from Comrade Jianfeng, simply by way of the Executive Yuan. On the one hand, the Communists must be dealt with, while on the other, the elements within the Kuomintang, the so-called Central Committee Clique, they have to be dealt with, too. Which is exactly what Comrade Jianfeng is doing. You could say he's taking the necessary steps. But let me tell you one thing, don't return to the police station. When the sun comes up, head to the offices that are managing the currency reforms for the Tianjin economic area. Focus your energies there."

"Understood."

―――

The clock in Fang's sitting room chimed two o'clock, but even at this hour, no one was asleep. The three people there had never before experienced a night quite like the one they were living through now. Fang Buting and Xie Peidong were seated but said nothing. The third person in their trio, Cheng Xiaoyun, periodically refilled their teapot with hot water. She didn't speak.

Finally, Fang Buting broke the silence: "Xiaoyun, I've been thinking... Would you care to hear?" Cheng Xiaoyun only looked at her husband, so Fang Buting continued: "I think I ought to transfer their uncle to the Bank of China. Afterwards, further arrangements could be made for him to be shifted to the New York branch. What do you think?"

Given what was being discussed, Fang ought to have asked for Xie Peidong's opinion on the matter, considering he was seated nearby. But it was clear, to Xie at least, that Fang Buting was merely trying to get her to talk. The more important, the more embarrassing issue between them was something Fang could not yet discuss.

In response to her husband, however, Cheng Xiaoyun only turned her attention to Xie Peidong.

"You don't need to worry yourselves about me," said Xie Peidong, avoiding making eye contact with Fang. "The first order of business ought to be making arrangements for Meng'ao to leave China. If you're truly worried I'm a Communist, sending me to New York will only serve to entangle you both in my affairs."

"You're still going on about that!" Fang Buting slapped the table. "Are we afraid of further entanglement? If I were, would I be here now, sitting down, talking to you! Xie Peidong, twenty years ago you came to tell me my sister had died. On the twelfth of August, you came to tell me Mulan had been sent to the liberated areas. Tell me, who was dragged down by you? Hmm? No answer? Then I'll answer for you. It was your wife, your daughter. Don't you understand that?" Fang Buting was trembling all over. His rage had bubbled up and exploded.

"How dare you!" said Cheng Xiaoyun. " How can you be certain things are not the way you think they are? How can you talk to your brother-in-law like this?"

"Then how should I speak to him?" retorted Fang Buting, directing his fury at his wife. "Should I wait for the Kuomintang to knock down the door and haul him away?"

"Brother," said Xie Peidong, "will you listen for a moment to what I have to say?"

Fang Buting turned and focused his full attention on Xie, but he didn't respond. Cheng Xiaoyun interjected: "Please, Husband, listen to him."

"For twenty years, you never once suspected me of being a Communist. And Xu Tieying, despite the considerable resources he drew upon in the government, couldn't find concrete proof either. This is the only thing I can say. If I really am a Communist, after I'm dead, make sure that word is nowhere carved into the tombstone that marks my grave. The two of us, we're old. We don't know who'll send whom off to whatever awaits after life. But Xiaoyun, she's younger than both of us. She's the only one we can ask to take care of the affairs we will undoubtedly leave behind…"

"Please, I don't want either of you to talk like this." Tears began to form and roll down her cheeks.

Xie continued: "Everyone dies. There's no avoiding it. When my time comes, I would ask that you see me buried next to Mulan's mum. And if… if Mulan's really… if they hurt her, then I would ask that the three of us be put together as a family should. Tomorrow, I'm leaving the bank, leaving Peking. I'm going home to Wuxi, to Jiangsu. Let's see if anyone tries to arrest me."

"Don't. Stop talking like this." Cheng Xiaoyun sat down on the sofa and wept silently.

Fang Buting couldn't hold back his tears either.

Xie Peidong's eyes looked like deep pools of water. Tears glistened, but they did not fall.

The only sound that could be heard in the entire house, throughout the entire compound, was the sound of bamboo blowing in the wind.

The phoenix-tailed bamboo that grew on both sides of the stone path that snaked through the Jingyuan Botanical Gardens enclosed the two men who now walked along it. The moon shone brilliantly in the night sky above them. As they came up to the gate, a young man pushed it open and saluted, although his voice was not much more than a whisper: "Secretary Zhang, sir. Hello!"

Zhang Yueyin took the young man's hand in his and shook it

vigorously. His companion, however, did not. A few seconds later, the two men had stepped inside. Zhang's companion finally spoke, issuing orders for the young man to bolt the gate. He complied without hesitation, and shortly after they could hear it being locked behind them.

In front of them was the familiar small room that faced north. To the left of it was another, perhaps even smaller room. Zhang and his companion walked towards it, but on the stone steps, the man in front of Zhang stopped suddenly. He turned to look at Zhang Yueyin, his hand holding onto the metal rail that ran along the steps. His voice was soft: "Comrade Liuyun is here." Zhang Yueyin was startled by the news. However, his companion, Director Fan of the University Housing Services, seemed not to be. He continued up the steps and knocked twice on the door. Seconds later, someone from inside opened it.

"Allow me to make the introductions." Despite what he said, there was little by way of cordiality in Liuyun's voice. He gestured towards the man who looked to be in his early thirties: "This here is Comrade Qi Mutang. He's assuming Comrade Liu Chuwu's duties."

"Greetings, comrade."

"The same to you, Comrade Yueyin."

Under the feeble lighting, it still seemed as though there was a greater sparkle in this young man's eyes than there had been in Old Liu. Unbeknownst to Zhang, the man had already been carrying out duties around the campus, for he was none other than the young electrician who had already had dealings with Liang Jinglun.

"Please, be seated." Liuyun sat first as he offered chairs to his guests.

The other men quickly obeyed.

"Comrade Zhang Yueyin." There was even more sternness in his eyes than there was in the tone of Liuyun's voice.

In spite of having just sat down, Zhang Yueyin now slowly stood up again.

Liuyun continued: "You know the orders. Xie Peidong was not to be contacted, nor was any comrade permitted to interfere in his work. So why did you, this very evening, reach out to him?"

"Comrade Liuyun…"

"I don't want an explanation," Liuyun interjected. "The Kuomintang's Secret Service has had Xie Peidong under surveillance for the last twenty-four hours at least. Were you aware of this? The current situation for both Comrade Xie and Comrade Fang Meng'ao is incredibly dangerous, didn't you know?"

Zhang could only answer in the affirmative.

"And yet while he was en route to the police station, you saw fit to waylay him? His driver, Young Li, was dispatched by the party to guarantee his safety. Who gave you the authority to change the character of his assignment? Who ordered you to contact He Xiaoyu, to send her the note that you did? Who authorised you to monitor Xie Peidong's actions? It was already made clear to you that the work Xie Peidong is carrying out is at the behest of Deputy Chair Zhou, who has the utmost faith in Xie Peidong's ability to see things through, as does the central leadership as a whole. So just what the hell are you up to?"

Zhang Yueyin hesitated, but he knew he had to provide some sort of explanation: "Xu Tieying had moved against Comrade Xie Peidong. Comrade Fang Meng'ao had commandeered a military plane. According to how our underground operations are supposed to be carried out, I thought, given the suddenness of the situation, the unexpectedness of it, well, I felt urgent measures were in order."

Liuyun stared at Zhang, and then a stern smile appeared on his face. "All right. Tell me, what urgent measures have you taken? And sit down."

Despite the instruction, Zhang Yueyin remained standing.

Qi Mutang, who had initially taken the seat next to Zhang Yueyin and had been watching him as he explained, now turned to Liuyun. "Comrade, I would suggest you pass on the direct orders from the central leadership."

Liuyun caught the meaning in Qi Mutang's eyes and then turned back to Zhang. "Would you agree with this suggestion?"

"Please, Comrade Liuyun, your orders."

"Then sit."

Reluctantly, Zhang Yueyin lowered himself down onto the chair.

"First, I shall raise a question. We all already know the Kuomintang has a secret operation in the works here in Peking, their so-called Operation Peacocks Flying Southeast. But does anyone know why it's called this? You're a learned fellow, aren't you Comrade Zhang. I remember it was your suggestion that allowed Comrade Yan Chunming to break their code. Jiao Zhongqing is none other than Comrade Fang Meng'ao, and Liu Lanzhi is Liang Jinglun. At the moment, the Kuomintang is holding Fang Meng'ao for his actions with the transport plane. As for Liang Jinglun, he's fallen under suspicion and a fair share of jealousy, because of the internal conflict and contradictions within the Kuomintang. Analyse the situation, then. Do you think the 'peacocks' will be able to fly?"

As before, the criticism held no small amount of irony and satire, only adding to the awkwardness of the situation and the heaviness of the mood.

Zhang Yueyin's trust in the character of the party, his firm belief in it, allowed him to answer earnestly: "In our previous meeting, the central leadership already issued instructions with regard to the Kuomintang's Peacocks Flying Southeast operation. They made it clear that the plan is important to Chiang Kai-shek as its aim is to safeguard military supplies for Fu Zuoyi's men in the north. Fang Meng'ao and Liang Jinglun were put in place by Chiang Ching-kuo to actually implement the plan, they're both key cogs. Now, if Fang Meng'ao leaves Peking, and if the internal strife in the Kuomintang makes Liang Jinglun's position untenable, then they'll have no other choice but to put someone else in charge of the operation."

"Excellent analysis, quite astute." Liuyun's attitude had noticeably warmed. "But let's carry things a little further. Do you think the central leadership will agree with Fang Meng'ao leaving Peking – leaving China altogether – or do you believe they'd rather have him stay?"

Zhang Yueyin thought this over for a moment. "Comrade Xie Peidong hopes Comrade Fang will be allowed to leave China."

"But in that case, do you believe the central leadership will agree with Comrade Xie's opinion on the matter?"

At that moment, Zhang Yueyin came to realise one crucial aspect of their entire conversation: "I believe they would agree."

"And why do you think this?"

"Deputy Chair Zhou has complete faith in Xie Peidong, and so does the central leadership. Since Comrade Xie has acted as he has, there must be a reason for it. There has to be certain logic behind what he's done."

Liuyun smiled. "I'm glad you've said this. Allow me to pass along the formal orders of the central leadership, a new article in the party's code of conduct. But this is restricted information. Only the three of you know."

The three men replied in unison: "Understood."

Liuyun continued: "What's the deal with these peacocks flying southeast? Who *is* the peacock? Where is the destination? And what about flying south, where would it end up?"

The three men held their breaths and stared at Liuyun.

"Well let me explain. The so-called 'peacock' is Fu Zuoyi. Fu has more than five hundred thousand men stationed in the north. This large force, if it moves eastward can be in the northeast quicker than a bird flies. There, it can join up with the men under Wei Lihuang's command and launch a two-pronged attack on our field army. If they head south, they can be on the central plains in no time, or in Shandong, or Xuzhou in order to join up with the Kuomintang's main forces and attack more of our field armies, either the ones on the central plains or in and around Shandong. But, and this is important, this 'peacock' is not one of Chiang Kai-shek's men. He's a Shanxi man. If Chiang thought to have him fly eastward or southward, then he had to train him well. To put things bluntly, Fu Zuoyi's logistical needs, his supply needs, the Kuomintang must make sure these are met… at all costs, too, I should say, no matter what. But, and again this is important, to ensure that they need their American assistance. This is the reason why Comrade Fang Meng'ao and Liang Jinglun were put in charge of the operation in the first place. He Qicang can lobby the American ambassador, Mr Stuart, to make sure the Americans pay what they need. Fang Buting can see to the Central Bank allocating the funds. The two Chiangs, father and son, their plans are coming to a head. Think of what Comrade Zhang just said. Comrade Xie must have a reason for supporting Fang Meng'ao's departure from China. So, now that I've told you all of this, do understand what that reason is?"

Zhang Yueyin was the first to speak: "To prevent Fu Zuoyi's

forces from getting their necessary supplies, Operation Peacocks Flying Southeast must be impeded, blocked."

"So is that Xie's reason? Comrade Qi Mutang, you've just come from Xibaipo. Discuss, if you will, your understanding of the instructions the central leadership has given."

"All right." Qi Mutang raised himself from his chair.

"There's no need to stand. Sit, please."

"If you insist." Qi returned to his seat and continued: "Their aim, their hope, is that the Kuomintang will be able to safeguard Fu Zuoyi's supply needs."

"Pass on the chairman's exact words if you will," Liuyun interjected.

"Yes. To quote the chairman: 'Why do birds fly? They fly because they're hungry, they're looking for something to eat. How can you stop a bird from flying? That's easy. If you feed it plenty, you'll make it lazy. In fact, the best thing to do is make it fat. Then, even if it wanted to fly, it wouldn't be able to.'"

"Let's not beat around the bush any longer, but rather relay directly Deputy Zhou's orders. There are four points in total. The first is that the party is in agreement with Mr Fang. Thus, Comrade Fang Meng'ao is permitted to leave China. Two, if Chiang Chingkuo persists in wanting to use Fang Meng'ao and Laing Jinglun to carry out his Operation Peacocks Flying Southeast, if he won't agree to Comrade Meng'ao leaving the country, then we are not to interfere, nor do anything that might hinder his plans. Third, orders must be conveyed to Comrade Xie Peidong to cease immediately any and all underground activities. His main task, his only task, is to stay safe. Fourth, the party consents to Comrades He Xiaoyu and Fang Meng'ao marrying. From here on, party orders will be passed to Comrade Fang Meng'ao via Comrade He Xiaoyu. Comrade Fan Yinong?"

"I'm here."

"Comrade Fan, if you will, relay to us what you have learned today, how the situation has changed, rather unexpectedly, and, finally, speculate on how this change impacts Deputy Zhou's instructions?"

"Yes…"

Liuyun looked at Fan. "Go ahead then, explain. But be brief."

"Understood. The changed situation relates to He Qicang, who, this evening, telephoned Ambassador Stuart to ask him to request a meeting with Chiang Kai-shek. Not long after, Chiang made contact with Fu Zuoyi who, in turn, lied about what happened earlier in the day regarding Captain Fang's commandeering of the airplane. In short, he said Fang was acting on his orders, that he didn't take the plane on his own authority and that he hasn't violated the military code of conduct. Consequently, at sunrise, the order to arrest Captain Fang will be rescinded, and he will return to duty as captain of the special Air Force detachment in Peking under the command of the Kuomintang."

Fan's words were noticeably cautious, and longwinded. But, given his age and position, this was not entirely unexpected. Liuyun laughed a little. "Could you be a little more concise?"

"Understood." Fan paused a moment, then continued: "The central leadership's analysis of these new developments is as wise as it is brilliant. The 'peacock' in question is undoubtedly Fu Zuoyi, as was mentioned a moment ago, and not Comrade Fang Meng'ao, nor, naturally enough, Liang Jinglun. He Qicang's efforts to get Stuart to appeal for Fang Meng'ao's release have allowed the Nanking Kuomintang government to seize the opportunity to make changes to their plans. Initially, Mr He did not agree, but, afterwards, in order to protect both Fang Meng'ao and his student Liang Jinglun…"

"Let me jump in here." Liuyun's patience at Fan's long-windedness had run out. "The Kuomintang have hastily organised a committee led by Wang Yunwu to lobby the Americans for even more aid. To see this succeed, they've asked for He Qicang to travel to the US to sell the idea in person. Mr He has agreed, but on one condition, that Liang Jinglun accompanies him as his assistant. Nanking consented. As they say, 'beat the dog to tame the lion'. It proves Liang Jinglun is no longer of any use to Chiang Ching-kuo. We assume, also, that once Liang is off to America, he'll never return." At this point, Liuyun paused and turned towards Fan. "Is this what you were getting at?"

Fan had a smile on his face, as always seemed to be the case. "Yes, Comrade Liuyun, you've summarised the salient points."

"Before too long, Comrade He Xiaoyu will be all alone on

Yenching campus. You will be her sole contact. You'll also be responsible for her safety. The orders I've just told you, all four points, you're to relay them to Comrade He, and tell her to pass them along to Comrade Fang Meng'ao. Make sure you emphasise that he must comply with whatever the Kuomintang orders him to do. He's to transport whatever they tell him to transport. We must make the 'peacock' as fat as possible."

"Understood."

Liuyun turned once more to Zhang Yueyin. "Comrade Yueyin, you're responsible for making contact with Comrade Xie Peidong."

"Understood."

Liuyun pulled out a pack of cigarettes. "These are a gift from Deputy Zhou to Comrade Xie," he said. "The third cigarette in the first row is not a smoke at all, but rather a letter. Fetch Young Li and tell him to give the cigarettes to Xie and no one else."

Zhang Yueyin accepted the pack of cigarettes with both hands. "May I also write a letter and get Li to pass it on to Comrade Xie as well? I would like to apologise."

Liuyun waved his hand to say 'no'. "Take care of Comrade Xie. That's the best way to make up for your mistake."

"Understood, comrade."

CHAPTER 14

Would his impending trip to the United States be like before? Would he be able to get even more aid from the Americans? Would his old, weary body stand up to the difficulties that lay ahead? Would he be able to ultimately return to his home, return to Yenching University? It was far, far too difficult for him to say. He Qicang was sitting in front of the telephone but slowly turned his eyes towards the nearby bed and his daughter standing beside it. His oversized leather case lay sprawled out on top of the bed. He'd bought it a lifetime ago when he had been in the US as an overseas student. The years seemed to be etched into its leather, it had seen so much, endured so much. He Xiaoyu was busy packing his clothes, all folded into neat piles. She lifted them off the bed sheets and placed them carefully inside the leather case. Tears rolled down her cheeks and fell in tiny droplets onto his immaculately clean, if old, shirts and jackets. He watched as she paused, and then reached for a handkerchief to wipe her face. A second later, he was standing just behind her.

"I'll be gone for a month, two at the most."

"Uh-huh." He Xiaoyu did her best to compose herself and then continued to pack his belongings. "The Kuomintang government has already sent so many officials to the United States to request more aid. Have they not sent enough that they have to drag you into this? Do you feel obligated to help, is that it?"

"What do you mean 'obligation'? I helped write the report on the need for currency reforms, so I suppose you could say that I added fuel to the fire. Right now, Nanking is discussing this very matter with your Uncle Stuart, they're fleshing out possible terms. They've also agreed not to pursue an investigation into Fang Meng'ao. That was one of the conditions, and besides, I long thought about a return trip to the US... a chance to see old friends and classmates. This is more a holiday than anything else."

He Xiaoyu looked at her father intently. "Dad, tell me the truth, are you really taking Liang Jinglun with you so that he can be your assistant? Or is there something else to it?"

"Why are you asking such a question?"

"I don't know. I just feel that the two of you... that you're hiding something from the rest of us. Are you trying to protect him from something?"

"I'm protecting Meng'ao. If Jinglun needed my help and protection, do you think I should give it?"

He Xiaoyu lowered her head and went back to packing his clothes. She answered, but her voice was uncertain: "I never said you shouldn't."

"When morning comes, I want you to go and fetch Meng'ao. We've got an open ticket to Nanking in any case. And you're nearly finished packing what I need. Besides which, he needs the help more than I do, you know. He's never had a person love him so dearly..."

He Xiaoyu placed his last shirt into the suitcase. "Sure, Dad, I will."

He Xiaoyu walked into Liang Jinglun's bedroom, intending to help him pack as well before Liang stopped her before she could begin. "I've finished already."

He Xiaoyu stopped in front of his table, her hand suspended in midair above his case. She turned to Liang and said: "Is there something in there you'd rather I didn't see?"

Liang was not expecting such a question but laughed nonetheless, if a little bitterly. "You're welcome to check and make sure I've got everything."

"I could, but I'd rather not look through someone else's personal belongings."

"I wouldn't pack private things in my suitcase. Come on, give me a hand and have a look through."

He Xiaoyu opened the suitcase and her eyes immediately fell on it: there, on top of his clothes, was a picture frame. Her father was standing in the middle. She was on one side, Liang Jinglun on the other. She felt a lump form in her throat, and she tried to swallow it down. Tears formed in her eyes and it took her a moment longer to calm the swirl of emotions she was feeling. Finally, she whispered: "Are you not coming back?"

"I'll be coming back with your father, of course."

"And if he doesn't?"

"I'm sure you know this, but I'll say it anyway. Your father needs someone to look after him."

"And what about the New China? You can't have forgotten what you told me at your precious Foreign Languages Bookstore, can you?"

Liang Jinglun was silent for more than a moment or two before he finally answered: "I think... I said so much to you in that bookstore."

"You described, in detail, what the New China would be. Thinking of what you said now, it was as though you were reciting something you had memorised, who you were then and who you are now. Aren't they the same person?"

"I've only ever been one person. I've never had the chance to be anyone else."

"Everyone gets the chance to choose."

"I've not chosen, I've not had the chance."

"I don't think I'd like to hear you wax philosophical right now." He Xiaoyu narrowed her eyes. "You're leaving in the morning. I think I'd rather like to hear you recite those same words you told me then, when we were at the bookstore. Can you?"

Liang Jinglun sighed deeply. "If that's what you'd like to hear, then that's what you shall."

He Xiaoyu closed her eyes.

"What will the New China be like?" Liang Jinglun looked out of the window, his voice getting louder the more he spoke: "It is like a ship far out at sea whose masthead can already be seen from shore. It is like the morning sun whose shimmering rays are visible from a high mountain top. It is like a child about to be born, moving restlessly in its mother's womb.'"

Liang's passion subsided. He Xiaoyu could hear hidden under the surface the lump growing in his throat. She opened her eyes and saw the back of his long gown just as it had been long ago. She walked up to him and tried to smooth out some of the fine wrinkles. "Take care of Father when you go. Be good company for him, and do the same when you come back."

Liang Jinglun turned around slowly. He made no attempt to hide the tears in his eyes. At the same time, he smiled, if only a little. "Oh my, I've just remembered, I've not offered my congratulations to you and Meng'ao. May I at least wish you good fortune?"

He Xiaoyu looked deeply into Liang's face but did not answer.

Liang switched to English: "God bless you and yours, and surround you evermore with his blessing."

"And to you as well."

The sun had risen above Nanyuan airbase, but it seemed to be hesitant, unsure whether it wished to be seen. Two Curtiss C-46s were parked near the runway, their metal spines washed in the sun's cautious, scarlet glow. Below the first plane, ten pilots raised their hands to salute. Ten more did the same below the second C-46.

He Xiaoyu stood beside the runaway, a bouquet of wild flowers in her hand, her eyes purposefully avoiding Fang Meng'ao.

In response to his men, Fang Meng'ao saluted in textbook fashion. Indeed, it seemed as though he had been charged with reviewing the troops, so perfect was his salutation.

A little further past the runway, Wang Kejun kept company with Fang Buting, Cheng Xiaoyun, and, perhaps surprisingly, Xie Peidong. Watching his son in full military attire, watching He Xiaoyu holding the bouquet, Fang Buting couldn't help but smile at the vicissitudes of life and its innate changeability. Cheng Xiaoyun smiled as well, albeit carefully; after all, Xie was standing closest to her.

Fang Meng'ao took He Xiaoyu's arm in his, and together they

walked towards the transport plane, and together they climbed into the cabin. Quickly after, Fang's men turned and boarded the aircraft as well, ten in each one. The cabin door was closed. The great propellers on each plane slowly came to life, the hum of their engines growing louder. The first transport began to taxi down the runway. The second did the same. Moments later, both C-46s were in the air, angling ever upwards. The sun finally broke through the clouds, bathing both aircraft and causing them to sparkle under its radiance.

Below, Fang Buting, Cheng Xiaoyun and Xie Peidong welcomed the sunlight and trained their eyes on the fast-receding planes. Both C-46s then circled and tipped their wings as though saying goodbye. Moments later they were gone, hidden behind the brilliance of the sun.

―――

Suddenly, the sun in the sky transformed into a ball of fire. The roar of the airplane engines became the roar of cannons.

On the vast map of China, artillery barrages spanned all across the northeast along the Peining line, from Changli in northeastern Hebei to Beidaihe on Bohai Bay; from Ningyuan to Yi County, all throughout Liaoning province; indeed, Jinzhou and its surrounding areas were the sight of continuous battles, explosions loud enough to make the heavens tremble. On 12 September 1948, the PLA's Northeast Field Army, seven hundred thousand stalwart men, launched the Liaoning campaign that saw the city of Jinzhou surrounded between 16 and 24 September, a prelude to the opening of the third theatre and the final battle between the Kuomintang and the CPC.

Hot on the heels of this campaign in the northeast, the northwestern parts of the country in and around Hohhot and the southern parts of Chahar province also erupted in open warfare. In the regions surrounding Ulanqab, Horinger and Hohhot itself, battles raged, again with explosions loud enough to make heaven shake. Before long, the barrage of artillery reached Peking and its neighbouring counties of Miyun, Huairou, and stretching down to Sanhe in Hebei. From 23 to 27 September, the PLA's Northern

Field Army, in their efforts to join up with forces in the Liaoning campaign, stretched their battle lines west, encircling Hohhot and finally cutting the railway line between Peking and Chengde. As a result, Fu Zuoyi's substantial military force was pinned down in the north, and unable to assist those Kuomintang forces in the northeast.

In the skies above Nanyuan airbase, the two transport aircraft had taken to the air and disappeared into the distance. Now they had returned and begun their descent.

On the ground, Fang Meng'ao's men hurried to the C-46 transport. Moments later, the plane was in the air again.

Once the C-46s landed, Fang and his men disembarked.

Out beyond the fence that encircled the airbase, massive tyres churned, ten in total, conveying canopied trucks and men. The men, having already disembarked, climbed aboard the transports. Fang Meng'ao sat behind the wheel of the first truck, Guo Jinyang beside him. Chen Changwu was in the driver's seat of the second vehicle, Shao Yuangang sitting next to him. The third truck was similarly manned, the fourth and so on. The sentry pole was raised and the motorcade hurtled past.

8 October 1948, on special orders to maintain the fighting readiness of Fu Zuoyi's Northern Army, Captain Fang Meng'ao and his men conveyed goods and supplies from Tianjin to Peking...

The Peking civilian storage loomed large in front of them as the motorcade pulled into the street that ran along the western side of it. Fang Meng'ao slammed on the brakes, bringing the first vehicle of their convoy to a sudden stop. The trucks following behind did the same.

There in front of the storage gate was a large group of civilians, seated on the road, blocking their path. There were men, women, seniors and children. Immediately in front of the gate were iron barriers, gendarmerie, police and young soldiers. There was no ruckus, nor did anyone say a word on either side.

Fang Meng'ao looked at the mass of people, then narrowed his eyes in surprise. There among the crowd was Ye Biyu. To her right was Boqin, and to her left Pingyang. He turned the key in the ignition and shut off the truck's engine. His hand trembled as he did so.

Fang climbed down. Seconds later, Chen Changwu walked up beside him. Fang did not move or speak, so it was up to Chen to ask what was wrong. "Captain, how are we going to get the convoy through?"

"Tell the men to stay in their vehicles."

"Yes sir." Chen turned around and strode back over towards the trucks.

Fang Meng'ao walked into the throng of people. So tightly pack was the crowd that he couldn't help but feel as though he were walking on people. Cold, hard stares greeted him as he made his way through. Many were holding the new Kuomintang currency in their hands, despite what little help it offered. Nearer the gate, Fang's eyes fell upon Commander Li, who raised his hand, preparing to salute. Fang Meng'ao's eyes, however, told him to stop, and Li let his hand fall back softly to his side. Fang half walked, half stumbled past a few more people until he reached Cui Zhongshi's widow. He looked down and met Ye Biyu's stare.

Pingyang leaned into her mother's breast, while Boqin stood up. "Uncle Fang…" His voice was soft, cautious.

Fang Meng'ao leaned down beside the boy's mother, grasping his hand as he did so, and then directing his gaze towards Ye Biyu. "Mrs Cui, why are you here? What's going on? What's the matter?"

Cui's widow looked around, then answered in little more than a whisper: "Early this morning, not a single shop was selling any groceries…"

"But why would that make you come here? What are you hoping to accomplish?"

"There were rumours that all the city's rations had been moved here, so we came along with everyone else. I never thought there'd be so many. Tell me, will we be able to buy something to eat here?"

Before he could stop them, tears filled Fang Meng'ao's eyes and rolled down his face. "Why didn't you call on Mr Fang or Mr Xie?"

"I saw the news in the papers. The pair of them already exchanged their valuables for this… this paper money. You know as well as I do it's the only legal tender. Trying to buy anything with gold or silver, or any other currency is against the law. I didn't want to bother them."

Fang pulled the young boy a little closer, held him a little tighter and then directed his attention towards the storage gate. Despite the glare of the sun, Fang was surprised by the hazy image of a man pacing back and forth in front of the door, a look of consternation on his face. He felt, too, a sense of astonishment for the man seemed to be none other than Ma Hanshan! Fang closed his eyes, but then from behind him he thought he heard Ma's voice telling him about Deputy Director Cui's grave, about a marker on the hill engraved with the words 'thirty-seventh year of the reign of Kangxi', and about how, underneath the marker, not buried very deep there were a dozen or so bars of gold, the only valuables his family had left. Fang remembered then, how Ma wanted him to give those bars to Ye Biyu, when the time was right, to help raise the two kids.

"Captain Fang." Ye Biyu's voice brought him out of his trance. "Go on, finish the work you have to do. If we can't buy anything to eat, we'll get going in a little bit."

Fang Meng'ao turned away and wiped the tears from his face. Then he smiled at Boqin and Pingyang. "Go on home with your mum. I'll call later with the food you need."

"Uncle, we've moved you know…"

"Don't talk nonsense, Boqin!" His mum's eyes brooked no protest from him.

Boqin didn't dare say another word. But what he had started to say was enough for Fang Meng'ao to suddenly turn back towards Ye Biyu. "When did you move?"

An abrupt disturbance rolled through the crowd. An enormous group of students emerged on both sides to stand at the mouth of the road.

Fang Meng'ao rose to his feet almost instantly.

The students to the east now formed a line and marched forward. The students to the west did the same. The people who had been sitting on the ground quietly began to stand up, and before long nearly everyone was on their feet. Underneath the sound of the rising commotion, Fang Meng'ao's sensitive ears picked up another, far more ominous sound: the ordered stomp of uniformed men.

"You must get out of here, now!" Fang lifted Ye Biyu to her feet, his eyes darting around for an escape route.

The gendarmerie and the police raised their weapons and began to rush towards the students who had emerged to the west and to the east. Only the young soldiers remained at the gate; not one had unsheathed his rifle.

Suddenly, Zeng Keda appeared in the doorway to the storage. As if fated, his eyes fell on Fang Meng'ao. Fang glanced back at his truck and then began to move towards the gate. As he drew close, he could see the sign now designating the storage as the Peking Administrative Office for the Tianjin Economic Area. Its original civilian designation was nowhere to be seen.

Zeng Keda was the first to walk into the storage office, with Fang Meng'ao following close behind. Before, in what seemed like a different time, the office had belonged to Ma Hanshan. Now it belonged to Zeng Keda, if only on a temporary, ad hoc basis.

Outside, on the other side of the gates, the sound of people shouting slogans reached them. The students were the first to start the chant: "The people want food!" They were soon followed by the rest of the crowd: "The people want food!"

Zeng Keda closed the office door gently.

"We want to buy provisions!"

"We want to buy provisions!"

Zeng Keda walked over to the window that opened onto the storage grounds and closed that, too.

"Oppose the rich who stockpile and hoard!"

"Oppose the rich who stockpile and hoard!"

Once he'd closed the window, Zeng Keda hesitated in front of it, leaving Fang Meng'ao to simply stare at his back. "Are you thinking about ordering them to fire?"

"I don't give the orders here. Besides, no one would dare to shoot."

Fang Meng'ao forced himself to look away. He grabbed a chair but didn't sit down. "The new currency's been issued. Why can't they buy the food and provisions they need?"

"There was looting, the shops in Peking have been cleared out."

"Is it that there's really no food left, or that those who have it are refusing to sell?"

"It's a little of both, I guess. There's not much left, and what there is, they aren't selling."

"Why aren't you trying to do something about this?"

"Well, the stockpiles are in Tianjin, which means there's nothing you or I can do about them."

"Isn't Zhang Lisheng in Tianjin? Can't he sort this out?"

"Today, you and your men made three trips. You transported sixty-seven tonnes of rations, all of which was what Inspector Zhang and his men confiscated yesterday."

Fang Meng'ao narrowed his eyes. "Are you trying to tell me that despite all of the cargo my men and I brought into Peking today, the city's inhabitants, a million-plus men, women and children, still can't buy anything to eat?"

"Yes."

Fang Meng'ao looked out the window and at the grain storage tower, and then he turned back to Zeng Keda. "So what are you planning to do with the grain stored here? There's got to be tens of thousands of tonnes. Will you be selling it to the people outside?"

Zeng Keda laughed bitterly. "You know as well as I do that the grain stored here is earmarked for the soldiers in the north, on special orders."

"Outside, the city's residents, the university students, they're surrounding my convoy. Why the hell did you ask me to come in here? What are you planning?"

A flash of something sparkled in Zeng's eyes. "I want you... you're going to sell the stuff you're carrying to those people out there!"

Fang Meng'ao was blown over by what Zeng said. It was completely unexpected, and he couldn't help but look the man over, wondering if he had ulterior motives.

Unbothered by Fang's reaction, Zeng continued: "I know what you're thinking. First, the rations, the grain, the food, all of it on those ten trucks outside... well, let me make things clear. Me giving orders to sell it to the city's residents has nothing to do with you. It's my responsibility, so you needn't think twice about it. Second, you know that selling the stuff will do little to alleviate the problem the city's inhabitants are facing. It certainly won't be enough to feed the millions who are going without right now. Then why am I doing it? Well, I'll tell you that later. Come on, let's go."

"I think I'd rather hear the explanation now, if you don't mind." Fang Meng'ao blocked the door with his arm and stared at Zeng Keda. "Tell me, and I'll help you."

Zeng Keda walked over to the window and pushed it open. The sounds of the students and people shouting slogans bombarded them. Zeng called out for his assistant: "Wang!"

As so many times before, the man appeared in mere seconds.

"Come here a little closer so I don't have to speak so loudly. Use the name of this office, find a bullhorn, and then tell the people outside the gates to settle themselves down, and to queue up to get ready to purchase the food they've been shouting about."

"Inspector..." said a surprised Wang.

"Go on, boy, do as I told you!"

"Sir, yes sir!"

Zeng Kede closed the window again and turned to face Fang Meng'ao. "When did we come to Peking? Do you remember?"

"It was the sixth of July."

"And what's today's date?"

Fang Meng'ao glanced at a calendar that was hanging near the window. To his own surprise, he realised it was already 8 October. Fang looked back to Zeng Keda but he didn't answer.

"It's the eighth of October. We've been in Peking for three months and two days. The five of us in our little band went to the Ministry of Defence to begin our investigations. We looked into the activities of the civilian government in Peking and we investigated the dealings of the bank. We killed a few Communists whom money wouldn't corrupt, and we murdered a number of students who didn't do anything wrong. They weren't even Communists. Then our little band was broken up, dissolved. Xu Tieying, once he was finished killing who he wanted, left, too. We certainly didn't root out all of the corruption. All we did was arrest Ma Hanshan, who was executed ten days ago in Nanking by firing squad. So, what the hell have we accomplished?"

Zeng paused and a look of bewilderment passed over his face. Then he continued: "The only thing we succeeded in doing, I guess, is pushing forward the currency reform plans. And what's been the result? Before two months have passed, markets and grocery stores in Peking, Tianjin, Chungking, Canton, and even in Shanghai, of all places, have closed one after the other. Department stores, even shops selling non-staple foods, all of them, their shelves are empty. And the people? They exchanged all their valuables for the new money, even their few remaining silver coins earmarked to buy their coffins, and for what? There's no food to purchase, nor is there even any coal to light their stoves, dammit all. They can't even use their *jinyuanquan* to buy a bar of soap since there isn't any! Prohibiting people to use gold, silver and foreign currencies only enabled those more unsavoury elements in Shanghai to use their ill-gotten monies to buy and hoard American goods. And they did this out in the open, too, all so they could flood the black market and make a bloody fortune for themselves! Shit, they even sailed a six-thousand-tonne cargo ship back and forth between Shanghai and Wuhan selling grain to people along the way, grain that should have been in the hands of the government, instead of in the hands of criminals who did nothing other than encourage panic buying! It's like no one gives a shit, no one is managing the store… nothing! Captain Fang, I arrested you, interrogated you. I also worked with you here in Peking. You've seen everything I've done, tried to do. It's all been to further Chiang Ching-kuo's efforts to win back the popular sentiment of the people from the CPC. Today, this might be our last chance to win back their hearts! I've played all my cards. I've placed my bets on Chiang Ching-kuo arresting that man in Shanghai. Everything's riding on it!"

"That man?"

"Kung Ling-kan!"

"What have you gambled?"

"Five days ago Chiang Ching-kuo halted all transactions of Kung's Yangtze Construction Company, but no other business out of the so many that are in Shanghai dared to move in on its holdings, all because that bastard Kung was still driving around

Shanghai in his fancy car, essentially ignoring the Kuomintang's actions and thus demonstrating his own power. I'm walking through that gate out there. I'm going to use my authority to make sure those ten trucks, the foodstuffs they're carrying, I'm going to see that the people have the chance to use their new currency to good effect, dammit! Didn't you just ask me why I was going to do this? Well, now I've told you."

Again there was that sparkle in Zeng Keda's eyes, but this time, Fang's eyes glimmered, too.

"The president is coming to Peking today. He's called a meeting. It'll take place in the Northern Command base. My selling of the grain has been my means to remonstrate the president! If he chooses to have me arrested, I'll know where he stands. If, however, he agrees with his own son, then that bastard Kung Ling-kan will be the one in chains!"

"What do you need me to do?"

"I've told you already, what I'm doing today has nothing to do with you. I only called you inside so that I could explain. Regardless of your loyalties, from now on I want you to be open with me. I want you to believe me when I say that there are those of us in the Kuomintang who truly wish to serve the people, and we'll fight whatever old tigers get in our way."

Zeng Keda made towards the door, and this time, Fang Meng'ao stepped aside to let him open it. Zeng pulled the handle, but then stopped abruptly and turned towards Fang. "Can I ask you about something completely unrelated... will you be willing to answer me?"

"Sure, go ahead."

"What's closer, the moon or Nanking?"

"Right now, I'm closest to you."

Zeng Keda smiled and marched outside, a new spring in his step. Fang Meng'ao followed right behind.

―――

Outside Fang Buting's home, a single gendarme jeep came to a screeching halt. Right behind it, two more jeeps, both sporting military police markings, stopped. Sun Chaozhong pushed open the door and leapt down. There were now two bars and two stars on the epaulettes of his uniform. He'd been promoted to deputy head of the Investigative Services.

"Emergency measures have been enacted!" Sun barked.

Helmeted soldiers, each bearing rifles, climbed out of the first vehicle and then marched towards the mouth of the hutong. More armed soldiers climbed out of the second and third jeeps and positioned themselves in the smaller street. It took only minutes for the hutong and the street leading to Fang Buting's home to be filled with armed men.

Fang Buting was now under house arrest!

Seconds after their deployment, another official vehicle appeared. After coming to a stop alongside Sun Chaozhong's, Fang Mengwei jumped out. He walked over to Sun who greeted him without hesitation: "Deputy Chief Fang…"

"That's Deputy Section Chief now."

Sun Chaozhong was surprised at this revelation, but only for a second. "Yes sir, Deputy Section Chief…"

"Are you here, at my home, to carry out an arrest?"

"I don't know, sir."

"Are you to make a search then, of my home, confiscate possessions?"

"I don't know that either, sir."

"Since you seem to not know anything, why the hell have you brought soldiers here with you?" Fang Mengwei's tone betrayed his growing frustration.

"I'm simply following orders, sir, and the order was to surround Mr Fang Buting's home."

Colour drained from Fang Mengwei's face. He looked down the street and to the mouth of the hutong, his eyes scanning the soldiers that stood alongside the neighbourhood walls. "Have I been dismissed from my position?" asked Fang Mengwei, now staring at Sun Chaozhong.

"I've not received that order, sir."

"All right then," Fang said as he stepped past Sun and went towards his father's home. As he walked, each soldier shifted to attention, their heels clicked and their hands rose to salute.

Fang Mengwei's heart skipped a beat as soon as he entered his father's sitting room. Indeed, he was so surprised he could only stand in the doorway. His eyes fell first on his uncle, who had changed out of his somewhat uncomfortable Zhongshan suit, and was now descending the stairs, a leather case in his hand. He then noticed his father, who had removed his Western suit and was reclining on the living room sofa. Seconds later, Xie Peidong was standing next to the sofa, his luggage placed on the floor. Fang Mengwei hesitated a little longer, but then regained his composure and moved slowly into the room, his eyes focused on his uncle.

Xie was staring at him, too, and now offered a thin smile. "Nothing's going on."

Fang had not asked any questions and had no idea what his uncle meant. All he could do was look to his father in the hope of seeing some explanation on his face.

Fang Buting looked at his wristwatch, turned to Xie and said: "The game's coming to an end. Let's finish things."

"I fear we won't be able to," said Xie, shifting his attention to the small tea table in front of Fang.

Fang Mengwei finally noticed the Go board on the table.

"We'll call it quits after the next few moves, yes?"

Xie Peidong moved a little closer and sat down opposite Fang Buting. The Go board lay between them.

Fang Mengwei could only stand and watch the two older men, unsure of what to say or do. A sound from the kitchen drew his attention in that direction, and he saw Cheng Xiaoyun emerge from the small stairwell that was tucked into the rear of the room. Fang Mengwei stared unblinkingly at his stepmother. He noticed the puzzled look on her face, the same one he was wearing. Xiaoyun only nodded in response.

Finally, Mengwei spoke to his father: "Dad, tell me, what's going on?" His voice trembled.

Despite holding a stone in his hand, Fang Buting glanced at his son: "Didn't the men outside tell you?"

Fang Mengwei did not respond.

"Well, if they didn't tell you, you needn't ask again."

Fang Mengwei rushed over to the table and their Go board: "Meng'ao is busy selling off the foodstuffs he brought from Tianjin, and they're outside to arrest Uncle Xie. Am I right?"

499

It was now Cheng Xiaoyun's turn to tremble and rush over to the men. She looked first to Xie Peidong, then to her husband.

Fang Buting tossed the stone onto the board. "In less than two months, I managed to arrange fifty thousand tonnes of provisions for Fu Zuoyi and his men, enough food for six months for the two hundred thousand men he has in Peking. They sure as hell will arrest people for selling those ten trucks-worth of supplies!"

"I don't think the Kuomintang has any secrets left," said Xie Peidong. "And I don't think we should help them keep secret whatever is left either. Go on, tell them right away."

"If we can't finish the game properly, there's no point continuing." Fang Buting stood up from the sofa. "Chiang Kai-shek has arrived. He's chairing a meeting up north. He's also informed us he wants to pay a visit to the treasury."

Fang Mengwei's eyes opened wide in surprise. "Is Uncle going, too?"

"Your uncle handles the bank's accounts, and I've no idea the scale of cash reserves held in the treasury. Your uncle knows much more than me. They still suspect him of being a Communist, don't they? Then I say let's allow this suspected Communist to tell Chiang Kai-shek in person how much gold, silver and foreign currency we were able to raise for him in less than two months."

Fang Mengwei relaxed. He looked at Cheng Xiaoyun, and saw the worry drain from her face, too. His eyes fell on the leather case still lying on the floor.

Before anyone said anything further, the doorbell rang.

"Wang Kejun's here." Fang Buting walked over to the door. Xie Peidong followed him, holding the leather case. Fang Mengwei rushed over to give him a hand.

Fang Mengwei's father stopped him before he could take hold of the leather case. "Let your uncle carry it. These blasted accounts... dirty money. For months I've been under investigation... my own son leading it... and all because of orders from *his* son. Our lives have been turned upside down. Today, I'm giving it all back to *his* old man. Let's let them sort this morass out!"

Military police had already been deployed around the Peking treasury. They lined both sides of the roads approaching the building, each helmeted, each holding a rifle, each decked out in long leather boots.

Wang Kejun was seated next to the driver in front. He leaned over a little and ordered in a low voice: "Reduce speed now!"

In the rear, Fang Buting's eyes were trained on the scene through the window. A bluish glare shone off the soldiers' helmets and off their rifles as well. Fang Buting turned away and looked at Xie Peidong seated next to him. Fang saw the leather case on his friend's lap, and then looked up to see Xie staring at him.

The vehicle slowed to a stop. Both men shifted. They were already outside the main gates to the treasury. An outstretched palm waved in front of the windscreen. The rank insignia on his uniform identified the man as a senior regimental officer from the Northern Command.

Wang Kejun stepped out of the jeep and saluted the man. "Secretary Wang here to report, sir. We ask permission to move inside, sir."

"I know," and he waved a hand at Wang Kejun.

At almost the same moment, two military police officers walked over to the jeep, each opening one of the rear doors. Fang Buting climbed out on the left. Xie Peidong, holding on to the leather case, climbed out on the right.

Wang Kejun was not permitted to drive his vehicle beyond the main gate, for inside the grounds of the treasury there were already two parked Buicks, as well as a medium-sized jeep. From the large sluice gates of the treasury to the high walls surrounding the structure, there were no military police, only soldiers wearing rough-hewn uniforms, Mauser pistols hung at their sides. They were Fu Zuoyi's personal guard.

The treasury guards were nowhere to be seen. Instead, there were eight strapping young men standing outside the steel doors that led into the main building. Each one wore a Zhongshan jacket, the Kuomintang emblem displayed prominently on the breast pocket.

Wang Kejun escorted Fang Buting and Xie Peidong in the direction of these men. When they got close, and without being prompted, Wang removed the pistol he had at his waist and handed it to one of the men, smiling as he did so. "This here is the governor of the Peking branch of the Central Bank, Mr Fang Buting, and this is his assistant, Mr Xie."

The man gave a perfunctory smile and then turned to Fang and Xie. "My pleasure in meeting both of you. If you'll wait here for a moment, I will ask the men to conduct a quick, routine inspection. I'm sure you understand."

Fang Buting raised his arms and opened both hands.

Xie Peidong put his leather case on the ground and did the same.

Two attendants walked over to them. They were professional and polite, and quickly patted the two men down.

The man who had greeted him never took his eyes off of the leather case.

Once he was finished being patted down, Xie lifted the keys out of his pocket, bent down and opened the lid so they could see what was inside. The man knelt down to inspect the contents. He flipped through the ledgers, felt around the edges of the case to make sure nothing was stuffed surreptitiously under the lining and then closed the lid. "Mr Fang, Mr Xie, you're free to proceed."

"There's something I'd like to ask, if I may?" Fang Buting asked the man in the Zhongshan suit.

"Please."

"How were the treasury gates opened?"

The man smiled again. "Your own Chairman Yu opened them for us. He has the keys, after all."

"Yes, of course, thank you."

The man gestured for them to enter. "Please, go on in."

Fang Buting was at the head of the line. Xie Peidong, his leather case in hand, came next. Wang Kejun was last.

———

Telegram machines clicked in rhythm like a great grandfather clock: tick, tock, tick, tock. No one in the Fuping County CPC detachment spoke. No one moved. The operators were all seated facing the wall, receiving transmissions, sending responses.

Enveloped in their own telegraphic-radioed worlds, they seemed disconnected from their immediate surroundings.

The only man standing was Liuyun. He was perched over the shoulder of the first operator, waiting anxiously for decoded messages to be passed to him. "Sir, I've got an urgent telegram from Peking!" said an operator.

Liuyun grabbed the message and in seconds a look of surprise washed over his face:

Zeng Keda and Fang Meng'ao have made sixty-seven tonnes of rations available to the residents of Peking for purchase <break> Chiang Kai-shek, Fu Zuoyi, Yu Hongjun are secretly inspecting the Peking branch treasury <break> Fang Buting and Xie Peidong are accompanying them <end transmission>

"Relay this information to the central leadership immediately!"
"Yes sir!"

In the recent past, the treasury had been essentially deserted, its shelves empty. Now, those very same shelves were weighed down with twenty-five-kilo bars of gold that glimmered and shone under the electric bulbs that flickered above.

Xie Peidong was the first to comment: "The count as of yesterday evening is 198,768 taels of gold, sir."

A distinctive Fenghua accented voice replied: "Excellent, yes, excellent indeed..."

Next to the shelves were specially made wooden boxes prepared by the Central Bank, each filled to capacity with silver dollars.

Again, Xie Peidong provided the total: "The count as of yesterday evening is 480,300,500 silver dollars."

"Excellent, excellent."

Next, there were purpose-built green tin boxes, each filled with silver ingots.

"As of yesterday evening, sir, we've got 800,000 taels."

"Excellent, excellent."

And then they were gone. The corridor that stretched down the length of the treasury was empty, as deserted as it was before. Chiang Kai-shek had left, and so too had Fu Zuoyi and Yu Hongjun. Outside the steel doors, under the dimmed lights, only Xie Peidong and Fang Buting remained.

But the Fenghua-accented voice lingered: "The nation's situation has come to a head. Its future will be decided soon. I leave it to you to stabilise things in the north and in Peking. You're responsible, also, for providing logistical support and supplies for Commander Fu's forces. No matter how financially strained the government might become, no matter the difficulties it faces, at least these cash reserves are here in Peking. They can be turned over to the people, to Commander Fu."

Gradually, the echo of the voice dissipated, leaving the treasury silent and still.

Fang Buting glanced down the corridor. "Peidong, what are your thoughts on that recent phone call?"

"What call are you talking about?"

"The call that came from Shanghai, from Madam Soong."

"No doubt it involves both their families, Kung's and Soong's. I reckon it's as you said earlier… it's time for father and son to sort out this mess."

"So, you think President Chiang is racing back to Shanghai? Where do you think he'll stand, on this side, or with his wife's family?"

"Didn't you hear what Commander Fu said?"

"What? What did he say?"

Xie Peidong cast his attention down the corridor towards his familiar office. "When President Chiang was leaving, Commander Fu didn't go with him, at least not right away. I actually heard him sigh, although I don't think he intended to actually do that out loud…"

"What sigh? What are you talking about?"

Xie Peidong hesitated a moment before saying: "You know the story of the Prince of Wales and the choice he made, don't you?"

"Did he really mention this?" Fang Buting couldn't disguise his growing confusion.

"I imagine we just didn't hear him."

The telegram machines continued to click nonstop; messages sent and transmissions received. Liuyun was still standing beside the first radio operator, watching as the man transcribed the message he had just received. His eyes flashed as the telegram was decoded:

Chiang Kai-shek answered a telephone call from Madam Soong <break> He immediately returned to Nanyuan airbase to board a plane bound for Shanghai <break> According to multiple sources, his urgent departure from Peking has to do with the emerging situation in Shanghai between Chiang Ching-kuo and Kung Ling-kan <break> Fu Zuoyi has apparently displayed exasperation at this turn of events <break> Chiang Kai-shek seems to be choosing to be Edward, Prince of Wales <break>

Liuyun slammed his hand down on the table, stunned by the report from Peking. He looked at the operator and said: "Relay immediately!"

"Sir, yes sir!"

It was past eight o'clock in the evening. The military police had stationed themselves at the mouth of the road that led east away from the Peking storage facility. They used the lights of their vehicles to illuminate the main gates. Another contingent of soldiers had taken up positions to the west of the storage facility. Their vehicle lights were also directed towards the main gates. Together, the military police and the special troops of the Fourth Corps had cut off the grounds immediately in front of the storage facility.

And there in front of those gates, Captain Fang had parked his truck. The crates his convoy had been responsible for were open and empty; everything had been sold.

The crowd, too, had mostly dispersed by this time.

Fortunately, there had been space enough for at least a thousand city residents to squeeze into the area around the main gates. They had queued up and waved their fresh *jinyuanquan* high in the air, desperate to use it to buy whatever food they could. The remainder of the masses had been cleared out already. The police and the soldiers had seen to that. They'd set up barriers, too, to make sure no one else got in or out.

Chen Changwu, Shao Yuangang, Guo Jinyang and the rest of Captain Fang's men stood calmly by their respective trucks. They'd seen the flailing arms, the new currency notes clutched tightly in anxious hands. Now they stood and stared at the police and soldiers.

To the east, in front of the military police barrier, a pair of dark, somewhat downtrodden, eyes watched them intently. The eyes belonged to none other than Sun Chaozhong. To the west, another set of eyes did the same. By contrast, the commander of the Fourth Corps had fury and rage on his face.

"Eh now, what's the matter with you? What's going on?" The voice had come from behind. When the commander turned to see who it was, he couldn't hide the shock on his face: Wang Puchen had come!

"Sir, Communists have incited the people to violence. Inspector Zeng and Captain Fang have sold off the food supplies to the city's inhabitants… on their own volition, sir. Are you here to arrest them?"

"Have you received orders to that effect?"

"Yes sir, according to the emergency measures, sir. Curfew, sir, is set at twenty-one hundred hours. Arrests will be made after then, sir."

"And who gave these orders?"

"Sir, the orders come from Deputy Commander-in-Chief Li, sir."

"It's twenty hundred twenty right now, hmm." Wang Puchen glanced at his watch and continued: "Report to Deputy Commander Li. I'm going to speak with Inspector Zeng and Captain Fang. I want to try to get to the bottom of things, see if this is what Nanking meant. If you're intending to make arrests, wait for me to come back first. Understood?"

"Yes sir!"

Before leaving, Wang Puchen looked towards Sun Chaozhong and then turned back to the commander. "Make sure you inform

Deputy Chief Sun. Tell him he's to wait until I return before proceeding with any arrests."

Careful to avoid the glare of the vehicle lights, Wang Puchen walked quietly to the storage facility gates.

———

Both Zeng Keda and Fang Meng'ao were waiting in the main office. Wang Puchen entered almost silently. He moved over to the head of the table both men were seated at and lowered his frame into a chair. "Are you waiting for Shanghai?"

Neither Zeng Keda nor Fang Meng'ao responded.

"You can't wait any longer," said Wang Puchen. "Emergency orders come into effect at twenty-one hundred hours. There are so many people outside on the streets. Are we to arrest them, or is there some alternative?"

"Originally, you were to arrest the PLA massing about the city!" Zeng Keda slammed his hand down on the table. "Originally, you were supposed to arrest Big-Eared Du's son, Du Weibing… and… and Hung Ling-kan, too!"

Wang Puchen rose abruptly from his chair, noticeably enraged.

Fang Meng'ao shot a forceful look at the man.

Wang did his best to calm himself before speaking: "Keda, my friend. There are only the three of us here. What you just said, I'll keep that between us. Captain Fang won't share it with anyone either, I'm sure. Let's forget it, yes?"

Fang continued to stare hard at Wang Puchen. "What the hell does that even mean?"

"I've news from Shanghai. After a thorough investigation, it's been determined that the Yangtze Construction Company is entirely legitimate. There is thus no reason for Mr Chiang to detain Kung Ling-kan."

Fang Meng'ao turned suddenly to Zeng Keda.

An unimaginable wave of astonishment washed over Zeng. He stood and looked at Wang Puchen. "Where to? Xishan? Escorted to Nanking?"

"Who's going to Xishan? Who's to be escorted to Nanking?"

Zeng Keda remained staring at Wang Puchen, but deep inside his heart, he could feel his life draining away.

"You two have sold ten trucks-worth of military rations. That's less than a tenth of the amount of food smuggled on one boat owned by the Yangtze Construction Company. In Shanghai, Kung Ling-kan is untouchable. In Peking, the same could be said of you, Inspector Zeng. There'll be no more talk of fighting or weeding out corruption. Those are the orders of the president. Your energies are to be directed solely towards rooting out Communist agents."

CHAPTER 15

On the vast map of China, the northeastern city of Yingkou in Liaoning Province is shaped much like a coffer used to hold valuables. The people swarmed around the city like ants, their roars and shouts echoing far and wide. In the last days of autumn, the town's dusty, dark walls, its main gates, the entire city itself, took on a red tinge. At first, the redness was no more than small flecks the size of leaves blowing in the wind, but the flecks grew larger and larger, the flags were raised higher and higher, and soon they enveloped all of Yingkou, then all of Liaoxi, and finally the entire northeast.

It was 2 November 1948. The PLA's Northeast Field Army had triumphed. Shenyang and Jinzhou were now in the hands of the CPC. The Liaoshen Campaign had been a roaring success, and a terrible defeat for the Kuomintang, leaving their forces in Tianjin and Peking under threat of direct attack.

The Red Flag had unfurled throughout the northeast, exhibiting as much brightness as the Shanghai Bund and the Central Bank once had in the past.

At nearly the same time, the Kuomintang acknowledged that the currency reforms had failed. Chiang Ching-kuo took to the airwaves to make the announcement, his voice echoing over the Bund, pained and dejected: "Over these past seventy days, I cannot help but feel deeply that I have not done all that I could have to fulfil the tasks I gave myself. Not only have my plans failed, my work left incomplete, but I have also caused no small amount of consternation among Shanghai's residents. I've added to your worries and hindered your attempts to make an honest living. In addition to submitting myself to the government to be disciplined, I would also like to express to the people of Shanghai my sincerest apologies..."

The Central Bank of the Republic of China had been torn from history's frame. The importance given to its great building in Shanghai had departed into the night sky, into the clouds. Attention shifted to the prize of Xuzhou, headquarters for the Kuomintang. Its defeat was the ultimate goal of the PLA's Huaihai Campaign. Artillery battles raged from Xi'nan to Pi County, from Wannianzha to Taierzhuang, from Hanzhuang to Dangshan in Suzhou. One after the other with barely a pause in between, finally the shells exploded above Xuzhou itself.

Chiang Ching-kuo's desolate voice now became his parting words as he exited this stage of history.

It was four days after the announcement of the failure of the currency reforms, on the night of 6 November, that the combined field armies from the northeast and the central plains launched their Huaihai Campaign. Then, as the sound of Chiang Ching-kuo's voice disappeared into the ether, the bombs and shells exploding over Xuzhou, over Hohhot, and over the central plains began to fade away as well, but not because the CPC had decided to abandon its plans to capture Xuzhou. From 15 to 16 November, the party called off its attacks against Kuomintang forces in northern Jiangsu, and in and around Hohhot as well, in order to contain Fu Zuoyi's retreating men from joining up with the Kuomintang in Xuzhou. It was decided that the encirclement of Peking took precedence.

Outside the Peking storage facility, border sentries had been set up on both roads leading to the main gate. All passage in and out was forbidden. A solitary jeep was parked in the middle of the road in front of the structure. Zeng Keda's aide-de-camp was seated behind the driver's wheel, quiet and unmoving. To one side, Commander Li stood watching. The men under his command queued in two rows behind him, not a single one making a sound.

Suddenly, Li's eyes were drawn to just inside the gate. Zeng Keda emerged from his office, his pace slow, deliberate. Commander Li and the young soldiers watched him as he walked beyond the main gate and came to a stop squarely in front of their formation. His eyes met theirs, and then he raised his hand in a sudden, abrupt salute. Commander Li and the men responded in kind.

Zeng Keda lowered his hand but kept his attention solely on the men. "From the sixth of July until today, that's nearly five months, I would like to thank you all for your service to the investigative arm of the Ministry of Defence. I would also like to express my appreciation for the hard work you've carried out in service to the economic reform efforts throughout the Tianjin economic area. From now on, the tens of thousands of tonnes of rations and military supplies, well, I would request that you men..."

Zeng Keda extended his hand towards Commander Li. Before Li could fully reciprocate, Zeng had already clasped his hand tightly. Li's eyes brimmed with tears of excitement.

Zeng released his hand, turned and walked to his jeep. He took only a few steps, however, before stopping, his face drawn to the sign that had been placed at the gate to the storage facility: the Peking Office for the Management of Tianjin Economic Area. His attention lingered for a moment, and then he strode over to the sign. With both hands, he removed it, wiped away the dust and placed it on the ground face down. To his mind, it seemed, there was no point hanging it back up.

Zeng then walked over to his jeep and climbed aboard. Moments later, they were passing through the sentry gate and motoring down the road heading east. Commander Li led his men in saluting Inspector Zeng as he departed.

Zeng's jeep pulled up and stopped in front of Fang Buting's home. Young Li opened the small door in the rear gate and greeted the inspector in the most respectful of tones. Zeng walked through the door and was stunned by what his eyes fell upon. A second later after regaining his composure, he hurried over. Fang Buting was standing in the garden seemingly waiting for him. He was dressed in a traditional long gown, immaculately clean and pressed. He was holding a walking stick to support his weight. As Zeng drew close, Fang reached out his hand. The two men shook and for a moment simply stared at each other. Finally, Fang Buting glanced towards the garden gate, gesturing for his driver to leave. Young Li understood his master's look and departed through the door Zeng had just come through. He closed it softly from the outside.

"Welcome, Inspector. Shall we go inside?"

Zeng Keda nodded and followed the older man into the house.

Once inside, Fang Buting gestured for Zeng Keda to sit on the sofa. He stood up almost immediately, however, when he saw Xie Peidong walk into the sitting room carrying a tray of tea. He turned to Fang Buting and said: "According to Mr Chiang's exhortation, his letter must be delivered to the bank governor... in private."

"Me and him," said Fang Buting, gesturing to Xie Peidong, "we've been through thick and thin together. Please, sit."

Zeng Keda had little choice but to lower himself once more onto the sofa.

Xie Peidong put the tray down carefully on the table and then stepped to one side. There in front of him was the same teapot, and the same teacups he'd recently gifted, on behalf of Chiang Ching-kuo, to Fang Buting. Fang poured one cup, and then with both hands passed it to Zeng, who accepted it in the same manner.

Fang poured tea into one of the other two cups and passed it to Xie. "Please, toast once with Inspector Zeng."

Xie Peidong lifted his cup and motioned to Zeng Keda.

Somewhat at a loss at this unexpected show of respect, Zeng responded despite the vacant look in his eyes.

"Inspector Zeng," said Xie, "I don't think I've said this before, but I'd like to thank you for coming out with me in that rain to look for my daughter. Even though we didn't find her, I still appreciate the gesture." Xie took a sip of his tea.

Zeng did the same, although his heart was plagued by a mixture of emotions.

Fang Buting now interjected, saying to his friend: "Inspector Zeng's not involved in what happened to Mulan. Let's not bring it up. Please, Peidong, sit with us." Xie Peidong lowered himself into a chair that seemed to have already been put in place for him to join them. Fang now turned to Zeng Keda and said: "So, Mr Chiang's letter?"

Zeng Keda reached into his pocket and drew out the letter. Holding it with both hands, he passed it to Fang Buting. Fang broke the seal over the lip of the envelope and pulled out its contents. His eyes scanned the words on the page, growing noticeably wet as he did so. He was silent for quite a while. Finally, he spoke: "I think you should have a look, too." He passed the letter to Xie Peidong.

Xie took hold of the letter:

Attn: Ministry of Foreign Affairs
 Right Honourable Minister Wang Shijie,
 I write this letter to recommend Colonel Fang Meng'ao of the Ministry of Defence, Bureau of Reserve Cadres (Youth League), to serve as military attaché for the Mission of the Republic of China in the United States of America. If such a special request can be accepted and reported to the president, I would be eternally grateful.
 Yours sincerely,
 Chiang Ching-kuo
 Thirty-Seventh Year of the Republic, 18 January

"Peidong." Fang Buting rose to his feet, his teacup in his hand.

Xie Peidong lifted himself up from his chair.

Fang continued: "Mr Chiang has kept his word, it seems. Meng'ao will be allowed to leave China and go to the US. We must entreat Inspector Zeng to pass on our greatest appreciation and gratitude."

It was now Zeng Keda's turn to rise to his feet.

"As Meng'ao's father, I can't say thank you enough to Mr Chiang… or to you, Inspector Zeng." He tipped his cup to his mouth and swallowed the tea in one gulp. Then he turned to Xie Peidong.

Zeng Keda looked towards Xie as well, his cup held safely in his hand.

"Yes, to echo Meng'ao's father, thank you!" And he similarly drained his teacup.

Zeng Keda followed suit and then placed the cup on the table. "I no longer have an official post in Peking," he said. "These last few months, I've not accomplished anything either. In truth, I've caused no small amount of trouble for the two of you, and for the rest of the city's residents, too… far too much trouble and bother. The last thing I've left to do is accompany Captain Fang back to Nanking and help him prepare to head to America. I'm staying in the Northern Command's guesthouse, a little out of the way, I admit. So please, would you be so kind to pass this recommendation letter on to Captain Fang, and tell him I will wait for him at the guesthouse? It'll be best if we depart tomorrow."

Zeng Keda stepped away from the sofa, removed his wide-brimmed cap and bowed deeply to Fang Buting and Xie Peidong. Once finished, he hurried towards the door. Neither Fang nor Xie made an effort to see him off. They merely stood where they were, silent and unmoving.

Fang was the first to speak: "Should I telephone, or you?"

"I'll tell Meng'ao to come." Xie walked over to the telephone and picked up the receiver.

———

The door to Fang Buting's study was open and the lights were on when Fang Meng'ao appeared. He walked over to the clothes hanger and removed his jacket, then turned to speak to his uncle: "So where's Dad?"

Xie Peidong stood up from where he was sitting on the balcony and answered: "Out among his bamboo."

Fang Meng'ao strode out onto the balcony and looked over the rail at the garden below. They were already ten days into winter, five days away from the first snow. The sun had just fallen and he could feel the chill in the air, the bite of the impending cold. But he couldn't see his father, not even a trace.

"The letter?" Fang Meng'ao turned away from the rail.

Xie passed it to him.

Fang scanned its contents and placed it back on the table: "Do you agree with me going?"

"I do."

"And Deputy Zhou, does he agree?" Fang stared hard at his uncle.

Xie met his gaze and returned it with equal intensity. "He does."

"And did anyone actually ask me if I bloody well want to go!"

Xie's face turned grave. "Are you asking me that question, or is that for Deputy Zhou?"

"I'm not asking anyone but myself, dammit!"

"Say what you want to say, yes? Come on, sit, tell me what's on your mind."

Fang did as his uncle suggested, and Xie sat down next to him. "Go ahead…"

"Do you know how long Cui Zhongshi groomed me to join the party? Do you know it's been two years, two months and eight days since I swore my loyalty? It was the tenth of September 1946, the Mid-Autumn Festival. And throughout these two years, two months and eight days the party has not given me one mission to complete. Nor have I done anything for it… no, that's not entirely true, I have done something. I've put those who introduced me to the party in the line of fire. I've brought pain and suffering to them. The twelfth of August, the day Mr Zhu Ziqing died. Comrade Liu Chuwu got close to me and ate a bullet for his troubles, and then… and then… Comrade Yan Chunming and a whole slew of students, including Mulan, were arrested, right before my very own eyes. Afterwards, you went out in the pouring rain to try to find her. We… we all knew they weren't coming back, but you put on a brave face. So did I. Why did we do that, why? And now, you and the party, you're working with the Kuomintang. To do what, send me away to become military attaché to the American Mission? Is that what you all think of me? That I'd rather drink whiskey and smoke cigars. Is that it? But you know what? Whenever I drink, whenever I close my eyes, it's not Uncle Cui who I see, it's… it's Mulan, that's who I see. Do you know what I'm telling you? Do you understand?"

Tears were streaming down Fang Meng'ao's face. His voice trembled and halted. He looked at Xie Peidong and saw his wet eyes, his tear-stained cheeks. But there was more to say: "Chiang Ching-kuo used me to try to win over public sentiment. And we've seen how that's worked out. It's gone, all of it, exhausted. Zhou Enlai used me in much the same way, so tell me who's better suited to talk about morals, about human sentiment? Do you have something, anything to say about that? Do you?"

"Shut up! Shut up! Shut up!" Xie Peidong's tears flowed even more than before. He even took to pounding his hand on the table.

Fang Meng'ao stared at the other man. A profound silence hung between them.

Finally, Xie spoke: "If this is how you understand us, how you think you know Deputy Zhou, then you can leave the party right now. It's as you say, you've not done anything for the party. Cui Zhongshi didn't properly groom you, so I guess you can do whatever the hell you want to."

"Fine. Then let me see Uncle Cui. Huh! Bring him out here!" It was Fang Meng'ao's turn to slam his hand on the table. "If I'm to leave the party, I should tell him. Can you get him here for me? Are you able to do that?"

Xie Peidong's spirit crumbled. He fell back into his chair and looked out of the window. The sky was dark, impenetrably so. When he gathered enough strength to speak again, his voice was low and hoarse: "Comrade Cui Zhongshi is gone… forever. I can't make decisions for you about what to do. And even if I agreed with you leaving the party, it's not for me to say. Chiang Ching-kuo wrote the recommendation. The party has no cause to disagree with it. If you're not willing to go yourself, well, all I can say is that your position with the Kuomintang Air Force will most likely be untenable… unless you can think of a reason, a good, solid reason, to stay. Have you thought about this at all?"

"No." Fang Meng'ao hesitated a moment. "I've not thought much about any of that. All I thought to tell you is that I can remain in Peking. I can continue in my current position."

Xie Peidong turned slowly to look at Fang Buting's eldest son.

Fang explained: "The Americans have announced a new programme to assist the Republic. You should already know this, I'm sure."

"The new programme," Fang continued. "Well, the Americans will implement it themselves. They'll be on the ground personally to oversee things. The first thing they're going to do is provide arms and munitions to the northern forces. The day after tomorrow, those supplies will be in Tanggu harbour."

"How do you know all of this?"

"I know who they've put in charge of transporting the supplies inland. His name's Chen Nade. It seems that the original air transport division has been disbanded. Chen's been tasked with organising a new group, but he doesn't have enough men. He knew I had a contingent of men in Peking, and so he telephoned me, hoping I could take on this mission for him."

"When is this supposed to happen? What did you tell him?"

"This morning, I told him I was willing to consider it."

Xie Peidong rose from his chair and looked unconsciously towards the cabinet that was behind Fang Buting's desk. His mind was racing.

Fang Meng'ao couldn't take his eyes off him. "Uncle Xie..."

"Eh..." Xie woke from his trance and looked at Fang Meng'ao.

"That day, the twelfth of August, the day before the rations were distributed, I asked you something, that if the final battle began, would Deputy Zhou and Chairman Mao agree or not with me transporting supplies to Fu Zuoyi's men, all to keep his forces well-fed and well-armed, and content to remain in the Pingjin area, and not venture southwards. You answered by saying you believed they would agree. Right now, the north's been won, and the Huaihai Campaign is heating up. Chairman Mao and Deputy Zhou believe they've got a handle on Fu Zuoyi's men. Do you think they'll let me join in, let me do something to aid the cause?"

Xie Peidong's eyes sparkled, and he turned to look out beyond the balcony again and towards the bamboo grove in the garden. It was as dark as the night sky above them. Xie then turned back and asked: "How will you explain things to your father?"

"It's been ten years. I should be here, should be with him, with my family."

Xie Peidong nodded and walked over to the clothes hanger. He lifted Fang Buting's jacket from the hook and passed it to the man's son. "Go on, out to the bamboo. Talk things over with your father."

"Yes, I know." Fang Meng'ao took hold of his father's coat and walked out of his study. Xie Peidong followed him to the door and stood there for a moment. He watched the younger man descend the stairs, before closing the door. Then he strode over to the cabinet behind the desk and opened it. He reached in behind the panel in the back and lifted out the radio. He dragged a chair over to sit on, and placed the headphones over his ears.

The winter of 1948 came a little early to Peking. The skies were mostly overcast, and whenever the winter wind decided to relent, snow threatened to fall. The guards who stood outside on the steps leading to the main conference hall in the Northern Command had already dug out their winter parkas, so frigid was the weather. By the rank and insignia on their winter jackets, it was easy to tell that Fu Zuoyi was inside. Military vehicles appeared intermittently, as did columns of soldiers. When they drove or marched in through the southern gates, they were the epitome of military rigour, orderly and neat. But in truth, their appearance illustrated more the growing chaos than anything else. The most pitiable of all was Zeng Keda. He arrived in Peking in midsummer, and although he had prepared long-sleeved uniforms, the cold was very nearly unbearable for him. Ultimately, he had to borrow a proper parka to ward off the chill.

And there he sat, in the main grounds, under a tree not too far away from the conference hall, waiting for the conference taking place inside to finish.

Fang Meng'ao had declined the posting to the US. Instead, he had agreed to take on the task proposed by Chen Nade: he was now in charge of transporting American supplies to the Northern Command. Zeng had made several attempts to contact Comrade Jianfeng, but they had all been unsuccessful. Finally, he reported to the Bureau of Reserve Cadres and received the following instructions: he was to meet Fu Zuoyi but keep the meeting secret from Chen. Afterwards, he was to return Captain Fang to Nanking.

Suddenly, the guards standing outside the conference hall straightened up and pulled open the doors.

Zeng Keda roused himself from where he was sitting and stood up.

Wang Kejun emerged first, followed by two men wearing Zhongshan suits. Zeng Keda recognised both. One was Li Wen, commander of the Fourth Corps in the Central Army, and the other was Shi Jue, commander of the Ninth Corps. Wang Kejun shook their hands and saw them off. At the same time, Zeng Keda hurried over to the steps of the conference hall, but as soon as he got close, the guards moved towards him to block his path. Several military jeeps pulled up in single file and stopped in front of the building. Li Wen climbed aboard the first vehicle and instructed his driver to leave. He was followed by two more jeeps: his protective detail. Shi Jue boarded the second jeep, and like Li Wen, two more jeeps followed his own as it departed.

Zeng Keda stood as close as he was allowed, his eyes fixed on the door to the conference hall, waiting for General Fu to appear. When he saw the guards turn and walk inside, however, he had no choice but to shout out: "Secretary-General Wang, sir!"

In truth, Wang Kejun had already seen Zeng Keda waiting nearby and had made no move to walk back inside. Now, he descended the stairs. Zeng Keda was permitted to move a little closer to the building. He saluted before speaking: "General Fu?"

"He left by the rear door." Wang Kejun's voice was matter-of-fact.

Zeng's tone betrayed his growing sense of urgency: "The Ministry of Defence's Bureau of Reserve Cadres…"

"You don't need to say anything," said Wang Kejun, cutting him off. "General Fu has already ordered me to consult Nanking about your request. Captain Fang is acting on orders from Chen Nada. He's the one who has organised things, tasked Captain Fang with transporting the American supplies. The orders didn't come from the Northern Command. If the Bureau of Reserve Cadres seeks to redeploy Fang and his men, I'm afraid you'll need to get US approval first."

"And which department am I to go through to contact the Americans?"

Wang Kejun shot a pitiable look at Zeng Keda. "You'll need to contact Madam Soong."

Zeng couldn't help but feel an overwhelming sense of despair.

Wang Kejun glanced at his wristwatch.

Zeng slowly saluted again. "Thank you, Secretary-General Wang. I'll take my leave."

"When you wish to leave Peking, please let me know. I'll arrange the flight." Wang Kejun extended his hand for Zeng to shake.

"There's no need for you to trouble yourself." Zeng was already turning away and descending the stairs.

The gates through which military transport vehicles moved in and out of Nanyuan airbase were well fortified and heavily guarded. Barbed wire extended in both directions from the main gate, and soldiers were stationed every five paces. The entire facility was encircled.

Zeng Keda's jeep pulled off to the left of the road and stopped about thirty metres from the base. Wang, Zeng's assistant, was behind the wheel. Zeng sat to his right. In the mirror, they could see the road that stretched behind them. Moments later, a small jeep came into view, followed by another, slightly larger one. Zeng Keda opened his passenger side door and climbed out to stand on the side of the road.

Fang Meng'ao was at the wheel of the first jeep. When he spied Zeng Keda, he reduced speed and parked his vehicle on the opposite side of the road. The jeep behind him did the same.

Fang Meng'ao hopped out and looked towards Chen Changwu, who was in the driver's seat of the second jeep. "Go on ahead. Get the plane ready."

"Yes sir." Chen put the vehicle into first gear and drove on towards the gate. The men seated in the back all saw Zeng Keda standing on the side of the road as they passed.

Fang walked up to Zeng and shook his hand. The two men stood for a moment, just looking at each other. Finally, Zeng spoke: "I promise to delay you no more than ten minutes."

"Fine."

Zeng did not release his grip on Fang's hand, but rather pulled the other man a little farther off from the side of the road and into the uncultivated land that spread out beneath them.

"It's been nearly six months, hasn't it? I wanted to say farewell." Zeng kept his eyes on Fang Meng'ao.

"You're going back to Nanking?"

"'Southeast flies the peacock, but every five *li*, it hesitates.' It doesn't matter where I'm going."

"Is there anything else you wish to tell me?"

"No, nothing important. It's just, I'd like to ask you something. There's no one else around. Are you willing to answer me straight?"

"Fire away."

"In the beginning, I had you arrested, interrogated. Afterwards, we both came to Peking and we worked together. I want to ask: what do you think of me?"

"Is my opinion important?"

"To me it is."

"You're a specialist in making things difficult for the rich and affluent."

Zeng smiled gratifyingly, but he didn't respond right away. He took a moment before he asked his next question: "And how do you see Mr Chiang Ching-kuo?"

"He's a devoted, filial son." A look of sadness crossed Zeng's face and he looked past Fang Meng'ao and to the airbase beyond. There were so many C-46s waiting to taxi onto the runway.

Zeng brought his attention back to the man in front of him: "One last question. You can answer it, or choose not to."

"I will answer."

"On the sixth of July, when I had you in front of the special tribunal in Nanking, I demanded you tell me whether or not you were a Communist, and you said you were. Right now, would you still respond the same way?"

Fang Meng'ao smiled. "If you ask me that same question, I can only give you the same response."

"Are you a Communist?"

"Yes, I am."

Zeng Keda laughed and so, too, did Fang Meng'ao. Their laughter was so loud, in fact, that the guards standing watching at the gate couldn't help but stare in their direction.

Zeng silenced his laugh but kept the smile on his lips. "Since you really are a Communist, take a guess: will I arrest you again?"

"I can't guess that."

"Then let me say goodbye." Zeng Keda reached out his hand once more to shake.

Fang Meng'ao clasped his hand tightly. "Goodbye."

Their handshake lingered a moment before each man let go.

Zeng ordered Wang to stop the jeep. They were in the grounds of Xishan prison. Zeng allowed himself a moment to look around, to scan the walls, the mountains that rose up beyond them, the withered and leafless trees. But no matter how far his eyes wandered, no matter what they saw, Xishan was still just a prison, and the Western Hills were just that. Nothing had changed, and perhaps it never would.

"Hold on a minute, Inspector Zeng." The wind blew fiercely, forcing the prison executive officer, who was standing next to the jeep, to shout: "We've just made a few dozen arrests. The warden will be out to see you as quickly as possible."

The rear door of the prison vehicle opened wide, and the Secret Police detainees filed out. Some had long hair, others had short. In the merciless wind, they were a muddled and undefined group of prisoners.

Zeng looked at the officer and said: "Go on, carry out your duties. You have your hands full by the look of it."

"Yes sir."

Zeng Keda turned his attention to his aide-de-camp and said: "I know your background is on file, but remind me again. You taught six months in elementary school, didn't you?"

"Yes sir. That was right after I graduated from secondary school."

"The Bureau of Reserve Cadres has been dissolved. You ought to go back to being a teacher." As he spoke, Zeng reached into his pocket and pulled out a pen. "You've been with me for so long. Here, take this... as a reminder of our time together. A souvenir, such as it is."

"Inspector..." Wang extended his hand but hesitated. His heart twisted and turned. "Sir, aren't we returning to Nanking?"

Zeng placed the pen in his outstretched hand. "Yes, we are. Once we get back in Nanking, there are a number of files that must be returned to the Ministry of Defence."

As they spoke, Zeng Keda noticed that Wang Puchen had appeared in the doorway. He saw him walk towards the parked jeep, his hand held across his face to ward off some of the wind. Zeng turned back to his assistant and saw his hand still open, the pen perched precariously on top of it. Zeng reached for it, clasped it between his fingers and then leaned forward to slip it into Wang's coat pocket. He straightened the young man's jacket and told him to wait in the vehicle.

Zeng climbed out of his jeep and went to greet Wang Puchen.

Wang Puchen flicked the lights on as the two men strode into his personal, secret office in Xishan prison. Zeng scanned the contents of the room, paying particular attention to the radio and telephone on the table. On top of the telephone, he noticed the words still designating it as the 'number two hotline'. Unsurprisingly, he couldn't help but ask Wang about it: "So when you make contact with Comrade Jianfeng, this is the machine you use, right?"

"Yes, it is."

Zeng Keda slowly extended his hand as though he were going to pick up the receiver.

"The line's already been cut…"

"I know." Zeng still reached for the phone, despite his eyes being drawn to the window high up in the rear wall. Thoughts of the past rumbled through his mind. He heard that familiar Fenghua accent and wondered if it had come via the telephone or via the window high up in the wall: "We've now failed…" "I have no idea as to what we should do…" "I can't be certain if we should continue to work together…" "Perhaps we'll know more in the future. We'll know to maintain party discipline and look after ourselves." Zeng Keda's eyes grew moist. Behind him, Wang Puchen pulled out a pack of cigarettes.

Despite keeping his back to Wang, Zeng issued an order: "Make a call for me."

Wang slowly returned the pack to his pocket without taking a cigarette out. "And what number would you like me to dial?"

"I want you to ring the Presidential Palace and ask for Director Chen Fang."

"Ahem. There's no line connected…"

"Don't," said Zeng Keda, spinning around. "I know that's not true. The Secret Service has the means to connect to the president. I make this request in the name of the Bureau of Reserve Cadres *and* in the name of the Iron and Blood Congress. Comrade Puchen, I ask for your cooperation."

"Comrade Keda, you ought to return to Nanking…"

"Don't say another word about Nanking or the blasted moon being closer!" Zeng Keda's eyes hardened. "My request concerns the Bureau of Reserve Cadres, the Iron and Blood Congress. It concerns Chiang Ching-kuo, too! What I want to say will one day be in the history books, dammit! Please…"

"Fine," Wang Puchen replied. "I will dial the number." He picked up the receiver, and the line connected immediately. "This is the Peking office of the Secret Service. I have something urgent to report. Please connect me right away to the Presidential Palace, to Director Chen Fang." The telephone went silent for a minute, and then Wang turned to Zeng: "Here." He passed him the phone.

Zeng Keda lifted the receiver to his ear to hear Chen Fang's voice: "Comrade Wang? Why are you calling me direct…"

"It's me, sir, Zeng Keda."

After a short pause, Chen responded: "Ah, Keda. You're still in Peking? Has something held up your return to Nanking?"

"Sir, I apologise, but I cannot return to the capital."

Chen's tone grew stern: "Is it something important?"

"Yes sir, it is. Our party sir, the Kuomintang, our government, too, we're about to be consigned to the history books, sir. You're responsible for handling all presidential paperwork. What I'm about to tell you, sir, will provide all the evidence you need to explain not just the failures of the party, but Mr Chiang Ching-kuo's failures, as well. Another man from Jiangxi said it best: 'In the State of Qi, the grand historian recorded simply the crime of regicide, but the historian Dong Hu of the State of Jin committed to posterity the truth of what happened.' Please, take down what I'm about to tell you…"

"Zeng Keda!" Chen Fang's voice was sterner and graver than before: "I'm but a simple secretary in the Presidential Palace. I don't record history. I'm no grand historian of the past, nor am I obliged to help you set the record straight. Also, from this day forward, don't go phoning here and using the name of famous countrymen. Please conduct yourself with some dignity, at least."

The sound of the receiver being slammed down echoed throughout Wang Puchen's office. Wang tried to make out Zeng's reaction, but there was nothing discernible. Zeng merely replaced the telephone on its base and slowly turned around. Wang stared at Zeng Keda, and in that moment he felt that the Jiangxi man in front of him was a far more extraordinary person than the Jiangxi man at the other end of the telephone could ever hope to be.

"Is there another number you'd like to dial?"

"No. There's no one worth calling anyway." Zeng Keda walked over towards the door but stopped in front of Wang Puchen. "I've put everything down on paper, in a letter. Will you please pass it on to Comrade Jianfeng when you next see him?" Zeng Keda reached into his jacket pocket, pulled out an envelope and gave it to Wang.

Wang Puchen seemed acutely aware of Zeng Keda's unique character traits. He did not accept the letter. "Return to Nanking, please. You can then make your report to the Ministry of Defence, and after that leave for Hangzhou. I've heard that's where Comrade Jianfeng is."

Zeng Keda held the letter in his outstretched hand. "No, I don't wish to see him face to face. That will only increase our sadness. This letter, I've written it in the form of a five-character quatrain." Zeng paused, and a look of bashfulness came over him. "I tried to use poetry as the ancients did... to express my deepest thoughts, my heart. But I don't think I've mastered the technique well enough. I should have studied more. I don't think I've succeeded. Give it to Comrade Jianfeng and tell him this, then please ask a gentleman who knows poetry much better than me to help explain it."

Wang Puchen was stunned by Zeng's words. He could do nothing else but accept the letter.

"I know the way. There's no need to see me off."

Seconds later and Zeng Keda was through the door. Wang Puchen turned and saw Zeng unholster his pistol. Wang closed his eyes and remained where he was. The sound of the gun echoed sharply in his ears, and down through the corridor. Zeng's body slumped onto the concrete floor. A pool of blood began to form around it.

By 13 December 1948, the Northeast Field Army had occupied the areas of Wanping and Fengtai on the outskirts of Peking. The following day, they pushed into Xiangshan, and headed straight towards Nanyuan airbase. As a result, the only southern route of retreat available to Fu Zuoyi's men had been cut off.

In the southwestern skies above Nanyuan, artillery shells exploded with such violence and with such great force that the entire facility seemed to shake. Unable to land, resupply planes could only circle high above. Eventually, they turned east, recalled by the Central Command in Nanking. On the ground, jeeps and other military vehicles were arranged as makeshift barriers. Alongside them, airbase guards, military police from Peking, troops from the Fourth and Ninth Corps, several hundred men at least, had taken up defensive positions.

Wang Puchen and Sun Chaozhong stood among the men and listened to the explosions draw nearer, their eyes trained on the sky above. Wang Kejun, Li Wen, Shi Jue, as well as their personal assistants and bodyguards, stood beside the runway, their faces all turned towards the sky.

An aeroplane appeared on the eastern horizon once more. Its wings dipped, twisted. The plane began its descent. Minutes later, although time seemed to drag on interminably, the wheels of the transport touched down on the far edges of the runway. The aeroplane taxied towards Wang Kejun and the men standing beside him.

The sound of cannon rang out and the plane came to a stop. In a flurried panic, a ramp was flung out from the aeroplane. Wang Kejun, Li Wen and Shi Jue walked over to greet the plane. Moments later, the cabin door opened and a four-star general emerged from within.

On 15 December 1948, Chiang Kai-shek dispatched General Hsu Yung-chang to Peking to consult confidentially with Fu Zuoyi...

Three jeeps drove towards the aeroplane. General Hsu, accompanied by Wang Kejun, climbed aboard the first vehicle. Li Wen sat in the second jeep, Shi Jue in the third. The vehicles turned and pulled away from the runway in the direction of the main gate. Two medium-sized jeeps raced in front of them to make sure the route ahead was clear. Three troop vehicles, each filled to capacity with military police, brought up the rear.

The cabin door was still wide open.

Only two jeeps remained. One carried Secret Service markings, the other those of the Peking Police headquarters. Wang Puchen stood in front, Sun Chaozhong in back. They lingered a short while, and then hurried over towards the aeroplane, only to be surprised by a familiar figure: Xu Tieying. He appeared on the ramp leading up into the bowels of the plane. Dressed as he had been before in a Zhongshan jacket, still with his departmental insignia, Xu carried a woollen parka over one arm. In his other, he held his familiar attaché case. His attention was on the sky above and the explosions that still rang out from the southwest. When he noticed the two of them approaching, he turned, smiled and stepped down the ramp.

The door to Fang Buting's sitting room was wide open. Xie Peidong stood in the porch, Xu Tieying just outside. A cold winter wind swirled through the garden, the bamboo grove and into the house. It whipped around them both, but neither man moved. Xie's face was stolid, although there was no hint of indignation or anger. In fact, the only emotion Xu displayed was a slight, apologetic smile. In the distance, but not all that far, artillery continued to explode, crackling like lightning in the frigid winter air.

Xu spoke first: "My word, you can hear the explosions even here."

Xie ignored the comment. "Mr Fang is upstairs in his study." He stepped aside to allow Xu Tieying to enter.

Xu, however, hesitated. "In truth, I'd like to speak with you alone, Mr Xie."

Xie turned and walked towards the sitting room sofa. Xu Tieying followed.

"Mr Fang is waiting upstairs. I'm sure you know the way."

Xu Tieying scanned the room, the stairwell and the familiar door above. Then he turned back to Xie Peidong. "I have something

I'd like you to take a look at." Xu reached into his attaché case and pulled out a single dossier.

"I suggest you give that to Mr Fang." Xie moved towards the exit.

"The dossier... it's the interrogation transcript from the special tribunal in Nanking. You're the accuser, I'm the defendant."

Xie Peidong halted his steps, but he did not turn to speak to Xu face to face. "And why do you have the special tribunal's transcript?"

"The justice department allowed me to borrow it. It concerns your daughter. It should explain things. Mr Xie, if you won't look at it, allow me to read one section..."

Xie Peidong moved again towards the exit.

"Listen to what he has to say." Fang Buting appeared at the top of the steps.

"Mr Fang..."

"Yes. Am I permitted to hear what you have to say?"

"Certainly, sir."

"Then please go ahead."

Xu Tieying opened the dossier and began to read: "'Thirty-seventh year of the Republic, sixteenth of September. Nanking Special Tribunal Interrogation Room Number Two. Interrogator, Qian Shiming, Interrogatee, Xu Tieying...'"

Xie Peidong picked up a dust cloth on a nearby cabinet and began to wipe its surface.

Xu Tieying continued: "'Question: Regarding the daughter of Mr Xie Peidong, assistant manager of the Peking branch of the Central Bank, a young Miss Xie Mulan of Yenching University, where is she being detained?' 'Answer: Miss Xie Mulan is not currently being detained.'"

Fang Buting glanced at Xie Peidong, but Xie said nothing. He continued to dust.

"'Question: In the Peking branch treasury, you told Mr Xie Peidong that his daughter was in your custody. Could you explain?'"

Xie moved on to another cabinet, this one beneath a framed picture on the wall. He continued to dust.

"'Answer: At that time, I suspected Mr Xie of being a Communist agent. I used the whereabouts of his daughter to test my suspicions, but I lied. His daughter was not in my custody.' 'Question: Is Mr Xie Peidong a Communist?' 'Answer: After close investigation, there is no evidence to suggest that he is.' 'Question: Is Miss Xie Mulan a Communist?' 'Answer: No, she isn't.' 'Question: Why was she arrested?' 'Answer: Because during the student protests, the scene was very chaotic. Several hundred were arrested.' 'Question: Where is Miss Xie Mulan now?' 'Answer: The detained students were released on the same day. To my knowledge, Miss Xie Mulan was mistakenly transported out of Peking and to the so-called 'liberated areas' along with those students who did not reside in the city.'"

"Mr Fang," said Xie Peidong, looking at his friend still on the first-floor landing. "Do you still want me to listen?"

"The problem is that if he doesn't continue, he won't come upstairs."

"In that case, I'll stop." Xu Tieying closed the dossier and walked over to Xie Peidong. "There are additional details inside, as well as follow-up investigations. Nanking has made it clear that anyone and everyone connected to the case will be investigated." He held the dossier up for Xie to take.

Xie still refused to look at it, but he did turn to face Xu Tieying: "You're still standing here."

"It's true, I did stand trial." Xu looked at Fang Buting. "Mr Fang…"

Fang met his gaze unflinchingly.

"The battle situation in Peking is critical, I'm sure you realise this. As we speak, General Hsu Yung-chang is consulting with General Fu Zuoyi. Nanking could have sent anyone here, but let me ask you, why did they send me? Neither of you might trust me, but I would ask you to have faith that Nanking is being sincere."

"I suppose we must make do in troubling times, eh?" said Fang Buting. "Come upstairs with him, let's listen to Nanking's… sincerity." Fang ambled back into his study.

Xu Tieying knew he could follow after Fang Buting, but he still held the dossier in his hand. He looked at Xie, almost pleadingly.

Xie accepted the file, placed it gently on top of the cabinet he'd dusted, lifted up the hem of his traditional gown and ascended the stairs.

Xu Tieying glanced at the dossier and then noticed the framed picture it lay in front of: on the left was Xie Peidong, on the right Fang Buting, and in the middle... Xie Mulan. The young girl stared back at him, a smile on her face.

Xu Tieying abruptly looked away towards the stairwell and Xie Peidong. The sound of his footsteps echoed in unison with the artillery fire outside. He simply had to go upstairs. He pulled his attaché case a little closer and followed after.

The three men were upstairs in Fang Buting's study, seated in the same chairs that looked out onto the balcony. On the other side of the window, winter had already come. "'The Central Bank of the Republic of China, hmm...Taipei branch manager.'" Fang Buting breathed the words out loud, letting them roll over his tongue. He held the appointment letter tightly, even removing his spectacles and passing them to Xie Peidong, before reciting further lines from the letter: "'Fifty years of Japanese occupation means there's a great deal to do.' Chairman Yu Hongjun wrote this, you know, but it reads more like a lyrical essay, along the lines of what Li Mi of the Jin wrote to that state's first emperor... you know, wherein he talked of his grandmother. Go ahead, have a look."

Xie Peidong accepted the letter and placed it on the table, along with Fang's spectacles. "I don't think I need to."

"If you don't read it, am I to assume you're unwilling to serve as my assistant manager again?"

"What do you think?"

"That I, too, have no desire to serve as bank manager in Taipei. But I am curious about one thing... perhaps Director Xu will be able to satisfy my curiosity..."

"I shall try, Mr Fang."

"We'll leave our particular entanglement unsaid, yes? The battle is at a crucial stage, the enemy is quite literally storming the castle, so the Central Bank's decided to up shop and leave Peking. An evacuation, a retreat. But let me ask you this: surely you're not the person qualified to do this, are you? I mean, your department has nothing to do with banking, does it?"

"Your question is certainly warranted, Mr Fang. And I have an answer. The situation in Peking is critical, as you say. As a result, Nanking has formed a committee to see to the evacuation of important persons and institutions from the city. Naturally, such a task falls to my department, given the reach of its connections throughout the country. As for why I, personally, am here, well, it was determined that my first-hand familiarity with what's going on in Peking made me the logical choice to head this evacuation plan. Its most important task, I might add, is seeing to yourselves and the bank."

"And how is that to be done, exactly? How do you evacuate a bank? Will it just be us, or will you relocate our homes and offices as well?"

"First, I had to present that appointment letter to you. Naturally, as manager of the Taipei branch, your property and holdings in Peking will serve as the foundation of the new branch in Taiwan."

"But the few of us here, well, we can't just start up a new branch. It will take more than a snap of the fingers to make that happen."

"We will of course be transporting the national reserves held in the Peking treasury."

"Aha! Now we've hit on it," said Fang Buting. "Battles are raging across the country, fighting every day, but surprise, surprise, Nanking hasn't forgotten about all that money held in the treasury. Tell me, Director Xu, how are you planning to move all of it?"

"Well, Mr Fang, as governor of the Peking branch, it's your responsibility to oversee the evacuation of its holdings, its people and accounts. All of it will have to be relocated to Taipei. My role is to assist you."

"But I just told you, Director Xu, I have no intention of being manager of the Taipei branch." Fang Buting rose from his chair. "I'm sorry to throw this spanner in the works, but you'll have to return to Nanking and request the Central Bank appoint a new governor of the Peking branch. I'll stay on long enough to hand things over to the new person. Once that's done, whomever they appoint will be in charge of the relocation."

"I'm sorry, too, Mr Fang, but this is something I cannot do. As I mentioned a little earlier, Generals Hsu and Fu are discussing right now the situation in Peking and the planned evacuation. The Peking branch is naturally a key component of these plans. That, I

531

should add, needs to be implemented immediately. I'm just, as they say, the messenger. Captain Fang and his men are to evacuate as well. If it's convenient, you're to leave along with him. Mengwei, too. Your entire family is to be relocated to Taipei. At least, this is the sincere wish of the Nanking government."

No one could be sure when the shelling had stopped, but the skies to the southwest had gone quiet. Security at Nanyuan airbase, however, tightened further. Not even Fang Mengwei in his official vehicle was allowed immediate access. Instead, he had to wait just beyond the sentry gate while the guard telephoned the tower to ask whether access would be permitted.

Within minutes of making the call, another jeep, this one on the other side of the sentry post, raced over to the gate. Fang Mengwei watched as it drew near and soon realised it was his elder brother behind the wheel. They exchanged a knowing look. Seconds later, Fang Meng'ao had parked his jeep, climbed out and was now walking over to his younger brother.

"Captain, sir!" The guard saluted and then proceeded to raise the sentry pole that barred the gate.

Fang Meng'ao saluted in return and crouched under the pole rather than wait for it to be fully lifted into the air.

Fang Mengwei looked at his brother.

Fang Meng'ao glanced in the direction of the wild grasses growing alongside the only road that led to the airbase; the same place he'd had that conversation with Zeng Keda not too long ago. He turned back to his brother. "Let's talk over there."

They walked off the road together.

Fang Mengwei spoke first: "Xu Tieying's returned."

"I know."

"They want Dad to take up management of the bank in Taipei."

"I know that, too."

"And what do you think?"

"Are you willing to go?" Fang Meng'ao responded with a question of his own.

"No."

"Then don't."

"Hsu Yung-chang's here on direct orders from Chiang Kai-shek. You know there are soldiers surrounding our home and the treasury, too. Xu Tieying is keeping a close watch on everything. Along with Wang Puchen."

Fang Meng'ao chuckled. "Then let them try and move the bank's holdings to Taipei."

Fang Mengwei's eyes flickered. "Haven't you made arrangements?"

"Arrangements for what?"

"To fly your planes into the liberated areas!"

Fang Meng'ao looked his brother up and down for what seemed like forever. He smiled, but his face was grave. "So you're a Communist, are you, here to incite the men to rebel?"

Fang Mengwei did not return the smile. "You're my big brother. Which one of us is a Communist? Well, only your heart knows that. The same is true for me, too."

"Tell me, what do you know? What do you understand?"

"Uncle Cui was a party member. Uncle Xie is, and so are you. What I don't understand is why they're allowing you to fly these planes, why they're letting Uncle Xie remain at the bank. That's what I don't get. Brother, the party has its plans. So does Uncle Xie. So do you. If you all agree, give me Xu Tieying, Wang Puchen and that bastard Sun Chaozhong… and I'll make sure they don't leave Peking alive."

"Listen." Fang Meng'ao put his hand on his brother's shoulder and pulled him a little closer. "In this family, everyone listens to Dad, yeah, and Dad listens to Uncle Xie. Are you willing to listen to me?"

"Of course, you're my elder brother."

"Don't repeat to anyone what you just told me. When the time comes to do whatever must be done, I'll come for you."

"All right…"

Suddenly, the commander of the airbase security came running into the field in the direction of the two brothers.

"Sir, Captain Fang," the commander said. "I've something to report, sir. We've received word from Northern Command. The motorcade carrying senior officials from Nanking is on its way back to the airbase. Your orders are to prepare the plane. Sir, I ask that you accompany me."

"Do you know who's coming?"

"Not exactly, sir, just that it's a senior official. I assume it must be General Hsu returning."

"Understood. I'll be there in a minute."

The commander saluted and ran back from where he'd come.

Fang Meng'ao looked deeply into his brother's face. "In what's to come, our enemy won't just be Xu Tieying, but Fu Zuoyi as well. Listen, don't go home. Don't go back to the police station, either. Return to headquarters and carry out your shift. We've got to play the long game here."

"Understood."

"Then go, quickly!"

The troops stationed in the streets around Fang Buting's home would not allow the Austin to pass. All routes in and out of the hutong were blocked by military police. There were secret servicemen in civilian clothes walking the alleyways, too. Li scanned the faces but could not recognise any of them.

Within seconds, a company commander marched up to stand in front of the vehicle. "Sir, my orders are to ensure the protection of Mr Fang's residence. No vehicles are permitted beyond the checkpoint."

Li glanced behind him at Cheng Xiaoyun seated in the back. She, in turn, looked to He Xiaoyu seated beside her. He Xiaoyu was first to speak: "Perhaps it's best if we get out of the car?"

"Get Miss He's things from the boot," Cheng Xiaoyun told Li in front.

"Yes ma'am." Li turned the handle and pushed the car door open.

Before he could climb out, however, the company commander stopped him. "You've come from outside the city limits, haven't you?" he said.

"Yes, that's right."

"Did you run into any Communists?"

"No, we didn't."

"Raise your arms. I need to pat you down."

Li looked straight into the other man's face. "I suppose you'll want to do the same with the women in the back, huh?"

"Just put them up, and shut up."

"Why you dirty fucking dog whelp!" Li countered. "Go home, why don't you? Here you are, not letting the car pass and patting people down. What is it huh, you don't trust us?" Li climbed back into the Austin and slammed the door. "Absolutely unreal! Ma'am, if you'll allow me." Li turned the key in the ignition, put his hand on the gearstick and pressed his foot down on the accelerator.

"What… what are you doing?"

"Ma'am, Miss, hold on!" Li shifted gears and stepped hard on the pedal.

The Austin lurched forward, past the guards and down into the hutong. Fortunately, the military police officers were quick enough to lunge out of the way, some pressing themselves against the walls of the narrow alleyways, others dodging to one side or the other. The look of rage on their faces was unmistakable.

Li brought the car to a sudden stop in front of the main door of Fang's residence.

The company commander regained his senses and pulled out his gun. With two other men, he raced after the Austin. Li pushed open the driver's seat door and stood straight, waiting for the police to come. Cheng Xiaoyun opened the left side door and climbed out. He Xiaoyu got out on the right. The company commander raced up, and then, with the other guards that had been stationed at the door to Fang's house, they encircled the Austin. Li made to move towards the main gate that led into the garden but was stopped by two guns pointed in his face.

Still gasping for breath, the commander walked up to Li and asked: "Where are your papers."

"Inside."

"Inside? Who are you to Mr Fang?"

"I'm his driver."

"Arrest him!" The commander shouted to his men, turned and was greeted by a fierce slap across the face.

535

Cheng Xiaoyun was standing in front of him. "Will you arrest me, too?"

The man was dumbstruck, his body rigid.

Finally, a familiar face came running up. Wang Puchen's officer shouted at the commander: "Stop what you're doing right now! You've made a mistake. They're to be allowed in. This is Mr Fang's wife and Captain Fang's fiancé. Step aside immediately!"

Cheng Xiaoyun turned to Li: "Go and open the door will you? We'll bring the luggage."

Cheng Xiaoyun guided He Xiaoyu inside. When Li opened the door to the sitting room, Fang Buting and Xie Peidong were waiting for them. Fang smiled at his wife. "I'll say, not much can stop the wife of the governor of the Taipei branch of the Central Bank, eh?" He turned to Xie and laughed. "All these years, and it never occurred to us that she could hit like that..."

"Having a laugh, are we?" Cheng Xiaoyun interjected. "Ten years ago, it was a challenge to get home. Now, I'm stopped at my door. Do you think I've any patience left? Xiaoyu, come on upstairs."

Holding a leather case, Cheng Xiaoyun moved towards the stairwell.

He Xiaoyu was clutching a small rattan box, and she looked at Fang Buting and Xie Peidong before following Cheng Xiaoyun. When both men nodded, she followed Xiaoyun up the stairs.

There were still two larger suitcases left on the floor. Li stood beside them, but his eyes were on Fang Buting.

"Go on, take them upstairs."

"Yes sir." Li lifted the bags, one suitcase in each hand, and hurried after the two women.

On the first-floor landing, Cheng Xiaoyun stopped and looked down at her husband. "Oh, let me tell you one thing: I'm no bloody wife of no bloody governor of the Taipei branch! You want a woman with you, you find one in Taiwan!" With that, she stormed into the room once used by Xie Mulan.

He Xiaoyu followed in after her.

Li brought the suitcases in, too.

Both men looked at each other, a noticeably sober gloss to their faces. Fang spoke: "Come on, let's go back up to the study and continue our chat."

Once inside, Fang Buting stared intently at Xie Peidong, and said: "If, and I do really mean 'if', you are a Communist, and if you speak directly with Zhou Enlai... now that you know the Kuomintang wishes to have me manage the bank in Taipei, they want me to make arrangements to transport all that money in the treasury, along with their dirty account, what advice would you give your precious Deputy Zhou?"

"There's no advice I would give."

The look in Fang's eyes changed. "What then, you'll take delight in the inevitable disaster?"

Xie shook his head. "If I were a real Communist, I might find myself up in the Yellow Crane Tower watching the disaster unfold below, but Zhou Enlai wouldn't be because the calamity he'd seen would be that of his own party. The conflict situation is clear. Sooner or later, the CPC will push into Peking. Their first order of business will be seeing to the two million inhabitants of the city, feeding them, clothing them. Once they're in charge, they'll realise how expensive firewood can be, how much rice costs. Zhou Enlai won't need to listen to any advice. He'll know already how important the money hoarded in the Peking treasury is."

Fang Buting's eyes flashed. "So what should I do to make sure the money stays where it is?"

"Brother, I kept you in the dark for twenty years. Do you blame me for the predicament we're in?"

"You helped me for twenty years, especially Meng'ao."

Xie Peidong straightened a little and shouted towards the door: "Li!"

In the hallway just outside Fang Buting's office, Li was holding a thermos of water he'd just brought from downstairs. He walked over to the room that used to belong to Xie Mulan, but turned his head and called back in response: "I'm here, sir."

Xie Peidong was standing in the doorway. "Come here."

Li put the thermos down beside the bedroom door and glanced inside.

Cheng Xiaoyun called out: "Go on, it's all right."

"Yes ma'am." Li stood up and walked down the hall to Fang's study.

"Mr Governor, Mr Xie." As usual, Li was polite, respectful and cautious. He stood in the doorway, wiping his hands on his trousers, trying to dry the little bit of water he had spilt.

Fang Buting looked the young man up and down, and turned to Xie: "He's a Com..." His voice trailed off, he couldn't finish saying the word.

Xie returned his look and nodded, tacitly understanding what and why his friend couldn't say the word.

Fang glanced towards the door and out beyond it. "Who else in this household is a..."

"No one," Xie answered quickly.

"Then go ahead, say what you have to say."

"There's no need to conceal anything from the governor. When you went to collect Miss He, what did your contact tell you?"

Li remained cautious: "I... I can be completely candid?"

"Yes."

"Understood. Comrade Zhang received a telephone call. You've been given permission to reveal your true identity."

"Reveal it to whom?"

"Sorry, but they didn't tell me that."

"All right, go. There's no need for you to expose your true identity to Madam Cheng and Miss He."

"Understood." Li turned to leave, but before doing so, he didn't forget to look in the direction of Fang Buting. "Governor, I'll take my leave, sir." He left the study and closed the door behind him.

Fang Buting turned his attention to his friend, his face filled with questions.

Xie pre-empted him: "Let's wait for that phone call."

Dusk had set on Nanyuan airbase. The weather had cleared in the afternoon, the cannons from the southwest had stopped their barrage, and now there was only a slight breeze blowing through the grounds. Wang Kejun, Li Wen, Shi Jue and Xu Tieying stood beside the runway, their faces trained upwards, following the aeroplane carrying General Hsu back to Nanking. The plane was flying east, getting smaller and smaller until it was no more than a black dot in the sky. Finally, it disappeared altogether.

The three jeeps belonging to Wang Kejun, Li Wen and Shi Jue, followed closely by their respective protection details, drove up to where the men were standing. Wang glanced at his driver and then at Xu Tieying. "Director Xu, you'll accompany Commander Li. Commander Shi, you can depart now. I have to wait a moment for Captain Fang to relay orders."

"My sincerest thanks, Secretary-General Wang." Xu shook the man's hand and walked over to Li Wen's waiting vehicle. Li was already sitting in the passenger seat. Shi Jue had climbed aboard his jeep as well. Once Xu was in the back, the small motorcade of vehicles hastily departed Nanyuan airbase.

Turning to his assistant and the guards standing beside him, Wang Kejun said: "Wait here."

"Yes sir."

Wang Kejun, followed by an Air Force colonel, walked towards the nearby hangar.

A temporary office had been set up inside the hangar for Fang Meng'ao to use. When he spied Wang Kejun and the colonel approaching, he saluted as he had done so many times before.

Wang Kejun did not reciprocate, however. Instead, he laughed. "Go on, sit down. We've things to discuss."

Fang Meng'ao waited for Wang to lower himself into a chair, and looked to the colonel who was closing the door to his office. Once he was seated, Fang finally took to his own chair directly opposite.

The colonel sitting beside Wang Kejun carried orders in his hand. He now opened these, confirming they had come from the Northern Command.

Fang Meng'ao stood up abruptly.

Wang remained in his chair, his eyes focused on the written orders. "They're specifically for you, Captain Fang, as commander of the special transport unit. They read thus: 'On the sixteenth and seventeenth, you are to transport goods from Tanggu port in Tianjin to the Thirty-Fifth Division of the new armed forces tasked with safeguarding Peking from the Communists. You are also ordered to make resupply airdrops to the 104th Regiment fighting in the Huailai region. When your mission is complete, you are to return to Nanyuan airbase on the eighteenth. Signed, Northern Command.'"

Once he had finished reading them, Wang Kejun passed the orders across the table to Fang.

Wang made no suggestion for Fang Meng'ao to return to his seat. He only smiled at the colonel sitting beside him and then smiled at Fang. "There are specific mission details, directly from Northern Command. Have either of you seen them?"

"No sir," Fang answered.

Wang leaned over towards the colonel and said: "I think you ought to introduce yourself."

The colonel rose from his chair and smiled slightly. "I'm an acquaintance, a friend of Xie Peidong." He extended his hand to Fang Meng'ao.

Fang hesitated, then slowly extended his own hand.

Unbeknownst to Fang Meng'ao, the man's hand he was shaking belonged to none other than Zhang Yueyin. While their hands were clasped together, Zhang glanced at the telephone on the table and then looked at Fang. "Mr Xie is awaiting our call. Would you like to dial the number, or should I?"

"You go ahead, please," Fang Meng'ao answered quickly.

Zhang released Fang's hand and picked up the receiver.

Xie and Fang Buting were patiently waiting for the telephone to ring. When it sounded, Fang Buting couldn't help but feel that the bell echoed throughout the entire house. Nervously, he looked at Xie Peidong. When it rang a third time, Xie finally lifted up the receiver and said: "Peking branch. May I ask who's speaking?"

Neither Fang Meng'ao nor Zhang Yueyin noticed when Wang Kejun rose from his chair, but he was now standing beside the door, lighting a cigarette. Zhang was still holding onto the telephone. "Mr Xie? I'm an officer with the Northern Command. Zhang's my name. We spoke not too long ago. Do you happen to recall, sir? We discussed the philosophy of Zhu Xi…"

At this point, Zhang Yueyin glanced at Fang Meng'ao. Fang was now staring at the table and the documents that lay on it.

At the other end of the telephone, Fang Buting could not take his eyes off of his friend. Xie seemed to be thinking something over, but what it was, Fang had no inkling. Finally, Xie said: "Ah, yes, Zhu Xi's idea of 'one principle, many manifestations'... is that it?"

Zhang Yueyin had the telephone up to his ear, and he chuckled as he said: "Mr Xie, I compliment you on your powers of recall. Yes, that was our topic exactly. Right now, I'm with Secretary-General Wang Kejun. We're in Captain Fang's office, Nanyuan airbase."

Zhang Yueyin was in the company of Wang Kejun! Xie Peidong couldn't hide the astonishment in his voice: "Eh, I see. Please go ahead."

Zhang Yueyin continued: "As I said, we're in Captain Fang's office. He's here, too, of course. The captain's been given new orders from Northern Command. He'll be leaving Peking in a few days. Secretary-General Wang will accompany him in order to make sure things go smoothly, but before they depart, the secretary-general would like to have a few words with Mr Fang. Is he in?"

Xie Peidong looked to Fang Buting, who had not taken his eyes off of his friend and long-time colleague. Xie spoke: "He's in, but he's downstairs at the moment. Shall I fetch him?"

Fang Meng'ao rose to his feet again. "You don't need to call my father. Let me…"

Fang Meng'ao had been listening to the conversation the entire time, had heard the voices on the other end. A brief look of amazement crossed Zhang Yueyin's face. "No, there's no need. Captain Fang, however, would like to speak to you." Zhang handed the receiver to Fang Meng'ao.

"Uncle Xie," said Fang, holding the phone close to his face. "These past two days I've been busy, quite a few flights. I'm sure you understand. It's also the reason why I haven't been home. Please let Father know."

"I understand. Carry out the orders given by the Northern Command. Pass along our gratitude to Mr Wang and Officer Zhang."

Fang Buting watched as Xie Peidong replaced the phone on its base and stood up. "Meng'ao is there together with those men?"

"Yes, with the Northern Command's Secretary-General Wang. There's nothing to worry about."

Zhang Yueyin hung up as well and returned to his seat. He

looked at Fang Meng'ao, who was still standing, his eyes focused on the back of Wang Kejun at the door. "You spoke well," said Zhang. "Now it's time for us to discuss things."

Slowly, Fang Meng'ao lowered himself back into his chair. "Spoke well to whom? To him? To General Fu?"

"There's an order to these things, discipline, protocol to uphold." Zhang put away the smile he had on his face and continued: "As for your question, I'm afraid I don't have an answer. I trust you understand."

Fang Meng'ao only stared at the other man.

"There are two hundred and fifty thousand men tasked with protecting Peking. Half of them belong to either the Central Army's Fourth or Ninth Corps. Nominally speaking, General Fu is in command of these troops, but in reality, they take their orders directly from Chiang Kai-shek. Do you understand what I'm saying?"

Fang Meng'ao was deliberately slow with his answer: "Yes, I understand."

"Excellent." Zhang Yueyin lowered his voice somewhat: "Xu Tieying's in Peking, ostensibly to see to the transport arrangements for all of that money holed up in the bank treasury. But his real purpose is to urge the Fourth and Ninth Corps to hold out and fight to the last man. Heh, he's like poor old Feng Fu from that Mencius story. You know the one, the old tiger hunter trying to relive past glories. Arrangements have been made for you to carry out airdrops today, to disrupt Nanking's plans. The day after tomorrow, our forces will have fully encircled Peking. At the same time, we'll be in control of this airbase. When the two of your return, you won't be able to land here."

Fang Meng'ao's eyes flickered. "Where am I to fly to, then?"

"That's why I'm here meeting with you now. Comrade Fang, this will be the first time the party is giving you direct orders. Please pay attention and commit to memory what I'm about to tell you. On the eighteenth, you must return to Peking, but you're to land at the temporary airstrip in Dongdan."

"The northeast's already been liberated. Why return to Peking?" Fang Meng'ao's sudden, unexpected question resulted in Zhang Yueyin wondering about the order as well, but his response was quick: "Only our superiors have the answer to that question. I'm just the messenger."

"And which superiors would that be?"

Facing this special operative for the first time, Zhang Yueyin realised how difficult it must have been for both Xie Peidong and Cui Zhongshi. He thought things over for a few seconds, raised himself from his chair and answered: "The central leadership."

CHAPTER 16

Two days later, on the morning of 17 August 1948, PLA artillery shells covered the skies as expected over the Nanyuan airbase. On the same day, the PLA Northeast Field Army formed ranks and pushed into Mentougou to the west of Peking proper. In quick succession, they occupied Shijingshan and advanced to capture Xizhimen and Deshengmen, ultimately encircling the entire city from the north and west. To the south and east, General Xiao Jinguang's forces seized Langfang and Wuqing districts just outside Tianjin, then eventually occupied Nanyuan airbase. The troop movements from the east and south completed the encirclement of Peking.

By this time, General Fu Zuoyi and his men had withdrawn into the city itself, swearing to defend it until their last breath.

At dusk, the cannons fell silent.

It was at this time that Fang Meng'ao's special transport unit returned to the skies over Peking. Landing at Nanyuan was of course no longer an option. From inside the cockpit of the first C-46, Fang peered down at the city. He couldn't escape the feeling he was looking at an aged black-and-white aerial photograph of Peking, something he had found in a long-lost history book.

Fang Meng'ao barked into his microphone in search of orders: "This is the captain of the special air transport unit, Captain Fang.

Whoever hears this, please respond. I repeat, this is Captain Fang of the special air transport unit, come in please."

"We're receiving you, captain. Please report your current position. I repeat, please report your current position."

"We're in the skies above Peking. We need instructions on where to land."

"Captain Fang, you're cleared to land. I repeat you're cleared to land. Instructions forthcoming."

"Acknowledged."

"Captain Fang, you're ordered to proceed to the temporary airstrip in Dongdan. I repeat, you're ordered to land at Dongdan. Be advised, the runway is only six hundred metres in length, thirty metres wide. It runs south to north. Be advised also, there are residential buildings in the area, three storeys high. You'll have to determine the correct altitude and approach. There is no ground crew available. Be aware, Communist bombardment continues. It'll be a rough ride. Repeat, be aware."

"Acknowledged." Fang Meng'ao adjusted his radio frequency. "This is Captain Fang aboard air transport zero-zero-one. Calling air transport zero-zero-two and zero-zero-three. Respond please."

Chen Changwu responded from the second C-46: "This is air transport zero-zero-two, awaiting instructions. Over."

Shao Yuangang responded from the third C-46: "This is zero-zero-three, sir, awaiting instructions. Over."

"The runway in Dongdan is only six hundred by thirty metres. Our descent won't be easy. I'll land first. You're to note my altitude and slope, and copy accordingly. Note my distance and speed from the runway, too."

"Roger that, sir," Chang and Shao replied nearly simultaneously.

The nose of Fang Meng'ao's C-46 arched upwards and the wings tipped. Seconds later, the aeroplane was headed south to Dongdan. The two other planes copied the manoeuvre and were soon heading south as well. Fang further adjusted his altitude, pitch and slope, pointing his aircraft in the direction of Dongdan. Chen and Shao did the same.

Fang Meng'ao's aeroplane had landed in Dongdan and taxied off the runway to the adjacent clearing. Chen had done the same with his plane. Inside his cabin, Fang's eyes were on the sky above.

Shao Yuangang began his descent.

Fang's voice echoed through the radio: "All right, Shao, bring her in."

Moments later, Fang and his men filed out of the C-46. A dozen or so metres away he spied Xu Tieying with an unexpected smile on his face. When Xu approached him, followed closely by several men wearing Zhongshan jackets, as well as a squad of soldiers from the Fourth Corps Special Unit, Fang Meng'ao walked forward, too.

All of a sudden, the sound of urgent footsteps rang out. Fang and the other men turned to see soldiers wearing Northwest Army winter parkas rushing towards them, weapons in hand. They were General Fu Zuoyi's special protective detail.

Soon the men split into three groups. One ran towards the planes and then formed ranks around them. The second group rushed to Fang Meng'ao, coming to a stop right in front of him. The third and final group moved towards Xu Tieying and his men, blocking his way. To bring the point home, their commander held his hand up to halt Xu in his place. All he could do was stand there, no more than ten metres away from Fang Meng'ao, a look of astonishment on his face.

There were no rank insignia on the winter parkas, but Xu noticed one of the men, a soldier well over thirty, leave the line to stand in front of Fang Meng'ao and salute. Fang responded in kind. The soldier then turned and shouted in a distinctive Shanxi accent: "General Fu's orders are that no one belonging to the military or the government is permitted to leave Peking. No exceptions. Violators will be caught and punished accordingly. Captain Fang, my men and I will take charge of your planes and cargo. You're to stand down and await further orders."

Fang Meng'ao smiled and turned to his men. "All right, boys, you're free to hit the showers and relax."

Fang's men hesitated a moment, then responded together: "Sir, yes sir!" Not one man, however, moved a muscle. They all remained standing where they were.

Fang gestured for Chen Changwu to come closer. "Chen, I'm

going to nip home for a bit. You take charge of the men. Shower and get something to eat. If anything happens, I'll be there, just come and get me."

"Understood, sir." Chen signalled to the men.

Fang Meng'ao removed his hat and looked in the direction of Xu Tieying. Xu met his gaze, and both men started to walk towards each other.

"I guess I'm grounded for now, hmm?" Fang Meng'ao said as he passed by Xu Tieying. He did not stop.

Seconds later, Chen Changwu, leading the rest of Fang's men, hurried past Xu Tieying on the other side. The men standing behind Xu could only stare. Xu turned abruptly to look at them: "Report back to the Northern Command."

He walked towards Xinhuamen by himself.

―――

Fang Buting was seated on the sofa in his sitting room, his eyes on his friend Xie Peidong. The sound of water gushing out of a tap in the adjacent bathroom echoed around them.

Moments later, the echo of the water ended and Fang Meng'ao emerged from the bathroom. He was wearing a thin white undershirt and khaki military trousers. In his hand, he held a towel that he was using to dry his hair.

At the same time, the sound of Cheng Xiaoyun and He Xiaoyu descending the stairs reached the sitting room.

Fang Meng'ao looked at the women who were each carrying a bundle of clothes, as he grabbed his jacket off the back of a dining table chair. "Auntie Cheng..." he said.

"Try one of these."

Fang glanced at the clothes they held as he pulled his jacket over his shoulders: "None of them fits."

His father called out from the sitting room: "Would it kill you to just try something on?"

"Your auntie had the coat stitched with your measurements in mind," said He Xiaoyu. "She knitted the sweater herself."

Fang Meng'ao stopped in response, one arm down the sleeve of his jacket. He Xiaoyu passed him the sweater. He pulled his arm out and passed the jacket to her in turn. He pulled the jumper over his head, paused for a moment as he thought of the work his stepmother had put into knitting it and tugged it gently the rest of the way down. "It fits perfectly."

Both women stared at him. The sweater was a dark green. Its low collar exposed the white shirt he was wearing underneath. It was a good match.

"Here, try this on." Cheng Xiaoyun handed him a black tweed jacket.

The look in Fang's eyes changed abruptly. He scrutinised the jacket she'd opened in her arms, but he didn't move to slip into it.

The atmosphere in the room grew still.

"I told your Aunt Cheng about this long ago, how, when you were a child, you got into several arguments with your mum. You wanted her to make you a Don Quixote cloak. I told her how I got angry with you, cursed you for your silliness. You know, your aunt put a lot into making this jacket for you... Ah, Xiaoyun, if he doesn't want it, just put it away."

Fang Meng'ao reached out and took hold of the jacket and put it on. "Thank you, Auntie. I've worn only military fatigues for the last ten years. From now on, I won't need to."

Fang Buting looked relieved and pleased at the same time. He rose from the sofa. "The old saying is true, eh? It's better for the future to be strong than for the past to be stronger. Have you finished Mengwei's clothes, too?"

"Yes."

Fang Meng'ao glanced at his father, then shifted his attention to Xie Peidong.

"Let's go upstairs. Your father has some things he'd like to speak to you about."

A deep silence had fallen over the three men in the first-floor study. The tea table had been moved next to the balcony window. Something had obviously been said. Fang Buting looked at his friend and at his son, one a longtime communist activist, the other a younger one.

Finally, Fang Buting spoke: "What does that Ming Dynasty primer for youth say? 'Social relations are no thicker than paper, they're so easily torn.' Heh, life's a chess match, isn't it? I think that's in the primer, too. Ah, Meng'ao, you've just asked me how I've got the money to have new clothes made for you and your brother, but nothing left to help your Uncle Cui's widow and his children. Peidong, weren't we talking earlier today about Meng'ao's situation? Human relations mightn't be much thicker than paper, true, but that doesn't mean I don't give a damn about my former employee's widow and his fatherless children. The problem is the Communist Party. They've got their hands all over Cui's family, but I have to make arrangements on my own."

Fang Meng'ao glanced back and forth between his uncle and his father.

"And now, even the old men who pull carts through the streets hawking cigarettes know the Kuomintang has lost. The CPC will control all under heaven. But how many people really know why the Kuomintang has lost, why the Communists have won? I worked for more than twenty years in their bank, I know the answer. It's a disease, one that's been around for thousands and thousands of years. The disease of inequality between rich and poor. While from time to time there have been efforts to eradicate it, they've proven to be unsuccessful. A Western-style financial system could only add fuel to that already blazing fire of inequity. I can't go to Taiwan and run the Kuomintang's bank, I won't be party to making the same mistakes, but what I've learnt of Communism, well, I don't think it will work either. So what can I do? What should I do? Fortunately, the small parcel of land my family had back in Wuxi was sold, and the money they got from that sale they exchanged for the new currency. As a result, whether I'm in the countryside or in the city, there's no way I could be classified as a member of the exploitative class. As soon as the battle for Peking is over, your stepmother and I are returning to our hometown. We're going to start a middle school, an elementary one, either would be fine. The only thing this family is worried about is its youngest son. Mengwei has always been a good boy, so obedient. I tried to set things up with the Youth League... with the Standing Committee of the Kuomintang, too. I even thought of reaching out to the CPC, but the hour is late, I know. Peidong, tell me, what arrangements can you and your people make?"

Fang Meng'ao regarded his uncle. What plans was his father talking about?

Xie hesitated before answering: "The central leadership has already agreed. They've made arrangements for Mengwei to accompany Cui Zhongshi's widow and his children to Hong Kong."

"What are you talking about? Arrangements could have been made for anywhere. Why Hong Kong?"

Xie Peidong grew contemplative, dark. "I worked for the Central Bank for twenty years. I kept your father in the dark for those same twenty years, the Kuomintang, too. The reason I was able to do so, to conceal things for so long, was that I'd already prepared myself to lie for a lifetime. History is written by people, but so many people, so many lives are simply forgotten. They're not recorded in any history book. People like me, like your Uncle Cui. Once Peking's liberated, the whole country will be. And you know what, our identities, our loyalty to the party, will probably go on being concealed. Your uncle's role will never be made public, that's for certain. To arrange for his widow and his children to remain in Peking, or even in Shanghai, that's near impossible. It just won't work. If they relocate to Hong Kong, we can set up a small shop for them, enough for his widow to make a living, and for his kids to go to school. Your dad's helped me for twenty years. In essence, he's helped the party for the same amount of time. Now he's come to me about Mengwei, about him going to Hong Kong, going to university. I couldn't find any reason not to agree to his request, so I passed it on to my superiors. They agreed. Mengwei can accompany Cui's widow to Hong Kong."

Fang Meng'ao was silent for a moment, his mind opposed to his heart, but then he spoke: "And Mengwei, is he willing to go?"

"We've not spoken to him. In fact, we'd like very much for you to do so."

"And how exactly am I to do that?"

"Mengwei feels things first. He's always been a sensitive boy, and his emotions run deepest for Uncle Cui's widow. Just tell him these plans have been made to ensure their safety. He'll agree."

Fang Meng'ao rose from his seat. "We can't keep Auntie Cui in the dark any longer. She has to know what happened to her husband. Before they leave, they ought to be given the chance to say a proper goodbye."

Xie Peidong stood up, and after a long pause, he spoke: "It's time to go. PLA troops are already stationed in Xishan prison. We'll make the arrangements ourselves. The key is to get out of the city. We'll have to ask Wang Kejun for a special pass… and make sure we don't run into Xu Tieying or Wang Puchen."

―――

A Yenching University car came to a stop at the end of the road that led to Xishan prison. The front door opened and Director Fan climbed out. He moved in front of the rear passenger door and pulled on the handle. "We're here. Be careful getting out."

He Xiaoyu exited first and then turned to extend her hand to help Ye Biyu. Fang Meng'ao, in civilian clothes, climbed out next. He was holding a shovel in one hand, and in the other, he had hold of Boqin. Finally, Fang Mengwei left the vehicle. Pingyang was in his arms. Mengwei turned to look back down the road they'd travelled. He could see the PLA soldiers in the distance, all of them armed. Then he directed his attention forwards and saw the vague outline of the prison.

Director Fan maintained his polite demeanour: "Miss He…" He reached into the car and lifted out a basket: "Here, you'll need this. The road up the hill is slippery. Please be careful. I will wait for you all here."

"Thank you, Director Fan."

"There's no need for thanks. This is as it should be."

―――

They trekked into the Western Hills behind the prison. Fang Meng'ao had held Boqin in his arms for part of the way, but now put him on the ground. His younger brother did the same with Pingyang. The four of them stood there and waited. The two Fangs looked further up the mountain towards Cui Zhongshi's grave and then turned to look at Ye Biyu and He Xiaoyu bringing up the rear.

Xiaoyu had her arm around Ye Biyu's waist, helping as best she could. They paused often. Tears stained Biyu's face.

He Xiaoyu leaned in closer and spoke gently to the older woman: "Auntie, you can't let the children know, at least not yet."

"I know, I know." Ye Biyu wiped the tears from her cheeks. She also twisted away from He Xiaoyu's arm, intent on walking the rest of the way on her own.

He Xiaoyu didn't protest. She simply held on a little tighter to the basket she'd been carrying and followed after. Once the two brothers saw the women walking again, they took hold of the children's hands and continued up the mountain as well.

There were so many graves along the mountainside that it almost seemed crowded. Some had tablets stuck into the ground to mark the identity of the grave, while others had nothing but a mound of earth. Finally, they came to a stop in front of an unmarked pile of raised soil. Fang Meng'ao and his younger brother looked back at Ye Biyu. Cui's widow looked at both and then at the ground beside them. It was high summer and the grave was covered in tall grass, much of it already dry and yellow. Fang Meng'ao drove the spade he'd been carrying into the earth in front of the mound. He shovelled once, twice, three times and stopped. Putting the spade to one side, he leaned down and picked up a dirt-encrusted bottle. He Xiaoyu recognised it almost immediately. It was a bottle of red wine gifted some time ago to Fang Meng'ao by Chen Nade. The two children stared at what their uncle held in his hand, their eyes wide with curiosity.

"We're here."

He Xiaoyu poked around inside the basket for a moment, lifted out several candles and passed them to Fang Meng'ao, who lit them promptly with his lighter.

Ye Biyu knelt on the ground. In her hand was hell money, which she now held over the burning candles. The joss paper caught and the flames danced, turning the money for the dead into ash. Boqin seemed to grasp something. Perhaps he understood what his mum was doing, but he did not dare to ask.

Pingyang walked closer to her mother to help with the hell money. Her voice was low: "Who are you burning this for?"

Ye Biyu's face was wet again with tears. "For a family relative. Call your brother over. He can burn a little of the money, too."

Pingyang signalled to Boqin, who walked over quietly to make the same offering to the dead his mum and sister were doing.

Fang Meng'ao glanced at He Xiaoyu. "You remain here with them, all right?"

He Xiaoyu nodded. Her face had become wet as well.

Fang Meng'ao turned to his brother. "Come with me."

The two men walked a little further up the hill, past the few pine trees that grew on the other side of Cui Zhongshi's burial mound.

The old, crumbling marker barely showed above the grass. The words inscribed into the stone drew Fang Meng'ao's attention: "Thirty-seventh year of the Kangxi reign". For a moment, Fang stood mesmerised. Finally, he turned to his younger brother and asked: "Do you know what's buried here?"

"No."

"Ma Hanshan."

Fang Mengwei's eyes grew wide as he looked back and forth between the broken stone marker and his older brother. "It can't be Ma Hanshan."

Fang Meng'ao looked off into the distance, then passed the spade to Mengwei. "Not Ma Hanshan himself, no, you're right about that. But he did bury something beneath this marker. He told me what it was. I want you to dig it up. I want you to take it with you to Hong Kong. I want you and Auntie Cui... Boqin and Pingyang... I want you all to live well."

Fang Mengwei's heart grew tight in his chest. He seemed to grasp what his brother was saying. He drove the shovel into the ground and flung a pile of dirt into the air. Before long, the spade clanged against something hard and still halfway buried. Mengwei knelt down and brushed the earth to one side, revealing the metal container Ma Hanshan had placed in the ground some time ago. He dug around the edges and finally lifted the box; its weight was considerable.

"What's in it?"

"Open it and see for yourself."

Fang Mengwei undid the latch. A golden hue made more brilliant by the afternoon sun enveloped his face. The box was filled with bars of gold.

Fang Meng'ao crouched down on his haunches. "Sit," he said.

Fang Mengwei lowered his backside onto the ground next to the box.

"Do you know why Ma Hanshan wants to give all of this to Uncle Cui's widow?"

"Because you released him."

Fang Meng'ao sighed, before explaining: "That's not the whole story, no. Mengwei, if you and I were born to a different family, if we'd been there in Shanghai, on the beach, do you think I would've become a man like Ma Hanshan?"

"No, I don't."

"How do you know?"

"If you'd been there, if you'd changed, you'd have ended up like Wang Yaqiao, leader of the Shanghai Axe Gang, an assassin, that kind of person."

Fang Meng'ao punched his young brother on the shoulder. "Heh, heh, I guess my brother still knows what kind of man I am, eh!"

"Meng'ao, tell me. People like us, what are we supposed to do? What are we doing? Are we doing what we can, what we should?"

Fang Meng'ao closed the lid and stood up. "I know some of what we're doing is a little confusing right now, but after today, and in the days to come, these things will make sense. I know, too, that there are other things that we'll never fully understand, not now, not ever. We've got one more place to go, come on."

Fang Mengwei turned slowly to face his brother. "Can we... can we not?"

"Eh? Yeah. You know what, if you don't want to go, we don't need to." Fang Meng'ao leaned over, took hold of the strongbox and hoisted it over his shoulder.

Fang Mengwei stood up, too. "No, let's go see."

They walked past several old, weathered trees until Mengwei came to an abrupt stop. A look of astonishment crossed his face as his eyes fell on a marker that had not been stuck in the ground all that long ago. The words inscribed into the stone drew him in: "Here lies Zeng Keda, originally from Jiangxi." Slowly, Fang Mengwei's senses returned and he looked at his brother. Meng'ao stared at his brother for a moment, then let his eyes fall on the grave. He placed the strongbox down beside the marker, reached into his jacket and pulled out a cigarette. Once it was lit, he dug into the ground in front of Zeng Keda's final resting place.

"You know he arrested me, interrogated me. Then he came to Peking and was hard on Uncle Cui, hard on our family, too. I seem to recall you argued with him as well."

Mengwei was silent.

"He never ceased working for the Kuomintang, one of the few to remain loyal and true, I suppose. But in the end, no one from the Kuomintang would talk to him. He was left out in the cold. He came especially to the airbase to say goodbye to me."

"What did he say?"

"He asked me what I thought of him. I told him he was a specialist in making things hard for the rich and affluent. I remember he smiled at that. Then he asked me, not for the first time, if I were a Communist. I said I was. He asked me to guess whether or not he'd arrest me again should I return to Nanking. I told him I couldn't. At the time, it never occurred to me he'd be… worm food like this. If I'd known, my appraisal of him would have risen for sure…"

"And what good would that have done him?"

Fang Meng'ao looked deeply into his brother's eyes and said: "When you get to Hong Kong, go and buy a copy of *Don Quixote*. I reckon you'll find the answer to that question in there, and a great many others, too."

Once they saw off Fang Mengwei and Cui's remaining family, Fang Meng'ao accompanied He Xiaoyu to the Yenching University Foreign Languages Bookstore. Miss Sophia escorted them upstairs to the first floor, unlocked the door and smiled as the seemingly unchanged chapel opened in front of them. "Mr Liang told me to expect you."

He Xiaoyu and Fang Meng'ao looked at each other.

Xiaoyu turned to Miss Sophia and smiled accordingly. "You're right, we're very grateful."

Miss Sophia remained smiling. "See you again soon."

As they walked into the room, they heard the older woman descend the stairs behind them.

Books were piled everywhere, on the table and on the chairs. He Xiaoyu stood just inside the door, unsure of what to do or say. Fang Meng'ao was equally perplexed. The winter sun arched in through the window, gradually shifting across the floor and illuminating the entire room as though a stage curtain were being pulled away.

Liang Jinglun and He Xiaoyu... Liang Jinglun and Fang Meng'ao... Liang Jinglun and Xie Mulan.

The sunlight fell on the books upon the table, and then as quickly as it had come it retreated back through the window, plunging the room into darkness again.

Fang Meng'ao turned on the light, walked over to the table, removed the books from a chair and sat down. "The second bookcase on the left, second shelf, first book."

He Xiaoyu walked slowly over towards the bookcase, her eyes drawn to the second shelf, first book: *Don Quixote*!

"Is this the one?"

Fang did not look up. "Yes. Turn to chapter two. A passage has been circled."

He Xiaoyu's heart pounded. She pulled the book slowly off of the shelf and opened it to chapter two. She found the paragraph, neatly circled. "I found the section."

"I'll recite it. See if I'm correct."

He Xiaoyu focused on the words on the page.

Fang Meng'ao's voice seemed to echo through the air: "'Happy the age, happy the time, in which shall be made known my deeds of fame, worthy to be moulded in brass, carved in marble, limned in pictures, for a memorial for ever. And thou, O sage magician, whoever thou art, to whom it shall fall to be the chronicler of this wondrous history, forget not, I entreat thee, my good Rocinante, the constant companion of my ways and wanderings.'"

Even though he had finished his recitation, his words hung about them. Minutes passed before he spoke again: "Come here."

He Xiaoyu did her best to rein in her racing heart. Turning the words over in her mind, she returned the book to where she'd found it. She wiped a chair and sat down opposite Fang Meng'ao.

"Do you know why Liang Jinglun has marked that passage?"

He Xiaoyu had no answer.

"When I first happened upon it, I was stumped for a good while, too. Right now, however, I think I understand. He wanted to see the currency reforms succeed, but at the same time, he realised they wouldn't. Just like Don Quixote. The hardest thing to do is to accept the reality one has done his best to refuse. Keeping one's head in the sand is easy, but we know that sooner or later we'll have to lift our heads up. Of course, the success or failure of the reforms had really nothing to do with him."

"Is that why you brought me here… you wanted to explain this?"

"We're here to talk about me."

"How does that passage fit in?"

"Don't you think we're both a lot like Don Quixote?"

"We're warring against windmills, too?"

Fang Meng'ao's eyes glimmered as he rose from his chair. "Do you know why I like you?"

He Xiaoyu remained seated. "You like me?"

"I like windmills!" Fang Meng'ao lifted his leg and untied his shoelace.

"Wh… what are you doing? Stop messing around."

Fang Meng'ao lifted his other leg and untied his other shoelace. He then pushed at the desk. "What's this doing here, huh?"

He Xiaoyu could not decide if she was confused and somewhat upset by Fang Meng'ao's outward recklessness, or excited by it. "Well, it's used for reading books isn't it?"

"Do you think we could sit on it?"

"No, I don't…"

With a grunt, Fang Meng'ao bounded up on top of the table, his legs crooked over the side. He extended his hand towards He Xiaoyu. "Look, it's fine. Come sit next to me."

"Just what are you up to?" Despite her confusion, she unconsciously reached out and allowed Fang Meng'ao to take hold of her hand.

"Both hands."

She did as he requested and held out her arms. Fang clasped them tightly and in one quick movement gently hoisted her onto the table next to him.

"I've not taken off my shoes…"

Before she could finish her statement, Fang Meng'ao was already removing her shoes for her.

The faces were close to each other, their knees were side by side. Each looked deeply into the other's eyes.

"So, do you think the table can hold us?"

"I guess it can."

"Can I say that I love you?"

He Xiaoyu closed her eyes, her body trembled. Quickly, deftly, Fang Meng'ao slipped his arms out of his overcoat and wrapped them around her quivering frame. She had no time to react before he slipped his arms underneath her legs and lifted her up, placing her on his lap. The hem of Fang Meng'ao's dark overcoat bunched up on the table behind them; He Xiaoyu was bundled up inside of it. She never imagined she would feel this comfortable, never dared to think of being here like this. Her worries melted away. All she could feel was Fang Meng'ao's hand about her waist.

She waited, her eyes closed.

But Fang Meng'ao only looked at her.

Slowly, she opened her eyes and saw the profound loneliness of the man who was holding her so close. She responded with her heart and moved her arms around Fang Meng'ao, pulling him even closer. Fang allowed his eyelids to close, and then his head to fall onto her shoulder. She could feel his breath on the nape of her neck, the static electricity tingling across his lips. The desk lamp flickered, popped and went dark. Books fell from their shelves, apparently of their own volition. The faint light coming in through the window was no longer visible.

The world outside had disappeared.

He Xiaoyu's face rested against his shoulder, her breath shallow and uneven. It echoed in his ears as he moved his mouth to her cheek. "Do you understand now why I brought you here, why I recited that passage?"

"No, I still don't understand."

"Would you like to?"

"I don't think so, no."

Fang Meng'ao went quiet.

He Xiaoyu felt the heaviness of the silence and lifted her head slightly. "Maybe I would like to know. Yes… please."

"'Happy the age, happy the time in which shall be made known my deeds of fame.' Peking is about to be liberated. The liberation of the rest of China will soon follow. But what I've done, my deeds, they'll be forgotten. What will you do then?"

He Xiaoyu reached up and put her hand over Fang Meng'ao's mouth. She looked into his face for a moment and then moved to get down from his lap. Standing in front of him, there was a particular seriousness in her voice. "The New China won't forget anyone, and certainly not you! Would you like to hear about what the New China will be like?"

Fang Meng'ao remained seated on the table, his face looking up to hers. "I would…"

In a soft voice, He Xiaoyu began her recitation: "'It is like a ship far out at sea whose masthead can already be seen from the shore. It is like the morning sun in the east whose shimmering rays are visible from a high mountain top. It is like a child about to be born moving restlessly in its mother's womb.'"

"That sounds really wonderful."

He Xiaoyu bent her waist and sat down again next to Fang Meng'ao. "We can both see that ship. We're watching the morning sun together……"

"We're having a child!" Fang Meng'ao cut her off with a laugh.

"Don't be silly!" Her embarrassment was barely concealed.

Fang Meng'ao retracted his smile. "I know your quotation. It's in a letter written by Chairman Mao, 'A Single Spark Can Start a Prairie Fire'. I think that was the title. He wrote it a few years after 1927, after the retreat into the Jinggang Mountains between Jiangxi and Hunan. With regard to history, it's proven to be quite prophetic. But history is written by men, and so, so many men are left out of it. If I don't see this New China with you, will you wait for me?"

"What do you mean? Has something happened? Have you received new orders from higher up? You're not allowed to scare me."

"Do you know why we saw Uncle Cui's family off to Hong Kong today? Have you thought about it at all?"

He Xiaoyu shook her head.

"It means that even after liberation, Uncle Cui's true identity will be kept secret. The same is true for Uncle Xie. Would you like to know why? I'll tell you. It's all to do with moving the Peking branch of the bank to Taiwan. All that money in the treasury needs to be moved. They need aeroplanes to do it."

He Xiaoyu was stunned by this admission. "Has the central leadership made arrangements?"

"Not yet, but I imagine they soon will."

"But why?"

"Because the liberation of Peking might in fact be peaceful."

He Xiaoyu reached out, took hold of his hand and squeezed it tightly. "But a peaceful liberation shouldn't mean that you all have to leave!"

"The peaceful surrender of the city to the PLA has already been confirmed. It was a condition of Fu Zuoyi when he began secret negotiations with the CPC, with us. The greatest worry has been Chiang Kai-shek's Fourth and Ninth Corps. In all likelihood, promises have been made to allow Chiang's men – and the money in the treasury – to be evacuated. At present, Chiang's planes can't land in the city. As a result, my men and I have become a bargaining chip in the discussions concerning Peking's surrender."

He Xiaoyu was growing visibly agitated. "And do you think the central leadership will agree to this?"

"The peaceful liberation of Peking would be a glorious achievement for the CPC, a real feather in their cap. Certainly something worthy of being memorialised forever in brass, or carved into marble, limned in pictures for all time."

He Xiaoyu threw her arms around him. "If this is how it will be, let me come with you."

"If you want me to come back, all you need to do is wait for me in Peking."

In the alleys that snaked around Fang Buting's home, all throughout the hutong, people could be heard singing the opera *In the Deep of the Night*. The drums reverberated out from the ground floor of Fang's residence, shattering the quiet of the night. The armed soldiers standing guard could almost feel the concussive force of the tune. But before they could grow accustomed to the thump of the drums, the ear-splitting twang of the two-stringed *jinghu* cut through whatever calm was left in the night air. Someone was playing a tune from Mei Lanfang's classic *Farewell My Concubine*.

Xu Tieying was assaulted by the high-pitched cords of the *jinghu* as soon as he walked into Fang Buting's garden. His eyes were drawn to a broom sweeping across the stone pathway just inside the gate. He allowed his eyes to run up the handle to see Xie Peidong busily cleaning away. Xu glanced at the house and the sitting room in particular. The door was wide open, allowing the ceiling lights to force their way outside. He could see the outline of Fang Meng'ao's frame. He appeared to be standing calmly, his arms crossed. Xu realised he was dressed in his pilot's attire. The sound of the *jinghu* continued to assault his ears. Xu looked at his watch.

As though he could hear the pained sound of the *jinghu* as well, Wang Puchen glanced at his watch and looked about the temporary airstrip in Dongdan. He saw Fang's men, all twenty of them, standing restlessly nearby. Just beyond them were the three C-46s, quiet and still in the cold winter wind. Alongside the planes were crates of military cargo, each filled to capacity. Soldiers from the Northwest Regiment watched the pilots, the planes and the cargo, all of them wearing hardy winter hats.

The distinctive strum of the *jinghu* and the percussion accompanying seemed even to reach as far as the Northern Command. Outside the conference chambers, General Fu Zuoyi's men, dressed in their winter parkas, had been standing to attention for what felt like forever. To the left of the central grounds, where Li Wen's Fourth Corps soldiers stood, and opposite them on the right were Shi Jue's men. They had all been standing for quite a while. General Fu's men kept their eyes on the other soldiers to the right and left. These men, in turn, kept their attention focused on the doors to the conference chambers.

The PLA had claimed victory in the Huaihai Campaign on 10 January 1949. Out of the three great theatres of battle between the Kuomintang and the CPC, only the north had yet to be decided. On 14 January, the PLA captured Tianjin. On 21 January, negotiations between General Fu Zuoyi and the Communists regarding Peking began. After a full night of intense talks, General Fu announced that an agreement had been reached concerning the peaceful liberation of Peking. Special attention was given to both the Fourth and

Ninth Corps, and how best to manage their departure from the field of battle. It was later announced that senior military advisors and high-ranking officers would be flown out of the city. The negotiations grew tense as each side confronted the other with demands and assurances well into the night.

The *jinghu*, the drums, each reached their crescendo. A jeep screeched to a halt at the mouth of the street that led to Fang Buting's residence. The armed soldiers stood to attention. Wang Kejun led a middle-aged man dressed in civilian attire down the alleyway and into the sounds of the thumping drums.

"Attention!" The sound of the command coming from just outside the garden brought the music of the *jinghu* and drums to a sudden stop. Moments later, Wang Kejun and the middle-aged man in plain clothes were standing just inside the door. Xie Peidong stopped sweeping. Xu Tieying was surprised at their appearance, but then rushed to greet them.

Wang Kejun spoke first: "Let me make the introductions. This is Commander Liu of the PLA."

Face to face with Liu Yun, leader of the CPC forces in Peking, Xu Tieying wasn't sure what to do. Finally, he stretched out both hands. "It's a pleasure!"

Liu Yun extended only one hand in return.

Taking hold of it, Xu spoke: "Your calls for peace have been heard throughout the country. My greatest hope is to end the hostilities and together strive to alleviate the dire straits the people face. With one heart and one mind, we can work together to establish a lasting peace."

Liu Yun chuckled. "Aren't those the same words President Chiang used in his resignation statement? How have you committed them to memory so quickly, Director Xu?"

"Eh... my apologies."

"Mr Xie, a senior official from the PLA has come." Wang Kejun gestured and moved together with Liu Yun towards Xie Peidong. Xu Tieying grovelled behind.

Xie turned slowly towards Liu Yun. "Greetings, sir."

Liu Yun smiled and responded: "We don't use that form of address in the PLA. There're no humble sirs, only soldiers."

"Please, can you take us in to see Mr Fang Buting?"

"Mr Fang is unwilling to leave Peking. There's no point in me trying to persuade him any more. Go on in yourselves."

Wang turned to Liu Yun and said: "Commander Liu, should we, you and I, and I guess Director Xu... should we go in and speak to him?"

"Yes, let's try at least."

The three men walked through the garden in the direction of the door that led to the sitting room. Fang Meng'ao saluted Wang Kejun and Liu Yun at the same time. Wang made the introductions: "This is Captain Fang. He's in charge of the special transport unit. He's the National Army's ace pilot. He's also Mr Fang Buting's eldest son."

"I know, he's a hero of the war against Japan, too." Liu Yun reached out a hand to shake Fang Meng'ao's. Fang reciprocated, stood to attention and moved to allow the men to enter his father's home.

Fang Buting was upstairs in his study. He wasn't sitting near the balcony, nor had he prepared water for tea. Liu Yun and Wang Kejun were seated on the sofa. Xu Tieying was in the smaller armchair. Fang Buting lowered the cover over the phonograph and pulled a chair over to face them. He was the first to speak: "To play with a line from the *Analects*: 'When a man may not be engaged in conversation, to speak to him is to err in reference to our words. When a man may be engaged in conversation, not to speak to him is to err in reference to the man.' May I ask this PLA commander what his specific position is?"

Wang Kejun looked at Liu Yun. So did Xu Tieying.

Liu Yun answered: "I was a deep-cover CPC agent in the labour offices in Peking, charged with disrupting their normal operations and sowing dissent."

"Ah, excuse my abruptness then. I do, however, have quite a few questions I'd like to ask you."

"Please."

"I am the governor of the Peking branch of the Central Bank. I am a free man. What I would like to be is beyond my control, I accept this, but what I will not accept is being deprived of my freedom to choose. It seems this freedom has been stripped away from me. The Kuomintang is forcing me to relocate to Taipei, but I would much prefer to stay in Peking. Fu Zuoyi, however, has deemed this to be impossible, so I must leave. I can accept that, so long as I can choose where to go. The problem is, the Communists are also advising me to relocate to Taipei. It seems everyone's telling me there is no place in China where I can squat to even take a shit – excuse my language. Now, Secretary-General Wang has tried to reason things out with me. He's told me that tomorrow the announcement concerning the peaceful surrender of Peking is to be made. Not one of the city's inhabitants is to be harmed, not one of its buildings is to be destroyed, and whosoever impedes upon the freedom of others will be called a criminal. But there's something I just don't understand. I don't want to go to Taipei, but how does that make *me* a criminal?"

"But Mr Fang, no one considers you to be a criminal."

"I know myself whether or not I'm a criminal." Fang Buting paused before continuing: "Before the nineteenth of August and the financial collapse of the nation's economy, there was no gold or silver left in the bank's treasury. The following day, the twentieth, the currency reforms were launched and everyone was forced into exchanging whatever gold and silver they had for the new legal tender, the *jinyuanquan*. In essence, I was responsible for robbing the people, plundering what little they had. If I do this again, if I see to the transport of all that's in the treasury to Taipei, won't I be a criminal?"

Wang Kejun had no answer. Xu Tieying was even more at a loss for words.

Fang Buting kept his focus on Liu Yun.

"May I quote something to you? Are you willing to listen?"

"I'll listen to sage advice."

"Allow me. 'In ancient times, Gun of Xia made a city wall twenty-four feet high, but the Lords of the Land turned against him and those who dwelled beyond the seas had deceitful hearts. His son Yu understood that the world had become rebellious and promptly knocked down the wall, filled in the moat surrounding the city, gave away their resources, burned their armour and weapons, and treated everyone with beneficence. And so the lands beyond the Four Seas respectfully submitted...' So, tell me, is there a crime in this?"

Fang Buting could barely disguise his surprise at hearing Liu Yun quote from the classics, but he gradually brought himself under control and relaxed. There was only admiration on Wang Kejun's face, which forced him to glance in the direction of Xu Tieying.

Finally, Fang Buting responded: "I must say, I'm surprised such a learned man could be a member of the Communist Party!" He narrowed his eyes and looked intently at Liu Yun. "It's from the *Huainanzi*, isn't it, that classic of governance from the early Han. Chapter one if I'm not mistaken, yes?"

Liu Yun smiled in reply. "You're a learned man yourself, Mr Fang."

"If you can, Commander Liu, might you put this ancient bit of advice into your own words and explain its significance to me?"

"That, I'm sorry to say, is something I cannot do. I can only give you his original words: 'Let the Kuomintang spirit the money away, and leave the hearts and minds of the people to us!'"

"And who said that?"

"Chairman Mao."

Li Wen was the first to emerge from the conference chamber, followed by Shi Jue. The two men stood on the steps for a moment, forming a neat square. They did not appear to speak to each other. A second later, and they both turned around; again in orderly, military fashion. Li's Fourth Corps responded first to the actions of their commander. The sound of their boots hitting the ground echoed about the clearing as they marched through the main gate. The Ninth Corps under the command of Shi Jue followed in an equally orderly fashion. According to the conditions of the peaceful surrender of Peking, both sides had agreed General Fu's 250,000 men of the Northern Command would be absorbed into the PLA. Any remaining military personnel or government officials affiliated with the Kuomintang were free to choose: they could stay in Peking or leave. Higher-ranking officers of the Fourth and Ninth Corps could also leave if they wished by boarding one of the transports that had been arranged to fly Kuomintang loyalists out of Peking.

Under no circumstances was any form of resistance or disruption of the peaceful handover permitted.

Captain Fang's men quickly boarded their aircraft. The rear cargo door of each C-46 was open. The military-marked crates that had been lying on the ground beside them were being loaded aboard with great urgency. To the side of the aeroplanes, the soldiers garbed in winter parkas were inspecting the transport passes, every one signed personally by General Fu Zuoyi. Butlers, drivers and other household assistants carried leather suitcases as shields for the families they were accompanying. Most were directed towards Chen Changwu's plane in the middle.

Liu Yun and Wang Kejun had already departed Fang Buting's home. Young Li was leaving the house with the last suitcase. Xie Peidong stood in the garden, facing Fang Buting and Cheng Xiaoyun. Fang Meng'ao and He Xiaoyu were just to the side.

"You're the only one left here in the garden, Peidong. Take care of it, please. Who knows, one day we might yet return. Xiaoyun?"

Cheng Xiaoyun moved a little closer and took hold of Xie Peidong's hand, squeezing it tightly. Words failed her, however. Tears were all she had to say goodbye with.

"Go on, tell him what you need to."

Cheng Xiaoyun pulled herself closer to Xie so that her face was nearly upon his shoulder. She'd stopped crying and now whispered into his ear: "Find someone to be with, OK, even someone a little younger. Just don't be alone."

Xie smiled. "And who would be willing to stay with someone like me?"

"I already mentioned a name once before, Ms Wei Yuying in the business department. I know she's interested."

Xie smiled more contemplatively this time. "She's a good person. Let's see if the fates bring us together."

The car horn just beyond the garden gate sounded. At first, only a single horn blew, but it was quickly followed by many, many others.

"Let Meng'ao and Xiaoyu have a few words." Fang Buting looked deeply into his friend's eyes, who returned the gaze with equal intensity. Tears began to pool. "Come on Xiaoyun, it's time."

"It's time." Tears had formed in Xie Peidong's eyes as well.

Fang Buting turned quickly, took hold of Cheng Xiaoyun's hand and left his home for perhaps the last time.

Fang Meng'ao and He Xiaoyu were left standing alongside Xie Peidong.

Xie extended his hand towards Xiaoyu. "May I give you a hug, please?" He Xiaoyu leaned in, allowing Xie to put his arms around her. He whispered into her ear: "Your dad's sent a telegram. He hopes you'll go with Meng'ao." Tears were already streaming down her face. Xie glanced at Fang Meng'ao. "Come here." The younger man obliged and moved forward. Xie released He Xiaoyu, passing her hand to Meng'ao. "Treat her well, and don't mess things up. Understand?"

Fang Meng'ao wrapped his free arm around Xie. "Uncle, let me take your place. I can stay behind, for you, for Uncle Cui… for Mulan."

Xie Peidong grasped immediately what Fang Meng'ao was saying and replied in a stern, if quiet voice: "That's not what the party has decided. No more nonsense!"

Fang released his grip around Xie's shoulders and stepped back. All of a sudden, he saluted, took Xiaoyu's hand in his and walked out of the garden. He didn't once look back.

———

On 21 January 1949, the thirty-eighth year of the Republic of China, the last day of the year on the lunar calendar, the night sky was completely free of clouds. The moon had risen high above the city, half of it glistening like a great disc in the heavens. It shone brightly down upon the Forbidden City, the home of China's many emperors.

Shao Yuangang's aeroplane had already taken off and was now circling above Dongdan airstrip waiting for the two other planes to lift themselves into the air. The propellers on Chen Changwu's C-46 started to turn, and as the plane gained speed, its nose arched into the sky.

There were now two planes circling above.

On the ground, Fang Meng'ao helped his stepmother climb up the ramp of the third and final C-46. Once inside, Guo Jinyang took her to one side to wait. Fang Meng'ao turned to help his father up next. As the older man scrambled aboard, both Guo Jinyan and Cheng Xiaoyun reached out their hands to help him inside. Safely onboard, Fang turned again and reached out his hand, this time to He Xiaoyu, who had just stepped up on the ramp. He pulled her up and then passed one of her hands to his father. Together, they made their way inside the cavernous body of the C-46 plane.

Standing beside the ramp was Xu Tieying, his forever companion, the attaché case tucked under his arm. Wang Puchen and Sun Chaozhong stood nearby. Xu extended his hand to Wang Puchen, and the two men shook. At the same time, he lifted a dossier out of his case and passed it to Wang. "This is a summons from the special court in Nanking. After I'm gone, give it to Sun Chaozhong."

Surprise washed over Wang's face. Sun seemed to shake.

"Whether the Standing Committee is more loyal or the Bureau of Reserve Cadres, that will depend on Secretary Sun accepting to stand trial or not."

Xu Tieying walked towards the ramp, surprised to see Fang Meng'ao apparently waiting for him. He smiled and called out: "Thank you."

But then, just as he was about to step up on the ramp, it shifted and moved away from him. Xu Tieying stared at Fang Meng'ao, a supreme look of astonishment on his face. Fang kicked at the ramp again, knocking it from the plane completely. With a few steps and a leap, Fang was able to climb into the aeroplane. Xu Tieying was left flabbergasted. All he could do was stare as the door to the aeroplane closed. Then he watched as the propellers spun faster and faster. He watched as the plane taxied to the runway. He watched as the C-46 lifted into the air.

Suddenly, he realised his attaché case was no longer under his arm, and so he turned, only to see Sun Chaozhong holding it.

"Director, I guess we'll show our loyalty together."

In the skies above Peking, three Curtiss C-46s circled. Fang Meng'ao looked down over the city, awash in a silvery hue cast by the moon. Again it reminded him of an old aerial photograph. Black and white, something lost to the recesses of time in an undiscovered history book. Fang Meng'ao raised his hand to his forehead and saluted the ancient city. He then pulled on the yoke. The wings of the aircraft tipped, and the great beast headed in the direction of the moon.

In the streets of Peking surrounding Deshengmen, a cacophony of voices rang out in a tidal wave of song: "Bright the sky in the Liberated Areas/ And happy the people there…"

Military vehicles and tanks emerged among the marching crowds. The first vehicle carried portraits of Mao Zedong and Zhu De proudly on their bonnets. The tide of people marched into the city, buoyed by the PLA troops marching along with them. Even more people were stuck behind the crowds that had already entered Deshengmen. And there in the crowd was Xie Peidong.

A tank passed by and the crowd grew tempestuous. Xie gave himself over to it and allowed himself to be swept up with the mass of people. A thunderous cheer rang out from an adjacent avenue. Xie looked and saw the students march proudly, a banner held high above them. They stomped their feet in unison as they passed. Xie was mesmerised, then startled. There in the crowd, arm in arm with the students, he spied the profile of Liang Jinglun. As the figure moved he caught sight of the student on the left and on the right.

Xie narrowed his vision.

The student to the right of Liang Jinglun looked like his beloved Xie Mulan!

In that moment, the roaring mass of people, the shouting, the gongs, the firecrackers, all of it went silent. Xie Peidong could no longer hear anything. His eyes were fixed on that young, female student. Then suddenly, finally, the girl turned around and smiled proudly at Xie Peidong.

It was Xie Mulan.

ABOUT THE AUTHOR

Liu Heping was born in Hunan Province, southern China in 1953. He spent his childhood in the theatre and went on to become an acclaimed screenwriter, novelist and historian known for his deep insights into the events of Chinese history. His pioneering historical drama about the Ming Dynasty, *Da Ming Wang Chao 1566*, was first published as a novel in 2006 and sold nearly a million copies. The following year, it was broadcast as a 46-episode TV series that garnered popular and critical acclaim in China. His Chinese Civil War TV drama, *All Quiet in Peking*, gained a cumulative 400 million online views in the month following its first broadcast in October 2014. The series made waves among China's intellectual circles and was picked up for international distribution by Netflix. Liu's realist approach to the historical and contemporary transformation of China has been hugely influential and well received in the Chinese-speaking world.

ABOUT THE TRANSLATOR

Christopher Payne has co-translated the award-winning novels *Decoded* and *In the Dark* by Mai Jia, and along with his frequent collaborator, Olivia Milburn, he's also brought Jiang Zilong's magnum opus, *Empires of Dust*, to an English-language audience. Christopher holds a PhD in Chinese literature from the School of Oriental and African Studies at the University of London, and he has spent more than a decade teaching at postsecondary institutions, most notably Sungkyunkwan University in Seoul, South Korea, and the University of Manchester in the UK. In 2020 he took up a position at the University of Toronto, where he has continued to champion Chinese literature in the English-speaking world.

ABOUT THE SERIES

The *All Quiet in Peking* series follows Fang Meng'ao, a Communist Party member working undercover in the Chinese Nationalist Air Force. It is 1948, and civil war is raging between the Communists and the Kuomintang, ravaging the economy of Peking. Fang is ordered to investigate a corruption case involving the Peking Citizens' Committee and the Peking branch of the Central Bank, the president of which is none other than his own father. Fang's desire for the peaceful liberation of Peking is a race against the clock. The nation doesn't know it yet, but the happiness and peace of the people depends on him.